Brontë Sisters

Jane Eyre

&

The Tenant of Wildfell Hall

This is a FLAME TREE Book

Publisher & Creative Director: Nick Wells
Project Editor: Laura Bulbeck
Early Life and Charlotte Brontë biography by Chris McNab & Judith John;
Anne Brontë biography by Flame Tree Studio

FLAME TREE PUBLISHING
6 Melbray Mews, Fulham,
London SW6 3NS, United Kingdom
www.flametreepublishing.com

First published 2017

The cover image is created by Flame Tree Studio
Typography based on Octavia Script, Will Sherring and ITC Garamond

A copy of the CIP data for this book is available from the British Library.

Printed and bound in Italy

Foreword by

Sophie Franklin

Brontë Sisters

Jane Eyre

The Tenant of Wildfell Hall

FLAME TREE
PUBLISHING

Romantic Fantasy

Contents

Charlotte Brontë
Jane Eyre

Anne Brontë
The Tenant of Wildfell Hall

Foreword

ON 16TH OCTOBER 1847, *Jane Eyre* by Currer Bell entered the literary circuit and became an overnight sensation. Two months later, *Wuthering Heights* by Ellis Bell and *Agnes Grey* by Acton Bell were published as a three-volume novel, gaining acclaim but also shocking critics and readers alike. In June 1848, Acton Bell's second novel, *The Tenant of Wildfell Hall*, was circulated, again receiving praise while also causing a stir for its depiction of debauchery and marital abuse. Several reviewers took exception to these novels largely because, as the *Spectator* remarked in 1848, there was an apparent 'coarseness of tone throughout the writing of all these Bells, that puts an offensive subject in its worst point of view'.

The 'Bells brothers' were, of course, the Brontë sisters. The Brontës wrote – often unflinchingly – of issues considered taboo in the 1840s, including female sexuality, domestic violence, and class struggles. This fascination with the 'coarser' side of life and the power with which their writing represented such topics often positioned them as outsiders, social anomalies out of touch with the world beyond the Haworth parsonage on the Yorkshire moors. As authors, they seemed to come from nowhere. In fact, the Brontës were fully engaged with the world around them and had been writing stories from an early age. They devoured newspapers as children and kept up-to-date with the latest poetry and novels; indeed, much of their writing was responding directly to contemporary concerns. Charlotte Brontë's *Jane Eyre* and Anne Brontë's *The Tenant of Wildfell Hall* exemplify this sensitivity to societal anxieties.

Despite being viewed predominantly as a romance, *Jane Eyre* is full of the spirit of revolution, something contemporary critics were again quick to denounce. In 1848, Elizabeth Rigby famously pinpointed the radicalism of Charlotte Brontë's first published work in the following terms: 'the tone of mind and thought which has overthrown authority and violated every code human and divine abroad, and fostered Chartism and rebellion at home, is the same which has also written *Jane Eyre*'. For a woman like Jane Eyre – 'poor, obscure, plain, and little' as she is – to win the heart of her employer, to climb her way up the social ladder, to come into a substantial inheritance, and, crucially, to assert her right to love and be happy loudly and vehemently: this was challenging and new. Jane's unwavering strength and the intimacy of her voice still resonate with readers. The novel is a clarion cry for the underdog, rallying against injustice while opening up conversations about human rights (particularly through Bertha Mason) and what it means to live a life of integrity.

Anne Brontë's *The Tenant of Wildfell Hall* was not an instant bestseller like *Jane Eyre* and its brilliance is still often underrated, especially when unfairly compared to Charlotte and Emily's novels. This is perhaps partly due to the didacticism of Anne's work. There is a clear moral agenda running through the book, but this only heightens its power. We feel the injustice of and the danger in Helen Huntingdon's situation as her husband becomes increasingly abusive and descends into profligacy, threatening to take their young son with him. Helen challenges convention by removing herself and her son from the destructive environment, thereby abandoning her wifely duties. It is this defiance against subordination and the clarity of Helen's voice that position *The Tenant of Wildfell Hall* as a proto-feminist text. In many ways, nineteenth-century audiences were not ready for the force of Anne Brontë's message.

The novels that follow continue to be read, reread (and, then, read again), adapted, and adored a hundred and seventy years after their initial publication. Not only are they beautifully crafted stories; they still speak to modern readers and many of the concerns articulated in these novels chime with our own today. As we celebrate the bicentenaries of the Brontë sisters' births, beginning with Charlotte Brontë last year in 2016 and culminating with Anne Brontë in 2020, revisiting or even reading *Jane Eyre* and *The Tenant of Wildfell Hall* for the first time feels more appropriate now than ever.

Sophie Franklin
Writer and Researcher

Publisher's Note

THE BRONTË SISTERS, though they originally published their works under male pseudonyms, have since earned their places amongst the most beloved of British authors. Selected here for your enjoyment are two of their great works: Charlotte Brontë's quintessential romantic novel *Jane Eyre*, and its very worthy companion *The Tenant of Wildfell Hall* by Anne Brontë. In *Jane Eyre*, Charlotte crafts an incredible love story between the heroine Jane and her employer Mr Rochester, whilst enshrouding us in the mystery of Thornfield Hall and the mad woman in the attic. Her sister Anne's *The Tenant of Wildfell Hall* meanwhile is a wrestless tale of romantic denial that grips the reader's attention from start to end. It is no wonder that the Brontës' masterpieces have become literary classics.

We have edited the original texts as little as possible, whilst still making choices about how to best present them for full enjoyment and ease of reading. Both of the novels were originally printed in either two or three volumes, and we have identified where these begin, for interest; but the chapter numbers continue to flow chronologically, for clarity. We hope you take great pleasure in either discovering or rediscovering the two stories collected here.

Charlotte Brontë

Jane Eyre

Volume One

Chapter One

THERE WAS NO possibility of taking a walk that day. We had been wandering, indeed, in the leafless shrubbery an hour in the morning; but since dinner (Mrs. Reed, when there was no company, dined early) the cold winter wind had brought with it clouds so sombre, and a rain so penetrating, that further out-door exercise was now out of the question.

I was glad of it: I never liked long walks, especially on chilly afternoons: dreadful to me was the coming home in the raw twilight, with nipped fingers and toes, and a heart saddened by the chidings of Bessie, the nurse, and humbled by the consciousness of my physical inferiority to Eliza, John, and Georgiana Reed.

The said Eliza, John, and Georgiana were now clustered round their mama in the drawing room: she lay reclined on a sofa by the fireside, and with her darlings about her (for the time neither quarrelling nor crying) looked perfectly happy. Me, she had dispensed from joining the group; saying, "She regretted to be under the necessity of keeping me at a distance; but that until she heard from Bessie, and could discover by her own observation, that I was endeavouring in good earnest to acquire a more sociable and childlike disposition, a more attractive and sprightly manner – something lighter, franker, more natural, as it were – she really must exclude me from privileges intended only for contented, happy, little children."

"What does Bessie say I have done?" I asked.

"Jane, I don't like cavillers or questioners; besides, there is something truly forbidding in a child taking up her elders in that manner. Be seated somewhere; and until you can speak pleasantly, remain silent."

A breakfast room adjoined the drawing room, I slipped in there. It contained a bookcase: I soon possessed myself of a volume, taking care that it should be one stored with pictures. I mounted into the window seat: gathering up my feet, I sat cross-legged, like a Turk; and, having drawn the red moreen curtain nearly close, I was shrined in double retirement.

Folds of scarlet drapery shut in my view to the right hand; to the left were the clear panes of glass, protecting, but not separating me from the drear November day. At intervals, while turning over the leaves of my book, I studied the aspect of that winter afternoon. Afar, it offered a pale blank of mist and cloud; near a scene of wet lawn and storm-beat shrub, with ceaseless rain sweeping away wildly before a long and lamentable blast.

I returned to my book – Bewick's *History of British Birds*: the letterpress thereof I cared little for, generally speaking; and yet there were certain introductory pages that, child as I was, I could not pass quite as a blank. They were those which treat of the haunts of sea-fowl; of 'the solitary rocks and promontories' by them only inhabited; of the coast of Norway, studded with isles from its southern extremity, the Lindeness, or Naze, to the North Cape:

> *Where the Northern Ocean, in vast whirls,*
> *Boils round the naked, melancholy isles*
> *Of farthest Thule; and the Atlantic surge*
> *Pours in among the stormy Hebrides.*

Nor could I pass unnoticed the suggestion of the bleak shores of Lapland, Siberia, Spitzbergen, Nova Zembla, Iceland, Greenland, with 'the vast sweep of the Arctic Zone, and those forlorn regions of dreary space, – that reservoir of frost and snow, where firm fields of ice, the accumulation of centuries of winters, glazed in Alpine heights above heights, surround the pole, and concentre the multiplied rigours of extreme cold.' Of these death-white realms I formed an idea of my own: shadowy, like all the half-comprehended notions that float dim through children's brains, but strangely impressive. The words in these introductory pages connected themselves with the succeeding vignettes, and gave significance to the rock standing up alone in a sea of billow and spray; to the broken boat stranded on a desolate coast; to the cold and ghastly moon glancing through bars of cloud at a wreck just sinking.

I cannot tell what sentiment haunted the quite solitary churchyard, with its inscribed headstone; its gate, its two trees, its low horizon, girdled by a broken wall, and its newly-risen crescent, attesting the hour of eventide.

The two ships becalmed on a torpid sea, I believed to be marine phantoms.

The fiend pinning down the thief's pack behind him, I passed over quickly: it was an object of terror.

So was the black horned thing seated aloof on a rock, surveying a distant crowd surrounding a gallows.

Each picture told a story; mysterious often to my undeveloped understanding and imperfect feelings, yet ever profoundly interesting: as interesting as the tales Bessie sometimes narrated on winter evenings, when she chanced to be in good humour; and when, having brought her ironing-table to the nursery hearth, she allowed us to sit about it, and while she got up Mrs. Reed's lace frills, and crimped her nightcap borders, fed our eager attention with passages of love and adventure taken from old fairy tales and other ballads; or (as at a later period I discovered) from the pages of *Pamela*, and *Henry, Earl of Moreland*.

With Bewick on my knee, I was then happy: happy at least in my way. I feared nothing but interruption, and that came too soon. The breakfast room door opened.

"Boh! Madam Mope!" cried the voice of John Reed; then he paused: he found the room apparently empty.

"Where the dickens is she!" he continued. "Lizzy! Georgy! (calling to his sisters) Joan is not here: tell mama she is run out into the rain – bad animal!"

"It is well I drew the curtain," thought I; and I wished fervently he might not discover my hiding-place: nor would John Reed have found it out himself; he was not quick either of vision or conception; but Eliza just put her head in at the door, and said at once:

"She is in the window seat, to be sure, Jack."

And I came out immediately, for I trembled at the idea of being dragged forth by the said Jack.

"What do you want?" I asked, with awkward diffidence.

"Say, 'What do you want, Master Reed?'" was the answer. "I want you to come here;" and seating himself in an armchair, he intimated by a gesture that I was to approach and stand before him.

John Reed was a schoolboy of fourteen years old; four years older than I, for I was but ten: large and stout for his age, with a dingy and unwholesome skin; thick lineaments in a spacious visage, heavy limbs and large extremities. He gorged himself habitually at table, which made him bilious, and gave him a dim and bleared eye and flabby cheeks. He ought now to have been at school; but his mama had taken him home for a month or two, "on account of his delicate health." Mr. Miles, the master, affirmed that he would do very well if he had fewer cakes and sweetmeats sent him from home; but the mother's heart turned from an opinion so harsh, and inclined rather to the more refined idea that John's sallowness was owing to over-application and, perhaps, to pining after home.

John had not much affection for his mother and sisters, and an antipathy to me. He bullied and punished me; not two or three times in the week, nor once or twice in the day, but continually: every nerve I had feared him, and every morsel of flesh in my bones shrank when he came near. There were moments when I was bewildered by the terror he inspired, because I had no appeal whatever against either his menaces or his inflictions; the servants did not like to offend their young master by taking my part against him, and Mrs. Reed was blind and deaf on the subject: she never saw him strike or heard him abuse me, though he did both now and then in her very presence, more frequently, however, behind her back.

Habitually obedient to John, I came up to his chair: he spent some three minutes in thrusting out his tongue at me as far as he could without damaging the roots: I knew he would soon strike, and while dreading the blow, I mused on the disgusting and ugly appearance of him who would presently deal it. I wonder if he read that notion in my face; for, all at once, without speaking, he struck suddenly and strongly. I tottered, and on regaining my equilibrium retired back a step or two from his chair.

"That is for your impudence in answering mama awhile since," said he, "and for your sneaking way of getting behind curtains, and for the look you had in your eyes two minutes since, you rat!"

Accustomed to John Reed's abuse, I never had an idea of replying to it; my care was how to endure the blow which would certainly follow the insult.

"What were you doing behind the curtain?" he asked.

"I was reading."

"Show the book."

I returned to the window and fetched it thence.

"You have no business to take our books; you are a dependent, mama says; you have no money; your father left you none; you ought to beg, and not to live here with gentlemen's children like us, and eat the same meals we do, and wear clothes at our mama's expense. Now, I'll teach you to rummage my bookshelves: for they *are* mine; all the house belongs to me, or will do in a few years. Go and stand by the door, out of the way of the mirror and the windows."

I did so, not at first aware what was his intention; but when I saw him lift and poise the book and stand in act to hurl it, I instinctively started aside with a cry of alarm: not soon enough, however; the volume was flung, it hit me, and I fell, striking my head against the door and cutting it. The cut bled, the pain was sharp: my terror had passed its climax; other feelings succeeded.

"Wicked and cruel boy!" I said. "You are like a murderer – you are like a slave-driver – you are like the Roman emperors!"

I had read Goldsmith's *History of Rome*, and had formed my opinion of Nero, Caligula, etc. Also I had drawn parallels in silence, which I never thought thus to have declared aloud.

"What! What!" he cried. "Did she say that to me? Did you hear her, Eliza and Georgiana? Won't I tell mama? but first –"

He ran headlong at me: I felt him grasp my hair and my shoulder: he had closed with a desperate thing. I really saw in him a tyrant, a murderer. I felt a drop or two of blood from my head trickle down my neck, and was sensible of somewhat pungent suffering: these sensations for the time predominated over fear, and I received him in frantic sort. I don't very well know what I did with my hands, but he called me "Rat! Rat!" and bellowed out aloud. Aid was near him: Eliza and Georgiana had run for Mrs. Reed, who was gone upstairs: she now came upon the scene, followed by Bessie and her maid Abbot. We were parted: I heard the words:

"Dear! Dear! What a fury to fly at Master John!"

"Did ever anybody see such a picture of passion!"

Then Mrs. Reed subjoined:

"Take her away to the red-room, and lock her in there." Four hands were immediately laid upon me, and I was borne upstairs.

Chapter Two

I RESISTED all the way: a new thing for me, and a circumstance which greatly strengthened the bad opinion Bessie and Miss Abbot were disposed to entertain of me. The fact is, I was a trifle beside myself; or rather *out* of myself, as the French would say: I was conscious that a moment's mutiny had already rendered me liable to strange penalties, and, like any other rebel slave, I felt resolved, in my desperation, to go all lengths.

"Hold her arms, Miss Abbot: she's like a mad cat."

"For shame! For shame!" cried the lady's-maid. "What shocking conduct, Miss Eyre, to strike a young gentleman, your benefactress's son! Your young master."

"Master! How is he my master? Am I a servant?"

"No; you are less than a servant, for you do nothing for your keep. There, sit down, and think over your wickedness."

They had got me by this time into the apartment indicated by Mrs. Reed, and had thrust me upon a stool: my impulse was to rise from it like a spring; their two pair of hands arrested me instantly.

"If you don't sit still, you must be tied down," said Bessie. "Miss Abbot, lend me your garters; she would break mine directly."

Miss Abbot turned to divest a stout leg of the necessary ligature. This preparation for bonds, and the additional ignominy it inferred, took a little of the excitement out of me.

"Don't take them off," I cried; "I will not stir."

In guarantee whereof, I attached myself to my seat by my hands.

"Mind you don't," said Bessie; and when she had ascertained that I was really subsiding, she loosened her hold of me; then she and Miss Abbot stood with folded arms, looking darkly and doubtfully on my face, as incredulous of my sanity.

"She never did so before," at last said Bessie, turning to the Abigail.

"But it was always in her," was the reply. "I've told Missis often my opinion about the child, and Missis agreed with me. She's an underhand little thing: I never saw a girl of her age with so much cover."

Bessie answered not; but ere long, addressing me, she said: "You ought to be aware, Miss, that you are under obligations to Mrs. Reed: she keeps you: if she were to turn you off, you would have to go to the poorhouse."

I had nothing to say to these words: they were not new to me: my very first recollections of existence included hints of the same kind. This reproach of my dependence had become a vague sing-song in my ear: very painful and crushing, but only half intelligible. Miss Abbot joined in:

"And you ought not to think yourself on an equality with the Misses Reed and Master Reed, because Missis kindly allows you to be brought up with them. They will have a great deal of money, and you will have none: it is your place to be humble, and to try to make yourself agreeable to them."

"What we tell you is for your good," added Bessie, in no harsh voice, "you should try to be useful and pleasant, then, perhaps, you would have a home here; but if you become passionate and rude, Missis will send you away, I am sure."

"Besides," said Miss Abbot, "God will punish her: He might strike her dead in the midst of her tantrums, and then where would she go? Come, Bessie, we will leave her: I wouldn't have her heart for anything. Say your prayers, Miss Eyre, when you are by yourself; for if you don't repent, something bad might be permitted to come down the chimney and fetch you away."

They went, shutting the door, and locking it behind them.

The red-room was a square chamber, very seldom slept in, I might say never, indeed, unless when a chance influx of visitors at Gateshead Hall rendered it necessary to turn to account all the accommodation it contained: yet it was one of the largest and stateliest chambers in the mansion. A bed supported on massive pillars of mahogany, hung with curtains of deep red damask, stood out like a tabernacle in the centre; the two large windows, with their blinds always drawn down, were half shrouded in festoons and falls of similar drapery; the carpet was red; the table at the foot of the bed was covered with a crimson cloth; the walls were a soft fawn colour with a blush of pink in it; the wardrobe, the toilet-table, the chairs were of darkly polished old mahogany. Out of these deep surrounding shades rose high, and glared white, the piled-up mattresses and pillows of the bed, spread with a snowy Marseilles counterpane. Scarcely less prominent was an ample cushioned easy chair near the head of the bed, also white, with a footstool before it; and looking, as I thought, like a pale throne.

This room was chill, because it seldom had a fire; it was silent, because remote from the nursery and kitchen; solemn, because it was known to be so seldom entered. The house-maid alone came here on Saturdays, to wipe from the mirrors and the furniture a week's quiet dust: and Mrs. Reed herself, at far intervals, visited it to review the contents of a certain secret drawer in the wardrobe, where were stored divers parchments, her jewel-casket, and a miniature of her deceased husband; and in those last words lies the secret of the red-room – the spell which kept it so lonely in spite of its grandeur.

Mr. Reed had been dead nine years: it was in this chamber he breathed his last; here he lay in state; hence his coffin was borne by the undertaker's men; and, since that day, a sense of dreary consecration had guarded it from frequent intrusion.

My seat, to which Bessie and the bitter Miss Abbot had left me riveted, was a low ottoman near the marble chimney-piece; the bed rose before me; to my right hand there was the high, dark wardrobe, with subdued, broken reflections varying the gloss of its panels; to my left were the muffled windows; a great looking-glass between them repeated the vacant majesty of the bed and room. I was not quite sure whether they had locked the door; and when I dared move, I got up and went to see. Alas! yes: no jail was ever more secure. Returning, I had to cross before the looking-glass; my fascinated glance involuntarily explored the depth it revealed. All looked colder and darker in that visionary hollow than in reality: and the strange little figure there gazing at me, with a white face and arms specking the gloom, and glittering eyes of fear moving where all else was still, had the effect of a real spirit: I thought it like one of the tiny phantoms, half fairy, half imp, Bessie's evening stories represented as coming out of lone, ferny dells in moors, and appearing before the eyes of belated travellers. I returned to my stool.

Superstition was with me at that moment; but it was not yet her hour for complete victory: my blood was still warm; the mood of the revolted slave was still bracing me with its bitter vigour; I had to stem a rapid rush of retrospective thought before I quailed to the dismal present.

All John Reed's violent tyrannies, all his sisters' proud indifference, all his mother's aversion, all the servants' partiality, turned up in my disturbed mind like a dark deposit in a turbid well. Why was I always suffering, always browbeaten, always accused, for ever condemned? Why could I never please? Why was it useless to try to win anyone's favour? Eliza, who was headstrong and selfish, was respected. Georgiana, who had a spoiled temper, a very acrid spite, a captious and insolent carriage, was universally indulged. Her beauty, her pink cheeks and golden curls, seemed to give delight to all who looked at her, and to purchase indemnity for every fault. John no one thwarted, much less punished; though he twisted the necks of the pigeons, killed the little pea-chicks, set the dogs at the sheep, stripped the hothouse vines of their fruit, and broke the buds off the choicest plants in the conservatory: he called his mother 'old girl', too; sometimes reviled her for her dark skin, similar to his own; bluntly disregarded her wishes; not unfrequently tore and spoiled her silk attire; and he was still 'her own darling'. I dared commit no fault: I strove to fulfil every duty; and I was termed naughty and tiresome, sullen and sneaking, from morning to noon, and from noon to night.

My head still ached and bled with the blow and fall I had received: no one had reproved John for wantonly striking me; and because I had turned against him to avert farther irrational violence, I was loaded with general opprobrium.

"Unjust! – Unjust!" said my reason, forced by the agonising stimulus into precocious though transitory power: and Resolve, equally wrought up, instigated some strange expedient to achieve escape from insupportable oppression – as running away, or, if that could not be effected, never eating or drinking more, and letting myself die.

What a consternation of soul was mine that dreary afternoon! How all my brain was in tumult, and all my heart in insurrection! Yet in what darkness, what dense ignorance, was the mental battle fought! I could not answer the ceaseless inward question – why I thus suffered; now, at the distance of – I will not say how many years, I see it clearly.

I was a discord in Gateshead Hall: I was like nobody there; I had nothing in harmony with Mrs. Reed or her children, or her chosen vassalage. If they did not love me, in fact, as little did I love them. They were not bound to regard with affection a thing that could not sympathise with one amongst them; a heterogeneous thing, opposed to them in temperament, in capacity, in propensities; a useless thing, incapable of serving their interest, or adding to their pleasure; a noxious thing, cherishing the germs of indignation at their treatment, of contempt of their judgment. I know that had I been a sanguine, brilliant, careless, exacting, handsome, romping child – though equally dependent and friendless – Mrs. Reed would have endured my presence more complacently; her children would have entertained for me more of the cordiality of fellow-feeling; the servants would have been less prone to make me the scapegoat of the nursery.

Daylight began to forsake the red-room; it was past four o'clock, and the beclouded afternoon was tending to drear twilight. I heard the rain still beating continuously on the staircase window, and the wind howling in the grove behind the hall; I grew by degrees cold as a stone, and then my courage sank. My habitual mood of humiliation, self-doubt, forlorn depression, fell damp on the embers of my decaying ire. All said I was wicked, and perhaps I might be so; what thought had I been but just conceiving of starving myself to death? That certainly was a crime: and was I fit to die? Or was the vault under the chancel of Gateshead Church an inviting bourne? In such vault I had been told did Mr. Reed lie buried; and led by this thought to recall his idea, I dwelt on it with gathering dread. I could not remember him; but I knew that he was my own uncle – my mother's brother – that he had taken me when a parentless infant to his house; and that in his last moments he had required a promise of Mrs. Reed that she would rear and maintain me as one of her own children. Mrs. Reed probably considered she had kept this promise; and so she had, I dare say, as well as her nature would permit her; but how could she really like an interloper not of her race, and unconnected with her, after her husband's death, by any tie? It must have been most irksome to find herself bound by a hard-wrung pledge to stand in the stead of a parent to a strange child she could not love, and to see an uncongenial alien permanently intruded on her own family group.

A singular notion dawned upon me. I doubted not – never doubted – that if Mr. Reed had been alive he would have treated me kindly; and now, as I sat looking at the white bed and overshadowed walls – occasionally also turning a fascinated eye towards the dimly gleaning mirror – I began to recall what I had heard of dead men, troubled in their graves by the violation of their last wishes, revisiting the earth to punish the perjured and avenge the oppressed; and I thought Mr. Reed's spirit, harassed by the wrongs of his sister's child, might quit its abode – whether in the church vault or in the unknown world of the departed – and rise before me in this chamber. I wiped my tears and hushed my sobs, fearful lest any sign of violent grief might waken a preternatural voice to comfort me, or elicit from the gloom some haloed face, bending over me with strange pity. This idea, consolatory in theory, I felt would be terrible if realised: with all my might I endeavoured to stifle it – I endeavoured to be firm. Shaking my hair from my eyes, I lifted my head and tried to look boldly round the dark room; at this moment a light gleamed on the wall. Was it, I asked myself, a ray from the moon penetrating some aperture in the blind? No; moonlight was still, and this stirred; while I gazed, it glided up to the ceiling and quivered over my head. I can now conjecture readily that this streak of light was, in all likelihood, a gleam from a lantern carried by some one across the lawn: but then, prepared as my mind was for horror, shaken as my nerves were by agitation, I thought the swift darting beam was a herald of some coming vision from another world. My heart beat thick, my head grew hot; a sound filled my ears, which I deemed the rushing of wings; something seemed near me; I was oppressed, suffocated: endurance broke down; I rushed to the door and shook the lock in desperate effort. Steps came running along the outer passage; the key turned, Bessie and Abbot entered.

"Miss Eyre, are you ill?" said Bessie.

"What a dreadful noise! It went quite through me!" exclaimed Abbot.

"Take me out! Let me go into the nursery!" was my cry.

"What for? Are you hurt? Have you seen something?" again demanded Bessie.

"Oh! I saw a light, and I thought a ghost would come." I had now got hold of Bessie's hand, and she did not snatch it from me.

"She has screamed out on purpose," declared Abbot, in some disgust. "And what a scream! If she had been in great pain one would have excused it, but she only wanted to bring us all here: I know her naughty tricks."

"What is all this?" demanded another voice peremptorily; and Mrs. Reed came along the corridor, her cap flying wide, her gown rustling stormily. "Abbot and Bessie, I believe I gave orders that Jane Eyre should be left in the red-room till I came to her myself."

"Miss Jane screamed so loud, ma'am," pleaded Bessie.

"Let her go," was the only answer. "Loose Bessie's hand, child: you cannot succeed in getting out by these means, be assured. I abhor artifice, particularly in children; it is my duty to show you that tricks will not answer: you will now stay here an hour longer, and it is only on condition of perfect submission and stillness that I shall liberate you then."

"O aunt! Have pity! Forgive me! I cannot endure it – let me be punished some other way! I shall be killed if –"

"Silence! This violence is all most repulsive:" and so, no doubt, she felt it. I was a precocious actress in her eyes; she sincerely looked on me as a compound of virulent passions, mean spirit, and dangerous duplicity.

Bessie and Abbot having retreated, Mrs. Reed, impatient of my now frantic anguish and wild sobs, abruptly thrust me back and locked me in, without farther parley. I heard her sweeping away; and soon after she was gone, I suppose I had a species of fit: unconsciousness closed the scene.

Chapter Three

THE NEXT THING I remember is, waking up with a feeling as if I had had a frightful nightmare, and seeing before me a terrible red glare, crossed with thick black bars. I heard voices, too, speaking with a hollow sound, and as if muffled by a rush of wind or water: agitation, uncertainty, and an all-predominating sense of terror confused my faculties. Ere long, I became aware that some one was handling me; lifting me up and supporting me in a sitting posture, and that more tenderly than I had ever been raised or upheld before. I rested my head against a pillow or an arm, and felt easy.

In five minutes more the cloud of bewilderment dissolved: I knew quite well that I was in my own bed, and that the red glare was the nursery fire. It was night: a candle burnt on the table; Bessie stood at the bed-foot with a basin in her hand, and a gentleman sat in a chair near my pillow, leaning over me.

I felt an inexpressible relief, a soothing conviction of protection and security, when I knew that there was a stranger in the room, an individual not belonging to Gateshead, and not related to Mrs. Reed. Turning from Bessie (though her presence was far less obnoxious to me than that of Abbot, for instance, would have been), I scrutinised the face of the gentleman: I knew him; it was Mr. Lloyd, an apothecary, sometimes called in by Mrs. Reed when the servants were ailing: for herself and the children she employed a physician.

"Well, who am I?" he asked.

I pronounced his name, offering him at the same time my hand: he took it, smiling and saying, "We shall do very well by-and-by." Then he laid me down, and addressing Bessie, charged her to be very careful that I was not disturbed during the night. Having given some further directions, and intimates that he should call again the next day, he departed; to my grief: I felt so sheltered and befriended while he sat in the chair near my pillow; and as he closed the door after him, all the room darkened and my heart again sank: inexpressible sadness weighed it down.

"Do you feel as if you should sleep, Miss?" asked Bessie, rather softly.

Scarcely dared I answer her; for I feared the next sentence might be rough. "I will try."

"Would you like to drink, or could you eat anything?"

"No, thank you, Bessie."

"Then I think I shall go to bed, for it is past twelve o'clock; but you may call me if you want anything in the night."

Wonderful civility this! It emboldened me to ask a question.

"Bessie, what is the matter with me? Am I ill?"

"You fell sick, I suppose, in the red-room with crying; you'll be better soon, no doubt."

Bessie went into the housemaid's apartment, which was near. I heard her say:

"Sarah, come and sleep with me in the nursery; I daren't for my life be alone with that poor child tonight: she might die; it's such a strange thing she should have that fit: I wonder if she saw anything. Missis was rather too hard."

Sarah came back with her; they both went to bed; they were whispering together for half an hour before they fell asleep. I caught scraps of their conversation, from which I was able only too distinctly to infer the main subject discussed.

"Something passed her, all dressed in white, and vanished" – "A great black dog behind him" – "Three loud raps on the chamber door" – "A light in the churchyard just over his grave," etc., etc.

At last both slept: the fire and the candle went out. For me, the watches of that long night passed in ghastly wakefulness; strained by dread: such dread as children only can feel.

No severe or prolonged bodily illness followed this incident of the red-room; it only gave my nerves a shock of which I feel the reverberation to this day. Yes, Mrs. Reed, to you I owe some fearful pangs of mental suffering, but I ought to forgive you, for you knew not what you did: while rending my heart strings, you thought you were only uprooting my bad propensities.

Next day, by noon, I was up and dressed, and sat wrapped in a shawl by the nursery hearth. I felt physically weak and broken down: but my worse ailment was an unutterable wretchedness of mind: a wretchedness which kept drawing from me silent tears; no sooner had I wiped one salt drop from my cheek than another followed. Yet, I thought, I ought to have been happy, for none of the Reeds were there, they were all gone out in the carriage with their mama. Abbot, too, was sewing in another room, and Bessie, as she moved hither and thither, putting away toys and arranging drawers, addressed to me every now and then a word of unwonted kindness. This state of things should have been to me a paradise of peace, accustomed as I was to a life of ceaseless reprimand and thankless fagging; but, in fact, my racked nerves were now in such a state that no calm could soothe, and no pleasure excite them agreeably.

Bessie had been down into the kitchen, and she brought up with her a tart on a certain brightly painted china plate, whose bird of paradise, nestling in a wreath of convolvuli and rosebuds, had been wont to stir in me a most enthusiastic sense of admiration; and which plate I had often petitioned to be allowed to take in my hand in order to examine it more closely, but had always hitherto been deemed unworthy of such a privilege. This precious vessel was now placed on my knee, and I was cordially invited to eat the circlet of delicate pastry upon it. Vain favour! Coming, like most other favours long deferred and often wished for, too late! I could not eat the tart; and the plumage of the bird, the tints of the flowers, seemed strangely faded: I put both plate and tart away. Bessie asked if I would have a book: the word *book* acted as a transient stimulus, and I begged her to fetch *Gulliver's Travels* from the library. This book I had again and again perused with delight. I considered it a narrative of facts, and discovered in it a vein of interest deeper than what I found in fairy tales: for as to the elves, having sought them in vain among foxglove leaves and bells, under mushrooms and beneath the ground-ivy mantling old wall-nooks, I had at length made up my mind to the sad truth, that they were all gone out of England to some savage country where the woods were wilder and thicker, and the population more scant; whereas, Lilliput and Brobdignag being, in my creed, solid parts of the earth's surface, I doubted not that I might one day, by taking a long voyage, see with my own eyes the little fields, houses, and trees, the diminutive people, the tiny cows, sheep, and birds of the one realm; and the corn-fields forest-high, the mighty mastiffs, the monster cats, the tower-like men and women, of the other. Yet, when this cherished volume was now placed in my hand – when I turned over its leaves, and sought in its marvellous pictures the charm I had, till now, never failed to find – all was eerie and dreary; the giants were gaunt goblins, the pigmies malevolent and fearful imps, Gulliver a most desolate wanderer in most dread and dangerous regions. I closed the book, which I dared no longer peruse, and put it on the table, beside the untasted tart.

Bessie had now finished dusting and tidying the room, and having washed her hands, she opened a certain little drawer, full of splendid shreds of silk and satin, and began making a new bonnet for Georgiana's doll. Meantime she sang: her song was:

> *"In the days when we went gipsying,*
> *A long time ago."*

I had often heard the song before, and always with lively delight; for Bessie had a sweet voice, – at least, I thought so. But now, though her voice was still sweet, I found in its melody an indescribable sadness. Sometimes, preoccupied with her work, she sang the refrain very low, very lingeringly; 'A long time ago' came out like the saddest cadence of a funeral hymn. She passed into another ballad, this time a really doleful one.

> *"My feet they are sore, and my limbs they are weary;*
> *Long is the way, and the mountains are wild;*
> *Soon will the twilight close moonless and dreary*
> *Over the path of the poor orphan child.*
> *Why did they send me so far and so lonely,*
> *Up where the moors spread and grey rocks are piled?*
> *Men are hard-hearted, and kind angels only*
> *Watch o'er the steps of a poor orphan child.*
> *Yet distant and soft the night breeze is blowing,*
> *Clouds there are none, and clear stars beam mild,*
> *God, in His mercy, protection is showing,*
> *Comfort and hope to the poor orphan child.*
> *Ev'n should I fall o'er the broken bridge passing,*

> *Or stray in the marshes, by false lights beguiled,*
> *Still will my Father, with promise and blessing,*
> *Take to His bosom the poor orphan child.*
> *There is a thought that for strength should avail me,*
> *Though both of shelter and kindred despoiled;*
> *Heaven is a home, and a rest will not fail me;*
> *God is a friend to the poor orphan child."*

"Come, Miss Jane, don't cry," said Bessie as she finished. She might as well have said to the fire, "don't burn!" but how could she divine the morbid suffering to which I was a prey? In the course of the morning Mr. Lloyd came again.

"What, already up!" said he, as he entered the nursery. "Well, nurse, how is she?"

Bessie answered that I was doing very well.

"Then she ought to look more cheerful. Come here, Miss Jane: your name is Jane, is it not?"

"Yes, sir, Jane Eyre."

"Well, you have been crying, Miss Jane Eyre; can you tell me what about? Have you any pain?"

"No, sir."

"Oh! I daresay she is crying because she could not go out with Missis in the carriage," interposed Bessie.

"Surely not! Why, she is too old for such pettishness."

I thought so too; and my self-esteem being wounded by the false charge, I answered promptly, "I never cried for such a thing in my life: I hate going out in the carriage. I cry because I am miserable."

"Oh fie, Miss!" said Bessie.

The good apothecary appeared a little puzzled. I was standing before him; he fixed his eyes on me very steadily: his eyes were small and grey; not very bright, but I dare say I should think them shrewd now: he had a hard-featured yet good-natured looking face. Having considered me at leisure, he said:

"What made you ill yesterday?"

"She had a fall," said Bessie, again putting in her word.

"Fall! Why, that is like a baby again! Can't she manage to walk at her age? She must be eight or nine years old."

"I was knocked down," was the blunt explanation, jerked out of me by another pang of mortified pride; "but that did not make me ill," I added; while Mr. Lloyd helped himself to a pinch of snuff.

As he was returning the box to his waistcoat pocket, a loud bell rang for the servants' dinner; he knew what it was. "That's for you, nurse," said he; "you can go down; I'll give Miss Jane a lecture till you come back."

Bessie would rather have stayed, but she was obliged to go, because punctuality at meals was rigidly enforced at Gateshead Hall.

"The fall did not make you ill; what did, then?" pursued Mr. Lloyd when Bessie was gone.

"I was shut up in a room where there is a ghost till after dark."

I saw Mr. Lloyd smile and frown at the same time.

"Ghost! What, you are a baby after all! You are afraid of ghosts?"

"Of Mr. Reed's ghost I am: he died in that room, and was laid out there. Neither Bessie nor anyone else will go into it at night, if they can help it; and it was cruel to shut me up alone without a candle, – so cruel that I think I shall never forget it."

"Nonsense! And is it that makes you so miserable? Are you afraid now in daylight?"

"No: but night will come again before long: and besides, – I am unhappy, – very unhappy, for other things."

"What other things? Can you tell me some of them?"

How much I wished to reply fully to this question! How difficult it was to frame any answer! Children can feel, but they cannot analyse their feelings; and if the analysis is partially effected in thought, they know not how to express the result of the process in words. Fearful, however, of losing this first and only opportunity of relieving my grief by imparting it, I, after a disturbed pause, contrived to frame a meagre, though, as far as it went, true response.

"For one thing, I have no father or mother, brothers or sisters."

"You have a kind aunt and cousins."

Again I paused; then bunglingly enounced:

"But John Reed knocked me down, and my aunt shut me up in the red-room."

Mr. Lloyd a second time produced his snuff-box.

"Don't you think Gateshead Hall a very beautiful house?" asked he. "Are you not very thankful to have such a fine place to live at?"

"It is not my house, sir; and Abbot says I have less right to be here than a servant."

"Pooh! You can't be silly enough to wish to leave such a splendid place?"

"If I had anywhere else to go, I should be glad to leave it; but I can never get away from Gateshead till I am a woman."

"Perhaps you may – who knows? Have you any relations besides Mrs. Reed?"

"I think not, sir."

"None belonging to your father?"

"I don't know. I asked Aunt Reed once, and she said possibly I might have some poor, low relations called Eyre, but she knew nothing about them."

"If you had such, would you like to go to them?"

I reflected. Poverty looks grim to grown people; still more so to children: they have not much idea of industrious, working, respectable poverty; they think of the word only as connected with ragged clothes, scanty food, fireless grates, rude manners, and debasing vices: poverty for me was synonymous with degradation.

"No; I should not like to belong to poor people," was my reply.

"Not even if they were kind to you?"

I shook my head: I could not see how poor people had the means of being kind; and then to learn to speak like them, to adopt their manners, to be uneducated, to grow up like one of the poor women I saw sometimes nursing their children or washing their clothes at the cottage doors of the village of Gateshead: no, I was not heroic enough to purchase liberty at the price of caste.

"But are your relatives so very poor? Are they working people?"

"I cannot tell; Aunt Reed says if I have any, they must be a beggarly set: I should not like to go a begging."

"Would you like to go to school?"

Again I reflected: I scarcely knew what school was: Bessie sometimes spoke of it as a place where young ladies sat in the stocks, wore backboards, and were expected to be exceedingly genteel and precise: John Reed hated his school, and abused his master; but John Reed's tastes were no rule for mine, and if Bessie's accounts of school-discipline (gathered from the young ladies of a family where she had lived before coming to Gateshead) were somewhat appalling, her details of certain accomplishments attained by these same young ladies were, I thought, equally attractive. She boasted of beautiful paintings of landscapes and flowers by them executed; of songs they could sing and pieces they could play, of purses they could net, of French books they could translate; till my spirit was moved to emulation as I listened. Besides, school would be a complete change: it implied a long journey, an entire separation from Gateshead, an entrance into a new life.

"I should indeed like to go to school," was the audible conclusion of my musings.

"Well, well! Who knows what may happen?" said Mr. Lloyd, as he got up. "The child ought to have change of air and scene," he added, speaking to himself; "nerves not in a good state."

Bessie now returned; at the same moment the carriage was heard rolling up the gravel-walk.

"Is that your mistress, nurse?" asked Mr. Lloyd. "I should like to speak to her before I go."

Bessie invited him to walk into the breakfast room, and led the way out. In the interview which followed between him and Mrs. Reed, I presume, from after-occurrences, that the apothecary ventured to recommend my being sent to school; and the recommendation was no doubt readily enough adopted; for as Abbot said, in discussing the subject with Bessie when both sat sewing in the nursery one night, after I was in bed, and, as they thought, asleep, "Missis was, she dared say, glad enough to get rid of such a tiresome, ill-conditioned child, who always looked as if she were watching everybody, and scheming plots underhand." Abbot, I think, gave me credit for being a sort of infantine Guy Fawkes.

On that same occasion I learned, for the first time, from Miss Abbot's communications to Bessie, that my father had been a poor clergyman; that my mother had married him against the wishes of her friends, who considered the match beneath her; that my grandfather Reed was so irritated at her disobedience, he cut her off without a shilling; that after my mother and father had been married a year, the latter caught the typhus fever while visiting among the poor of a large manufacturing town where his curacy was situated, and where that disease was then prevalent: that my mother took the infection from him, and both died within a month of each other.

Bessie, when she heard this narrative, sighed and said, "Poor Miss Jane is to be pitied, too, Abbot."

"Yes," responded Abbot; "if she were a nice, pretty child, one might compassionate her forlornness; but one really cannot care for such a little toad as that."

"Not a great deal, to be sure," agreed Bessie: "at any rate, a beauty like Miss Georgiana would be more moving in the same condition."

"Yes, I doat on Miss Georgiana!" cried the fervent Abbot. "Little darling! – With her long curls and her blue eyes, and such a sweet colour as she has; just as if she were painted! – Bessie, I could fancy a Welsh rabbit for supper."

"So could I – with a roast onion. Come, we'll go down." They went.

Chapter Four

FROM MY DISCOURSE with Mr. Lloyd, and from the above reported conference between Bessie and Abbot, I gathered enough of hope to suffice as a motive for wishing to get well: a change seemed near, – I desired and waited it in silence. It tarried, however: days and weeks passed: I had regained my normal state of health, but no new allusion was made to the subject over which I brooded. Mrs. Reed surveyed me at times with a severe eye, but seldom addressed me: since my illness, she had drawn a more marked line of separation than ever between me and her own children; appointing me a small closet to sleep in by myself, condemning me to take my meals alone, and pass all my time in the nursery, while my cousins were constantly in the drawing room. Not a hint, however, did she drop about sending me to school: still I felt an instinctive certainty that she would not long endure me under the same roof with her; for her glance, now more than ever, when turned on me, expressed an insuperable and rooted aversion.

Eliza and Georgiana, evidently acting according to orders, spoke to me as little as possible: John thrust his tongue in his cheek whenever he saw me, and once attempted chastisement; but as I instantly turned against him, roused by the same sentiment of deep ire and desperate revolt which had stirred my corruption before, he thought it better to desist, and ran from me tittering execrations, and vowing I had burst his nose. I had indeed levelled at that prominent feature as hard a blow as my knuckles could inflict; and when I saw that either that or my look daunted him, I had the greatest inclination to follow up my advantage to purpose; but he was already with his mama. I heard him in a blubbering tone commence the tale of how "that nasty Jane Eyre" had flown at him like a mad cat: he was stopped rather harshly:

"Don't talk to me about her, John: I told you not to go near her; she is not worthy of notice; I do not choose that either you or your sisters should associate with her."

Here, leaning over the banister, I cried out suddenly, and without at all deliberating on my words:

"They are not fit to associate with me."

Mrs. Reed was rather a stout woman; but, on hearing this strange and audacious declaration, she ran nimbly up the stair, swept me like a whirlwind into the nursery, and crushing me down on the edge of my crib, dared me in an emphatic voice to rise from that place, or utter one syllable during the remainder of the day.

"What would Uncle Reed say to you, if he were alive?" was my scarcely voluntary demand. I say scarcely voluntary, for it seemed as if my tongue pronounced words without my will consenting to their utterance: something spoke out of me over which I had no control.

"What?" said Mrs. Reed under her breath: her usually cold composed grey eye became troubled with a look like fear; she took her hand from my arm, and gazed at me as if she really did not know whether I were child or fiend. I was now in for it.

"My Uncle Reed is in heaven, and can see all you do and think; and so can papa and mama: they know how you shut me up all day long, and how you wish me dead."

Mrs. Reed soon rallied her spirits: she shook me most soundly, she boxed both my ears, and then left me without a word. Bessie supplied the hiatus by a homily of an hour's length, in which she proved beyond a doubt that I was the most wicked and abandoned child ever reared under a roof. I half believed her; for I felt indeed only bad feelings surging in my breast.

November, December, and half of January passed away. Christmas and the New Year had been celebrated at Gateshead with the usual festive cheer; presents had been interchanged, dinners and evening parties given. From every enjoyment I was, of course, excluded: my share of the gaiety consisted in witnessing the daily apparelling of Eliza and Georgiana, and seeing them descend to the drawing room, dressed out in thin muslin frocks and scarlet sashes, with hair elaborately ringletted; and afterwards, in listening to the sound of the piano or the harp played below, to the passing to and fro of the butler and footman, to the jingling of glass and china as refreshments were handed, to the broken hum of conversation as the drawing room door opened and closed. When tired of this occupation, I would retire from the stairhead to the solitary and silent nursery: there, though somewhat sad, I was not miserable.

To speak truth, I had not the least wish to go into company, for in company I was very rarely noticed; and if Bessie had but been kind and companionable, I should have deemed it a treat to spend the evenings quietly with her, instead of passing them under the formidable eye of Mrs. Reed, in a room full of ladies and gentlemen. But Bessie, as soon as she had dressed her young ladies, used to take herself off to the lively regions of the kitchen and housekeeper's room, generally bearing the candle along with her. I then sat with my doll on my knee till the fire got low, glancing round occasionally to make sure that nothing worse than myself haunted the shadowy room; and when the embers sank to a dull red, I undressed hastily, tugging at knots and strings as I best might, and sought shelter from cold and darkness in my crib. To this crib I always took my doll; human beings must love something, and, in the dearth of worthier objects of affection, I contrived to find a pleasure in loving and cherishing a faded graven image, shabby as a miniature scarecrow. It puzzles me now to remember with what absurd sincerity I doated on this little toy, half fancying it alive and capable of sensation. I could not sleep unless it was folded in my night-gown; and when it lay there safe and warm, I was comparatively happy, believing it to be happy likewise.

Long did the hours seem while I waited the departure of the company, and listened for the sound of Bessie's step on the stairs: sometimes she would come up in the interval to seek her thimble or her scissors, or perhaps to bring me something by way of supper – a bun or a cheese-cake – then she would sit on the bed while I ate it, and when I had finished, she would tuck the clothes round me, and twice she kissed me, and said, "Goodnight, Miss Jane." When thus gentle, Bessie seemed to me the best, prettiest, kindest being in the world; and I wished most intensely that she would always be so pleasant and amiable, and never push me about, or scold, or task me unreasonably, as she was too often wont to do. Bessie Lee must, I think, have been a girl of good natural capacity, for she was smart in all she did, and had a remarkable knack of narrative; so, at least, I judge from the impression made on me by her nursery tales. She was pretty too, if my recollections of her face and person are correct. I remember her as a slim young woman, with black hair, dark eyes, very nice features, and good, clear complexion; but she had a capricious and hasty temper, and indifferent ideas of principle or justice: still, such as she was, I preferred her to anyone else at Gateshead Hall.

It was the fifteenth of January, about nine o'clock in the morning: Bessie was gone down to breakfast; my cousins had not yet been summoned to their mama; Eliza was putting on her bonnet and warm garden-coat to go and feed her poultry, an occupation of which she was fond: and not less so of selling the eggs to the housekeeper and hoarding up the money she thus obtained. She had a turn for traffic, and a marked propensity for saving; shown not only in the vending of eggs and chickens, but also in driving hard bargains with the gardener about flower-roots, seeds, and slips of plants; that functionary having orders from Mrs. Reed to buy of his young lady all the products of her parterre she wished to sell: and Eliza would have sold the hair off her head if she could have made a handsome profit thereby. As to her money, she first secreted it in odd corners, wrapped in a rag or an old curl-paper; but some of these hoards having been discovered by the housemaid, Eliza, fearful of one day losing her valued treasure, consented to intrust it to her mother, at a usurious rate of interest – fifty or sixty per cent; which interest she exacted every quarter, keeping her accounts in a little book with anxious accuracy.

Georgiana sat on a high stool, dressing her hair at the glass, and interweaving her curls with artificial flowers and faded feathers, of which she had found a store in a drawer in the attic. I was making my bed, having received strict orders from Bessie to get it arranged before she returned (for Bessie now frequently employed me as a sort of under nursery-maid, to tidy the room, dust the chairs, etc.). Having spread the quilt and folded my night-dress, I went to the window seat to put in order some picture-books and doll's house furniture scattered there; an abrupt command from Georgiana to let her playthings alone (for the tiny chairs and mirrors, the fairy plates and cups, were her property) stopped my proceedings; and then, for lack of other occupation, I fell to breathing on the frost-flowers with which the window was fretted, and thus clearing a space in the glass through which I might look out on the grounds, where all was still and petrified under the influence of a hard frost.

From this window were visible the porter's lodge and the carriage-road, and just as I had dissolved so much of the silver-white foliage veiling the panes as left room to look out, I saw the gates thrown open and a carriage roll through. I watched it ascending the drive with indifference; carriages often came to Gateshead, but none ever brought visitors in whom I was interested; it stopped in front of the house, the doorbell rang loudly, the newcomer was admitted. All this being nothing to me, my vacant attention soon found livelier attraction in the spectacle of a little hungry robin, which came and chirruped on the twigs of the leafless cherry-tree nailed against the wall near the casement. The remains of my breakfast of bread and milk stood on the table, and having crumbled a morsel of roll, I was tugging at the sash to put out the crumbs on the window-sill, when Bessie came running upstairs into the nursery.

"Miss Jane, take off your pinafore; what are you doing there? Have you washed your hands and face this morning?" I gave another tug before I answered, for I wanted the bird to be secure of its bread: the sash yielded; I scattered the crumbs, some on the stone sill, some on the cherry-tree bough, then, closing the window, I replied:

"No, Bessie; I have only just finished dusting."

"Troublesome, careless child! And what are you doing now? You look quite red, as if you had been about some mischief: what were you opening the window for?"

I was spared the trouble of answering, for Bessie seemed in too great a hurry to listen to explanations; she hauled me to the washstand, inflicted a merciless, but happily brief scrub on my face and hands with soap, water, and a coarse towel; disciplined my head with a bristly brush, denuded me of my pinafore, and then hurrying me to the top of the stairs, bid me go down directly, as I was wanted in the breakfast room.

I would have asked who wanted me: I would have demanded if Mrs. Reed was there; but Bessie was already gone, and had closed the nursery-door upon me. I slowly descended. For nearly three months, I had never been called to Mrs. Reed's presence; restricted so long to the nursery, the breakfast, dining, and drawing rooms were become for me awful regions, on which it dismayed me to intrude.

I now stood in the empty hall; before me was the breakfast room door, and I stopped, intimidated and trembling. What a miserable little poltroon had fear, engendered of unjust punishment, made of me in those days! I feared to return to the nursery, and feared to go forward to the parlour; ten minutes I stood in agitated hesitation; the vehement ringing of the breakfast room bell decided me; I *must* enter.

"Who could want me?" I asked inwardly, as with both hands I turned the stiff door-handle, which, for a second or two, resisted my efforts. "What should I see besides Aunt Reed in the apartment? – A man or a woman?" The handle turned, the door unclosed, and passing through and curtseying low, I looked up at – a black pillar! – such, at least, appeared to me, at first sight, the straight, narrow, sable-clad shape standing erect on the rug: the grim face at the top was like a carved mask, placed above the shaft by way of capital.

Mrs. Reed occupied her usual seat by the fireside; she made a signal to me to approach; I did so, and she introduced me to the stony stranger with the words: "This is the little girl respecting whom I applied to you."

He, for it was a man, turned his head slowly towards where I stood, and having examined me with the two inquisitive-looking grey eyes which twinkled under a pair of bushy brows, said solemnly, and in a bass voice, "Her size is small: what is her age?"

"Ten years."

"So much?" was the doubtful answer; and he prolonged his scrutiny for some minutes. Presently he addressed me – "Your name, little girl?"

"Jane Eyre, sir."

In uttering these words I looked up: he seemed to me a tall gentleman; but then I was very little; his features were large, and they and all the lines of his frame were equally harsh and prim.

"Well, Jane Eyre, and are you a good child?"

Impossible to reply to this in the affirmative: my little world held a contrary opinion: I was silent. Mrs. Reed answered for me by an expressive shake of the head, adding soon, "Perhaps the less said on that subject the better, Mr. Brocklehurst."

"Sorry indeed to hear it! She and I must have some talk;" and bending from the perpendicular, he installed his person in the armchair opposite Mrs. Reed's. "Come here," he said.

I stepped across the rug; he placed me square and straight before him. What a face he had, now that it was almost on a level with mine! What a great nose! And what a mouth! And what large prominent teeth!

"No sight so sad as that of a naughty child," he began, "especially a naughty little girl. Do you know where the wicked go after death?"

"They go to hell," was my ready and orthodox answer.

"And what is hell? Can you tell me that?"

"A pit full of fire."

"And should you like to fall into that pit, and to be burning there for ever?"

"No, sir."

"What must you do to avoid it?"

I deliberated a moment; my answer, when it did come, was objectionable: "I must keep in good health, and not die."

"How can you keep in good health? Children younger than you die daily. I buried a little child of five years old only a day or two since, – a good little child, whose soul is now in heaven. It is to be feared the same could not be said of you were you to be called hence."

Not being in a condition to remove his doubt, I only cast my eyes down on the two large feet planted on the rug, and sighed, wishing myself far enough away.

"I hope that sigh is from the heart, and that you repent of ever having been the occasion of discomfort to your excellent benefactress."

"Benefactress! Benefactress!" said I inwardly: "they all call Mrs. Reed my benefactress; if so, a benefactress is a disagreeable thing."

"Do you say your prayers night and morning?" continued my interrogator.

"Yes, sir."

"Do you read your Bible?"

"Sometimes."

"With pleasure? Are you fond of it?"

"I like Revelations, and the book of Daniel, and Genesis and Samuel, and a little bit of Exodus, and some parts of Kings and Chronicles, and Job and Jonah."

"And the Psalms? I hope you like them?"

"No, sir."

"No? Oh, shocking! I have a little boy, younger than you, who knows six Psalms by heart: and when you ask him which he would rather have, a gingerbread-nut to eat or a verse of a Psalm to learn, he says: 'Oh! The verse of a Psalm! Angels sing Psalms;' says he, 'I wish to be a little angel here below;' he then gets two nuts in recompense for his infant piety."

"Psalms are not interesting," I remarked.

"That proves you have a wicked heart; and you must pray to God to change it: to give you a new and clean one: to take away your heart of stone and give you a heart of flesh."

I was about to propound a question, touching the manner in which that operation of changing my heart was to be performed, when Mrs. Reed interposed, telling me to sit down; she then proceeded to carry on the conversation herself.

"Mr. Brocklehurst, I believe I intimated in the letter which I wrote to you three weeks ago, that this little girl has not quite the character and disposition I could wish: should you admit her into Lowood school, I should be glad if the superintendent and teachers were requested to keep a strict eye on her, and, above all, to guard against her worst fault, a tendency to deceit. I mention this in your hearing, Jane, that you may not attempt to impose on Mr. Brocklehurst."

Well might I dread, well might I dislike Mrs. Reed; for it was her nature to wound me cruelly; never was I happy in her presence; however carefully I obeyed, however strenuously I strove to please her, my efforts were still repulsed and repaid by such sentences as the above. Now, uttered before a stranger, the accusation cut me to the heart; I dimly perceived that she was already obliterating hope from the new phase of existence which she destined me to enter; I felt, though I could not have expressed the feeling, that she was sowing aversion and unkindness along my future path; I saw myself transformed under Mr. Brocklehurst's eye into an artful, noxious child, and what could I do to remedy the injury?

"Nothing, indeed," thought I, as I struggled to repress a sob, and hastily wiped away some tears, the impotent evidences of my anguish.

"Deceit is, indeed, a sad fault in a child," said Mr. Brocklehurst; "it is akin to falsehood, and all liars will have their portion in the lake burning with fire and brimstone; she shall, however, be watched, Mrs. Reed. I will speak to Miss Temple and the teachers."

"I should wish her to be brought up in a manner suiting her prospects," continued my benefactress; "to be made useful, to be kept humble: as for the vacations, she will, with your permission, spend them always at Lowood."

"Your decisions are perfectly judicious, madam," returned Mr. Brocklehurst. "Humility is a Christian grace, and one peculiarly appropriate to the pupils of Lowood; I, therefore, direct that especial care shall be bestowed on its cultivation amongst them. I have studied how best to mortify in them the worldly sentiment of pride; and, only the other day, I had a pleasing proof of my success. My second daughter, Augusta, went with her mama to visit the school, and on her return she exclaimed: 'Oh, dear papa, how quiet and plain all the girls at Lowood look, with their hair combed behind their ears, and their long pinafores, and those little holland pockets outside their frocks – they are almost like poor people's children! and,' said she, 'they looked at my dress and mama's, as if they had never seen a silk gown before.'"

"This is the state of things I quite approve," returned Mrs. Reed; "had I sought all England over, I could scarcely have found a system more exactly fitting a child like Jane Eyre. Consistency, my dear Mr. Brocklehurst; I advocate consistency in all things."

"Consistency, madam, is the first of Christian duties; and it has been observed in every arrangement connected with the establishment of Lowood: plain fare, simple attire, unsophisticated accommodations, hardy and active habits; such is the order of the day in the house and its inhabitants."

"Quite right, sir. I may then depend upon this child being received as a pupil at Lowood, and there being trained in conformity to her position and prospects?"

"Madam, you may: she shall be placed in that nursery of chosen plants, and I trust she will show herself grateful for the inestimable privilege of her election."

"I will send her, then, as soon as possible, Mr. Brocklehurst; for, I assure you, I feel anxious to be relieved of a responsibility that was becoming too irksome."

"No doubt, no doubt, madam; and now I wish you good morning. I shall return to Brocklehurst Hall in the course of a week or two: my good friend, the Archdeacon, will not permit me to leave him sooner. I shall send Miss Temple notice that she is to expect a new girl, so that there will be no difficulty about receiving her. Goodbye."

"Goodbye, Mr. Brocklehurst; remember me to Mrs. and Miss Brocklehurst, and to Augusta and Theodore, and Master Broughton Brocklehurst."

"I will, madam. Little girl, here is a book entitled the *Child's Guide*, read it with prayer, especially that part containing 'An account of the awfully sudden death of Martha G—, a naughty child addicted to falsehood and deceit.'"

With these words Mr. Brocklehurst put into my hand a thin pamphlet sewn in a cover, and having rung for his carriage, he departed.

Mrs. Reed and I were left alone: some minutes passed in silence; she was sewing, I was watching her. Mrs. Reed might be at that time some six or seven and thirty; she was a woman of robust frame, square-shouldered and strong-limbed, not tall, and, though stout, not obese: she had a somewhat large face, the under jaw being much developed and very solid; her brow was low, her chin large and prominent, mouth and nose sufficiently regular; under her light eyebrows glimmered an eye devoid of ruth; her skin was dark and opaque, her hair nearly flaxen; her constitution was sound as a bell – illness never came near her; she was an exact, clever manager; her household and tenantry were thoroughly under her control; her children only at times defied her authority and laughed it to scorn; she dressed well, and had a presence and port calculated to set off handsome attire.

Sitting on a low stool, a few yards from her armchair, I examined her figure; I perused her features. In my hand I held the tract containing the sudden death of the Liar, to which narrative my attention had been pointed as to an appropriate warning. What had just passed; what Mrs. Reed had said concerning me to Mr. Brocklehurst; the whole tenor of their conversation, was recent, raw, and stinging in my mind; I had felt every word as acutely as I had heard it plainly, and a passion of resentment fomented now within me.

Mrs. Reed looked up from her work; her eye settled on mine, her fingers at the same time suspended their nimble movements.

"Go out of the room; return to the nursery," was her mandate. My look or something else must have struck her as offensive, for she spoke with extreme though suppressed irritation. I got up, I went to the door; I came back again; I walked to the window, across the room, then close up to her.

Speak I must: I had been trodden on severely, and *must* turn: but how? What strength had I to dart retaliation at my antagonist? I gathered my energies and launched them in this blunt sentence:

"I am not deceitful: if I were, I should say I loved you; but I declare I do not love you: I dislike you the worst of anybody in the world except John Reed; and this book about the liar, you may give to your girl, Georgiana, for it is she who tells lies, and not I."

Mrs. Reed's hands still lay on her work inactive: her eye of ice continued to dwell freezingly on mine.

"What more have you to say?" she asked, rather in the tone in which a person might address an opponent of adult age than such as is ordinarily used to a child.

That eye of hers, that voice stirred every antipathy I had. Shaking from head to foot, thrilled with ungovernable excitement, I continued:

"I am glad you are no relation of mine: I will never call you aunt again as long as I live. I will never come to see you when I am grown up; and if anyone asks me how I liked you, and how you treated me, I will say the very thought of you makes me sick, and that you treated me with miserable cruelty."

"How dare you affirm that, Jane Eyre?"

"How dare I, Mrs. Reed? How dare I? Because it is the *truth*. You think I have no feelings, and that I can do without one bit of love or kindness; but I cannot live so: and you have no pity. I shall remember how you thrust me back – roughly and violently thrust me back – into the red-room, and locked me up there, to my dying day; though I was in agony; though I cried out, while suffocating with distress, 'Have mercy! Have mercy, Aunt Reed!' And that punishment you made me suffer because your wicked boy struck me – knocked me down for nothing. I will tell anybody who asks me questions, this exact tale. People think you a good woman, but you are bad, hard-hearted. *You* are deceitful!"

Ere I had finished this reply, my soul began to expand, to exult, with the strangest sense of freedom, of triumph, I ever felt. It seemed as if an invisible bond had burst, and that I had struggled out into unhoped-for liberty. Not without cause was this sentiment: Mrs. Reed looked frightened; her work had slipped from her knee; she was lifting up her hands, rocking herself to and fro, and even twisting her face as if she would cry.

"Jane, you are under a mistake: what is the matter with you? Why do you tremble so violently? Would you like to drink some water?"

"No, Mrs. Reed."

"Is there anything else you wish for, Jane? I assure you, I desire to be your friend."

"Not you. You told Mr. Brocklehurst I had a bad character, a deceitful disposition; and I'll let everybody at Lowood know what you are, and what you have done."

"Jane, you don't understand these things: children must be corrected for their faults."

"Deceit is not my fault!" I cried out in a savage, high voice.

"But you are passionate, Jane, that you must allow: and now return to the nursery – there's a dear – and lie down a little."

"I am not your dear; I cannot lie down: send me to school soon, Mrs. Reed, for I hate to live here."

"I will indeed send her to school soon," murmured Mrs. Reed *sotto voce*; and gathering up her work, she abruptly quitted the apartment.

I was left there alone – winner of the field. It was the hardest battle I had fought, and the first victory I had gained: I stood awhile on the rug, where Mr. Brocklehurst had stood, and I enjoyed my conqueror's solitude. First, I smiled to myself and felt elate; but this fierce pleasure subsided in me as fast as did the accelerated throb of my pulses. A child cannot quarrel with its elders, as I had done; cannot give its furious feelings uncontrolled play, as I had given mine, without experiencing afterwards the pang of remorse and the chill of reaction. A ridge of lighted heath, alive, glancing, devouring, would have been a meet emblem of my mind when I accused and menaced Mrs. Reed: the same ridge, black and blasted after the flames are dead, would have represented as meetly my subsequent condition, when half an hour's silence and reflection had shown me the madness of my conduct, and the dreariness of my hated and hating position.

Something of vengeance I had tasted for the first time; as aromatic wine it seemed, on swallowing, warm and racy: its after-flavour, metallic and corroding, gave me a sensation as if I had been poisoned. Willingly would I now have gone and asked Mrs. Reed's pardon; but I knew, partly from experience and partly from instinct, that was the way to make her repulse me with double scorn, thereby re-exciting every turbulent impulse of my nature.

I would fain exercise some better faculty than that of fierce speaking; fain find nourishment for some less fiendish feeling than that of sombre indignation. I took a book – some Arabian tales; I sat down and endeavoured to read. I could make no sense of the subject; my own thoughts swam always between me and the page I had usually found fascinating. I opened the glass-door in the breakfast room: the shrubbery was quite still: the black frost reigned, unbroken by sun or breeze, through the grounds. I covered my head and arms with the skirt of my frock, and went out to walk in a part of the plantation which was quite sequestrated; but I found no pleasure in the silent trees, the falling fir-cones, the congealed relics of autumn, russet leaves, swept by past winds in heaps, and now stiffened together. I leaned against a gate, and looked into an empty field where no sheep were feeding, where the short grass was nipped and blanched. It was a very grey day; a most opaque sky, 'onding on snaw', [1] canopied all; thence flakes felt it intervals, which settled on the hard path and on the hoary lea without melting. I stood, a wretched child enough, whispering to myself over and over again, "What shall I do? – What shall I do?"

All at once I heard a clear voice call, "Miss Jane! Where are you? Come to lunch!"

It was Bessie, I knew well enough; but I did not stir; her light step came tripping down the path.

"You naughty little thing!" she said. "Why don't you come when you are called?"

Bessie's presence, compared with the thoughts over which I had been brooding, seemed cheerful; even though, as usual, she was somewhat cross. The fact is, after my conflict with and victory over Mrs. Reed, I was not disposed to care much for the nursemaid's transitory anger; and I *was* disposed to bask in her youthful lightness of heart. I just put my two arms round her and said, "Come, Bessie! Don't scold."

The action was more frank and fearless than any I was habituated to indulge in: somehow it pleased her.

"You are a strange child, Miss Jane," she said, as she looked down at me; "a little roving, solitary thing: and you are going to school, I suppose?"

I nodded.

"And won't you be sorry to leave poor Bessie?"

"What does Bessie care for me? She is always scolding me."

"Because you're such a queer, frightened, shy little thing. You should be bolder."

"What! To get more knocks?"

"Nonsense! But you are rather put upon, that's certain. My mother said, when she came to see me last week, that she would not like a little one of her own to be in your place. – Now, come in, and I've some good news for you."

"I don't think you have, Bessie."

"Child! What do you mean? What sorrowful eyes you fix on me! Well, but Missis and the young ladies and Master John are going out to tea this afternoon, and you shall have tea with me. I'll ask cook to bake you a little cake, and then you shall help me to look over your drawers; for I am soon to pack your trunk. Missis intends you to leave Gateshead in a day or two, and you shall choose what toys you like to take with you."

"Bessie, you must promise not to scold me any more till I go."

"Well, I will; but mind you are a very good girl, and don't be afraid of me. Don't start when I chance to speak rather sharply; it's so provoking."

"I don't think I shall ever be afraid of you again, Bessie, because I have got used to you, and I shall soon have another set of people to dread."

"If you dread them they'll dislike you."

"As you do, Bessie?"

"I don't dislike you, Miss; I believe I am fonder of you than of all the others."

"You don't show it."

"You little sharp thing! You've got quite a new way of talking. What makes you so venturesome and hardy?"

"Why, I shall soon be away from you, and besides" – I was going to say something about what had passed between me and Mrs. Reed, but on second thoughts I considered it better to remain silent on that head.

"And so you're glad to leave me?"

"Not at all, Bessie; indeed, just now I'm rather sorry."

"Just now! And rather! How coolly my little lady says it! I dare say now if I were to ask you for a kiss you wouldn't give it me: you'd say you'd *rather* not."

"I'll kiss you and welcome: bend your head down." Bessie stooped; we mutually embraced, and I followed her into the house quite comforted. That afternoon lapsed in peace and harmony; and in the evening Bessie told me some of her most enchanting stories, and sang me some of her sweetest songs. Even for me life had its gleams of sunshine.

Chapter Five

FIVE O'CLOCK had hardly struck on the morning of the 19th of January, when Bessie brought a candle into my closet and found me already up and nearly dressed. I had risen half an hour before her entrance, and had washed my face, and put on my clothes by the light of a half-moon just setting, whose rays streamed through the narrow window near my crib. I was to leave Gateshead that day by a coach which passed the lodge gates at six a.m. Bessie was the only person yet risen; she had lit a fire in the nursery, where she now proceeded to make my breakfast. Few children can eat when excited with the thoughts of a journey; nor could I. Bessie, having pressed me in vain to take a few spoonfuls of the boiled milk and bread she had prepared for me, wrapped up some biscuits in a paper and put them into my bag; then she helped me on with my pelisse and bonnet, and wrapping herself in a shawl, she and I left the nursery. As we passed Mrs. Reed's bedroom, she said, "Will you go in and bid Missis goodbye?"

"No, Bessie: she came to my crib last night when you were gone down to supper, and said I need not disturb her in the morning, or my cousins either; and she told me to remember that she had always been my best friend, and to speak of her and be grateful to her accordingly."

"What did you say, Miss?"

"Nothing: I covered my face with the bedclothes, and turned from her to the wall."

"That was wrong, Miss Jane."

"It was quite right, Bessie. Your Missis has not been my friend: she has been my foe."

"O Miss Jane! Don't say so!"

"Goodbye to Gateshead!" cried I, as we passed through the hall and went out at the front door.

The moon was set, and it was very dark; Bessie carried a lantern, whose light glanced on wet steps and gravel road sodden by a recent thaw. Raw and chill was the winter morning: my teeth chattered as I hastened down the drive. There was a light in the porter's lodge: when we reached it, we found the porter's wife just kindling her fire: my trunk, which had been carried down the evening before, stood corded at the door. It wanted but a few minutes of six, and shortly after that hour had struck, the distant roll of wheels announced the coming coach; I went to the door and watched its lamps approach rapidly through the gloom.

"Is she going by herself?" asked the porter's wife.

"Yes."

"And how far is it?"

"Fifty miles."

"What a long way! I wonder Mrs. Reed is not afraid to trust her so far alone."

The coach drew up; there it was at the gates with its four horses and its top laden with passengers: the guard and coachman loudly urged haste; my trunk was hoisted up; I was taken from Bessie's neck, to which I clung with kisses.

"Be sure and take good care of her," cried she to the guard, as he lifted me into the inside.

"Ay, ay!" was the answer: the door was slapped to, a voice exclaimed "All right," and on we drove. Thus was I severed from Bessie and Gateshead; thus whirled away to unknown, and, as I then deemed, remote and mysterious regions.

I remember but little of the journey; I only know that the day seemed to me of a preternatural length, and that we appeared to travel over hundreds of miles of road. We passed through several towns, and in one, a very large one, the coach stopped; the horses were taken out, and the passengers alighted to dine. I was carried into an inn, where the guard wanted me to have some dinner; but, as I had no appetite, he left me in an immense room with a fireplace at each end, a chandelier pendent from the ceiling, and a little red gallery high up against the wall filled with musical instruments. Here I walked about for a long time, feeling very strange, and mortally apprehensive of some one coming in and kidnapping me; for I believed in kidnappers, their exploits having frequently figured in Bessie's fireside chronicles. At last the guard returned; once more I was stowed away in the coach, my protector mounted his own seat, sounded his hollow horn, and away we rattled over the 'stony street' [2] of L—.

The afternoon came on wet and somewhat misty: as it waned into dusk, I began to feel that we were getting very far indeed from Gateshead: we ceased to pass through towns; the country changed; great grey hills heaved up round the horizon: as twilight deepened, we descended a valley, dark with wood, and long after night had overclouded the prospect, I heard a wild wind rushing amongst trees.

Lulled by the sound, I at last dropped asleep; I had not long slumbered when the sudden cessation of motion awoke me; the coach-door was open, and a person like a servant was standing at it: I saw her face and dress by the light of the lamps.

"Is there a little girl called Jane Eyre here?" she asked. I answered "Yes," and was then lifted out; my trunk was handed down, and the coach instantly drove away.

I was stiff with long sitting, and bewildered with the noise and motion of the coach: Gathering my faculties, I looked about me. Rain, wind, and darkness filled the air; nevertheless, I dimly discerned a wall before me and a door open in it; through this door I passed with my new guide: she shut and locked it behind her. There was now visible a house or houses – for the building spread far – with many windows, and lights burning in some; we went up a broad pebbly path, splashing wet, and were admitted at a door; then the servant led me through a passage into a room with a fire, where she left me alone.

I stood and warmed my numbed fingers over the blaze, then I looked round; there was no candle, but the uncertain light from the hearth showed, by intervals, papered walls, carpet, curtains, shining mahogany furniture: it was a parlour, not so spacious or splendid as the drawing room at Gateshead, but comfortable enough. I was puzzling to make out the subject of a picture on the wall, when the door opened, and an individual carrying a light entered; another followed close behind.

The first was a tall lady with dark hair, dark eyes, and a pale and large forehead; her figure was partly enveloped in a shawl, her countenance was grave, her bearing erect.

"The child is very young to be sent alone," said she, putting her candle down on the table. She considered me attentively for a minute or two, then further added:

"She had better be put to bed soon; she looks tired: are you tired?" she asked, placing her hand on my shoulder.

"A little, ma'am."

"And hungry too, no doubt: let her have some supper before she goes to bed, Miss Miller. Is this the first time you have left your parents to come to school, my little girl?"

I explained to her that I had no parents. She inquired how long they had been dead: then how old I was, what was my name, whether I could read, write, and sew a little: then she touched my cheek gently with her forefinger, and saying, "She hoped I should be a good child," dismissed me along with Miss Miller.

The lady I had left might be about twenty-nine; the one who went with me appeared some years younger: the first impressed me by her voice, look, and air. Miss Miller was more ordinary; ruddy in complexion, though of a careworn countenance; hurried in gait and action, like one who had always a multiplicity of tasks on hand: she looked, indeed, what I afterwards found she really was, an under-teacher. Led by her, I passed from compartment to compartment, from passage to passage, of a large and irregular building; till, emerging from the total and somewhat dreary silence pervading that portion of the house we had traversed, we came upon the hum of many voices, and presently entered a wide, long room, with great deal tables, two at each end, on each of which burnt a pair of candles, and seated all round on benches, a congregation of girls of every age, from nine or ten to twenty. Seen by the dim light of the dips, their number to me appeared countless, though not in reality exceeding eighty; they were uniformly dressed in brown stuff frocks of quaint fashion, and long holland pinafores. It was the hour of study; they were engaged in conning over their tomorrow's task, and the hum I had heard was the combined result of their whispered repetitions.

Miss Miller signed to me to sit on a bench near the door, then walking up to the top of the long room she cried out:

"Monitors, collect the lesson-books and put them away!"

Four tall girls arose from different tables, and going round, gathered the books and removed them. Miss Miller again gave the word of command:

"Monitors, fetch the supper-trays!"

The tall girls went out and returned presently, each bearing a tray, with portions of something, I knew not what, arranged thereon, and a pitcher of water and mug in the middle of each tray. The portions were handed round; those who liked took a draught of the water, the mug being common to all. When it came to my turn, I drank, for I was thirsty, but did not touch the food, excitement and fatigue rendering me incapable of eating: I now saw, however, that it was a thin oaten cake shared into fragments.

The meal over, prayers were read by Miss Miller, and the classes filed off, two and two, upstairs. Overpowered by this time with weariness, I scarcely noticed what sort of a place the bedroom was, except that, like the schoolroom, I saw it was very long. Tonight I was to be Miss Miller's bed-fellow; she helped me to undress: when laid down I glanced at the long rows of beds, each of which was quickly filled with two occupants; in ten minutes the single light was extinguished, and amidst silence and complete darkness I fell asleep.

The night passed rapidly. I was too tired even to dream; I only once awoke to hear the wind rave in furious gusts, and the rain fall in torrents, and to be sensible that Miss Miller had taken her place by my side. When I again unclosed my eyes, a loud bell was ringing; the girls were up and dressing; day had not yet begun to dawn, and a rushlight or two burned in the room. I too rose reluctantly; it was bitter cold, and I dressed as well as I could for shivering, and washed when there was a basin at liberty, which did not occur soon, as there was but one basin to six girls, on the stands down the middle of the room. Again the bell rang: all formed in file, two and two, and in that order descended the stairs and entered the cold and dimly lit schoolroom: here prayers were read by Miss Miller; afterwards she called out:

"Form classes!"

A great tumult succeeded for some minutes, during which Miss Miller repeatedly exclaimed, "Silence!" and "Order!" When it subsided, I saw them all drawn up in four semicircles, before four chairs, placed at the four tables; all held books in their hands, and a great book, like a Bible, lay on each table, before the vacant seat. A pause of some seconds succeeded, filled up by the low, vague hum of numbers; Miss Miller walked from class to class, hushing this indefinite sound.

A distant bell tinkled: immediately three ladies entered the room, each walked to a table and took her seat. Miss Miller assumed the fourth vacant chair, which was that nearest the door, and around which the smallest of the children were assembled: to this inferior class I was called, and placed at the bottom of it.

Business now began, the day's Collect was repeated, then certain texts of Scripture were said, and to these succeeded a protracted reading of chapters in the Bible, which lasted an hour. By the time that exercise was terminated, day had fully dawned. The indefatigable bell now sounded for the fourth time: the classes were marshalled and marched into another room to breakfast: how glad I was to behold a prospect of getting something to eat! I was now nearly sick from inanition, having taken so little the day before.

The refectory was a great, low-ceiled, gloomy room; on two long tables smoked basins of something hot, which, however, to my dismay, sent forth an odour far from inviting. I saw a universal manifestation of discontent when the fumes of the repast met the nostrils of those destined to swallow it; from the van of the procession, the tall girls of the first class, rose the whispered words:

"Disgusting! The porridge is burnt again!"

"Silence!" ejaculated a voice; not that of Miss Miller, but one of the upper teachers, a little and dark personage, smartly dressed, but of somewhat morose aspect, who installed herself at the top of one table, while a more buxom lady presided at the other. I looked in vain for her I had first seen the night before; she was not visible: Miss Miller occupied the foot of the table where I sat, and a strange, foreign-looking, elderly lady, the French teacher, as I afterwards found, took the corresponding seat at the other board. A long grace was said and a hymn sung; then a servant brought in some tea for the teachers, and the meal began.

Ravenous, and now very faint, I devoured a spoonful or two of my portion without thinking of its taste; but the first edge of hunger blunted, I perceived I had got in hand a nauseous mess; burnt porridge is almost as bad as rotten potatoes; famine itself soon sickens over it. The spoons were moved slowly: I saw each girl taste her food and try to swallow it; but in most cases the effort was soon relinquished. Breakfast was over, and none had breakfasted. Thanks being returned for what we had not got, and a second hymn chanted, the refectory was evacuated for the schoolroom. I was one of the last to go out, and in passing the tables, I saw one teacher take a basin of the porridge and taste it; she looked at the others; all their countenances expressed displeasure, and one of them, the stout one, whispered:

"Abominable stuff! How shameful!"

A quarter of an hour passed before lessons again began, during which the schoolroom was in a glorious tumult; for that space of time it seemed to be permitted to talk loud and more freely, and they used their privilege. The whole conversation ran on the breakfast, which one and all abused roundly. Poor things! It was the sole consolation they had. Miss Miller was now the only teacher in the room: a group of great girls standing about her spoke with serious and sullen gestures. I heard the name of Mr. Brocklehurst pronounced by some lips; at which Miss Miller shook her head disapprovingly; but she made no great effort to check the general wrath; doubtless she shared in it.

A clock in the schoolroom struck nine; Miss Miller left her circle, and standing in the middle of the room, cried:

"Silence! To your seats!"

Discipline prevailed: in five minutes the confused throng was resolved into order, and comparative silence quelled the Babel clamour of tongues. The upper teachers now punctually resumed their posts: but still, all seemed to wait. Ranged on benches down the sides of the room, the eighty girls sat motionless and erect; a quaint assemblage they appeared, all with plain locks combed from their faces, not a curl visible; in brown dresses, made high and surrounded by a narrow tucker about the throat, with little pockets of holland (shaped something like a Highlander's purse) tied in front of their frocks, and destined to serve the purpose of a work-bag: all, too, wearing woollen stockings and country-made shoes, fastened with brass buckles. Above twenty of those clad in this costume were full-grown girls, or rather young women; it suited them ill, and gave an air of oddity even to the prettiest.

I was still looking at them, and also at intervals examining the teachers – none of whom precisely pleased me; for the stout one was a little coarse, the dark one not a little fierce, the foreigner harsh and grotesque, and Miss Miller, poor thing!, looked purple, weather-beaten, and over-worked – when, as my eye wandered from face to face, the whole school rose simultaneously, as if moved by a common spring.

What was the matter? I had heard no order given: I was puzzled. Ere I had gathered my wits, the classes were again seated: but as all eyes were now turned to one point, mine followed the general direction, and encountered the personage who had received me last night. She stood at the bottom of the long room, on the hearth; for there was a fire at each end; she surveyed the two rows of girls silently and gravely. Miss Miller approaching, seemed to ask her a question, and having received her answer, went back to her place, and said aloud:

"Monitor of the first class, fetch the globes!"

While the direction was being executed, the lady consulted moved slowly up the room. I suppose I have a considerable organ of veneration, for I retain yet the sense of admiring awe with which my eyes traced her steps. Seen now, in broad daylight, she looked tall, fair, and shapely; brown eyes with a benignant light in their irids, [3] and a fine pencilling of long lashes round, relieved the whiteness of her large front; on each of her temples her hair, of a very dark brown, was clustered in round curls, according to the fashion of those times, when neither smooth bands nor long ringlets were in vogue; her dress, also in the mode of the day, was of purple cloth, relieved by a sort of Spanish trimming of black velvet; a gold watch (watches were not so common then as now) shone at her girdle. Let the reader add, to complete the picture, refined features; a complexion, if pale, clear; and a stately air and carriage, and he will have, at least, as clearly as words can give it, a correct idea of the exterior of Miss Temple – Maria Temple, as I afterwards saw the name written in a prayer book intrusted to me to carry to church.

The superintendent of Lowood (for such was this lady) having taken her seat before a pair of globes placed on one of the tables, summoned the first class round her, and commenced giving a lesson on geography; the lower classes were called by the teachers: repetitions in history, grammar, etc., went on for an hour; writing and arithmetic succeeded, and music lessons were given by Miss Temple to some of the elder girls. The duration of each lesson was measured by the clock, which at last struck twelve. The superintendent rose:

"I have a word to address to the pupils," said she.

The tumult of cessation from lessons was already breaking forth, but it sank at her voice. She went on:

"You had this morning a breakfast which you could not eat; you must be hungry: I have ordered that a lunch of bread and cheese shall be served to all."

The teachers looked at her with a sort of surprise.

"It is to be done on my responsibility," she added, in an explanatory tone to them, and immediately afterwards left the room.

The bread and cheese was presently brought in and distributed, to the high delight and refreshment of the whole school. The order was now given "To the garden!" Each put on a coarse straw bonnet, with strings of coloured calico, and a cloak of grey frieze. I was similarly equipped, and, following the stream, I made my way into the open air.

The garden was a wide enclosure, surrounded with walls so high as to exclude every glimpse of prospect; a covered verandah ran down one side, and broad walks bordered a middle space divided into scores of little beds: these beds were assigned as gardens for the pupils to cultivate, and each bed had an owner. When full of flowers they would doubtless look pretty; but now, at the latter end of January, all was wintry blight and brown decay. I shuddered as I stood and looked round me: it was an inclement day for outdoor exercise; not positively rainy, but darkened by a drizzling yellow fog; all under foot was still soaking wet with the floods of yesterday. The stronger among the girls ran about and engaged in active games, but sundry pale and thin ones herded together for shelter and warmth in the verandah; and amongst these, as the dense mist penetrated to their shivering frames, I heard frequently the sound of a hollow cough.

As yet I had spoken to no one, nor did anybody seem to take notice of me; I stood lonely enough: but to that feeling of isolation I was accustomed; it did not oppress me much. I leant against a pillar of the verandah, drew my grey mantle close about me, and, trying to forget the cold which nipped me without, and the unsatisfied hunger which gnawed me within, delivered myself up to the employment of watching and thinking. My reflections were too undefined and fragmentary to merit record: I hardly yet knew where I was; Gateshead and my past life seemed floated away to an immeasurable distance; the present was vague and strange, and of the future I could form no conjecture. I looked round the convent-like garden, and then up at the house – a large building, half of which seemed grey and old, the other half quite new. The new part, containing the schoolroom and dormitory, was lit by mullioned and latticed windows, which gave it a church-like aspect; a stone tablet over the door bore this inscription:

Lowood Institution. – This portion was rebuilt A.D. —, by Naomi Brocklehurst, of Brocklehurst Hall, in this county.
'Let your light so shine before men, that they may see your good works, and glorify your Father which is in heaven.' – St. Matt. v. 16.

I read these words over and over again: I felt that an explanation belonged to them, and was unable fully to penetrate their import. I was still pondering the signification of 'Institution', and endeavouring to make out a connection between the first words and the verse of Scripture, when the sound of a cough close behind me made me turn my head. I saw a girl sitting on a stone bench near; she was bent over a book, on the perusal of which she seemed intent: from where I stood I could see the title – it was *Rasselas*; a name that struck me as strange, and consequently attractive. In turning a leaf she happened to look up, and I said to her directly:

"Is your book interesting?" I had already formed the intention of asking her to lend it to me some day.

"I like it," she answered, after a pause of a second or two, during which she examined me.

"What is it about?" I continued. I hardly know where I found the hardihood thus to open a conversation with a stranger; the step was contrary to my nature and habits: but I think her occupation touched a chord of sympathy somewhere; for I too liked reading, though of a frivolous and childish kind; I could not digest or comprehend the serious or substantial.

"You may look at it," replied the girl, offering me the book.

I did so; a brief examination convinced me that the contents were less taking than the title: *Rasselas* looked dull to my trifling taste; I saw nothing about fairies, nothing about genii; no bright variety seemed spread over the closely-printed pages. I returned it to her; she received it quietly, and without saying anything she was about to relapse into her former studious mood: again I ventured to disturb her:

"Can you tell me what the writing on that stone over the door means? What is Lowood Institution?"

"This house where you are come to live."

"And why do they call it Institution? Is it in any way different from other schools?"

"It is partly a charity-school: you and I, and all the rest of us, are charity-children. I suppose you are an orphan: are not either your father or your mother dead?"

"Both died before I can remember."

"Well, all the girls here have lost either one or both parents, and this is called an institution for educating orphans."

"Do we pay no money? Do they keep us for nothing?"

"We pay, or our friends pay, fifteen pounds a year for each."

"Then why do they call us charity-children?"

"Because fifteen pounds is not enough for board and teaching, and the deficiency is supplied by subscription."

"Who subscribes?"

"Different benevolent-minded ladies and gentlemen in this neighbourhood and in London."

"Who was Naomi Brocklehurst?"

"The lady who built the new part of this house as that tablet records, and whose son overlooks and directs everything here."

"Why?"

"Because he is treasurer and manager of the establishment."

"Then this house does not belong to that tall lady who wears a watch, and who said we were to have some bread and cheese?"

"To Miss Temple? Oh, no! I wish it did: she has to answer to Mr. Brocklehurst for all she does. Mr. Brocklehurst buys all our food and all our clothes."

"Does he live here?"

"No – two miles off, at a large hall."

"Is he a good man?"

"He is a clergyman, and is said to do a great deal of good."

"Did you say that tall lady was called Miss Temple?"

"Yes."

"And what are the other teachers called?"

"The one with red cheeks is called Miss Smith; she attends to the work, and cuts out – for we make our own clothes, our frocks, and pelisses, and everything; the little one with black hair is Miss Scatcherd; she teaches history and grammar, and hears the second class repetitions; and the one who wears a shawl, and has a pocket-handkerchief tied to her side with a yellow ribband, is Madame Pierrot: she comes from Lisle, in France, and teaches French."

"Do you like the teachers?"

"Well enough."

"Do you like the little black one, and the Madame —? – I cannot pronounce her name as you do."

"Miss Scatcherd is hasty – you must take care not to offend her; Madame Pierrot is not a bad sort of person."

"But Miss Temple is the best – isn't she?"

"Miss Temple is very good and very clever; she is above the rest, because she knows far more than they do."

"Have you been long here?"

"Two years."

"Are you an orphan?"

"My mother is dead."

"Are you happy here?"

"You ask rather too many questions. I have given you answers enough for the present: now I want to read."

But at that moment the summons sounded for dinner; all re-entered the house. The odour which now filled the refectory was scarcely more appetising than that which had regaled our nostrils at breakfast: the dinner was served in two huge tin-plated vessels, whence rose a strong steam redolent of rancid fat. I found the mess to consist of indifferent potatoes and strange shreds of rusty meat, mixed and cooked together. Of this preparation a tolerably abundant plateful was apportioned to each pupil. I ate what I could, and wondered within myself whether every day's fare would be like this.

After dinner, we immediately adjourned to the schoolroom: lessons recommenced, and were continued till five o'clock.

The only marked event of the afternoon was, that I saw the girl with whom I had conversed in the verandah dismissed in disgrace by Miss Scatcherd from a history class, and sent to stand in the middle of the large schoolroom. The punishment seemed to me in a high degree ignominious, especially for so great a girl – she looked thirteen or upwards. I expected she would show signs of great distress and shame; but to my surprise she neither wept nor blushed: composed, though grave, she stood, the central mark of all eyes. "How can she bear it so quietly – so firmly?" I asked of myself. "Were I in her place, it seems to me I should wish the earth to open and swallow me up. She looks as if she were thinking of something beyond her punishment – beyond her situation: of something not round her nor before her. I have heard of daydreams – is she in a daydream now? Her eyes are fixed on the floor, but I am sure they do not see it – her sight seems turned in, gone down into her heart: she is looking at what she can remember, I believe; not at what is really present. I wonder what sort of a girl she is – whether good or naughty."

Soon after five p.m. we had another meal, consisting of a small mug of coffee, and half-a-slice of brown bread. I devoured my bread and drank my coffee with relish; but I should have been glad of as much more – I was still hungry. Half an hour's recreation succeeded, then study; then the glass of water and the piece of oat-cake, prayers, and bed. Such was my first day at Lowood.

Chapter Six

THE NEXT DAY commenced as before, getting up and dressing by rushlight; but this morning we were obliged to dispense with the ceremony of washing; the water in the pitchers was frozen. A change had taken place in the weather the preceding evening, and a keen north-east wind, whistling through the crevices of our bedroom windows all night long, had made us shiver in our beds, and turned the contents of the ewers to ice.

Before the long hour and a half of prayers and Bible-reading was over, I felt ready to perish with cold. Breakfast-time came at last, and this morning the porridge was not burnt; the quality was eatable, the quantity small. How small my portion seemed! I wished it had been doubled.

In the course of the day I was enrolled a member of the fourth class, and regular tasks and occupations were assigned me: hitherto, I had only been a spectator of the proceedings at Lowood; I was now to become an actor therein. At first, being little accustomed to learn by heart, the lessons appeared to me both long and difficult; the frequent change from task to task, too, bewildered me; and I was glad when, about three o'clock in the afternoon, Miss Smith put into my hands a border of muslin two yards long, together with needle, thimble, etc., and sent me to sit in a quiet corner of the schoolroom, with directions to hem the same. At that hour most of the others were sewing likewise; but one class still stood round Miss Scatcherd's chair reading, and as all was quiet, the subject of their lessons could be heard, together with the manner in which each girl acquitted herself, and the animadversions or commendations of Miss Scatcherd on the performance. It was English history: among the readers I observed my acquaintance of the verandah: at the commencement of the lesson, her place had been at the top of the class, but for some error of pronunciation, or some inattention to stops, she was suddenly sent to the very bottom. Even in that obscure position, Miss Scatcherd continued to make her an object of constant notice: she was continually addressing to her such phrases as the following:

"Burns" (such it seems was her name: the girls here were all called by their surnames, as boys are elsewhere), "Burns, you are standing on the side of your shoe; turn your toes out immediately." "Burns, you poke your chin most unpleasantly; draw it in." "Burns, I insist on your holding your head up; I will not have you before me in that attitude," etc. etc.

A chapter having been read through twice, the books were closed and the girls examined. The lesson had comprised part of the reign of Charles I, and there were sundry questions about tonnage and poundage and ship-money, which most of them appeared unable to answer; still, every little difficulty was solved instantly when it reached Burns: her memory seemed to have retained the substance of the whole lesson, and she was ready with answers on every point. I kept expecting that Miss Scatcherd would praise her attention; but, instead of that, she suddenly cried out:

"You dirty, disagreeable girl! You have never cleaned your nails this morning!"

Burns made no answer: I wondered at her silence. "Why," thought I, "does she not explain that she could neither clean her nails nor wash her face, as the water was frozen?"

My attention was now called off by Miss Smith desiring me to hold a skein of thread: while she was winding it, she talked to me from time to time, asking whether I had ever been at school before, whether I could mark, stitch, knit, etc.; till she dismissed me, I could not pursue my observations on Miss Scatcherd's movements. When I returned to my seat, that lady was just delivering an order of which I did not catch the import; but Burns immediately left the class, and going into the small inner room where the books were kept, returned in half a minute, carrying in her hand a bundle of twigs tied together at one end. This ominous tool she presented to Miss Scatcherd with a respectful curtesy; then she quietly, and without being told, unloosed her pinafore, and the teacher instantly and sharply inflicted on her neck a dozen strokes with the bunch of twigs. Not a tear rose to Burns' eye; and, while I paused from my sewing, because my fingers quivered at this spectacle with a sentiment of unavailing and impotent anger, not a feature of her pensive face altered its ordinary expression.

"Hardened girl!" exclaimed Miss Scatcherd; "nothing can correct you of your slatternly habits: carry the rod away."

Burns obeyed: I looked at her narrowly as she emerged from the book-closet; she was just putting back her handkerchief into her pocket, and the trace of a tear glistened on her thin cheek.

The play-hour in the evening I thought the pleasantest fraction of the day at Lowood: the bit of bread, the draught of coffee swallowed at five o'clock had revived vitality, if it had not satisfied hunger: the long restraint of the day was slackened; the schoolroom felt warmer than in the morning – its fires being allowed to burn a little more brightly, to supply, in some measure, the place of candles, not yet introduced: the ruddy gloaming, the licensed uproar, the confusion of many voices gave one a welcome sense of liberty.

On the evening of the day on which I had seen Miss Scatcherd flog her pupil, Burns, I wandered as usual among the forms and tables and laughing groups without a companion, yet not feeling lonely: when I passed the windows, I now and then lifted a blind, and looked out; it snowed fast, a drift was already forming against the lower panes; putting my ear close to the window, I could distinguish from the gleeful tumult within, the disconsolate moan of the wind outside.

Probably, if I had lately left a good home and kind parents, this would have been the hour when I should most keenly have regretted the separation; that wind would then have saddened my heart; this obscure chaos would have disturbed my peace! As it was, I derived from both a strange excitement, and reckless and feverish, I wished the wind to howl more wildly, the gloom to deepen to darkness, and the confusion to rise to clamour.

Jumping over forms, and creeping under tables, I made my way to one of the fire-places; there, kneeling by the high wire fender, I found Burns, absorbed, silent, abstracted from all round her by the companionship of a book, which she read by the dim glare of the embers.

"Is it still *Rasselas*?" I asked, coming behind her.

"Yes," she said, "and I have just finished it."

And in five minutes more she shut it up. I was glad of this. "Now," thought I, "I can perhaps get her to talk." I sat down by her on the floor.

"What is your name besides Burns?"

"Helen."

"Do you come a long way from here?"

"I come from a place farther north, quite on the borders of Scotland."

"Will you ever go back?"

"I hope so; but nobody can be sure of the future."

"You must wish to leave Lowood?"

"No! Why should I? I was sent to Lowood to get an education; and it would be of no use going away until I have attained that object."

"But that teacher, Miss Scatcherd, is so cruel to you?"

"Cruel? Not at all! She is severe: she dislikes my faults."

"And if I were in your place I should dislike her; I should resist her. If she struck me with that rod, I should get it from her hand; I should break it under her nose."

"Probably you would do nothing of the sort: but if you did, Mr. Brocklehurst would expel you from the school; that would be a great grief to your relations. It is far better to endure patiently a smart which nobody feels but yourself, than to commit a hasty action whose evil consequences will extend to all connected with you; and besides, the Bible bids us return good for evil."

"But then it seems disgraceful to be flogged, and to be sent to stand in the middle of a room full of people; and you are such a great girl: I am far younger than you, and I could not bear it."

"Yet it would be your duty to bear it, if you could not avoid it: it is weak and silly to say you *cannot bear* what it is your fate to be required to bear."

I heard her with wonder: I could not comprehend this doctrine of endurance; and still less could I understand or sympathise with the forbearance she expressed for her chastiser. Still I felt that Helen Burns considered things by a light invisible to my eyes. I suspected she might be right and I wrong; but I would not ponder the matter deeply; like Felix, I put it off to a more convenient season.

"You say you have faults, Helen: what are they? To me you seem very good."

"Then learn from me, not to judge by appearances: I am, as Miss Scatcherd said, slatternly; I seldom put, and never keep, things, in order; I am careless; I forget rules; I read when I should learn my lessons; I have no method; and sometimes I say, like you, I cannot *bear* to be subjected to systematic arrangements. This is all very provoking to Miss Scatcherd, who is naturally neat, punctual, and particular."

"And cross and cruel," I added; but Helen Burns would not admit my addition: she kept silence.

"Is Miss Temple as severe to you as Miss Scatcherd?"

At the utterance of Miss Temple's name, a soft smile flitted over her grave face.

"Miss Temple is full of goodness; it pains her to be severe to anyone, even the worst in the school: she sees my errors, and tells me of them gently; and, if I do anything worthy of praise, she gives me my meed liberally. One strong proof of my wretchedly defective nature is, that even her expostulations, so mild, so rational, have not influence to cure me of my faults; and even her praise, though I value it most highly, cannot stimulate me to continued care and foresight."

"That is curious," said I, "it is so easy to be careful."

"For *you* I have no doubt it is. I observed you in your class this morning, and saw you were closely attentive: your thoughts never seemed to wander while Miss Miller explained the lesson and questioned you. Now, mine continually rove away; when I should be listening to Miss Scatcherd, and collecting all she says with assiduity, often I lose the very sound of her voice; I fall into a sort of dream. Sometimes I think I am in Northumberland, and that the noises I hear round me are the bubbling of a little brook which runs through Deepden, near our house; – then, when it comes to my turn to reply, I have to be awakened; and having heard nothing of what was read for listening to the visionary brook, I have no answer ready."

"Yet how well you replied this afternoon."

"It was mere chance; the subject on which we had been reading had interested me. This afternoon, instead of dreaming of Deepden, I was wondering how a man who wished to do right could act so unjustly and unwisely as Charles the First sometimes did; and I thought what a pity it was that, with his integrity and conscientiousness, he could see no farther than the prerogatives of the crown. If he had but been able to look to a distance, and see how what they call the spirit of the age was tending! Still, I like Charles – I respect him – I pity him, poor murdered king! Yes, his enemies were the worst: they shed blood they had no right to shed. How dared they kill him!"

Helen was talking to herself now: she had forgotten I could not very well understand her – that I was ignorant, or nearly so, of the subject she discussed. I recalled her to my level.

"And when Miss Temple teaches you, do your thoughts wander then?"

"No, certainly, not often; because Miss Temple has generally something to say which is newer than my own reflections; her language is singularly agreeable to me, and the information she communicates is often just what I wished to gain."

"Well, then, with Miss Temple you are good?"

"Yes, in a passive way: I make no effort; I follow as inclination guides me. There is no merit in such goodness."

"A great deal: you are good to those who are good to you. It is all I ever desire to be. If people were always kind and obedient to those who are cruel and unjust, the wicked people would have it all their own way: they would never feel afraid, and so they would never alter, but would grow worse and worse. When we are struck at without a reason, we should strike back again very hard; I am sure we should – so hard as to teach the person who struck us never to do it again."

"You will change your mind, I hope, when you grow older: as yet you are but a little untaught girl."

"But I feel this, Helen; I must dislike those who, whatever I do to please them, persist in disliking me; I must resist those who punish me unjustly. It is as natural as that I should love those who show me affection, or submit to punishment when I feel it is deserved."

"Heathens and savage tribes hold that doctrine, but Christians and civilised nations disown it."

"How? I don't understand."

"It is not violence that best overcomes hate – nor vengeance that most certainly heals injury."

"What then?"

"Read the New Testament, and observe what Christ says, and how He acts; make His word your rule, and His conduct your example."

"What does He say?"

"Love your enemies; bless them that curse you; do good to them that hate you and despitefully use you."

"Then I should love Mrs. Reed, which I cannot do; I should bless her son John, which is impossible."

In her turn, Helen Burns asked me to explain, and I proceeded forthwith to pour out, in my own way, the tale of my sufferings and resentments. Bitter and truculent when excited, I spoke as I felt, without reserve or softening.

Helen heard me patiently to the end: I expected she would then make a remark, but she said nothing.

"Well," I asked impatiently, "is not Mrs. Reed a hard-hearted, bad woman?"

"She has been unkind to you, no doubt; because you see, she dislikes your cast of character, as Miss Scatcherd does mine; but how minutely you remember all she has done and said to you! What a singularly deep impression her injustice seems to have made on your heart! No ill-usage so brands its record on my feelings. Would you not be happier if you tried to forget her severity, together with the passionate emotions it excited? Life appears to me too short to be spent in nursing animosity or registering wrongs. We are, and must be, one and all, burdened with faults in this world: but the time will soon come when, I trust, we shall put them off in putting off our corruptible bodies; when debasement and sin will fall from us with this cumbrous frame of flesh, and only the spark of the spirit will remain, – the impalpable principle of light and thought, pure as when it left the Creator to inspire the creature: whence it came it will return; perhaps again to be communicated to some being higher than man – perhaps to pass through gradations of glory, from the pale human soul to brighten to the seraph! Surely it will never, on the contrary, be suffered to degenerate from man to fiend? No; I cannot believe that: I hold another creed: which no one ever taught me, and which I seldom mention; but in which I delight, and to which I cling: for it extends hope to all: it makes Eternity a rest – a mighty home, not a terror and an abyss. Besides, with this creed, I can so clearly distinguish between the criminal and his crime; I can so sincerely forgive the first while I abhor the last: with this creed revenge never worries my heart, degradation never too deeply disgusts me, injustice never crushes me too low: I live in calm, looking to the end."

Helen's head, always drooping, sank a little lower as she finished this sentence. I saw by her look she wished no longer to talk to me, but rather to converse with her own thoughts. She was not allowed much time for meditation: a monitor, a great rough girl, presently came up, exclaiming in a strong Cumberland accent:

"Helen Burns, if you don't go and put your drawer in order, and fold up your work this minute, I'll tell Miss Scatcherd to come and look at it!"

Helen sighed as her reverie fled, and getting up, obeyed the monitor without reply as without delay.

Chapter Seven

MY FIRST QUARTER at Lowood seemed an age; and not the golden age either; it comprised an irksome struggle with difficulties in habituating myself to new rules and unwonted tasks. The fear of failure in these points harassed me worse than the physical hardships of my lot; though these were no trifles.

During January, February, and part of March, the deep snows, and, after their melting, the almost impassable roads, prevented our stirring beyond the garden walls, except to go to church; but within these limits we had to pass an hour every day in the open air. Our clothing was insufficient to protect us from the severe cold: we had no boots, the snow got into our shoes and melted there: our ungloved hands became numbed and covered with chilblains, as were our feet: I remember well the distracting irritation I endured from this cause every evening, when my feet inflamed; and the torture of thrusting the swelled, raw, and stiff toes into my shoes in the morning. Then the scanty supply of food was distressing: with the keen appetites of growing children, we had scarcely sufficient to keep alive a delicate invalid. From this deficiency of nourishment resulted an abuse, which pressed hardly on the younger pupils: whenever the famished great girls had an opportunity, they would coax or menace the little ones out of their portion. Many a time I have shared between two claimants the precious morsel of brown bread distributed at tea time; and after relinquishing to a third half the contents of my mug of coffee, I have swallowed the remainder with an accompaniment of secret tears, forced from me by the exigency of hunger.

Sundays were dreary days in that wintry season. We had to walk two miles to Brocklebridge Church, where our patron officiated. We set out cold, we arrived at church colder: during the morning service we became almost paralysed. It was too far to return to dinner, and an allowance of cold meat and bread, in the same penurious proportion observed in our ordinary meals, was served round between the services.

At the close of the afternoon service we returned by an exposed and hilly road, where the bitter winter wind, blowing over a range of snowy summits to the north, almost flayed the skin from our faces.

I can remember Miss Temple walking lightly and rapidly along our drooping line, her plaid cloak, which the frosty wind fluttered, gathered close about her, and encouraging us, by precept and example, to keep up our spirits, and march forward, as she said, "like stalwart soldiers." The other teachers, poor things, were generally themselves too much dejected to attempt the task of cheering others.

How we longed for the light and heat of a blazing fire when we got back! But, to the little ones at least, this was denied: each hearth in the schoolroom was immediately surrounded by a double row of great girls, and behind them the younger children crouched in groups, wrapping their starved arms in their pinafores.

A little solace came at tea time, in the shape of a double ration of bread – a whole, instead of a half, slice – with the delicious addition of a thin scrape of butter: it was the hebdomadal treat to which we all looked forward from Sabbath to Sabbath. I generally contrived to reserve a moiety of this bounteous repast for myself; but the remainder I was invariably obliged to part with.

The Sunday evening was spent in repeating, by heart, the Church Catechism, and the fifth, sixth, and seventh chapters of St. Matthew; and in listening to a long sermon, read by Miss Miller, whose irrepressible yawns attested her weariness. A frequent interlude of these performances was the enactment of the part of Eutychus by some half-dozen little girls, who, overpowered with sleep, would fall down, if not out of the third loft, yet off the fourth form, and be taken up half dead. The remedy was, to thrust them forward into the centre of the schoolroom, and oblige them to stand there till the sermon was finished. Sometimes their feet failed them, and they sank together in a heap; they were then propped up with the monitors' high stools.

I have not yet alluded to the visits of Mr. Brocklehurst; and indeed that gentleman was from home during the greater part of the first month after my arrival; perhaps prolonging his stay with his friend the archdeacon: his absence was a relief to me. I need not say that I had my own reasons for dreading his coming: but come he did at last.

One afternoon (I had then been three weeks at Lowood), as I was sitting with a slate in my hand, puzzling over a sum in long division, my eyes, raised in abstraction to the window, caught sight of a figure just passing: I recognised almost instinctively that gaunt outline; and when, two minutes after, all the school, teachers included, rose *en masse*, it was not necessary for me to look up in order to ascertain whose entrance they thus greeted. A long stride measured the schoolroom, and presently beside Miss Temple, who herself had risen, stood the same black column which had frowned on me so ominously from the hearthrug of Gateshead. I now glanced sideways at this piece of architecture. Yes, I was right: it was Mr. Brocklehurst, buttoned up in a surtout, and looking longer, narrower, and more rigid than ever.

I had my own reasons for being dismayed at this apparition; too well I remembered the perfidious hints given by Mrs. Reed about my disposition, etc.; the promise pledged by Mr. Brocklehurst to apprise Miss Temple and the teachers of my vicious nature. All along I had been dreading the fulfilment of this promise, – I had been looking out daily for the 'Coming Man', whose information respecting my past life and conversation was to brand me as a bad child for ever: now there he was.

He stood at Miss Temple's side; he was speaking low in her ear: I did not doubt he was making disclosures of my villainy; and I watched her eye with painful anxiety, expecting every moment to see its dark orb turn on me a glance of repugnance and contempt. I listened too; and as I happened to be seated quite at the top of the room, I caught most of what he said: its import relieved me from immediate apprehension.

"I suppose, Miss Temple, the thread I bought at Lowton will do; it struck me that it would be just of the quality for the calico chemises, and I sorted the needles to match. You may tell Miss Smith that I forgot to make a memorandum of the darning needles, but she shall have some papers sent in next week; and she is not, on any account, to give out more than one at a time to each pupil: if they have more, they are apt to be careless and lose them. And, O ma'am! I wish the woollen stockings were better looked to! – when I was here last, I went into the kitchen-garden and examined the clothes drying on the line; there was a quantity of black hose in a very bad state of repair: from the size of the holes in them I was sure they had not been well mended from time to time."

He paused.

"Your directions shall be attended to, sir," said Miss Temple.

"And, ma'am," he continued, "the laundress tells me some of the girls have two clean tuckers in the week: it is too much; the rules limit them to one."

"I think I can explain that circumstance, sir. Agnes and Catherine Johnstone were invited to take tea with some friends at Lowton last Thursday, and I gave them leave to put on clean tuckers for the occasion."

Mr. Brocklehurst nodded.

"Well, for once it may pass; but please not to let the circumstance occur too often. And there is another thing which surprised me; I find, in settling accounts with the housekeeper, that a lunch, consisting of bread and cheese, has twice been served out to the girls during the past fortnight. How is this? I looked over the regulations, and I find no such meal as lunch mentioned. Who introduced this innovation? And by what authority?"

"I must be responsible for the circumstance, sir," replied Miss Temple: "the breakfast was so ill prepared that the pupils could not possibly eat it; and I dared not allow them to remain fasting till dinner-time."

"Madam, allow me an instant. You are aware that my plan in bringing up these girls is, not to accustom them to habits of luxury and indulgence, but to render them hardy, patient, self-denying. Should any little accidental disappointment of the appetite occur, such as the spoiling of a meal, the under or the over dressing of a dish, the incident ought not to be neutralised by replacing with something more delicate the comfort lost, thus pampering the body and obviating the aim of this institution; it ought to be improved to the spiritual edification of the pupils, by encouraging them to evince fortitude under temporary privation. A brief address on those occasions would not be mistimed, wherein a judicious instructor would take the opportunity of referring to the sufferings of the primitive Christians; to the torments of martyrs; to the exhortations of our blessed Lord Himself, calling upon His disciples to take up their cross and follow Him; to His warnings that man shall not live by bread alone, but by every word that proceedeth out of the mouth of God; to His divine consolations, 'If ye suffer hunger or thirst for My sake, happy are ye.' Oh, madam, when you put bread and cheese, instead of burnt porridge, into these children's mouths, you may indeed feed their vile bodies, but you little think how you starve their immortal souls!"

Mr. Brocklehurst again paused – perhaps overcome by his feelings. Miss Temple had looked down when he first began to speak to her; but she now gazed straight before her, and her face, naturally pale as marble, appeared to be assuming also the coldness and fixity of that material; especially her mouth, closed as if it would have required a sculptor's chisel to open it, and her brow settled gradually into petrified severity.

Meantime, Mr. Brocklehurst, standing on the hearth with his hands behind his back, majestically surveyed the whole school. Suddenly his eye gave a blink, as if it had met something that either dazzled or shocked its pupil; turning, he said in more rapid accents than he had hitherto used:

"Miss Temple, Miss Temple, what – *what* is that girl with curled hair? Red hair, ma'am, curled – curled all over?" And extending his cane he pointed to the awful object, his hand shaking as he did so.

"It is Julia Severn," replied Miss Temple, very quietly.

"Julia Severn, ma'am! And why has she, or any other, curled hair? Why, in defiance of every precept and principle of this house, does she conform to the world so openly – here in an evangelical, charitable establishment – as to wear her hair one mass of curls?"

"Julia's hair curls naturally," returned Miss Temple, still more quietly.

"Naturally! Yes, but we are not to conform to nature; I wish these girls to be the children of Grace: and why that abundance? I have again and again intimated that I desire the hair to be arranged closely, modestly, plainly. Miss Temple, that girl's hair must be cut off entirely; I will send a barber tomorrow: and I see others who have far too much of the excrescence – that tall girl, tell her to turn round. Tell all the first form to rise up and direct their faces to the wall."

Miss Temple passed her handkerchief over her lips, as if to smooth away the involuntary smile that curled them; she gave the order, however, and when the first class could take in what was required of them, they obeyed. Leaning a little back on my bench, I could see the looks and grimaces with which they commented on this manoeuvre: it was a pity Mr. Brocklehurst could not see them too; he would perhaps have felt that, whatever he might do with the outside of the cup and platter, the inside was further beyond his interference than he imagined.

He scrutinised the reverse of these living medals some five minutes, then pronounced sentence. These words fell like the knell of doom:

"All those top-knots must be cut off."

Miss Temple seemed to remonstrate.

"Madam," he pursued, "I have a Master to serve whose kingdom is not of this world: my mission is to mortify in these girls the lusts of the flesh; to teach them to clothe themselves with shame-facedness and sobriety, not with braided hair and costly apparel; and each of the young persons before us has a string of hair twisted in plaits which vanity itself might have woven; these, I repeat, must be cut off; think of the time wasted, of –"

Mr. Brocklehurst was here interrupted: three other visitors, ladies, now entered the room. They ought to have come a little sooner to have heard his lecture on dress, for they were splendidly attired in velvet, silk, and furs. The two younger of the trio (fine girls of sixteen and seventeen) had grey beaver hats, then in fashion, shaded with ostrich plumes, and from under the brim of this graceful head-dress fell a profusion of light tresses, elaborately curled; the elder lady was enveloped in a costly velvet shawl, trimmed with ermine, and she wore a false front of French curls.

These ladies were deferentially received by Miss Temple, as Mrs. and the Misses Brocklehurst, and conducted to seats of honour at the top of the room. It seems they had come in the carriage with their reverend relative, and had been conducting a rummaging scrutiny of the room upstairs, while he transacted business with the housekeeper, questioned the laundress, and lectured the superintendent. They now proceeded to address divers remarks and reproofs to Miss Smith, who was charged with the care of the linen and the inspection of the dormitories: but I had no time to listen to what they said; other matters called off and enchanted my attention.

Hitherto, while gathering up the discourse of Mr. Brocklehurst and Miss Temple, I had not, at the same time, neglected precautions to secure my personal safety; which I thought would be effected, if I could only elude observation. To this end, I had sat well back on the form, and while seeming to be busy with my sum, had held my slate in such a manner as to conceal my face: I might have escaped notice, had not my treacherous slate somehow happened to slip from my hand, and falling with an obtrusive crash, directly drawn every eye upon me; I knew it was all over now, and, as I stooped to pick up the two fragments of slate, I rallied my forces for the worst. It came.

"A careless girl!" said Mr. Brocklehurst, and immediately after – "It is the new pupil, I perceive." And before I could draw breath, "I must not forget I have a word to say respecting her." Then aloud: how loud it seemed to me! "Let the child who broke her slate come forward!"

Of my own accord I could not have stirred; I was paralysed: but the two great girls who sit on each side of me, set me on my legs and pushed me towards the dread judge, and then Miss Temple gently assisted me to his very feet, and I caught her whispered counsel:

"Don't be afraid, Jane, I saw it was an accident; you shall not be punished."

The kind whisper went to my heart like a dagger.

"Another minute, and she will despise me for a hypocrite," thought I; and an impulse of fury against Reed, Brocklehurst, and Co. bounded in my pulses at the conviction. I was no Helen Burns.

"Fetch that stool," said Mr. Brocklehurst, pointing to a very high one from which a monitor had just risen: it was brought.

"Place the child upon it."

And I was placed there, by whom I don't know: I was in no condition to note particulars; I was only aware that they had hoisted me up to the height of Mr. Brocklehurst's nose, that he was within a yard of me, and that a spread of shot orange and purple silk pelisses and a cloud of silvery plumage extended and waved below me.

Mr. Brocklehurst hemmed.

"Ladies," said he, turning to his family, "Miss Temple, teachers, and children, you all see this girl?"

Of course they did; for I felt their eyes directed like burning-glasses against my scorched skin.

"You see she is yet young; you observe she possesses the ordinary form of childhood; God has graciously given her the shape that He has given to all of us; no signal deformity points her out as a marked character. Who would think that the Evil One had already found a servant and agent in her? Yet such, I grieve to say, is the case."

A pause – in which I began to steady the palsy of my nerves, and to feel that the Rubicon was passed; and that the trial, no longer to be shirked, must be firmly sustained.

"My dear children," pursued the black marble clergyman, with pathos, "this is a sad, a melancholy occasion; for it becomes my duty to warn you, that this girl, who might be one of God's own lambs, is a little castaway: not a member of the true flock, but evidently an interloper and an alien. You must be on your guard against her; you must shun her example; if necessary, avoid her company, exclude her from your sports, and shut her out from your converse. Teachers, you must watch her: keep your eyes on her movements, weigh well her words, scrutinise her actions, punish her body to save her soul: if, indeed, such salvation be possible, for (my tongue falters while I tell it) this girl, this child, the native of a Christian land, worse than many a little heathen who says its prayers to Brahma and kneels before Juggernaut – this girl is – a liar!"

Now came a pause of ten minutes, during which I, by this time in perfect possession of my wits, observed all the female Brocklehursts produce their pocket-handkerchiefs and apply them to their optics, while the elderly lady swayed herself to and fro, and the two younger ones whispered, "How shocking!" Mr. Brocklehurst resumed.

"This I learned from her benefactress; from the pious and charitable lady who adopted her in her orphan state, reared her as her own daughter, and whose kindness, whose generosity the unhappy girl repaid by an ingratitude so bad, so dreadful, that at last her excellent patroness was obliged to separate her from her own young ones, fearful lest her vicious example should contaminate their purity: she has sent her here to be healed, even as the Jews of old sent their diseased to the troubled pool of Bethesda; and, teachers, superintendent, I beg of you not to allow the waters to stagnate round her."

With this sublime conclusion, Mr. Brocklehurst adjusted the top button of his surtout, muttered something to his family, who rose, bowed to Miss Temple, and then all the great people sailed in state from the room. Turning at the door, my judge said:

"Let her stand half an hour longer on that stool, and let no one speak to her during the remainder of the day."

There was I, then, mounted aloft; I, who had said I could not bear the shame of standing on my natural feet in the middle of the room, was now exposed to general view on a pedestal of infamy. What my sensations were no language can describe; but just as they all rose, stifling my breath and constricting my throat, a girl came up and passed me: in passing, she lifted her eyes. What a strange light inspired them! What an extraordinary sensation that ray sent through me! How the new feeling bore me up! It was as if a martyr, a hero, had passed a slave or victim, and imparted strength in the transit. I mastered the rising hysteria, lifted up my head, and took a firm stand on the stool. Helen Burns asked some slight question about her work of Miss Smith, was chidden for the triviality of the inquiry, returned to her place, and smiled at me as she again went by. What a smile! I remember it now, and I know that it was the effluence of fine intellect, of true courage; it lit up her marked lineaments, her thin face, her sunken grey eye, like a reflection from the aspect of an angel. Yet at that moment Helen Burns wore on her arm 'the untidy badge'; scarcely an hour ago I had heard her condemned by Miss Scatcherd to a dinner of bread and water on the morrow because she had blotted an exercise in copying it out. Such is the imperfect nature of man! Such spots are there on the disc of the clearest planet; and eyes like Miss Scatcherd's can only see those minute defects, and are blind to the full brightness of the orb.

Chapter Eight

ERE THE HALF-HOUR ended, five o'clock struck; school was dismissed, and all were gone into the refectory to tea. I now ventured to descend: it was deep dusk; I retired into a corner and sat down on the floor. The spell by which I had been so far supported began to dissolve; reaction took place, and soon, so overwhelming was the grief that seized me, I sank prostrate with my face to the ground. Now I wept: Helen Burns was not here; nothing sustained me; left to myself I abandoned myself, and my tears watered the boards. I had meant to be so good, and to do so much at Lowood: to make so many friends, to earn respect and win affection. Already I had made visible progress: that very morning I had reached the head of my class; Miss Miller had praised me warmly; Miss Temple had smiled approbation; she had promised to teach me drawing, and to let me learn French, if I continued to make similar improvement two months longer: and then I was well received by my fellow-pupils; treated as an equal by those of my own age, and not molested by any; now, here I lay again crushed and trodden on; and could I ever rise more?

"Never," I thought; and ardently I wished to die. While sobbing out this wish in broken accents, some one approached: I started up – again Helen Burns was near me; the fading fires just showed her coming up the long, vacant room; she brought my coffee and bread.

"Come, eat something," she said; but I put both away from me, feeling as if a drop or a crumb would have choked me in my present condition. Helen regarded me, probably with surprise: I could not now abate my agitation, though I tried hard; I continued to weep aloud. She sat down on the ground near me, embraced her knees with her arms, and rested her head upon them; in that attitude she remained silent as an Indian. I was the first who spoke:

"Helen, why do you stay with a girl whom everybody believes to be a liar?"

"Everybody, Jane? Why, there are only eighty people who have heard you called so, and the world contains hundreds of millions."

"But what have I to do with millions? The eighty, I know, despise me."

"Jane, you are mistaken: probably not one in the school either despises or dislikes you: many, I am sure, pity you much."

"How can they pity me after what Mr. Brocklehurst has said?"

"Mr. Brocklehurst is not a god: nor is he even a great and admired man: he is little liked here; he never took steps to make himself liked. Had he treated you as an especial favourite, you would have found enemies, declared or covert, all around you; as it is, the greater number would offer you sympathy if they dared. Teachers and pupils may look coldly on you for a day or two, but friendly feelings are concealed in their hearts; and if you persevere in doing well, these feelings will ere long appear so much the more evidently for their temporary suppression. Besides, Jane" – she paused.

"Well, Helen?" said I, putting my hand into hers: she chafed my fingers gently to warm them, and went on:

"If all the world hated you, and believed you wicked, while your own conscience approved you, and absolved you from guilt, you would not be without friends."

"No; I know I should think well of myself; but that is not enough: if others don't love me I would rather die than live – I cannot bear to be solitary and hated, Helen. Look here; to gain some real affection from you, or Miss Temple, or any other whom I truly love, I would willingly submit to have the bone of my arm broken, or to let a bull toss me, or to stand behind a kicking horse, and let it dash its hoof at my chest –"

"Hush, Jane! You think too much of the love of human beings; you are too impulsive, too vehement; the sovereign hand that created your frame, and put life into it, has provided you with other resources than your feeble self, or than creatures feeble as you. Besides this earth, and besides the race of men, there is an invisible world and a kingdom of spirits: that world is round us, for it is everywhere; and those spirits watch us, for they are commissioned to guard us; and if we were dying in pain and shame, if scorn smote us on all sides, and hatred crushed us, angels see our tortures, recognise our innocence (if innocent we be: as I know you are of this charge which Mr. Brocklehurst has weakly and pompously repeated at second-hand from Mrs. Reed; for I read a sincere nature in your ardent eyes and on your clear front), and God waits only the separation of spirit from flesh to crown us with a full reward. Why, then, should we ever sink overwhelmed with distress, when life is so soon over, and death is so certain an entrance to happiness – to glory?"

I was silent; Helen had calmed me; but in the tranquillity she imparted there was an alloy of inexpressible sadness. I felt the impression of woe as she spoke, but I could not tell whence it came; and when, having done speaking, she breathed a little fast and coughed a short cough, I momentarily forgot my own sorrows to yield to a vague concern for her.

Resting my head on Helen's shoulder, I put my arms round her waist; she drew me to her, and we reposed in silence. We had not sat long thus, when another person came in. Some heavy clouds, swept from the sky by a rising wind, had left the moon bare; and her light, streaming in through a window near, shone full both on us and on the approaching figure, which we at once recognised as Miss Temple.

"I came on purpose to find you, Jane Eyre," said she; "I want you in my room; and as Helen Burns is with you, she may come too."

We went; following the superintendent's guidance, we had to thread some intricate passages, and mount a staircase before we reached her apartment; it contained a good fire, and looked cheerful. Miss Temple told Helen Burns to be seated in a low armchair on one side of the hearth, and herself taking another, she called me to her side.

"Is it all over?" she asked, looking down at my face. "Have you cried your grief away?"

"I am afraid I never shall do that."

"Why?"

"Because I have been wrongly accused; and you, ma'am, and everybody else, will now think me wicked."

"We shall think you what you prove yourself to be, my child. Continue to act as a good girl, and you will satisfy us."

"Shall I, Miss Temple?"

"You will," said she, passing her arm round me. "And now tell me who is the lady whom Mr. Brocklehurst called your benefactress?"

"Mrs. Reed, my uncle's wife. My uncle is dead, and he left me to her care."

"Did she not, then, adopt you of her own accord?"

"No, ma'am; she was sorry to have to do it: but my uncle, as I have often heard the servants say, got her to promise before he died that she would always keep me."

"Well now, Jane, you know, or at least I will tell you, that when a criminal is accused, he is always allowed to speak in his own defence. You have been charged with falsehood; defend yourself to me as well as you can. Say whatever your memory suggests is true; but add nothing and exaggerate nothing."

I resolved, in the depth of my heart, that I would be most moderate – most correct; and, having reflected a few minutes in order to arrange coherently what I had to say, I told her all the story of my sad childhood. Exhausted by emotion, my language was more subdued than it generally was when it developed that sad theme; and mindful of Helen's warnings against the indulgence of resentment, I infused into the narrative far less of gall and wormwood than ordinary. Thus restrained and simplified, it sounded more credible: I felt as I went on that Miss Temple fully believed me.

In the course of the tale I had mentioned Mr. Lloyd as having come to see me after the fit: for I never forgot the, to me, frightful episode of the red-room: in detailing which, my excitement was sure, in some degree, to break bounds; for nothing could soften in my recollection the spasm of agony which clutched my heart when Mrs. Reed spurned my wild supplication for pardon, and locked me a second time in the dark and haunted chamber.

I had finished: Miss Temple regarded me a few minutes in silence; she then said:

"I know something of Mr. Lloyd; I shall write to him; if his reply agrees with your statement, you shall be publicly cleared from every imputation; to me, Jane, you are clear now."

She kissed me, and still keeping me at her side (where I was well contented to stand, for I derived a child's pleasure from the contemplation of her face, her dress, her one or two ornaments, her white forehead, her clustered and shining curls, and beaming dark eyes), she proceeded to address Helen Burns.

"How are you tonight, Helen? Have you coughed much today?"

"Not quite so much, I think, ma'am."

"And the pain in your chest?"

"It is a little better."

Miss Temple got up, took her hand and examined her pulse; then she returned to her own seat: as she resumed it, I heard her sigh low. She was pensive a few minutes, then rousing herself, she said cheerfully:

"But you two are my visitors tonight; I must treat you as such." She rang her bell.

"Barbara," she said to the servant who answered it, "I have not yet had tea; bring the tray and place cups for these two young ladies."

And a tray was soon brought. How pretty, to my eyes, did the china cups and bright teapot look, placed on the little round table near the fire! How fragrant was the steam of the beverage, and the scent of the toast! Of which, however, I, to my dismay (for I was beginning to be hungry) discerned only a very small portion: Miss Temple discerned it too.

"Barbara," said she, "can you not bring a little more bread and butter? There is not enough for three."

Barbara went out: she returned soon:

"Madam, Mrs. Harden says she has sent up the usual quantity."

Mrs. Harden, be it observed, was the housekeeper: a woman after Mr. Brocklehurst's own heart, made up of equal parts of whalebone and iron.

"Oh, very well!" returned Miss Temple; "we must make it do, Barbara, I suppose." And as the girl withdrew she added, smiling, "Fortunately, I have it in my power to supply deficiencies for this once."

Having invited Helen and me to approach the table, and placed before each of us a cup of tea with one delicious but thin morsel of toast, she got up, unlocked a drawer, and taking from it a parcel wrapped in paper, disclosed presently to our eyes a good-sized seed-cake.

"I meant to give each of you some of this to take with you," said she, "but as there is so little toast, you must have it now," and she proceeded to cut slices with a generous hand.

We feasted that evening as on nectar and ambrosia; and not the least delight of the entertainment was the smile of gratification with which our hostess regarded us, as we satisfied our famished appetites on the delicate fare she liberally supplied.

Tea over and the tray removed, she again summoned us to the fire; we sat one on each side of her, and now a conversation followed between her and Helen, which it was indeed a privilege to be admitted to hear.

Miss Temple had always something of serenity in her air, of state in her mien, of refined propriety in her language, which precluded deviation into the ardent, the excited, the eager: something which chastened the pleasure of those who looked on her and listened to her, by a controlling sense of awe; and such was my feeling now: but as to Helen Burns, I was struck with wonder.

The refreshing meal, the brilliant fire, the presence and kindness of her beloved instructress, or, perhaps, more than all these, something in her own unique mind, had roused her powers within her. They woke, they kindled: first, they glowed in the bright tint of her cheek, which till this hour I had never seen but pale and bloodless; then they shone in the liquid lustre of her eyes, which had suddenly acquired a beauty more singular than that of Miss Temple's – a beauty neither of fine colour nor long eyelash, nor pencilled brow, but of meaning, of movement, of radiance. Then her soul sat on her lips, and language flowed, from what source I cannot tell. Has a girl of fourteen a heart large enough, vigorous enough, to hold the swelling spring of pure, full, fervid eloquence? Such was the characteristic of Helen's discourse on that, to me, memorable evening; her spirit seemed hastening to live within a very brief span as much as many live during a protracted existence.

They conversed of things I had never heard of; of nations and times past; of countries far away; of secrets of nature discovered or guessed at: they spoke of books: how many they had read! What stores of knowledge they possessed! Then they seemed so familiar with French names and French authors: but my amazement reached its climax when Miss Temple asked Helen if she sometimes snatched a moment to recall the Latin her father had taught her, and taking a book from a shelf, bade her read and construe a page of Virgil; and Helen obeyed, my organ of veneration expanding at every sounding line. She had scarcely finished ere the bell announced bedtime! No delay could be admitted; Miss Temple embraced us both, saying, as she drew us to her heart:

"God bless you, my children!"

Helen she held a little longer than me: she let her go more reluctantly; it was Helen her eye followed to the door; it was for her she a second time breathed a sad sigh; for her she wiped a tear from her cheek.

On reaching the bedroom, we heard the voice of Miss Scatcherd: she was examining drawers; she had just pulled out Helen Burns's, and when we entered Helen was greeted with a sharp reprimand, and told that tomorrow she should have half-a-dozen of untidily folded articles pinned to her shoulder.

"My things were indeed in shameful disorder," murmured Helen to me, in a low voice: "I intended to have arranged them, but I forgot."

Next morning, Miss Scatcherd wrote in conspicuous characters on a piece of pasteboard the word "Slattern," and bound it like a phylactery round Helen's large, mild, intelligent, and benign-looking forehead. She wore it till evening, patient, unresentful, regarding it as a deserved punishment. The moment Miss Scatcherd withdrew after afternoon school, I ran to Helen, tore it off, and thrust it into the fire: the fury of which she was incapable had been burning in my soul all day, and tears, hot and large, had continually been scalding my cheek; for the spectacle of her sad resignation gave me an intolerable pain at the heart.

About a week subsequently to the incidents above narrated, Miss Temple, who had written to Mr. Lloyd, received his answer: it appeared that what he said went to corroborate my account. Miss Temple, having assembled the whole school, announced that inquiry had been made into the charges alleged against Jane Eyre, and that she was most happy to be able to pronounce her completely cleared from every imputation. The teachers then shook hands with me and kissed me, and a murmur of pleasure ran through the ranks of my companions.

Thus relieved of a grievous load, I from that hour set to work afresh, resolved to pioneer my way through every difficulty: I toiled hard, and my success was proportionate to my efforts; my memory, not naturally tenacious, improved with practice; exercise sharpened my wits; in a few weeks I was promoted to a higher class; in less than two months I was allowed to commence French and drawing. I learned the first two tenses of the verb *Être*, and sketched my first cottage (whose walls, by-the-bye, outrivalled in slope those of the leaning tower of Pisa), on the same day. That night, on going to bed, I forgot to prepare in imagination the Barmecide supper [4] of hot roast potatoes, or white bread and new milk, with which I was wont to amuse my inward cravings: I feasted instead on the spectacle of ideal drawings, which I saw in the dark; all the work of my own hands: freely pencilled houses and trees, picturesque rocks and ruins, Cuyp-like groups of cattle, sweet paintings of butterflies hovering over unblown roses, of birds picking at ripe cherries, of wren's nests enclosing pearl-like eggs, wreathed about with young ivy sprays. I examined, too, in thought, the possibility of my ever being able to translate currently a certain little French story which Madame Pierrot had that day shown me; nor was that problem solved to my satisfaction ere I fell sweetly asleep.

Well has Solomon said: "Better is a dinner of herbs where love is, than a stalled ox and hatred therewith."

I would not now have exchanged Lowood with all its privations for Gateshead and its daily luxuries.

Chapter Nine

BUT THE PRIVATIONS, or rather the hardships, of Lowood lessened. Spring drew on: she was indeed already come; the frosts of winter had ceased; its snows were melted, its cutting winds ameliorated. My wretched feet, flayed and swollen to lameness by the sharp air of January, began to heal and subside under the gentler breathings of April; the nights and mornings no longer by their Canadian temperature froze the very blood in our veins; we could now endure the play-hour passed in the garden: sometimes on a sunny day it began even to be pleasant and genial, and a greenness grew over those brown beds, which, freshening daily, suggested the thought that Hope traversed them at night, and left each morning brighter traces of her steps. Flowers peeped out amongst the leaves; snow-drops, crocuses, purple auriculas, and golden-eyed pansies. On Thursday afternoons (half-holidays) we now took walks, and found still sweeter flowers opening by the wayside, under the hedges.

I discovered, too, that a great pleasure, an enjoyment which the horizon only bounded, lay all outside the high and spike-guarded walls of our garden: this pleasure consisted in prospect of noble summits girdling a great hill-hollow, rich in verdure and shadow; in a bright beck, full of dark stones and sparkling eddies. How different had this scene looked when I viewed it laid out beneath the iron sky of winter, stiffened in frost, shrouded with snow! When mists as chill as death wandered to the impulse of east winds along those purple peaks, and rolled down 'ing' and holm [5] till they blended with the frozen fog of the beck! That beck itself was then a torrent, turbid and curbless: it tore asunder the wood, and sent a raving sound through the air, often thickened with wild rain or whirling sleet; and for the forest on its banks, *that* showed only ranks of skeletons.

April advanced to May: a bright serene May it was; days of blue sky, placid sunshine, and soft western or southern gales filled up its duration. And now vegetation matured with vigour; Lowood shook loose its tresses; it became all green, all flowery; its great elm, ash, and oak skeletons were restored to majestic life; woodland plants sprang up profusely in its recesses; unnumbered varieties of moss filled its hollows, and it made a strange ground-sunshine out of the wealth of its wild primrose plants: I have seen their pale gold gleam in overshadowed spots like scatterings of the sweetest lustre. All this I enjoyed often and fully, free, unwatched, and almost alone: for this unwonted liberty and pleasure there was a cause, to which it now becomes my task to advert.

Have I not described a pleasant site for a dwelling, when I speak of it as bosomed in hill and wood, and rising from the verge of a stream? Assuredly, pleasant enough: but whether healthy or not is another question.

That forest-dell, where Lowood lay, was the cradle of fog and fog-bred pestilence; which, quickening with the quickening spring, crept into the Orphan Asylum, breathed typhus through its crowded schoolroom and dormitory, and, ere May arrived, transformed the seminary into an hospital.

Semi-starvation and neglected colds had predisposed most of the pupils to receive infection: forty-five out of the eighty girls lay ill at one time. Classes were broken up, rules relaxed. The few who continued well were allowed almost unlimited license; because the medical attendant insisted on the necessity of frequent exercise to keep them in health: and had it been otherwise, no one had leisure to watch or restrain them. Miss Temple's whole attention was absorbed by the patients: she lived in the sick-room, never quitting it except to snatch a few hours' rest at night. The teachers were fully occupied with packing up and making other necessary preparations for the departure of those girls who were fortunate enough to have friends and relations able and willing to remove them from the seat of contagion. Many, already smitten, went home only to die: some died at the school, and were buried quietly and quickly, the nature of the malady forbidding delay.

While disease had thus become an inhabitant of Lowood, and death its frequent visitor; while there was gloom and fear within its walls; while its rooms and passages steamed with hospital smells, the drug and the pastille striving vainly to overcome the effluvia of mortality, that bright May shone unclouded over the bold hills and beautiful woodland out of doors. Its garden, too, glowed with flowers: hollyhocks had sprung up tall as trees, lilies had opened, tulips and roses were in bloom; the borders of the little beds were gay with pink thrift and crimson double daisies; the sweetbriars gave out, morning and evening, their scent of spice and apples; and these fragrant treasures were all useless for most of the inmates of Lowood, except to furnish now and then a handful of herbs and blossoms to put in a coffin.

But I, and the rest who continued well, enjoyed fully the beauties of the scene and season; they let us ramble in the wood, like gipsies, from morning till night; we did what we liked, went where we liked: we lived better too. Mr. Brocklehurst and his family never came near Lowood now: household matters were not scrutinised into; the cross housekeeper was gone, driven away by the fear of infection; her successor, who had been matron at the Lowton Dispensary, unused to the ways of her new abode, provided with comparative liberality. Besides, there were fewer to feed; the sick could eat little; our breakfast-basins were better filled; when there was no time to prepare a regular dinner, which often happened, she would give us a large piece of cold pie, or a thick slice of bread and cheese, and this we carried away with us to the wood, where we each chose the spot we liked best, and dined sumptuously.

My favourite seat was a smooth and broad stone, rising white and dry from the very middle of the beck, and only to be got at by wading through the water; a feat I accomplished barefoot. The stone was just broad enough to accommodate, comfortably, another girl and me, at that time my chosen comrade – one Mary Ann Wilson; a shrewd, observant personage, whose society I took pleasure in, partly because she was witty and original, and partly because she had a manner which set me at my ease. Some years older than I, she knew more of the world, and could tell me many things I liked to hear: with her my curiosity found gratification: to my faults also she gave ample indulgence, never imposing curb or rein on anything I said. She had a turn for narrative, I for analysis; she liked to inform, I to question; so we got on swimmingly together, deriving much entertainment, if not much improvement, from our mutual intercourse.

And where, meantime, was Helen Burns? Why did I not spend these sweet days of liberty with her? Had I forgotten her? Or was I so worthless as to have grown tired of her pure society? Surely the Mary Ann Wilson I have mentioned was inferior to my first acquaintance: she could only tell me amusing stories, and reciprocate any racy and pungent gossip I chose to indulge in; while, if I have spoken truth of Helen, she was qualified to give those who enjoyed the privilege of her converse a taste of far higher things.

True, reader; and I knew and felt this: and though I am a defective being, with many faults and few redeeming points, yet I never tired of Helen Burns; nor ever ceased to cherish for her a sentiment of attachment, as strong, tender, and respectful as any that ever animated my heart. How could it be otherwise, when Helen, at all times and under all circumstances, evinced for me a quiet and faithful friendship, which ill-humour never soured, nor irritation never troubled? But Helen was ill at present: for some weeks she had been removed from my sight to I knew not what room upstairs. She was not, I was told, in the hospital portion of the house with the fever patients; for her complaint was consumption, not typhus: and by consumption I, in my ignorance, understood something mild, which time and care would be sure to alleviate.

I was confirmed in this idea by the fact of her once or twice coming downstairs on very warm sunny afternoons, and being taken by Miss Temple into the garden; but, on these occasions, I was not allowed to go and speak to her; I only saw her from the schoolroom window, and then not distinctly; for she was much wrapped up, and sat at a distance under the verandah.

One evening, in the beginning of June, I had stayed out very late with Mary Ann in the wood; we had, as usual, separated ourselves from the others, and had wandered far; so far that we lost our way, and had to ask it at a lonely cottage, where a man and woman lived, who looked after a herd of half-wild swine that fed on the mast in the wood. When we got back, it was after moonrise: a pony, which we knew to be the surgeon's, was standing at the garden door. Mary Ann remarked that she supposed some one must be very ill, as Mr. Bates had been sent for at that time of the evening. She went into the house; I stayed behind a few minutes to plant in my garden a handful of roots I had dug up in the forest, and which I feared would wither if I left them till the morning. This done, I lingered yet a little longer: the flowers smelt so sweet as the dew fell; it was such a pleasant evening, so serene, so warm; the still glowing west promised so fairly another fine day on the morrow; the moon rose with such majesty in the grave east. I was noting these things and enjoying them as a child might, when it entered my mind as it had never done before:

"How sad to be lying now on a sick bed, and to be in danger of dying! This world is pleasant – it would be dreary to be called from it, and to have to go who knows where?"

And then my mind made its first earnest effort to comprehend what had been infused into it concerning heaven and hell; and for the first time it recoiled, baffled; and for the first time glancing behind, on each side, and before it, it saw all round an unfathomed gulf: it felt the one point where it stood – the present; all the rest was formless cloud and vacant depth; and it shuddered at the thought of tottering, and plunging amid that chaos. While pondering this new idea, I heard the front door open; Mr. Bates came out, and with him was a nurse. After she had seen him mount his horse and depart, she was about to close the door, but I ran up to her.

"How is Helen Burns?"

"Very poorly," was the answer.

"Is it her Mr. Bates has been to see?"

"Yes."

"And what does he say about her?"

"He says she'll not be here long."

This phrase, uttered in my hearing yesterday, would have only conveyed the notion that she was about to be removed to Northumberland, to her own home. I should not have suspected that it meant she was dying; but I knew instantly now! It opened clear on my comprehension that Helen Burns was numbering her last days in this world, and that she was going to be taken to the region of spirits, if such region there were. I experienced a shock of horror, then a strong thrill of grief, then a desire – a necessity to see her; and I asked in what room she lay.

"She is in Miss Temple's room," said the nurse.

"May I go up and speak to her?"

"Oh no, child! It is not likely; and now it is time for you to come in; you'll catch the fever if you stop out when the dew is falling."

The nurse closed the front door; I went in by the side entrance which led to the schoolroom: I was just in time; it was nine o'clock, and Miss Miller was calling the pupils to go to bed.

It might be two hours later, probably near eleven, when I – not having been able to fall asleep, and deeming, from the perfect silence of the dormitory, that my companions were all wrapt in profound repose – rose softly, put on my frock over my night-dress, and, without shoes, crept from the apartment, and set off in quest of Miss Temple's room. It was quite at the other end of the house; but I knew my way; and the light of the unclouded summer moon, entering here and there at passage windows, enabled me to find it without difficulty. An odour of camphor and burnt vinegar warned me when I came near the fever room: and I passed its door quickly, fearful lest the nurse who sat up all night should hear me. I dreaded being discovered and sent back; for I *must* see Helen, – I must embrace her before she died, – I must give her one last kiss, exchange with her one last word.

Having descended a staircase, traversed a portion of the house below, and succeeded in opening and shutting, without noise, two doors, I reached another flight of steps; these I mounted, and then just opposite to me was Miss Temple's room. A light shone through the keyhole and from under the door; a profound stillness pervaded the vicinity. Coming near, I found the door slightly ajar; probably to admit some fresh air into the close abode of sickness. Indisposed to hesitate, and full of impatient impulses – soul and senses quivering with keen throes – I put it back and looked in. My eye sought Helen, and feared to find death.

Close by Miss Temple's bed, and half covered with its white curtains, there stood a little crib. I saw the outline of a form under the clothes, but the face was hid by the hangings: the nurse I had spoken to in the garden sat in an easy chair asleep; an unsnuffed candle burnt dimly on the table. Miss Temple was not to be seen: I knew afterwards that she had been called to a delirious patient in the fever-room. I advanced; then paused by the crib side: my hand was on the curtain, but I preferred speaking before I withdrew it. I still recoiled at the dread of seeing a corpse.

"Helen!" I whispered softly, "are you awake?"

She stirred herself, put back the curtain, and I saw her face, pale, wasted, but quite composed: she looked so little changed that my fear was instantly dissipated.

"Can it be you, Jane?" she asked, in her own gentle voice.

"Oh!" I thought, "she is not going to die; they are mistaken: she could not speak and look so calmly if she were."

I got on to her crib and kissed her: her forehead was cold, and her cheek both cold and thin, and so were her hand and wrist; but she smiled as of old.

"Why are you come here, Jane? It is past eleven o'clock: I heard it strike some minutes since."

"I came to see you, Helen: I heard you were very ill, and I could not sleep till I had spoken to you."

"You came to bid me goodbye, then: you are just in time probably."

"Are you going somewhere, Helen? Are you going home?"

"Yes; to my long home – my last home."

"No, no, Helen!" I stopped, distressed. While I tried to devour my tears, a fit of coughing seized Helen; it did not, however, wake the nurse; when it was over, she lay some minutes exhausted; then she whispered:

"Jane, your little feet are bare; lie down and cover yourself with my quilt."

I did so: she put her arm over me, and I nestled close to her. After a long silence, she resumed, still whispering:

"I am very happy, Jane; and when you hear that I am dead, you must be sure and not grieve: there is nothing to grieve about. We all must die one day, and the illness which is removing me is not painful; it is gentle and gradual: my mind is at rest. I leave no one to regret me much: I have only a father; and he is lately married, and will not miss me. By dying young, I shall escape great sufferings. I had not qualities or talents to make my way very well in the world: I should have been continually at fault."

"But where are you going to, Helen? Can you see? Do you know?"

"I believe; I have faith: I am going to God."

"Where is God? What is God?"

"My Maker and yours, who will never destroy what He created. I rely implicitly on His power, and confide wholly in His goodness: I count the hours till that eventful one arrives which shall restore me to Him, reveal Him to me."

"You are sure, then, Helen, that there is such a place as heaven, and that our souls can get to it when we die?"

"I am sure there is a future state; I believe God is good; I can resign my immortal part to Him without any misgiving. God is my father; God is my friend: I love Him; I believe He loves me."

"And shall I see you again, Helen, when I die?"

"You will come to the same region of happiness: be received by the same mighty, universal Parent, no doubt, dear Jane."

Again I questioned, but this time only in thought. "Where is that region? Does it exist?" And I clasped my arms closer round Helen; she seemed dearer to me than ever; I felt as if I could not let her go; I lay with my face hidden on her neck. Presently she said, in the sweetest tone:

"How comfortable I am! That last fit of coughing has tired me a little; I feel as if I could sleep: but don't leave me, Jane; I like to have you near me."

"I'll stay with you, *dear* Helen: no one shall take me away."

"Are you warm, darling?"

"Yes."

"Goodnight, Jane."

"Goodnight, Helen."

She kissed me, and I her, and we both soon slumbered.

When I awoke it was day: an unusual movement roused me; I looked up; I was in somebody's arms; the nurse held me; she was carrying me through the passage back to the dormitory. I was not reprimanded for leaving my bed; people had something else to think about; no explanation was afforded then to my many questions; but a day or two afterwards I learned that Miss Temple, on returning to her own room at dawn, had found me laid in the little crib; my face against Helen Burns's shoulder, my arms round her neck. I was asleep, and Helen was – dead.

Her grave is in Brocklebridge churchyard: for fifteen years after her death it was only covered by a grassy mound; but now a grey marble tablet marks the spot, inscribed with her name, and the word 'Resurgam'.

Chapter Ten

HITHERTO I HAVE recorded in detail the events of my insignificant existence: to the first ten years of my life I have given almost as many chapters. But this is not to be a regular autobiography. I am only bound to invoke Memory where I know her responses will possess some degree of interest; therefore I now pass a space of eight years almost in silence: a few lines only are necessary to keep up the links of connection.

When the typhus fever had fulfilled its mission of devastation at Lowood, it gradually disappeared from thence; but not till its virulence and the number of its victims had drawn public attention on the school. Inquiry was made into the origin of the scourge, and by degrees various facts came out which excited public indignation in a high degree. The unhealthy nature of the site; the quantity and quality of the children's food; the brackish, fetid water used in its preparation; the pupils' wretched clothing and accommodations – all these things were discovered, and the discovery produced a result mortifying to Mr. Brocklehurst, but beneficial to the institution.

Several wealthy and benevolent individuals in the county subscribed largely for the erection of a more convenient building in a better situation; new regulations were made; improvements in diet and clothing introduced; the funds of the school were intrusted to the management of a committee. Mr. Brocklehurst, who, from his wealth and family connections, could not be overlooked, still retained the post of treasurer; but he was aided in the discharge of his duties by gentlemen of rather more enlarged and sympathising minds: his office of inspector, too, was shared by those who knew how to combine reason with strictness, comfort with economy, compassion with uprightness. The school, thus improved, became in time a truly useful and noble institution. I remained an inmate of its walls, after its regeneration, for eight years: six as pupil, and two as teacher; and in both capacities I bear my testimony to its value and importance.

During these eight years my life was uniform: but not unhappy, because it was not inactive. I had the means of an excellent education placed within my reach; a fondness for some of my studies, and a desire to excel in all, together with a great delight in pleasing my teachers, especially such as I loved, urged me on: I availed myself fully of the advantages offered me. In time I rose to be the first girl of the first class; then I was invested with the office of teacher; which I discharged with zeal for two years: but at the end of that time I altered.

Miss Temple, through all changes, had thus far continued superintendent of the seminary: to her instruction I owed the best part of my acquirements; her friendship and society had been my continual solace; she had stood me in the stead of mother, governess, and, latterly, companion. At this period she married, removed with her husband (a clergyman, an excellent man, almost worthy of such a wife) to a distant county, and consequently was lost to me.

From the day she left I was no longer the same: with her was gone every settled feeling, every association that had made Lowood in some degree a home to me. I had imbibed from her something of her nature and much of her habits: more harmonious thoughts: what seemed better regulated feelings had become the inmates of my mind. I had given in allegiance to duty and order; I was quiet; I believed I was content: to the eyes of others, usually even to my own, I appeared a disciplined and subdued character.

But destiny, in the shape of the Rev. Mr. Nasmyth, came between me and Miss Temple: I saw her in her travelling dress step into a post-chaise, shortly after the marriage ceremony; I watched the chaise mount the hill and disappear beyond its brow; and then retired to my own room, and there spent in solitude the greatest part of the half-holiday granted in honour of the occasion.

I walked about the chamber most of the time. I imagined myself only to be regretting my loss, and thinking how to repair it; but when my reflections were concluded, and I looked up and found that the afternoon was gone, and evening far advanced, another discovery dawned on me, namely, that in the interval I had undergone a transforming process; that my mind had put off all it had borrowed of Miss Temple – or rather that she had taken with her the serene atmosphere I had been breathing in her vicinity – and that now I was left in my natural element, and beginning to feel the stirring of old emotions. It did not seem as if a prop were withdrawn, but rather as if a motive were gone: it was not the power to be tranquil which had failed me, but the reason for tranquillity was no more. My world had for some years been in Lowood:

my experience had been of its rules and systems; now I remembered that the real world was wide, and that a varied field of hopes and fears, of sensations and excitements, awaited those who had courage to go forth into its expanse, to seek real knowledge of life amidst its perils.

I went to my window, opened it, and looked out. There were the two wings of the building; there was the garden; there were the skirts of Lowood; there was the hilly horizon. My eye passed all other objects to rest on those most remote, the blue peaks; it was those I longed to surmount; all within their boundary of rock and heath seemed prison-ground, exile limits. I traced the white road winding round the base of one mountain, and vanishing in a gorge between two; how I longed to follow it farther! I recalled the time when I had travelled that very road in a coach; I remembered descending that hill at twilight; an age seemed to have elapsed since the day which brought me first to Lowood, and I had never quitted it since. My vacations had all been spent at school: Mrs. Reed had never sent for me to Gateshead; neither she nor any of her family had ever been to visit me. I had had no communication by letter or message with the outer world: school-rules, school-duties, school-habits and notions, and voices, and faces, and phrases, and costumes, and preferences, and antipathies – such was what I knew of existence. And now I felt that it was not enough; I tired of the routine of eight years in one afternoon. I desired liberty; for liberty I gasped; for liberty I uttered a prayer; it seemed scattered on the wind then faintly blowing. I abandoned it and framed a humbler supplication; for change, stimulus: that petition, too, seemed swept off into vague space: "Then," I cried, half desperate, "grant me at least a new servitude!"

Here a bell, ringing the hour of supper, called me downstairs.

I was not free to resume the interrupted chain of my reflections till bedtime: even then a teacher who occupied the same room with me kept me from the subject to which I longed to recur, by a prolonged effusion of small talk. How I wished sleep would silence her. It seemed as if, could I but go back to the idea which had last entered my mind as I stood at the window, some inventive suggestion would rise for my relief.

Miss Gryce snored at last; she was a heavy Welshwoman, and till now her habitual nasal strains had never been regarded by me in any other light than as a nuisance; tonight I hailed the first deep notes with satisfaction; I was debarrassed of interruption; my half-effaced thought instantly revived.

"A new servitude! There is something in that," I soliloquised (mentally, be it understood; I did not talk aloud), "I know there is, because it does not sound too sweet; it is not like such words as Liberty, Excitement, Enjoyment: delightful sounds truly; but no more than sounds for me; and so hollow and fleeting that it is mere waste of time to listen to them. But Servitude! That must be matter of fact. Any one may serve: I have served here eight years; now all I want is to serve elsewhere. Can I not get so much of my own will? Is not the thing feasible? Yes – yes – the end is not so difficult; if I had only a brain active enough to ferret out the means of attaining it."

I sat up in bed by way of arousing this said brain: it was a chilly night; I covered my shoulders with a shawl, and then I proceeded *to think* again with all my might.

"What do I want? A new place, in a new house, amongst new faces, under new circumstances: I want this because it is of no use wanting anything better. How do people do to get a new place? They apply to friends, I suppose: I have no friends. There are many others who have no friends, who must look about for themselves and be their own helpers; and what is their resource?"

I could not tell: nothing answered me; I then ordered my brain to find a response, and quickly. It worked and worked faster: I felt the pulses throb in my head and temples; but for nearly an hour it worked in chaos; and no result came of its efforts. Feverish with vain labour, I got up and took a turn in the room; undrew the curtain, noted a star or two, shivered with cold, and again crept to bed.

A kind fairy, in my absence, had surely dropped the required suggestion on my pillow; for as I lay down, it came quietly and naturally to my mind. – "Those who want situations advertise; you must advertise in the —shire *Herald*."

"How? I know nothing about advertising."

Replies rose smooth and prompt now:

"You must enclose the advertisement and the money to pay for it under a cover directed to the Editor of the *Herald*; you must put it, the first opportunity you have, into the post at Lowton; answers must be addressed to J.E., at the post office there; you can go and inquire in about a week after you send your letter, if any are come, and act accordingly."

This scheme I went over twice, thrice; it was then digested in my mind; I had it in a clear practical form: I felt satisfied, and fell asleep.

With earliest day, I was up: I had my advertisement written, enclosed, and directed before the bell rang to rouse the school; it ran thus:

A young lady accustomed to tuition [had I not been a teacher two years?] *is desirous of meeting with a situation in a private family where the children are under fourteen* [I thought that as I was barely eighteen, it would not do to undertake the guidance of pupils nearer my own age]. *She is qualified to teach the usual branches of a good English education, together with French, Drawing, and Music* [in those days, reader, this now narrow catalogue of accomplishments, would have been held tolerably comprehensive]. *Address, J.E., Post office, Lowton, —shire.*

This document remained locked in my drawer all day: after tea, I asked leave of the new superintendent to go to Lowton, in order to perform some small commissions for myself and one or two of my fellow-teachers; permission was readily granted; I went. It was a walk of two miles, and the evening was wet, but the days were still long; I visited a shop or two, slipped the letter into the post office, and came back through heavy rain, with streaming garments, but with a relieved heart.

The succeeding week seemed long: it came to an end at last, however, like all sublunary things, and once more, towards the close of a pleasant autumn day, I found myself afoot on the road to Lowton. A picturesque track it was, by the way; lying along the side of the beck and through the sweetest curves of the dale: but that day I thought more of the letters, that might or might not be awaiting me at the little burgh whither I was bound, than of the charms of lea and water.

My ostensible errand on this occasion was to get measured for a pair of shoes; so I discharged that business first, and when it was done, I stepped across the clean and quiet little street from the shoemaker's to the post office: it was kept by an old dame, who wore horn spectacles on her nose, and black mittens on her hands.

"Are there any letters for J.E.?" I asked.

She peered at me over her spectacles, and then she opened a drawer and fumbled among its contents for a long time, so long that my hopes began to falter. At last, having held a document before her glasses for nearly five minutes, she presented it across the counter, accompanying the act by another inquisitive and mistrustful glance – it was for J.E.

"Is there only one?" I demanded.

"There are no more," said she; and I put it in my pocket and turned my face homeward: I could not open it then; rules obliged me to be back by eight, and it was already half-past seven.

Various duties awaited me on my arrival. I had to sit with the girls during their hour of study; then it was my turn to read prayers; to see them to bed: afterwards I supped with the other teachers. Even when we finally retired for the night, the inevitable Miss Gryce was still my companion: we had only a short end of candle in our candlestick, and I dreaded lest she should talk till it was all burnt out; fortunately, however, the heavy supper she had eaten produced a soporific effect: she was already snoring before I had finished undressing. There still remained an inch of candle: I now took out my letter; the seal was an initial F.; I broke it; the contents were brief:

If J.E., who advertised in the —shire Herald *of last Thursday, possesses the acquirements mentioned, and if she is in a position to give satisfactory references as to character and competency, a situation can be offered her where there is but one pupil, a little girl, under ten years of age; and where the salary is thirty pounds per annum. J.E. is requested to send references, name, address, and all particulars to the direction:*
Mrs. Fairfax, Thornfield, near Millcote, —shire.

I examined the document long: the writing was old-fashioned and rather uncertain, like that of an elderly lady. This circumstance was satisfactory: a private fear had haunted me, that in thus acting for myself, and by my own guidance, I ran the risk of getting into some scrape; and, above all things, I wished the result of my endeavours to be respectable, proper, *en règle*. I now felt that an elderly lady was no bad ingredient in the business I had on hand. Mrs. Fairfax! I saw her in a black gown and widow's cap; frigid, perhaps, but not uncivil: a model of elderly English respectability. Thornfield! that, doubtless, was the name of her house: a neat orderly spot, I was sure; though I failed in my efforts to conceive a correct plan of the premises. Millcote, —shire; I brushed up my recollections of the map of England, yes, I saw it; both the shire and the town. —shire was seventy miles nearer London than the remote county where I now resided: that was a recommendation to me. I longed to go where there was life and movement: Millcote was a large manufacturing town on the banks of the A—; a busy place enough, doubtless: so much the better; it would be a complete change at least. Not that my fancy was much captivated by the idea of long chimneys and clouds of smoke – "but," I argued, "Thornfield will, probably, be a good way from the town."

Here the socket of the candle dropped, and the wick went out.

Next day new steps were to be taken; my plans could no longer be confined to my own breast; I must impart them in order to achieve their success. Having sought and obtained an audience of the superintendent during the noontide recreation, I told her I had a prospect of getting a new situation where the salary would be double what I now received (for at Lowood I only got £15 per annum); and requested she would break the matter for me to Mr. Brocklehurst, or some of the committee, and ascertain whether they would permit me to mention them as references. She obligingly consented to act as mediatrix in the matter. The next day she laid the affair before Mr. Brocklehurst, who said that Mrs. Reed must be written to, as she was my natural guardian. A note was accordingly addressed to that lady, who returned for answer, that "I might do as I pleased: she had long relinquished all interference in my affairs." This note went the round of the committee, and at last, after what appeared to me most tedious delay, formal leave was given me to better my condition if I could; and an assurance added, that as I had always conducted myself well, both as teacher and pupil, at Lowood, a testimonial of character and capacity, signed by the inspectors of that institution, should forthwith be furnished me.

This testimonial I accordingly received in about a month, forwarded a copy of it to Mrs. Fairfax, and got that lady's reply, stating that she was satisfied, and fixing that day fortnight as the period for my assuming the post of governess in her house.

I now busied myself in preparations: the fortnight passed rapidly. I had not a very large wardrobe, though it was adequate to my wants; and the last day sufficed to pack my trunk, – the same I had brought with me eight years ago from Gateshead.

The box was corded, the card nailed on. In half an hour the carrier was to call for it to take it to Lowton, whither I myself was to repair at an early hour the next morning to meet the coach. I had brushed my black stuff travelling-dress, prepared my bonnet, gloves, and muff; sought in all my drawers to see that no article was left behind; and now having nothing more to do, I sat down and tried to rest. I could not; though I had been on foot all day, I could not now repose an instant; I was too much excited. A phase of my life was closing tonight, a new one opening tomorrow: impossible to slumber in the interval; I must watch feverishly while the change was being accomplished.

"Miss," said a servant who met me in the lobby, where I was wandering like a troubled spirit, "a person below wishes to see you."

"The carrier, no doubt," I thought, and ran downstairs without inquiry. I was passing the back-parlour or teachers' sitting-room, the door of which was half open, to go to the kitchen, when some one ran out:

"It's her, I am sure! – I could have told her anywhere!" cried the individual who stopped my progress and took my hand.

I looked: I saw a woman attired like a well-dressed servant, matronly, yet still young; very good-looking, with black hair and eyes, and lively complexion.

"Well, who is it?" she asked, in a voice and with a smile I half recognised; "you've not quite forgotten me, I think, Miss Jane?"

In another second I was embracing and kissing her rapturously: "Bessie! Bessie! Bessie!" that was all I said; whereat she half laughed, half cried, and we both went into the parlour. By the fire stood a little fellow of three years old, in plaid frock and trousers.

"That is my little boy," said Bessie directly.

"Then you are married, Bessie?"

"Yes; nearly five years since to Robert Leaven, the coachman; and I've a little girl besides Bobby there, that I've christened Jane."

"And you don't live at Gateshead?"

"I live at the lodge: the old porter has left."

"Well, and how do they all get on? Tell me everything about them, Bessie: but sit down first; and, Bobby, come and sit on my knee, will you?" but Bobby preferred sidling over to his mother.

"You're not grown so very tall, Miss Jane, nor so very stout," continued Mrs. Leaven. "I dare say they've not kept you too well at school: Miss Reed is the head and shoulders taller than you are; and Miss Georgiana would make two of you in breadth."

"Georgiana is handsome, I suppose, Bessie?"

"Very. She went up to London last winter with her mama, and there everybody admired her, and a young lord fell in love with her: but his relations were against the match; and – what do you think? – he and Miss Georgiana made it up to run away; but they were found out and stopped. It was Miss Reed that found them out: I believe she was envious; and now she and her sister lead a cat and dog life together; they are always quarrelling –"

"Well, and what of John Reed?"

"Oh, he is not doing so well as his mama could wish. He went to college, and he got – plucked, I think they call it: and then his uncles wanted him to be a barrister, and study the law: but he is such a dissipated young man, they will never make much of him, I think."

"What does he look like?"

"He is very tall: some people call him a fine-looking young man; but he has such thick lips."

"And Mrs. Reed?"

"Missis looks stout and well enough in the face, but I think she's not quite easy in her mind: Mr. John's conduct does not please her – he spends a deal of money."

"Did she send you here, Bessie?"

"No, indeed: but I have long wanted to see you, and when I heard that there had been a letter from you, and that you were going to another part of the country, I thought I'd just set off, and get a look at you before you were quite out of my reach."

"I am afraid you are disappointed in me, Bessie." I said this laughing: I perceived that Bessie's glance, though it expressed regard, did in no shape denote admiration.

"No, Miss Jane, not exactly: you are genteel enough; you look like a lady, and it is as much as ever I expected of you: you were no beauty as a child."

I smiled at Bessie's frank answer: I felt that it was correct, but I confess I was not quite indifferent to its import: at eighteen most people wish to please, and the conviction that they have not an exterior likely to second that desire brings anything but gratification.

"I dare say you are clever, though," continued Bessie, by way of solace. "What can you do? Can you play on the piano?"

"A little."

There was one in the room; Bessie went and opened it, and then asked me to sit down and give her a tune: I played a waltz or two, and she was charmed.

"The Miss Reeds could not play as well!" said she exultingly. "I always said you would surpass them in learning: and can you draw?"

"That is one of my paintings over the chimney-piece." It was a landscape in water colours, of which I had made a present to the superintendent, in acknowledgment of her obliging mediation with the committee on my behalf, and which she had framed and glazed.

"Well, that is beautiful, Miss Jane! It is as fine a picture as any Miss Reed's drawing-master could paint, let alone the young ladies themselves, who could not come near it: and have you learnt French?"

"Yes, Bessie, I can both read it and speak it."

"And you can work on muslin and canvas?"

"I can."

"Oh, you are quite a lady, Miss Jane! I knew you would be: you will get on whether your relations notice you or not. There was something I wanted to ask you. Have you ever heard anything from your father's kinsfolk, the Eyres?"

"Never in my life."

"Well, you know Missis always said they were poor and quite despicable: and they may be poor; but I believe they are as much gentry as the Reeds are; for one day, nearly seven years ago, a Mr. Eyre came to Gateshead and wanted to see you; Missis said you were at school fifty miles off; he seemed so much disappointed, for he could not stay: he was going on a voyage to a foreign country, and the ship was to sail from London in a day or two. He looked quite a gentleman, and I believe he was your father's brother."

"What foreign country was he going to, Bessie?"

"An island thousands of miles off, where they make wine – the butler did tell me –"

"Madeira?" I suggested.

"Yes, that is it – that is the very word."

"So he went?"

"Yes; he did not stay many minutes in the house: Missis was very high with him; she called him afterwards a 'sneaking tradesman.' My Robert believes he was a wine-merchant."

"Very likely," I returned; "or perhaps clerk or agent to a wine-merchant."

Bessie and I conversed about old times an hour longer, and then she was obliged to leave me: I saw her again for a few minutes the next morning at Lowton, while I was waiting for the coach. We parted finally at the door of the Brocklehurst Arms there: each went her separate way; she set off for the brow of Lowood Fell to meet the conveyance which was to take her back to Gateshead, I mounted the vehicle which was to bear me to new duties and a new life in the unknown environs of Millcote.

Chapter Eleven

A NEW CHAPTER in a novel is something like a new scene in a play; and when I draw up the curtain this time, reader, you must fancy you see a room in the George Inn at Millcote, with such large figured papering on the walls as inn rooms have; such a carpet, such furniture, such ornaments on the mantelpiece, such prints, including a portrait of George the Third, and another of the Prince of Wales, and a representation of the death of Wolfe. All this is visible to you by the light of an oil lamp hanging from the ceiling, and by that of an excellent fire, near which I sit in my cloak and bonnet; my muff and umbrella lie on the table, and I am warming away the numbness and chill contracted by sixteen hours' exposure to the rawness of an October day: I left Lowton at four o'clock a.m., and the Millcote town clock is now just striking eight.

Reader, though I look comfortably accommodated, I am not very tranquil in my mind. I thought when the coach stopped here there would be some one to meet me; I looked anxiously round as I descended the wooden steps the 'boots' placed for my convenience, expecting to hear my name pronounced, and to see some description of carriage waiting to convey me to Thornfield. Nothing of the sort was visible; and when I asked a waiter if anyone had been to inquire after a Miss Eyre, I was answered in the negative: so I had no resource but to request to be shown into a private room: and here I am waiting, while all sorts of doubts and fears are troubling my thoughts.

It is a very strange sensation to inexperienced youth to feel itself quite alone in the world, cut adrift from every connection, uncertain whether the port to which it is bound can be reached, and prevented by many impediments from returning to that it has quitted. The charm of adventure sweetens that sensation, the glow of pride warms it; but then the throb of fear disturbs it; and fear with me became predominant when half an hour elapsed and still I was alone. I bethought myself to ring the bell.

"Is there a place in this neighbourhood called Thornfield?" I asked of the waiter who answered the summons.

"Thornfield? I don't know, ma'am; I'll inquire at the bar." He vanished, but reappeared instantly:

"Is your name Eyre, Miss?"

"Yes."

"Person here waiting for you."

I jumped up, took my muff and umbrella, and hastened into the inn-passage: a man was standing by the open door, and in the lamp-lit street I dimly saw a one-horse conveyance.

"This will be your luggage, I suppose?" said the man rather abruptly when he saw me, pointing to my trunk in the passage.

"Yes." He hoisted it on to the vehicle, which was a sort of car, and then I got in; before he shut me up, I asked him how far it was to Thornfield.

"A matter of six miles."

"How long shall we be before we get there?"

"Happen an hour and a half."

He fastened the car door, climbed to his own seat outside, and we set off. Our progress was leisurely, and gave me ample time to reflect; I was content to be at length so near the end of my journey; and as I leaned back in the comfortable though not elegant conveyance, I meditated much at my ease.

"I suppose," thought I, "judging from the plainness of the servant and carriage, Mrs. Fairfax is not a very dashing person: so much the better; I never lived amongst fine people but once, and I was very miserable with them. I wonder if she lives alone except this little girl; if so, and if she is in any degree amiable, I shall surely be able to get on with her; I will do my best; it is a pity that doing one's best does not always answer. At Lowood, indeed, I took that resolution, kept it, and succeeded in pleasing; but with Mrs. Reed, I remember my best was always spurned with scorn. I pray God Mrs. Fairfax may not turn out a second Mrs. Reed; but if she does, I am not bound to stay with her! let the worst come to the worst, I can advertise again. How far are we on our road now, I wonder?"

I let down the window and looked out; Millcote was behind us; judging by the number of its lights, it seemed a place of considerable magnitude, much larger than Lowton. We were now, as far as I could see, on a sort of common; but there were houses scattered all over the district; I felt we were in a different region to Lowood, more populous, less picturesque; more stirring, less romantic.

The roads were heavy, the night misty; my conductor let his horse walk all the way, and the hour and a half extended, I verily believe, to two hours; at last he turned in his seat and said:

"You're noan so far fro' Thornfield now."

Again I looked out: we were passing a church; I saw its low broad tower against the sky, and its bell was tolling a quarter; I saw a narrow galaxy of lights too, on a hillside, marking a village or hamlet. About ten minutes after, the driver got down and opened a pair of gates: we passed through, and they clashed to behind us. We now slowly ascended a drive, and came upon the long front of a house: candlelight gleamed from one curtained bow-window; all the rest were dark. The car stopped at the front door; it was opened by a maid-servant; I alighted and went in.

"Will you walk this way, ma'am?" said the girl; and I followed her across a square hall with high doors all round: she ushered me into a room whose double illumination of fire and candle at first dazzled me, contrasting as it did with the darkness to which my eyes had been for two hours inured; when I could see, however, a cosy and agreeable picture presented itself to my view.

A snug small room; a round table by a cheerful fire; an armchair high-backed and old-fashioned, wherein sat the neatest imaginable little elderly lady, in widow's cap, black silk gown, and snowy muslin apron; exactly like what I had fancied Mrs. Fairfax, only less stately and milder looking. She was occupied in knitting; a large cat sat demurely at her feet; nothing in short was wanting to complete the beau-ideal of domestic comfort. A more reassuring introduction for a new governess could scarcely be conceived; there was no grandeur to overwhelm, no stateliness to embarrass; and then, as I entered, the old lady got up and promptly and kindly came forward to meet me.

"How do you do, my dear? I am afraid you have had a tedious ride; John drives so slowly; you must be cold, come to the fire."

"Mrs. Fairfax, I suppose?" said I.

"Yes, you are right: do sit down."

She conducted me to her own chair, and then began to remove my shawl and untie my bonnet-strings; I begged she would not give herself so much trouble.

"Oh, it is no trouble; I dare say your own hands are almost numbed with cold. Leah, make a little hot negus and cut a sandwich or two: here are the keys of the storeroom."

And she produced from her pocket a most housewifely bunch of keys, and delivered them to the servant.

"Now, then, draw nearer to the fire," she continued. "You've brought your luggage with you, haven't you, my dear?"

"Yes, ma'am."

"I'll see it carried into your room," she said, and bustled out.

"She treats me like a visitor," thought I. "I little expected such a reception; I anticipated only coldness and stiffness: this is not like what I have heard of the treatment of governesses; but I must not exult too soon."

She returned; with her own hands cleared her knitting apparatus and a book or two from the table, to make room for the tray which Leah now brought, and then herself handed me the refreshments. I felt rather confused at being the object of more attention than I had ever before received, and, that too, shown by my employer and superior; but as she did not herself seem to consider she was doing anything out of her place, I thought it better to take her civilities quietly.

"Shall I have the pleasure of seeing Miss Fairfax tonight?" I asked, when I had partaken of what she offered me.

"What did you say, my dear? I am a little deaf," returned the good lady, approaching her ear to my mouth.

I repeated the question more distinctly.

"Miss Fairfax? Oh, you mean Miss Varens! Varens is the name of your future pupil."

"Indeed! Then she is not your daughter?"

"No, – I have no family."

I should have followed up my first inquiry, by asking in what way Miss Varens was connected with her; but I recollected it was not polite to ask too many questions: besides, I was sure to hear in time.

"I am so glad," she continued, as she sat down opposite to me, and took the cat on her knee; "I am so glad you are come; it will be quite pleasant living here now with a companion. To be sure it is pleasant at any time; for Thornfield is a fine old hall, rather neglected of late years perhaps, but still it is a respectable place; yet you know in winter-time one feels dreary quite alone in the best quarters. I say alone – Leah is a nice girl to be sure, and John and his wife are very decent people; but then you see they are only servants, and one can't converse with them on terms of equality: one must keep them at due distance, for fear of losing one's authority. I'm sure last winter (it was a very severe one, if you recollect, and when it did not snow, it rained and blew), not a creature but the butcher and postman came to the house, from November till February; and I really got quite melancholy with sitting night after night alone; I had Leah in to read to me sometimes; but I don't think the poor girl liked the task much: she felt it confining. In spring and summer one got on better: sunshine and long days make such a difference; and then, just at the commencement of this autumn, little Adela Varens came and her nurse: a child makes a house alive all at once; and now you are here I shall be quite gay."

My heart really warmed to the worthy lady as I heard her talk; and I drew my chair a little nearer to her, and expressed my sincere wish that she might find my company as agreeable as she anticipated.

"But I'll not keep you sitting up late tonight," said she; "it is on the stroke of twelve now, and you have been travelling all day: you must feel tired. If you have got your feet well warmed, I'll show you your bedroom. I've had the room next to mine prepared for you; it is only a small apartment, but I thought you would like it better than one of the large front chambers: to be sure they have finer furniture, but they are so dreary and solitary, I never sleep in them myself."

I thanked her for her considerate choice, and as I really felt fatigued with my long journey, expressed my readiness to retire. She took her candle, and I followed her from the room. First she went to see if the hall-door was fastened; having taken the key from the lock, she led the way upstairs. The steps and banisters were of oak; the staircase window was high and latticed; both it and the long gallery into which the bedroom doors opened looked as if they belonged to a church rather than a house. A very chill and vault-like air pervaded the stairs and gallery, suggesting cheerless ideas of space and solitude; and I was glad, when finally ushered into my chamber, to find it of small dimensions, and furnished in ordinary, modern style.

When Mrs. Fairfax had bidden me a kind goodnight, and I had fastened my door, gazed leisurely round, and in some measure effaced the eerie impression made by that wide hall, that dark and spacious staircase, and that long, cold gallery, by the livelier aspect of my little room, I remembered that, after a day of bodily fatigue and mental anxiety, I was now at last in safe haven. The impulse of gratitude swelled my heart, and I knelt down at the bedside, and offered up thanks where thanks were due; not forgetting, ere I rose, to implore aid on my further path, and the power of meriting the kindness which seemed so frankly offered me before it was earned. My couch had no thorns in it that night; my solitary room no fears. At once weary and content, I slept soon and soundly: when I awoke it was broad day.

The chamber looked such a bright little place to me as the sun shone in between the gay blue chintz window curtains, showing papered walls and a carpeted floor, so unlike the bare planks and stained plaster of Lowood, that my spirits rose at the view. Externals have a great effect on the young: I thought that a fairer era of life was beginning for me, one that was to have its flowers and pleasures, as well as its thorns and toils. My faculties, roused by the change of scene, the new field offered to hope, seemed all astir. I cannot precisely define what they expected, but it was something pleasant: not perhaps that day or that month, but at an indefinite future period.

I rose; I dressed myself with care: obliged to be plain – for I had no article of attire that was not made with extreme simplicity – I was still by nature solicitous to be neat. It was not my habit to be disregardful of appearance or careless of the impression I made: on the contrary, I ever wished to look as well as I could, and to please as much as my want of beauty would permit. I sometimes regretted that I was not handsomer; I sometimes wished to have rosy cheeks, a straight nose, and small cherry mouth; I desired to be tall, stately, and finely developed in figure; I felt it a misfortune that I was so little, so pale, and had features so irregular and so marked. And why had I these aspirations and these regrets? It would be difficult to say: I could not then distinctly say it to myself; yet I had a reason, and a logical, natural reason too. However, when I had brushed my hair very smooth, and put on my black frock – which, Quakerlike as it was, at least had the merit of fitting to a nicety – and adjusted my clean white tucker, I thought I should do respectably enough to appear before Mrs. Fairfax, and that my new pupil would not at least recoil from me with antipathy. Having opened my chamber window, and seen that I left all things straight and neat on the toilet table, I ventured forth.

Traversing the long and matted gallery, I descended the slippery steps of oak; then I gained the hall: I halted there a minute; I looked at some pictures on the walls (one, I remember, represented a grim man in a cuirass, and one a lady with powdered hair and a pearl necklace), at a bronze lamp pendent from the ceiling, at a great clock whose case was of oak curiously carved, and ebon black with time and rubbing. Everything appeared very stately and imposing to me; but then I was so little accustomed to grandeur. The hall-door, which was half of glass, stood open; I stepped over the threshold. It was a fine autumn morning; the early sun shone serenely on embrowned groves and still green fields; advancing on to the lawn, I looked up and surveyed the front of the mansion. It was three storeys high, of proportions not vast, though considerable: a gentleman's manor-house, not a nobleman's seat: battlements round the top gave it a picturesque look. Its grey front stood out well from the background of a rookery, whose cawing tenants were now on the wing: they flew over the lawn and grounds to alight in a great meadow, from which these were separated by a sunk fence, and where an array of mighty old thorn trees, strong, knotty, and broad as oaks, at once explained the etymology of the mansion's designation. Farther off were hills: not so lofty as those round Lowood, nor so craggy, nor so like barriers of separation from the living world; but yet quiet and lonely hills enough, and seeming to embrace Thornfield with a seclusion I had not expected to find existent so near the stirring locality of Millcote. A little hamlet, whose roofs were blent with trees, straggled up the side of one of these hills; the church of the district stood nearer Thornfield: its old tower-top looked over a knoll between the house and gates.

I was yet enjoying the calm prospect and pleasant fresh air, yet listening with delight to the cawing of the rooks, yet surveying the wide, hoary front of the hall, and thinking what a great place it was for one lonely little dame like Mrs. Fairfax to inhabit, when that lady appeared at the door.

"What! Out already?" said she. "I see you are an early riser." I went up to her, and was received with an affable kiss and shake of the hand.

"How do you like Thornfield?" she asked. I told her I liked it very much.

"Yes," she said, "it is a pretty place; but I fear it will be getting out of order, unless Mr. Rochester should take it into his head to come and reside here permanently; or, at least, visit it rather oftener: great houses and fine grounds require the presence of the proprietor."

"Mr. Rochester!" I exclaimed. "Who is he?"

"The owner of Thornfield," she responded quietly. "Did you not know he was called Rochester?"

Of course I did not – I had never heard of him before; but the old lady seemed to regard his existence as a universally understood fact, with which everybody must be acquainted by instinct.

"I thought," I continued, "Thornfield belonged to you."

"To me? Bless you, child; what an idea! To me! I am only the housekeeper – the manager. To be sure I am distantly related to the Rochesters by the mother's side, or at least my husband was; he was a clergyman, incumbent of Hay – that little village yonder on the hill – and that church near the gates was his. The present Mr. Rochester's mother was a Fairfax, and second cousin to my husband: but I never presume on the connection – in fact, it is nothing to me; I consider myself quite in the light of an ordinary housekeeper: my employer is always civil, and I expect nothing more."

"And the little girl – my pupil?"

"She is Mr. Rochester's ward; he commissioned me to find a governess for her. He intended to have her brought up in —shire, I believe. Here she comes, with her 'bonne', as she calls her nurse." The enigma then was explained: this affable and kind little widow was no great dame; but a dependant like myself. I did not like her the worse for that; on the contrary, I felt better pleased than ever. The equality between her and me was real; not the mere result of condescension on her part: so much the better – my position was all the freer.

As I was meditating on this discovery, a little girl, followed by her attendant, came running up the lawn. I looked at my pupil, who did not at first appear to notice me: she was quite a child, perhaps seven or eight years old, slightly built, with a pale, small-featured face, and a redundancy of hair falling in curls to her waist.

"Good morning, Miss Adela," said Mrs. Fairfax. "Come and speak to the lady who is to teach you, and to make you a clever woman some day." She approached.

"C'est là ma gouvernante!" said she, pointing to me, and addressing her nurse; who answered:

"Mais oui, certainement."

"Are they foreigners?" I inquired, amazed at hearing the French language.

"The nurse is a foreigner, and Adela was born on the Continent; and, I believe, never left it till within six months ago. When she first came here she could speak no English; now she can make shift to talk it a little: I don't understand her, she mixes it so with French; but you will make out her meaning very well, I dare say."

Fortunately I had had the advantage of being taught French by a French lady; and as I had always made a point of conversing with Madame Pierrot as often as I could, and had besides, during the last seven years, learnt a portion of French by heart daily – applying myself to take pains with my accent, and imitating as closely as possible the pronunciation of my teacher, I had acquired a certain degree of readiness and correctness in the language, and was not likely to be much at a loss with Mademoiselle Adela. She came and shook hands with me when she heard that I was her governess; and as I led her in to breakfast, I addressed some phrases to her in her own tongue: she replied briefly at first, but after we were seated at the table, and she had examined me some ten minutes with her large hazel eyes, she suddenly commenced chattering fluently.

"Ah!" cried she, in French, "you speak my language as well as Mr. Rochester does: I can talk to you as I can to him, and so can Sophie. She will be glad: nobody here understands her: Madame Fairfax is all English. Sophie is my nurse; she came with me over the sea in a great ship with a chimney that smoked – how it did smoke! – and I was sick, and so was Sophie, and so was Mr. Rochester. Mr. Rochester lay down on a sofa in a pretty room called the salon, and Sophie and I had little beds in another place. I nearly fell out of mine; it was like a shelf. And Mademoiselle – what is your name?"

"Eyre – Jane Eyre."

"Aire? Bah! I cannot say it. Well, our ship stopped in the morning, before it was quite daylight, at a great city – a huge city, with very dark houses and all smoky; not at all like the pretty clean town I came from; and Mr. Rochester carried me in his arms over a plank to the land, and Sophie came after, and we all got into a coach, which took us to a beautiful large house, larger than this and finer, called an hotel. We stayed there nearly a week: I and Sophie used to walk every day in a great green place full of trees, called the Park; and there were many children there besides me, and a pond with beautiful birds in it, that I fed with crumbs."

"Can you understand her when she runs on so fast?" asked Mrs. Fairfax.

I understood her very well, for I had been accustomed to the fluent tongue of Madame Pierrot.

"I wish," continued the good lady, "you would ask her a question or two about her parents: I wonder if she remembers them?"

"Adèle," I inquired, "with whom did you live when you were in that pretty clean town you spoke of?"

"I lived long ago with mama; but she is gone to the Holy Virgin. Mama used to teach me to dance and sing, and to say verses. A great many gentlemen and ladies came to see mama, and I used to dance before them, or to sit on their knees and sing to them: I liked it. Shall I let you hear me sing now?"

She had finished her breakfast, so I permitted her to give a specimen of her accomplishments. Descending from her chair, she came and placed herself on my knee; then, folding her little hands demurely before her, shaking back her curls and lifting her eyes to the ceiling, she commenced singing a song from some opera. It was the strain of a forsaken lady, who, after bewailing the perfidy of her lover, calls pride to her aid; desires her attendant to deck her in her brightest jewels and richest robes, and resolves to meet the false one that night at a ball, and prove to him, by the gaiety of her demeanour, how little his desertion has affected her.

The subject seemed strangely chosen for an infant singer; but I suppose the point of the exhibition lay in hearing the notes of love and jealousy warbled with the lisp of childhood; and in very bad taste that point was: at least I thought so.

Adèle sang the canzonette tunefully enough, and with the *naïveté* of her age. This achieved, she jumped from my knee and said, "Now, Mademoiselle, I will repeat you some poetry."

Assuming an attitude, she began, "La Ligue des Rats: fable de La Fontaine." [6] She then declaimed the little piece with an attention to punctuation and emphasis, a flexibility of voice and an appropriateness of gesture, very unusual indeed at her age, and which proved she had been carefully trained.

"Was it your mama who taught you that piece?" I asked.

"Yes, and she just used to say it in this way: 'Qu' avez vous donc? Lui dit un de ces rats; parlez!' She made me lift my hand – so – to remind me to raise my voice at the question. Now shall I dance for you?"

"No, that will do: but after your mama went to the Holy Virgin, as you say, with whom did you live then?"

"With Madame Frédéric and her husband: she took care of me, but she is nothing related to me. I think she is poor, for she had not so fine a house as mama. I was not long there. Mr. Rochester asked me if I would like to go and live with him in England, and I said yes; for I knew Mr. Rochester before I knew Madame Frédéric, and he was always kind to me and gave me pretty dresses and toys: but you see he has not kept his word, for he has brought me to England, and now he is gone back again himself, and I never see him."

After breakfast, Adèle and I withdrew to the library, which room, it appears, Mr. Rochester had directed should be used as the schoolroom. Most of the books were locked up behind glass doors; but there was one bookcase left open containing everything that could be needed in the way of elementary works, and several volumes of light literature, poetry, biography, travels, a few romances, etc. I suppose he had considered that these were all the governess would require for her private perusal; and, indeed, they contented me amply for the present; compared with the scanty pickings I had now and then been able to glean at Lowood, they seemed to offer an abundant harvest of entertainment and information. In this room, too, there was a cabinet piano, quite new and of superior tone; also an easel for painting and a pair of globes.

I found my pupil sufficiently docile, though disinclined to apply: she had not been used to regular occupation of any kind. I felt it would be injudicious to confine her too much at first; so, when I had talked to her a great deal, and got her to learn a little, and when the morning had advanced to noon, I allowed her to return to her nurse. I then proposed to occupy myself till dinnertime in drawing some little sketches for her use.

As I was going upstairs to fetch my portfolio and pencils, Mrs. Fairfax called to me: "Your morning school hours are over now, I suppose," said she. She was in a room the folding doors of which stood open: I went in when she addressed me. It was a large, stately apartment, with purple chairs and curtains, a Turkey carpet, walnut-panelled walls, one vast window rich in slanted glass, and a lofty ceiling, nobly moulded. Mrs. Fairfax was dusting some vases of fine purple spar, which stood on a sideboard.

"What a beautiful room!" I exclaimed, as I looked round; for I had never before seen any half so imposing.

"Yes; this is the dining room. I have just opened the window, to let in a little air and sunshine; for everything gets so damp in apartments that are seldom inhabited; the drawing room yonder feels like a vault."

She pointed to a wide arch corresponding to the window, and hung like it with a Tyrian-dyed curtain, now looped up. Mounting to it by two broad steps, and looking through, I thought I caught a glimpse of a fairy place, so bright to my novice-eyes appeared the view beyond. Yet it was merely a very pretty drawing room, and within it a boudoir, both spread with white carpets, on which seemed laid brilliant garlands of flowers; both ceiled with snowy mouldings of white grapes and vine leaves, beneath which glowed in rich contrast crimson couches and ottomans; while the ornaments on the pale Parian mantelpiece were of sparkling Bohemian glass, ruby red; and between the windows large mirrors repeated the general blending of snow and fire.

"In what order you keep these rooms, Mrs. Fairfax!" said I. "No dust, no canvas coverings: except that the air feels chilly, one would think they were inhabited daily."

"Why, Miss Eyre, though Mr. Rochester's visits here are rare, they are always sudden and unexpected; and as I observed that it put him out to find everything swathed up, and to have a bustle of arrangement on his arrival, I thought it best to keep the rooms in readiness."

"Is Mr. Rochester an exacting, fastidious sort of man?"

"Not particularly so; but he has a gentleman's tastes and habits, and he expects to have things managed in conformity to them."

"Do you like him? Is he generally liked?"

"Oh, yes; the family have always been respected here. Almost all the land in this neighbourhood, as far as you can see, has belonged to the Rochesters time out of mind."

"Well, but, leaving his land out of the question, do you like him? Is he liked for himself?"

"I have no cause to do otherwise than like him; and I believe he is considered a just and liberal landlord by his tenants: but he has never lived much amongst them."

"But has he no peculiarities? What, in short, is his character?"

"Oh! His character is unimpeachable, I suppose. He is rather peculiar, perhaps: he has travelled a great deal, and seen a great deal of the world, I should think. I dare say he is clever, but I never had much conversation with him."

"In what way is he peculiar?"

"I don't know – it is not easy to describe – nothing striking, but you feel it when he speaks to you; you cannot be always sure whether he is in jest or earnest, whether he is pleased or the contrary; you don't thoroughly understand him, in short – at least, I don't: but it is of no consequence, he is a very good master."

This was all the account I got from Mrs. Fairfax of her employer and mine. There are people who seem to have no notion of sketching a character, or observing and describing salient points, either in persons or things: the good lady evidently belonged to this class; my queries puzzled, but did not draw her out. Mr. Rochester was Mr. Rochester in her eyes; a gentleman, a landed proprietor – nothing more: she inquired and searched no further, and evidently wondered at my wish to gain a more definite notion of his identity.

When we left the dining room, she proposed to show me over the rest of the house; and I followed her upstairs and downstairs, admiring as I went; for all was well arranged and handsome. The large front chambers I thought especially grand: and some of the third-storey rooms, though dark and low, were interesting from their air of antiquity. The furniture once appropriated to the lower apartments had from time to time been removed here, as fashions changed: and the imperfect light entering by their narrow casement showed bedsteads of a hundred years old; chests in oak or walnut, looking, with their strange carvings of palm branches and cherubs' heads, like types of the Hebrew ark; rows of venerable chairs, high-backed and narrow; stools still more antiquated, on whose cushioned tops were yet apparent traces of half-effaced embroideries, wrought by fingers that for two generations had been coffin dust. All these relics gave to the third storey of Thornfield Hall the aspect of a home of the past: a shrine of memory. I liked the hush, the gloom, the quaintness of these retreats in the day; but I by no means coveted a night's repose on one of those wide and heavy beds: shut in, some of them, with doors of oak; shaded, others, with wrought old English hangings crusted with thick work, portraying effigies of strange flowers, and stranger birds, and strangest human beings, – all which would have looked strange, indeed, by the pallid gleam of moonlight.

"Do the servants sleep in these rooms?" I asked.

"No; they occupy a range of smaller apartments to the back; no one ever sleeps here: one would almost say that, if there were a ghost at Thornfield Hall, this would be its haunt."

"So I think: you have no ghost, then?"

"None that I ever heard of," returned Mrs. Fairfax, smiling.

"Nor any traditions of one? No legends or ghost stories?"

"I believe not. And yet it is said the Rochesters have been rather a violent than a quiet race in their time: perhaps, though, that is the reason they rest tranquilly in their graves now."

"Yes – 'after life's fitful fever they sleep well',"⁷ I muttered. "Where are you going now, Mrs. Fairfax?" for she was moving away.

"On to the leads; will you come and see the view from thence?" I followed still, up a very narrow staircase to the attics, and thence by a ladder and through a trapdoor to the roof of the hall. I was now on a level with the crow colony, and could see into their nests. Leaning over the battlements and looking far down, I surveyed the grounds laid out like a map: the bright and velvet lawn closely girdling the grey base of the mansion; the field, wide as a park, dotted with its ancient timber; the wood, dun and sere, divided by a path visibly overgrown, greener with moss than the trees were with foliage; the church at the gates, the road, the tranquil hills, all reposing in the autumn day's sun; the horizon bounded by a propitious sky, azure, marbled with pearly white. No feature in the scene was extraordinary, but all was pleasing. When I turned from it and repassed the trapdoor, I could scarcely see my way down the ladder; the attic seemed black as a vault compared with that arch of blue air to which I had been looking up, and to that sunlit scene of grove, pasture, and green hill, of which the hall was the centre, and over which I had been gazing with delight.

Mrs. Fairfax stayed behind a moment to fasten the trapdoor; I, by drift of groping, found the outlet from the attic, and proceeded to descend the narrow garret staircase. I lingered in the long passage to which this led, separating the front and back rooms of the third storey: narrow, low, and dim, with only one little window at the far end, and looking, with its two rows of small black doors all shut, like a corridor in some Bluebeard's castle.

While I paced softly on, the last sound I expected to hear in so still a region, a laugh, struck my ear. It was a curious laugh; distinct, formal, mirthless. I stopped: the sound ceased, only for an instant; it began again, louder: for at first, though distinct, it was very low. It passed off in a clamorous peal that seemed to wake an echo in every lonely chamber; though it originated but in one, and I could have pointed out the door whence the accents issued.

"Mrs. Fairfax!" I called out: for I now heard her descending the great stairs. "Did you hear that loud laugh? Who is it?"

"Some of the servants, very likely," she answered: "perhaps Grace Poole."

"Did you hear it?" I again inquired.

"Yes, plainly: I often hear her: she sews in one of these rooms. Sometimes Leah is with her; they are frequently noisy together."

The laugh was repeated in its low, syllabic tone, and terminated in an odd murmur.

"Grace!" exclaimed Mrs. Fairfax.

I really did not expect any Grace to answer; for the laugh was as tragic, as preternatural a laugh as any I ever heard; and, but that it was high noon, and that no circumstance of ghostliness accompanied the curious cachinnation; but that neither scene nor season favoured fear, I should have been superstitiously afraid. However, the event showed me I was a fool for entertaining a sense even of surprise.

The door nearest me opened, and a servant came out, – a woman of between thirty and forty; a set, square-made figure, red-haired, and with a hard, plain face: any apparition less romantic or less ghostly could scarcely be conceived.

"Too much noise, Grace," said Mrs. Fairfax. "Remember directions!" Grace curtseyed silently and went in.

"She is a person we have to sew and assist Leah in her housemaid's work," continued the widow; "not altogether unobjectionable in some points, but she does well enough. By-the-bye, how have you got on with your new pupil this morning?"

The conversation, thus turned on Adèle, continued till we reached the light and cheerful region below. Adèle came running to meet us in the hall, exclaiming:

"Mesdames, vous êtes servies!" adding, "J'ai bien faim, moi!"

We found dinner ready, and waiting for us in Mrs. Fairfax's room.

Chapter Twelve

THE PROMISE OF a smooth career, which my first calm introduction to Thornfield Hall seemed to pledge, was not belied on a longer acquaintance with the place and its inmates. Mrs. Fairfax turned out to be what she appeared, a placid-tempered, kind-natured woman, of competent education and average intelligence. My pupil was a lively child, who had been spoilt and indulged, and therefore was sometimes wayward; but as she was committed entirely to my care, and no injudicious interference from any quarter ever thwarted my plans for her improvement, she soon forgot her little freaks, and became obedient and teachable. She had no great talents, no marked traits of character, no peculiar development of feeling or taste which raised her one inch above the ordinary level of childhood; but neither had she any deficiency or vice which sunk her below it. She made reasonable progress, entertained for me a vivacious, though perhaps not very profound, affection; and by her simplicity, gay prattle, and efforts to please, inspired me, in return, with a degree of attachment sufficient to make us both content in each other's society.

This, *par parenthèse*, will be thought cool language by persons who entertain solemn doctrines about the angelic nature of children, and the duty of those charged with their education to conceive for them an idolatrous devotion: but I am not writing to flatter parental egotism, to echo cant, or prop up humbug; I am merely telling the truth. I felt a conscientious solicitude for Adèle's welfare and progress, and a quiet liking for her little self: just as I cherished towards Mrs. Fairfax a thankfulness for her kindness, and a pleasure in her society proportionate to the tranquil regard she had for me, and the moderation of her mind and character.

Anybody may blame me who likes, when I add further, that, now and then, when I took a walk by myself in the grounds; when I went down to the gates and looked through them along the road; or when, while Adèle played with her nurse, and Mrs. Fairfax made jellies in the storeroom, I climbed the three staircases, raised the trapdoor of the attic, and having reached the leads, looked out afar over sequestered field and hill, and along dim skyline – that then I longed for a power of vision which might overpass that limit; which might reach the busy world, towns, regions full of life I had heard of but never seen – that then I desired more of practical experience than I possessed; more of intercourse with my kind, of acquaintance with variety of character, than was here within my reach. I valued what was good in Mrs. Fairfax, and what was good in Adèle; but I believed in the existence of other and more vivid kinds of goodness, and what I believed in I wished to behold.

Who blames me? Many, no doubt; and I shall be called discontented. I could not help it: the restlessness was in my nature; it agitated me to pain sometimes. Then my sole relief was to walk along the corridor of the third storey, backwards and forwards, safe in the silence and solitude of the spot, and allow my mind's eye to dwell on whatever bright visions rose before it – and, certainly, they were many and glowing; to let my heart be heaved by the exultant movement, which, while it swelled it in trouble, expanded it with life; and, best of all, to open my inward ear to a tale that was never ended – a tale my imagination created, and narrated continuously; quickened with all of incident, life, fire, feeling, that I desired and had not in my actual existence.

It is in vain to say human beings ought to be satisfied with tranquillity: they must have action; and they will make it if they cannot find it. Millions are condemned to a stiller doom than mine, and millions are in silent revolt against their lot. Nobody knows how many rebellions besides political rebellions ferment in the masses of life which people earth. Women are supposed to be very calm generally: but women feel just as men feel; they need exercise for their faculties, and a field for their efforts, as much as their brothers do; they suffer from too rigid a restraint, too absolute a stagnation, precisely as men would suffer; and it is narrow-minded in their more privileged fellow creatures to say that they ought to confine themselves to making puddings and knitting stockings, to playing on the piano and embroidering bags. It is thoughtless to condemn them, or laugh at them, if they seek to do more or learn more than custom has pronounced necessary for their sex.

When thus alone, I not unfrequently heard Grace Poole's laugh: the same peal, the same low, slow ha! ha! which, when first heard, had thrilled me: I heard, too, her eccentric murmurs; stranger than her laugh. There were days when she was quite silent;

but there were others when I could not account for the sounds she made. Sometimes I saw her: she would come out of her room with a basin, or a plate, or a tray in her hand, go down to the kitchen and shortly return, generally (oh, romantic reader, forgive me for telling the plain truth!) bearing a pot of porter. Her appearance always acted as a damper to the curiosity raised by her oral oddities: hard-featured and staid, she had no point to which interest could attach. I made some attempts to draw her into conversation, but she seemed a person of few words: a monosyllabic reply usually cut short every effort of that sort.

The other members of the household, viz., John and his wife, Leah the housemaid, and Sophie the French nurse, were decent people; but in no respect remarkable; with Sophie I used to talk French, and sometimes I asked her questions about her native country; but she was not of a descriptive or narrative turn, and generally gave such vapid and confused answers as were calculated rather to check than encourage inquiry.

October, November, December passed away. One afternoon in January, Mrs. Fairfax had begged a holiday for Adèle, because she had a cold; and, as Adèle seconded the request with an ardour that reminded me how precious occasional holidays had been to me in my own childhood, I accorded it, deeming that I did well in showing pliability on the point. It was a fine, calm day, though very cold; I was tired of sitting still in the library through a whole long morning: Mrs. Fairfax had just written a letter which was waiting to be posted, so I put on my bonnet and cloak and volunteered to carry it to Hay; the distance, two miles, would be a pleasant winter afternoon walk. Having seen Adèle comfortably seated in her little chair by Mrs. Fairfax's parlour fireside, and given her her best wax doll (which I usually kept enveloped in silver paper in a drawer) to play with, and a story-book for change of amusement; and having replied to her "Revenez bientôt, ma bonne amie, ma chère Mdlle. Jeannette," with a kiss I set out.

The ground was hard, the air was still, my road was lonely; I walked fast till I got warm, and then I walked slowly to enjoy and analyse the species of pleasure brooding for me in the hour and situation. It was three o'clock; the church bell tolled as I passed under the belfry: the charm of the hour lay in its approaching dimness, in the low-gliding and pale-beaming sun. I was a mile from Thornfield, in a lane noted for wild roses in summer, for nuts and blackberries in autumn, and even now possessing a few coral treasures in hips and haws, but whose best winter delight lay in its utter solitude and leafless repose. If a breath of air stirred, it made no sound here; for there was not a holly, not an evergreen to rustle, and the stripped hawthorn and hazel bushes were as still as the white, worn stones which causewayed the middle of the path. Far and wide, on each side, there were only fields, where no cattle now browsed; and the little brown birds, which stirred occasionally in the hedge, looked like single russet leaves that had forgotten to drop.

This lane inclined uphill all the way to Hay; having reached the middle, I sat down on a stile which led thence into a field. Gathering my mantle about me, and sheltering my hands in my muff, I did not feel the cold, though it froze keenly; as was attested by a sheet of ice covering the causeway, where a little brooklet, now congealed, had overflowed after a rapid thaw some days since. From my seat I could look down on Thornfield: the grey and battlemented hall was the principal object in the vale below me; its woods and dark rookery rose against the west. I lingered till the sun went down amongst the trees, and sank crimson and clear behind them. I then turned eastward.

On the hilltop above me sat the rising moon; pale yet as a cloud, but brightening momentarily, she looked over Hay, which, half lost in trees, sent up a blue smoke from its few chimneys: it was yet a mile distant, but in the absolute hush I could hear plainly its thin murmurs of life. My ear, too, felt the flow of currents; in what dales and depths I could not tell: but there were many hills beyond Hay, and doubtless many becks threading their passes. That evening calm betrayed alike the tinkle of the nearest streams, the sough of the most remote.

A rude noise broke on these fine ripplings and whisperings, at once so far away and so clear: a positive tramp, tramp, a metallic clatter, which effaced the soft wave-wanderings; as, in a picture, the solid mass of a crag, or the rough boles of a great oak, drawn in dark and strong on the foreground, efface the aerial distance of azure hill, sunny horizon, and blended clouds where tint melts into tint.

The din was on the causeway: a horse was coming; the windings of the lane yet hid it, but it approached. I was just leaving the stile; yet, as the path was narrow, I sat still to let it go by. In those days I was young, and all sorts of fancies bright and dark tenanted my mind: the memories of nursery stories were there amongst other rubbish; and when they recurred, maturing youth added to them a vigour and vividness beyond what childhood could give. As this horse approached, and as I watched for it to appear through the dusk, I remembered certain of Bessie's tales, wherein figured a North-of-England spirit called a 'Gytrash', which, in the form of horse, mule, or large dog, haunted solitary ways, and sometimes came upon belated travellers, as this horse was now coming upon me.

It was very near, but not yet in sight; when, in addition to the tramp, tramp, I heard a rush under the hedge, and close down by the hazel stems glided a great dog, whose black and white colour made him a distinct object against the trees. It was exactly one form of Bessie's Gytrash – a lion-like creature with long hair and a huge head: it passed me, however, quietly enough; not staying to look up, with strange pretercanine eyes, in my face, as I half expected it would. The horse followed, – a tall steed, and on its back a rider. The man, the human being, broke the spell at once. Nothing ever rode the Gytrash: it was always alone; and goblins, to my notions, though they might tenant the dumb carcasses of beasts, could scarce covet shelter in the commonplace human form. No Gytrash was this, – only a traveller taking the short cut to Millcote. He passed, and I went on; a few steps, and I turned: a sliding sound and an exclamation of "What the deuce is to do now?" and a clattering tumble, arrested my attention. Man and horse were down; they had slipped on the sheet of ice which glazed the causeway. The dog came bounding back, and seeing his master in a predicament, and hearing the horse groan, barked till the evening hills echoed the sound, which was deep in proportion to his magnitude. He snuffed round the prostrate group, and then he ran up to me; it was all he could do, – there was no other help at hand to summon. I obeyed him, and walked down to the traveller, by this time struggling himself free of his steed. His efforts were so vigorous, I thought he could not be much hurt; but I asked him the question:

"Are you injured, sir?"

I think he was swearing, but am not certain; however, he was pronouncing some formula which prevented him from replying to me directly.

"Can I do anything?" I asked again.

"You must just stand on one side," he answered as he rose, first to his knees, and then to his feet. I did; whereupon began a heaving, stamping, clattering process, accompanied by a barking and baying which removed me effectually some yards' distance; but I would not be driven quite away till I saw the event. This was finally fortunate; the horse was re-established, and the dog was silenced with a "Down, Pilot!" The traveller now, stooping, felt his foot and leg, as if trying whether they were sound; apparently something ailed them, for he halted to the stile whence I had just risen, and sat down.

I was in the mood for being useful, or at least officious, I think, for I now drew near him again.

"If you are hurt, and want help, sir, I can fetch some one either from Thornfield Hall or from Hay."

"Thank you: I shall do: I have no broken bones, – only a sprain;" and again he stood up and tried his foot, but the result extorted an involuntary "Ugh!"

Something of daylight still lingered, and the moon was waxing bright: I could see him plainly. His figure was enveloped in a riding cloak, fur collared and steel clasped; its details were not apparent, but I traced the general points of middle height and considerable breadth of chest. He had a dark face, with stern features and a heavy brow; his eyes and gathered eyebrows looked ireful and thwarted just now; he was past youth, but had not reached middle-age; perhaps he might be thirty-five. I felt no fear of him, and but little shyness. Had he been a handsome, heroic-looking young gentleman, I should not have dared to stand thus questioning him against his will, and offering my services unasked. I had hardly ever seen a handsome youth; never in my life spoken to one. I had a theoretical reverence and homage for beauty, elegance, gallantry, fascination; but had I met those qualities incarnate in masculine shape, I should have known instinctively that they neither had nor could have sympathy with anything in me, and should have shunned them as one would fire, lightning, or anything else that is bright but antipathetic.

If even this stranger had smiled and been good-humoured to me when I addressed him; if he had put off my offer of assistance gaily and with thanks, I should have gone on my way and not felt any vocation to renew inquiries: but the frown, the roughness of the traveller, set me at my ease: I retained my station when he waved to me to go, and announced:

"I cannot think of leaving you, sir, at so late an hour, in this solitary lane, till I see you are fit to mount your horse."

He looked at me when I said this; he had hardly turned his eyes in my direction before.

"I should think you ought to be at home yourself," said he, "if you have a home in this neighbourhood: where do you come from?"

"From just below; and I am not at all afraid of being out late when it is moonlight: I will run over to Hay for you with pleasure, if you wish it: indeed, I am going there to post a letter."

"You live just below – do you mean at that house with the battlements?" pointing to Thornfield Hall, on which the moon cast a hoary gleam, bringing it out distinct and pale from the woods that, by contrast with the western sky, now seemed one mass of shadow.

"Yes, sir."

"Whose house is it?"

"Mr. Rochester's."

"Do you know Mr. Rochester?"

"No, I have never seen him."

"He is not resident, then?"

"No."

"Can you tell me where he is?"

"I cannot."

"You are not a servant at the hall, of course. You are –" He stopped, ran his eye over my dress, which, as usual, was quite simple: a black merino cloak, a black beaver bonnet; neither of them half fine enough for a lady's-maid. He seemed puzzled to decide what I was; I helped him.

"I am the governess."

"Ah, the governess!" he repeated; "deuce take me, if I had not forgotten! The governess!" and again my raiment underwent scrutiny. In two minutes he rose from the stile: his face expressed pain when he tried to move.

"I cannot commission you to fetch help," he said; "but you may help me a little yourself, if you will be so kind."

"Yes, sir."

"You have not an umbrella that I can use as a stick?"

"No."

"Try to get hold of my horse's bridle and lead him to me: you are not afraid?"

I should have been afraid to touch a horse when alone, but when told to do it, I was disposed to obey. I put down my muff on the stile, and went up to the tall steed; I endeavoured to catch the bridle, but it was a spirited thing, and would not let me come near its head; I made effort on effort, though in vain: meantime, I was mortally afraid of its trampling fore-feet. The traveller waited and watched for some time, and at last he laughed.

"I see," he said, "the mountain will never be brought to Mahomet, so all you can do is to aid Mahomet to go to the mountain; I must beg of you to come here."

I came. "Excuse me," he continued: "necessity compels me to make you useful." He laid a heavy hand on my shoulder, and leaning on me with some stress, limped to his horse. Having once caught the bridle, he mastered it directly and sprang to his saddle; grimacing grimly as he made the effort, for it wrenched his sprain.

"Now," said he, releasing his under lip from a hard bite, "just hand me my whip; it lies there under the hedge."

I sought it and found it.

"Thank you; now make haste with the letter to Hay, and return as fast as you can."

A touch of a spurred heel made his horse first start and rear, and then bound away; the dog rushed in his traces; all three vanished

Like heath that, in the wilderness,
The wild wind whirls away. [8]

I took up my muff and walked on. The incident had occurred and was gone for me: it *was* an incident of no moment, no romance, no interest in a sense; yet it marked with change one single hour of a monotonous life. My help had been needed and claimed; I had given it: I was pleased to have done something; trivial, transitory though the deed was, it was yet an active thing, and I was weary of an existence all passive. The new face, too, was like a new picture introduced to the gallery of memory; and it was dissimilar to all the others hanging there: firstly, because it was masculine; and, secondly, because it was dark, strong, and stern. I had it still before me when I entered Hay, and slipped the letter into the post office; I saw it as I walked fast downhill all the way home. When I came to the stile, I stopped a minute, looked round and listened, with an idea that a horse's hoofs might ring on the causeway again, and that a rider in a cloak, and a Gytrash-like Newfoundland dog, might be again apparent: I saw only the hedge and a pollard willow before me, rising up still and straight to meet the moonbeams; I heard only the faintest waft of wind roaming fitful among the trees round Thornfield, a mile distant; and when I glanced down in the direction of the murmur, my eye, traversing the hall-front, caught a light kindling in a window: it reminded me that I was late, and I hurried on.

I did not like re-entering Thornfield. To pass its threshold was to return to stagnation; to cross the silent hall, to ascend the darksome staircase, to seek my own lonely little room, and then to meet tranquil Mrs. Fairfax, and spend the long winter evening with her, and her only, was to quell wholly the faint excitement wakened by my walk, – to slip again over my faculties the viewless fetters of an uniform and too still existence; of an existence whose very privileges of security and ease I was becoming incapable of appreciating. What good it would have done me at that time to have been tossed in the storms of an uncertain struggling life, and to have been taught by rough and bitter experience to long for the calm amidst which I now repined! Yes, just as much good as it would do a man tired of sitting still in a 'too easy chair' to take a long walk: and just as natural was the wish to stir, under my circumstances, as it would be under his.

I lingered at the gates; I lingered on the lawn; I paced backwards and forwards on the pavement; the shutters of the glass door were closed; I could not see into the interior; and both my eyes and spirit seemed drawn from the gloomy house – from the grey-hollow filled with rayless cells, as it appeared to me – to that sky expanded before me, – a blue sea absolved from taint of cloud; the moon ascending it in solemn march; her orb seeming to look up as she left the hilltops, from behind which she had come, far and farther below her, and aspired to the zenith, midnight dark in its fathomless depth and measureless distance; and for those trembling stars that followed her course; they made my heart tremble, my veins glow when I viewed them. Little things recall us to earth; the clock struck in the hall; that sufficed; I turned from moon and stars, opened a side-door, and went in.

The hall was not dark, nor yet was it lit, only by the high-hung bronze lamp; a warm glow suffused both it and the lower steps of the oak staircase. This ruddy shine issued from the great dining room, whose two-leaved door stood open, and showed a genial fire in the grate, glancing on marble hearth and brass fire irons, and revealing purple draperies and polished furniture, in the most pleasant radiance. It revealed, too, a group near the mantelpiece: I had scarcely caught it, and scarcely become aware of a cheerful mingling of voices, amongst which I seemed to distinguish the tones of Adèle, when the door closed.

I hastened to Mrs. Fairfax's room; there was a fire there too, but no candle, and no Mrs. Fairfax. Instead, all alone, sitting upright on the rug, and gazing with gravity at the blaze, I beheld a great black and white long-haired dog, just like the Gytrash of the lane. It was so like it that I went forward and said – "Pilot" and the thing got up and came to me and snuffed me. I caressed him, and he wagged his great tail; but he looked an eerie creature to be alone with, and I could not tell whence he had come. I rang the bell, for I wanted a candle; and I wanted, too, to get an account of this visitant. Leah entered.

"What dog is this?"

"He came with master."

"With whom?"

"With master – Mr. Rochester – he is just arrived."

"Indeed! And is Mrs. Fairfax with him?"

"Yes, and Miss Adèle; they are in the dining room, and John is gone for a surgeon; for master has had an accident; his horse fell and his ankle is sprained."

"Did the horse fall in Hay Lane?"

"Yes, coming downhill; it slipped on some ice."

"Ah! Bring me a candle will you Leah?"

Leah brought it; she entered, followed by Mrs. Fairfax, who repeated the news; adding that Mr. Carter the surgeon was come, and was now with Mr. Rochester: then she hurried out to give orders about tea, and I went upstairs to take off my things.

Chapter Thirteen

MR. ROCHESTER, it seems, by the surgeon's orders, went to bed early that night; nor did he rise soon next morning. When he did come down, it was to attend to business: his agent and some of his tenants were arrived, and waiting to speak with him.

Adèle and I had now to vacate the library: it would be in daily requisition as a reception room for callers. A fire was lit in an apartment upstairs, and there I carried our books, and arranged it for the future schoolroom. I discerned in the course of the morning that Thornfield Hall was a changed place: no longer silent as a church, it echoed every hour or two to a knock at the door, or a clang of the bell; steps, too, often traversed the hall, and new voices spoke in different keys below; a rill from the outer world was flowing through it; it had a master: for my part, I liked it better.

Adèle was not easy to teach that day; she could not apply: she kept running to the door and looking over the banisters to see if she could get a glimpse of Mr. Rochester; then she coined pretexts to go downstairs, in order, as I shrewdly suspected, to visit the library, where I knew she was not wanted; then, when I got a little angry, and made her sit still, she continued to talk incessantly of her "ami, Monsieur Edouard Fairfax *de* Rochester," as she dubbed him (I had not before heard his prenomens), ⁹ and to conjecture what presents he had brought her: for it appears he had intimated the night before, that when his luggage came from Millcote, there would be found amongst it a little box in whose contents she had an interest.

"Et cela doit signifier," said she, "qu'il y aura là dedans un cadeau pour moi, et peut-être pour vous aussi, mademoiselle. Monsieur a parlé de vous: il m'a demandé le nom de ma gouvernante, et si elle n'était pas une petite personne, assez mince et un peu pâle. J'ai dit qu'oui: car c'est vrai, n'est-ce pas, mademoiselle?"

I and my pupil dined as usual in Mrs. Fairfax's parlour; the afternoon was wild and snowy, and we passed it in the schoolroom. At dark I allowed Adèle to put away books and work, and to run downstairs; for, from the comparative silence below, and from the cessation of appeals to the doorbell, I conjectured that Mr. Rochester was now at liberty. Left alone, I walked to the window; but nothing was to be seen thence: twilight and snowflakes together thickened the air, and hid the very shrubs on the lawn. I let down the curtain and went back to the fireside.

In the clear embers I was tracing a view, not unlike a picture I remembered to have seen of the castle of Heidelberg, on the Rhine, when Mrs. Fairfax came in, breaking up by her entrance the fiery mosaic I had been piercing together, and scattering too some heavy unwelcome thoughts that were beginning to throng on my solitude.

"Mr. Rochester would be glad if you and your pupil would take tea with him in the drawing room this evening," said she: "he has been so much engaged all day that he could not ask to see you before."

"When is his tea time?" I inquired.

"Oh, at six o'clock: he keeps early hours in the country. You had better change your frock now; I will go with you and fasten it. Here is a candle."

"Is it necessary to change my frock?"

"Yes, you had better: I always dress for the evening when Mr. Rochester is here."

This additional ceremony seemed somewhat stately; however, I repaired to my room, and, with Mrs. Fairfax's aid, replaced my black stuff dress by one of black silk; the best and the only additional one I had, except one of light grey, which, in my Lowood notions of the toilette, I thought too fine to be worn, except on first-rate occasions.

"You want a brooch," said Mrs. Fairfax. I had a single little pearl ornament which Miss Temple gave me as a parting keepsake: I put it on, and then we went downstairs. Unused as I was to strangers, it was rather a trial to appear thus formally summoned in Mr. Rochester's presence. I let Mrs. Fairfax precede me into the dining room, and kept in her shade as we crossed that apartment; and, passing the arch, whose curtain was now dropped, entered the elegant recess beyond.

Two wax candles stood lighted on the table, and two on the mantelpiece; basking in the light and heat of a superb fire, lay Pilot – Adèle knelt near him. Half reclined on a couch appeared Mr. Rochester, his foot supported by the cushion; he was looking at Adèle and the dog: the fire shone full on his face. I knew my traveller with his broad and jetty eyebrows;

his square forehead, made squarer by the horizontal sweep of his black hair. I recognised his decisive nose, more remarkable for character than beauty; his full nostrils, denoting, I thought, choler; his grim mouth, chin, and jaw – yes, all three were very grim, and no mistake. His shape, now divested of cloak, I perceived harmonised in squareness with his physiognomy: I suppose it was a good figure in the athletic sense of the term – broad chested and thin flanked, though neither tall nor graceful.

Mr. Rochester must have been aware of the entrance of Mrs. Fairfax and myself; but it appeared he was not in the mood to notice us, for he never lifted his head as we approached.

"Here is Miss Eyre, sir," said Mrs. Fairfax, in her quiet way. He bowed, still not taking his eyes from the group of the dog and child.

"Let Miss Eyre be seated," said he: and there was something in the forced stiff bow, in the impatient yet formal tone, which seemed further to express, "What the deuce is it to me whether Miss Eyre be there or not? At this moment I am not disposed to accost her."

I sat down quite disembarrassed. A reception of finished politeness would probably have confused me: I could not have returned or repaid it by answering grace and elegance on my part; but harsh caprice laid me under no obligation; on the contrary, a decent quiescence, under the freak of manner, gave me the advantage. Besides, the eccentricity of the proceeding was piquant: I felt interested to see how he would go on.

He went on as a statue would, that is, he neither spoke nor moved. Mrs. Fairfax seemed to think it necessary that some one should be amiable, and she began to talk. Kindly, as usual – and, as usual, rather trite – she condoled with him on the pressure of business he had had all day; on the annoyance it must have been to him with that painful sprain: then she commended his patience and perseverance in going through with it.

"Madam, I should like some tea," was the sole rejoinder she got. She hastened to ring the bell; and when the tray came, she proceeded to arrange the cups, spoons, etc., with assiduous celerity. I and Adèle went to the table; but the master did not leave his couch.

"Will you hand Mr. Rochester's cup?" said Mrs. Fairfax to me; "Adèle might perhaps spill it."

I did as requested. As he took the cup from my hand, Adèle, thinking the moment propitious for making a request in my favour, cried out:

"N'est-ce pas, monsieur, qu'il y a un cadeau pour Mademoiselle Eyre dans votre petit coffre?"

"Who talks of cadeaux?" said he gruffly. "Did you expect a present, Miss Eyre? Are you fond of presents?" and he searched my face with eyes that I saw were dark, irate, and piercing.

"I hardly know, sir; I have little experience of them: they are generally thought pleasant things."

"Generally thought? But what do *you* think?"

"I should be obliged to take time, sir, before I could give you an answer worthy of your acceptance: a present has many faces to it, has it not? And one should consider all, before pronouncing an opinion as to its nature."

"Miss Eyre, you are not so unsophisticated as Adèle: she demands a 'cadeau', clamorously, the moment she sees me: you beat about the bush."

"Because I have less confidence in my deserts than Adèle has: she can prefer the claim of old acquaintance, and the right too of custom; for she says you have always been in the habit of giving her playthings; but if I had to make out a case I should be puzzled, since I am a stranger, and have done nothing to entitle me to an acknowledgment."

"Oh, don't fall back on over-modesty! I have examined Adèle, and find you have taken great pains with her: she is not bright, she has no talents; yet in a short time she has made much improvement."

"Sir, you have now given me my 'cadeau'; I am obliged to you: it is the meed teachers most covet – praise of their pupils' progress."

"Humph!" said Mr. Rochester, and he took his tea in silence.

"Come to the fire," said the master, when the tray was taken away, and Mrs. Fairfax had settled into a corner with her knitting; while Adèle was leading me by the hand round the room, showing me the beautiful books and ornaments on the consoles and chiffonnières. We obeyed, as in duty bound; Adèle wanted to take a seat on my knee, but she was ordered to amuse herself with Pilot.

"You have been resident in my house three months?"

"Yes, sir."

"And you came from –?"

"From Lowood school, in —shire."

"Ah! A charitable concern. How long were you there?"

"Eight years."

"Eight years! You must be tenacious of life. I thought half the time in such a place would have done up any constitution! No wonder you have rather the look of another world. I marvelled where you had got that sort of face. When you came on me in Hay Lane last night, I thought unaccountably of fairy tales, and had half a mind to demand whether you had bewitched my horse: I am not sure yet. Who are your parents?"

"I have none."

"Nor ever had, I suppose: do you remember them?"

"No."

"I thought not. And so you were waiting for your people when you sat on that stile?"

"For whom, sir?"

"For the men in green: it was a proper moonlight evening for them. Did I break through one of your rings, that you spread that damned ice on the causeway?"

I shook my head. "The men in green all forsook England a hundred years ago," said I, speaking as seriously as he had done. "And not even in Hay Lane, or the fields about it, could you find a trace of them. I don't think either summer or harvest, or winter moon, will ever shine on their revels more."

Mrs. Fairfax had dropped her knitting, and, with raised eyebrows, seemed wondering what sort of talk this was.

"Well," resumed Mr. Rochester, "if you disown parents, you must have some sort of kinsfolk: uncles and aunts?"

"No; none that I ever saw."

"And your home?"

"I have none."

"Where do your brothers and sisters live?"

"I have no brothers or sisters."

"Who recommended you to come here?"

"I advertised, and Mrs. Fairfax answered my advertisement."

"Yes," said the good lady, who now knew what ground we were upon, "and I am daily thankful for the choice Providence led me to make. Miss Eyre has been an invaluable companion to me, and a kind and careful teacher to Adèle."

"Don't trouble yourself to give her a character," returned Mr. Rochester: "eulogiums will not bias me; I shall judge for myself. She began by felling my horse."

"Sir?" said Mrs. Fairfax.

"I have to thank her for this sprain."

The widow looked bewildered.

"Miss Eyre, have you ever lived in a town?"

"No, sir."

"Have you seen much society?"

"None but the pupils and teachers of Lowood, and now the inmates of Thornfield."

"Have you read much?"

"Only such books as came in my way; and they have not been numerous or very learned."

"You have lived the life of a nun: no doubt you are well drilled in religious forms; – Brocklehurst, who I understand directs Lowood, is a parson, is he not?"

"Yes, sir."

"And you girls probably worshipped him, as a convent full of religieuses would worship their director."

"Oh, no."

"You are very cool! No! What! A novice not worship her priest! That sounds blasphemous."

"I disliked Mr. Brocklehurst; and I was not alone in the feeling. He is a harsh man; at once pompous and meddling; he cut off our hair; and for economy's sake bought us bad needles and thread, with which we could hardly sew."

"That was very false economy," remarked Mrs. Fairfax, who now again caught the drift of the dialogue.

"And was that the head and front of his offending?" demanded Mr. Rochester.

"He starved us when he had the sole superintendence of the provision department, before the committee was appointed; and he bored us with long lectures once a week, and with evening readings from books of his own inditing, about sudden deaths and judgments, which made us afraid to go to bed."

"What age were you when you went to Lowood?"

"About ten."

"And you stayed there eight years: you are now, then, eighteen?"

I assented.

"Arithmetic, you see, is useful; without its aid, I should hardly have been able to guess your age. It is a point difficult to fix where the features and countenance are so much at variance as in your case. And now what did you learn at Lowood? Can you play?"

"A little."

"Of course: that is the established answer. Go into the library – I mean, if you please. – (Excuse my tone of command; I am used to say, 'Do this', and it is done: I cannot alter my customary habits for one new inmate.) – Go, then, into the library; take a candle with you; leave the door open; sit down to the piano, and play a tune."

I departed, obeying his directions.

"Enough!" he called out in a few minutes. "You play *a little*, I see; like any other English schoolgirl; perhaps rather better than some, but not well."

I closed the piano and returned. Mr. Rochester continued – "Adèle showed me some sketches this morning, which she said were yours. I don't know whether they were entirely of your doing; probably a master aided you?"

"No, indeed!" I interjected.

"Ah! That pricks pride. Well, fetch me your portfolio, if you can vouch for its contents being original; but don't pass your word unless you are certain: I can recognise patchwork."

"Then I will say nothing, and you shall judge for yourself, sir."

I brought the portfolio from the library.

"Approach the table," said he; and I wheeled it to his couch. Adèle and Mrs. Fairfax drew near to see the pictures.

"No crowding," said Mr. Rochester: "take the drawings from my hand as I finish with them; but don't push your faces up to mine."

He deliberately scrutinised each sketch and painting. Three he laid aside; the others, when he had examined them, he swept from him.

"Take them off to the other table, Mrs. Fairfax," said he, "and look at them with Adèle; – you" (glancing at me) "resume your seat, and answer my questions. I perceive those pictures were done by one hand: was that hand yours?"

"Yes."

"And when did you find time to do them? They have taken much time, and some thought."

"I did them in the last two vacations I spent at Lowood, when I had no other occupation."

"Where did you get your copies?"

"Out of my head."

"That head I see now on your shoulders?"

"Yes, sir."

"Has it other furniture of the same kind within?"

"I should think it may have: I should hope – better."

He spread the pictures before him, and again surveyed them alternately.

While he is so occupied, I will tell you, reader, what they are: and first, I must premise that they are nothing wonderful. The subjects had, indeed, risen vividly on my mind. As I saw them with the spiritual eye, before I attempted to embody them, they were striking; but my hand would not second my fancy, and in each case it had wrought out but a pale portrait of the thing I had conceived.

These pictures were in water colours. The first represented clouds low and livid, rolling over a swollen sea: all the distance was in eclipse; so, too, was the foreground; or rather, the nearest billows, for there was no land. One gleam of light lifted into relief a half-submerged mast, on which sat a cormorant, dark and large, with wings flecked with foam; its beak held a gold bracelet set with gems, that I had touched with as brilliant tints as my palette could yield, and as glittering distinctness as my pencil could impart. Sinking below the bird and mast, a drowned corpse glanced through the green water; a fair arm was the only limb clearly visible, whence the bracelet had been washed or torn.

The second picture contained for foreground only the dim peak of a hill, with grass and some leaves slanting as if by a breeze. Beyond and above spread an expanse of sky, dark blue as at twilight: rising into the sky was a woman's shape to the bust, portrayed in tints as dusk and soft as I could combine. The dim forehead was crowned with a star; the lineaments below were seen as through the suffusion of vapour; the eyes shone dark and wild; the hair streamed shadowy, like a beamless cloud torn by storm or by electric travail. On the neck lay a pale reflection like moonlight; the same faint lustre touched the train of thin clouds from which rose and bowed this vision of the Evening Star.

The third showed the pinnacle of an iceberg piercing a polar winter sky: a muster of northern lights reared their dim lances, close serried, along the horizon. Throwing these into distance, rose, in the foreground, a head, – a colossal head, inclined towards the iceberg, and resting against it. Two thin hands, joined under the forehead, and supporting it, drew up before the lower features a sable veil, a brow quite bloodless, white as bone, and an eye hollow and fixed, blank of meaning but for the glassiness of despair, alone were visible. Above the temples, amidst wreathed turban folds of black drapery, vague in its character and consistency as cloud, gleamed a ring of white flame, gemmed with sparkles of a more lurid tinge. This pale crescent was 'the likeness of a kingly crown'; what it diademed was 'the shape which shape had none'. [10]

"Were you happy when you painted these pictures?" asked Mr. Rochester presently.

"I was absorbed, sir: yes, and I was happy. To paint them, in short, was to enjoy one of the keenest pleasures I have ever known."

"That is not saying much. Your pleasures, by your own account, have been few; but I daresay you did exist in a kind of artist's dreamland while you blent and arranged these strange tints. Did you sit at them long each day?"

"I had nothing else to do, because it was the vacation, and I sat at them from morning till noon, and from noon till night: the length of the midsummer days favoured my inclination to apply."

"And you felt self-satisfied with the result of your ardent labours?"

"Far from it. I was tormented by the contrast between my idea and my handiwork: in each case I had imagined something which I was quite powerless to realise."

"Not quite: you have secured the shadow of your thought; but no more, probably. You had not enough of the artist's skill and science to give it full being: yet the drawings are, for a schoolgirl, peculiar. As to the thoughts, they are elfish. These eyes in the Evening Star you must have seen in a dream. How could you make them look so clear, and yet not at all brilliant? For the planet above quells their rays. And what meaning is that in their solemn depth? And who taught you to paint wind? There is a high gale in that sky, and on this hilltop. Where did you see Latmos? For that is Latmos. There! Put the drawings away!"

I had scarce tied the strings of the portfolio, when, looking at his watch, he said abruptly:

"It is nine o'clock: what are you about, Miss Eyre, to let Adèle sit up so long? Take her to bed."

Adèle went to kiss him before quitting the room: he endured the caress, but scarcely seemed to relish it more than Pilot would have done, nor so much.

"I wish you all goodnight, now," said he, making a movement of the hand towards the door, in token that he was tired of our company, and wished to dismiss us. Mrs. Fairfax folded up her knitting: I took my portfolio: we curtseyed to him, received a frigid bow in return, and so withdrew.

"You said Mr. Rochester was not strikingly peculiar, Mrs. Fairfax," I observed, when I rejoined her in her room, after putting Adèle to bed.

"Well, is he?"

"I think so: he is very changeful and abrupt."

"True: no doubt he may appear so to a stranger, but I am so accustomed to his manner, I never think of it; and then, if he has peculiarities of temper, allowance should be made."

"Why?"

"Partly because it is his nature – and we can none of us help our nature; and partly because he has painful thoughts, no doubt, to harass him, and make his spirits unequal."

"What about?"

"Family troubles, for one thing."

"But he has no family."

"Not now, but he has had – or, at least, relatives. He lost his elder brother a few years since."

"His *elder* brother?"

"Yes. The present Mr. Rochester has not been very long in possession of the property; only about nine years."

"Nine years is a tolerable time. Was he so very fond of his brother as to be still inconsolable for his loss?"

"Why, no – perhaps not. I believe there were some misunderstandings between them. Mr. Rowland Rochester was not quite just to Mr. Edward; and perhaps he prejudiced his father against him. The old gentleman was fond of money, and anxious to keep the family estate together. He did not like to diminish the property by division, and yet he was anxious that Mr. Edward should have wealth, too, to keep up the consequence of the name; and, soon after he was of age, some steps were taken that were not quite fair, and made a great deal of mischief. Old Mr. Rochester and Mr. Rowland combined to bring Mr. Edward into what he considered a painful position, for the sake of making his fortune: what the precise nature of that position was I never clearly knew, but his spirit could not brook what he had to suffer in it. He is not very forgiving: he broke with his family, and now for many years he has led an unsettled kind of life. I don't think he has ever been resident at Thornfield for a fortnight together, since the death of his brother without a will left him master of the estate; and, indeed, no wonder he shuns the old place."

"Why should he shun it?"

"Perhaps he thinks it gloomy."

The answer was evasive. I should have liked something clearer; but Mrs. Fairfax either could not, or would not, give me more explicit information of the origin and nature of Mr. Rochester's trials. She averred they were a mystery to herself, and that what she knew was chiefly from conjecture. It was evident, indeed, that she wished me to drop the subject, which I did accordingly.

Chapter Fourteen

FOR SEVERAL subsequent days I saw little of Mr. Rochester. In the mornings he seemed much engaged with business, and, in the afternoon, gentlemen from Millcote or the neighbourhood called, and sometimes stayed to dine with him. When his sprain was well enough to admit of horse exercise, he rode out a good deal; probably to return these visits, as he generally did not come back till late at night.

During this interval, even Adèle was seldom sent for to his presence, and all my acquaintance with him was confined to an occasional rencontre in the hall, on the stairs, or in the gallery, when he would sometimes pass me haughtily and coldly, just acknowledging my presence by a distant nod or a cool glance, and sometimes bow and smile with gentlemanlike affability. His changes of mood did not offend me, because I saw that I had nothing to do with their alternation; the ebb and flow depended on causes quite disconnected with me.

One day he had had company to dinner, and had sent for my portfolio; in order, doubtless, to exhibit its contents: the gentlemen went away early, to attend a public meeting at Millcote, as Mrs. Fairfax informed me; but the night being wet and inclement, Mr. Rochester did not accompany them. Soon after they were gone he rang the bell: a message came that I and Adèle were to go downstairs. I brushed Adèle's hair and made her neat, and having ascertained that I was myself in my usual Quaker trim, where there was nothing to retouch – all being too close and plain, braided locks included, to admit of disarrangement – we descended, Adèle wondering whether the *petit coffre* was at length come; for, owing to some mistake, its arrival had hitherto been delayed. She was gratified: there it stood, a little carton, on the table when we entered the dining room. She appeared to know it by instinct.

"Ma boite! Ma boite!" exclaimed she, running towards it.

"Yes, there is your 'boite' at last: take it into a corner, you genuine daughter of Paris, and amuse yourself with disembowelling it," said the deep and rather sarcastic voice of Mr. Rochester, proceeding from the depths of an immense easy chair at the fireside. "And mind," he continued, "don't bother me with any details of the anatomical process, or any notice of the condition of the entrails: let your operation be conducted in silence: tiens-toi tranquille, enfant; comprends-tu?"

Adèle seemed scarcely to need the warning – she had already retired to a sofa with her treasure, and was busy untying the cord which secured the lid. Having removed this impediment, and lifted certain silvery envelopes of tissue paper, she merely exclaimed:

"Oh ciel! Que c'est beau!" and then remained absorbed in ecstatic contemplation.

"Is Miss Eyre there?" now demanded the master, half rising from his seat to look round to the door, near which I still stood.

"Ah! Well, come forward; be seated here." He drew a chair near his own. "I am not fond of the prattle of children," he continued; "for, old bachelor as I am, I have no pleasant associations connected with their lisp. It would be intolerable to me to pass a whole evening *tête-à-tête* with a brat. Don't draw that chair farther off, Miss Eyre; sit down exactly where I placed it – if you please, that is. Confound these civilities! I continually forget them. Nor do I particularly affect simple-minded old ladies. By-the-bye, I must have mine in mind; it won't do to neglect her; she is a Fairfax, or wed to one; and blood is said to be thicker than water."

He rang, and despatched an invitation to Mrs. Fairfax, who soon arrived, knitting-basket in hand.

"Good evening, madam; I sent to you for a charitable purpose. I have forbidden Adèle to talk to me about her presents, and she is bursting with repletion: have the goodness to serve her as auditress and interlocutrice; it will be one of the most benevolent acts you ever performed."

Adèle, indeed, no sooner saw Mrs. Fairfax, than she summoned her to her sofa, and there quickly filled her lap with the porcelain, the ivory, the waxen contents of her 'boite'; pouring out, meantime, explanations and raptures in such broken English as she was mistress of.

"Now I have performed the part of a good host," pursued Mr. Rochester, "put my guests into the way of amusing each other, I ought to be at liberty to attend to my own pleasure. Miss Eyre, draw your chair still a little farther forward:

you are yet too far back; I cannot see you without disturbing my position in this comfortable chair, which I have no mind to do."

I did as I was bid, though I would much rather have remained somewhat in the shade; but Mr. Rochester had such a direct way of giving orders, it seemed a matter of course to obey him promptly.

We were, as I have said, in the dining room: the lustre, which had been lit for dinner, filled the room with a festal breadth of light; the large fire was all red and clear; the purple curtains hung rich and ample before the lofty window and loftier arch; everything was still, save the subdued chat of Adèle (she dared not speak loud), and, filling up each pause, the beating of winter rain against the panes.

Mr. Rochester, as he sat in his damask-covered chair, looked different to what I had seen him look before; not quite so stern – much less gloomy. There was a smile on his lips, and his eyes sparkled, whether with wine or not, I am not sure; but I think it very probable. He was, in short, in his after-dinner mood; more expanded and genial, and also more self-indulgent than the frigid and rigid temper of the morning; still he looked preciously grim, cushioning his massive head against the swelling back of his chair, and receiving the light of the fire on his granite-hewn features, and in his great, dark eyes; for he had great, dark eyes, and very fine eyes, too – not without a certain change in their depths sometimes, which, if it was not softness, reminded you, at least, of that feeling.

He had been looking two minutes at the fire, and I had been looking the same length of time at him, when, turning suddenly, he caught my gaze fastened on his physiognomy.

"You examine me, Miss Eyre," said he: "do you think me handsome?"

I should, if I had deliberated, have replied to this question by something conventionally vague and polite; but the answer somehow slipped from my tongue before I was aware – "No, sir."

"Ah! By my word! There is something singular about you," said he: "you have the air of a little *nonnette*; [11] quaint, quiet, grave, and simple, as you sit with your hands before you, and your eyes generally bent on the carpet (except, by-the-bye, when they are directed piercingly to my face; as just now, for instance); and when one asks you a question, or makes a remark to which you are obliged to reply, you rap out a round rejoinder, which, if not blunt, is at least brusque. What do you mean by it?"

"Sir, I was too plain; I beg your pardon. I ought to have replied that it was not easy to give an impromptu answer to a question about appearances; that tastes mostly differ; and that beauty is of little consequence, or something of that sort."

"You ought to have replied no such thing. Beauty of little consequence, indeed! And so, under pretence of softening the previous outrage, of stroking and soothing me into placidity, you stick a sly penknife under my ear! Go on: what fault do you find with me, pray? I suppose I have all my limbs and all my features like any other man?"

"Mr. Rochester, allow me to disown my first answer: I intended no pointed repartee: it was only a blunder."

"Just so: I think so: and you shall be answerable for it. Criticise me: does my forehead not please you?"

He lifted up the sable waves of hair which lay horizontally over his brow, and showed a solid enough mass of intellectual organs, but an abrupt deficiency where the suave sign of benevolence should have risen.

"Now, ma'am, am I a fool?"

"Far from it, sir. You would, perhaps, think me rude if I inquired in return whether you are a philanthropist?"

"There again! Another stick of the penknife, when she pretended to pat my head: and that is because I said I did not like the society of children and old women (low be it spoken!). No, young lady, I am not a general philanthropist; but I bear a conscience;" and he pointed to the prominences which are said to indicate that faculty, and which, fortunately for him, were sufficiently conspicuous; giving, indeed, a marked breadth to the upper part of his head: "and, besides, I once had a kind of rude tenderness of heart. When I was as old as you, I was a feeling fellow enough, partial to the unfledged, unfostered, and unlucky; but Fortune has knocked me about since: she has even kneaded me with her knuckles, and now I flatter myself I am hard and tough as an India-rubber ball; pervious, though, through a chink or two still, and with one sentient point in the middle of the lump. Yes: does that leave hope for me?"

"Hope of what, sir?"

"Of my final re-transformation from India-rubber back to flesh?"

"Decidedly he has had too much wine," I thought; and I did not know what answer to make to his queer question: how could I tell whether he was capable of being re-transformed?

"You looked very much puzzled, Miss Eyre; and though you are not pretty any more than I am handsome, yet a puzzled air becomes you; besides, it is convenient, for it keeps those searching eyes of yours away from my physiognomy, and busies them with the worsted flowers of the rug; so puzzle on. Young lady, I am disposed to be gregarious and communicative tonight."

With this announcement he rose from his chair, and stood, leaning his arm on the marble mantelpiece: in that attitude his shape was seen plainly as well as his face; his unusual breadth of chest, disproportionate almost to his length of limb. I am sure most people would have thought him an ugly man; yet there was so much unconscious pride in his port; so much ease in his demeanour; such a look of complete indifference to his own external appearance; so haughty a reliance on the power of other qualities, intrinsic or adventitious, to atone for the lack of mere personal attractiveness, that, in looking at him, one inevitably shared the indifference, and, even in a blind, imperfect sense, put faith in the confidence.

"I am disposed to be gregarious and communicative tonight," he repeated, "and that is why I sent for you: the fire and the chandelier were not sufficient company for me; nor would Pilot have been, for none of these can talk. Adèle is a degree better, but still far below the mark; Mrs. Fairfax ditto; you, I am persuaded, can suit me if you will: you puzzled me the first evening I invited you down here. I have almost forgotten you since: other ideas have driven yours from my head; but tonight I am resolved to be at ease; to dismiss what importunes, and recall what pleases. It would please me now to draw you out – to learn more of you – therefore speak."

Instead of speaking, I smiled; and not a very complacent or submissive smile either.

"Speak," he urged.

"What about, sir?"

"Whatever you like. I leave both the choice of subject and the manner of treating it entirely to yourself."

Accordingly I sat and said nothing: "If he expects me to talk for the mere sake of talking and showing off, he will find he has addressed himself to the wrong person," I thought.

"You are dumb, Miss Eyre."

I was dumb still. He bent his head a little towards me, and with a single hasty glance seemed to dive into my eyes.

"Stubborn?" he said, "and annoyed. Ah! It is consistent. I put my request in an absurd, almost insolent form. Miss Eyre, I beg your pardon. The fact is, once for all, I don't wish to treat you like an inferior: that is" (correcting himself), "I claim only such superiority as must result from twenty years' difference in age and a century's advance in experience. This is legitimate, *et j'y tiens*, [12] as Adèle would say; and it is by virtue of this superiority, and this alone, that I desire you to have the goodness to talk to me a little now, and divert my thoughts, which are galled with dwelling on one point – cankering as a rusty nail."

He had deigned an explanation, almost an apology, and I did not feel insensible to his condescension, and would not seem so.

"I am willing to amuse you, if I can, sir – quite willing; but I cannot introduce a topic, because how do I know what will interest you? Ask me questions, and I will do my best to answer them."

"Then, in the first place, do you agree with me that I have a right to be a little masterful, abrupt, perhaps exacting, sometimes, on the grounds I stated, namely, that I am old enough to be your father, and that I have battled through a varied experience with many men of many nations, and roamed over half the globe, while you have lived quietly with one set of people in one house?"

"Do as you please, sir."

"That is no answer; or rather it is a very irritating, because a very evasive one. Reply clearly."

"I don't think, sir, you have a right to command me, merely because you are older than I, or because you have seen more of the world than I have; your claim to superiority depends on the use you have made of your time and experience."

"Humph! Promptly spoken. But I won't allow that, seeing that it would never suit my case, as I have made an indifferent, not to say a bad, use of both advantages. Leaving superiority out of the question, then, you must still agree to receive my orders now and then, without being piqued or hurt by the tone of command. Will you?"

I smiled: I thought to myself Mr. Rochester *is* peculiar – he seems to forget that he pays me £30 per annum for receiving his orders.

"The smile is very well," said he, catching instantly the passing expression; "but speak too."

"I was thinking, sir, that very few masters would trouble themselves to inquire whether or not their paid subordinates were piqued and hurt by their orders."

"Paid subordinates! What! You are my paid subordinate, are you? Oh yes, I had forgotten the salary! Well then, on that mercenary ground, will you agree to let me hector a little?"

"No, sir, not on that ground; but, on the ground that you did forget it, and that you care whether or not a dependent is comfortable in his dependency, I agree heartily."

"And will you consent to dispense with a great many conventional forms and phrases, without thinking that the omission arises from insolence?"

"I am sure, sir, I should never mistake informality for insolence: one I rather like, the other nothing free-born would submit to, even for a salary."

"Humbug! Most things free-born will submit to anything for a salary; therefore, keep to yourself, and don't venture on generalities of which you are intensely ignorant. However, I mentally shake hands with you for your answer, despite its inaccuracy; and as much for the manner in which it was said, as for the substance of the speech; the manner was frank and sincere; one does not often see such a manner: no, on the contrary, affectation, or coldness, or stupid, coarse-minded misapprehension of one's meaning are the usual rewards of candour. Not three in three thousand raw schoolgirl-governesses would have answered me as you have just done. But I don't mean to flatter you: if you are cast in a different mould to the majority, it is no merit of yours: nature did it. And then, after all, I go too fast in my conclusions: for what I yet know, you may be no better than the rest; you may have intolerable defects to counterbalance your few good points."

"And so may you," I thought. My eye met his as the idea crossed my mind: he seemed to read the glance, answering as if its import had been spoken as well as imagined:

"Yes, yes, you are right," said he; "I have plenty of faults of my own: I know it, and I don't wish to palliate them, I assure you. God wot I need not be too severe about others; I have a past existence, a series of deeds, a colour of life to contemplate within my own breast, which might well call my sneers and censures from my neighbours to myself. I started, or rather (for like other defaulters, I like to lay half the blame on ill fortune and adverse circumstances) was thrust on to a wrong tack at the age of one-and-twenty, and have never recovered the right course since: but I might have been very different; I might have been as good as you – wiser – almost as stainless. I envy you your peace of mind, your clean conscience, your unpolluted memory. Little girl, a memory without blot or contamination must be an exquisite treasure – an inexhaustible source of pure refreshment: is it not?"

"How was your memory when you were eighteen, sir?"

"All right then; limpid, salubrious: no gush of bilge water had turned it to fetid puddle. I was your equal at eighteen – quite your equal. Nature meant me to be, on the whole, a good man, Miss Eyre; one of the better kind, and you see I am not so. You would say you don't see it; at least I flatter myself I read as much in your eye (beware, by-the-bye, what you express with that organ; I am quick at interpreting its language). Then take my word for it, – I am not a villain: you are not to suppose that – not to attribute to me any such bad eminence; but, owing, I verily believe, rather to circumstances than to my natural bent, I am a trite commonplace sinner, hackneyed in all the poor petty dissipations with which the rich and worthless try to put on life. Do you wonder that I avow this to you? Know, that in the course of your future life you will often find yourself elected the involuntary confidant of your acquaintances' secrets: people will instinctively find out, as I have done, that it is not your forte to tell of yourself, but to listen while others talk of themselves; they will feel, too, that you listen with no malevolent scorn of their indiscretion, but with a kind of innate sympathy; not the less comforting and encouraging because it is very unobtrusive in its manifestations."

"How do you know? – How can you guess all this, sir?"

"I know it well; therefore I proceed almost as freely as if I were writing my thoughts in a diary. You would say, I should have been superior to circumstances; so I should – so I should; but you see I was not. When fate wronged me, I had not the wisdom to remain cool: I turned desperate; then I degenerated. Now, when any vicious simpleton excites my disgust by his paltry ribaldry, I cannot flatter myself that I am better than he: I am forced to confess that he and I are on a level. I wish I had stood firm – God knows I do! Dread remorse when you are tempted to err, Miss Eyre; remorse is the poison of life."

"Repentance is said to be its cure, sir."

"It is not its cure. Reformation may be its cure; and I could reform – I have strength yet for that – if – but where is the use of thinking of it, hampered, burdened, cursed as I am? Besides, since happiness is irrevocably denied me, I have a right to get pleasure out of life: and I *will* get it, cost what it may."

"Then you will degenerate still more, sir."

"Possibly: yet why should I, if I can get sweet, fresh pleasure? And I may get it as sweet and fresh as the wild honey the bee gathers on the moor."

"It will sting – it will taste bitter, sir."

"How do you know? – You never tried it. How very serious – how very solemn you look: and you are as ignorant of the matter as this cameo head" (taking one from the mantelpiece). "You have no right to preach to me, you neophyte, that have not passed the porch of life, and are absolutely unacquainted with its mysteries."

"I only remind you of your own words, sir: you said error brought remorse, and you pronounced remorse the poison of existence."

"And who talks of error now? I scarcely think the notion that flittered across my brain was an error. I believe it was an inspiration rather than a temptation: it was very genial, very soothing – I know that. Here it comes again! It is no devil, I assure you; or if it be, it has put on the robes of an angel of light. I think I must admit so fair a guest when it asks entrance to my heart."

"Distrust it, sir; it is not a true angel."

"Once more, how do you know? By what instinct do you pretend to distinguish between a fallen seraph of the abyss and a messenger from the eternal throne – between a guide and a seducer?"

"I judged by your countenance, sir, which was troubled when you said the suggestion had returned upon you. I feel sure it will work you more misery if you listen to it."

"Not at all – it bears the most gracious message in the world: for the rest, you are not my conscience-keeper, so don't make yourself uneasy. Here, come in, bonny wanderer!"

He said this as if he spoke to a vision, viewless to any eye but his own; then, folding his arms, which he had half extended, on his chest, he seemed to enclose in their embrace the invisible being.

"Now," he continued, again addressing me, "I have received the pilgrim – a disguised deity, as I verily believe. Already it has done me good: my heart was a sort of charnel; it will now be a shrine."

"To speak truth, sir, I don't understand you at all: I cannot keep up the conversation, because it has got out of my depth. Only one thing, I know: you said you were not as good as you should like to be, and that you regretted your own imperfection; – one thing I can comprehend: you intimated that to have a sullied memory was a perpetual bane. It seems to me, that if you tried hard, you would in time find it possible to become what you yourself would approve; and that if from this day you began with resolution to correct your thoughts and actions, you would in a few years have laid up a new and stainless store of recollections, to which you might revert with pleasure."

"Justly thought; rightly said, Miss Eyre; and, at this moment, I am paving hell with energy."

"Sir?"

"I am laying down good intentions, which I believe durable as flint. Certainly, my associates and pursuits shall be other than they have been."

"And better?"

"And better – so much better as pure ore is than foul dross. You seem to doubt me; I don't doubt myself: I know what my aim is, what my motives are; and at this moment I pass a law, unalterable as that of the Medes and Persians, that both are right."

"They cannot be, sir, if they require a new statute to legalise them."

"They are, Miss Eyre, though they absolutely require a new statute: unheard-of combinations of circumstances demand unheard-of rules."

"That sounds a dangerous maxim, sir; because one can see at once that it is liable to abuse."

"Sententious sage! So it is: but I swear by my household gods not to abuse it."

"You are human and fallible."

"I am: so are you – what then?"

"The human and fallible should not arrogate a power with which the divine and perfect alone can be safely intrusted."

"What power?"

"That of saying of any strange, unsanctioned line of action, – 'Let it be right.'"

"'Let it be right' – the very words: you have pronounced them."

"*May* it be right then," I said, as I rose, deeming it useless to continue a discourse which was all darkness to me; and, besides, sensible that the character of my interlocutor was beyond my penetration; at least, beyond its present reach; and feeling the uncertainty, the vague sense of insecurity, which accompanies a conviction of ignorance.

"Where are you going?"

"To put Adèle to bed: it is past her bedtime."

"You are afraid of me, because I talk like a Sphynx."

"Your language is enigmatical, sir: but though I am bewildered, I am certainly not afraid."

"You *are* afraid – your self-love dreads a blunder."

"In that sense I do feel apprehensive – I have no wish to talk nonsense."

"If you did, it would be in such a grave, quiet manner, I should mistake it for sense. Do you never laugh, Miss Eyre? Don't trouble yourself to answer – I see you laugh rarely; but you can laugh very merrily: believe me, you are not naturally austere, any more than I am naturally vicious. The Lowood constraint still clings to you somewhat; controlling your features, muffling your voice, and restricting your limbs; and you fear in the presence of a man and a brother – or father, or master, or what you will – to smile too gaily, speak too freely, or move too quickly: but, in time, I think you will learn to be natural with me, as I find it impossible to be conventional with you; and then your looks and movements will have more vivacity and variety than they dare offer now. I see at intervals the glance of a curious sort of bird through the close-set bars of a cage: a vivid, restless, resolute captive is there; were it but free, it would soar cloud-high. You are still bent on going?"

"It has struck nine, sir."

"Never mind, – wait a minute: Adèle is not ready to go to bed yet. My position, Miss Eyre, with my back to the fire, and my face to the room, favours observation. While talking to you, I have also occasionally watched Adèle (I have my own reasons for thinking her a curious study, – reasons that I may, nay, that I shall, impart to you some day). She pulled out of her box, about ten minutes ago, a little pink silk frock; rapture lit her face as she unfolded it; coquetry runs in her blood, blends with her brains, and seasons the marrow of her bones. 'Il faut que je l'essaie!' cried she, 'et à l'instant même!' and she rushed out of the room. She is now with Sophie, undergoing a robing process: in a few minutes she will re-enter; and I know what I shall see, – a miniature of Céline Varens, as she used to appear on the boards at the rising of – But never mind that. However, my tenderest feelings are about to receive a shock: such is my presentiment; stay now, to see whether it will be realised."

Ere long, Adèle's little foot was heard tripping across the hall. She entered, transformed as her guardian had predicted. A dress of rose-coloured satin, very short, and as full in the skirt as it could be gathered, replaced the brown frock she had previously worn; a wreath of rosebuds circled her forehead; her feet were dressed in silk stockings and small white satin sandals.

"Est-ce que ma robe va bien?" cried she, bounding forwards; "et mes souliers? et mes bas? Tenez, je crois que je vais danser!"

And spreading out her dress, she chasséed across the room till, having reached Mr. Rochester, she wheeled lightly round before him on tip-toe, then dropped on one knee at his feet, exclaiming:

"Monsieur, je vous remercie mille fois de votre bonté;" then rising, she added, "C'est comme cela que maman faisait, n'est-ce pas, monsieur?" [13]

"Pre-cise-ly!" was the answer; "and, 'comme cela', she charmed my English gold out of my British breeches' pocket. I have been green, too, Miss Eyre, – ay, grass green: not a more vernal tint freshens you now than once freshened me. My Spring is gone, however, but it has left me that French floweret on my hands, which, in some moods, I would fain be rid of. Not valuing now the root whence it sprang; having found that it was of a sort which nothing but gold dust could manure, I have but half a liking to the blossom, especially when it looks so artificial as just now. I keep it and rear it rather on the Roman Catholic principle of expiating numerous sins, great or small, by one good work. I'll explain all this some day. Goodnight."

Chapter Fifteen

MR. ROCHESTER did, on a future occasion, explain it. It was one afternoon, when he chanced to meet me and Adèle in the grounds: and while she played with Pilot and her shuttlecock, he asked me to walk up and down a long beech avenue within sight of her.

He then said that she was the daughter of a French opera-dancer, Céline Varens, towards whom he had once cherished what he called a *'grande passion'*. This passion Céline had professed to return with even superior ardour. He thought himself her idol, ugly as he was: he believed, as he said, that she preferred his *'taille d'athlète'* to the elegance of the Apollo Belvidere.

"And, Miss Eyre, so much was I flattered by this preference of the Gallic sylph for her British gnome, that I installed her in an hotel; [14] gave her a complete establishment of servants, a carriage, cashmeres, diamonds, dentelles, [15] etc. In short, I began the process of ruining myself in the received style, like any other spoony. [16] I had not, it seems, the originality to chalk out a new road to shame and destruction, but trode the old track with stupid exactness not to deviate an inch from the beaten centre. I had – as I deserved to have – the fate of all other spoonies. Happening to call one evening when Céline did not expect me, I found her out; but it was a warm night, and I was tired with strolling through Paris, so I sat down in her boudoir; happy to breathe the air consecrated so lately by her presence. No, – I exaggerate; I never thought there was any consecrating virtue about her: it was rather a sort of pastille perfume she had left; a scent of musk and amber, than an odour of sanctity. I was just beginning to stifle with the fumes of conservatory flowers and sprinkled essences, when I bethought myself to open the window and step out on to the balcony. It was moonlight and gaslight besides, and very still and serene. The balcony was furnished with a chair or two; I sat down, and took out a cigar, – I will take one now, if you will excuse me."

Here ensued a pause, filled up by the producing and lighting of a cigar; having placed it to his lips and breathed a trail of Havannah incense on the freezing and sunless air, he went on:

"I liked bonbons too in those days, Miss Eyre, and I was *croquant* – (overlook the barbarism) – *croquant* chocolate comfits, and smoking alternately, watching meantime the equipages that rolled along the fashionable streets towards the neighbouring opera-house, when in an elegant close carriage drawn by a beautiful pair of English horses, and distinctly seen in the brilliant city-night, I recognised the 'voiture' I had given Céline. She was returning: of course my heart thumped with impatience against the iron rails I leant upon. The carriage stopped, as I had expected, at the hotel door; my flame (that is the very word for an opera inamorata) alighted: though muffed in a cloak – an unnecessary encumbrance, by-the-bye, on so warm a June evening – I knew her instantly by her little foot, seen peeping from the skirt of her dress, as she skipped from the carriage-step. Bending over the balcony, I was about to murmur 'Mon ange' – in a tone, of course, which should be audible to the ear of love alone – when a figure jumped from the carriage after her; cloaked also; but that was a spurred heel which had rung on the pavement, and that was a hatted head which now passed under the arched *porte cochère* of the hotel.

"You never felt jealousy, did you, Miss Eyre? Of course not: I need not ask you; because you never felt love. You have both sentiments yet to experience: your soul sleeps; the shock is yet to be given which shall waken it. You think all existence lapses in as quiet a flow as that in which your youth has hitherto slid away. Floating on with closed eyes and muffled ears, you neither see the rocks bristling not far off in the bed of the flood, nor hear the breakers boil at their base. But I tell you – and you may mark my words – you will come some day to a craggy pass in the channel, where the whole of life's stream will be broken up into whirl and tumult, foam and noise: either you will be dashed to atoms on crag points, or lifted up and borne on by some master-wave into a calmer current – as I am now.

"I like this day; I like that sky of steel; I like the sternness and stillness of the world under this frost. I like Thornfield, its antiquity, its retirement, its old crow-trees and thorn-trees, its grey façade, and lines of dark windows reflecting that metal welkin: and yet how long have I abhorred the very thought of it, shunned it like a great plague-house? How I do still abhor –"

He ground his teeth and was silent: he arrested his step and struck his boot against the hard ground. Some hated thought seemed to have him in its grip, and to hold him so tightly that he could not advance.

We were ascending the avenue when he thus paused; the hall was before us. Lifting his eye to its battlements, he cast over them a glare such as I never saw before or since. Pain, shame, ire, impatience, disgust, detestation, seemed momentarily to hold a quivering conflict in the large pupil dilating under his ebon eyebrow. Wild was the wrestle which should be paramount; but another feeling rose and triumphed: something hard and cynical: self-willed and resolute: it settled his passion and petrified his countenance: he went on:

"During the moment I was silent, Miss Eyre, I was arranging a point with my destiny. She stood there, by that beech-trunk – a hag like one of those who appeared to Macbeth on the heath of Forres. 'You like Thornfield?' she said, lifting her finger; and then she wrote in the air a memento, which ran in lurid hieroglyphics all along the house-front, between the upper and lower row of windows, 'Like it if you can! Like it if you dare!'

"'I will like it', said I; 'I dare like it;' and" (he subjoined moodily) "I will keep my word; I will break obstacles to happiness, to goodness – yes, goodness. I wish to be a better man than I have been, than I am; as Job's leviathan broke the spear, the dart, and the habergeon, hindrances which others count as iron and brass, I will esteem but straw and rotten wood."

Adèle here ran before him with her shuttlecock. "Away!" he cried harshly; "keep at a distance, child; or go in to Sophie!" Continuing then to pursue his walk in silence, I ventured to recall him to the point whence he had abruptly diverged:

"Did you leave the balcony, sir," I asked, "when Mdlle. Varens entered?"

I almost expected a rebuff for this hardly well-timed question, but, on the contrary, waking out of his scowling abstraction, he turned his eyes towards me, and the shade seemed to clear off his brow. "Oh, I had forgotten Céline! Well, to resume. When I saw my charmer thus come in accompanied by a cavalier, I seemed to hear a hiss, and the green snake of jealousy, rising on undulating coils from the moonlit balcony, glided within my waistcoat, and ate its way in two minutes to my heart's core. Strange!" he exclaimed, suddenly starting again from the point. "Strange that I should choose you for the confidant of all this, young lady; passing strange that you should listen to me quietly, as if it were the most usual thing in the world for a man like me to tell stories of his opera-mistresses to a quaint, inexperienced girl like you! But the last singularity explains the first, as I intimated once before: you, with your gravity, considerateness, and caution were made to be the recipient of secrets. Besides, I know what sort of a mind I have placed in communication with my own: I know it is one not liable to take infection: it is a peculiar mind: it is a unique one. Happily I do not mean to harm it: but, if I did, it would not take harm from me. The more you and I converse, the better; for while I cannot blight you, you may refresh me." After this digression he proceeded:

"I remained in the balcony. 'They will come to her boudoir, no doubt', thought I: 'let me prepare an ambush.' So putting my hand in through the open window, I drew the curtain over it, leaving only an opening through which I could take observations; then I closed the casement, all but a chink just wide enough to furnish an outlet to lovers' whispered vows: then I stole back to my chair; and as I resumed it the pair came in. My eye was quickly at the aperture. Céline's chamber-maid entered, lit a lamp, left it on the table, and withdrew. The couple were thus revealed to me clearly: both removed their cloaks, and there was 'the Varens', shining in satin and jewels, – my gifts of course, – and there was her companion in an officer's uniform; and I knew him for a young roué of a vicomte – a brainless and vicious youth whom I had sometimes met in society, and had never thought of hating because I despised him so absolutely. On recognising him, the fang of the snake Jealousy was instantly broken; because at the same moment my love for Céline sank under an extinguisher. A woman who could betray me for such a rival was not worth contending for; she deserved only scorn; less, however, than I, who had been her dupe.

"They began to talk; their conversation eased me completely: frivolous, mercenary, heartless, and senseless, it was rather calculated to weary than enrage a listener. A card of mine lay on the table; this being perceived, brought my name under discussion. Neither of them possessed energy or wit to belabour me soundly, but they insulted me as coarsely as they could in their little way: especially Céline, who even waxed rather brilliant on my personal defects – deformities she termed them. Now it had been her custom to launch out into fervent admiration of what she called my '*beauté mâle*': wherein she differed diametrically from you, who told me point-blank, at the second interview, that you did not think me handsome. The contrast struck me at the time and –"

Adèle here came running up again.

"Monsieur, John has just been to say that your agent has called and wishes to see you."

"Ah! In that case I must abridge. Opening the window, I walked in upon them; liberated Céline from my protection; gave her notice to vacate her hotel; offered her a purse for immediate exigencies; disregarded screams, hysterics, prayers, protestations, convulsions; made an appointment with the vicomte for a meeting at the Bois de Boulogne. Next morning I had the pleasure of encountering him; left a bullet in one of his poor etiolated arms, feeble as the wing of a chicken in the pip, and then thought I had done with the whole crew. But unluckily the Varens, six months before, had given me this *filette* Adèle, who, she affirmed, was my daughter; and perhaps she may be, though I see no proofs of such grim paternity written in her countenance: Pilot is more like me than she. Some years after I had broken with the mother, she abandoned her child, and ran away to Italy with a musician or singer. I acknowledged no natural claim on Adèle's part to be supported by me, nor do I now acknowledge any, for I am not her father; but hearing that she was quite destitute, I e'en took the poor thing out of the slime and mud of Paris, and transplanted it here, to grow up clean in the wholesome soil of an English country garden. Mrs. Fairfax found you to train it; but now you know that it is the illegitimate offspring of a French opera-girl, you will perhaps think differently of your post and protégée: you will be coming to me some day with notice that you have found another place – that you beg me to look out for a new governess, etc. – Eh?"

"No: Adèle is not answerable for either her mother's faults or yours: I have a regard for her; and now that I know she is, in a sense, parentless – forsaken by her mother and disowned by you, sir – I shall cling closer to her than before. How could I possibly prefer the spoilt pet of a wealthy family, who would hate her governess as a nuisance, to a lonely little orphan, who leans towards her as a friend?"

"Oh, that is the light in which you view it! Well, I must go in now; and you too: it darkens."

But I stayed out a few minutes longer with Adèle and Pilot – ran a race with her, and played a game of battledore and shuttlecock. When we went in, and I had removed her bonnet and coat, I took her on my knee; kept her there an hour, allowing her to prattle as she liked: not rebuking even some little freedoms and trivialities into which she was apt to stray when much noticed, and which betrayed in her a superficiality of character, inherited probably from her mother, hardly congenial to an English mind. Still she had her merits; and I was disposed to appreciate all that was good in her to the utmost. I sought in her countenance and features a likeness to Mr. Rochester, but found none: no trait, no turn of expression announced relationship. It was a pity: if she could but have been proved to resemble him, he would have thought more of her.

It was not till after I had withdrawn to my own chamber for the night, that I steadily reviewed the tale Mr. Rochester had told me. As he had said, there was probably nothing at all extraordinary in the substance of the narrative itself: a wealthy Englishman's passion for a French dancer, and her treachery to him, were every-day matters enough, no doubt, in society; but there was something decidedly strange in the paroxysm of emotion which had suddenly seized him when he was in the act of expressing the present contentment of his mood, and his newly revived pleasure in the old hall and its environs. I meditated wonderingly on this incident; but gradually quitting it, as I found it for the present inexplicable, I turned to the consideration of my master's manner to myself. The confidence he had thought fit to repose in me seemed a tribute to my discretion: I regarded and accepted it as such. His deportment had now for some weeks been more uniform towards me than at the first. I never seemed in his way; he did not take fits of chilling hauteur: when he met me unexpectedly, the encounter seemed welcome; he had always a word and sometimes a smile for me: when summoned by formal invitation to his presence, I was honoured by a cordiality of reception that made me feel I really possessed the power to amuse him, and that these evening conferences were sought as much for his pleasure as for my benefit.

I, indeed, talked comparatively little, but I heard him talk with relish. It was his nature to be communicative; he liked to open to a mind unacquainted with the world glimpses of its scenes and ways (I do not mean its corrupt scenes and wicked ways, but such as derived their interest from the great scale on which they were acted, the strange novelty by which they were characterised); and I had a keen delight in receiving the new ideas he offered, in imagining the new pictures he portrayed, and following him in thought through the new regions he disclosed, never startled or troubled by one noxious allusion.

The ease of his manner freed me from painful restraint: the friendly frankness, as correct as cordial, with which he treated me, drew me to him. I felt at times as if he were my relation rather than my master: yet he was imperious sometimes still; but I did not mind that; I saw it was his way. So happy, so gratified did I become with this new interest added to life, that I ceased to pine after kindred: my thin crescent-destiny seemed to enlarge; the blanks of existence were filled up; my bodily health improved; I gathered flesh and strength.

And was Mr. Rochester now ugly in my eyes? No, reader: gratitude, and many associations, all pleasurable and genial, made his face the object I best liked to see; his presence in a room was more cheering than the brightest fire. Yet I had not forgotten his faults; indeed, I could not, for he brought them frequently before me. He was proud, sardonic, harsh to inferiority of every description: in my secret soul I knew that his great kindness to me was balanced by unjust severity to many others. He was moody, too; unaccountably so; I more than once, when sent for to read to him, found him sitting in his library alone, with his head bent on his folded arms; and, when he looked up, a morose, almost a malignant, scowl blackened his features. But I believed that his moodiness, his harshness, and his former faults of morality (I say *former*, for now he seemed corrected of them) had their source in some cruel cross of fate. I believed he was naturally a man of better tendencies, higher principles, and purer tastes than such as circumstances had developed, education instilled, or destiny encouraged. I thought there were excellent materials in him; though for the present they hung together somewhat spoiled and tangled. I cannot deny that I grieved for his grief, whatever that was, and would have given much to assuage it.

Though I had now extinguished my candle and was laid down in bed, I could not sleep for thinking of his look when he paused in the avenue, and told how his destiny had risen up before him, and dared him to be happy at Thornfield.

"Why not?" I asked myself. "What alienates him from the house? Will he leave it again soon? Mrs. Fairfax said he seldom stayed here longer than a fortnight at a time; and he has now been resident eight weeks. If he does go, the change will be doleful. Suppose he should be absent spring, summer, and autumn: how joyless sunshine and fine days will seem!"

I hardly know whether I had slept or not after this musing; at any rate, I started wide awake on hearing a vague murmur, peculiar and lugubrious, which sounded, I thought, just above me. I wished I had kept my candle burning: the night was drearily dark; my spirits were depressed. I rose and sat up in bed, listening. The sound was hushed.

I tried again to sleep; but my heart beat anxiously: my inward tranquillity was broken. The clock, far down in the hall, struck two. Just then it seemed my chamber-door was touched; as if fingers had swept the panels in groping a way along the dark gallery outside. I said, "Who is there?" Nothing answered. I was chilled with fear.

All at once I remembered that it might be Pilot, who, when the kitchen door chanced to be left open, not unfrequently found his way up to the threshold of Mr. Rochester's chamber: I had seen him lying there myself in the mornings. The idea calmed me somewhat: I lay down. Silence composes the nerves; and as an unbroken hush now reigned again through the whole house, I began to feel the return of slumber. But it was not fated that I should sleep that night. A dream had scarcely approached my ear, when it fled affrighted, scared by a marrow-freezing incident enough.

This was a demoniac laugh – low, suppressed, and deep – uttered, as it seemed, at the very keyhole of my chamber door. The head of my bed was near the door, and I thought at first the goblin-laugher stood at my bedside – or rather, crouched by my pillow: but I rose, looked round, and could see nothing; while, as I still gazed, the unnatural sound was reiterated: and I knew it came from behind the panels. My first impulse was to rise and fasten the bolt; my next, again to cry out, "Who is there?"

Something gurgled and moaned. Ere long, steps retreated up the gallery towards the third-storey staircase: a door had lately been made to shut in that staircase; I heard it open and close, and all was still.

"Was that Grace Poole? And is she possessed with a devil?" thought I. Impossible now to remain longer by myself: I must go to Mrs. Fairfax. I hurried on my frock and a shawl; I withdrew the bolt and opened the door with a trembling hand. There was a candle burning just outside, and on the matting in the gallery. I was surprised at this circumstance: but still more was I amazed to perceive the air quite dim, as if filled with smoke; and, while looking to the right hand and left, to find whence these blue wreaths issued, I became further aware of a strong smell of burning.

Something creaked: it was a door ajar; and that door was Mr. Rochester's, and the smoke rushed in a cloud from thence. I thought no more of Mrs. Fairfax; I thought no more of Grace Poole, or the laugh: in an instant, I was within the chamber. Tongues of flame darted round the bed: the curtains were on fire. In the midst of blaze and vapour, Mr. Rochester lay stretched motionless, in deep sleep.

"Wake! wake!" I cried. I shook him, but he only murmured and turned: the smoke had stupefied him. Not a moment could be lost: the very sheets were kindling, I rushed to his basin and ewer; fortunately, one was wide and the other deep, and both were filled with water. I heaved them up, deluged the bed and its occupant, flew back to my own room, brought my own water-jug, baptized the couch afresh, and, by God's aid, succeeded in extinguishing the flames which were devouring it.

The hiss of the quenched element, the breakage of a pitcher which I flung from my hand when I had emptied it, and, above all, the splash of the shower-bath I had liberally bestowed, roused Mr. Rochester at last. Though it was now dark, I knew he was awake; because I heard him fulminating strange anathemas at finding himself lying in a pool of water.

"Is there a flood?" he cried.

"No, sir," I answered; "but there has been a fire: get up, do; you are quenched now; I will fetch you a candle."

"In the name of all the elves in Christendom, is that Jane Eyre?" he demanded. "What have you done with me, witch, sorceress? Who is in the room besides you? Have you plotted to drown me?"

"I will fetch you a candle, sir; and, in Heaven's name, get up. Somebody has plotted something: you cannot too soon find out who and what it is."

"There! I am up now; but at your peril you fetch a candle yet: wait two minutes till I get into some dry garments, if any dry there be – yes, here is my dressing-gown. Now run!"

I did run; I brought the candle which still remained in the gallery. He took it from my hand, held it up, and surveyed the bed, all blackened and scorched, the sheets drenched, the carpet round swimming in water.

"What is it? And who did it?" he asked. I briefly related to him what had transpired: the strange laugh I had heard in the gallery: the step ascending to the third storey; the smoke, – the smell of fire which had conducted me to his room; in what state I had found matters there, and how I had deluged him with all the water I could lay hands on.

He listened very gravely; his face, as I went on, expressed more concern than astonishment; he did not immediately speak when I had concluded.

"Shall I call Mrs. Fairfax?" I asked.

"Mrs. Fairfax? No; what the deuce would you call her for? What can she do? Let her sleep unmolested."

"Then I will fetch Leah, and wake John and his wife."

"Not at all: just be still. You have a shawl on. If you are not warm enough, you may take my cloak yonder; wrap it about you, and sit down in the armchair: there, – I will put it on. Now place your feet on the stool, to keep them out of the wet. I am going to leave you a few minutes. I shall take the candle. Remain where you are till I return; be as still as a mouse. I must pay a visit to the second storey. Don't move, remember, or call anyone."

He went: I watched the light withdraw. He passed up the gallery very softly, unclosed the staircase door with as little noise as possible, shut it after him, and the last ray vanished. I was left in total darkness. I listened for some noise, but heard nothing. A very long time elapsed. I grew weary: it was cold, in spite of the cloak; and then I did not see the use of staying, as I was not to rouse the house. I was on the point of risking Mr. Rochester's displeasure by disobeying his orders, when the light once more gleamed dimly on the gallery wall, and I heard his unshod feet tread the matting. "I hope it is he," thought I, "and not something worse."

He re-entered, pale and very gloomy. "I have found it all out," said he, setting his candle down on the washstand; "it is as I thought."

"How, sir?"

He made no reply, but stood with his arms folded, looking on the ground. At the end of a few minutes he inquired in rather a peculiar tone:

"I forget whether you said you saw anything when you opened your chamber door."

"No, sir, only the candlestick on the ground."

"But you heard an odd laugh? You have heard that laugh before, I should think, or something like it?"

"Yes, sir: there is a woman who sews here, called Grace Poole, – she laughs in that way. She is a singular person."

"Just so. Grace Poole – you have guessed it. She is, as you say, singular – very. Well, I shall reflect on the subject. Meantime, I am glad that you are the only person, besides myself, acquainted with the precise details of tonight's incident. You are no talking fool: say nothing about it. I will account for this state of affairs" (pointing to the bed): "and now return to your own room. I shall do very well on the sofa in the library for the rest of the night. It is near four: – in two hours the servants will be up."

"Goodnight, then, sir," said I, departing.

He seemed surprised – very inconsistently so, as he had just told me to go.

"What!" he exclaimed, "are you quitting me already, and in that way?"

"You said I might go, sir."

"But not without taking leave; not without a word or two of acknowledgment and good will: not, in short, in that brief, dry fashion. Why, you have saved my life! – snatched me from a horrible and excruciating death! And you walk past me as if we were mutual strangers! At least shake hands."

He held out his hand; I gave him mine: he took it first in one, them in both his own.

"You have saved my life: I have a pleasure in owing you so immense a debt. I cannot say more. Nothing else that has being would have been tolerable to me in the character of creditor for such an obligation: but you: it is different; – I feel your benefits no burden, Jane."

He paused; gazed at me: words almost visible trembled on his lips, – but his voice was checked.

"Goodnight again, sir. There is no debt, benefit, burden, obligation, in the case."

"I knew," he continued, "you would do me good in some way, at some time; – I saw it in your eyes when I first beheld you: their expression and smile did not" – (again he stopped) – "did not" (he proceeded hastily) "strike delight to my very inmost heart so for nothing. People talk of natural sympathies; I have heard of good genii: there are grains of truth in the wildest fable. My cherished preserver, goodnight!"

Strange energy was in his voice, strange fire in his look.

"I am glad I happened to be awake," I said: and then I was going.

"What! You *will* go?"

"I am cold, sir."

"Cold? Yes, – and standing in a pool! Go, then, Jane; go!" But he still retained my hand, and I could not free it. I bethought myself of an expedient.

"I think I hear Mrs. Fairfax move, sir," said I.

"Well, leave me:" he relaxed his fingers, and I was gone.

I regained my couch, but never thought of sleep. Till morning dawned I was tossed on a buoyant but unquiet sea, where billows of trouble rolled under surges of joy. I thought sometimes I saw beyond its wild waters a shore, sweet as the hills of Beulah; and now and then a freshening gale, wakened by hope, bore my spirit triumphantly towards the bourne: but I could not reach it, even in fancy – a counteracting breeze blew off land, and continually drove me back. Sense would resist delirium: judgment would warn passion. Too feverish to rest, I rose as soon as day dawned.

Volume Two

Chapter Sixteen

I BOTH WISHED and feared to see Mr. Rochester on the day which followed this sleepless night: I wanted to hear his voice again, yet feared to meet his eye. During the early part of the morning, I momentarily expected his coming; he was not in the frequent habit of entering the schoolroom, but he did step in for a few minutes sometimes, and I had the impression that he was sure to visit it that day.

But the morning passed just as usual: nothing happened to interrupt the quiet course of Adèle's studies; only soon after breakfast, I heard some bustle in the neighbourhood of Mr. Rochester's chamber, Mrs. Fairfax's voice, and Leah's, and the cook's – that is, John's wife – and even John's own gruff tones. There were exclamations of "What a mercy master was not burnt in his bed!" "It is always dangerous to keep a candle lit at night." "How providential that he had presence of mind to think of the water-jug!" "I wonder he waked nobody!" "It is to be hoped he will not take cold with sleeping on the library sofa," etc.

To much confabulation succeeded a sound of scrubbing and setting to rights; and when I passed the room, in going downstairs to dinner, I saw through the open door that all was again restored to complete order; only the bed was stripped of its hangings. Leah stood up in the window seat, rubbing the panes of glass dimmed with smoke. I was about to address her, for I wished to know what account had been given of the affair: but, on advancing, I saw a second person in the chamber – a woman sitting on a chair by the bedside, and sewing rings to new curtains. That woman was no other than Grace Poole.

There she sat, staid and taciturn-looking, as usual, in her brown stuff gown, her check apron, white handkerchief, and cap. She was intent on her work, in which her whole thoughts seemed absorbed: on her hard forehead, and in her commonplace features, was nothing either of the paleness or desperation one would have expected to see marking the countenance of a woman who had attempted murder, and whose intended victim had followed her last night to her lair, and (as I believed), charged her with the crime she wished to perpetrate. I was amazed – confounded. She looked up, while I still gazed at her: no start, no increase or failure of colour betrayed emotion, consciousness of guilt, or fear of detection. She said "Good morning, Miss," in her usual phlegmatic and brief manner; and taking up another ring and more tape, went on with her sewing.

"I will put her to some test," thought I: "such absolute impenetrability is past comprehension."

"Good morning, Grace," I said. "Has anything happened here? I thought I heard the servants all talking together a while ago."

"Only master had been reading in his bed last night; he fell asleep with his candle lit, and the curtains got on fire; but, fortunately, he awoke before the bed clothes or the woodwork caught, and contrived to quench the flames with the water in the ewer."

"A strange affair!" I said, in a low voice: then, looking at her fixedly – "Did Mr. Rochester wake nobody? Did no one hear him move?"

She again raised her eyes to me, and this time there was something of consciousness in their expression. She seemed to examine me warily; then she answered:

"The servants sleep so far off, you know, Miss, they would not be likely to hear. Mrs. Fairfax's room and yours are the nearest to master's; but Mrs. Fairfax said she heard nothing: when people get elderly, they often sleep heavy." She paused, and then added, with a sort of assumed indifference, but still in a marked and significant tone – "But you are young, Miss; and I should say a light sleeper: perhaps you may have heard a noise?"

"I did," said I, dropping my voice, so that Leah, who was still polishing the panes, could not hear me, "and at first I thought it was Pilot: but Pilot cannot laugh; and I am certain I heard a laugh, and a strange one."

She took a new needleful of thread, waxed it carefully, threaded her needle with a steady hand, and then observed, with perfect composure:

"It is hardly likely master would laugh, I should think, Miss, when he was in such danger: You must have been dreaming."

"I was not dreaming," I said, with some warmth, for her brazen coolness provoked me. Again she looked at me; and with the same scrutinising and conscious eye.

"Have you told master that you heard a laugh?" she inquired.

"I have not had the opportunity of speaking to him this morning."

"You did not think of opening your door and looking out into the gallery?" she further asked.

She appeared to be cross-questioning me, attempting to draw from me information unawares. The idea struck me that if she discovered I knew or suspected her guilt, she would be playing off some of her malignant pranks on me; I thought it advisable to be on my guard.

"On the contrary," said I, "I bolted my door."

"Then you are not in the habit of bolting your door every night before you get into bed?"

"Fiend! She wants to know my habits, that she may lay her plans accordingly!" Indignation again prevailed over prudence: I replied sharply, "Hitherto I have often omitted to fasten the bolt: I did not think it necessary. I was not aware any danger or annoyance was to be dreaded at Thornfield Hall: but in future" (and I laid marked stress on the words) "I shall take good care to make all secure before I venture to lie down."

"It will be wise so to do," was her answer: "this neighbourhood is as quiet as any I know, and I never heard of the hall being attempted by robbers since it was a house; though there are hundreds of pounds' worth of plate in the plate-closet, as is well known. And you see, for such a large house, there are very few servants, because master has never lived here much; and when he does come, being a bachelor, he needs little waiting on: but I always think it best to err on the safe side; a door is soon fastened, and it is as well to have a drawn bolt between one and any mischief that may be about. A deal of people, Miss, are for trusting all to Providence; but I say Providence will not dispense with the means, though He often blesses them when they are used discreetly." And here she closed her harangue: a long one for her, and uttered with the demureness of a Quakeress.

I still stood absolutely dumfoundered at what appeared to me her miraculous self-possession and most inscrutable hypocrisy, when the cook entered.

"Mrs. Poole," said she, addressing Grace, "the servants' dinner will soon be ready: will you come down?"

"No; just put my pint of porter and bit of pudding on a tray, and I'll carry it upstairs."

"You'll have some meat?"

"Just a morsel, and a taste of cheese, that's all."

"And the sago?"

"Never mind it at present: I shall be coming down before teatime: I'll make it myself."

The cook here turned to me, saying that Mrs. Fairfax was waiting for me: so I departed.

I hardly heard Mrs. Fairfax's account of the curtain conflagration during dinner, so much was I occupied in puzzling my brains over the enigmatical character of Grace Poole, and still more in pondering the problem of her position at Thornfield and questioning why she had not been given into custody that morning, or, at the very least, dismissed from her master's service. He had almost as much as declared his conviction of her criminality last night: what mysterious cause withheld him from accusing her? Why had he enjoined me, too, to secrecy? It was strange: a bold, vindictive, and haughty gentleman seemed somehow in the power of one of the meanest of his dependants; so much in her power, that even when she lifted her hand against his life, he dared not openly charge her with the attempt, much less punish her for it.

Had Grace been young and handsome, I should have been tempted to think that tenderer feelings than prudence or fear influenced Mr. Rochester in her behalf; but, hard-favoured and matronly as she was, the idea could not be admitted. "Yet," I reflected, "she has been young once; her youth would be contemporary with her master's: Mrs. Fairfax told me once, she had lived here many years. I don't think she can ever have been pretty; but, for aught I know, she may possess originality and strength of character to compensate for the want of personal advantages. Mr. Rochester is an amateur of the decided and eccentric: Grace is eccentric at least. What if a former caprice (a freak very possible to a nature so sudden and headstrong as his) has delivered him into her power, and she now exercises over his actions a secret influence, the result of his own indiscretion, which he cannot shake off, and dare not disregard?" But, having reached this point of conjecture, Mrs. Poole's square, flat figure, and uncomely, dry, even coarse face, recurred so distinctly to my mind's eye, that I thought, "No; impossible! My supposition cannot be correct. Yet," suggested the secret voice which talks to us in our own hearts, "you are not beautiful either, and perhaps Mr. Rochester approves you: at any rate, you have often felt as if he did; and last night – remember his words; remember his look; remember his voice!"

I well remembered all; language, glance, and tone seemed at the moment vividly renewed. I was now in the schoolroom; Adèle was drawing; I bent over her and directed her pencil. She looked up with a sort of start.

"Qu'avez-vous, mademoiselle?" said she. "Vos doigts tremblent comme la feuille, et vos joues sont rouges: mais, rouges comme des cerises!"

"I am hot, Adèle, with stooping!" She went on sketching; I went on thinking.

I hastened to drive from my mind the hateful notion I had been conceiving respecting Grace Poole; it disgusted me. I compared myself with her, and found we were different. Bessie Leaven had said I was quite a lady; and she spoke truth – I was a lady. And now I looked much better than I did when Bessie saw me; I had more colour and more flesh, more life, more vivacity, because I had brighter hopes and keener enjoyments.

"Evening approaches," said I, as I looked towards the window. "I have never heard Mr. Rochester's voice or step in the house today; but surely I shall see him before night: I feared the meeting in the morning; now I desire it, because expectation has been so long baffled that it is grown impatient."

When dusk actually closed, and when Adèle left me to go and play in the nursery with Sophie, I did most keenly desire it. I listened for the bell to ring below; I listened for Leah coming up with a message; I fancied sometimes I heard Mr. Rochester's own tread, and I turned to the door, expecting it to open and admit him. The door remained shut; darkness only came in through the window. Still it was not late; he often sent for me at seven and eight o'clock, and it was yet but six. Surely I should not be wholly disappointed tonight, when I had so many things to say to him! I wanted again to introduce the subject of Grace Poole, and to hear what he would answer; I wanted to ask him plainly if he really believed it was she who had made last night's hideous attempt; and if so, why he kept her wickedness a secret. It little mattered whether my curiosity irritated him; I knew the pleasure of vexing and soothing him by turns; it was one I chiefly delighted in, and a sure instinct always prevented me from going too far; beyond the verge of provocation I never ventured; on the extreme brink I liked well to try my skill. Retaining every minute form of respect, every propriety of my station, I could still meet him in argument without fear or uneasy restraint; this suited both him and me.

A tread creaked on the stairs at last. Leah made her appearance; but it was only to intimate that tea was ready in Mrs. Fairfax's room. Thither I repaired, glad at least to go downstairs; for that brought me, I imagined, nearer to Mr. Rochester's presence.

"You must want your tea," said the good lady, as I joined her; "you ate so little at dinner. I am afraid," she continued, "you are not well today: you look flushed and feverish."

"Oh, quite well! I never felt better."

"Then you must prove it by evincing a good appetite; will you fill the teapot while I knit off this needle?" Having completed her task, she rose to draw down the blind, which she had hitherto kept up, by way, I suppose, of making the most of daylight, though dusk was now fast deepening into total obscurity.

"It is fair tonight," said she, as she looked through the panes, "though not starlight; Mr. Rochester has, on the whole, had a favourable day for his journey."

"Journey! – Is Mr. Rochester gone anywhere? I did not know he was out."

"Oh, he set off the moment he had breakfasted! He is gone to the Leas, Mr. Eshton's place, ten miles on the other side Millcote. I believe there is quite a party assembled there; Lord Ingram, Sir George Lynn, Colonel Dent, and others."

"Do you expect him back tonight?"

"No – nor tomorrow either; I should think he is very likely to stay a week or more: when these fine, fashionable people get together, they are so surrounded by elegance and gaiety, so well provided with all that can please and entertain, they are in no hurry to separate. Gentlemen especially are often in request on such occasions; and Mr. Rochester is so talented and so lively in society, that I believe he is a general favourite: the ladies are very fond of him; though you would not think his appearance calculated to recommend him particularly in their eyes: but I suppose his acquirements and abilities, perhaps his wealth and good blood, make amends for any little fault of look."

"Are there ladies at the Leas?"

"There are Mrs. Eshton and her three daughters – very elegant young ladies indeed; and there are the Honourable Blanche and Mary Ingram, most beautiful women, I suppose: indeed I have seen Blanche, six or seven years since, when she was a girl of eighteen. She came here to a Christmas ball and party Mr. Rochester gave. You should have seen the dining room that day – how richly it was decorated, how brilliantly lit up! I should think there were fifty ladies and gentlemen present – all of the first county families; and Miss Ingram was considered the belle of the evening."

"You saw her, you say, Mrs. Fairfax: what was she like?"

"Yes, I saw her. The dining room doors were thrown open; and, as it was Christmas-time, the servants were allowed to assemble in the hall, to hear some of the ladies sing and play. Mr. Rochester would have me to come in, and I sat down in a quiet corner and watched them. I never saw a more splendid scene: the ladies were magnificently dressed; most of them – at least most of the younger ones – looked handsome; but Miss Ingram was certainly the queen."

"And what was she like?"

"Tall, fine bust, sloping shoulders; long, graceful neck: olive complexion, dark and clear; noble features; eyes rather like Mr. Rochester's: large and black, and as brilliant as her jewels. And then she had such a fine head of hair; raven-black and so becomingly arranged: a crown of thick plaits behind, and in front the longest, the glossiest curls I ever saw. She was dressed in pure white; an amber-coloured scarf was passed over her shoulder and across her breast, tied at the side, and descending in long, fringed ends below her knee. She wore an amber-coloured flower, too, in her hair: it contrasted well with the jetty mass of her curls."

"She was greatly admired, of course?"

"Yes, indeed: and not only for her beauty, but for her accomplishments. She was one of the ladies who sang: a gentleman accompanied her on the piano. She and Mr. Rochester sang a duet."

"Mr. Rochester? I was not aware he could sing."

"Oh! He has a fine bass voice, and an excellent taste for music."

"And Miss Ingram: what sort of a voice had she?"

"A very rich and powerful one: she sang delightfully; it was a treat to listen to her; – and she played afterwards. I am no judge of music, but Mr. Rochester is; and I heard him say her execution was remarkably good."

"And this beautiful and accomplished lady, she is not yet married?"

"It appears not: I fancy neither she nor her sister have very large fortunes. Old Lord Ingram's estates were chiefly entailed, and the eldest son came in for everything almost."

"But I wonder no wealthy nobleman or gentleman has taken a fancy to her: Mr. Rochester, for instance. He is rich, is he not?"

"Oh! Yes. But you see there is a considerable difference in age: Mr. Rochester is nearly forty; she is but twenty-five."

"What of that? More unequal matches are made every day."

"True: yet I should scarcely fancy Mr. Rochester would entertain an idea of the sort. But you eat nothing: you have scarcely tasted since you began tea."

"No: I am too thirsty to eat. Will you let me have another cup?"

I was about again to revert to the probability of a union between Mr. Rochester and the beautiful Blanche; but Adèle came in, and the conversation was turned into another channel.

When once more alone, I reviewed the information I had got; looked into my heart, examined its thoughts and feelings, and endeavoured to bring back with a strict hand such as had been straying through imagination's boundless and trackless waste, into the safe fold of common sense.

Arraigned at my own bar, Memory having given her evidence of the hopes, wishes, sentiments I had been cherishing since last night – of the general state of mind in which I had indulged for nearly a fortnight past; Reason having come forward and told, in her own quiet way a plain, unvarnished tale, showing how I had rejected the real, and rabidly devoured the ideal; – I pronounced judgment to this effect:

That a greater fool than Jane Eyre had never breathed the breath of life; that a more fantastic idiot had never surfeited herself on sweet lies, and swallowed poison as if it were nectar.

"You," I said, "a favourite with Mr. Rochester? You gifted with the power of pleasing him? You of importance to him in any way? Go! Your folly sickens me. And you have derived pleasure from occasional tokens of preference – equivocal tokens shown by a gentleman of family and a man of the world to a dependent and a novice. How dared you? Poor stupid dupe! – Could not even self-interest make you wiser? You repeated to yourself this morning the brief scene of last night? – Cover your face and be ashamed! He said something in praise of your eyes, did he? Blind puppy! Open their bleared lids and look on your own accursed senselessness! It does good to no woman to be flattered by her superior, who cannot possibly intend to marry her; and it is madness in all women to let a secret love kindle within them, which, if unreturned and unknown, must devour the life that feeds it; and, if discovered and responded to, must lead, *ignis-fatuus*-like, into miry wilds whence there is no extrication.

"Listen, then, Jane Eyre, to your sentence: tomorrow, place the glass before you, and draw in chalk your own picture, faithfully, without softening one defect; omit no harsh line, smooth away no displeasing irregularity; write under it, 'Portrait of a Governess, disconnected, poor, and plain.'

"Afterwards, take a piece of smooth ivory – you have one prepared in your drawing-box: take your palette, mix your freshest, finest, clearest tints; choose your most delicate camel-hair pencils; delineate carefully the loveliest face you can imagine; paint it in your softest shades and sweetest lines, according to the description given by Mrs. Fairfax of Blanche Ingram; remember the raven ringlets, the oriental eye; – What! you revert to Mr. Rochester as a model! Order! No snivel! – No sentiment! – No regret! I will endure only sense and resolution. Recall the august yet harmonious lineaments, the Grecian neck and bust; let the round and dazzling arm be visible, and the delicate hand; omit neither diamond ring nor gold bracelet; portray faithfully the attire, aerial lace and glistening satin, graceful scarf and golden rose; call it 'Blanche, an accomplished lady of rank.'

"Whenever, in future, you should chance to fancy Mr. Rochester thinks well of you, take out these two pictures and compare them: say, 'Mr. Rochester might probably win that noble lady's love, if he chose to strive for it; is it likely he would waste a serious thought on this indigent and insignificant plebeian?'"

"I'll do it," I resolved: and having framed this determination, I grew calm, and fell asleep.

I kept my word. An hour or two sufficed to sketch my own portrait in crayons; and in less than a fortnight I had completed an ivory miniature of an imaginary Blanche Ingram. It looked a lovely face enough, and when compared with the real head in chalk, the contrast was as great as self-control could desire. I derived benefit from the task: it had kept my head and hands employed, and had given force and fixedness to the new impressions I wished to stamp indelibly on my heart.

Ere long, I had reason to congratulate myself on the course of wholesome discipline to which I had thus forced my feelings to submit. Thanks to it, I was able to meet subsequent occurrences with a decent calm, which, had they found me unprepared, I should probably have been unequal to maintain, even externally.

Chapter Seventeen

A WEEK PASSED, and no news arrived of Mr. Rochester: ten days, and still he did not come. Mrs. Fairfax said she should not be surprised if he were to go straight from the Leas to London, and thence to the Continent, and not show his face again at Thornfield for a year to come; he had not unfrequently quitted it in a manner quite as abrupt and unexpected. When I heard this, I was beginning to feel a strange chill and failing at the heart. I was actually permitting myself to experience a sickening sense of disappointment; but rallying my wits, and recollecting my principles, I at once called my sensations to order; and it was wonderful how I got over the temporary blunder – how I cleared up the mistake of supposing Mr. Rochester's movements a matter in which I had any cause to take a vital interest. Not that I humbled myself by a slavish notion of inferiority: on the contrary, I just said:

"You have nothing to do with the master of Thornfield, further than to receive the salary he gives you for teaching his protégée, and to be grateful for such respectful and kind treatment as, if you do your duty, you have a right to expect at his hands. Be sure that is the only tie he seriously acknowledges between you and him; so don't make him the object of your fine feelings, your raptures, agonies, and so forth. He is not of your order: keep to your caste, and be too self-respecting to lavish the love of the whole heart, soul, and strength, where such a gift is not wanted and would be despised."

I went on with my day's business tranquilly; but ever and anon vague suggestions kept wandering across my brain of reasons why I should quit Thornfield; and I kept involuntarily framing advertisements and pondering conjectures about new situations: these thoughts I did not think to check; they might germinate and bear fruit if they could.

Mr. Rochester had been absent upwards of a fortnight, when the post brought Mrs. Fairfax a letter.

"It is from the master," said she, as she looked at the direction. "Now I suppose we shall know whether we are to expect his return or not."

And while she broke the seal and perused the document, I went on taking my coffee (we were at breakfast): it was hot, and I attributed to that circumstance a fiery glow which suddenly rose to my face. Why my hand shook, and why I involuntarily spilt half the contents of my cup into my saucer, I did not choose to consider.

"Well, I sometimes think we are too quiet; but we run a chance of being busy enough now: for a little while at least," said Mrs. Fairfax, still holding the note before her spectacles.

Ere I permitted myself to request an explanation, I tied the string of Adèle's pinafore, which happened to be loose: having helped her also to another bun and refilled her mug with milk, I said, nonchalantly:

"Mr. Rochester is not likely to return soon, I suppose?"

"Indeed he is – in three days, he says: that will be next Thursday; and not alone either. I don't know how many of the fine people at the Leas are coming with him: he sends directions for all the best bedrooms to be prepared; and the library and drawing rooms are to be cleaned out; I am to get more kitchen hands from the George Inn, at Millcote, and from wherever else I can; and the ladies will bring their maids and the gentlemen their valets: so we shall have a full house of it." And Mrs. Fairfax swallowed her breakfast and hastened away to commence operations.

The three days were, as she had foretold, busy enough. I had thought all the rooms at Thornfield beautifully clean and well arranged; but it appears I was mistaken. Three women were got to help; and such scrubbing, such brushing, such washing of paint and beating of carpets, such taking down and putting up of pictures, such polishing of mirrors and lustres, such lighting of fires in bedrooms, such airing of sheets and feather-beds on hearths, I never beheld, either before or since. Adèle ran quite wild in the midst of it: the preparations for company and the prospect of their arrival, seemed to throw her into ecstasies. She would have Sophie to look over all her 'toilettes', as she called frocks; to furbish up any that were *'passées'*, and to air and arrange the new. For herself, she did nothing but caper about in the front chambers, jump on and off the bedsteads, and lie on the mattresses and piled-up bolsters and pillows before the enormous fires roaring in the chimneys. From school duties she was exonerated: Mrs. Fairfax had pressed me into her service, and I was all day in the storeroom, helping (or hindering) her and the cook; learning to make custards and cheesecakes and French pastry, to truss game and garnish desert-dishes.

The party were expected to arrive on Thursday afternoon, in time for dinner at six. During the intervening period I had no time to nurse chimeras; and I believe I was as active and gay as anybody – Adèle excepted. Still, now and then, I received a damping check to my cheerfulness; and was, in spite of myself, thrown back on the region of doubts and portents, and dark conjectures. This was when I chanced to see the third-storey staircase door (which of late had always been kept locked) open slowly, and give passage to the form of Grace Poole, in prim cap, white apron, and handkerchief; when I watched her glide along the gallery, her quiet tread muffled in a list slipper; when I saw her look into the bustling, topsy-turvy bedrooms, – just say a word, perhaps, to the charwoman about the proper way to polish a grate, or clean a marble mantelpiece, or take stains from papered walls, and then pass on. She would thus descend to the kitchen once a day, eat her dinner, smoke a moderate pipe on the hearth, and go back, carrying her pot of porter with her, for her private solace, in her own gloomy, upper haunt. Only one hour in the twenty-four did she pass with her fellow-servants below; all the rest of her time was spent in some low-ceiled, oaken chamber of the second storey: there she sat and sewed – and probably laughed drearily to herself, – as companionless as a prisoner in his dungeon.

The strangest thing of all was, that not a soul in the house, except me, noticed her habits, or seemed to marvel at them: no one discussed her position or employment; no one pitied her solitude or isolation. I once, indeed, overheard part of a dialogue between Leah and one of the charwomen, of which Grace formed the subject. Leah had been saying something I had not caught, and the charwoman remarked:

"She gets good wages, I guess?"

"Yes," said Leah; "I wish I had as good; not that mine are to complain of, – there's no stinginess at Thornfield; but they're not one fifth of the sum Mrs. Poole receives. And she is laying by: she goes every quarter to the bank at Millcote. I should not wonder but she has saved enough to keep her independent if she liked to leave; but I suppose she's got used to the place; and then she's not forty yet, and strong and able for anything. It is too soon for her to give up business."

"She is a good hand, I daresay," said the charwoman.

"Ah! – She understands what she has to do, – nobody better," rejoined Leah significantly; "and it is not every one could fill her shoes – not for all the money she gets."

"That it is not!" was the reply. "I wonder whether the master –"

The charwoman was going on; but here Leah turned and perceived me, and she instantly gave her companion a nudge.

"Doesn't she know?" I heard the woman whisper.

Leah shook her head, and the conversation was of course dropped. All I had gathered from it amounted to this, – that there was a mystery at Thornfield; and that from participation in that mystery I was purposely excluded.

Thursday came: all work had been completed the previous evening; carpets were laid down, bed-hangings festooned, radiant white counterpanes spread, toilet tables arranged, furniture rubbed, flowers piled in vases: both chambers and saloons looked as fresh and bright as hands could make them. The hall, too, was scoured; and the great carved clock, as well as the steps and banisters of the staircase, were polished to the brightness of glass; in the dining room, the sideboard flashed resplendent with plate; in the drawing room and boudoir, vases of exotics bloomed on all sides.

Afternoon arrived: Mrs. Fairfax assumed her best black satin gown, her gloves, and her gold watch; for it was her part to receive the company, – to conduct the ladies to their rooms, etc. Adèle, too, would be dressed: though I thought she had little chance of being introduced to the party that day at least. However, to please her, I allowed Sophie to apparel her in one of her short, full muslin frocks. For myself, I had no need to make any change; I should not be called upon to quit my sanctum of the schoolroom; for a sanctum it was now become to me, – 'a very pleasant refuge in time of trouble'. [17]

It had been a mild, serene spring day – one of those days which, towards the end of March or the beginning of April, rise shining over the earth as heralds of summer. It was drawing to an end now; but the evening was even warm, and I sat at work in the schoolroom with the window open.

"It gets late," said Mrs. Fairfax, entering in rustling state. "I am glad I ordered dinner an hour after the time Mr. Rochester mentioned; for it is past six now. I have sent John down to the gates to see if there is anything on the road: one can see a long way from thence in the direction of Millcote." She went to the window. "Here he is!" said she. "Well, John" (leaning out), "any news?"

"They're coming, ma'am," was the answer. "They'll be here in ten minutes."

Adèle flew to the window. I followed, taking care to stand on one side, so that, screened by the curtain, I could see without being seen.

The ten minutes John had given seemed very long, but at last wheels were heard; four equestrians galloped up the drive, and after them came two open carriages. Fluttering veils and waving plumes filled the vehicles; two of the cavaliers were young, dashing-looking gentlemen; the third was Mr. Rochester, on his black horse, Mesrour, Pilot bounding before him; at his side rode a lady, and he and she were the first of the party. Her purple riding-habit almost swept the ground, her veil streamed long on the breeze; mingling with its transparent folds, and gleaming through them, shone rich raven ringlets.

"Miss Ingram!" exclaimed Mrs. Fairfax, and away she hurried to her post below.

The cavalcade, following the sweep of the drive, quickly turned the angle of the house, and I lost sight of it. Adèle now petitioned to go down; but I took her on my knee, and gave her to understand that she must not on any account think of venturing in sight of the ladies, either now or at any other time, unless expressly sent for: that Mr. Rochester would be very angry, etc. 'Some natural tears she shed' [18] on being told this; but as I began to look very grave, she consented at last to wipe them.

A joyous stir was now audible in the hall: gentlemen's deep tones and ladies' silvery accents blent harmoniously together, and distinguishable above all, though not loud, was the sonorous voice of the master of Thornfield Hall, welcoming his fair and gallant guests under its roof. Then light steps ascended the stairs; and there was a tripping through the gallery, and soft cheerful laughs, and opening and closing doors, and, for a time, a hush.

"Elles changent de toilettes," said Adèle; who, listening attentively, had followed every movement; and she sighed.

"Chez maman," said she, "quand il y avait du monde, je le suivais partout, au salon et à leurs chambres; souvent je regardais les femmes de chambre coiffer et habiller les dames, et c'était si amusant: comme cela on apprend." [19]

"Don't you feel hungry, Adèle?"

"Mais oui, mademoiselle: voilà cinq ou six heures que nous n'avons pas mangé."

"Well now, while the ladies are in their rooms, I will venture down and get you something to eat."

And issuing from my asylum with precaution, I sought a back-stairs which conducted directly to the kitchen. All in that region was fire and commotion; the soup and fish were in the last stage of projection, and the cook hung over her crucibles in a frame of mind and body threatening spontaneous combustion. In the servants' hall two coachmen and three gentlemen's gentlemen stood or sat round the fire; the Abigails, I suppose, were upstairs with their mistresses; the new servants, that had been hired from Millcote, were bustling about everywhere. Threading this chaos, I at last reached the larder; there I took possession of a cold chicken, a roll of bread, some tarts, a plate or two and a knife and fork: with this booty I made a hasty retreat. I had regained the gallery, and was just shutting the back door behind me, when an accelerated hum warned me that the ladies were about to issue from their chambers. I could not proceed to the schoolroom without passing some of their doors, and running the risk of being surprised with my cargo of victualage; so I stood still at this end, which, being windowless, was dark: quite dark now, for the sun was set and twilight gathering.

Presently the chambers gave up their fair tenants one after another: each came out gaily and airily, with dress that gleamed lustrous through the dusk. For a moment they stood grouped together at the other extremity of the gallery, conversing in a key of sweet subdued vivacity: they then descended the staircase almost as noiselessly as a bright mist rolls down a hill. Their collective appearance had left on me an impression of high-born elegance, such as I had never before received.

I found Adèle peeping through the schoolroom door, which she held ajar. "What beautiful ladies!" cried she in English. "Oh, I wish I might go to them! Do you think Mr. Rochester will send for us by-and-bye, after dinner?"

"No, indeed, I don't; Mr. Rochester has something else to think about. Never mind the ladies tonight; perhaps you will see them tomorrow: here is your dinner."

She was really hungry, so the chicken and tarts served to divert her attention for a time. It was well I secured this forage, or both she, I, and Sophie, to whom I conveyed a share of our repast, would have run a chance of getting no dinner at all: every one downstairs was too much engaged to think of us. The dessert was not carried out till after nine and at ten footmen were still running to and fro with trays and coffee cups. I allowed Adèle to sit up much later than usual; for she declared she could not possibly go to sleep while the doors kept opening and shutting below, and people bustling about. Besides, she added, a message might possibly come from Mr. Rochester when she was undressed; "et alors quel dommage!"

I told her stories as long as she would listen to them; and then for a change I took her out into the gallery. The hall lamp was now lit, and it amused her to look over the balustrade and watch the servants passing backwards and forwards. When the evening was far advanced, a sound of music issued from the drawing room, whither the piano had been removed; Adèle and I sat down on the top step of the stairs to listen. Presently a voice blent with the rich tones of the instrument; it was a lady who sang, and very sweet her notes were. The solo over, a duet followed, and then a glee: a joyous conversational murmur filled up the intervals. I listened long: suddenly I discovered that my ear was wholly intent on analysing the mingled sounds, and trying to discriminate amidst the confusion of accents those of Mr. Rochester; and when it caught them, which it soon did, it found a further task in framing the tones, rendered by distance inarticulate, into words.

The clock struck eleven. I looked at Adèle, whose head leant against my shoulder; her eyes were waxing heavy, so I took her up in my arms and carried her off to bed. It was near one before the gentlemen and ladies sought their chambers.

The next day was as fine as its predecessor: it was devoted by the party to an excursion to some site in the neighbourhood. They set out early in the forenoon, some on horseback, the rest in carriages; I witnessed both the departure and the return. Miss Ingram, as before, was the only lady equestrian; and, as before, Mr. Rochester galloped at her side; the two rode a little apart from the rest. I pointed out this circumstance to Mrs. Fairfax, who was standing at the window with me:

"You said it was not likely they should think of being married," said I, "but you see Mr. Rochester evidently prefers her to any of the other ladies."

"Yes, I daresay: no doubt he admires her."

"And she him," I added; "look how she leans her head towards him as if she were conversing confidentially; I wish I could see her face; I have never had a glimpse of it yet."

"You will see her this evening," answered Mrs. Fairfax. "I happened to remark to Mr. Rochester how much Adèle wished to be introduced to the ladies, and he said: 'Oh! let her come into the drawing room after dinner; and request Miss Eyre to accompany her.'"

"Yes; he said that from mere politeness: I need not go, I am sure," I answered.

"Well, I observed to him that as you were unused to company, I did not think you would like appearing before so gay a party – all strangers; and he replied, in his quick way – 'Nonsense! If she objects, tell her it is my particular wish; and if she resists, say I shall come and fetch her in case of contumacy.'"

"I will not give him that trouble," I answered. "I will go, if no better may be; but I don't like it. Shall you be there, Mrs. Fairfax?"

"No; I pleaded off, and he admitted my plea. I'll tell you how to manage so as to avoid the embarrassment of making a formal entrance, which is the most disagreeable part of the business. You must go into the drawing room while it is empty, before the ladies leave the dinner-table; choose your seat in any quiet nook you like; you need not stay long after the gentlemen come in, unless you please: just let Mr. Rochester see you are there and then slip away – nobody will notice you."

"Will these people remain long, do you think?"

"Perhaps two or three weeks, certainly not more. After the Easter recess, Sir George Lynn, who was lately elected member for Millcote, will have to go up to town and take his seat; I daresay Mr. Rochester will accompany him: it surprises me that he has already made so protracted a stay at Thornfield."

It was with some trepidation that I perceived the hour approach when I was to repair with my charge to the drawing room. Adèle had been in a state of ecstasy all day, after hearing she was to be presented to the ladies in the evening; and it was not till Sophie commenced the operation of dressing her that she sobered down. Then the importance of the process quickly steadied her, and by the time she had her curls arranged in well-smoothed, drooping clusters, her pink satin frock put on, her long sash tied, and her lace mittens adjusted, she looked as grave as any judge. No need to warn her not to disarrange her attire: when she was dressed, she sat demurely down in her little chair, taking care previously to lift up the satin skirt for fear she should crease it, and assured me she would not stir thence till I was ready. This I quickly was: my best dress (the silver-grey one, purchased for Miss Temple's wedding, and never worn since) was soon put on; my hair was soon smoothed; my sole ornament, the pearl brooch, soon assumed. We descended.

Fortunately there was another entrance to the drawing room than that through the saloon where they were all seated at dinner. We found the apartment vacant; a large fire burning silently on the marble hearth, and wax candles shining in bright solitude, amid the exquisite flowers with which the tables were adorned. The crimson curtain hung before the arch: slight as was the separation this drapery formed from the party in the adjoining saloon, they spoke in so low a key that nothing of their conversation could be distinguished beyond a soothing murmur.

Adèle, who appeared to be still under the influence of a most solemnising impression, sat down, without a word, on the footstool I pointed out to her. I retired to a window seat, and taking a book from a table near, endeavoured to read. Adèle brought her stool to my feet; ere long she touched my knee.

"What is it, Adèle?"

"Est-ce que je ne puis pas prendre une seule de ces fleurs magnifiques, mademoiselle? Seulement pour completer ma toilette."

"You think too much of your 'toilette', Adèle: but you may have a flower." And I took a rose from a vase and fastened it in her sash. She sighed a sigh of ineffable satisfaction, as if her cup of happiness were now full. I turned my face away to conceal a smile I could not suppress: there was something ludicrous as well as painful in the little Parisienne's earnest and innate devotion to matters of dress.

A soft sound of rising now became audible; the curtain was swept back from the arch; through it appeared the dining room, with its lit lustre pouring down light on the silver and glass of a magnificent dessert-service covering a long table; a band of ladies stood in the opening; they entered, and the curtain fell behind them.

There were but eight; yet, somehow, as they flocked in, they gave the impression of a much larger number. Some of them were very tall; many were dressed in white; and all had a sweeping amplitude of array that seemed to magnify their persons as a mist magnifies the moon. I rose and curtseyed to them: one or two bent their heads in return, the others only stared at me.

They dispersed about the room, reminding me, by the lightness and buoyancy of their movements, of a flock of white plumy birds. Some of them threw themselves in half-reclining positions on the sofas and ottomans: some bent over the tables and examined the flowers and books: the rest gathered in a group round the fire: all talked in a low but clear tone which seemed habitual to them. I knew their names afterwards, and may as well mention them now.

First, there was Mrs. Eshton and two of her daughters. She had evidently been a handsome woman, and was well preserved still. Of her daughters, the eldest, Amy, was rather little: naive, and child-like in face and manner, and piquant in form; her white muslin dress and blue sash became her well. The second, Louisa, was taller and more elegant in figure; with a very pretty face, of that order the French term *minois chiffoné*: [20] both sisters were fair as lilies.

Lady Lynn was a large and stout personage of about forty, very erect, very haughty-looking, richly dressed in a satin robe of changeful sheen: her dark hair shone glossily under the shade of an azure plume, and within the circlet of a band of gems.

Mrs. Colonel Dent was less showy; but, I thought, more lady-like. She had a slight figure, a pale, gentle face, and fair hair. Her black satin dress, her scarf of rich foreign lace, and her pearl ornaments, pleased me better than the rainbow radiance of the titled dame.

But the three most distinguished – partly, perhaps, because the tallest figures of the band – were the Dowager Lady Ingram and her daughters, Blanche and Mary. They were all three of the loftiest stature of women. The Dowager might be between forty and fifty: her shape was still fine; her hair (by candle-light at least) still black; her teeth, too, were still apparently perfect. Most people would have termed her a splendid woman of her age: and so she was, no doubt, physically speaking; but then there was an expression of almost insupportable haughtiness in her bearing and countenance. She had Roman features and a double chin, disappearing into a throat like a pillar: these features appeared to me not only inflated and darkened, but even furrowed with pride; and the chin was sustained by the same principle, in a position of almost preternatural erectness. She had, likewise, a fierce and a hard eye: it reminded me of Mrs. Reed's; she mouthed her words in speaking; her voice was deep, its inflections very pompous, very dogmatical, – very intolerable, in short. A crimson velvet robe, and a shawl turban of some gold-wrought Indian fabric, invested her (I suppose she thought) with a truly imperial dignity.

Blanche and Mary were of equal stature, – straight and tall as poplars. Mary was too slim for her height, but Blanche was moulded like a Dian. I regarded her, of course, with special interest. First, I wished to see whether her appearance accorded with Mrs. Fairfax's description; secondly, whether it at all resembled the fancy miniature I had painted of her; and thirdly – it will out! – whether it were such as I should fancy likely to suit Mr. Rochester's taste.

As far as person went, she answered point for point, both to my picture and Mrs. Fairfax's description. The noble bust, the sloping shoulders, the graceful neck, the dark eyes and black ringlets were all there; – but her face? Her face was like her mother's; a youthful unfurrowed likeness: the same low brow, the same high features, the same pride. It was not, however, so saturnine a pride! She laughed continually; her laugh was satirical, and so was the habitual expression of her arched and haughty lip.

Genius is said to be self-conscious. I cannot tell whether Miss Ingram was a genius, but she was self-conscious – remarkably self-conscious indeed. She entered into a discourse on botany with the gentle Mrs. Dent. It seemed Mrs. Dent had not studied that science: though, as she said, she liked flowers, "especially wild ones;" Miss Ingram had, and she ran over its vocabulary with an air. I presently perceived she was (what is vernacularly termed) *trailing* Mrs. Dent; that is, playing on her ignorance – her *trail* might be clever, but it was decidedly not good-natured. She played: her execution was brilliant; she sang: her voice was fine; she talked French apart to her mamma; and she talked it well, with fluency and with a good accent.

Mary had a milder and more open countenance than Blanche; softer features too, and a skin some shades fairer (Miss Ingram was dark as a Spaniard) – but Mary was deficient in life: her face lacked expression, her eye lustre; she had nothing to say, and having once taken her seat, remained fixed like a statue in its niche. The sisters were both attired in spotless white.

And did I now think Miss Ingram such a choice as Mr. Rochester would be likely to make? I could not tell – I did not know his taste in female beauty. If he liked the majestic, she was the very type of majesty: then she was accomplished, sprightly. Most gentlemen would admire her, I thought; and that he *did* admire her, I already seemed to have obtained proof: to remove the last shade of doubt, it remained but to see them together.

You are not to suppose, reader, that Adèle has all this time been sitting motionless on the stool at my feet: no; when the ladies entered, she rose, advanced to meet them, made a stately reverence, and said with gravity:

"Bon jour, mesdames."

And Miss Ingram had looked down at her with a mocking air, and exclaimed, "Oh, what a little puppet!"

Lady Lynn had remarked, "It is Mr. Rochester's ward, I suppose – the little French girl he was speaking of."

Mrs. Dent had kindly taken her hand, and given her a kiss.

Amy and Louisa Eshton had cried out simultaneously – "What a love of a child!"

And then they had called her to a sofa, where she now sat, ensconced between them, chattering alternately in French and broken English; absorbing not only the young ladies' attention, but that of Mrs. Eshton and Lady Lynn, and getting spoilt to her heart's content.

At last coffee is brought in, and the gentlemen are summoned. I sit in the shade – if any shade there be in this brilliantly lit apartment; the window-curtain half hides me. Again the arch yawns; they come. The collective appearance of the gentlemen, like that of the ladies, is very imposing: they are all costumed in black; most of them are tall, some young. Henry and Frederick Lynn are very dashing sparks indeed; and Colonel Dent is a fine soldierly man. Mr. Eshton, the magistrate of the district, is gentleman-like: his hair is quite white, his eyebrows and whiskers still dark, which gives him something of the appearance of a 'père noble de théâtre'. Lord Ingram, like his sisters, is very tall; like them, also, he is handsome; but he shares Mary's apathetic and listless look: he seems to have more length of limb than vivacity of blood or vigour of brain.

And where is Mr. Rochester?

He comes in last: I am not looking at the arch, yet I see him enter. I try to concentrate my attention on those netting-needles, on the meshes of the purse I am forming – I wish to think only of the work I have in my hands, to see only the silver beads and silk threads that lie in my lap; whereas, I distinctly behold his figure, and I inevitably recall the moment when I last saw it; just after I had rendered him, what he deemed, an essential service, and he, holding my hand, and looking down on my face, surveyed me with eyes that revealed a heart full and eager to overflow; in whose emotions I had a part. How near had I approached him at that moment! What had occurred since, calculated to change his and my relative positions? Yet now, how distant, how far estranged we were! So far estranged, that I did not expect him to come and speak to me. I did not wonder, when, without looking at me, he took a seat at the other side of the room, and began conversing with some of the ladies.

No sooner did I see that his attention was riveted on them, and that I might gaze without being observed, than my eyes were drawn involuntarily to his face; I could not keep their lids under control: they would rise, and the irids would fix on him. I looked, and had an acute pleasure in looking, – a precious yet poignant pleasure; pure gold, with a steely point of agony: a pleasure like what the thirst-perishing man might feel who knows the well to which he has crept is poisoned, yet stoops and drinks divine draughts nevertheless.

Most true is it that 'beauty is in the eye of the gazer'. My master's colourless, olive face, square, massive brow, broad and jetty eyebrows, deep eyes, strong features, firm, grim mouth, – all energy, decision, will, – were not beautiful, according to rule; but they were more than beautiful to me; they were full of an interest, an influence that quite mastered me, – that took my feelings from my own power and fettered them in his. I had not intended to love him; the reader knows I had wrought hard to extirpate from my soul the germs of love there detected; and now, at the first renewed view of him, they spontaneously arrived, green and strong! He made me love him without looking at me.

I compared him with his guests. What was the gallant grace of the Lynns, the languid elegance of Lord Ingram, – even the military distinction of Colonel Dent, contrasted with his look of native pith and genuine power? I had no sympathy in their appearance, their expression: yet I could imagine that most observers would call them attractive, handsome, imposing; while they would pronounce Mr. Rochester at once harsh-featured and melancholy-looking. I saw them smile, laugh – it was nothing; the light of the candles had as much soul in it as their smile; the tinkle of the bell as much significance as their laugh. I saw Mr. Rochester smile: – his stern features softened; his eye grew both brilliant and gentle, its ray both searching and sweet. He was talking, at the moment, to Louisa and Amy Eshton. I wondered to see them receive with calm that look which seemed to me so penetrating: I expected their eyes to fall, their colour to rise under it; yet I was glad when I found they were in no sense moved. "He is not to them what he is to me," I thought: "he is not of their kind. I believe he is of mine; – I am sure he is – I feel akin to him – I understand the language of his countenance and movements: though rank and wealth sever us widely, I have something in my brain and heart, in my blood and nerves, that assimilates me mentally to him. Did I say, a few days since, that I had nothing to do with him but to receive my salary at his hands? Did I forbid myself to think of him in any other light than as a paymaster? Blasphemy against nature! Every good, true, vigorous feeling I have gathers impulsively round him. I know I must conceal my sentiments: I must smother hope; I must remember that he cannot care much for me. For when I say that I am of his kind, I do not mean that I have his force to influence, and his spell to attract; I mean only that I have certain tastes and feelings in common with him. I must, then, repeat continually that we are for ever sundered: – and yet, while I breathe and think, I must love him."

Coffee is handed. The ladies, since the gentlemen entered, have become lively as larks; conversation waxes brisk and merry. Colonel Dent and Mr. Eshton argue on politics; their wives listen. The two proud dowagers, Lady Lynn and Lady Ingram, confabulate together. Sir George – whom, by-the-bye, I have forgotten to describe, – a very big, and very fresh-looking country gentleman, stands before their sofa, coffee-cup in hand, and occasionally puts in a word. Mr. Frederick Lynn has taken a seat beside Mary Ingram, and is showing her the engravings of a splendid volume: she looks, smiles now and then, but apparently says little. The tall and phlegmatic Lord Ingram leans with folded arms on the chair-back of the little and lively Amy Eshton; she glances up at him, and chatters like a wren: she likes him better than she does Mr. Rochester. Henry Lynn has taken possession of an ottoman at the feet of Louisa: Adèle shares it with him: he is trying to talk French with her, and Louisa laughs at his blunders. With whom will Blanche Ingram pair? She is standing alone at the table, bending gracefully over an album. She seems waiting to be sought; but she will not wait too long: she herself selects a mate.

Mr. Rochester, having quitted the Eshtons, stands on the hearth as solitary as she stands by the table: she confronts him, taking her station on the opposite side of the mantelpiece.

"Mr. Rochester, I thought you were not fond of children?"

"Nor am I."

"Then, what induced you to take charge of such a little doll as that?" (pointing to Adèle). "Where did you pick her up?"

"I did not pick her up; she was left on my hands."

"You should have sent her to school."

"I could not afford it: schools are so dear."

"Why, I suppose you have a governess for her: I saw a person with her just now – is she gone? Oh, no! There she is still, behind the window-curtain. You pay her, of course; I should think it quite as expensive, – more so; for you have them both to keep in addition."

I feared – or should I say, hoped? – the allusion to me would make Mr. Rochester glance my way; and I involuntarily shrank farther into the shade: but he never turned his eyes.

"I have not considered the subject," said he indifferently, looking straight before him.

"No, you men never do consider economy and common sense. You should hear mama on the chapter of governesses: Mary and I have had, I should think, a dozen at least in our day; half of them detestable and the rest ridiculous, and all incubi – were they not, mama?"

"Did you speak, my own?"

The young lady thus claimed as the dowager's special property, reiterated her question with an explanation.

"My dearest, don't mention governesses; the word makes me nervous. I have suffered a martyrdom from their incompetency and caprice. I thank Heaven I have now done with them!"

Mrs. Dent here bent over to the pious lady and whispered something in her ear; I suppose, from the answer elicited, it was a reminder that one of the anathematised race was present.

"Tant pis!" said her Ladyship, "I hope it may do her good!" Then, in a lower tone, but still loud enough for me to hear, "I noticed her; I am a judge of physiognomy, and in hers I see all the faults of her class."

"What are they, madam?" inquired Mr. Rochester aloud.

"I will tell you in your private ear," replied she, wagging her turban three times with portentous significancy.

"But my curiosity will be past its appetite; it craves food now."

"Ask Blanche; she is nearer you than I."

"Oh, don't refer him to me, mama! I have just one word to say of the whole tribe; they are a nuisance. Not that I ever suffered much from them; I took care to turn the tables. What tricks Theodore and I used to play on our Miss Wilsons, and Mrs. Greys, and Madame Jouberts! Mary was always too sleepy to join in a plot with spirit. The best fun was with Madame Joubert: Miss Wilson was a poor sickly thing, lachrymose and low-spirited, not worth the trouble of vanquishing, in short; and Mrs. Grey was coarse and insensible; no blow took effect on her. But poor Madame Joubert! I see her yet in her raging passions, when we had driven her to extremities – spilt our tea, crumbled our bread and butter, tossed our books up to the ceiling, and played a charivari with the ruler and desk, the fender and fire irons. Theodore, do you remember those merry days?"

"Yaas, to be sure I do," drawled Lord Ingram; "and the poor old stick used to cry out 'Oh you villains childs!' – and then we sermonised her on the presumption of attempting to teach such clever blades as we were, when she was herself so ignorant."

"We did; and, Tedo, you know, I helped you in prosecuting (or persecuting) your tutor, whey-faced Mr. Vining – the parson in the pip, as we used to call him. He and Miss Wilson took the liberty of falling in love with each other – at least Tedo and I thought so; we surprised sundry tender glances and sighs which we interpreted as tokens of 'la belle passion', and I promise you the public soon had the benefit of our discovery; we employed it as a sort of lever to hoist our deadweights from the house. Dear mama, there, as soon as she got an inkling of the business, found out that it was of an immoral tendency. Did you not, my lady-mother?"

"Certainly, my best. And I was quite right: depend on that: there are a thousand reasons why liaisons between governesses and tutors should never be tolerated a moment in any well-regulated house; firstly –"

"Oh, gracious, mama! Spare us the enumeration! *Au reste*, we all know them: danger of bad example to innocence of childhood; distractions and consequent neglect of duty on the part of the attached – mutual alliance and reliance; confidence thence resulting – insolence accompanying – mutiny and general blow-up. Am I right, Baroness Ingram, of Ingram Park?"

"My lily-flower, you are right now, as always."

"Then no more need be said: change the subject."

Amy Eshton, not hearing or not heeding this dictum, joined in with her soft, infantine tone: "Louisa and I used to quiz our governess too; but she was such a good creature, she would bear anything: nothing put her out. She was never cross with us; was she, Louisa?"

"No, never: we might do what we pleased; ransack her desk and her workbox, and turn her drawers inside out; and she was so good-natured, she would give us anything we asked for."

"I suppose, now," said Miss Ingram, curling her lip sarcastically, "we shall have an abstract of the memoirs of all the governesses extant: in order to avert such a visitation, I again move the introduction of a new topic. Mr. Rochester, do you second my motion?"

"Madam, I support you on this point, as on every other."

"Then on me be the onus of bringing it forward. Signior Eduardo, are you in voice tonight?"

"Donna Bianca, if you command it, I will be."

"Then, signior, I lay on you my sovereign behest to furbish up your lungs and other vocal organs, as they will be wanted on my royal service."

"Who would not be the Rizzio of so divine a Mary?"

"A fig for Rizzio!" cried she, tossing her head with all its curls, as she moved to the piano. "It is my opinion the fiddler David must have been an insipid sort of fellow; I like black Bothwell better: to my mind a man is nothing without a spice of the devil in him; and history may say what it will of James Hepburn, but I have a notion, he was just the sort of wild, fierce, bandit hero whom I could have consented to gift with my hand."

"Gentlemen, you hear! Now which of you most resembles Bothwell?" cried Mr. Rochester.

"I should say the preference lies with you," responded Colonel Dent.

"On my honour, I am much obliged to you," was the reply.

Miss Ingram, who had now seated herself with proud grace at the piano, spreading out her snowy robes in queenly amplitude, commenced a brilliant prelude; talking meantime. She appeared to be on her high horse tonight; both her words and her air seemed intended to excite not only the admiration, but the amazement of her auditors: she was evidently bent on striking them as something very dashing and daring indeed.

"Oh, I am so sick of the young men of the present day!" exclaimed she, rattling away at the instrument. "Poor, puny things, not fit to stir a step beyond papa's park gates: nor to go even so far without mama's permission and guardianship! Creatures so absorbed in care about their pretty faces, and their white hands, and their small feet; as if a man had anything to do with beauty! As if loveliness were not the special prerogative of woman – her legitimate appanage and heritage! I grant an ugly *woman* is a blot on the fair face of creation; but as to the *gentlemen*, let them be solicitous to possess only strength and valour: let their motto be: – Hunt, shoot, and fight: the rest is not worth a fillip. Such should be my device, were I a man."

"Whenever I marry," she continued after a pause which none interrupted, "I am resolved my husband shall not be a rival, but a foil to me. I will suffer no competitor near the throne; I shall exact an undivided homage: his devotions shall not be shared between me and the shape he sees in his mirror. Mr. Rochester, now sing, and I will play for you."

"I am all obedience," was the response.

"Here then is a Corsair-song. Know that I doat on Corsairs; and for that reason, sing it *con spirito*."

"Commands from Miss Ingram's lips would put spirit into a mug of milk and water."

"Take care, then: if you don't please me, I will shame you by showing how such things *should* be done."

"That is offering a premium on incapacity: I shall now endeavour to fail."

"Gardez-vous en bien! If you err wilfully, I shall devise a proportionate punishment."

"Miss Ingram ought to be clement, for she has it in her power to inflict a chastisement beyond mortal endurance."

"Ha! Explain!" commanded the lady.

"Pardon me, madam: no need of explanation; your own fine sense must inform you that one of your frowns would be a sufficient substitute for capital punishment."

"Sing!" said she, and again touching the piano, she commenced an accompaniment in spirited style.

"Now is my time to slip away," thought I: but the tones that then severed the air arrested me. Mrs. Fairfax had said Mr. Rochester possessed a fine voice: he did – a mellow, powerful bass, into which he threw his own feeling, his own force; finding a way through the ear to the heart, and there waking sensation strangely. I waited till the last deep and full vibration had expired – till the tide of talk, checked an instant, had resumed its flow; I then quitted my sheltered corner and made my exit by the side-door, which was fortunately near. Thence a narrow passage led into the hall: in crossing it, I perceived my sandal was loose; I stopped to tie it, kneeling down for that purpose on the mat at the foot of the staircase. I heard the dining room door unclose; a gentleman came out; rising hastily, I stood face to face with him: it was Mr. Rochester.

"How do you do?" he asked.

"I am very well, sir."

"Why did you not come and speak to me in the room?"

I thought I might have retorted the question on him who put it: but I would not take that freedom. I answered:

"I did not wish to disturb you, as you seemed engaged, sir."

"What have you been doing during my absence?"

"Nothing particular; teaching Adèle as usual."

"And getting a good deal paler than you were – as I saw at first sight. What is the matter?"

"Nothing at all, sir."

"Did you take any cold that night you half drowned me?"

"Not the least."

"Return to the drawing room: you are deserting too early."

"I am tired, sir."

He looked at me for a minute.

"And a little depressed," he said. "What about? Tell me."

"Nothing – nothing, sir. I am not depressed."

"But I affirm that you are: so much depressed that a few more words would bring tears to your eyes – indeed, they are there now, shining and swimming; and a bead has slipped from the lash and fallen on to the flag. If I had time, and was not in mortal dread of some prating prig of a servant passing, I would know what all this means. Well, tonight I excuse you; but understand that so long as my visitors stay, I expect you to appear in the drawing room every evening; it is my wish; don't neglect it. Now go, and send Sophie for Adèle. Goodnight, my –" He stopped, bit his lip, and abruptly left me.

Chapter Eighteen

MERRY DAYS were these at Thornfield Hall; and busy days too: how different from the first three months of stillness, monotony, and solitude I had passed beneath its roof! All sad feelings seemed now driven from the house, all gloomy associations forgotten: there was life everywhere, movement all day long. You could not now traverse the gallery, once so hushed, nor enter the front chambers, once so tenantless, without encountering a smart lady's-maid or a dandy valet.

The kitchen, the butler's pantry, the servants' hall, the entrance hall, were equally alive; and the saloons were only left void and still when the blue sky and halcyon sunshine of the genial spring weather called their occupants out into the grounds. Even when that weather was broken, and continuous rain set in for some days, no damp seemed cast over enjoyment: indoor amusements only became more lively and varied, in consequence of the stop put to outdoor gaiety.

I wondered what they were going to do the first evening a change of entertainment was proposed: they spoke of 'playing charades', but in my ignorance I did not understand the term. The servants were called in, the dining room tables wheeled away, the lights otherwise disposed, the chairs placed in a semicircle opposite the arch. While Mr. Rochester and the other gentlemen directed these alterations, the ladies were running up and down stairs ringing for their maids. Mrs. Fairfax was summoned to give information respecting the resources of the house in shawls, dresses, draperies of any kind; and certain wardrobes of the third storey were ransacked, and their contents, in the shape of brocaded and hooped petticoats, satin sacques, black modes, lace lappets, etc., were brought down in armfuls by the Abigails; then a selection was made, and such things as were chosen were carried to the boudoir within the drawing room.

Meantime, Mr. Rochester had again summoned the ladies round him, and was selecting certain of their number to be of his party. "Miss Ingram is mine, of course," said he: afterwards he named the two Misses Eshton, and Mrs. Dent. He looked at me: I happened to be near him, as I had been fastening the clasp of Mrs. Dent's bracelet, which had got loose.

"Will you play?" he asked. I shook my head. He did not insist, which I rather feared he would have done; he allowed me to return quietly to my usual seat.

He and his aids now withdrew behind the curtain: the other party, which was headed by Colonel Dent, sat down on the crescent of chairs. One of the gentlemen, Mr. Eshton, observing me, seemed to propose that I should be asked to join them; but Lady Ingram instantly negatived the notion.

"No," I heard her say: "she looks too stupid for any game of the sort."

Ere long a bell tinkled, and the curtain drew up. Within the arch, the bulky figure of Sir George Lynn, whom Mr. Rochester had likewise chosen, was seen enveloped in a white sheet: before him, on a table, lay open a large book; and at his side stood Amy Eshton, draped in Mr. Rochester's cloak, and holding a book in her hand. Somebody, unseen, rang the bell merrily; then Adèle (who had insisted on being one of her guardian's party), bounded forward, scattering round her the contents of a basket of flowers she carried on her arm. Then appeared the magnificent figure of Miss Ingram, clad in white, a long veil on her head, and a wreath of roses round her brow; by her side walked Mr. Rochester, and together they drew near the table. They knelt; while Mrs. Dent and Louisa Eshton, dressed also in white, took up their stations behind them. A ceremony followed, in dumb show, in which it was easy to recognise the pantomime of a marriage. At its termination, Colonel Dent and his party consulted in whispers for two minutes, then the Colonel called out:

"Bride!" Mr. Rochester bowed, and the curtain fell.

A considerable interval elapsed before it again rose. Its second rising displayed a more elaborately prepared scene than the last. The drawing room, as I have before observed, was raised two steps above the dining room, and on the top of the upper step, placed a yard or two back within the room, appeared a large marble basin – which I recognised as an ornament of the conservatory – where it usually stood, surrounded by exotics, and tenanted by gold fish – and whence it must have been transported with some trouble, on account of its size and weight.

Seated on the carpet, by the side of this basin, was seen Mr. Rochester, costumed in shawls, with a turban on his head. His dark eyes and swarthy skin and Paynim features suited the costume exactly: he looked the very model of an Eastern emir, an agent or a victim of the bowstring. Presently advanced into view Miss Ingram. She, too, was attired in oriental fashion: a crimson scarf tied sash-like round the waist: an embroidered handkerchief knotted about her temples; her beautifully-moulded arms bare, one of them upraised in the act of supporting a pitcher, poised gracefully on her head. Both her cast of form and feature, her complexion and her general air, suggested the idea of some Israelitish princess of the patriarchal days; and such was doubtless the character she intended to represent.

She approached the basin, and bent over it as if to fill her pitcher; she again lifted it to her head. The personage on the well-brink now seemed to accost her; to make some request: – 'She hasted, let down her pitcher on her hand, and gave him to drink.' [21] From the bosom of his robe he then produced a casket, opened it and showed magnificent bracelets and earrings; she acted astonishment and admiration; kneeling, he laid the treasure at her feet; incredulity and delight were expressed by her looks and gestures; the stranger fastened the bracelets on her arms and the rings in her ears. It was Eliezer and Rebecca: the camels only were wanting.

The divining party again laid their heads together: apparently they could not agree about the word or syllable the scene illustrated. Colonel Dent, their spokesman, demanded "the tableau of the whole;" whereupon the curtain again descended.

On its third rising only a portion of the drawing room was disclosed; the rest being concealed by a screen, hung with some sort of dark and coarse drapery. The marble basin was removed; in its place, stood a deal table and a kitchen chair: these objects were visible by a very dim light proceeding from a horn lantern, the wax candles being all extinguished.

Amidst this sordid scene, sat a man with his clenched hands resting on his knees, and his eyes bent on the ground. I knew Mr. Rochester; though the begrimed face, the disordered dress (his coat hanging loose from one arm, as if it had been almost torn from his back in a scuffle), the desperate and scowling countenance, the rough, bristling hair might well have disguised him. As he moved, a chain clanked; to his wrists were attached fetters.

"Bridewell!" exclaimed Colonel Dent, and the charade was solved.

A sufficient interval having elapsed for the performers to resume their ordinary costume, they re-entered the dining room. Mr. Rochester led in Miss Ingram; she was complimenting him on his acting.

"Do you know," said she, "that, of the three characters, I liked you in the last best? Oh, had you but lived a few years earlier, what a gallant gentleman-highwayman you would have made!"

"Is all the soot washed from my face?" he asked, turning it towards her.

"Alas! Yes: the more's the pity! Nothing could be more becoming to your complexion than that ruffian's rouge."

"You would like a hero of the road then?"

"An English hero of the road would be the next best thing to an Italian bandit; and that could only be surpassed by a Levantine pirate."

"Well, whatever I am, remember you are my wife; we were married an hour since, in the presence of all these witnesses." She giggled, and her colour rose.

"Now, Dent," continued Mr. Rochester, "it is your turn." And as the other party withdrew, he and his band took the vacated seats. Miss Ingram placed herself at her leader's right hand; the other diviners filled the chairs on each side of him and her. I did not now watch the actors; I no longer waited with interest for the curtain to rise; my attention was absorbed by the spectators; my eyes, erewhile fixed on the arch, were now irresistibly attracted to the semicircle of chairs. What charade Colonel Dent and his party played, what word they chose, how they acquitted themselves, I no longer remember; but I still see the consultation which followed each scene: I see Mr. Rochester turn to Miss Ingram, and Miss Ingram to him; I see her incline her head towards him, till the jetty curls almost touch his shoulder and wave against his cheek; I hear their mutual whisperings; I recall their interchanged glances; and something even of the feeling roused by the spectacle returns in memory at this moment.

I have told you, reader, that I had learnt to love Mr. Rochester: I could not unlove him now, merely because I found that he had ceased to notice me – because I might pass hours in his presence, and he would never once turn his eyes in my direction – because I saw all his attentions appropriated by a great lady, who scorned to touch me with the hem of her robes as she passed; who, if ever her dark and imperious eye fell on me by chance, would withdraw it instantly as from an object too mean to merit observation. I could not unlove him, because I felt sure he would soon marry this very lady – because I read daily in her a proud security in his intentions respecting her – because I witnessed hourly in him a style of courtship which, if careless and choosing rather to be sought than to seek, was yet, in its very carelessness, captivating, and in its very pride, irresistible.

There was nothing to cool or banish love in these circumstances, though much to create despair. Much too, you will think, reader, to engender jealousy: if a woman, in my position, could presume to be jealous of a woman in Miss Ingram's. But I was not jealous: or very rarely; – the nature of the pain I suffered could not be explained by that word. Miss Ingram was a mark beneath jealousy: she was too inferior to excite the feeling. Pardon the seeming paradox; I mean what I say. She was very showy, but she was not genuine: she had a fine person, many brilliant attainments; but her mind was poor, her heart barren by nature: nothing bloomed spontaneously on that soil; no unforced natural fruit delighted by its freshness. She was not good; she was not original: she used to repeat sounding phrases from books: she never offered, nor had, an opinion of her own. She advocated a high tone of sentiment; but she did not know the sensations of sympathy and pity; tenderness and truth were not in her. Too often she betrayed this, by the undue vent she gave to a spiteful antipathy she had conceived against little Adèle: pushing her away with some contumelious epithet if she happened to approach her; sometimes ordering her from the room, and always treating her with coldness and acrimony. Other eyes besides mine watched these manifestations of character – watched them closely, keenly, shrewdly. Yes; the future bridegroom, Mr. Rochester himself, exercised over his intended a ceaseless surveillance; and it was from this sagacity – this guardedness of his – this perfect, clear consciousness of his fair one's defects – this obvious absence of passion in his sentiments towards her, that my ever-torturing pain arose.

I saw he was going to marry her, for family, perhaps political reasons, because her rank and connections suited him; I felt he had not given her his love, and that her qualifications were ill adapted to win from him that treasure. This was the point – this was where the nerve was touched and teased – this was where the fever was sustained and fed: *she could not charm him.*

If she had managed the victory at once, and he had yielded and sincerely laid his heart at her feet, I should have covered my face, turned to the wall, and (figuratively) have died to them. If Miss Ingram had been a good and noble woman, endowed with force, fervour, kindness, sense, I should have had one vital struggle with two tigers – jealousy and despair: then, my heart torn out and devoured, I should have admired her – acknowledged her excellence, and been quiet for the rest of my days: and the more absolute her superiority, the deeper would have been my admiration – the more truly tranquil my quiescence. But as matters really stood, to watch Miss Ingram's efforts at fascinating Mr. Rochester, to witness their repeated failure – herself unconscious that they did fail; vainly fancying that each shaft launched hit the mark, and infatuatedly pluming herself on success, when her pride and self-complacency repelled further and further what she wished to allure – to witness *this*, was to be at once under ceaseless excitation and ruthless restraint.

Because, when she failed, I saw how she might have succeeded. Arrows that continually glanced off from Mr. Rochester's breast and fell harmless at his feet, might, I knew, if shot by a surer hand, have quivered keen in his proud heart – have called love into his stern eye, and softness into his sardonic face; or, better still, without weapons a silent conquest might have been won.

"Why can she not influence him more, when she is privileged to draw so near to him?" I asked myself. "Surely she cannot truly like him, or not like him with true affection! If she did, she need not coin her smiles so lavishly, flash her glances so unremittingly, manufacture airs so elaborate, graces so multitudinous. It seems to me that she might, by merely sitting quietly at his side, saying little and looking less, get nigher his heart. I have seen in his face a far different expression from that which hardens it now while she is so vivaciously accosting him; but then it came of itself: it was not elicited by meretricious arts and calculated manoeuvres; and one had but to accept it – to answer what he asked without pretension, to address him when needful without grimace – and it increased and grew kinder and more genial, and warmed one like a fostering sunbeam. How will she manage to please him when they are married? I do not think she will manage it; and yet it might be managed; and his wife might, I verily believe, be the very happiest woman the sun shines on."

I have not yet said anything condemnatory of Mr. Rochester's project of marrying for interest and connections. It surprised me when I first discovered that such was his intention: I had thought him a man unlikely to be influenced by motives so commonplace in his choice of a wife; but the longer I considered the position, education, etc., of the parties, the less I felt justified in judging and blaming either him or Miss Ingram for acting in conformity to ideas and principles instilled into them, doubtless, from their childhood. All their class held these principles: I supposed, then, they had reasons for holding them such as I could not fathom. It seemed to me that, were I a gentleman like him, I would take to my bosom only such a wife as I could love; but the very obviousness of the advantages to the husband's own happiness offered by this plan convinced me that there must be arguments against its general adoption of which I was quite ignorant: otherwise I felt sure all the world would act as I wished to act.

But in other points, as well as this, I was growing very lenient to my master: I was forgetting all his faults, for which I had once kept a sharp look-out. It had formerly been my endeavour to study all sides of his character: to take the bad with the good; and from the just weighing of both, to form an equitable judgment. Now I saw no bad. The sarcasm that had repelled, the harshness that had startled me once, were only like keen condiments in a choice dish: their presence was pungent, but their absence would be felt as comparatively insipid. And as for the vague something – was it a sinister or a sorrowful, a designing or a desponding expression? – that opened upon a careful observer, now and then, in his eye, and closed again before one could fathom the strange depth partially disclosed; that something which used to make me fear and shrink, as if I had been wandering amongst volcanic-looking hills, and had suddenly felt the ground quiver and seen it gape: that something, I, at intervals, beheld still; and with throbbing heart, but not with palsied nerves. Instead of wishing to shun, I longed only to dare – to divine it; and I thought Miss Ingram happy, because one day she might look into the abyss at her leisure, explore its secrets and analyse their nature.

Meantime, while I thought only of my master and his future bride – saw only them, heard only their discourse, and considered only their movements of importance – the rest of the party were occupied with their own separate interests and pleasures. The Ladies Lynn and Ingram continued to consort in solemn conferences, where they nodded their two turbans at each other, and held up their four hands in confronting gestures of surprise, or mystery, or horror, according to the theme on which their gossip ran, like a pair of magnified puppets. Mild Mrs. Dent talked with good-natured Mrs. Eshton; and the two sometimes bestowed a courteous word or smile on me. Sir George Lynn, Colonel Dent, and Mr. Eshton discussed politics, or county affairs, or justice business. Lord Ingram flirted with Amy Eshton; Louisa played and sang to and with one of the Messrs. Lynn; and Mary Ingram listened languidly to the gallant speeches of the other. Sometimes all, as with one consent, suspended their by-play to observe and listen to the principal actors: for, after all, Mr. Rochester and – because closely connected with him – Miss Ingram were the life and soul of the party. If he was absent from the room an hour, a perceptible dulness seemed to steal over the spirits of his guests; and his re-entrance was sure to give a fresh impulse to the vivacity of conversation.

The want of his animating influence appeared to be peculiarly felt one day that he had been summoned to Millcote on business, and was not likely to return till late. The afternoon was wet: a walk the party had proposed to take to see a gipsy camp, lately pitched on a common beyond Hay, was consequently deferred. Some of the gentlemen were gone to the stables: the younger ones, together with the younger ladies, were playing billiards in the billiard-room. The dowagers Ingram and Lynn sought solace in a quiet game at cards. Blanche Ingram, after having repelled, by supercilious taciturnity, some efforts of Mrs. Dent and Mrs. Eshton to draw her into conversation, had first murmured over some sentimental tunes and airs on the piano, and then, having fetched a novel from the library, had flung herself in haughty listlessness on a sofa, and prepared to beguile, by the spell of fiction, the tedious hours of absence. The room and the house were silent: only now and then the merriment of the billiard players was heard from above.

It was verging on dusk, and the clock had already given warning of the hour to dress for dinner, when little Adèle, who knelt by me in the drawing room window seat, suddenly exclaimed:

"Voilà, Monsieur Rochester, qui revient!"

I turned, and Miss Ingram darted forwards from her sofa: the others, too, looked up from their several occupations; for at the same time a crunching of wheels and a splashing tramp of horse hoofs became audible on the wet gravel. A post-chaise was approaching.

"What can possess him to come home in that style?" said Miss Ingram. "He rode Mesrour (the black horse), did he not, when he went out? And Pilot was with him: – what has he done with the animals?"

As she said this, she approached her tall person and ample garments so near the window, that I was obliged to bend back almost to the breaking of my spine: in her eagerness she did not observe me at first, but when she did, she curled her lip and moved to another casement. The post-chaise stopped; the driver rang the doorbell, and a gentleman alighted attired in travelling garb; but it was not Mr. Rochester; it was a tall, fashionable-looking man, a stranger.

"How provoking!" exclaimed Miss Ingram: "you tiresome monkey!" (apostrophising Adèle), "who perched you up in the window to give false intelligence?" and she cast on me an angry glance, as if I were in fault.

Some parleying was audible in the hall, and soon the newcomer entered. He bowed to Lady Ingram, as deeming her the eldest lady present.

"It appears I come at an inopportune time, madam," said he, "when my friend, Mr. Rochester, is from home; but I arrive from a very long journey, and I think I may presume so far on old and intimate acquaintance as to instal myself here till he returns."

His manner was polite; his accent, in speaking, struck me as being somewhat unusual, – not precisely foreign, but still not altogether English: his age might be about Mr. Rochester's, – between thirty and forty; his complexion was singularly sallow: otherwise he was a fine-looking man, at first sight especially. On closer examination, you detected something in his face that displeased, or rather that failed to please. His features were regular, but too relaxed: his eye was large and well cut, but the life looking out of it was a tame, vacant life – at least so I thought.

The sound of the dressing-bell dispersed the party. It was not till after dinner that I saw him again: he then seemed quite at his ease. But I liked his physiognomy even less than before: it struck me as being at the same time unsettled and inanimate. His eye wandered, and had no meaning in its wandering: this gave him an odd look, such as I never remembered to have seen. For a handsome and not an unamiable-looking man, he repelled me exceedingly: there was no power in that smooth-skinned face of a full oval shape: no firmness in that aquiline nose and small cherry mouth; there was no thought on the low, even forehead; no command in that blank, brown eye.

As I sat in my usual nook, and looked at him with the light of the girandoles on the mantelpiece beaming full over him – for he occupied an armchair drawn close to the fire, and kept shrinking still nearer, as if he were cold, I compared him with Mr. Rochester. I think (with deference be it spoken) the contrast could not be much greater between a sleek gander and a fierce falcon: between a meek sheep and the rough-coated keen-eyed dog, its guardian.

He had spoken of Mr. Rochester as an old friend. A curious friendship theirs must have been: a pointed illustration, indeed, of the old adage that 'extremes meet'.

Two or three of the gentlemen sat near him, and I caught at times scraps of their conversation across the room. At first I could not make much sense of what I heard; for the discourse of Louisa Eshton and Mary Ingram, who sat nearer to me, confused the fragmentary sentences that reached me at intervals. These last were discussing the stranger; they both called him "a beautiful man". Louisa said he was "a love of a creature," and she "adored him;" and Mary instanced his "pretty little mouth, and nice nose," as her ideal of the charming.

"And what a sweet-tempered forehead he has!" cried Louisa, – "so smooth – none of those frowning irregularities I dislike so much; and such a placid eye and smile!"

And then, to my great relief, Mr. Henry Lynn summoned them to the other side of the room, to settle some point about the deferred excursion to Hay Common.

I was now able to concentrate my attention on the group by the fire, and I presently gathered that the new-comer was called Mr. Mason; then I learned that he was but just arrived in England, and that he came from some hot country: which was the reason, doubtless, his face was so sallow, and that he sat so near the hearth, and wore a surtout in the house. Presently the words Jamaica, Kingston, Spanish Town, indicated the West Indies as his residence; and it was with no little surprise I gathered, ere long, that he had there first seen and become acquainted with Mr. Rochester. He spoke of his friend's dislike of the burning heats, the hurricanes, and rainy seasons of that region. I knew Mr. Rochester had been a traveller: Mrs. Fairfax had said so; but I thought the continent of Europe had bounded his wanderings; till now I had never heard a hint given of visits to more distant shores.

I was pondering these things, when an incident, and a somewhat unexpected one, broke the thread of my musings. Mr. Mason, shivering as some one chanced to open the door, asked for more coal to be put on the fire, which had burnt out its flame, though its mass of cinder still shone hot and red. The footman who brought the coal, in going out, stopped near Mr. Eshton's chair, and said something to him in a low voice, of which I heard only the words, "old woman," – "quite troublesome".

"Tell her she shall be put in the stocks if she does not take herself off," replied the magistrate.

"No – stop!" interrupted Colonel Dent. "Don't send her away, Eshton; we might turn the thing to account; better consult the ladies." And speaking aloud, he continued – "Ladies, you talked of going to Hay Common to visit the gipsy camp; Sam here says that one of the old Mother Bunches is in the servants' hall at this moment, and insists upon being brought in before 'the quality', to tell them their fortunes. Would you like to see her?"

"Surely, colonel," cried Lady Ingram, "you would not encourage such a low impostor? Dismiss her, by all means, at once!"

"But I cannot persuade her to go away, my lady," said the footman; "nor can any of the servants: Mrs. Fairfax is with her just now, entreating her to be gone; but she has taken a chair in the chimney corner, and says nothing shall stir her from it till she gets leave to come in here."

"What does she want?" asked Mrs. Eshton.

"'To tell the gentry their fortunes', she says, ma'am; and she swears she must and will do it."

"What is she like?" inquired the Misses Eshton, in a breath.

"A shockingly ugly old creature, miss; almost as black as a crock."

"Why, she's a real sorceress!" cried Frederick Lynn. "Let us have her in, of course."

"To be sure," rejoined his brother; "it would be a thousand pities to throw away such a chance of fun."

"My dear boys, what are you thinking about?" exclaimed Mrs. Lynn.

"I cannot possibly countenance any such inconsistent proceeding," chimed in the Dowager Ingram.

"Indeed, mama, but you can – and will," pronounced the haughty voice of Blanche, as she turned round on the piano stool; where till now she had sat silent, apparently examining sundry sheets of music. "I have a curiosity to hear my fortune told: therefore, Sam, order the beldame forward."

"My darling Blanche! Recollect –"

"I do – I recollect all you can suggest; and I must have my will – quick, Sam!"

"Yes – yes – yes!" cried all the juveniles, both ladies and gentlemen. "Let her come – it will be excellent sport!"

The footman still lingered. "She looks such a rough one," said he.

"Go!" ejaculated Miss Ingram, and the man went.

Excitement instantly seized the whole party: a running fire of raillery and jests was proceeding when Sam returned.

"She won't come now," said he. "She says it's not her mission to appear before the 'vulgar herd' (them's her words). I must show her into a room by herself, and then those who wish to consult her must go to her one by one."

"You see now, my queenly Blanche," began Lady Ingram, "she encroaches. Be advised, my angel girl – and –"

"Show her into the library, of course," cut in the 'angel girl'. "It is not my mission to listen to her before the vulgar herd either: I mean to have her all to myself. Is there a fire in the library?"

"Yes, ma'am – but she looks such a tinkler."

"Cease that chatter, blockhead! And do my bidding."

Again Sam vanished; and mystery, animation, expectation rose to full flow once more.

"She's ready now," said the footman, as he reappeared. "She wishes to know who will be her first visitor."

"I think I had better just look in upon her before any of the ladies go," said Colonel Dent.

"Tell her, Sam, a gentleman is coming."

Sam went and returned.

"She says, sir, that she'll have no gentlemen; they need not trouble themselves to come near her; nor," he added, with difficulty suppressing a titter, "any ladies either, except the young, and single."

"By Jove, she has taste!" exclaimed Henry Lynn.

Miss Ingram rose solemnly: "I go first," she said, in a tone which might have befitted the leader of a forlorn hope, mounting a breach in the van of his men.

"Oh, my best! Oh, my dearest! Pause – reflect!" was her mama's cry; but she swept past her in stately silence, passed through the door which Colonel Dent held open, and we heard her enter the library.

A comparative silence ensued. Lady Ingram thought it 'le cas' [22] to wring her hands: which she did accordingly. Miss Mary declared she felt, for her part, she never dared venture. Amy and Louisa Eshton tittered under their breath, and looked a little frightened.

The minutes passed very slowly: fifteen were counted before the library door again opened. Miss Ingram returned to us through the arch.

Would she laugh? Would she take it as a joke? All eyes met her with a glance of eager curiosity, and she met all eyes with one of rebuff and coldness; she looked neither flurried nor merry: she walked stiffly to her seat, and took it in silence.

"Well, Blanche?" said Lord Ingram.

"What did she say, sister?" asked Mary.

"What did you think? How do you feel? – Is she a real fortune-teller?" demanded the Misses Eshton.

"Now, now, good people," returned Miss Ingram, "don't press upon me. Really your organs of wonder and credulity are easily excited: you seem, by the importance of you all – my good mama included – ascribe to this matter, absolutely to believe we have a genuine witch in the house, who is in close alliance with the old gentleman. I have seen a gipsy vagabond; she has practised in hackneyed fashion the science of palmistry and told me what such people usually tell. My whim is gratified; and now I think Mr. Eshton will do well to put the hag in the stocks tomorrow morning, as he threatened."

Miss Ingram took a book, leant back in her chair, and so declined further conversation. I watched her for nearly half an hour: during all that time she never turned a page, and her face grew momently darker, more dissatisfied, and more sourly expressive of disappointment. She had obviously not heard anything to her advantage: and it seemed to me, from her prolonged fit of gloom and taciturnity, that she herself, notwithstanding her professed indifference, attached undue importance to whatever revelations had been made her.

Meantime, Mary Ingram, Amy and Louisa Eshton, declared they dared not go alone; and yet they all wished to go. A negotiation was opened through the medium of the ambassador, Sam; and after much pacing to and fro, till, I think, the said Sam's calves must have ached with the exercise, permission was at last, with great difficulty, extorted from the rigorous Sibyl, for the three to wait upon her in a body.

Their visit was not so still as Miss Ingram's had been: we heard hysterical giggling and little shrieks proceeding from the library; and at the end of about twenty minutes they burst the door open, and came running across the hall, as if they were half-scared out of their wits.

"I am sure she is something not right!" they cried, one and all. "She told us such things! She knows all about us!" and they sank breathless into the various seats the gentlemen hastened to bring them.

Pressed for further explanation, they declared she had told them of things they had said and done when they were mere children; described books and ornaments they had in their boudoirs at home: keepsakes that different relations had presented to them. They affirmed that she had even divined their thoughts, and had whispered in the ear of each the name of the person she liked best in the world, and informed them of what they most wished for.

Here the gentlemen interposed with earnest petitions to be further enlightened on these two last-named points; but they got only blushes, ejaculations, tremors, and titters, in return for their importunity. The matrons, meantime, offered vinaigrettes and wielded fans; and again and again reiterated the expression of their concern that their warning had not been taken in time; and the elder gentlemen laughed, and the younger urged their services on the agitated fair ones.

In the midst of the tumult, and while my eyes and ears were fully engaged in the scene before me, I heard a hem close at my elbow: I turned, and saw Sam.

"If you please, miss, the gipsy declares that there is another young single lady in the room who has not been to her yet, and she swears she will not go till she has seen all. I thought it must be you: there is no one else for it. What shall I tell her?"

"Oh, I will go by all means," I answered: and I was glad of the unexpected opportunity to gratify my much-excited curiosity. I slipped out of the room, unobserved by any eye – for the company were gathered in one mass about the trembling trio just returned – and I closed the door quietly behind me.

"If you like, miss," said Sam, "I'll wait in the hall for you; and if she frightens you, just call and I'll come in."

"No, Sam, return to the kitchen: I am not in the least afraid." Nor was I; but I was a good deal interested and excited.

Chapter Nineteen

THE LIBRARY LOOKED tranquil enough as I entered it, and the Sibyl – if Sibyl she were – was seated snugly enough in an easy chair at the chimney corner. She had on a red cloak and a black bonnet: or rather, a broad-brimmed gipsy hat, tied down with a striped handkerchief under her chin. An extinguished candle stood on the table; she was bending over the fire, and seemed reading in a little black book, like a prayer book, by the light of the blaze: she muttered the words to herself, as most old women do, while she read; she did not desist immediately on my entrance: it appeared she wished to finish a paragraph.

I stood on the rug and warmed my hands, which were rather cold with sitting at a distance from the drawing room fire. I felt now as composed as ever I did in my life: there was nothing indeed in the gipsy's appearance to trouble one's calm. She shut her book and slowly looked up; her hat-brim partially shaded her face, yet I could see, as she raised it, that it was a strange one. It looked all brown and black: elf-locks bristled out from beneath a white band which passed under her chin, and came half over her cheeks, or rather jaws: her eye confronted me at once, with a bold and direct gaze.

"Well, and you want your fortune told?" she said, in a voice as decided as her glance, as harsh as her features.

"I don't care about it, mother; you may please yourself: but I ought to warn you, I have no faith."

"It's like your impudence to say so: I expected it of you; I heard it in your step as you crossed the threshold."

"Did you? You've a quick ear."

"I have; and a quick eye and a quick brain."

"You need them all in your trade."

"I do; especially when I've customers like you to deal with. Why don't you tremble?"

"I'm not cold."

"Why don't you turn pale?"

"I am not sick."

"Why don't you consult my art?"

"I'm not silly."

The old crone 'nichered' [23] a laugh under her bonnet and bandage; she then drew out a short black pipe, and lighting it began to smoke. Having indulged a while in this sedative, she raised her bent body, took the pipe from her lips, and while gazing steadily at the fire, said very deliberately – "You are cold; you are sick; and you are silly."

"Prove it," I rejoined.

"I will, in few words. You are cold, because you are alone: no contact strikes the fire from you that is in you. You are sick; because the best of feelings, the highest and the sweetest given to man, keeps far away from you. You are silly, because, suffer as you may, you will not beckon it to approach, nor will you stir one step to meet it where it waits you."

She again put her short black pipe to her lips, and renewed her smoking with vigour.

"You might say all that to almost anyone who you knew lived as a solitary dependent in a great house."

"I might say it to almost anyone: but would it be true of almost anyone?"

"In my circumstances."

"Yes; just so, in *your* circumstances: but find me another precisely placed as you are."

"It would be easy to find you thousands."

"You could scarcely find me one. If you knew it, you are peculiarly situated: very near happiness; yes, within reach of it. The materials are all prepared; there only wants a movement to combine them. Chance laid them somewhat apart; let them be once approached and bliss results."

"I don't understand enigmas. I never could guess a riddle in my life."

"If you wish me to speak more plainly, show me your palm."

"And I must cross it with silver, I suppose?"

"To be sure."

I gave her a shilling: she put it into an old stocking-foot which she took out of her pocket, and having tied it round and returned it, she told me to hold out my hand. I did. She approached her face to the palm, and pored over it without touching it.

"It is too fine," said she. "I can make nothing of such a hand as that; almost without lines: besides, what is in a palm? Destiny is not written there."

"I believe you," said I.

"No," she continued, "it is in the face: on the forehead, about the eyes, in the lines of the mouth. Kneel, and lift up your head."

"Ah! Now you are coming to reality," I said, as I obeyed her. "I shall begin to put some faith in you presently."

I knelt within half a yard of her. She stirred the fire, so that a ripple of light broke from the disturbed coal: the glare, however, as she sat, only threw her face into deeper shadow: mine, it illumined.

"I wonder with what feelings you came to me tonight," she said, when she had examined me a while. "I wonder what thoughts are busy in your heart during all the hours you sit in yonder room with the fine people flitting before you like shapes in a magic lantern: just as little sympathetic communion passing between you and them as if they were really mere shadows of human forms, and not the actual substance."

"I feel tired often, sleepy sometimes, but seldom sad."

"Then you have some secret hope to buoy you up and please you with whispers of the future?"

"Not I. The utmost I hope is, to save money enough out of my earnings to set up a school some day in a little house rented by myself."

"A mean nutriment for the spirit to exist on: and sitting in that window seat (you see I know your habits) –"

"You have learned them from the servants."

"Ah! You think yourself sharp. Well, perhaps I have: to speak truth, I have an acquaintance with one of them, Mrs. Poole –"

I started to my feet when I heard the name.

"You have – have you?" thought I; "there is diablerie in the business after all, then!"

"Don't be alarmed," continued the strange being; "she's a safe hand is Mrs. Poole: close and quiet; anyone may repose confidence in her. But, as I was saying: sitting in that window seat, do you think of nothing but your future school? Have you no present interest in any of the company who occupy the sofas and chairs before you? Is there not one face you study? One figure whose movements you follow with at least curiosity?"

"I like to observe all the faces and all the figures."

"But do you never single one from the rest – or it may be, two?"

"I do frequently; when the gestures or looks of a pair seem telling a tale: it amuses me to watch them."

"What tale do you like best to hear?"

"Oh, I have not much choice! They generally run on the same theme – courtship; and promise to end in the same catastrophe – marriage."

"And do you like that monotonous theme?"

"Positively, I don't care about it: it is nothing to me."

"Nothing to you? When a lady, young and full of life and health, charming with beauty and endowed with the gifts of rank and fortune, sits and smiles in the eyes of a gentleman you –"

"I what?"

"You know – and perhaps think well of."

"I don't know the gentlemen here. I have scarcely interchanged a syllable with one of them; and as to thinking well of them, I consider some respectable, and stately, and middle-aged, and others young, dashing, handsome, and lively: but certainly they are all at liberty to be the recipients of whose smiles they please, without my feeling disposed to consider the transaction of any moment to me."

"You don't know the gentlemen here? You have not exchanged a syllable with one of them? Will you say that of the master of the house!"

"He is not at home."

"A profound remark! A most ingenious quibble! He went to Millcote this morning, and will be back here tonight or tomorrow: does that circumstance exclude him from the list of your acquaintance – blot him, as it were, out of existence?"

"No; but I can scarcely see what Mr. Rochester has to do with the theme you had introduced."

"I was talking of ladies smiling in the eyes of gentlemen; and of late so many smiles have been shed into Mr. Rochester's eyes that they overflow like two cups filled above the brim: have you never remarked that?"

"Mr. Rochester has a right to enjoy the society of his guests."

"No question about his right: but have you never observed that, of all the tales told here about matrimony, Mr. Rochester has been favoured with the most lively and the most continuous?"

"The eagerness of a listener quickens the tongue of a narrator." I said this rather to myself than to the gipsy, whose strange talk, voice, manner, had by this time wrapped me in a kind of dream. One unexpected sentence came from her lips after another, till I got involved in a web of mystification; and wondered what unseen spirit had been sitting for weeks by my heart watching its workings and taking record of every pulse.

"Eagerness of a listener!" repeated she: "yes; Mr. Rochester has sat by the hour, his ear inclined to the fascinating lips that took such delight in their task of communicating; and Mr. Rochester was so willing to receive and looked so grateful for the pastime given him; you have noticed this?"

"Grateful! I cannot remember detecting gratitude in his face."

"Detecting! You have analysed, then. And what did you detect, if not gratitude?"

I said nothing.

"You have seen love: have you not? – and, looking forward, you have seen him married, and beheld his bride happy?"

"Humph! Not exactly. Your witch's skill is rather at fault sometimes."

"What the devil have you seen, then?"

"Never mind: I came here to inquire, not to confess. Is it known that Mr. Rochester is to be married?"

"Yes; and to the beautiful Miss Ingram."

"Shortly?"

"Appearances would warrant that conclusion: and, no doubt (though, with an audacity that wants chastising out of you, you seem to question it), they will be a superlatively happy pair. He must love such a handsome, noble, witty, accomplished lady; and probably she loves him, or, if not his person, at least his purse. I know she considers the Rochester estate eligible to the last degree; though (God pardon me!) I told her something on that point about an hour ago which made her look wondrous grave: the corners of her mouth fell half an inch. I would advise her blackaviced [24] suitor to look out: if another comes, with a longer or clearer rent-roll, – he's dished –"

"But, mother, I did not come to hear Mr. Rochester's fortune: I came to hear my own; and you have told me nothing of it."

"Your fortune is yet doubtful: when I examined your face, one trait contradicted another. Chance has meted you a measure of happiness: that I know. I knew it before I came here this evening. She has laid it carefully on one side for you. I saw her do it. It depends on yourself to stretch out your hand, and take it up: but whether you will do so, is the problem I study. Kneel again on the rug."

"Don't keep me long; the fire scorches me."

I knelt. She did not stoop towards me, but only gazed, leaning back in her chair. She began muttering:

"The flame flickers in the eye; the eye shines like dew; it looks soft and full of feeling; it smiles at my jargon: it is susceptible; impression follows impression through its clear sphere; where it ceases to smile, it is sad; an unconscious lassitude weighs on the lid: that signifies melancholy resulting from loneliness. It turns from me; it will not suffer further scrutiny; it seems to deny, by a mocking glance, the truth of the discoveries I have already made, – to disown the charge both of sensibility and chagrin: its pride and reserve only confirm me in my opinion. The eye is favourable.

"As to the mouth, it delights at times in laughter; it is disposed to impart all that the brain conceives; though I daresay it would be silent on much the heart experiences. Mobile and flexible, it was never intended to be compressed in the eternal silence of solitude: it is a mouth which should speak much and smile often, and have human affection for its interlocutor. That feature too is propitious.

"I see no enemy to a fortunate issue but in the brow; and that brow professes to say, – 'I can live alone, if self-respect, and circumstances require me so to do. I need not sell my soul to buy bliss. I have an inward treasure born with me, which can keep me alive if all extraneous delights should be withheld, or offered only at a price I cannot afford to give.' The forehead declares, 'Reason sits firm and holds the reins, and she will not let the feelings burst away and hurry her to wild chasms. The passions may rage furiously, like true heathens, as they are; and the desires may imagine all sorts of vain things: but judgment shall still have the last word in every argument, and the casting vote in every decision. Strong wind, earthquake-shock, and fire may pass by: but I shall follow the guiding of that still small voice which interprets the dictates of conscience.'

"Well said, forehead; your declaration shall be respected. I have formed my plans – right plans I deem them – and in them I have attended to the claims of conscience, the counsels of reason. I know how soon youth would fade and bloom perish, if, in the cup of bliss offered, but one dreg of shame, or one flavour of remorse were detected; and I do not want sacrifice, sorrow, dissolution – such is not my taste. I wish to foster, not to blight – to earn gratitude, not to wring tears of blood – no, nor of brine: my harvest must be in smiles, in endearments, in sweet – That will do. I think I rave in a kind of exquisite delirium. I should wish now to protract this moment *ad infinitum*; but I dare not. So far I have governed myself thoroughly. I have acted as I inwardly swore I would act; but further might try me beyond my strength. Rise, Miss Eyre: leave me; the play is played out'."

Where was I? Did I wake or sleep? Had I been dreaming? Did I dream still? The old woman's voice had changed: her accent, her gesture, and all were familiar to me as my own face in a glass – as the speech of my own tongue. I got up, but did not go. I looked; I stirred the fire, and I looked again: but she drew her bonnet and her bandage closer about her face, and again beckoned me to depart. The flame illuminated her hand stretched out: roused now, and on the alert for discoveries, I at once noticed that hand. It was no more the withered limb of eld than my own; it was a rounded supple member, with smooth fingers, symmetrically turned; a broad ring flashed on the little finger, and stooping forward, I looked at it, and saw a gem I had seen a hundred times before. Again I looked at the face; which was no longer turned from me – on the contrary, the bonnet was doffed, the bandage displaced, the head advanced.

"Well, Jane, do you know me?" asked the familiar voice.

"Only take off the red cloak, sir, and then –"

"But the string is in a knot – help me."

"Break it, sir."

"There, then – 'Off, ye lendings!'" And Mr. Rochester stepped out of his disguise.

"Now, sir, what a strange idea!"

"But well carried out, eh? Don't you think so?"

"With the ladies you must have managed well."

"But not with you?"

"You did not act the character of a gipsy with me."

"What character did I act? My own?"

"No; some unaccountable one. In short, I believe you have been trying to draw me out – or in; you have been talking nonsense to make me talk nonsense. It is scarcely fair, sir."

"Do you forgive me, Jane?"

"I cannot tell till I have thought it all over. If, on reflection, I find I have fallen into no great absurdity, I shall try to forgive you; but it was not right."

"Oh, you have been very correct – very careful, very sensible."

I reflected, and thought, on the whole, I had. It was a comfort; but, indeed, I had been on my guard almost from the beginning of the interview. Something of masquerade I suspected. I knew gipsies and fortune-tellers did not express themselves as this seeming old woman had expressed herself; besides I had noted her feigned voice, her anxiety to conceal her features. But my mind had been running on Grace Poole – that living enigma, that mystery of mysteries, as I considered her. I had never thought of Mr. Rochester.

"Well," said he, "what are you musing about? What does that grave smile signify?"

"Wonder and self-congratulation, sir. I have your permission to retire now, I suppose?"

"No; stay a moment; and tell me what the people in the drawing room yonder are doing."

"Discussing the gipsy, I daresay."

"Sit down! – Let me hear what they said about me."

"I had better not stay long, sir; it must be near eleven o'clock. Oh, are you aware, Mr. Rochester, that a stranger has arrived here since you left this morning?"

"A stranger! – No; who can it be? I expected no one; is he gone?"

"No; he said he had known you long, and that he could take the liberty of installing himself here till you returned."

"The devil he did! Did he give his name?"

"His name is Mason, sir; and he comes from the West Indies; from Spanish Town, in Jamaica, I think."

Mr. Rochester was standing near me; he had taken my hand, as if to lead me to a chair. As I spoke he gave my wrist a convulsive grip; the smile on his lips froze: apparently a spasm caught his breath.

"Mason! – The West Indies!" he said, in the tone one might fancy a speaking automaton to enounce its single words; "Mason! – The West Indies!" he reiterated; and he went over the syllables three times, growing, in the intervals of speaking, whiter than ashes: he hardly seemed to know what he was doing.

"Do you feel ill, sir?" I inquired.

"Jane, I've got a blow; I've got a blow, Jane!" He staggered.

"Oh, lean on me, sir."

"Jane, you offered me your shoulder once before; let me have it now."

"Yes, sir, yes; and my arm."

He sat down, and made me sit beside him. Holding my hand in both his own, he chafed it; gazing on me, at the same time, with the most troubled and dreary look.

"My little friend!" said he, "I wish I were in a quiet island with only you; and trouble, and danger, and hideous recollections removed from me."

"Can I help you, sir? – I'd give my life to serve you."

"Jane, if aid is wanted, I'll seek it at your hands; I promise you that."

"Thank you, sir. Tell me what to do, – I'll try, at least, to do it."

"Fetch me now, Jane, a glass of wine from the dining room: they will be at supper there; and tell me if Mason is with them, and what he is doing."

I went. I found all the party in the dining room at supper, as Mr. Rochester had said; they were not seated at table, – the supper was arranged on the sideboard; each had taken what he chose, and they stood about here and there in groups, their plates and glasses in their hands. Every one seemed in high glee; laughter and conversation were general and animated. Mr. Mason stood near the fire, talking to Colonel and Mrs. Dent, and appeared as merry as any of them. I filled a wine glass (I saw Miss Ingram watch me frowningly as I did so: she thought I was taking a liberty, I daresay), and I returned to the library.

Mr. Rochester's extreme pallor had disappeared, and he looked once more firm and stern. He took the glass from my hand.

"Here is to your health, ministrant spirit!" he said. He swallowed the contents and returned it to me. "What are they doing, Jane?"

"Laughing and talking, sir."

"They don't look grave and mysterious, as if they had heard something strange?"

"Not at all: they are full of jests and gaiety."

"And Mason?"

"He was laughing too."

"If all these people came in a body and spat at me, what would you do, Jane?"

"Turn them out of the room, sir, if I could."

He half smiled. "But if I were to go to them, and they only looked at me coldly, and whispered sneeringly amongst each other, and then dropped off and left me one by one, what then? Would you go with them?"

"I rather think not, sir: I should have more pleasure in staying with you."

"To comfort me?"

"Yes, sir, to comfort you, as well as I could."

"And if they laid you under a ban for adhering to me?"

"I, probably, should know nothing about their ban; and if I did, I should care nothing about it."

"Then, you could dare censure for my sake?"

"I could dare it for the sake of any friend who deserved my adherence; as you, I am sure, do."

"Go back now into the room; step quietly up to Mason, and whisper in his ear that Mr. Rochester is come and wishes to see him: show him in here and then leave me."

"Yes, sir."

I did his behest. The company all stared at me as I passed straight among them. I sought Mr. Mason, delivered the message, and preceded him from the room: I ushered him into the library, and then I went upstairs.

At a late hour, after I had been in bed some time, I heard the visitors repair to their chambers: I distinguished Mr. Rochester's voice, and heard him say, "This way, Mason; this is your room."

He spoke cheerfully: the gay tones set my heart at ease. I was soon asleep.

Chapter Twenty

I HAD FORGOTTEN to draw my curtain, which I usually did, and also to let down my window-blind. The consequence was, that when the moon, which was full and bright (for the night was fine), came in her course to that space in the sky opposite my casement, and looked in at me through the unveiled panes, her glorious gaze roused me. Awaking in the dead of night, I opened my eyes on her disk – silver-white and crystal clear. It was beautiful, but too solemn; I half rose, and stretched my arm to draw the curtain.

Good God! What a cry!

The night – its silence – its rest, was rent in twain by a savage, a sharp, a shrilly sound that ran from end to end of Thornfield Hall.

My pulse stopped: my heart stood still; my stretched arm was paralysed. The cry died, and was not renewed. Indeed, whatever being uttered that fearful shriek could not soon repeat it: not the widest-winged condor on the Andes could, twice in succession, send out such a yell from the cloud shrouding his eyrie. The thing delivering such utterance must rest ere it could repeat the effort.

It came out of the third storey; for it passed overhead. And overhead – yes, in the room just above my chamber-ceiling – I now heard a struggle: a deadly one it seemed from the noise; and a half-smothered voice shouted:

"Help! Help! Help!" three times rapidly.

"Will no one come?" it cried; and then, while the staggering and stamping went on wildly, I distinguished through plank and plaster:

"Rochester! Rochester! For God's sake, come!"

A chamber door opened: some one ran, or rushed, along the gallery. Another step stamped on the flooring above and something fell; and there was silence.

I had put on some clothes, though horror shook all my limbs; I issued from my apartment. The sleepers were all aroused: ejaculations, terrified murmurs sounded in every room; door after door unclosed; one looked out and another looked out; the gallery filled. Gentlemen and ladies alike had quitted their beds; and "Oh! What is it?" – "Who is hurt?" – "What has happened?" – "Fetch a light!" – "Is it fire?" – "Are there robbers?" – "Where shall we run?" was demanded confusedly on all hands. But for the moonlight they would have been in complete darkness. They ran to and fro; they crowded together: some sobbed, some stumbled: the confusion was inextricable.

"Where the devil is Rochester?" cried Colonel Dent. "I cannot find him in his bed."

"Here! Here!" was shouted in return. "Be composed, all of you: I'm coming."

And the door at the end of the gallery opened, and Mr. Rochester advanced with a candle: he had just descended from the upper storey. One of the ladies ran to him directly; she seized his arm: it was Miss Ingram.

"What awful event has taken place?" said she. "Speak! Let us know the worst at once!"

"But don't pull me down or strangle me," he replied: for the Misses Eshton were clinging about him now; and the two dowagers, in vast white wrappers, were bearing down on him like ships in full sail.

"All's right! – All's right!" he cried. "It's a mere rehearsal of *Much Ado about Nothing*. Ladies, keep off, or I shall wax dangerous."

And dangerous he looked: his black eyes darted sparks. Calming himself by an effort, he added:

"A servant has had the nightmare; that is all. She's an excitable, nervous person: she construed her dream into an apparition, or something of that sort, no doubt; and has taken a fit with fright. Now, then, I must see you all back into your rooms; for, till the house is settled, she cannot be looked after. Gentlemen, have the goodness to set the ladies the example. Miss Ingram, I am sure you will not fail in evincing superiority to idle terrors. Amy and Louisa, return to your nests like a pair of doves, as you are. Mesdames" (to the dowagers), "you will take cold to a dead certainty, if you stay in this chill gallery any longer."

And so, by dint of alternate coaxing and commanding, he contrived to get them all once more enclosed in their separate dormitories. I did not wait to be ordered back to mine, but retreated unnoticed, as unnoticed I had left it.

Not, however, to go to bed: on the contrary, I began and dressed myself carefully. The sounds I had heard after the scream, and the words that had been uttered, had probably been heard only by me; for they had proceeded from the room above mine: but they assured me that it was not a servant's dream which had thus struck horror through the house; and that the explanation Mr. Rochester had given was merely an invention framed to pacify his guests. I dressed, then, to be ready for emergencies. When dressed, I sat a long time by the window looking out over the silent grounds and silvered fields and waiting for I knew not what. It seemed to me that some event must follow the strange cry, struggle, and call.

No: stillness returned: each murmur and movement ceased gradually, and in about an hour Thornfield Hall was again as hushed as a desert. It seemed that sleep and night had resumed their empire. Meantime the moon declined: she was about to set. Not liking to sit in the cold and darkness, I thought I would lie down on my bed, dressed as I was. I left the window, and moved with little noise across the carpet; as I stooped to take off my shoes, a cautious hand tapped low at the door.

"Am I wanted?" I asked.

"Are you up?" asked the voice I expected to hear, viz., my master's.

"Yes, sir."

"And dressed?"

"Yes."

"Come out, then, quietly."

I obeyed. Mr. Rochester stood in the gallery holding a light.

"I want you," he said: "come this way: take your time, and make no noise."

My slippers were thin: I could walk the matted floor as softly as a cat. He glided up the gallery and up the stairs, and stopped in the dark, low corridor of the fateful third storey: I had followed and stood at his side.

"Have you a sponge in your room?" he asked in a whisper.

"Yes, sir."

"Have you any salts – volatile salts?"

"Yes."

"Go back and fetch both."

I returned, sought the sponge on the washstand, the salts in my drawer, and once more retraced my steps. He still waited; he held a key in his hand: approaching one of the small, black doors, he put it in the lock; he paused, and addressed me again.

"You don't turn sick at the sight of blood?"

"I think I shall not: I have never been tried yet."

I felt a thrill while I answered him; but no coldness, and no faintness.

"Just give me your hand," he said: "it will not do to risk a fainting fit."

I put my fingers into his. "Warm and steady," was his remark: he turned the key and opened the door.

I saw a room I remembered to have seen before, the day Mrs. Fairfax showed me over the house: it was hung with tapestry; but the tapestry was now looped up in one part, and there was a door apparent, which had then been concealed. This door was open; a light shone out of the room within: I heard thence a snarling, snatching sound, almost like a dog quarrelling. Mr. Rochester, putting down his candle, said to me, "Wait a minute," and he went forward to the inner apartment. A shout of laughter greeted his entrance; noisy at first, and terminating in Grace Poole's own goblin ha! ha! *She* then was there. He made some sort of arrangement without speaking, though I heard a low voice address him: he came out and closed the door behind him.

"Here, Jane!" he said; and I walked round to the other side of a large bed, which with its drawn curtains concealed a considerable portion of the chamber. An easy chair was near the bedhead: a man sat in it, dressed with the exception of his coat; he was still; his head leant back; his eyes were closed. Mr. Rochester held the candle over him; I recognised in his pale and seemingly lifeless face – the stranger, Mason: I saw too that his linen on one side, and one arm, was almost soaked in blood.

"Hold the candle," said Mr. Rochester, and I took it: he fetched a basin of water from the washstand: "Hold that," said he. I obeyed. He took the sponge, dipped it in, and moistened the corpse-like face; he asked for my smelling-bottle, and applied it to the nostrils. Mr. Mason shortly unclosed his eyes; he groaned. Mr. Rochester opened the shirt of the wounded man, whose arm and shoulder were bandaged: he sponged away blood, trickling fast down.

"Is there immediate danger?" murmured Mr. Mason.

"Pooh! No – a mere scratch. Don't be so overcome, man: bear up! I'll fetch a surgeon for you now, myself: you'll be able to be removed by morning, I hope. Jane," he continued.

"Sir?"

"I shall have to leave you in this room with this gentleman, for an hour, or perhaps two hours: you will sponge the blood as I do when it returns: if he feels faint, you will put the glass of water on that stand to his lips, and your salts to his nose. You will not speak to him on any pretext – and – Richard, it will be at the peril of your life if you speak to her: open your lips – agitate yourself – and I'll not answer for the consequences."

Again the poor man groaned; he looked as if he dared not move; fear, either of death or of something else, appeared almost to paralyse him. Mr. Rochester put the now bloody sponge into my hand, and I proceeded to use it as he had done. He watched me a second, then saying, "Remember! – No conversation," he left the room. I experienced a strange feeling as the key grated in the lock, and the sound of his retreating step ceased to be heard.

Here then I was in the third storey, fastened into one of its mystic cells; night around me; a pale and bloody spectacle under my eyes and hands; a murderess hardly separated from me by a single door: yes – that was appalling – the rest I could bear; but I shuddered at the thought of Grace Poole bursting out upon me.

I must keep to my post, however. I must watch this ghastly countenance – these blue, still lips forbidden to unclose – these eyes now shut, now opening, now wandering through the room, now fixing on me, and ever glazed with the dulness of horror. I must dip my hand again and again in the basin of blood and water, and wipe away the trickling gore. I must see the light of the unsnuffed candle wane on my employment; the shadows darken on the wrought, antique tapestry round me, and grow black under the hangings of the vast old bed, and quiver strangely over the doors of a great cabinet opposite – whose front, divided into twelve panels, bore, in grim design, the heads of the twelve apostles, each enclosed in its separate panel as in a frame; while above them at the top rose an ebon crucifix and a dying Christ.

According as the shifting obscurity and flickering gleam hovered here or glanced there, it was now the bearded physician, Luke, that bent his brow; now St. John's long hair that waved; and anon the devilish face of Judas, that grew out of the panel, and seemed gathering life and threatening a revelation of the arch-traitor – of Satan himself – in his subordinate's form.

Amidst all this, I had to listen as well as watch: to listen for the movements of the wild beast or the fiend in yonder side den. But since Mr. Rochester's visit it seemed spellbound: all the night I heard but three sounds at three long intervals, – a step creak, a momentary renewal of the snarling, canine noise, and a deep human groan.

Then my own thoughts worried me. What crime was this that lived incarnate in this sequestered mansion, and could neither be expelled nor subdued by the owner? – What mystery, that broke out now in fire and now in blood, at the deadest hours of night? What creature was it, that, masked in an ordinary woman's face and shape, uttered the voice, now of a mocking demon, and anon of a carrion-seeking bird of prey?

And this man I bent over – this commonplace, quiet stranger – how had he become involved in the web of horror? And why had the Fury flown at him? What made him seek this quarter of the house at an untimely season, when he should have been asleep in bed? I had heard Mr. Rochester assign him an apartment below – what brought him here! And why, now, was he so tame under the violence or treachery done him? Why did he so quietly submit to the concealment Mr. Rochester enforced? Why *did* Mr. Rochester enforce this concealment? His guest had been outraged, his own life on a former occasion had been hideously plotted against; and both attempts he smothered in secrecy and sank in oblivion! Lastly, I saw Mr. Mason was submissive to Mr. Rochester; that the impetuous will of the latter held complete sway over the inertness of the former: the few words which had passed between them assured me of this. It was evident that in their former intercourse, the passive disposition of the one had been habitually influenced by the active energy of the other: whence then had arisen Mr. Rochester's dismay when he heard of Mr. Mason's arrival? Why had the mere name of this unresisting individual – whom his word now sufficed to control like a child – fallen on him, a few hours since, as a thunderbolt might fall on an oak?

Oh! I could not forget his look and his paleness when he whispered: "Jane, I have got a blow – I have got a blow, Jane." I could not forget how the arm had trembled which he rested on my shoulder: and it was no light matter which could thus bow the resolute spirit and thrill the vigorous frame of Fairfax Rochester.

"When will he come? When will he come?" I cried inwardly, as the night lingered and lingered – as my bleeding patient drooped, moaned, sickened: and neither day nor aid arrived. I had, again and again, held the water to Mason's white lips; again and again offered him the stimulating salts: my efforts seemed ineffectual: either bodily or mental suffering, or loss of blood, or all three combined, were fast prostrating his strength. He moaned so, and looked so weak, wild, and lost, I feared he was dying; and I might not even speak to him.

The candle, wasted at last, went out; as it expired, I perceived streaks of grey light edging the window curtains: dawn was then approaching. Presently I heard Pilot bark far below, out of his distant kennel in the courtyard: hope revived. Nor was it unwarranted: in five minutes more the grating key, the yielding lock, warned me my watch was relieved. It could not have lasted more than two hours: many a week has seemed shorter.

Mr. Rochester entered, and with him the surgeon he had been to fetch.

"Now, Carter, be on the alert," he said to this last: "I give you but half an hour for dressing the wound, fastening the bandages, getting the patient downstairs and all."

"But is he fit to move, sir?"

"No doubt of it; it is nothing serious; he is nervous, his spirits must be kept up. Come, set to work."

Mr. Rochester drew back the thick curtain, drew up the holland blind, let in all the daylight he could; and I was surprised and cheered to see how far dawn was advanced: what rosy streaks were beginning to brighten the east. Then he approached Mason, whom the surgeon was already handling.

"Now, my good fellow, how are you?" he asked.

"She's done for me, I fear," was the faint reply.

"Not a whit! – Courage! This day fortnight you'll hardly be a pin the worse of it: you've lost a little blood; that's all. Carter, assure him there's no danger."

"I can do that conscientiously," said Carter, who had now undone the bandages; "only I wish I could have got here sooner: he would not have bled so much – but how is this? The flesh on the shoulder is torn as well as cut. This wound was not done with a knife: there have been teeth here!"

"She bit me," he murmured. "She worried me like a tigress, when Rochester got the knife from her."

"You should not have yielded: you should have grappled with her at once," said Mr. Rochester.

"But under such circumstances, what could one do?" returned Mason. "Oh, it was frightful!" he added, shuddering. "And I did not expect it: she looked so quiet at first."

"I warned you," was his friend's answer; "I said – be on your guard when you go near her. Besides, you might have waited till tomorrow, and had me with you: it was mere folly to attempt the interview tonight, and alone."

"I thought I could have done some good."

"You thought! You thought! Yes, it makes me impatient to hear you: but, however, you have suffered, and are likely to suffer enough for not taking my advice; so I'll say no more. Carter – hurry! – hurry! The sun will soon rise, and I must have him off."

"Directly, sir; the shoulder is just bandaged. I must look to this other wound in the arm: she has had her teeth here too, I think."

"She sucked the blood: she said she'd drain my heart," said Mason.

I saw Mr. Rochester shudder: a singularly marked expression of disgust, horror, hatred, warped his countenance almost to distortion; but he only said:

"Come, be silent, Richard, and never mind her gibberish: don't repeat it."

"I wish I could forget it," was the answer.

"You will when you are out of the country: when you get back to Spanish Town, you may think of her as dead and buried – or rather, you need not think of her at all."

"Impossible to forget this night!"

"It is not impossible: have some energy, man. You thought you were as dead as a herring two hours since, and you are all alive and talking now. There! – Carter has done with you or nearly so; I'll make you decent in a trice. Jane" (he turned to me for the first time since his re-entrance), "take this key: go down into my bedroom, and walk straight forward into my dressing-room: open the top drawer of the wardrobe and take out a clean shirt and neck-handkerchief: bring them here; and be nimble."

I went; sought the repository he had mentioned, found the articles named, and returned with them.

"Now," said he, "go to the other side of the bed while I order his toilet; but don't leave the room: you may be wanted again."

I retired as directed.

"Was anybody stirring below when you went down, Jane?" inquired Mr. Rochester presently.

"No, sir; all was very still."

"We shall get you off cannily, Dick: and it will be better, both for your sake, and for that of the poor creature in yonder. I have striven long to avoid exposure, and I should not like it to come at last. Here, Carter, help him on with his waistcoat. Where did you leave your furred cloak? You can't travel a mile without that, I know, in this damned cold climate. In your room? – Jane, run down to Mr. Mason's room, – the one next mine, – and fetch a cloak you will see there."

Again I ran, and again returned, bearing an immense mantle lined and edged with fur.

"Now, I've another errand for you," said my untiring master; "you must away to my room again. What a mercy you are shod with velvet, Jane! – a clod-hopping messenger would never do at this juncture. You must open the middle drawer of my toilet table and take out a little phial and a little glass you will find there, – quick!"

I flew thither and back, bringing the desired vessels.

"That's well! Now, doctor, I shall take the liberty of administering a dose myself, on my own responsibility. I got this cordial at Rome, of an Italian charlatan – a fellow you would have kicked, Carter. It is not a thing to be used indiscriminately, but it is good upon occasion: as now, for instance. Jane, a little water."

He held out the tiny glass, and I half filled it from the water bottle on the washstand.

"That will do; – now wet the lip of the phial."

I did so; he measured twelve drops of a crimson liquid, and presented it to Mason.

"Drink, Richard: it will give you the heart you lack, for an hour or so."

"But will it hurt me? – is it inflammatory?"

"Drink! Drink! Drink!"

Mr. Mason obeyed, because it was evidently useless to resist. He was dressed now: he still looked pale, but he was no longer gory and sullied. Mr. Rochester let him sit three minutes after he had swallowed the liquid; he then took his arm:

"Now I am sure you can get on your feet," he said – "try."

The patient rose.

"Carter, take him under the other shoulder. Be of good cheer, Richard; step out – that's it!"

"I do feel better," remarked Mr. Mason.

"I am sure you do. Now, Jane, trip on before us away to the backstairs; unbolt the side-passage door, and tell the driver of the post-chaise you will see in the yard – or just outside, for I told him not to drive his rattling wheels over the pavement – to be ready; we are coming: and, Jane, if anyone is about, come to the foot of the stairs and hem."

It was by this time half-past five, and the sun was on the point of rising; but I found the kitchen still dark and silent. The side-passage door was fastened; I opened it with as little noise as possible: all the yard was quiet; but the gates stood wide open, and there was a post-chaise, with horses ready harnessed, and driver seated on the box, stationed outside. I approached him, and said the gentlemen were coming; he nodded: then I looked carefully round and listened. The stillness of early morning slumbered everywhere; the curtains were yet drawn over the servants' chamber windows; little birds were just twittering in the blossom-blanched orchard trees, whose boughs drooped like white garlands over the wall enclosing one side of the yard; the carriage horses stamped from time to time in their closed stables: all else was still.

The gentlemen now appeared. Mason, supported by Mr. Rochester and the surgeon, seemed to walk with tolerable ease: they assisted him into the chaise; Carter followed.

"Take care of him," said Mr. Rochester to the latter, "and keep him at your house till he is quite well: I shall ride over in a day or two to see how he gets on. Richard, how is it with you?"

"The fresh air revives me, Fairfax."

"Leave the window open on his side, Carter; there is no wind – goodbye, Dick."

"Fairfax –"

"Well what is it?"

"Let her be taken care of; let her be treated as tenderly as may be: let her –" he stopped and burst into tears.

"I do my best; and have done it, and will do it," was the answer: he shut up the chaise door, and the vehicle drove away.

"Yet would to God there was an end of all this!" added Mr. Rochester, as he closed and barred the heavy yard gates.

This done, he moved with slow step and abstracted air towards a door in the wall bordering the orchard. I, supposing he had done with me, prepared to return to the house; again, however, I heard him call "Jane!" He had opened the portal and stood at it, waiting for me.

"Come where there is some freshness, for a few moments," he said; "that house is a mere dungeon: don't you feel it so?"

"It seems to me a splendid mansion, sir."

"The glamour of inexperience is over your eyes," he answered; "and you see it through a charmed medium: you cannot discern that the gilding is slime and the silk draperies cobwebs; that the marble is sordid slate, and the polished woods mere refuse chips and scaly bark. Now *here*" (he pointed to the leafy enclosure we had entered) "all is real, sweet, and pure."

He strayed down a walk edged with box, with apple trees, pear trees, and cherry trees on one side, and a border on the other full of all sorts of old-fashioned flowers, stocks, sweet williams, primroses, pansies, mingled with southernwood, sweetbriar, and various fragrant herbs. They were fresh now as a succession of April showers and gleams, followed by a lovely spring morning, could make them: the sun was just entering the dappled east, and his light illumined the wreathed and dewy orchard trees and shone down the quiet walks under them.

"Jane, will you have a flower?"

He gathered a half-blown rose, the first on the bush, and offered it to me.

"Thank you, sir."

"Do you like this sunrise, Jane? That sky with its high and light clouds which are sure to melt away as the day waxes warm – this placid and balmly atmosphere?"

"I do, very much."

"You have passed a strange night, Jane."

"Yes, sir."

"And it has made you look pale – were you afraid when I left you alone with Mason?"

"I was afraid of someone coming out of the inner room."

"But I had fastened the door – I had the key in my pocket: I should have been a careless shepherd if I had left a lamb – my pet lamb – so near a wolf's den, unguarded: you were safe."

"Will Grace Poole live here still, sir?"

"Oh yes! Don't trouble your head about her – put the thing out of your thoughts."

"Yet it seems to me your life is hardly secure while she stays."

"Never fear – I will take care of myself."

"Is the danger you apprehended last night gone by now, sir?"

"I cannot vouch for that till Mason is out of England: nor even then. To live, for me, Jane, is to stand on a crater-crust which may crack and spue fire any day."

"But Mr. Mason seems a man easily led. Your influence, sir, is evidently potent with him: he will never set you at defiance or wilfully injure you."

"Oh, no! Mason will not defy me; nor, knowing it, will he hurt me – but, unintentionally, he might in a moment, by one careless word, deprive me, if not of life, yet for ever of happiness."

"Tell him to be cautious, sir: let him know what you fear, and show him how to avert the danger."

He laughed sardonically, hastily took my hand, and as hastily threw it from him.

"If I could do that, simpleton, where would the danger be? Annihilated in a moment. Ever since I have known Mason, I have only had to say to him 'Do that', and the thing has been done. But I cannot give him orders in this case: I cannot say 'Beware of harming me, Richard;' for it is imperative that I should keep him ignorant that harm to me is possible. Now you look puzzled; and I will puzzle you further. You are my little friend, are you not?"

"I like to serve you, sir, and to obey you in all that is right."

"Precisely: I see you do. I see genuine contentment in your gait and mien, your eye and face, when you are helping me and pleasing me – working for me, and with me, in, as you characteristically say, '*all that is right*:' for if I bid you do what you thought wrong, there would be no light-footed running, no neat-handed alacrity, no lively glance and animated complexion. My friend would then turn to me, quiet and pale, and would say, 'No, sir; that is impossible: I cannot do it, because it is wrong;' and would become immutable as a fixed star. Well, you too have power over me, and may injure me: yet I dare not show you where I am vulnerable, lest, faithful and friendly as you are, you should transfix me at once."

"If you have no more to fear from Mr. Mason than you have from me, sir, you are very safe."

"God grant it may be so! Here, Jane, is an arbour; sit down."

The arbour was an arch in the wall, lined with ivy; it contained a rustic seat. Mr. Rochester took it, leaving room, however, for me: but I stood before him.

"Sit," he said; "the bench is long enough for two. You don't hesitate to take a place at my side, do you? Is that wrong, Jane?"

I answered him by assuming it: to refuse would, I felt, have been unwise.

"Now, my little friend, while the sun drinks the dew – while all the flowers in this old garden awake and expand, and the birds fetch their young ones' breakfast out of the Thornfield, and the early bees do their first spell of work – I'll put a case to you, which you must endeavour to suppose your own: but first, look at me, and tell me you are at ease, and not fearing that I err in detaining you, or that you err in staying."

"No, sir; I am content."

"Well then, Jane, call to aid your fancy: suppose you were no longer a girl well reared and disciplined, but a wild boy indulged from childhood upwards; imagine yourself in a remote foreign land; conceive that you there commit a capital error, no matter of what nature or from what motives, but one whose consequences must follow you through life and taint all your existence. Mind, I don't say a *crime*; I am not speaking of shedding of blood or any other guilty act, which might make the perpetrator amenable to the law: my word is *error*. The results of what you have done become in time to you utterly insupportable; you take measures to obtain relief: unusual measures, but neither unlawful nor culpable. Still you are miserable; for hope has quitted you on the very confines of life: your sun at noon darkens in an eclipse, which you feel will not leave it till the time of setting. Bitter and base associations have become the sole food of your memory: you wander here and there, seeking rest in exile: happiness in pleasure – I mean in heartless, sensual pleasure – such as dulls intellect and blights feeling. Heart-weary and soul-withered, you come home after years of voluntary banishment: you make a new acquaintance – how or where no matter: you find in this stranger much of the good and bright qualities which you have sought for twenty years, and never before encountered; and they are all fresh, healthy, without soil and without taint. Such society revives, regenerates: you feel better days come back – higher wishes, purer feelings; you desire to recommence your life, and to spend what remains to you of days in a way more worthy of an immortal being. To attain this end, are you justified in overleaping an obstacle of custom – a mere conventional impediment which neither your conscience sanctifies nor your judgment approves?"

He paused for an answer: and what was I to say? Oh, for some good spirit to suggest a judicious and satisfactory response! Vain aspiration! The west wind whispered in the ivy round me; but no gentle Ariel borrowed its breath as a medium of speech: the birds sang in the tree-tops; but their song, however sweet, was inarticulate.

Again Mr. Rochester propounded his query:

"Is the wandering and sinful, but now rest-seeking and repentant, man justified in daring the world's opinion, in order to attach to him for ever this gentle, gracious, genial stranger, thereby securing his own peace of mind and regeneration of life?"

"Sir," I answered, "a wanderer's repose or a sinner's reformation should never depend on a fellow creature. Men and women die; philosophers falter in wisdom, and Christians in goodness: if anyone you know has suffered and erred, let him look higher than his equals for strength to amend and solace to heal."

"But the instrument – the instrument! God, who does the work, ordains the instrument. I have myself – I tell it you without parable – been a worldly, dissipated, restless man; and I believe I have found the instrument for my cure in –"

He paused: the birds went on carolling, the leaves lightly rustling. I almost wondered they did not check their songs and whispers to catch the suspended revelation; but they would have had to wait many minutes – so long was the silence protracted. At last I looked up at the tardy speaker: he was looking eagerly at me.

"Little friend," said he, in quite a changed tone – while his face changed too, losing all its softness and gravity, and becoming harsh and sarcastic – "you have noticed my tender penchant for Miss Ingram: don't you think if I married her she would regenerate me with a vengeance?"

He got up instantly, went quite to the other end of the walk, and when he came back he was humming a tune.

"Jane, Jane," said he, stopping before me, "you are quite pale with your vigils: don't you curse me for disturbing your rest?"

"Curse you? No, sir."

"Shake hands in confirmation of the word. What cold fingers! They were warmer last night when I touched them at the door of the mysterious chamber. Jane, when will you watch with me again?"

"Whenever I can be useful, sir."

"For instance, the night before I am married! I am sure I shall not be able to sleep. Will you promise to sit up with me to bear me company? To you I can talk of my lovely one: for now you have seen her and know her."

"Yes, sir."

"She's a rare one, is she not, Jane?"

"Yes, sir."

"A strapper – a real strapper, Jane: big, brown, and buxom; with hair just such as the ladies of Carthage must have had. Bless me! There's Dent and Lynn in the stables! Go in by the shrubbery, through that wicket."

As I went one way, he went another, and I heard him in the yard, saying cheerfully:

"Mason got the start of you all this morning; he was gone before sunrise: I rose at four to see him off."

Chapter Twenty-One

PRESENTIMENTS are strange things! And so are sympathies; and so are signs; and the three combined make one mystery to which humanity has not yet found the key. I never laughed at presentiments in my life, because I have had strange ones of my own. Sympathies, I believe, exist (for instance, between far-distant, long-absent, wholly estranged relatives asserting, notwithstanding their alienation, the unity of the source to which each traces his origin) whose workings baffle mortal comprehension. And signs, for aught we know, may be but the sympathies of Nature with man.

When I was a little girl, only six years old, I one night heard Bessie Leaven say to Martha Abbot that she had been dreaming about a little child; and that to dream of children was a sure sign of trouble, either to one's self or one's kin. The saying might have worn out of my memory, had not a circumstance immediately followed which served indelibly to fix it there. The next day Bessie was sent for home to the deathbed of her little sister.

Of late I had often recalled this saying and this incident; for during the past week scarcely a night had gone over my couch that had not brought with it a dream of an infant, which I sometimes hushed in my arms, sometimes dandled on my knee, sometimes watched playing with daisies on a lawn, or again, dabbling its hands in running water. It was a wailing child this night, and a laughing one the next: now it nestled close to me, and now it ran from me; but whatever mood the apparition evinced, whatever aspect it wore, it failed not for seven successive nights to meet me the moment I entered the land of slumber.

I did not like this iteration of one idea – this strange recurrence of one image, and I grew nervous as bedtime approached and the hour of the vision drew near. It was from companionship with this baby-phantom I had been roused on that moonlight night when I heard the cry; and it was on the afternoon of the day following I was summoned downstairs by a message that some one wanted me in Mrs. Fairfax's room. On repairing thither, I found a man waiting for me, having the appearance of a gentleman's servant: he was dressed in deep mourning, and the hat he held in his hand was surrounded with a crape band.

"I daresay you hardly remember me, Miss," he said, rising as I entered; "but my name is Leaven: I lived coachman with Mrs. Reed when you were at Gateshead, eight or nine years since, and I live there still."

"Oh, Robert! How do you do? I remember you very well: you used to give me a ride sometimes on Miss Georgiana's bay pony. And how is Bessie? You are married to Bessie?"

"Yes, Miss: my wife is very hearty, thank you; she brought me another little one about two months since – we have three now – and both mother and child are thriving."

"And are the family well at the house, Robert?"

"I am sorry I can't give you better news of them, Miss: they are very badly at present – in great trouble."

"I hope no one is dead," I said, glancing at his black dress. He too looked down at the crape round his hat and replied:

"Mr. John died yesterday was a week, at his chambers in London."

"Mr. John?"

"Yes."

"And how does his mother bear it?"

"Why, you see, Miss Eyre, it is not a common mishap: his life has been very wild: these last three years he gave himself up to strange ways, and his death was shocking."

"I heard from Bessie he was not doing well."

"Doing well! He could not do worse: he ruined his health and his estate amongst the worst men and the worst women. He got into debt and into jail: his mother helped him out twice, but as soon as he was free he returned to his old companions and habits. His head was not strong: the knaves he lived amongst fooled him beyond anything I ever heard. He came down to Gateshead about three weeks ago and wanted missis to give up all to him. Missis refused: her means have long been much reduced by his extravagance; so he went back again, and the next news was that he was dead. How he died, God knows! – They say he killed himself."

I was silent: the things were frightful. Robert Leaven resumed:

"Missis had been out of health herself for some time: she had got very stout, but was not strong with it; and the loss of money and fear of poverty were quite breaking her down. The information about Mr. John's death and the manner of it came too suddenly: it brought on a stroke. She was three days without speaking; but last Tuesday she seemed rather better: she appeared as if she wanted to say something, and kept making signs to my wife and mumbling. It was only yesterday morning, however, that Bessie understood she was pronouncing your name; and at last she made out the words, 'Bring Jane – fetch Jane Eyre: I want to speak to her.' Bessie is not sure whether she is in her right mind, or means anything by the words; but she told Miss Reed and Miss Georgiana, and advised them to send for you. The young ladies put it off at first; but their mother grew so restless, and said, 'Jane, Jane', so many times, that at last they consented. I left Gateshead yesterday: and if you can get ready, Miss, I should like to take you back with me early tomorrow morning."

"Yes, Robert, I shall be ready: it seems to me that I ought to go."

"I think so too, Miss. Bessie said she was sure you would not refuse: but I suppose you will have to ask leave before you can get off?"

"Yes; and I will do it now;" and having directed him to the servants' hall, and recommended him to the care of John's wife, and the attentions of John himself, I went in search of Mr. Rochester.

He was not in any of the lower rooms; he was not in the yard, the stables, or the grounds. I asked Mrs. Fairfax if she had seen him; – yes: she believed he was playing billiards with Miss Ingram. To the billiard-room I hastened: the click of balls and the hum of voices resounded thence; Mr. Rochester, Miss Ingram, the two Misses Eshton, and their admirers, were all busied in the game. It required some courage to disturb so interesting a party; my errand, however, was one I could not defer, so I approached the master where he stood at Miss Ingram's side. She turned as I drew near, and looked at me haughtily: her eyes seemed to demand, "What can the creeping creature want now?" and when I said, in a low voice, "Mr. Rochester," she made a movement as if tempted to order me away. I remember her appearance at the moment – it was very graceful and very striking: she wore a morning robe of sky-blue crape; a gauzy azure scarf was twisted in her hair. She had been all animation with the game, and irritated pride did not lower the expression of her haughty lineaments.

"Does that person want you?" she inquired of Mr. Rochester; and Mr. Rochester turned to see who the 'person' was. He made a curious grimace – one of his strange and equivocal demonstrations – threw down his cue and followed me from the room.

"Well, Jane?" he said, as he rested his back against the schoolroom door, which he had shut.

"If you please, sir, I want leave of absence for a week or two."

"What to do? – where to go?"

"To see a sick lady who has sent for me."

"What sick lady? – where does she live?"

"At Gateshead; in —shire."

"—shire? That is a hundred miles off! Who may she be that sends for people to see her that distance?"

"Her name is Reed, sir – Mrs. Reed."

"Reed of Gateshead? There was a Reed of Gateshead, a magistrate."

"It is his widow, sir."

"And what have you to do with her? How do you know her?"

"Mr. Reed was my uncle – my mother's brother."

"The deuce he was! You never told me that before: you always said you had no relations."

"None that would own me, sir. Mr. Reed is dead, and his wife cast me off."

"Why?"

"Because I was poor, and burdensome, and she disliked me."

"But Reed left children? – You must have cousins? Sir George Lynn was talking of a Reed of Gateshead yesterday, who, he said, was one of the veriest rascals on town; and Ingram was mentioning a Georgiana Reed of the same place, who was much admired for her beauty a season or two ago in London."

"John Reed is dead, too, sir: he ruined himself and half-ruined his family, and is supposed to have committed suicide. The news so shocked his mother that it brought on an apoplectic attack."

"And what good can you do her? Nonsense, Jane! I would never think of running a hundred miles to see an old lady who will, perhaps, be dead before you reach her: besides, you say she cast you off."

"Yes, sir, but that is long ago; and when her circumstances were very different: I could not be easy to neglect her wishes now."

"How long will you stay?"

"As short a time as possible, sir."

"Promise me only to stay a week –"

"I had better not pass my word: I might be obliged to break it."

"At all events you *will* come back: you will not be induced under any pretext to take up a permanent residence with her?"

"Oh, no! I shall certainly return if all be well."

"And who goes with you? You don't travel a hundred miles alone."

"No, sir, she has sent her coachman."

"A person to be trusted?"

"Yes, sir, he has lived ten years in the family."

Mr. Rochester meditated. "When do you wish to go?"

"Early tomorrow morning, sir."

"Well, you must have some money; you can't travel without money, and I daresay you have not much: I have given you no salary yet. How much have you in the world, Jane?" he asked, smiling.

I drew out my purse; a meagre thing it was. "Five shillings, sir." He took the purse, poured the hoard into his palm, and chuckled over it as if its scantiness amused him. Soon he produced his pocket book: "Here," said he, offering me a note; it was fifty pounds, and he owed me but fifteen. I told him I had no change.

"I don't want change; you know that. Take your wages."

I declined accepting more than was my due. He scowled at first; then, as if recollecting something, he said:

"Right, right! Better not give you all now: you would, perhaps, stay away three months if you had fifty pounds. There are ten; is it not plenty?"

"Yes, sir, but now you owe me five."

"Come back for it, then; I am your banker for forty pounds."

"Mr. Rochester, I may as well mention another matter of business to you while I have the opportunity."

"Matter of business? I am curious to hear it."

"You have as good as informed me, sir, that you are going shortly to be married?"

"Yes; what then?"

"In that case, sir, Adèle ought to go to school: I am sure you will perceive the necessity of it."

"To get her out of my bride's way, who might otherwise walk over her rather too emphatically? There's sense in the suggestion; not a doubt of it. Adèle, as you say, must go to school; and you, of course, must march straight to – the devil?"

"I hope not, sir; but I must seek another situation somewhere."

"In course!" he exclaimed, with a twang of voice and a distortion of features equally fantastic and ludicrous. He looked at me some minutes.

"And old Madam Reed, or the Misses, her daughters, will be solicited by you to seek a place, I suppose?"

"No, sir; I am not on such terms with my relatives as would justify me in asking favours of them – but I shall advertise."

"You shall walk up the pyramids of Egypt!" he growled. "At your peril you advertise! I wish I had only offered you a sovereign instead of ten pounds. Give me back nine pounds, Jane; I've a use for it."

"And so have I, sir," I returned, putting my hands and my purse behind me. "I could not spare the money on any account."

"Little niggard!" said he, "refusing me a pecuniary request! Give me five pounds, Jane."

"Not five shillings, sir; nor five pence."

"Just let me look at the cash."

"No, sir; you are not to be trusted."

"Jane!"

"Sir?"

"Promise me one thing."

"I'll promise you anything, sir, that I think I am likely to perform."

"Not to advertise: and to trust this quest of a situation to me. I'll find you one in time."

"I shall be glad so to do, sir, if you, in your turn, will promise that I and Adèle shall be both safe out of the house before your bride enters it."

"Very well! Very well! I'll pledge my word on it. You go tomorrow, then?"

"Yes, sir; early."

"Shall you come down to the drawing room after dinner?"

"No, sir, I must prepare for the journey."

"Then you and I must bid goodbye for a little while?"

"I suppose so, sir."

"And how do people perform that ceremony of parting, Jane? Teach me; I'm not quite up to it."

"They say, Farewell, or any other form they prefer."

"Then say it."

"Farewell, Mr. Rochester, for the present."

"What must I say?"

"The same, if you like, sir."

"Farewell, Miss Eyre, for the present; is that all?"

"Yes?"

"It seems stingy, to my notions, and dry, and unfriendly. I should like something else: a little addition to the rite. If one shook hands, for instance; but no – that would not content me either. So you'll do no more than say Farewell, Jane?"

"It is enough, sir: as much good will may be conveyed in one hearty word as in many."

"Very likely; but it is blank and cool – 'Farewell.'"

"How long is he going to stand with his back against that door?" I asked myself; "I want to commence my packing." The dinner bell rang, and suddenly away he bolted, without another syllable: I saw him no more during the day, and was off before he had risen in the morning.

I reached the lodge at Gateshead about five o'clock in the afternoon of the first of May: I stepped in there before going up to the hall. It was very clean and neat: the ornamental windows were hung with little white curtains; the floor was spotless; the grate and fire irons were burnished bright, and the fire burnt clear. Bessie sat on the hearth, nursing her last-born, and Robert and his sister played quietly in a corner.

"Bless you! – I knew you would come!" exclaimed Mrs. Leaven, as I entered.

"Yes, Bessie," said I, after I had kissed her; "and I trust I am not too late. How is Mrs. Reed? – Alive still, I hope."

"Yes, she is alive; and more sensible and collected than she was. The doctor says she may linger a week or two yet; but he hardly thinks she will finally recover."

"Has she mentioned me lately?"

"She was talking of you only this morning, and wishing you would come, but she is sleeping now, or was ten minutes ago, when I was up at the house. She generally lies in a kind of lethargy all the afternoon, and wakes up about six or seven. Will you rest yourself here an hour, Miss, and then I will go up with you?"

Robert here entered, and Bessie laid her sleeping child in the cradle and went to welcome him: afterwards she insisted on my taking off my bonnet and having some tea; for she said I looked pale and tired. I was glad to accept her hospitality; and I submitted to be relieved of my travelling garb just as passively as I used to let her undress me when a child.

Old times crowded fast back on me as I watched her bustling about – setting out the tea-tray with her best china, cutting bread and butter, toasting a tea-cake, and, between whiles, giving little Robert or Jane an occasional tap or push, just as she used to give me in former days. Bessie had retained her quick temper as well as her light foot and good looks.

Tea ready, I was going to approach the table; but she desired me to sit still, quite in her old peremptory tones. I must be served at the fireside, she said; and she placed before me a little round stand with my cup and a plate of toast, absolutely as she used to accommodate me with some privately purloined dainty on a nursery chair: and I smiled and obeyed her as in bygone days.

She wanted to know if I was happy at Thornfield Hall, and what sort of a person the mistress was; and when I told her there was only a master, whether he was a nice gentleman, and if I liked him. I told her he was rather an ugly man, but quite a gentleman; and that he treated me kindly, and I was content. Then I went on to describe to her the gay company that had lately been staying at the house; and to these details Bessie listened with interest: they were precisely of the kind she relished.

In such conversation an hour was soon gone: Bessie restored to me my bonnet, etc., and, accompanied by her, I quitted the lodge for the hall. It was also accompanied by her that I had, nearly nine years ago, walked down the path I was now ascending. On a dark, misty, raw morning in January, I had left a hostile roof with a desperate and embittered heart – a sense of outlawry and almost of reprobation – to seek the chilly harbourage of Lowood: that bourne so far away and unexplored. The same hostile roof now again rose before me: my prospects were doubtful yet; and I had yet an aching heart. I still felt as a wanderer on the face of the earth; but I experienced firmer trust in myself and my own powers, and less withering dread of oppression. The gaping wound of my wrongs, too, was now quite healed; and the flame of resentment extinguished.

"You shall go into the breakfast room first," said Bessie, as she preceded me through the hall; "the young ladies will be there."

In another moment I was within that apartment. There was every article of furniture looking just as it did on the morning I was first introduced to Mr. Brocklehurst: the very rug he had stood upon still covered the hearth. Glancing at the bookcases, I thought I could distinguish the two volumes of Bewick's *British Birds* occupying their old place on the third shelf, and *Gulliver's Travels* and the *Arabian Nights* ranged just above. The inanimate objects were not changed; but the living things had altered past recognition.

Two young ladies appeared before me; one very tall, almost as tall as Miss Ingram – very thin too, with a sallow face and severe mien. There was something ascetic in her look, which was augmented by the extreme plainness of a straight-skirted, black, stuff dress, a starched linen collar, hair combed away from the temples, and the nun-like ornament of a string of ebony beads and a crucifix. This I felt sure was Eliza, though I could trace little resemblance to her former self in that elongated and colourless visage.

The other was as certainly Georgiana: but not the Georgiana I remembered – the slim and fairy-like girl of eleven. This was a full-blown, very plump damsel, fair as waxwork, with handsome and regular features, languishing blue eyes, and ringleted yellow hair. The hue of her dress was black too; but its fashion was so different from her sister's – so much more flowing and becoming – it looked as stylish as the other's looked puritanical.

In each of the sisters there was one trait of the mother – and only one; the thin and pallid elder daughter had her parent's Cairngorm eye: the blooming and luxuriant younger girl had her contour of jaw and chin – perhaps a little softened, but still imparting an indescribable hardness to the countenance otherwise so voluptuous and buxom.

Both ladies, as I advanced, rose to welcome me, and both addressed me by the name of "Miss Eyre." Eliza's greeting was delivered in a short, abrupt voice, without a smile; and then she sat down again, fixed her eyes on the fire, and seemed to forget me. Georgiana added to her "How d'ye do?" several commonplaces about my journey, the weather, and so on, uttered in rather a drawling tone: and accompanied by sundry side-glances that measured me from head to foot – now traversing the folds of my drab merino pelisse, and now lingering on the plain trimming of my cottage bonnet. Young ladies have a remarkable way of letting you know that they think you a 'quiz' [25] without actually saying the words. A certain superciliousness of look, coolness of manner, nonchalance of tone, express fully their sentiments on the point, without committing them by any positive rudeness in word or deed.

A sneer, however, whether covert or open, had now no longer that power over me it once possessed: as I sat between my cousins, I was surprised to find how easy I felt under the total neglect of the one and the semi-sarcastic attentions of the other – Eliza did not mortify, nor Georgiana ruffle me. The fact was, I had other things to think about; within the last few months feelings had been stirred in me so much more potent than any they could raise – pains and pleasures so much more acute and exquisite had been excited than any it was in their power to inflict or bestow – that their airs gave me no concern either for good or bad.

"How is Mrs. Reed?" I asked soon, looking calmly at Georgiana, who thought fit to bridle at the direct address, as if it were an unexpected liberty.

"Mrs. Reed? Ah! Mama, you mean; she is extremely poorly: I doubt if you can see her tonight."

"If," said I, "you would just step upstairs and tell her I am come, I should be much obliged to you."

Georgiana almost started, and she opened her blue eyes wild and wide. "I know she had a particular wish to see me," I added, "and I would not defer attending to her desire longer than is absolutely necessary."

"Mama dislikes being disturbed in an evening," remarked Eliza. I soon rose, quietly took off my bonnet and gloves, uninvited, and said I would just step out to Bessie – who was, I dared say, in the kitchen – and ask her to ascertain whether Mrs. Reed was disposed to receive me or not tonight. I went, and having found Bessie and despatched her on my errand, I proceeded to take further measures. It had heretofore been my habit always to shrink from arrogance: received as I had been today, I should, a year ago, have resolved to quit Gateshead the very next morning; now, it was disclosed to me all at once that that would be a foolish plan. I had taken a journey of a hundred miles to see my aunt, and I must stay with her till she was better – or dead: as to her daughters' pride or folly, I must put it on one side, make myself independent of it. So I addressed the housekeeper; asked her to show me a room, told her I should probably be a visitor here for a week or two, had my trunk conveyed to my chamber, and followed it thither myself: I met Bessie on the landing.

"Missis is awake," said she; "I have told her you are here: come and let us see if she will know you."

I did not need to be guided to the well-known room, to which I had so often been summoned for chastisement or reprimand in former days. I hastened before Bessie; I softly opened the door: a shaded light stood on the table, for it was now getting dark. There was the great four-post bed with amber hangings as of old; there the toilet-table, the armchair, and the footstool, at which I had a hundred times been sentenced to kneel, to ask pardon for offences by me uncommitted. I looked into a certain corner near, half-expecting to see the slim outline of a once dreaded switch which used to lurk there, waiting to leap out imp-like and lace my quivering palm or shrinking neck. I approached the bed; I opened the curtains and leant over the high-piled pillows.

Well did I remember Mrs. Reed's face, and I eagerly sought the familiar image. It is a happy thing that time quells the longings of vengeance and hushes the promptings of rage and aversion. I had left this woman in bitterness and hate, and I came back to her now with no other emotion than a sort of ruth for her great sufferings, and a strong yearning to forget and forgive all injuries – to be reconciled and clasp hands in amity.

The well-known face was there: stern, relentless as ever – there was that peculiar eye which nothing could melt, and the somewhat raised, imperious, despotic eyebrow. How often had it lowered on me menace and hate! And how the recollection of childhood's terrors and sorrows revived as I traced its harsh line now! And yet I stooped down and kissed her: she looked at me.

"Is this Jane Eyre?" she said.

"Yes, Aunt Reed. How are you, dear aunt?"

I had once vowed that I would never call her aunt again: I thought it no sin to forget and break that vow now. My fingers had fastened on her hand which lay outside the sheet: had she pressed mine kindly, I should at that moment have experienced true pleasure. But unimpressionable natures are not so soon softened, nor are natural antipathies so readily eradicated. Mrs. Reed took her hand away, and, turning her face rather from me, she remarked that the night was warm. Again she regarded me so icily, I felt at once that her opinion of me – her feeling towards me – was unchanged and unchangeable. I knew by her stony eye – opaque to tenderness, indissoluble to tears – that she was resolved to consider me bad to the last; because to believe me good would give her no generous pleasure: only a sense of mortification.

I felt pain, and then I felt ire; and then I felt a determination to subdue her – to be her mistress in spite both of her nature and her will. My tears had risen, just as in childhood: I ordered them back to their source. I brought a chair to the bedhead: I sat down and leaned over the pillow.

"You sent for me," I said, "and I am here; and it is my intention to stay till I see how you get on."

"Oh, of course! You have seen my daughters?"

"Yes."

"Well, you may tell them I wish you to stay till I can talk some things over with you I have on my mind: tonight it is too late, and I have a difficulty in recalling them. But there was something I wished to say – let me see –"

The wandering look and changed utterance told what wreck had taken place in her once vigorous frame. Turning restlessly, she drew the bedclothes round her; my elbow, resting on a corner of the quilt, fixed it down: she was at once irritated.

"Sit up!" said she; "don't annoy me with holding the clothes fast. Are you Jane Eyre?"

"I am Jane Eyre."

"I have had more trouble with that child than anyone would believe. Such a burden to be left on my hands – and so much annoyance as she caused me, daily and hourly, with her incomprehensible disposition, and her sudden starts of temper, and her continual, unnatural watchings of one's movements! I declare she talked to me once like something mad, or like a fiend – no child ever spoke or looked as she did; I was glad to get her away from the house. What did they do with her at Lowood? The fever broke out there, and many of the pupils died. She, however, did not die: but I said she did – I wish she had died!"

"A strange wish, Mrs. Reed; why do you hate her so?"

"I had a dislike to her mother always; for she was my husband's only sister, and a great favourite with him: he opposed the family's disowning her when she made her low marriage; and when news came of her death, he wept like a simpleton. He would send for the baby; though I entreated him rather to put it out to nurse and pay for its maintenance. I hated it the first time I set my eyes on it – a sickly, whining, pining thing! It would wail in its cradle all night long – not screaming heartily like any other child, but whimpering and moaning. Reed pitied it; and he used to nurse it and notice it as if it had been his own: more, indeed, than he ever noticed his own at that age. He would try to make my children friendly to the little beggar: the darlings could not bear it, and he was angry with them when they showed their dislike. In his last illness, he had it brought continually to his bedside; and but an hour before he died, he bound me by vow to keep the creature. I would as soon have been charged with a pauper brat out of a workhouse: but he was weak, naturally weak. John does not at all resemble his father, and I am glad of it: John is like me and like my brothers – he is quite a Gibson. Oh, I wish he would cease tormenting me with letters for money? I have no more money to give him: we are getting poor. I must send away half the servants and shut up part of the house; or let it off. I can never submit to do that – yet how are we to get on? Two-thirds of my income goes in paying the interest of mortgages. John gambles dreadfully, and always loses – poor boy! He is beset by sharpers: John is sunk and degraded – his look is frightful – I feel ashamed for him when I see him."

She was getting much excited. "I think I had better leave her now," said I to Bessie, who stood on the other side of the bed.

"Perhaps you had, Miss: but she often talks in this way towards night – in the morning she is calmer."

I rose. "Stop!" exclaimed Mrs. Reed, "there is another thing I wished to say. He threatens me – he continually threatens me with his own death, or mine: and I dream sometimes that I see him laid out with a great wound in his throat, or with a swollen and blackened face. I am come to a strange pass: I have heavy troubles. What is to be done? How is the money to be had?"

Bessie now endeavoured to persuade her to take a sedative draught: she succeeded with difficulty. Soon after, Mrs. Reed grew more composed, and sank into a dozing state. I then left her.

More than ten days elapsed before I had again any conversation with her. She continued either delirious or lethargic; and the doctor forbade everything which could painfully excite her. Meantime, I got on as well as I could with Georgiana and Eliza. They were very cold, indeed, at first. Eliza would sit half the day sewing, reading, or writing, and scarcely utter a word either to me or her sister. Georgiana would chatter nonsense to her canary bird by the hour, and take no notice of me. But I was determined not to seem at a loss for occupation or amusement: I had brought my drawing materials with me, and they served me for both.

Provided with a case of pencils, and some sheets of paper, I used to take a seat apart from them, near the window, and busy myself in sketching fancy vignettes, representing any scene that happened momentarily to shape itself in the ever-shifting kaleidoscope of imagination: a glimpse of sea between two rocks; the rising moon, and a ship crossing its disk; a group of reeds and water-flags, and a naiad's head, crowned with lotus-flowers, rising out of them; an elf sitting in a hedge-sparrow's nest, under a wreath of hawthorn bloom.

One morning I fell to sketching a face: what sort of a face it was to be, I did not care or know. I took a soft black pencil, gave it a broad point, and worked away. Soon I had traced on the paper a broad and prominent forehead and a square lower outline of visage: that contour gave me pleasure; my fingers proceeded actively to fill it with features. Strongly-marked horizontal eyebrows must be traced under that brow; then followed, naturally, a well-defined nose, with a straight ridge and full nostrils; then a flexible-looking mouth, by no means narrow; then a firm chin, with a decided cleft down the middle of it: of course, some black whiskers were wanted, and some jetty hair, tufted on the temples, and waved above the forehead. Now for the eyes: I had left them to the last, because they required the most careful working. I drew them large; I shaped them well: the eyelashes I traced long and sombre; the irids lustrous and large. "Good! But not quite the thing," I thought, as I surveyed the effect: "they want more force and spirit;" and I wrought the shades blacker, that the lights might flash more brilliantly – a happy touch or two secured success. There, I had a friend's face under my gaze; and what did it signify that those young ladies turned their backs on me? I looked at it; I smiled at the speaking likeness: I was absorbed and content.

"Is that a portrait of some one you know?" asked Eliza, who had approached me unnoticed. I responded that it was merely a fancy head, and hurried it beneath the other sheets. Of course, I lied: it was, in fact, a very faithful representation of Mr. Rochester. But what was that to her, or to anyone but myself? Georgiana also advanced to look. The other drawings pleased her much, but she called that "an ugly man." They both seemed surprised at my skill. I offered to sketch their portraits; and each, in turn, sat for a pencil outline. Then Georgiana produced her album. I promised to contribute a watercolour drawing: this put her at once into good humour. She proposed a walk in the grounds. Before we had been out two hours, we were deep in a confidential conversation: she had favoured me with a description of the brilliant winter she had spent in London two seasons ago – of the admiration she had there excited – the attention she had received; and I even got hints of the titled conquest she had made. In the course of the afternoon and evening these hints were enlarged on: various soft conversations were reported, and sentimental scenes represented; and, in short, a volume of a novel of fashionable life was that day improvised by her for my benefit. The communications were renewed from day to day: they always ran on the same theme – herself, her loves, and woes. It was strange she never once adverted either to her mother's illness, or her brother's death, or the present gloomy state of the family prospects. Her mind seemed wholly taken up with reminiscences of past gaiety, and aspirations after dissipations to come. She passed about five minutes each day in her mother's sick room, and no more.

Eliza still spoke little: she had evidently no time to talk. I never saw a busier person than she seemed to be; yet it was difficult to say what she did: or rather, to discover any result of her diligence. She had an alarm to call her up early. I know not how she occupied herself before breakfast, but after that meal she divided her time into regular portions, and each hour had its allotted task. Three times a day she studied a little book, which I found, on inspection, was a Common Prayer Book. I asked her once what was the great attraction of that volume, and she said, "the Rubric." Three hours she gave to stitching, with gold thread, the border of a square crimson cloth, almost large enough for a carpet. In answer to my inquiries after the use of this article, she informed me it was a covering for the altar of a new church lately erected near Gateshead. Two hours she devoted to her diary; two to working by herself in the kitchen garden; and one to the regulation of her accounts. She seemed to want no company; no conversation. I believe she was happy in her way: this routine sufficed for her; and nothing annoyed her so much as the occurrence of any incident which forced her to vary its clockwork regularity.

She told me one evening, when more disposed to be communicative than usual, that John's conduct, and the threatened ruin of the family, had been a source of profound affliction to her: but she had now, she said, settled her mind, and formed her resolution. Her own fortune she had taken care to secure; and when her mother died – and it was wholly improbable, she tranquilly remarked, that she should either recover or linger long – she would execute a long-cherished project: seek a retirement where punctual habits would be permanently secured from disturbance, and place safe barriers between herself and a frivolous world. I asked if Georgiana would accompany her.

"Of course not. Georgiana and she had nothing in common: they never had had. She would not be burdened with her society for any consideration. Georgiana should take her own course; and she, Eliza, would take hers."

Georgiana, when not unburdening her heart to me, spent most of her time in lying on the sofa, fretting about the dulness of the house, and wishing over and over again that her aunt Gibson would send her an invitation up to town. "It would be so much better," she said, "if she could only get out of the way for a month or two, till all was over." I did not ask what she meant by "all being over," but I suppose she referred to the expected decease of her mother and the gloomy sequel of funeral rites. Eliza generally took no more notice of her sister's indolence and complaints than if no such murmuring, lounging object had been before her. One day, however, as she put away her account-book and unfolded her embroidery, she suddenly took her up thus:

"Georgiana, a more vain and absurd animal than you was certainly never allowed to cumber the earth. You had no right to be born, for you make no use of life. Instead of living for, in, and with yourself, as a reasonable being ought, you seek only to fasten your feebleness on some other person's strength: if no one can be found willing to burden her or himself with such a fat, weak, puffy, useless thing, you cry out that you are ill-treated, neglected, miserable. Then, too, existence for you must be a scene of continual change and excitement, or else the world is a dungeon: you must be admired, you must be courted, you must be flattered – you must have music, dancing, and society – or you languish, you die away. Have you no sense to devise a system which will make you independent of all efforts, and all wills, but your own? Take one day; share it into sections; to each section apportion its task: leave no stray unemployed quarters of an hour, ten minutes, five minutes – include all; do each piece of business in its turn with method, with rigid regularity. The day will close almost before you are aware it has begun; and you are indebted to no one for helping you to get rid of one vacant moment: you have had to seek no one's company, conversation, sympathy, forbearance; you have lived, in short, as an independent being ought to do. Take this advice: the first and last I shall offer you; then you will not want me or anyone else, happen what may. Neglect it – go on as heretofore, craving, whining, and idling – and suffer the results of your idiocy, however bad and insuperable they may be. I tell you this plainly; and listen: for though I shall no more repeat what I am now about to say, I shall steadily act on it. After my mother's death, I wash my hands of you: from the day her coffin is carried to the vault in Gateshead Church, you and I will be as separate as if we had never known each other. You need not think that because we chanced to be born of the same parents, I shall suffer you to fasten me down by even the feeblest claim: I can tell you this – if the whole human race, ourselves excepted, were swept away, and we two stood alone on the earth, I would leave you in the old world, and betake myself to the new."

She closed her lips.

"You might have spared yourself the trouble of delivering that tirade," answered Georgiana. "Everybody knows you are the most selfish, heartless creature in existence: and *I* know your spiteful hatred towards me: I have had a specimen of it before in the trick you played me about Lord Edwin Vere: you could not bear me to be raised above you, to have a title, to be received into circles where you dare not show your face, and so you acted the spy and informer, and ruined my prospects for ever." Georgiana took out her handkerchief and blew her nose for an hour afterwards; Eliza sat cold, impassable, and assiduously industrious.

True, generous feeling is made small account of by some, but here were two natures rendered, the one intolerably acrid, the other despicably savourless for the want of it. Feeling without judgment is a washy draught indeed; but judgment untempered by feeling is too bitter and husky a morsel for human deglutition.

It was a wet and windy afternoon: Georgiana had fallen asleep on the sofa over the perusal of a novel; Eliza was gone to attend a saint's-day service at the new church – for in matters of religion she was a rigid formalist: no weather ever prevented the punctual discharge of what she considered her devotional duties; fair or foul, she went to church thrice every Sunday, and as often on week-days as there were prayers.

I bethought myself to go upstairs and see how the dying woman sped, who lay there almost unheeded: the very servants paid her but a remittent attention: the hired nurse, being little looked after, would slip out of the room whenever she could. Bessie was faithful; but she had her own family to mind, and could only come occasionally to the hall. I found the sick room unwatched, as I had expected: no nurse was there; the patient lay still, and seemingly lethargic; her livid face sunk in the pillows: the fire was dying in the grate. I renewed the fuel, re-arranged the bedclothes, gazed awhile on her who could not now gaze on me, and then I moved away to the window.

The rain beat strongly against the panes, the wind blew tempestuously: "One lies there," I thought, "who will soon be beyond the war of earthly elements. Whither will that spirit – now struggling to quit its material tenement – flit when at length released?"

In pondering the great mystery, I thought of Helen Burns, recalled her dying words – her faith – her doctrine of the equality of disembodied souls. I was still listening in thought to her well-remembered tones – still picturing her pale and spiritual aspect, her wasted face and sublime gaze, as she lay on her placid deathbed, and whispered her longing to be restored to her divine Father's bosom – when a feeble voice murmured from the couch behind: "Who is that?"

I knew Mrs. Reed had not spoken for days: was she reviving? I went up to her.

"It is I, Aunt Reed."

"Who – I?" was her answer. "Who are you?" looking at me with surprise and a sort of alarm, but still not wildly. "You are quite a stranger to me – where is Bessie?"

"She is at the lodge, aunt."

"Aunt," she repeated. "Who calls me aunt? You are not one of the Gibsons; and yet I know you – that face, and the eyes and forehead, are quiet familiar to me: you are like – why, you are like Jane Eyre!"

I said nothing: I was afraid of occasioning some shock by declaring my identity.

"Yet," said she, "I am afraid it is a mistake: my thoughts deceive me. I wished to see Jane Eyre, and I fancy a likeness where none exists: besides, in eight years she must be so changed." I now gently assured her that I was the person she supposed and desired me to be: and seeing that I was understood, and that her senses were quite collected, I explained how Bessie had sent her husband to fetch me from Thornfield.

"I am very ill, I know," she said ere long. "I was trying to turn myself a few minutes since, and find I cannot move a limb. It is as well I should ease my mind before I die: what we think little of in health, burdens us at such an hour as the present is to me. Is the nurse here? Or is there no one in the room but you?"

I assured her we were alone.

"Well, I have twice done you a wrong which I regret now. One was in breaking the promise which I gave my husband to bring you up as my own child; the other –" she stopped. "After all, it is of no great importance, perhaps," she murmured to herself: "and then I may get better; and to humble myself so to her is painful."

She made an effort to alter her position, but failed: her face changed; she seemed to experience some inward sensation – the precursor, perhaps, of the last pang.

"Well, I must get it over. Eternity is before me: I had better tell her. – Go to my dressing-case, open it, and take out a letter you will see there."

I obeyed her directions. "Read the letter," she said.

It was short, and thus conceived:

> *Madam, – Will you have the goodness to send me the address of my niece, Jane Eyre, and to tell me how she is? It is my intention to write shortly and desire her to come to me at Madeira. Providence has blessed my endeavours to secure a competency; and as I am unmarried and childless, I wish to adopt her during my life, and bequeath her at my death whatever I may have to leave. – I am, Madam, etc., etc.,*
> *John Eyre, Madeira.*

It was dated three years back.

"Why did I never hear of this?" I asked.

"Because I disliked you too fixedly and thoroughly ever to lend a hand in lifting you to prosperity. I could not forget your conduct to me, Jane – the fury with which you once turned on me; the tone in which you declared you abhorred me the worst of anybody in the world; the unchildlike look and voice with which you affirmed that the very thought of me made you sick, and asserted that I had treated you with miserable cruelty. I could not forget my own sensations when you thus started up and poured out the venom of your mind: I felt fear as if an animal that I had struck or pushed had looked up at me with human eyes and cursed me in a man's voice. – Bring me some water! Oh, make haste!"

"Dear Mrs. Reed," said I, as I offered her the draught she required, "think no more of all this, let it pass away from your mind. Forgive me for my passionate language: I was a child then; eight, nine years have passed since that day."

She heeded nothing of what I said; but when she had tasted the water and drawn breath, she went on thus:

"I tell you I could not forget it; and I took my revenge: for you to be adopted by your uncle, and placed in a state of ease and comfort, was what I could not endure. I wrote to him; I said I was sorry for his disappointment, but Jane Eyre was dead: she had died of typhus fever at Lowood. Now act as you please: write and contradict my assertion – expose my falsehood as soon as you like. You were born, I think, to be my torment: my last hour is racked by the recollection of a deed which, but for you, I should never have been tempted to commit."

"If you could but be persuaded to think no more of it, aunt, and to regard me with kindness and forgiveness –"

"You have a very bad disposition," said she, "and one to this day I feel it impossible to understand: how for nine years you could be patient and quiescent under any treatment, and in the tenth break out all fire and violence, I can never comprehend."

"My disposition is not so bad as you think: I am passionate, but not vindictive. Many a time, as a little child, I should have been glad to love you if you would have let me; and I long earnestly to be reconciled to you now: kiss me, aunt."

I approached my cheek to her lips: she would not touch it. She said I oppressed her by leaning over the bed, and again demanded water. As I laid her down – for I raised her and supported her on my arm while she drank – I covered her ice-cold and clammy hand with mine: the feeble fingers shrank from my touch – the glazing eyes shunned my gaze.

"Love me, then, or hate me, as you will," I said at last, "you have my full and free forgiveness: ask now for God's, and be at peace."

Poor, suffering woman! It was too late for her to make now the effort to change her habitual frame of mind: living, she had ever hated me – dying, she must hate me still.

The nurse now entered, and Bessie followed. I yet lingered half an hour longer, hoping to see some sign of amity: but she gave none. She was fast relapsing into stupor; nor did her mind again rally: at twelve o'clock that night she died. I was not present to close her eyes, nor were either of her daughters. They came to tell us the next morning that all was over. She was by that time laid out. Eliza and I went to look at her: Georgiana, who had burst out into loud weeping, said she dared not go. There was stretched Sarah Reed's once robust and active frame, rigid and still: her eye of flint was covered with its cold lid; her brow and strong traits wore yet the impress of her inexorable soul. A strange and solemn object was that corpse to me. I gazed on it with gloom and pain: nothing soft, nothing sweet, nothing pitying, or hopeful, or subduing did it inspire; only a grating anguish for *her* woes – not *my* loss – and a sombre tearless dismay at the fearfulness of death in such a form.

Eliza surveyed her parent calmly. After a silence of some minutes she observed:

"With her constitution she should have lived to a good old age: her life was shortened by trouble." And then a spasm constricted her mouth for an instant: as it passed away she turned and left the room, and so did I. Neither of us had dropt a tear.

Chapter Twenty-Two

MR. ROCHESTER HAD given me but one week's leave of absence: yet a month elapsed before I quitted Gateshead. I wished to leave immediately after the funeral, but Georgiana entreated me to stay till she could get off to London, whither she was now at last invited by her uncle, Mr. Gibson, who had come down to direct his sister's interment and settle the family affairs. Georgiana said she dreaded being left alone with Eliza; from her she got neither sympathy in her dejection, support in her fears, nor aid in her preparations; so I bore with her feeble-minded wailings and selfish lamentations as well as I could, and did my best in sewing for her and packing her dresses. It is true, that while I worked, she would idle; and I thought to myself, "If you and I were destined to live always together, cousin, we would commence matters on a different footing. I should not settle tamely down into being the forbearing party; I should assign you your share of labour, and compel you to accomplish it, or else it should be left undone: I should insist, also, on your keeping some of those drawling, half-insincere complaints hushed in your own breast. It is only because our connection happens to be very transitory, and comes at a peculiarly mournful season, that I consent thus to render it so patient and compliant on my part."

At last I saw Georgiana off; but now it was Eliza's turn to request me to stay another week. Her plans required all her time and attention, she said; she was about to depart for some unknown bourne; and all day long she stayed in her own room, her door bolted within, filling trunks, emptying drawers, burning papers, and holding no communication with anyone. She wished me to look after the house, to see callers, and answer notes of condolence.

One morning she told me I was at liberty. "And," she added, "I am obliged to you for your valuable services and discreet conduct! There is some difference between living with such a one as you and with Georgiana: you perform your own part in life and burden no one. Tomorrow," she continued, "I set out for the Continent. I shall take up my abode in a religious house near Lisle – a nunnery you would call it; there I shall be quiet and unmolested. I shall devote myself for a time to the examination of the Roman Catholic dogmas, and to a careful study of the workings of their system: if I find it to be, as I half suspect it is, the one best calculated to ensure the doing of all things decently and in order, I shall embrace the tenets of Rome and probably take the veil."

I neither expressed surprise at this resolution nor attempted to dissuade her from it. "The vocation will fit you to a hair," I thought: "much good may it do you!"

When we parted, she said: "Goodbye, cousin Jane Eyre; I wish you well: you have some sense."

I then returned: "You are not without sense, cousin Eliza; but what you have, I suppose, in another year will be walled up alive in a French convent. However, it is not my business, and so it suits you, I don't much care."

"You are in the right," said she; and with these words we each went our separate way. As I shall not have occasion to refer either to her or her sister again, I may as well mention here, that Georgiana made an advantageous match with a wealthy worn-out man of fashion, and that Eliza actually took the veil, and is at this day superior of the convent where she passed the period of her novitiate, and which she endowed with her fortune.

How people feel when they are returning home from an absence, long or short, I did not know: I had never experienced the sensation. I had known what it was to come back to Gateshead when a child after a long walk, to be scolded for looking cold or gloomy; and later, what it was to come back from church to Lowood, to long for a plenteous meal and a good fire, and to be unable to get either. Neither of these returnings was very pleasant or desirable: no magnet drew me to a given point, increasing in its strength of attraction the nearer I came. The return to Thornfield was yet to be tried.

My journey seemed tedious – very tedious: fifty miles one day, a night spent at an inn; fifty miles the next day. During the first twelve hours I thought of Mrs. Reed in her last moments; I saw her disfigured and discoloured face, and heard her strangely altered voice. I mused on the funeral day, the coffin, the hearse, the black train of tenants and servants – few was the number of relatives – the gaping vault, the silent church, the solemn service. Then I thought of Eliza and Georgiana; I beheld one the cynosure of a ballroom, the other the inmate of a convent cell; and I dwelt on and analysed their separate peculiarities of person and character. The evening arrival at the great town of — scattered these thoughts; night gave them quite another turn: laid down on my traveller's bed, I left reminiscence for anticipation.

I was going back to Thornfield: but how long was I to stay there? Not long; of that I was sure. I had heard from Mrs. Fairfax in the interim of my absence: the party at the hall was dispersed; Mr. Rochester had left for London three weeks ago, but he was then expected to return in a fortnight. Mrs. Fairfax surmised that he was gone to make arrangements for his wedding, as he had talked of purchasing a new carriage: she said the idea of his marrying Miss Ingram still seemed strange to her; but from what everybody said, and from what she had herself seen, she could no longer doubt that the event would shortly take place. "You would be strangely incredulous if you did doubt it," was my mental comment. "I don't doubt it."

The question followed, "Where was I to go?" I dreamt of Miss Ingram all the night: in a vivid morning dream I saw her closing the gates of Thornfield against me and pointing me out another road; and Mr. Rochester looked on with his arms folded – smiling sardonically, as it seemed, at both her and me.

I had not notified to Mrs. Fairfax the exact day of my return; for I did not wish either car or carriage to meet me at Millcote. I proposed to walk the distance quietly by myself; and very quietly, after leaving my box in the ostler's care, did I slip away from the George Inn, about six o'clock of a June evening, and take the old road to Thornfield: a road which lay chiefly through fields, and was now little frequented.

It was not a bright or splendid summer evening, though fair and soft: the haymakers were at work all along the road; and the sky, though far from cloudless, was such as promised well for the future: its blue – where blue was visible – was mild and settled, and its cloud strata high and thin. The west, too, was warm: no watery gleam chilled it – it seemed as if there was a fire lit, an altar burning behind its screen of marbled vapour, and out of apertures shone a golden redness.

I felt glad as the road shortened before me: so glad that I stopped once to ask myself what that joy meant: and to remind reason that it was not to my home I was going, or to a permanent resting-place, or to a place where fond friends looked out for me and waited my arrival. "Mrs. Fairfax will smile you a calm welcome, to be sure," said I; "and little Adèle will clap her hands and jump to see you: but you know very well you are thinking of another than they, and that he is not thinking of you."

But what is so headstrong as youth? What so blind as inexperience? These affirmed that it was pleasure enough to have the privilege of again looking on Mr. Rochester, whether he looked on me or not; and they added – "Hasten! hasten! Be with him while you may: but a few more days or weeks, at most, and you are parted from him for ever!" And then I strangled a newborn agony – a deformed thing which I could not persuade myself to own and rear – and ran on.

They are making hay, too, in Thornfield meadows: or rather, the labourers are just quitting their work, and returning home with their rakes on their shoulders, now, at the hour I arrive. I have but a field or two to traverse, and then I shall cross the road and reach the gates. How full the hedges are of roses! But I have no time to gather any; I want to be at the house. I passed a tall briar, shooting leafy and flowery branches across the path; I see the narrow stile with stone steps; and I see – Mr. Rochester sitting there, a book and a pencil in his hand; he is writing.

Well, he is not a ghost; yet every nerve I have is unstrung: for a moment I am beyond my own mastery. What does it mean? I did not think I should tremble in this way when I saw him, or lose my voice or the power of motion in his presence. I will go back as soon as I can stir: I need not make an absolute fool of myself. I know another way to the house. It does not signify if I knew twenty ways; for he has seen me.

"Hillo!" he cries; and he puts up his book and his pencil. "There you are! Come on, if you please."

I suppose I do come on; though in what fashion I know not; being scarcely cognisant of my movements, and solicitous only to appear calm; and, above all, to control the working muscles of my face – which I feel rebel insolently against my will, and struggle to express what I had resolved to conceal. But I have a veil – it is down: I may make shift yet to behave with decent composure.

"And this is Jane Eyre? Are you coming from Millcote, and on foot? Yes – just one of your tricks: not to send for a carriage, and come clattering over street and road like a common mortal, but to steal into the vicinage of your home along with twilight, just as if you were a dream or a shade. What the deuce have you done with yourself this last month?"

"I have been with my aunt, sir, who is dead."

"A true Janian reply! Good angels be my guard! She comes from the other world – from the abode of people who are dead; and tells me so when she meets me alone here in the gloaming! If I dared, I'd touch you, to see if you are substance or shadow, you elf! – but I'd as soon offer to take hold of a blue *ignis fatuus* [26] light in a marsh. Truant! Truant!" he added, when he had paused an instant. "Absent from me a whole month, and forgetting me quite, I'll be sworn!"

I knew there would be pleasure in meeting my master again, even though broken by the fear that he was so soon to cease to be my master, and by the knowledge that I was nothing to him: but there was ever in Mr. Rochester (so at least I thought) such a wealth of the power of communicating happiness, that to taste but of the crumbs he scattered to stray and stranger birds like me, was to feast genially. His last words were balm: they seemed to imply that it imported something to him whether I forgot him or not. And he had spoken of Thornfield as my home – would that it were my home!

He did not leave the stile, and I hardly liked to ask to go by. I inquired soon if he had not been to London.

"Yes; I suppose you found that out by second-sight."

"Mrs. Fairfax told me in a letter."

"And did she inform you what I went to do?"

"Oh, yes, sir! Everybody knew your errand."

"You must see the carriage, Jane, and tell me if you don't think it will suit Mrs. Rochester exactly; and whether she won't look like Queen Boadicea, leaning back against those purple cushions. I wish, Jane, I were a trifle better adapted to match with her externally. Tell me now, fairy as you are – can't you give me a charm, or a philter, or something of that sort, to make me a handsome man?"

"It would be past the power of magic, sir;" and, in thought, I added, "A loving eye is all the charm needed: to such you are handsome enough; or rather your sternness has a power beyond beauty."

Mr. Rochester had sometimes read my unspoken thoughts with an acumen to me incomprehensible: in the present instance he took no notice of my abrupt vocal response; but he smiled at me with a certain smile he had of his own, and which he used but on rare occasions. He seemed to think it too good for common purposes: it was the real sunshine of feeling – he shed it over me now.

"Pass, Janet," said he, making room for me to cross the stile: "go up home, and stay your weary little wandering feet at a friend's threshold."

All I had now to do was to obey him in silence: no need for me to colloquise further. I got over the stile without a word, and meant to leave him calmly. An impulse held me fast – a force turned me round. I said – or something in me said for me, and in spite of me:

"Thank you, Mr. Rochester, for your great kindness. I am strangely glad to get back again to you: and wherever you are is my home – my only home."

I walked on so fast that even he could hardly have overtaken me had he tried. Little Adèle was half wild with delight when she saw me. Mrs. Fairfax received me with her usual plain friendliness. Leah smiled, and even Sophie bid me "bon soir" with glee. This was very pleasant; there is no happiness like that of being loved by your fellow creatures, and feeling that your presence is an addition to their comfort.

I that evening shut my eyes resolutely against the future: I stopped my ears against the voice that kept warning me of near separation and coming grief. When tea was over and Mrs. Fairfax had taken her knitting, and I had assumed a low seat near her, and Adèle, kneeling on the carpet, had nestled close up to me, and a sense of mutual affection seemed to surround us with a ring of golden peace, I uttered a silent prayer that we might not be parted far or soon; but when, as we thus sat, Mr. Rochester entered, unannounced, and looking at us, seemed to take pleasure in the spectacle of a group so amicable – when he said he supposed the old lady was all right now that she had got her adopted daughter back again, and added that he saw Adèle was "prête à croquer sa petite maman Anglaise" [27] – I half ventured to hope that he would, even after his marriage, keep us together somewhere under the shelter of his protection, and not quite exiled from the sunshine of his presence.

A fortnight of dubious calm succeeded my return to Thornfield Hall. Nothing was said of the master's marriage, and I saw no preparation going on for such an event. Almost every day I asked Mrs. Fairfax if she had yet heard anything decided: her answer was always in the negative. Once she said she had actually put the question to Mr. Rochester as to when he was going to bring his bride home; but he had answered her only by a joke and one of his queer looks, and she could not tell what to make of him.

One thing specially surprised me, and that was, there were no journeyings backward and forward, no visits to Ingram Park: to be sure it was twenty miles off, on the borders of another county; but what was that distance to an ardent lover? To so practised and indefatigable a horseman as Mr. Rochester, it would be but a morning's ride. I began to cherish hopes I had no right to conceive: that the match was broken off; that rumour had been mistaken; that one or both parties had changed their minds. I used to look at my master's face to see if it were sad or fierce; but I could not remember the time when it had been so uniformly clear of clouds or evil feelings. If, in the moments I and my pupil spent with him, I lacked spirits and sank into inevitable dejection, he became even gay. Never had he called me more frequently to his presence; never been kinder to me when there – and, alas! Never had I loved him so well.

Chapter Twenty-Three

A SPLENDID MIDSUMMER shone over England: skies so pure, suns so radiant as were then seen in long succession, seldom favour even singly, our wave-girt land. It was as if a band of Italian days had come from the South, like a flock of glorious passenger birds, and lighted to rest them on the cliffs of Albion. The hay was all got in; the fields round Thornfield were green and shorn; the roads white and baked; the trees were in their dark prime; hedge and wood, full-leaved and deeply tinted, contrasted well with the sunny hue of the cleared meadows between.

On Midsummer-eve, Adèle, weary with gathering wild strawberries in Hay Lane half the day, had gone to bed with the sun. I watched her drop asleep, and when I left her, I sought the garden.

It was now the sweetest hour of the twenty-four: – "Day its fervid fires had wasted," and dew fell cool on panting plain and scorched summit. Where the sun had gone down in simple state – pure of the pomp of clouds – spread a solemn purple, burning with the light of red jewel and furnace flame at one point, on one hill peak, and extending high and wide, soft and still softer, over half heaven. The east had its own charm or fine deep blue, and its own modest gem, a casino and solitary star: soon it would boast the moon; but she was yet beneath the horizon.

I walked a while on the pavement; but a subtle, well-known scent – that of a cigar – stole from some window; I saw the library casement open a handbreadth; I knew I might be watched thence; so I went apart into the orchard. No nook in the grounds more sheltered and more Eden-like; it was full of trees, it bloomed with flowers: a very high wall shut it out from the court, on one side; on the other, a beech avenue screened it from the lawn. At the bottom was a sunk fence; its sole separation from lonely fields: a winding walk, bordered with laurels and terminating in a giant horse-chestnut, circled at the base by a seat, led down to the fence. Here one could wander unseen. While such honeydew fell, such silence reigned, such gloaming gathered, I felt as if I could haunt such shade for ever; but in threading the flower and fruit parterres at the upper part of the enclosure, enticed there by the light the now rising moon cast on this more open quarter, my step is stayed – not by sound, not by sight, but once more by a warning fragrance.

Sweetbriar and southernwood, jasmine, pink, and rose have long been yielding their evening sacrifice of incense: this new scent is neither of shrub nor flower; it is – I know it well – it is Mr. Rochester's cigar. I look round and I listen. I see trees laden with ripening fruit. I hear a nightingale warbling in a wood half a mile off; no moving form is visible, no coming step audible; but that perfume increases: I must flee. I make for the wicket leading to the shrubbery, and I see Mr. Rochester entering. I step aside into the ivy recess; he will not stay long: he will soon return whence he came, and if I sit still he will never see me.

But no – eventide is as pleasant to him as to me, and this antique garden as attractive; and he strolls on, now lifting the gooseberry-tree branches to look at the fruit, large as plums, with which they are laden; now taking a ripe cherry from the wall; now stooping towards a knot of flowers, either to inhale their fragrance or to admire the dew-beads on their petals. A great moth goes humming by me; it alights on a plant at Mr. Rochester's foot: he sees it, and bends to examine it.

"Now, he has his back towards me," thought I, "and he is occupied too; perhaps, if I walk softly, I can slip away unnoticed."

I trode on an edging of turf that the crackle of the pebbly gravel might not betray me: he was standing among the beds at a yard or two distant from where I had to pass; the moth apparently engaged him. "I shall get by very well," I meditated. As I crossed his shadow, thrown long over the garden by the moon, not yet risen high, he said quietly, without turning:

"Jane, come and look at this fellow."

I had made no noise: he had not eyes behind – could his shadow feel? I started at first, and then I approached him.

"Look at his wings," said he, "he reminds me rather of a West Indian insect; one does not often see so large and gay a night-rover in England; there! He is flown."

The moth roamed away. I was sheepishly retreating also; but Mr. Rochester followed me, and when we reached the wicket, he said:

"Turn back: on so lovely a night it is a shame to sit in the house; and surely no one can wish to go to bed while sunset is thus at meeting with moonrise."

It is one of my faults, that though my tongue is sometimes prompt enough at an answer, there are times when it sadly fails me in framing an excuse; and always the lapse occurs at some crisis, when a facile word or plausible pretext is specially wanted to get me out of painful embarrassment. I did not like to walk at this hour alone with Mr. Rochester in the shadowy orchard; but I could not find a reason to allege for leaving him. I followed with lagging step, and thoughts busily bent on discovering a means of extrication; but he himself looked so composed and so grave also, I became ashamed of feeling any confusion: the evil – if evil existent or prospective there was – seemed to lie with me only; his mind was unconscious and quiet.

"Jane," he recommenced, as we entered the laurel walk, and slowly strayed down in the direction of the sunk fence and the horse-chestnut, "Thornfield is a pleasant place in summer, is it not?"

"Yes, sir."

"You must have become in some degree attached to the house, – you, who have an eye for natural beauties, and a good deal of the organ of Adhesiveness?"

"I am attached to it, indeed."

"And though I don't comprehend how it is, I perceive you have acquired a degree of regard for that foolish little child Adèle, too; and even for simple dame Fairfax?"

"Yes, sir; in different ways, I have an affection for both."

"And would be sorry to part with them?"

"Yes."

"Pity!" he said, and sighed and paused. "It is always the way of events in this life," he continued presently: "no sooner have you got settled in a pleasant resting-place, than a voice calls out to you to rise and move on, for the hour of repose is expired."

"Must I move on, sir?" I asked. "Must I leave Thornfield?"

"I believe you must, Jane. I am sorry, Janet, but I believe indeed you must."

This was a blow: but I did not let it prostrate me.

"Well, sir, I shall be ready when the order to march comes."

"It is come now – I must give it tonight."

"Then you *are* going to be married, sir?"

"Ex-act-ly – pre-cise-ly: with your usual acuteness, you have hit the nail straight on the head."

"Soon, sir?"

"Very soon, my – that is, Miss Eyre: and you'll remember, Jane, the first time I, or Rumour, plainly intimated to you that it was my intention to put my old bachelor's neck into the sacred noose, to enter into the holy estate of matrimony – to take Miss Ingram to my bosom, in short (she's an extensive armful: but that's not to the point – one can't have too much of such a very excellent thing as my beautiful Blanche): well, as I was saying – listen to me, Jane! You're not turning your head to look after more moths, are you? That was only a lady-clock, child, 'flying away home.' I wish to remind you that it was you who first said to me, with that discretion I respect in you – with that foresight, prudence, and humility which befit your responsible and dependent position – that in case I married Miss Ingram, both you and little Adèle had better trot forthwith. I pass over the sort of slur conveyed in this suggestion on the character of my beloved; indeed, when you are far away, Janet, I'll try to forget it: I shall notice only its wisdom; which is such that I have made it my law of action. Adèle must go to school; and you, Miss Eyre, must get a new situation."

"Yes, sir, I will advertise immediately: and meantime, I suppose –" I was going to say, "I suppose I may stay here, till I find another shelter to betake myself to:" but I stopped, feeling it would not do to risk a long sentence, for my voice was not quite under command.

"In about a month I hope to be a bridegroom," continued Mr. Rochester; "and in the interim, I shall myself look out for employment and an asylum for you."

"Thank you, sir; I am sorry to give –"

"Oh, no need to apologise! I consider that when a dependent does her duty as well as you have done yours, she has a sort of claim upon her employer for any little assistance he can conveniently render her; indeed I have already, through my future mother-in-law, heard of a place that I think will suit: it is to undertake the education of the five daughters of Mrs. Dionysius O'Gall of Bitternutt Lodge, Connaught, Ireland. You'll like Ireland, I think: they're such warm-hearted people there, they say."

"It is a long way off, sir."

"No matter – a girl of your sense will not object to the voyage or the distance."

"Not the voyage, but the distance: and then the sea is a barrier –"

"From what, Jane?"

"From England and from Thornfield: and –"

"Well?"

"From *you*, sir."

I said this almost involuntarily, and, with as little sanction of free will, my tears gushed out. I did not cry so as to be heard, however; I avoided sobbing. The thought of Mrs. O'Gall and Bitternutt Lodge struck cold to my heart; and colder the thought of all the brine and foam, destined, as it seemed, to rush between me and the master at whose side I now walked, and coldest the remembrance of the wider ocean – wealth, caste, custom intervened between me and what I naturally and inevitably loved.

"It is a long way," I again said.

"It is, to be sure; and when you get to Bitternutt Lodge, Connaught, Ireland, I shall never see you again, Jane: that's morally certain. I never go over to Ireland, not having myself much of a fancy for the country. We have been good friends, Jane; have we not?"

"Yes, sir."

"And when friends are on the eve of separation, they like to spend the little time that remains to them close to each other. Come! We'll talk over the voyage and the parting quietly half an hour or so, while the stars enter into their shining life up in heaven yonder: here is the chestnut tree: here is the bench at its old roots. Come, we will sit there in peace tonight, though we should never more be destined to sit there together." He seated me and himself.

"It is a long way to Ireland, Janet, and I am sorry to send my little friend on such weary travels: but if I can't do better, how is it to be helped? Are you anything akin to me, do you think, Jane?"

I could risk no sort of answer by this time: my heart was still.

"Because," he said, "I sometimes have a queer feeling with regard to you – especially when you are near me, as now: it is as if I had a string somewhere under my left ribs, tightly and inextricably knotted to a similar string situated in the corresponding quarter of your little frame. And if that boisterous Channel, and two hundred miles or so of land come broad between us, I am afraid that cord of communion will be snapt; and then I've a nervous notion I should take to bleeding inwardly. As for you, – you'd forget me."

"That I *never* should, sir: you know –" Impossible to proceed.

"Jane, do you hear that nightingale singing in the wood? Listen!"

In listening, I sobbed convulsively; for I could repress what I endured no longer; I was obliged to yield, and I was shaken from head to foot with acute distress. When I did speak, it was only to express an impetuous wish that I had never been born, or never come to Thornfield.

"Because you are sorry to leave it?"

The vehemence of emotion, stirred by grief and love within me, was claiming mastery, and struggling for full sway, and asserting a right to predominate, to overcome, to live, rise, and reign at last: yes, – and to speak.

"I grieve to leave Thornfield: I love Thornfield: – I love it, because I have lived in it a full and delightful life, – momentarily at least. I have not been trampled on. I have not been petrified. I have not been buried with inferior minds, and excluded from every glimpse of communion with what is bright and energetic and high. I have talked, face to face, with what I reverence, with what I delight in, – with an original, a vigorous, an expanded mind. I have known you, Mr. Rochester; and it strikes me with terror and anguish to feel I absolutely must be torn from you for ever. I see the necessity of departure; and it is like looking on the necessity of death."

"Where do you see the necessity?" he asked suddenly.

"Where? You, sir, have placed it before me."

"In what shape?"

"In the shape of Miss Ingram; a noble and beautiful woman, – your bride."

"My bride! What bride? I have no bride!"

"But you will have."

"Yes; – I will! – I will!" He set his teeth.

"Then I must go: – you have said it yourself."

"No: you must stay! I swear it – and the oath shall be kept."

"I tell you I must go!" I retorted, roused to something like passion. "Do you think I can stay to become nothing to you? Do you think I am an automaton? – A machine without feelings? And can bear to have my morsel of bread snatched from my lips, and my drop of living water dashed from my cup? Do you think, because I am poor, obscure, plain, and little, I am soulless and heartless? You think wrong! – I have as much soul as you, – and full as much heart! And if God had gifted me with some beauty and much wealth, I should have made it as hard for you to leave me, as it is now for me to leave you. I am not talking to you now through the medium of custom, conventionalities, nor even of mortal flesh; – it is my spirit that addresses your spirit; just as if both had passed through the grave, and we stood at God's feet, equal, – as we are!"

"As we are!" repeated Mr. Rochester – "so," he added, enclosing me in his arms. Gathering me to his breast, pressing his lips on my lips: "so, Jane!"

"Yes, so, sir," I rejoined: "and yet not so; for you are a married man – or as good as a married man, and wed to one inferior to you – to one with whom you have no sympathy – whom I do not believe you truly love; for I have seen and heard you sneer at her. I would scorn such a union: therefore I am better than you – let me go!"

"Where, Jane? To Ireland?"

"Yes – to Ireland. I have spoken my mind, and can go anywhere now."

"Jane, be still; don't struggle so, like a wild frantic bird that is rending its own plumage in its desperation."

"I am no bird; and no net ensnares me; I am a free human being with an independent will, which I now exert to leave you." Another effort set me at liberty, and I stood erect before him.

"And your will shall decide your destiny," he said: "I offer you my hand, my heart, and a share of all my possessions."

"You play a farce, which I merely laugh at."

"I ask you to pass through life at my side – to be my second self, and best earthly companion."

"For that fate you have already made your choice, and must abide by it."

"Jane, be still a few moments: you are over-excited: I will be still too."

A waft of wind came sweeping down the laurel-walk, and trembled through the boughs of the chestnut: it wandered away – away – to an indefinite distance – it died. The nightingale's song was then the only voice of the hour: in listening to it, I again wept. Mr. Rochester sat quiet, looking at me gently and seriously. Some time passed before he spoke; he at last said:

"Come to my side, Jane, and let us explain and understand one another."

"I will never again come to your side: I am torn away now, and cannot return."

"But, Jane, I summon you as my wife: it is you only I intend to marry."

I was silent: I thought he mocked me.

"Come, Jane – come hither."

"Your bride stands between us."

He rose, and with a stride reached me.

"My bride is here," he said, again drawing me to him, "because my equal is here, and my likeness. Jane, will you marry me?"

Still I did not answer, and still I writhed myself from his grasp: for I was still incredulous.

"Do you doubt me, Jane?"

"Entirely."

"You have no faith in me?"

"Not a whit."

"Am I a liar in your eyes?" he asked passionately. "Little sceptic, you *shall* be convinced. What love have I for Miss Ingram? None: and that you know. What love has she for me? None: as I have taken pains to prove: I caused a rumour to reach her that my fortune was not a third of what was supposed, and after that I presented myself to see the result; it was coldness both from her and her mother. I would not – I could not – marry Miss Ingram. You – you strange, you almost unearthly thing! – I love as my own flesh. You – poor and obscure, and small and plain as you are – I entreat to accept me as a husband."

"What, me!" I ejaculated, beginning in his earnestness – and especially in his incivility – to credit his sincerity: "me who have not a friend in the world but you – if you are my friend: not a shilling but what you have given me?"

"You, Jane, I must have you for my own – entirely my own. Will you be mine? Say yes, quickly."

"Mr. Rochester, let me look at your face: turn to the moonlight."

"Why?"

"Because I want to read your countenance – turn!"

"There! You will find it scarcely more legible than a crumpled, scratched page. Read on: only make haste, for I suffer."

His face was very much agitated and very much flushed, and there were strong workings in the features, and strange gleams in the eyes.

"Oh, Jane, you torture me!" he exclaimed. "With that searching and yet faithful and generous look, you torture me!"

"How can I do that? If you are true, and your offer real, my only feelings to you must be gratitude and devotion – they cannot torture."

"Gratitude!" he ejaculated; and added wildly – "Jane accept me quickly. Say, Edward – give me my name – Edward – I will marry you."

"Are you in earnest? Do you truly love me? Do you sincerely wish me to be your wife?"

"I do; and if an oath is necessary to satisfy you, I swear it."

"Then, sir, I will marry you."

"Edward – my little wife!"

"Dear Edward!"

"Come to me – come to me entirely now," said he; and added, in his deepest tone, speaking in my ear as his cheek was laid on mine, "Make my happiness – I will make yours."

"God pardon me!" he subjoined ere long; "and man meddle not with me: I have her, and will hold her."

"There is no one to meddle, sir. I have no kindred to interfere."

"No – that is the best of it," he said. And if I had loved him less I should have thought his accent and look of exultation savage; but, sitting by him, roused from the nightmare of parting – called to the paradise of union – I thought only of the bliss given me to drink in so abundant a flow. Again and again he said, "Are you happy, Jane?" And again and again I answered, "Yes." After which he murmured, "It will atone – it will atone. Have I not found her friendless, and cold, and comfortless? Will I not guard, and cherish, and solace her? Is there not love in my heart, and constancy in my resolves? It will expiate at God's tribunal. I know my Maker sanctions what I do. For the world's judgment – I wash my hands thereof. For man's opinion – I defy it."

But what had befallen the night? The moon was not yet set, and we were all in shadow: I could scarcely see my master's face, near as I was. And what ailed the chestnut tree? It writhed and groaned; while wind roared in the laurel walk, and came sweeping over us.

"We must go in," said Mr. Rochester: "the weather changes. I could have sat with thee till morning, Jane."

"And so," thought I, "could I with you." I should have said so, perhaps, but a livid, vivid spark leapt out of a cloud at which I was looking, and there was a crack, a crash, and a close rattling peal; and I thought only of hiding my dazzled eyes against Mr. Rochester's shoulder.

The rain rushed down. He hurried me up the walk, through the grounds, and into the house; but we were quite wet before we could pass the threshold. He was taking off my shawl in the hall, and shaking the water out of my loosened hair, when Mrs. Fairfax emerged from her room. I did not observe her at first, nor did Mr. Rochester. The lamp was lit. The clock was on the stroke of twelve.

"Hasten to take off your wet things," said he; "and before you go, goodnight – goodnight, my darling!"

He kissed me repeatedly. When I looked up, on leaving his arms, there stood the widow, pale, grave, and amazed. I only smiled at her, and ran upstairs. "Explanation will do for another time," thought I. Still, when I reached my chamber, I felt a pang at the idea she should even temporarily misconstrue what she had seen. But joy soon effaced every other feeling; and loud as the wind blew, near and deep as the thunder crashed, fierce and frequent as the lightning gleamed, cataract-like as the rain fell during a storm of two hours' duration, I experienced no fear and little awe. Mr. Rochester came thrice to my door in the course of it, to ask if I was safe and tranquil: and that was comfort, that was strength for anything.

Before I left my bed in the morning, little Adèle came running in to tell me that the great horse-chestnut at the bottom of the orchard had been struck by lightning in the night, and half of it split away.

Chapter Twenty-Four

AS I ROSE and dressed, I thought over what had happened, and wondered if it were a dream. I could not be certain of the reality till I had seen Mr. Rochester again, and heard him renew his words of love and promise.

While arranging my hair, I looked at my face in the glass, and felt it was no longer plain: there was hope in its aspect and life in its colour; and my eyes seemed as if they had beheld the fount of fruition, and borrowed beams from the lustrous ripple. I had often been unwilling to look at my master, because I feared he could not be pleased at my look; but I was sure I might lift my face to his now, and not cool his affection by its expression. I took a plain but clean and light summer dress from my drawer and put it on: it seemed no attire had ever so well become me, because none had I ever worn in so blissful a mood.

I was not surprised, when I ran down into the hall, to see that a brilliant June morning had succeeded to the tempest of the night; and to feel, through the open glass door, the breathing of a fresh and fragrant breeze. Nature must be gladsome when I was so happy. A beggar-woman and her little boy – pale, ragged objects both – were coming up the walk, and I ran down and gave them all the money I happened to have in my purse – some three or four shillings: good or bad, they must partake of my jubilee. The rooks cawed, and blither birds sang; but nothing was so merry or so musical as my own rejoicing heart.

Mrs. Fairfax surprised me by looking out of the window with a sad countenance, and saying gravely – "Miss Eyre, will you come to breakfast?" During the meal she was quiet and cool: but I could not undeceive her then. I must wait for my master to give explanations; and so must she. I ate what I could, and then I hastened upstairs. I met Adèle leaving the schoolroom.

"Where are you going? It is time for lessons."

"Mr. Rochester has sent me away to the nursery."

"Where is he?"

"In there," pointing to the apartment she had left; and I went in, and there he stood.

"Come and bid me good morning," said he. I gladly advanced; and it was not merely a cold word now, or even a shake of the hand that I received, but an embrace and a kiss. It seemed natural: it seemed genial to be so well loved, so caressed by him.

"Jane, you look blooming, and smiling, and pretty," said he: "truly pretty this morning. Is this my pale, little elf? Is this my mustard-seed? This little sunny-faced girl with the dimpled cheek and rosy lips; the satin-smooth hazel hair, and the radiant hazel eyes?" (I had green eyes, reader; but you must excuse the mistake: for him they were new-dyed, I suppose.)

"It is Jane Eyre, sir."

"Soon to be Jane Rochester," he added: "in four weeks, Janet; not a day more. Do you hear that?"

I did, and I could not quite comprehend it: it made me giddy. The feeling, the announcement sent through me, was something stronger than was consistent with joy – something that smote and stunned. It was, I think almost fear.

"You blushed, and now you are white, Jane: what is that for?"

"Because you gave me a new name – Jane Rochester; and it seems so strange."

"Yes, Mrs. Rochester," said he; "young Mrs. Rochester – Fairfax Rochester's girl-bride."

"It can never be, sir; it does not sound likely. Human beings never enjoy complete happiness in this world. I was not born for a different destiny to the rest of my species: to imagine such a lot befalling me is a fairy tale – a daydream."

"Which I can and will realise. I shall begin today. This morning I wrote to my banker in London to send me certain jewels he has in his keeping, – heirlooms for the ladies of Thornfield. In a day or two I hope to pour them into your lap: for every privilege, every attention shall be yours that I would accord a peer's daughter, if about to marry her."

"Oh, sir! – Never rain jewels! I don't like to hear them spoken of. Jewels for Jane Eyre sounds unnatural and strange: I would rather not have them."

"I will myself put the diamond chain round your neck, and the circlet on your forehead, – which it will become: for nature, at least, has stamped her patent of nobility on this brow, Jane; and I will clasp the bracelets on these fine wrists, and load these fairy-like fingers with rings."

"No, no, sir! Think of other subjects, and speak of other things, and in another strain. Don't address me as if I were a beauty; I am your plain, Quakerish governess."

"You are a beauty in my eyes, and a beauty just after the desire of my heart, – delicate and aerial."

"Puny and insignificant, you mean. You are dreaming, sir, – or you are sneering. For God's sake don't be ironical!"

"I will make the world acknowledge you a beauty, too," he went on, while I really became uneasy at the strain he had adopted, because I felt he was either deluding himself or trying to delude me. "I will attire my Jane in satin and lace, and she shall have roses in her hair; and I will cover the head I love best with a priceless veil."

"And then you won't know me, sir; and I shall not be your Jane Eyre any longer, but an ape in a harlequin's jacket – a jay in borrowed plumes. I would as soon see you, Mr. Rochester, tricked out in stage-trappings, as myself clad in a court-lady's robe; and I don't call you handsome, sir, though I love you most dearly: far too dearly to flatter you. Don't flatter me."

He pursued his theme, however, without noticing my deprecation. "This very day I shall take you in the carriage to Millcote, and you must choose some dresses for yourself. I told you we shall be married in four weeks. The wedding is to take place quietly, in the church down below yonder; and then I shall waft you away at once to town. After a brief stay there, I shall bear my treasure to regions nearer the sun: to French vineyards and Italian plains; and she shall see whatever is famous in old story and in modern record: she shall taste, too, of the life of cities; and she shall learn to value herself by just comparison with others."

"Shall I travel? – And with you, sir?"

"You shall sojourn at Paris, Rome, and Naples: at Florence, Venice, and Vienna: all the ground I have wandered over shall be re-trodden by you: wherever I stamped my hoof, your sylph's foot shall step also. Ten years since, I flew through Europe half mad; with disgust, hate, and rage as my companions: now I shall revisit it healed and cleansed, with a very angel as my comforter."

I laughed at him as he said this. "I am not an angel," I asserted; "and I will not be one till I die: I will be myself. Mr. Rochester, you must neither expect nor exact anything celestial of me – for you will not get it, any more than I shall get it of you: which I do not at all anticipate."

"What do you anticipate of me?"

"For a little while you will perhaps be as you are now, – a very little while; and then you will turn cool; and then you will be capricious; and then you will be stern, and I shall have much ado to please you: but when you get well used to me, you will perhaps like me again, – *like* me, I say, not *love* me. I suppose your love will effervesce in six months, or less. I have observed in books written by men, that period assigned as the farthest to which a husband's ardour extends. Yet, after all, as a friend and companion, I hope never to become quite distasteful to my dear master."

"Distasteful! And like you again! I think I shall like you again, and yet again: and I will make you confess I do not only *like*, but *love* you – with truth, fervour, constancy."

"Yet are you not capricious, sir?"

"To women who please me only by their faces, I am the very devil when I find out they have neither souls nor hearts – when they open to me a perspective of flatness, triviality, and perhaps imbecility, coarseness, and ill-temper: but to the clear eye and eloquent tongue, to the soul made of fire, and the character that bends but does not break – at once supple and stable, tractable and consistent – I am ever tender and true."

"Had you ever experience of such a character, sir? Did you ever love such an one?"

"I love it now."

"But before me: if I, indeed, in any respect come up to your difficult standard?"

"I never met your likeness. Jane, you please me, and you master me – you seem to submit, and I like the sense of pliancy you impart; and while I am twining the soft, silken skein round my finger, it sends a thrill up my arm to my heart. I am influenced – conquered; and the influence is sweeter than I can express; and the conquest I undergo has a witchery beyond any triumph I can win. Why do you smile, Jane? What does that inexplicable, that uncanny turn of countenance mean?"

"I was thinking, sir (you will excuse the idea; it was involuntary), I was thinking of Hercules and Samson with their charmers –"

"You were, you little elfish –"

"Hush, sir! You don't talk very wisely just now; any more than those gentlemen acted very wisely. However, had they been married, they would no doubt by their severity as husbands have made up for their softness as suitors; and so will you, I fear. I wonder how you will answer me a year hence, should I ask a favour it does not suit your convenience or pleasure to grant."

"Ask me something now, Jane, – the least thing: I desire to be entreated –"

"Indeed I will, sir; I have my petition all ready."

"Speak! But if you look up and smile with that countenance, I shall swear concession before I know to what, and that will make a fool of me."

"Not at all, sir; I ask only this: don't send for the jewels, and don't crown me with roses: you might as well put a border of gold lace round that plain pocket handkerchief you have there."

"I might as well 'gild refined gold'. I know it: your request is granted then – for the time. I will remand the order I despatched to my banker. But you have not yet asked for anything; you have prayed a gift to be withdrawn: try again."

"Well then, sir, have the goodness to gratify my curiosity, which is much piqued on one point."

He looked disturbed. "What? What?" he said hastily. "Curiosity is a dangerous petition: it is well I have not taken a vow to accord every request –"

"But there can be no danger in complying with this, sir."

"Utter it, Jane: but I wish that instead of a mere inquiry into, perhaps, a secret, it was a wish for half my estate."

"Now, King Ahasuerus! What do I want with half your estate? Do you think I am a Jew-usurer, seeking good investment in land? I would much rather have all your confidence. You will not exclude me from your confidence if you admit me to your heart?"

"You are welcome to all my confidence that is worth having, Jane; but for God's sake, don't desire a useless burden! Don't long for poison – don't turn out a downright Eve on my hands!"

"Why not, sir? You have just been telling me how much you liked to be conquered, and how pleasant over-persuasion is to you. Don't you think I had better take advantage of the confession, and begin and coax and entreat – even cry and be sulky if necessary – for the sake of a mere essay of my power?"

"I dare you to any such experiment. Encroach, presume, and the game is up."

"Is it, sir? You soon give in. How stern you look now! Your eyebrows have become as thick as my finger, and your forehead resembles what, in some very astonishing poetry, I once saw styled, 'a blue-piled thunderloft.' **28** That will be your married look, sir, I suppose?"

"If that will be *your* married look, I, as a Christian, will soon give up the notion of consorting with a mere sprite or salamander. But what had you to ask, thing, – out with it?"

"There, you are less than civil now; and I like rudeness a great deal better than flattery. I had rather be a *thing* than an angel. This is what I have to ask, – Why did you take such pains to make me believe you wished to marry Miss Ingram?"

"Is that all? Thank God it is no worse!" And now he unknit his black brows; looked down, smiling at me, and stroked my hair, as if well pleased at seeing a danger averted. "I think I may confess," he continued, "even although I should make you a little indignant, Jane – and I have seen what a fire-spirit you can be when you are indignant. You glowed in the cool moonlight last night, when you mutinied against fate, and claimed your rank as my equal. Janet, by-the-bye, it was you who made me the offer."

"Of course I did. But to the point if you please, sir – Miss Ingram?"

"Well, I feigned courtship of Miss Ingram, because I wished to render you as madly in love with me as I was with you; and I knew jealousy would be the best ally I could call in for the furtherance of that end."

"Excellent! Now you are small – not one whit bigger than the end of my little finger. It was a burning shame and a scandalous disgrace to act in that way. Did you think nothing of Miss Ingram's feelings, sir?"

"Her feelings are concentrated in one – pride; and that needs humbling. Were you jealous, Jane?"

"Never mind, Mr. Rochester: it is in no way interesting to you to know that. Answer me truly once more. Do you think Miss Ingram will not suffer from your dishonest coquetry? Won't she feel forsaken and deserted?"

"Impossible! – When I told you how she, on the contrary, deserted me: the idea of my insolvency cooled, or rather extinguished, her flame in a moment."

"You have a curious, designing mind, Mr. Rochester. I am afraid your principles on some points are eccentric."

"My principles were never trained, Jane: they may have grown a little awry for want of attention."

"Once again, seriously; may I enjoy the great good that has been vouchsafed to me, without fearing that anyone else is suffering the bitter pain I myself felt a while ago?"

"That you may, my good little girl: there is not another being in the world has the same pure love for me as yourself – for I lay that pleasant unction to my soul, Jane, a belief in your affection."

I turned my lips to the hand that lay on my shoulder. I loved him very much – more than I could trust myself to say – more than words had power to express.

"Ask something more," he said presently; "it is my delight to be entreated, and to yield."

I was again ready with my request. "Communicate your intentions to Mrs. Fairfax, sir: she saw me with you last night in the hall, and she was shocked. Give her some explanation before I see her again. It pains me to be misjudged by so good a woman."

"Go to your room, and put on your bonnet," he replied. "I mean you to accompany me to Millcote this morning; and while you prepare for the drive, I will enlighten the old lady's understanding. Did she think, Janet, you had given the world for love, and considered it well lost?"

"I believe she thought I had forgotten my station, and yours, sir."

"Station! Station! – Your station is in my heart, and on the necks of those who would insult you, now or hereafter. – Go."

I was soon dressed; and when I heard Mr. Rochester quit Mrs. Fairfax's parlour, I hurried down to it. The old lady, had been reading her morning portion of Scripture – the Lesson for the day; her Bible lay open before her, and her spectacles were upon it. Her occupation, suspended by Mr. Rochester's announcement, seemed now forgotten: her eyes, fixed on the blank wall opposite, expressed the surprise of a quiet mind stirred by unwonted tidings. Seeing me, she roused herself: she made a sort of effort to smile, and framed a few words of congratulation; but the smile expired, and the sentence was abandoned unfinished. She put up her spectacles, shut the Bible, and pushed her chair back from the table.

"I feel so astonished," she began, "I hardly know what to say to you, Miss Eyre. I have surely not been dreaming, have I? Sometimes I half fall asleep when I am sitting alone and fancy things that have never happened. It has seemed to me more than once when I have been in a doze, that my dear husband, who died fifteen years since, has come in and sat down beside me; and that I have even heard him call me by my name, Alice, as he used to do. Now, can you tell me whether it is actually true that Mr. Rochester has asked you to marry him? Don't laugh at me. But I really thought he came in here five minutes ago, and said that in a month you would be his wife."

"He has said the same thing to me," I replied.

"He has! Do you believe him? Have you accepted him?"

"Yes."

She looked at me bewildered. "I could never have thought it. He is a proud man: all the Rochesters were proud: and his father, at least, liked money. He, too, has always been called careful. He means to marry you?"

"He tells me so."

She surveyed my whole person: in her eyes I read that they had there found no charm powerful enough to solve the enigma.

"It passes me!" she continued; "but no doubt, it is true since you say so. How it will answer, I cannot tell: I really don't know. Equality of position and fortune is often advisable in such cases; and there are twenty years of difference in your ages. He might almost be your father."

"No, indeed, Mrs. Fairfax!" exclaimed I, nettled; "he is nothing like my father! No one, who saw us together, would suppose it for an instant. Mr. Rochester looks as young, and is as young, as some men at five-and-twenty."

"Is it really for love he is going to marry you?" she asked.

I was so hurt by her coldness and scepticism, that the tears rose to my eyes.

"I am sorry to grieve you," pursued the widow; "but you are so young, and so little acquainted with men, I wished to put you on your guard. It is an old saying that 'all is not gold that glitters'; and in this case I do fear there will be something found to be different to what either you or I expect."

"Why? – Am I a monster?" I said: "is it impossible that Mr. Rochester should have a sincere affection for me?"

"No: you are very well; and much improved of late; and Mr. Rochester, I daresay, is fond of you. I have always noticed that you were a sort of pet of his. There are times when, for your sake, I have been a little uneasy at his marked preference, and have wished to put you on your guard: but I did not like to suggest even the possibility of wrong. I knew such an idea would shock, perhaps offend you; and you were so discreet, and so thoroughly modest and sensible, I hoped you might be trusted to protect yourself. Last night I cannot tell you what I suffered when I sought all over the house, and could find you nowhere, nor the master either; and then, at twelve o'clock, saw you come in with him."

"Well, never mind that now," I interrupted impatiently; "it is enough that all was right."

"I hope all will be right in the end," she said: "but believe me, you cannot be too careful. Try and keep Mr. Rochester at a distance: distrust yourself as well as him. Gentlemen in his station are not accustomed to marry their governesses."

I was growing truly irritated: happily, Adèle ran in.

"Let me go, – let me go to Millcote too!" she cried. "Mr. Rochester won't: though there is so much room in the new carriage. Beg him to let me go mademoiselle."

"That I will, Adèle;" and I hastened away with her, glad to quit my gloomy monitress. The carriage was ready: they were bringing it round to the front, and my master was pacing the pavement, Pilot following him backwards and forwards.

"Adèle may accompany us, may she not, sir?"

"I told her no. I'll have no brats! – I'll have only you."

"Do let her go, Mr. Rochester, if you please: it would be better."

"Not it: she will be a restraint."

He was quite peremptory, both in look and voice. The chill of Mrs. Fairfax's warnings, and the damp of her doubts were upon me: something of unsubstantiality and uncertainty had beset my hopes. I half lost the sense of power over him. I was about mechanically to obey him, without further remonstrance; but as he helped me into the carriage, he looked at my face.

"What is the matter?" he asked; "all the sunshine is gone. Do you really wish the bairn to go? Will it annoy you if she is left behind?"

"I would far rather she went, sir."

"Then off for your bonnet, and back like a flash of lightning!" cried he to Adèle.

She obeyed him with what speed she might.

"After all, a single morning's interruption will not matter much," said he, "when I mean shortly to claim you – your thoughts, conversation, and company – for life."

Adèle, when lifted in, commenced kissing me, by way of expressing her gratitude for my intercession: she was instantly stowed away into a corner on the other side of him. She then peeped round to where I sat; so stern a neighbour was too restrictive to him, in his present fractious mood, she dared whisper no observations, nor ask of him any information.

"Let her come to me," I entreated: "she will, perhaps, trouble you, sir: there is plenty of room on this side."

He handed her over as if she had been a lapdog. "I'll send her to school yet," he said, but now he was smiling.

Adèle heard him, and asked if she was to go to school "sans mademoiselle?"

"Yes," he replied, "absolutely sans mademoiselle; for I am to take mademoiselle to the moon, and there I shall seek a cave in one of the white valleys among the volcano-tops, and mademoiselle shall live with me there, and only me."

"She will have nothing to eat: you will starve her," observed Adèle.

"I shall gather manna for her morning and night: the plains and hillsides in the moon are bleached with manna, Adèle."

"She will want to warm herself: what will she do for a fire?"

"Fire rises out of the lunar mountains: when she is cold, I'll carry her up to a peak, and lay her down on the edge of a crater."

"Oh, qu'elle y sera mal – peu comfortable! And her clothes, they will wear out: how can she get new ones?"

Mr. Rochester professed to be puzzled. "Hem!" said he. "What would you do, Adèle? Cudgel your brains for an expedient. How would a white or a pink cloud answer for a gown, do you think? And one could cut a pretty enough scarf out of a rainbow."

"She is far better as she is," concluded Adèle, after musing some time: "besides, she would get tired of living with only you in the moon. If I were mademoiselle, I would never consent to go with you."

"She has consented: she has pledged her word."

"But you can't get her there; there is no road to the moon: it is all air; and neither you nor she can fly."

"Adèle, look at that field." We were now outside Thornfield gates, and bowling lightly along the smooth road to Millcote, where the dust was well laid by the thunderstorm, and, where the low hedges and lofty timber trees on each side glistened green and rain-refreshed.

"In that field, Adèle, I was walking late one evening about a fortnight since – the evening of the day you helped me to make hay in the orchard meadows; and, as I was tired with raking swaths, I sat down to rest me on a stile; and there I took out a little book and a pencil, and began to write about a misfortune that befell me long ago, and a wish I had for happy days to come: I was writing away very fast, though daylight was fading from the leaf, when something came up the path and stopped two yards off me. I looked at it. It was a little thing with a veil of gossamer on its head. I beckoned it to come near me; it stood soon at my knee. I never spoke to it, and it never spoke to me, in words; but I read its eyes, and it read mine; and our speechless colloquy was to this effect:

"It was a fairy, and come from Elf-land, it said; and its errand was to make me happy: I must go with it out of the common world to a lonely place – such as the moon, for instance – and it nodded its head towards her horn, rising over Hay-hill: it told me of the alabaster cave and silver vale where we might live. I said I should like to go; but reminded it, as you did me, that I had no wings to fly.

"'Oh', returned the fairy, 'that does not signify! Here is a talisman will remove all difficulties;' and she held out a pretty gold ring. 'Put it', she said, 'on the fourth finger of my left hand, and I am yours, and you are mine; and we shall leave earth, and make our own heaven yonder.' She nodded again at the moon. The ring, Adèle, is in my breeches-pocket, under the disguise of a sovereign: but I mean soon to change it to a ring again."

"But what has mademoiselle to do with it? I don't care for the fairy: you said it was mademoiselle you would take to the moon?"

"Mademoiselle is a fairy," he said, whispering mysteriously. Whereupon I told her not to mind his badinage; and she, on her part, evinced a fund of genuine French scepticism: denominating Mr. Rochester "un vrai menteur," and assuring him that she made no account whatever of his "contes de fée," and that "du reste, il n'y avait pas de fées, et quand même il y en avait:" she was sure they would never appear to him, nor ever give him rings, or offer to live with him in the moon.

The hour spent at Millcote was a somewhat harassing one to me. Mr. Rochester obliged me to go to a certain silk warehouse: there I was ordered to choose half a dozen dresses. I hated the business, I begged leave to defer it: no – it should be gone through with now. By dint of entreaties expressed in energetic whispers, I reduced the half-dozen to two: these however, he vowed he would select himself. With anxiety I watched his eye rove over the gay stores: he fixed on a rich silk of the most brilliant amethyst dye, and a superb pink satin. I told him in a new series of whispers, that he might as well buy me a gold gown and a silver bonnet at once: I should certainly never venture to wear his choice. With infinite difficulty, for he was stubborn as a stone, I persuaded him to make an exchange in favour of a sober black satin and pearl-grey silk. "It might pass for the present," he said; "but he would yet see me glittering like a parterre."

Glad was I to get him out of the silk warehouse, and then out of a jewellers shop: the more he bought me, the more my cheek burned with a sense of annoyance and degradation. As we re-entered the carriage, and I sat back feverish and fagged, I remembered what, in the hurry of events, dark and bright, I had wholly forgotten – the letter of my uncle, John Eyre, to Mrs. Reed: his intention to adopt me and make me his legatee. "It would, indeed, be a relief," I thought, "if I had ever so small an independency; I never can bear being dressed like a doll by Mr. Rochester, or sitting like a second Danae with the golden shower falling daily round me. I will write to Madeira the moment I get home, and tell my uncle John I am going to be married, and to whom: if I had but a prospect of one day bringing Mr. Rochester an accession of fortune, I could better endure to be kept by him now." And somewhat relieved by this idea (which I failed not to execute that day), I ventured once more to meet my master's and lover's eye, which most pertinaciously sought mine, though I averted both face and gaze. He smiled; and I thought his smile was such as a sultan might, in a blissful and fond moment, bestow on a slave his gold and gems had enriched: I crushed his hand, which was ever hunting mine, vigorously, and thrust it back to him red with the passionate pressure.

"You need not look in that way," I said; "if you do, I'll wear nothing but my old Lowood frocks to the end of the chapter. I'll be married in this lilac gingham: you may make a dressing-gown for yourself out of the pearl-grey silk, and an infinite series of waistcoats out of the black satin."

He chuckled; he rubbed his hands. "Oh, it is rich to see and hear her!" he exclaimed. "Is she original? Is she piquant? I would not exchange this one little English girl for the Grand Turk's whole seraglio, gazelle-eyes, houri forms, and all!"

The Eastern allusion bit me again. "I'll not stand you an inch in the stead of a seraglio," I said; "so don't consider me an equivalent for one. If you have a fancy for anything in that line, away with you, sir, to the bazaars of Stamboul without delay, and lay out in extensive slave-purchases some of that spare cash you seem at a loss to spend satisfactorily here."

"And what will you do, Janet, while I am bargaining for so many tons of flesh and such an assortment of black eyes?"

"I'll be preparing myself to go out as a missionary to preach liberty to them that are enslaved – your harem inmates amongst the rest. I'll get admitted there, and I'll stir up mutiny; and you, three-tailed bashaw as you are, sir, shall in a trice find yourself fettered amongst our hands: nor will I, for one, consent to cut your bonds till you have signed a charter, the most liberal that despot ever yet conferred."

"I would consent to be at your mercy, Jane."

"I would have no mercy, Mr. Rochester, if you supplicated for it with an eye like that. While you looked so, I should be certain that whatever charter you might grant under coercion, your first act, when released, would be to violate its conditions."

"Why, Jane, what would you have? I fear you will compel me to go through a private marriage ceremony, besides that performed at the altar. You will stipulate, I see, for peculiar terms – what will they be?"

"I only want an easy mind, sir; not crushed by crowded obligations. Do you remember what you said of Céline Varens? – of the diamonds, the cashmeres you gave her? I will not be your English Céline Varens. I shall continue to act as Adèle's governess; by that I shall earn my board and lodging, and thirty pounds a year besides. I'll furnish my own wardrobe out of that money, and you shall give me nothing but –"

"Well, but what?"

"Your regard; and if I give you mine in return, that debt will be quit."

"Well, for cool native impudence and pure innate pride, you haven't your equal," said he. We were now approaching Thornfield. "Will it please you to dine with me today?" he asked, as we re-entered the gates.

"No, thank you, sir."

"And what for, 'no, thank you?' if one may inquire."

"I never have dined with you, sir: and I see no reason why I should now: till –"

"Till what? You delight in half-phrases."

"Till I can't help it."

"Do you suppose I eat like an ogre or a ghoul, that you dread being the companion of my repast?"

"I have formed no supposition on the subject, sir; but I want to go on as usual for another month."

"You will give up your governessing slavery at once."

"Indeed, begging your pardon, sir, I shall not. I shall just go on with it as usual. I shall keep out of your way all day, as I have been accustomed to do: you may send for me in the evening, when you feel disposed to see me, and I'll come then; but at no other time."

"I want a smoke, Jane, or a pinch of snuff, to comfort me under all this, 'pour me donner une contenance', as Adèle would say; and unfortunately I have neither my cigar-case, nor my snuff-box. But listen – whisper. It is your time now, little tyrant, but it will be mine presently; and when once I have fairly seized you, to have and to hold, I'll just – figuratively speaking – attach you to a chain like this" (touching his watch-guard). "Yes, bonny wee thing, I'll wear you in my bosom, lest my jewel I should tyne."

He said this as he helped me to alight from the carriage, and while he afterwards lifted out Adèle, I entered the house, and made good my retreat upstairs.

He duly summoned me to his presence in the evening. I had prepared an occupation for him; for I was determined not to spend the whole time in a *tête-à-tête* conversation. I remembered his fine voice; I knew he liked to sing – good singers generally do. I was no vocalist myself, and, in his fastidious judgment, no musician, either; but I delighted in listening when the performance was good. No sooner had twilight, that hour of romance, began to lower her blue and starry banner over the lattice, than I rose, opened the piano, and entreated him, for the love of heaven, to give me a song. He said I was a capricious witch, and that he would rather sing another time; but I averred that no time was like the present.

"Did I like his voice?" he asked.

"Very much." I was not fond of pampering that susceptible vanity of his; but for once, and from motives of expediency, I would e'en soothe and stimulate it.

"Then, Jane, you must play the accompaniment."

"Very well, sir, I will try."

I did try, but was presently swept off the stool and denominated "a little bungler." Being pushed unceremoniously to one side – which was precisely what I wished – he usurped my place, and proceeded to accompany himself: for he could play as well as sing. I hied me to the window-recess. And while I sat there and looked out on the still trees and dim lawn, to a sweet air was sung in mellow tones the following strain:

> *"The truest love that ever heart*
> *Felt at its kindled core,*
> *Did through each vein, in quickened start,*
> *The tide of being pour.*
>
> *Her coming was my hope each day,*
> *Her parting was my pain;*
> *The chance that did her steps delay*
> *Was ice in every vein.*
>
> *I dreamed it would be nameless bliss,*
> *As I loved, loved to be;*
> *And to this object did I press*
> *As blind as eagerly.*
>
> *But wide as pathless was the space*
> *That lay our lives between,*
> *And dangerous as the foamy race*
> *Of ocean-surges green.*
>
> *And haunted as a robber-path*
> *Through wilderness or wood;*
> *For Might and Right, and Woe and Wrath,*
> *Between our spirits stood.*
>
> *I dangers dared; I hindrance scorned;*
> *I omens did defy:*
> *Whatever menaced, harassed, warned,*
> *I passed impetuous by.*
>
> *On sped my rainbow, fast as light;*
> *I flew as in a dream;*
> *For glorious rose upon my sight*
> *That child of Shower and Gleam.*

> *Still bright on clouds of suffering dim*
> *Shines that soft, solemn joy;*
> *Nor care I now, how dense and grim*
> *Disasters gather nigh.*
>
> *I care not in this moment sweet,*
> *Though all I have rushed o'er*
> *Should come on pinion, strong and fleet,*
> *Proclaiming vengeance sore:*
>
> *Though haughty Hate should strike me down,*
> *Right, bar approach to me,*
> *And grinding Might, with furious frown,*
> *Swear endless enmity.*
>
> *My love has placed her little hand*
> *With noble faith in mine,*
> *And vowed that wedlock's sacred band*
> *Our nature shall entwine.*
>
> *My love has sworn, with sealing kiss,*
> *With me to live – to die;*
> *I have at last my nameless bliss.*
> *As I love – loved am I!"*

He rose and came towards me, and I saw his face all kindled, and his full falcon-eye flashing, and tenderness and passion in every lineament. I quailed momentarily – then I rallied. Soft scene, daring demonstration, I would not have; and I stood in peril of both: a weapon of defence must be prepared – I whetted my tongue: as he reached me, I asked with asperity, "whom he was going to marry now?"

"That was a strange question to be put by his darling Jane."

"Indeed! I considered it a very natural and necessary one: he had talked of his future wife dying with him. What did he mean by such a pagan idea? *I* had no intention of dying with him – he might depend on that."

"Oh, all he longed, all he prayed for, was that I might live with him! Death was not for such as I."

"Indeed it was: I had as good a right to die when my time came as he had: but I should bide that time, and not be hurried away in a suttee."

"Would I forgive him for the selfish idea, and prove my pardon by a reconciling kiss?"

"No: I would rather be excused."

Here I heard myself apostrophised as a "hard little thing;" and it was added, "any other woman would have been melted to marrow at hearing such stanzas crooned in her praise."

I assured him I was naturally hard – very flinty, and that he would often find me so; and that, moreover, I was determined to show him divers rugged points in my character before the ensuing four weeks elapsed: he should know fully what sort of a bargain he had made, while there was yet time to rescind it.

"Would I be quiet and talk rationally?"

"I would be quiet if he liked, and as to talking rationally, I flattered myself I was doing that now."

He fretted, pished, and pshawed. "Very good," I thought; "you may fume and fidget as you please: but this is the best plan to pursue with you, I am certain. I like you more than I can say; but I'll not sink into a bathos of sentiment: and with this needle of repartee I'll keep you from the edge of the gulf too; and, moreover, maintain by its pungent aid that distance between you and myself most conducive to our real mutual advantage."

From less to more, I worked him up to considerable irritation; then, after he had retired, in dudgeon, quite to the other end of the room, I got up, and saying, "I wish you goodnight, sir," in my natural and wonted respectful manner, I slipped out by the side-door and got away.

The system thus entered on, I pursued during the whole season of probation; and with the best success. He was kept, to be sure, rather cross and crusty; but on the whole I could see he was excellently entertained, and that a lamb-like submission and turtle-dove sensibility, while fostering his despotism more, would have pleased his judgment, satisfied his common-sense, and even suited his taste less.

In other people's presence I was, as formerly, deferential and quiet; any other line of conduct being uncalled for: it was only in the evening conferences I thus thwarted and afflicted him. He continued to send for me punctually the moment the clock struck seven; though when I appeared before him now, he had no such honeyed terms as "love" and "darling" on his lips: the best words at my service were "provoking puppet," "malicious elf," "sprite," "changeling," etc. For caresses, too, I now got grimaces; for a pressure of the hand, a pinch on the arm; for a kiss on the cheek, a severe tweak of the ear. It was all right: at present I decidedly preferred these fierce favours to anything more tender. Mrs. Fairfax, I saw, approved me: her anxiety on my account vanished; therefore I was certain I did well. Meantime, Mr. Rochester affirmed I was wearing him to skin and bone, and threatened awful vengeance for my present conduct at some period fast coming. I laughed in my sleeve at his menaces. "I can keep you in reasonable check now," I reflected; "and I don't doubt to be able to do it hereafter: if one expedient loses its virtue, another must be devised."

Yet after all my task was not an easy one; often I would rather have pleased than teased him. My future husband was becoming to me my whole world; and more than the world: almost my hope of heaven. He stood between me and every thought of religion, as an eclipse intervenes between man and the broad sun. I could not, in those days, see God for His creature: of whom I had made an idol.

Chapter Twenty-Five

THE MONTH OF COURTSHIP had wasted: its very last hours were being numbered. There was no putting off the day that advanced – the bridal day; and all preparations for its arrival were complete. *I*, at least, had nothing more to do: there were my trunks, packed, locked, corded, ranged in a row along the wall of my little chamber; tomorrow, at this time, they would be far on their road to London: and so should I (D.V.), – or rather, not I, but one Jane Rochester, a person whom as yet I knew not. The cards of address alone remained to nail on: they lay, four little squares, in the drawer. Mr. Rochester had himself written the direction, "Mrs. Rochester, — Hotel, London," on each: I could not persuade myself to affix them, or to have them affixed. Mrs. Rochester! She did not exist: she would not be born till tomorrow, some time after eight o'clock a.m.; and I would wait to be assured she had come into the world alive before I assigned to her all that property. It was enough that in yonder closet, opposite my dressing-table, garments said to be hers had already displaced my black stuff Lowood frock and straw bonnet: for not to me appertained that suit of wedding raiment; the pearl-coloured robe, the vapoury veil pendent from the usurped portmanteau. I shut the closet to conceal the strange, wraith-like apparel it contained; which, at this evening hour – nine o'clock – gave out certainly a most ghostly shimmer through the shadow of my apartment. "I will leave you by yourself, white dream," I said. "I am feverish: I hear the wind blowing: I will go out of doors and feel it."

It was not only the hurry of preparation that made me feverish; not only the anticipation of the great change – the new life which was to commence tomorrow: both these circumstances had their share, doubtless, in producing that restless, excited mood which hurried me forth at this late hour into the darkening grounds: but a third cause influenced my mind more than they.

I had at heart a strange and anxious thought. Something had happened which I could not comprehend; no one knew of or had seen the event but myself: it had taken place the preceding night. Mr. Rochester that night was absent from home; nor was he yet returned: business had called him to a small estate of two or three farms he possessed thirty miles off – business it was requisite he should settle in person, previous to his meditated departure from England. I waited now his return; eager to disburthen my mind, and to seek of him the solution of the enigma that perplexed me. Stay till he comes, reader; and, when I disclose my secret to him, you shall share the confidence.

I sought the orchard, driven to its shelter by the wind, which all day had blown strong and full from the south, without, however, bringing a speck of rain. Instead of subsiding as night drew on, it seemed to augment its rush and deepen its roar: the trees blew steadfastly one way, never writhing round, and scarcely tossing back their boughs once in an hour; so continuous was the strain bending their branchy heads northward – the clouds drifted from pole to pole, fast following, mass on mass: no glimpse of blue sky had been visible that July day.

It was not without a certain wild pleasure I ran before the wind, delivering my trouble of mind to the measureless air-torrent thundering through space. Descending the laurel walk, I faced the wreck of the chestnut-tree; it stood up black and riven: the trunk, split down the centre, gasped ghastly. The cloven halves were not broken from each other, for the firm base and strong roots kept them unsundered below; though community of vitality was destroyed – the sap could flow no more: their great boughs on each side were dead, and next winter's tempests would be sure to fell one or both to earth: as yet, however, they might be said to form one tree – a ruin, but an entire ruin.

"You did right to hold fast to each other," I said: as if the monster-splinters were living things, and could hear me. "I think, scathed as you look, and charred and scorched, there must be a little sense of life in you yet, rising out of that adhesion at the faithful, honest roots: you will never have green leaves more – never more see birds making nests and singing idyls in your boughs; the time of pleasure and love is over with you: but you are not desolate: each of you has a comrade to sympathise with him in his decay." As I looked up at them, the moon appeared momentarily in that part of the sky which filled their fissure; her disk was blood-red and half overcast; she seemed to throw on me one bewildered, dreary glance, and buried herself again instantly in the deep drift of cloud. The wind fell, for a second, round Thornfield; but far away over wood and water, poured a wild, melancholy wail: it was sad to listen to, and I ran off again.

Here and there I strayed through the orchard, gathered up the apples with which the grass round the tree roots was thickly strewn; then I employed myself in dividing the ripe from the unripe; I carried them into the house and put them away in the store room. Then I repaired to the library to ascertain whether the fire was lit, for, though summer, I knew on such a gloomy evening Mr. Rochester would like to see a cheerful hearth when he came in: yes, the fire had been kindled some time, and burnt well. I placed his armchair by the chimney corner: I wheeled the table near it: I let down the curtain, and had the candles brought in ready for lighting. More restless than ever, when I had completed these arrangements I could not sit still, nor even remain in the house: a little time-piece in the room and the old clock in the hall simultaneously struck ten.

"How late it grows!" I said. "I will run down to the gates: it is moonlight at intervals; I can see a good way on the road. He may be coming now, and to meet him will save some minutes of suspense."

The wind roared high in the great trees which embowered the gates; but the road as far as I could see, to the right hand and the left, was all still and solitary: save for the shadows of clouds crossing it at intervals as the moon looked out, it was but a long pale line, unvaried by one moving speck.

A puerile tear dimmed my eye while I looked – a tear of disappointment and impatience; ashamed of it, I wiped it away. I lingered; the moon shut herself wholly within her chamber, and drew close her curtain of dense cloud: the night grew dark; rain came driving fast on the gale.

"I wish he would come! I wish he would come!" I exclaimed, seized with hypochondriac foreboding. I had expected his arrival before tea; now it was dark: what could keep him? Had an accident happened? The event of last night again recurred to me. I interpreted it as a warning of disaster. I feared my hopes were too bright to be realised; and I had enjoyed so much bliss lately that I imagined my fortune had passed its meridian, and must now decline.

"Well, I cannot return to the house," I thought; "I cannot sit by the fireside, while he is abroad in inclement weather: better tire my limbs than strain my heart; I will go forward and meet him."

I set out; I walked fast, but not far: ere I had measured a quarter of a mile, I heard the tramp of hoofs; a horseman came on, full gallop; a dog ran by his side. Away with evil presentiment! It was he: here he was, mounted on Mesrour, followed by Pilot. He saw me; for the moon had opened a blue field in the sky, and rode in it watery bright: he took his hat off, and waved it round his head. I now ran to meet him.

"There!" he exclaimed, as he stretched out his hand and bent from the saddle: "You can't do without me, that is evident. Step on my boot-toe; give me both hands: mount!"

I obeyed: joy made me agile: I sprang up before him. A hearty kissing I got for a welcome, and some boastful triumph, which I swallowed as well as I could. He checked himself in his exultation to demand, "But is there anything the matter, Janet, that you come to meet me at such an hour? Is there anything wrong?"

"No, but I thought you would never come. I could not bear to wait in the house for you, especially with this rain and wind."

"Rain and wind, indeed! Yes, you are dripping like a mermaid; pull my cloak round you: but I think you are feverish, Jane: both your cheek and hand are burning hot. I ask again, is there anything the matter?"

"Nothing now; I am neither afraid nor unhappy."

"Then you have been both?"

"Rather: but I'll tell you all about it by-and-bye, sir; and I daresay you will only laugh at me for my pains."

"I'll laugh at you heartily when tomorrow is past; till then I dare not: my prize is not certain. This is you, who have been as slippery as an eel this last month, and as thorny as a briar-rose? I could not lay a finger anywhere but I was pricked; and now I seem to have gathered up a stray lamb in my arms. You wandered out of the fold to seek your shepherd, did you, Jane?"

"I wanted you: but don't boast. Here we are at Thornfield: now let me get down."

He landed me on the pavement. As John took his horse, and he followed me into the hall, he told me to make haste and put something dry on, and then return to him in the library; and he stopped me, as I made for the staircase, to extort a promise that I would not be long: nor was I long; in five minutes I rejoined him. I found him at supper.

"Take a seat and bear me company, Jane: please God, it is the last meal but one you will eat at Thornfield Hall for a long time."

I sat down near him, but told him I could not eat. "Is it because you have the prospect of a journey before you, Jane? Is it the thoughts of going to London that takes away your appetite?"

"I cannot see my prospects clearly tonight, sir; and I hardly know what thoughts I have in my head. Everything in life seems unreal."

"Except me: I am substantial enough – touch me."

"You, sir, are the most phantom-like of all: you are a mere dream."

He held out his hand, laughing. "Is that a dream?" said he, placing it close to my eyes. He had a rounded, muscular, and vigorous hand, as well as a long, strong arm.

"Yes; though I touch it, it is a dream," said I, as I put it down from before my face. "Sir, have you finished supper?"

"Yes, Jane."

I rang the bell and ordered away the tray. When we were again alone, I stirred the fire, and then took a low seat at my master's knee.

"It is near midnight," I said.

"Yes: but remember, Jane, you promised to wake with me the night before my wedding."

"I did; and I will keep my promise, for an hour or two at least: I have no wish to go to bed."

"Are all your arrangements complete?"

"All, sir."

"And on my part likewise," he returned, "I have settled everything; and we shall leave Thornfield tomorrow, within half an hour after our return from church."

"Very well, sir."

"With what an extraordinary smile you uttered that word – 'very well', Jane! What a bright spot of colour you have on each cheek! And how strangely your eyes glitter! Are you well?"

"I believe I am."

"Believe! What is the matter? Tell me what you feel."

"I could not, sir: no words could tell you what I feel. I wish this present hour would never end: who knows with what fate the next may come charged?"

"This is hypochondria, Jane. You have been over-excited, or over-fatigued."

"Do you, sir, feel calm and happy?"

"Calm? – No: but happy – to the heart's core."

I looked up at him to read the signs of bliss in his face: it was ardent and flushed.

"Give me your confidence, Jane," he said: "relieve your mind of any weight that oppresses it, by imparting it to me. What do you fear? – that I shall not prove a good husband?"

"It is the idea farthest from my thoughts."

"Are you apprehensive of the new sphere you are about to enter? – of the new life into which you are passing?"

"No."

"You puzzle me, Jane: your look and tone of sorrowful audacity perplex and pain me. I want an explanation."

"Then, sir, listen. You were from home last night?"

"I was: I know that; and you hinted a while ago at something which had happened in my absence: – nothing, probably, of consequence; but, in short, it has disturbed you. Let me hear it. Mrs. Fairfax has said something, perhaps? Or you have overheard the servants talk? – your sensitive self-respect has been wounded?"

"No, sir." It struck twelve – I waited till the timepiece had concluded its silver chime, and the clock its hoarse, vibrating stroke, and then I proceeded.

"All day yesterday I was very busy, and very happy in my ceaseless bustle; for I am not, as you seem to think, troubled by any haunting fears about the new sphere, et cetera: I think it a glorious thing to have the hope of living with you, because I love you. No, sir, don't caress me now – let me talk undisturbed. Yesterday I trusted well in Providence, and believed that events were working together for your good and mine: it was a fine day, if you recollect – the calmness of the air and sky forbade apprehensions respecting your safety or comfort on your journey. I walked a little while on the pavement after tea, thinking of you; and I beheld you in imagination so near me, I scarcely missed your actual presence. I thought of the life that lay before me – *your* life, sir – an existence more expansive and stirring than my own: as much more so as the depths of the sea to which the brook runs are than the shallows of its own strait channel. I wondered why moralists call this world a dreary wilderness: for me it blossomed like a rose. Just at sunset, the air turned cold and the sky cloudy: I went in, Sophie called me upstairs to look at my wedding dress, which they had just brought; and under it in the box I found your present – the veil which, in your princely extravagance, you sent for from London: resolved, I suppose, since I would not have jewels, to cheat me into accepting something as costly. I smiled as I unfolded it, and devised how I would tease you about your aristocratic tastes, and your efforts to masque your plebeian bride in the attributes of a peeress. I thought how I would carry down to you the square of unembroidered blond I had myself prepared as a covering for my low-born head, and ask if that was not good enough for a woman who could bring her husband neither fortune, beauty, nor connections. I saw plainly how you would look; and heard your impetuous republican answers, and your haughty disavowal of any necessity on your part to augment your wealth, or elevate your standing, by marrying either a purse or a coronet."

"How well you read me, you witch!" interposed Mr. Rochester: "but what did you find in the veil besides its embroidery? Did you find poison, or a dagger, that you look so mournful now?"

"No, no, sir; besides the delicacy and richness of the fabric, I found nothing save Fairfax Rochester's pride; and that did not scare me, because I am used to the sight of the demon. But, sir, as it grew dark, the wind rose: it blew yesterday evening, not as it blows now – wild and high – but 'with a sullen, moaning sound' far more eerie. I wished you were at home. I came into this room, and the sight of the empty chair and fireless hearth chilled me. For some time after I went to bed, I could not sleep – a sense of anxious excitement distressed me. The gale still rising, seemed to my ear to muffle a mournful under-sound; whether in the house or abroad I could not at first tell, but it recurred, doubtful yet doleful at every lull; at last I made out it must be some dog howling at a distance. I was glad when it ceased. On sleeping, I continued in dreams the idea of a dark and gusty night. I continued also the wish to be with you, and experienced a strange, regretful consciousness of some barrier dividing us. During all my first sleep, I was following the windings of an unknown road; total obscurity environed me; rain pelted me; I was burdened with the charge of a little child: a very small creature, too young and feeble to walk, and which shivered in my cold arms, and wailed piteously in my ear. I thought, sir, that you were on the road a long way before me; and I strained every nerve to overtake you, and made effort on effort to utter your name and entreat you to stop – but my movements were fettered, and my voice still died away inarticulate; while you, I felt, withdrew farther and farther every moment."

"And these dreams weigh on your spirits now, Jane, when I am close to you? Little nervous subject! Forget visionary woe, and think only of real happiness! You say you love me, Janet: yes – I will not forget that; and you cannot deny it. *Those* words did not die inarticulate on your lips. I heard them clear and soft: a thought too solemn perhaps, but sweet as music – 'I think it is a glorious thing to have the hope of living with you, Edward, because I love you.' Do you love me, Jane? – repeat it."

"I do, sir – I do, with my whole heart."

"Well," he said, after some minutes' silence, "it is strange; but that sentence has penetrated my breast painfully. Why? I think because you said it with such an earnest, religious energy, and because your upward gaze at me now is the very sublime of faith, truth, and devotion: it is too much as if some spirit were near me. Look wicked, Jane: as you know well how to look: coin one of your wild, shy, provoking smiles; tell me you hate me – tease me, vex me; do anything but move me: I would rather be incensed than saddened."

"I will tease you and vex you to your heart's content, when I have finished my tale: but hear me to the end."

"I thought, Jane, you had told me all. I thought I had found the source of your melancholy in a dream."

I shook my head. "What! Is there more? But I will not believe it to be anything important. I warn you of incredulity beforehand. Go on."

The disquietude of his air, the somewhat apprehensive impatience of his manner, surprised me: but I proceeded.

"I dreamt another dream, sir: that Thornfield Hall was a dreary ruin, the retreat of bats and owls. I thought that of all the stately front nothing remained but a shell-like wall, very high and very fragile-looking. I wandered, on a moonlight night, through the grass-grown enclosure within: here I stumbled over a marble hearth, and there over a fallen fragment of cornice. Wrapped up in a shawl, I still carried the unknown little child: I might not lay it down anywhere, however tired were my arms – however much its weight impeded my progress, I must retain it. I heard the gallop of a horse at a distance on the road; I was sure it was you; and you were departing for many years and for a distant country. I climbed the thin wall with frantic perilous haste, eager to catch one glimpse of you from the top: the stones rolled from under my feet, the ivy branches I grasped gave way, the child clung round my neck in terror, and almost strangled me; at last I gained the summit. I saw you like a speck on a white track, lessening every moment. The blast blew so strong I could not stand. I sat down on the narrow ledge; I hushed the scared infant in my lap: you turned an angle of the road: I bent forward to take a last look; the wall crumbled; I was shaken; the child rolled from my knee, I lost my balance, fell, and woke."

"Now, Jane, that is all."

"All the preface, sir; the tale is yet to come. On waking, a gleam dazzled my eyes; I thought – Oh, it is daylight! But I was mistaken; it was only candlelight. Sophie, I supposed, had come in. There was a light in the dressing-table, and the door of the closet, where, before going to bed, I had hung my wedding dress and veil, stood open; I heard a rustling there. I asked, 'Sophie, what are you doing?' No one answered; but a form emerged from the closet; it took the light, held it aloft, and surveyed the garments pendent from the portmanteau. 'Sophie! Sophie!' I again cried: and still it was silent. I had risen up in bed, I bent forward: first surprise, then bewilderment, came over me; and then my blood crept cold through my veins. Mr. Rochester, this was not Sophie, it was not Leah, it was not Mrs. Fairfax: it was not – no, I was sure of it, and am still – it was not even that strange woman, Grace Poole."

"It must have been one of them," interrupted my master.

"No, sir, I solemnly assure you to the contrary. The shape standing before me had never crossed my eyes within the precincts of Thornfield Hall before; the height, the contour were new to me."

"Describe it, Jane."

"It seemed, sir, a woman, tall and large, with thick and dark hair hanging long down her back. I know not what dress she had on: it was white and straight; but whether gown, sheet, or shroud, I cannot tell."

"Did you see her face?"

"Not at first. But presently she took my veil from its place; she held it up, gazed at it long, and then she threw it over her own head, and turned to the mirror. At that moment I saw the reflection of the visage and features quite distinctly in the dark oblong glass."

"And how were they?"

"Fearful and ghastly to me – oh, sir, I never saw a face like it! It was a discoloured face – it was a savage face. I wish I could forget the roll of the red eyes and the fearful blackened inflation of the lineaments!"

"Ghosts are usually pale, Jane."

"This, sir, was purple: the lips were swelled and dark; the brow furrowed: the black eyebrows widely raised over the bloodshot eyes. Shall I tell you of what it reminded me?"

"You may."

"Of the foul German spectre – the Vampyre."

"Ah! – What did it do?"

"Sir, it removed my veil from its gaunt head, rent it in two parts, and flinging both on the floor, trampled on them."

"Afterwards?"

"It drew aside the window-curtain and looked out; perhaps it saw dawn approaching, for, taking the candle, it retreated to the door. Just at my bedside, the figure stopped: the fiery eyes glared upon me – she thrust up her candle close to my face, and extinguished it under my eyes. I was aware her lurid visage flamed over mine, and I lost consciousness: for the second time in my life – only the second time – I became insensible from terror."

"Who was with you when you revived?"

"No one, sir, but the broad day. I rose, bathed my head and face in water, drank a long draught; felt that though enfeebled I was not ill, and determined that to none but you would I impart this vision. Now, sir, tell me who and what that woman was?"

"The creature of an over-stimulated brain; that is certain. I must be careful of you, my treasure: nerves like yours were not made for rough handling."

"Sir, depend on it, my nerves were not in fault; the thing was real: the transaction actually took place."

"And your previous dreams, were they real too? Is Thornfield Hall a ruin? Am I severed from you by insuperable obstacles? Am I leaving you without a tear – without a kiss – without a word?"

"Not yet."

"Am I about to do it? Why, the day is already commenced which is to bind us indissolubly; and when we are once united, there shall be no recurrence of these mental terrors: I guarantee that."

"Mental terrors, sir! I wish I could believe them to be only such: I wish it more now than ever; since even you cannot explain to me the mystery of that awful visitant."

"And since I cannot do it, Jane, it must have been unreal."

"But, sir, when I said so to myself on rising this morning, and when I looked round the room to gather courage and comfort from the cheerful aspect of each familiar object in full daylight, there – on the carpet – I saw what gave the distinct lie to my hypothesis, – the veil, torn from top to bottom in two halves!"

I felt Mr. Rochester start and shudder; he hastily flung his arms round me. "Thank God!" he exclaimed, "that if anything malignant did come near you last night, it was only the veil that was harmed. Oh, to think what might have happened!"

He drew his breath short, and strained me so close to him, I could scarcely pant. After some minutes' silence, he continued, cheerily:

"Now, Janet, I'll explain to you all about it. It was half dream, half reality. A woman did, I doubt not, enter your room: and that woman was – must have been – Grace Poole. You call her a strange being yourself: from all you know, you have reason so to call her – what did she do to me? What to Mason? In a state between sleeping and waking, you noticed her entrance and her actions; but feverish, almost delirious as you were, you ascribed to her a goblin appearance different from her own: the long dishevelled hair, the swelled black face, the exaggerated stature, were figments of imagination; results of nightmare: the spiteful tearing of the veil was real: and it is like her. I see you would ask why I keep such a woman in my house: when we have been married a year and a day, I will tell you; but not now. Are you satisfied, Jane? Do you accept my solution of the mystery?"

I reflected, and in truth it appeared to me the only possible one: satisfied I was not, but to please him I endeavoured to appear so – relieved, I certainly did feel; so I answered him with a contented smile. And now, as it was long past one, I prepared to leave him.

"Does not Sophie sleep with Adèle in the nursery?" he asked, as I lit my candle.

"Yes, sir."

"And there is room enough in Adèle's little bed for you. You must share it with her tonight, Jane: it is no wonder that the incident you have related should make you nervous, and I would rather you did not sleep alone: promise me to go to the nursery."

"I shall be very glad to do so, sir."

"And fasten the door securely on the inside. Wake Sophie when you go upstairs, under pretence of requesting her to rouse you in good time tomorrow; for you must be dressed and have finished breakfast before eight. And now, no more sombre thoughts: chase dull care away, Janet. Don't you hear to what soft whispers the wind has fallen? And there is no more beating of rain against the window-panes: look here" (he lifted up the curtain) – "it is a lovely night!"

It was. Half heaven was pure and stainless: the clouds, now trooping before the wind, which had shifted to the west, were filing off eastward in long, silvered columns. The moon shone peacefully.

"Well," said Mr. Rochester, gazing inquiringly into my eyes, "how is my Janet now?"

"The night is serene, sir; and so am I."

"And you will not dream of separation and sorrow tonight; but of happy love and blissful union."

This prediction was but half fulfilled: I did not indeed dream of sorrow, but as little did I dream of joy; for I never slept at all. With little Adèle in my arms, I watched the slumber of childhood – so tranquil, so passionless, so innocent – and waited for the coming day: all my life was awake and astir in my frame: and as soon as the sun rose I rose too. I remember Adèle clung to me as I left her: I remember I kissed her as I loosened her little hands from my neck; and I cried over her with strange emotion, and quitted her because I feared my sobs would break her still sound repose. She seemed the emblem of my past life; and here I was now to array myself to meet, the dread, but adored, type of my unknown future day.

Chapter Twenty-Six

SOPHIE CAME AT SEVEN to dress me: she was very long indeed in accomplishing her task; so long that Mr. Rochester, grown, I suppose, impatient of my delay, sent up to ask why I did not come. She was just fastening my veil (the plain square of blond after all) to my hair with a brooch; I hurried from under her hands as soon as I could.

"Stop!" she cried in French. "Look at yourself in the mirror: you have not taken one peep."

So I turned at the door: I saw a robed and veiled figure, so unlike my usual self that it seemed almost the image of a stranger. "Jane!" called a voice, and I hastened down. I was received at the foot of the stairs by Mr. Rochester.

"Lingerer!" he said, "my brain is on fire with impatience, and you tarry so long!"

He took me into the dining room, surveyed me keenly all over, pronounced me "fair as a lily, and not only the pride of his life, but the desire of his eyes," and then telling me he would give me but ten minutes to eat some breakfast, he rang the bell. One of his lately hired servants, a footman, answered it.

"Is John getting the carriage ready?"

"Yes, sir."

"Is the luggage brought down?"

"They are bringing it down, sir."

"Go you to the church: see if Mr. Wood (the clergyman) and the clerk are there: return and tell me."

The church, as the reader knows, was but just beyond the gates; the footman soon returned.

"Mr. Wood is in the vestry, sir, putting on his surplice."

"And the carriage?"

"The horses are harnessing."

"We shall not want it to go to church; but it must be ready the moment we return: all the boxes and luggage arranged and strapped on, and the coachman in his seat."

"Yes, sir."

"Jane, are you ready?"

I rose. There were no groomsmen, no bridesmaids, no relatives to wait for or marshal: none but Mr. Rochester and I. Mrs. Fairfax stood in the hall as we passed. I would fain have spoken to her, but my hand was held by a grasp of iron: I was hurried along by a stride I could hardly follow; and to look at Mr. Rochester's face was to feel that not a second of delay would be tolerated for any purpose. I wonder what other bridegroom ever looked as he did – so bent up to a purpose, so grimly resolute: or who, under such steadfast brows, ever revealed such flaming and flashing eyes.

I know not whether the day was fair or foul; in descending the drive, I gazed neither on sky nor earth: my heart was with my eyes; and both seemed migrated into Mr. Rochester's frame. I wanted to see the invisible thing on which, as we went along, he appeared to fasten a glance fierce and fell. I wanted to feel the thoughts whose force he seemed breasting and resisting.

At the churchyard wicket he stopped: he discovered I was quite out of breath. "Am I cruel in my love?" he said. "Delay an instant: lean on me, Jane."

And now I can recall the picture of the grey old house of God rising calm before me, of a rook wheeling round the steeple, of a ruddy morning sky beyond. I remember something, too, of the green grave-mounds; and I have not forgotten, either, two figures of strangers straying amongst the low hillocks and reading the mementoes graven on the few mossy headstones. I noticed them, because, as they saw us, they passed round to the back of the church; and I doubted not they were going to enter by the side-aisle door and witness the ceremony. By Mr. Rochester they were not observed; he was earnestly looking at my face from which the blood had, I daresay, momentarily fled: for I felt my forehead dewy, and my cheeks and lips cold. When I rallied, which I soon did, he walked gently with me up the path to the porch.

We entered the quiet and humble temple; the priest waited in his white surplice at the lowly altar, the clerk beside him. All was still: two shadows only moved in a remote corner. My conjecture had been correct: the strangers had slipped in before us, and they now stood by the vault of the Rochesters, their backs towards us, viewing through the rails the old time-stained marble tomb, where a kneeling angel guarded the remains of Damer de Rochester, slain at Marston Moor in the time of the civil wars, and of Elizabeth, his wife.

Our place was taken at the communion rails. Hearing a cautious step behind me, I glanced over my shoulder: one of the strangers – a gentleman, evidently – was advancing up the chancel. The service began. The explanation of the intent of matrimony was gone through; and then the clergyman came a step further forward, and, bending slightly towards Mr. Rochester, went on.

"I require and charge you both (as ye will answer at the dreadful day of judgment, when the secrets of all hearts shall be disclosed), that if either of you know any impediment why ye may not lawfully be joined together in matrimony, ye do now confess it; for be ye well assured that so many as are coupled together otherwise than God's Word doth allow, are not joined together by God, neither is their matrimony lawful."

He paused, as the custom is. When is the pause after that sentence ever broken by reply? Not, perhaps, once in a hundred years. And the clergyman, who had not lifted his eyes from his book, and had held his breath but for a moment, was proceeding: his hand was already stretched towards Mr. Rochester, as his lips unclosed to ask, "Wilt thou have this woman for thy wedded wife?" – when a distinct and near voice said:

"The marriage cannot go on: I declare the existence of an impediment."

The clergyman looked up at the speaker and stood mute; the clerk did the same; Mr. Rochester moved slightly, as if an earthquake had rolled under his feet: taking a firmer footing, and not turning his head or eyes, he said, "Proceed."

Profound silence fell when he had uttered that word, with deep but low intonation. Presently Mr. Wood said:

"I cannot proceed without some investigation into what has been asserted, and evidence of its truth or falsehood."

"The ceremony is quite broken off," subjoined the voice behind us. "I am in a condition to prove my allegation: an insuperable impediment to this marriage exists."

Mr. Rochester heard, but heeded not: he stood stubborn and rigid, making no movement but to possess himself of my hand. What a hot and strong grasp he had! And how like quarried marble was his pale, firm, massive front at this moment! How his eye shone, still watchful, and yet wild beneath!

Mr. Wood seemed at a loss. "What is the nature of the impediment?" he asked. "Perhaps it may be got over – explained away?"

"Hardly," was the answer. "I have called it insuperable, and I speak advisedly."

The speaker came forward and leaned on the rails. He continued, uttering each word distinctly, calmly, steadily, but not loudly:

"It simply consists in the existence of a previous marriage. Mr. Rochester has a wife now living."

My nerves vibrated to those low-spoken words as they had never vibrated to thunder – my blood felt their subtle violence as it had never felt frost or fire; but I was collected, and in no danger of swooning. I looked at Mr. Rochester: I made him look at me. His whole face was colourless rock: his eye was both spark and flint. He disavowed nothing: he seemed as if he would defy all things. Without speaking, without smiling, without seeming to recognise in me a human being, he only twined my waist with his arm and riveted me to his side.

"Who are you?" he asked of the intruder.

"My name is Briggs, a solicitor of — Street, London."

"And you would thrust on me a wife?"

"I would remind you of your lady's existence, sir, which the law recognises, if you do not."

"Favour me with an account of her – with her name, her parentage, her place of abode."

"Certainly." Mr. Briggs calmly took a paper from his pocket, and read out in a sort of official, nasal voice:

"'I affirm and can prove that on the 20th of October A.D. — (a date of fifteen years back), Edward Fairfax Rochester, of Thornfield Hall, in the county of —, and of Ferndean Manor, in —shire, England, was married to my sister, Bertha Antoinetta Mason, daughter of Jonas Mason, merchant, and of Antoinetta his wife, a Creole, at — church, Spanish Town, Jamaica. The record of the marriage will be found in the register of that church – a copy of it is now in my possession. Signed, Richard Mason.'"

"That – if a genuine document – may prove I have been married, but it does not prove that the woman mentioned therein as my wife is still living."

"She was living three months ago," returned the lawyer.

"How do you know?"

"I have a witness to the fact, whose testimony even you, sir, will scarcely controvert."

"Produce him – or go to hell."

"I will produce him first – he is on the spot. Mr. Mason, have the goodness to step forward."

Mr. Rochester, on hearing the name, set his teeth; he experienced, too, a sort of strong convulsive quiver; near to him as I was, I felt the spasmodic movement of fury or despair run through his frame. The second stranger, who had hitherto lingered in the background, now drew near; a pale face looked over the solicitor's shoulder – yes, it was Mason himself. Mr. Rochester turned and glared at him. His eye, as I have often said, was a black eye: it had now a tawny, nay, a bloody light in its gloom; and his face flushed – olive cheek and hueless forehead received a glow as from spreading, ascending heart-fire: and he stirred, lifted his strong arm – he could have struck Mason, dashed him on the church-floor, shocked by ruthless blow the breath from his body – but Mason shrank away, and cried faintly, "Good God!" Contempt fell cool on Mr. Rochester – his passion died as if a blight had shrivelled it up: he only asked – "What have *you* to say?"

An inaudible reply escaped Mason's white lips.

"The devil is in it if you cannot answer distinctly. I again demand, what have you to say?"

"Sir – sir," interrupted the clergyman, "do not forget you are in a sacred place." Then addressing Mason, he inquired gently, "Are you aware, sir, whether or not this gentleman's wife is still living?"

"Courage," urged the lawyer, – "speak out."

"She is now living at Thornfield Hall," said Mason, in more articulate tones: "I saw her there last April. I am her brother."

"At Thornfield Hall!" ejaculated the clergyman. "Impossible! I am an old resident in this neighbourhood, sir, and I never heard of a Mrs. Rochester at Thornfield Hall."

I saw a grim smile contort Mr. Rochester's lips, and he muttered:

"No, by God! I took care that none should hear of it – or of her under that name." He mused – for ten minutes he held counsel with himself: he formed his resolve, and announced it:

"Enough! All shall bolt out at once, like the bullet from the barrel. Wood, close your book and take off your surplice; John Green (to the clerk), leave the church: there will be no wedding today." The man obeyed.

Mr. Rochester continued, hardily and recklessly: "Bigamy is an ugly word! – I meant, however, to be a bigamist; but fate has out-manoeuvred me, or Providence has checked me, – perhaps the last. I am little better than a devil at this moment; and, as my pastor there would tell me, deserve no doubt the sternest judgments of God, even to the quenchless fire and deathless worm. Gentlemen, my plan is broken up: – what this lawyer and his client say is true: I have been married, and the woman to whom I was married lives! You say you never heard of a Mrs. Rochester at the house up yonder, Wood; but I daresay you have many a time inclined your ear to gossip about the mysterious lunatic kept there under watch and ward. Some have whispered to you that she is my bastard half-sister: some, my cast-off mistress. I now inform you that she is my wife, whom I married fifteen years ago, – Bertha Mason by name; sister of this resolute personage, who is now, with his quivering limbs and white cheeks, showing you what a stout heart men may bear. Cheer up, Dick! – Never fear me! – I'd almost as soon strike a woman as you. Bertha Mason is mad; and she came of a mad family; idiots and maniacs through three generations! Her mother, the Creole, was both a madwoman and a drunkard! – As I found out after I had wed the daughter: for they were silent on family secrets before. Bertha, like a dutiful child, copied her parent in both points. I had a charming partner – pure, wise, modest: you can fancy I was a happy man. I went through rich scenes! Oh! My experience has been heavenly, if you only knew it! But I owe you no further explanation. Briggs, Wood, Mason, I invite you all to come up to the house and visit Mrs. Poole's patient, and *my wife*! You shall see what sort of a being I was cheated into espousing, and judge whether or not I had a right to break the compact, and seek sympathy with something at least human. This girl," he continued, looking at me, "knew no more than you, Wood, of the disgusting secret: she thought all was fair and legal and never dreamt she was going to be entrapped into a feigned union with a defrauded wretch, already bound to a bad, mad, and embruted partner! Come all of you – follow!"

Still holding me fast, he left the church: the three gentlemen came after. At the front door of the hall we found the carriage.

"Take it back to the coach-house, John," said Mr. Rochester coolly; "it will not be wanted today."

At our entrance, Mrs. Fairfax, Adèle, Sophie, Leah, advanced to meet and greet us.

"To the right-about – every soul!" cried the master; "away with your congratulations! Who wants them? Not I! – they are fifteen years too late!"

He passed on and ascended the stairs, still holding my hand, and still beckoning the gentlemen to follow him, which they did. We mounted the first staircase, passed up the gallery, proceeded to the third storey: the low, black door, opened by Mr. Rochester's master-key, admitted us to the tapestried room, with its great bed and its pictorial cabinet.

"You know this place, Mason," said our guide; "she bit and stabbed you here."

He lifted the hangings from the wall, uncovering the second door: this, too, he opened. In a room without a window, there burnt a fire guarded by a high and strong fender, and a lamp suspended from the ceiling by a chain. Grace Poole bent over the fire, apparently cooking something in a saucepan. In the deep shade, at the farther end of the room, a figure ran backwards and forwards. What it was, whether beast or human being, one could not, at first sight, tell: it grovelled, seemingly, on all fours; it snatched and growled like some strange wild animal: but it was covered with clothing, and a quantity of dark, grizzled hair, wild as a mane, hid its head and face.

"Good-morrow, Mrs. Poole!" said Mr. Rochester. "How are you? And how is your charge today?"

"We're tolerable, sir, I thank you," replied Grace, lifting the boiling mess carefully on to the hob: "rather snappish, but not 'rageous."

A fierce cry seemed to give the lie to her favourable report: the clothed hyena rose up, and stood tall on its hind-feet.

"Ah! Sir, she sees you!" exclaimed Grace: "you'd better not stay."

"Only a few moments, Grace: you must allow me a few moments."

"Take care then, sir! – for God's sake, take care!"

The maniac bellowed: she parted her shaggy locks from her visage, and gazed wildly at her visitors. I recognised well that purple face, – those bloated features. Mrs. Poole advanced.

"Keep out of the way," said Mr. Rochester, thrusting her aside: "she has no knife now, I suppose, and I'm on my guard."

"One never knows what she has, sir: she is so cunning: it is not in mortal discretion to fathom her craft."

"We had better leave her," whispered Mason.

"Go to the devil!" was his brother-in-law's recommendation.

"'Ware!" cried Grace. The three gentlemen retreated simultaneously. Mr. Rochester flung me behind him: the lunatic sprang and grappled his throat viciously, and laid her teeth to his cheek: they struggled. She was a big woman, in stature almost equalling her husband, and corpulent besides: she showed virile force in the contest – more than once she almost throttled him, athletic as he was. He could have settled her with a well-planted blow; but he would not strike: he would only wrestle. At last he mastered her arms; Grace Poole gave him a cord, and he pinioned them behind her: with more rope, which was at hand, he bound her to a chair. The operation was performed amidst the fiercest yells and the most convulsive plunges. Mr. Rochester then turned to the spectators: he looked at them with a smile both acrid and desolate.

"That is *my wife*," said he. "Such is the sole conjugal embrace I am ever to know – such are the endearments which are to solace my leisure hours! And *this* is what I wished to have" (laying his hand on my shoulder): "this young girl, who stands so grave and quiet at the mouth of hell, looking collectedly at the gambols of a demon, I wanted her just as a change after that fierce ragout. Wood and Briggs, look at the difference! Compare these clear eyes with the red balls yonder – this face with that mask – this form with that bulk; then judge me, priest of the gospel and man of the law, and remember with what judgment ye judge ye shall be judged! Off with you now. I must shut up my prize."

We all withdrew. Mr. Rochester stayed a moment behind us, to give some further order to Grace Poole. The solicitor addressed me as he descended the stair.

"You, madam," said he, "are cleared from all blame: your uncle will be glad to hear it – if, indeed, he should be still living – when Mr. Mason returns to Madeira."

"My uncle! What of him? Do you know him?"

"Mr. Mason does. Mr. Eyre has been the Funchal correspondent of his house for some years. When your uncle received your letter intimating the contemplated union between yourself and Mr. Rochester, Mr. Mason, who was staying at Madeira to recruit his health, on his way back to Jamaica, happened to be with him. Mr. Eyre mentioned the intelligence; for he knew that my client here was acquainted with a gentleman of the name of Rochester. Mr. Mason, astonished and distressed as you may suppose, revealed the real state of matters. Your uncle, I am sorry to say, is now on a sick bed; from which, considering the nature of his disease – decline – and the stage it has reached, it is unlikely he will ever rise. He could not then hasten to England himself, to extricate you from the snare into which you had fallen, but he implored Mr. Mason to lose no time in taking steps to prevent the false marriage. He referred him to me for assistance. I used all despatch, and am thankful I was not too late: as you, doubtless, must be also. Were I not morally certain that your uncle will be dead ere you reach Madeira, I would advise you to accompany Mr. Mason back; but as it is, I think you had better remain in England till you can hear further, either from or of Mr. Eyre. Have we anything else to stay for?" he inquired of Mr. Mason.

"No, no – let us be gone," was the anxious reply; and without waiting to take leave of Mr. Rochester, they made their exit at the hall door. The clergyman stayed to exchange a few sentences, either of admonition or reproof, with his haughty parishioner; this duty done, he too departed.

I heard him go as I stood at the half-open door of my own room, to which I had now withdrawn. The house cleared, I shut myself in, fastened the bolt that none might intrude, and proceeded – not to weep, not to mourn, I was yet too calm for that, but – mechanically to take off the wedding dress, and replace it by the stuff gown I had worn yesterday, as I thought, for the last time. I then sat down: I felt weak and tired. I leaned my arms on a table, and my head dropped on them. And now I thought: till now I had only heard, seen, moved – followed up and down where I was led or dragged – watched event rush on event, disclosure open beyond disclosure: but *now, I thought*.

The morning had been a quiet morning enough – all except the brief scene with the lunatic: the transaction in the church had not been noisy; there was no explosion of passion, no loud altercation, no dispute, no defiance or challenge, no tears, no sobs: a few words had been spoken, a calmly pronounced objection to the marriage made; some stern, short questions put by Mr. Rochester; answers, explanations given, evidence adduced; an open admission of the truth had been uttered by my master; then the living proof had been seen; the intruders were gone, and all was over.

I was in my own room as usual – just myself, without obvious change: nothing had smitten me, or scathed me, or maimed me. And yet where was the Jane Eyre of yesterday? – Where was her life? – Where were her prospects?

Jane Eyre, who had been an ardent, expectant woman – almost a bride, was a cold, solitary girl again: her life was pale; her prospects were desolate. A Christmas frost had come at midsummer; a white December storm had whirled over June; ice glazed the ripe apples, drifts crushed the blowing roses; on hayfield and cornfield lay a frozen shroud: lanes which last night blushed full of flowers, today were pathless with untrodden snow; and the woods, which twelve hours since waved leafy and flagrant as groves between the tropics, now spread, waste, wild, and white as pine-forests in wintry Norway. My hopes were all dead – struck with a subtle doom, such as, in one night, fell on all the first-born in the land of Egypt. I looked on my cherished wishes, yesterday so blooming and glowing; they lay stark, chill, livid corpses that could never revive. I looked at my love: that feeling which was my master's – which he had created; it shivered in my heart, like a suffering child in a cold cradle; sickness and anguish had seized it; it could not seek Mr. Rochester's arms – it could not derive warmth from his breast. Oh, never more could it turn to him; for faith was blighted – confidence destroyed! Mr. Rochester was not to me what he had been; for he was not what I had thought him. I would not ascribe vice to him; I would not say he had betrayed me; but the attribute of stainless truth was gone from his idea, and from his presence I must go: *that* I perceived well. When – how – whither, I could not yet discern; but he himself, I doubted not, would hurry me from Thornfield. Real affection, it seemed, he could not have for me; it had been only fitful passion: that was balked; he would want me no more. I should fear even to cross his path now: my view must be hateful to him. Oh, how blind had been my eyes! How weak my conduct!

My eyes were covered and closed: eddying darkness seemed to swim round me, and reflection came in as black and confused a flow. Self-abandoned, relaxed, and effortless, I seemed to have laid me down in the dried-up bed of a great river; I heard a flood loosened in remote mountains, and felt the torrent come: to rise I had no will, to flee I had no strength. I lay faint, longing to be dead. One idea only still throbbed life-like within me – a remembrance of God: it begot an unuttered prayer: these words went wandering up and down in my rayless mind, as something that should be whispered, but no energy was found to express them:

"Be not far from me, for trouble is near: there is none to help."

It was near: and as I had lifted no petition to Heaven to avert it – as I had neither joined my hands, nor bent my knees, nor moved my lips – it came: in full heavy swing the torrent poured over me. The whole consciousness of my life lorn, my love lost, my hope quenched, my faith death-struck, swayed full and mighty above me in one sullen mass. That bitter hour cannot be described: in truth, "the waters came into my soul; I sank in deep mire: I felt no standing; I came into deep waters; the floods overflowed me."

Volume Three

Chapter Twenty-Seven

SOME TIME IN the afternoon I raised my head, and looking round and seeing the western sun gilding the sign of its decline on the wall, I asked, "What am I to do?"

But the answer my mind gave – "Leave Thornfield at once" – was so prompt, so dread, that I stopped my ears. I said I could not bear such words now. "That I am not Edward Rochester's bride is the least part of my woe," I alleged: "that I have wakened out of most glorious dreams, and found them all void and vain, is a horror I could bear and master; but that I must leave him decidedly, instantly, entirely, is intolerable. I cannot do it."

But, then, a voice within me averred that I could do it and foretold that I should do it. I wrestled with my own resolution: I wanted to be weak that I might avoid the awful passage of further suffering I saw laid out for me; and Conscience, turned tyrant, held Passion by the throat, told her tauntingly, she had yet but dipped her dainty foot in the slough, and swore that with that arm of iron he would thrust her down to unsounded depths of agony.

"Let me be torn away," then I cried. "Let another help me!"

"No; you shall tear yourself away, none shall help you: you shall yourself pluck out your right eye; yourself cut off your right hand: your heart shall be the victim, and you the priest to transfix it."

I rose up suddenly, terror-struck at the solitude which so ruthless a judge haunted, – at the silence which so awful a voice filled. My head swam as I stood erect. I perceived that I was sickening from excitement and inanition; neither meat nor drink had passed my lips that day, for I had taken no breakfast. And, with a strange pang, I now reflected that, long as I had been shut up here, no message had been sent to ask how I was, or to invite me to come down: not even little Adèle had tapped at the door; not even Mrs. Fairfax had sought me. "Friends always forget those whom fortune forsakes," I murmured, as I undrew the bolt and passed out. I stumbled over an obstacle: my head was still dizzy, my sight was dim, and my limbs were feeble. I could not soon recover myself. I fell, but not on to the ground: an outstretched arm caught me. I looked up – I was supported by Mr. Rochester, who sat in a chair across my chamber threshold.

"You come out at last," he said. "Well, I have been waiting for you long, and listening: yet not one movement have I heard, nor one sob: five minutes more of that death-like hush, and I should have forced the lock like a burglar. So you shun me? – you shut yourself up and grieve alone! I would rather you had come and upbraided me with vehemence. You are passionate. I expected a scene of some kind. I was prepared for the hot rain of tears; only I wanted them to be shed on my breast: now a senseless floor has received them, or your drenched handkerchief. But I err: you have not wept at all! I see a white cheek and a faded eye, but no trace of tears. I suppose, then, your heart has been weeping blood?"

"Well, Jane! Not a word of reproach? Nothing bitter – nothing poignant? Nothing to cut a feeling or sting a passion? You sit quietly where I have placed you, and regard me with a weary, passive look."

"Jane, I never meant to wound you thus. If the man who had but one little ewe lamb that was dear to him as a daughter, that ate of his bread and drank of his cup, and lay in his bosom, had by some mistake slaughtered it at the shambles, he would not have rued his bloody blunder more than I now rue mine. Will you ever forgive me?"

Reader, I forgave him at the moment and on the spot. There was such deep remorse in his eye, such true pity in his tone, such manly energy in his manner; and besides, there was such unchanged love in his whole look and mien – I forgave him all: yet not in words, not outwardly; only at my heart's core.

"You know I am a scoundrel, Jane?" ere long he inquired wistfully – wondering, I suppose, at my continued silence and tameness, the result rather of weakness than of will.

"Yes, sir."

"Then tell me so roundly and sharply – don't spare me."

"I cannot: I am tired and sick. I want some water." He heaved a sort of shuddering sigh, and taking me in his arms, carried me downstairs. At first I did not know to what room he had borne me; all was cloudy to my glazed sight: presently I felt the reviving warmth of a fire; for, summer as it was, I had become icy cold in my chamber. He put wine to my lips; I tasted it and revived; then I ate something he offered me, and was soon myself. I was in the library – sitting in his chair

– he was quite near. "If I could go out of life now, without too sharp a pang, it would be well for me," I thought; "then I should not have to make the effort of cracking my heart-strings in rending them from among Mr. Rochester's. I must leave him, it appears. I do not want to leave him – I cannot leave him."

"How are you now, Jane?"

"Much better, sir; I shall be well soon."

"Taste the wine again, Jane."

I obeyed him; then he put the glass on the table, stood before me, and looked at me attentively. Suddenly he turned away, with an inarticulate exclamation, full of passionate emotion of some kind; he walked fast through the room and came back; he stooped towards me as if to kiss me; but I remembered caresses were now forbidden. I turned my face away and put his aside.

"What! – How is this?" he exclaimed hastily. "Oh, I know! You won't kiss the husband of Bertha Mason? You consider my arms filled and my embraces appropriated?"

"At any rate, there is neither room nor claim for me, sir."

"Why, Jane? I will spare you the trouble of much talking; I will answer for you – Because I have a wife already, you would reply. – I guess rightly?"

"Yes."

"If you think so, you must have a strange opinion of me; you must regard me as a plotting profligate – a base and low rake who has been simulating disinterested love in order to draw you into a snare deliberately laid, and strip you of honour and rob you of self-respect. What do you say to that? I see you can say nothing in the first place, you are faint still, and have enough to do to draw your breath; in the second place, you cannot yet accustom yourself to accuse and revile me, and besides, the flood-gates of tears are opened, and they would rush out if you spoke much; and you have no desire to expostulate, to upbraid, to make a scene: you are thinking how *to act* – *talking* you consider is of no use. I know you – I am on my guard."

"Sir, I do not wish to act against you," I said; and my unsteady voice warned me to curtail my sentence.

"Not in your sense of the word, but in mine you are scheming to destroy me. You have as good as said that I am a married man – as a married man you will shun me, keep out of my way: just now you have refused to kiss me. You intend to make yourself a complete stranger to me: to live under this roof only as Adèle's governess; if ever I say a friendly word to you, if ever a friendly feeling inclines you again to me, you will say, – 'That man had nearly made me his mistress: I must be ice and rock to him;' and ice and rock you will accordingly become."

I cleared and steadied my voice to reply: "All is changed about me, sir; I must change too – there is no doubt of that; and to avoid fluctuations of feeling, and continual combats with recollections and associations, there is only one way – Adèle must have a new governess, sir."

"Oh, Adèle will go to school – I have settled that already; nor do I mean to torment you with the hideous associations and recollections of Thornfield Hall – this accursed place – this tent of Achan – this insolent vault, offering the ghastliness of living death to the light of the open sky – this narrow stone hell, with its one real fiend, worse than a legion of such as we imagine. Jane, you shall not stay here, nor will I. I was wrong ever to bring you to Thornfield Hall, knowing as I did how it was haunted. I charged them to conceal from you, before I ever saw you, all knowledge of the curse of the place; merely because I feared Adèle never would have a governess to stay if she knew with what inmate she was housed, and my plans would not permit me to remove the maniac elsewhere – though I possess an old house, Ferndean Manor, even more retired and hidden than this, where I could have lodged her safely enough, had not a scruple about the unhealthiness of the situation, in the heart of a wood, made my conscience recoil from the arrangement. Probably those damp walls would soon have eased me of her charge: but to each villain his own vice; and mine is not a tendency to indirect assassination, even of what I most hate.

"Concealing the mad woman's neighbourhood from you, however, was something like covering a child with a cloak and laying it down near a upas-tree: that demon's vicinage is poisoned, and always was. But I'll shut up Thornfield Hall: I'll nail up the front door and board the lower windows: I'll give Mrs. Poole two hundred a year to live here with *my wife*, as you term that fearful hag: Grace will do much for money, and she shall have her son, the keeper at Grimsby Retreat, to bear her company and be at hand to give her aid in the paroxysms, when *my wife* is prompted by her familiar to burn people in their beds at night, to stab them, to bite their flesh from their bones, and so on –"

"Sir," I interrupted him, "you are inexorable for that unfortunate lady: you speak of her with hate – with vindictive antipathy. It is cruel – she cannot help being mad."

"Jane, my little darling (so I will call you, for so you are), you don't know what you are talking about; you misjudge me again: it is not because she is mad I hate her. If you were mad, do you think I should hate you?"

"I do indeed, sir."

"Then you are mistaken, and you know nothing about me, and nothing about the sort of love of which I am capable. Every atom of your flesh is as dear to me as my own: in pain and sickness it would still be dear. Your mind is my treasure, and if it were broken, it would be my treasure still: if you raved, my arms should confine you, and not a strait waistcoat – your grasp, even in fury, would have a charm for me: if you flew at me as wildly as that woman did this morning, I should receive you in an embrace, at least as fond as it would be restrictive. I should not shrink from you with disgust as I did from her: in your quiet moments you should have no watcher and no nurse but me; and I could hang over you with untiring tenderness, though you gave me no smile in return; and never weary of gazing into your eyes, though they had no longer a ray of recognition for me. – But why do I follow that train of ideas? I was talking of removing you from Thornfield. All, you know, is prepared for prompt departure: tomorrow you shall go. I only ask you to endure one more night under this roof, Jane; and then, farewell to its miseries and terrors for ever! I have a place to repair to, which will be a secure sanctuary from hateful reminiscences, from unwelcome intrusion – even from falsehood and slander."

"And take Adèle with you, sir," I interrupted; "she will be a companion for you."

"What do you mean, Jane? I told you I would send Adèle to school; and what do I want with a child for a companion, and not my own child, – a French dancer's bastard? Why do you importune me about her! I say, why do you assign Adèle to me for a companion?"

"You spoke of a retirement, sir; and retirement and solitude are dull: too dull for you."

"Solitude! Solitude!" he reiterated with irritation. "I see I must come to an explanation. I don't know what sphynx-like expression is forming in your countenance. You are to share my solitude. Do you understand?"

I shook my head: it required a degree of courage, excited as he was becoming, even to risk that mute sign of dissent. He had been walking fast about the room, and he stopped, as if suddenly rooted to one spot. He looked at me long and hard: I turned my eyes from him, fixed them on the fire, and tried to assume and maintain a quiet, collected aspect.

"Now for the hitch in Jane's character," he said at last, speaking more calmly than from his look I had expected him to speak. "The reel of silk has run smoothly enough so far; but I always knew there would come a knot and a puzzle: here it is. Now for vexation, and exasperation, and endless trouble! By God! I long to exert a fraction of Samson's strength, and break the entanglement like tow!"

He recommenced his walk, but soon again stopped, and this time just before me.

"Jane! Will you hear reason?" (He stooped and approached his lips to my ear); "because, if you won't, I'll try violence." His voice was hoarse; his look that of a man who is just about to burst an insufferable bond and plunge headlong into wild license. I saw that in another moment, and with one impetus of frenzy more, I should be able to do nothing with him. The present – the passing second of time – was all I had in which to control and restrain him – a movement of repulsion, flight, fear would have sealed my doom, – and his. But I was not afraid: not in the least. I felt an inward power; a sense of influence, which supported me. The crisis was perilous; but not without its charm: such as the Indian, perhaps, feels when he slips over the rapid in his canoe. I took hold of his clenched hand, loosened the contorted fingers, and said to him, soothingly:

"Sit down; I'll talk to you as long as you like, and hear all you have to say, whether reasonable or unreasonable."

He sat down: but he did not get leave to speak directly. I had been struggling with tears for some time: I had taken great pains to repress them, because I knew he would not like to see me weep. Now, however, I considered it well to let them flow as freely and as long as they liked. If the flood annoyed him, so much the better. So I gave way and cried heartily.

Soon I heard him earnestly entreating me to be composed. I said I could not while he was in such a passion.

"But I am not angry, Jane: I only love you too well; and you had steeled your little pale face with such a resolute, frozen look, I could not endure it. Hush, now, and wipe your eyes."

His softened voice announced that he was subdued; so I, in my turn, became calm. Now he made an effort to rest his head on my shoulder, but I would not permit it. Then he would draw me to him: no.

"Jane! Jane!" he said, in such an accent of bitter sadness it thrilled along every nerve I had; "you don't love me, then? It was only my station, and the rank of my wife, that you valued? Now that you think me disqualified to become your husband, you recoil from my touch as if I were some toad or ape."

These words cut me: yet what could I do or I say? I ought probably to have done or said nothing; but I was so tortured by a sense of remorse at thus hurting his feelings, I could not control the wish to drop balm where I had wounded.

"I *do* love you," I said, "more than ever: but I must not show or indulge the feeling: and this is the last time I must express it."

"The last time, Jane! What! Do you think you can live with me, and see me daily, and yet, if you still love me, be always cold and distant?"

"No, sir; that I am certain I could not; and therefore I see there is but one way: but you will be furious if I mention it."

"Oh, mention it! If I storm, you have the art of weeping."

"Mr. Rochester, I must leave you."

"For how long, Jane? For a few minutes, while you smooth your hair – which is somewhat dishevelled; and bathe your face – which looks feverish?"

"I must leave Adèle and Thornfield. I must part with you for my whole life: I must begin a new existence among strange faces and strange scenes."

"Of course: I told you you should. I pass over the madness about parting from me. You mean you must become a part of me. As to the new existence, it is all right: you shall yet be my wife: I am not married. You shall be Mrs. Rochester – both virtually and nominally. I shall keep only to you so long as you and I live. You shall go to a place I have in the south of France: a whitewashed villa on the shores of the Mediterranean. There you shall live a happy, and guarded, and most innocent life. Never fear that I wish to lure you into error – to make you my mistress. Why did you shake your head? Jane, you must be reasonable, or in truth I shall again become frantic."

His voice and hand quivered: his large nostrils dilated; his eye blazed: still I dared to speak.

"Sir, your wife is living: that is a fact acknowledged this morning by yourself. If I lived with you as you desire, I should then be your mistress: to say otherwise is sophistical – is false."

"Jane, I am not a gentle-tempered man – you forget that: I am not long-enduring; I am not cool and dispassionate. Out of pity to me and yourself, put your finger on my pulse, feel how it throbs, and – beware!"

He bared his wrist, and offered it to me: the blood was forsaking his cheek and lips, they were growing livid; I was distressed on all hands. To agitate him thus deeply, by a resistance he so abhorred, was cruel: to yield was out of the question. I did what human beings do instinctively when they are driven to utter extremity – looked for aid to one higher than man: the words "God help me!" burst involuntarily from my lips.

"I am a fool!" cried Mr. Rochester suddenly. "I keep telling her I am not married, and do not explain to her why. I forget she knows nothing of the character of that woman, or of the circumstances attending my infernal union with her. Oh, I am certain Jane will agree with me in opinion, when she knows all that I know! Just put your hand in mine, Janet – that I may have the evidence of touch as well as sight, to prove you are near me – and I will in a few words show you the real state of the case. Can you listen to me?"

"Yes, sir; for hours if you will."

"I ask only minutes. Jane, did you ever hear or know that I was not the eldest son of my house: that I had once a brother older than I?"

"I remember Mrs. Fairfax told me so once."

"And did you ever hear that my father was an avaricious, grasping man?"

"I have understood something to that effect."

"Well, Jane, being so, it was his resolution to keep the property together; he could not bear the idea of dividing his estate and leaving me a fair portion: all, he resolved, should go to my brother, Rowland. Yet as little could he endure that a son of his should be a poor man. I must be provided for by a wealthy marriage. He sought me a partner betimes. Mr.

Mason, a West India planter and merchant, was his old acquaintance. He was certain his possessions were real and vast: he made inquiries. Mr. Mason, he found, had a son and daughter; and he learned from him that he could and would give the latter a fortune of thirty thousand pounds: that sufficed. When I left college, I was sent out to Jamaica, to espouse a bride already courted for me. My father said nothing about her money; but he told me Miss Mason was the boast of Spanish Town for her beauty: and this was no lie. I found her a fine woman, in the style of Blanche Ingram: tall, dark, and majestic. Her family wished to secure me because I was of a good race; and so did she. They showed her to me in parties, splendidly dressed. I seldom saw her alone, and had very little private conversation with her. She flattered me, and lavishly displayed for my pleasure her charms and accomplishments. All the men in her circle seemed to admire her and envy me. I was dazzled, stimulated: my senses were excited; and being ignorant, raw, and inexperienced, I thought I loved her. There is no folly so besotted that the idiotic rivalries of society, the prurience, the rashness, the blindness of youth, will not hurry a man to its commission. Her relatives encouraged me; competitors piqued me; she allured me: a marriage was achieved almost before I knew where I was. Oh, I have no respect for myself when I think of that act! – an agony of inward contempt masters me. I never loved, I never esteemed, I did not even know her. I was not sure of the existence of one virtue in her nature: I had marked neither modesty, nor benevolence, nor candour, nor refinement in her mind or manners – and, I married her: – gross, grovelling, mole-eyed blockhead that I was! With less sin I might have – But let me remember to whom I am speaking."

"My bride's mother I had never seen: I understood she was dead. The honeymoon over, I learned my mistake; she was only mad, and shut up in a lunatic asylum. There was a younger brother, too – a complete dumb idiot. The elder one, whom you have seen (and whom I cannot hate, whilst I abhor all his kindred, because he has some grains of affection in his feeble mind, shown in the continued interest he takes in his wretched sister, and also in a dog-like attachment he once bore me), will probably be in the same state one day. My father and my brother Rowland knew all this; but they thought only of the thirty thousand pounds, and joined in the plot against me."

"These were vile discoveries; but except for the treachery of concealment, I should have made them no subject of reproach to my wife, even when I found her nature wholly alien to mine, her tastes obnoxious to me, her cast of mind common, low, narrow, and singularly incapable of being led to anything higher, expanded to anything larger – when I found that I could not pass a single evening, nor even a single hour of the day with her in comfort; that kindly conversation could not be sustained between us, because whatever topic I started, immediately received from her a turn at once coarse and trite, perverse and imbecile – when I perceived that I should never have a quiet or settled household, because no servant would bear the continued outbreaks of her violent and unreasonable temper, or the vexations of her absurd, contradictory, exacting orders – even then I restrained myself: I eschewed upbraiding, I curtailed remonstrance; I tried to devour my repentance and disgust in secret; I repressed the deep antipathy I felt.

"Jane, I will not trouble you with abominable details: some strong words shall express what I have to say. I lived with that woman upstairs four years, and before that time she had tried me indeed: her character ripened and developed with frightful rapidity; her vices sprang up fast and rank: they were so strong, only cruelty could check them, and I would not use cruelty. What a pigmy intellect she had, and what giant propensities! How fearful were the curses those propensities entailed on me! Bertha Mason, the true daughter of an infamous mother, dragged me through all the hideous and degrading agonies which must attend a man bound to a wife at once intemperate and unchaste.

"My brother in the interval was dead, and at the end of the four years my father died too. I was rich enough now – yet poor to hideous indigence: a nature the most gross, impure, depraved I ever saw, was associated with mine, and called by the law and by society a part of me. And I could not rid myself of it by any legal proceedings: for the doctors now discovered that *my wife* was mad – her excesses had prematurely developed the germs of insanity. Jane, you don't like my narrative; you look almost sick – shall I defer the rest to another day?"

"No, sir, finish it now; I pity you – I do earnestly pity you."

"Pity, Jane, from some people is a noxious and insulting sort of tribute, which one is justified in hurling back in the teeth of those who offer it; but that is the sort of pity native to callous, selfish hearts; it is a hybrid, egotistical pain at hearing of woes, crossed with ignorant contempt for those who have endured them. But that is not your pity, Jane; it is not the feeling of which your whole face is full at this moment – with which your eyes are now almost overflowing – with which your heart is heaving – with which your hand is trembling in mine. Your pity, my darling, is the suffering mother of love: its anguish is the very natal pang of the divine passion. I accept it, Jane; let the daughter have free advent – my arms wait to receive her."

"Now, sir, proceed; what did you do when you found she was mad?"

"Jane, I approached the verge of despair; a remnant of self-respect was all that intervened between me and the gulf. In the eyes of the world, I was doubtless covered with grimy dishonour; but I resolved to be clean in my own sight – and to the last I repudiated the contamination of her crimes, and wrenched myself from connection with her mental defects. Still, society associated my name and person with hers; I yet saw her and heard her daily: something of her breath (faugh!) mixed with the air I breathed; and besides, I remembered I had once been her husband – that recollection was then, and is now, inexpressibly odious to me; moreover, I knew that while she lived I could never be the husband of another and better wife; and, though five years my senior (her family and her father had lied to me even in the particular of her age), she was likely to live as long as I, being as robust in frame as she was infirm in mind. Thus, at the age of twenty-six, I was hopeless.

"One night I had been awakened by her yells – (since the medical men had pronounced her mad, she had, of course, been shut up) – it was a fiery West Indian night; one of the description that frequently precede the hurricanes of those climates. Being unable to sleep in bed, I got up and opened the window. The air was like sulphur-steams – I could find no refreshment anywhere. Mosquitoes came buzzing in and hummed sullenly round the room; the sea, which I could hear from thence, rumbled dull like an earthquake – black clouds were casting up over it; the moon was setting in the waves, broad and red, like a hot cannon-ball – she threw her last bloody glance over a world quivering with the ferment of tempest. I was physically influenced by the atmosphere and scene, and my ears were filled with the curses the maniac still shrieked out; wherein she momentarily mingled my name with such a tone of demon-hate, with such language! – No professed harlot ever had a fouler vocabulary than she: though two rooms off, I heard every word – the thin partitions of the West India house opposing but slight obstruction to her wolfish cries.

"'This life', said I at last, 'is hell: this is the air – those are the sounds of the bottomless pit! I have a right to deliver myself from it if I can. The sufferings of this mortal state will leave me with the heavy flesh that now cumbers my soul. Of the fanatic's burning eternity I have no fear: there is not a future state worse than this present one – let me break away, and go home to God!'

"I said this whilst I knelt down at, and unlocked a trunk which contained a brace of loaded pistols: I mean to shoot myself. I only entertained the intention for a moment; for, not being insane, the crisis of exquisite and unalloyed despair, which had originated the wish and design of self-destruction, was past in a second.

"A wind fresh from Europe blew over the ocean and rushed through the open casement: the storm broke, streamed, thundered, blazed, and the air grew pure. I then framed and fixed a resolution. While I walked under the dripping orange-trees of my wet garden, and amongst its drenched pomegranates and pine-apples, and while the refulgent dawn of the tropics kindled round me – I reasoned thus, Jane – and now listen; for it was true Wisdom that consoled me in that hour, and showed me the right path to follow.

"The sweet wind from Europe was still whispering in the refreshed leaves, and the Atlantic was thundering in glorious liberty; my heart, dried up and scorched for a long time, swelled to the tone, and filled with living blood – my being longed for renewal – my soul thirsted for a pure draught. I saw hope revive – and felt regeneration possible. From a flowery arch at the bottom of my garden I gazed over the sea – bluer than the sky: the old world was beyond; clear prospects opened thus:

"'Go', said Hope, 'and live again in Europe: there it is not known what a sullied name you bear, nor what a filthy burden is bound to you. You may take the maniac with you to England; confine her with due attendance and precautions at Thornfield: then travel yourself to what clime you will, and form what new tie you like. That woman, who has so abused your long-suffering, so sullied your name, so outraged your honour, so blighted your youth, is not your wife, nor are you her husband. See that she is cared for as her condition demands, and you have done all that God and humanity require of you. Let her identity, her connection with yourself, be buried in oblivion: you are bound to impart them to no living being. Place her in safety and comfort: shelter her degradation with secrecy, and leave her.'

"I acted precisely on this suggestion. My father and brother had not made my marriage known to their acquaintance; because, in the very first letter I wrote to apprise them of the union – having already begun to experience extreme disgust of its consequences, and, from the family character and constitution, seeing a hideous future opening to me – I added an urgent charge to keep it secret: and very soon the infamous conduct of the wife my father had selected for me was such as to make him blush to own her as his daughter-in-law. Far from desiring to publish the connection, he became as anxious to conceal it as myself.

"To England, then, I conveyed her; a fearful voyage I had with such a monster in the vessel. Glad was I when I at last got her to Thornfield, and saw her safely lodged in that third-storey room, of whose secret inner cabinet she has now for ten years made a wild beast's den – a goblin's cell. I had some trouble in finding an attendant for her, as it was necessary to select one on whose fidelity dependence could be placed; for her ravings would inevitably betray my secret: besides, she had lucid intervals of days – sometimes weeks – which she filled up with abuse of me. At last I hired Grace Poole from the Grimsby Retreat. She and the surgeon, Carter (who dressed Mason's wounds that night he was stabbed and worried), are the only two I have ever admitted to my confidence. Mrs. Fairfax may indeed have suspected something, but she could have gained no precise knowledge as to facts. Grace has, on the whole, proved a good keeper; though, owing partly to a fault of her own, of which it appears nothing can cure her, and which is incident to her harassing profession, her vigilance has been more than once lulled and baffled. The lunatic is both cunning and malignant; she has never failed to take advantage of her guardian's temporary lapses; once to secrete the knife with which she stabbed her brother, and twice to possess herself of the key of her cell, and issue therefrom in the nighttime. On the first of these occasions, she perpetrated the attempt to burn me in my bed; on the second, she paid that ghastly visit to you. I thank Providence, who watched over you, that she then spent her fury on your wedding apparel, which perhaps brought back vague reminiscences of her own bridal days: but on what might have happened, I cannot endure to reflect. When I think of the thing which flew at my throat this morning, hanging its black and scarlet visage over the nest of my dove, my blood curdles –"

"And what, sir," I asked, while he paused, "did you do when you had settled her here? Where did you go?"

"What did I do, Jane? I transformed myself into a will-o'-the-wisp. Where did I go? I pursued wanderings as wild as those of the March-spirit. I sought the Continent, and went devious through all its lands. My fixed desire was to seek and find a good and intelligent woman, whom I could love: a contrast to the fury I left at Thornfield –"

"But you could not marry, sir."

"I had determined and was convinced that I could and ought. It was not my original intention to deceive, as I have deceived you. I meant to tell my tale plainly, and make my proposals openly: and it appeared to me so absolutely rational that I should be considered free to love and be loved, I never doubted some woman might be found willing and able to understand my case and accept me, in spite of the curse with which I was burdened."

"Well, sir?"

"When you are inquisitive, Jane, you always make me smile. You open your eyes like an eager bird, and make every now and then a restless movement, as if answers in speech did not flow fast enough for you, and you wanted to read the tablet of one's heart. But before I go on, tell me what you mean by your 'Well, sir?' It is a small phrase very frequent with you; and which many a time has drawn me on and on through interminable talk: I don't very well know why."

"I mean, – What next? How did you proceed? What came of such an event?"

"Precisely! And what do you wish to know now?"

"Whether you found anyone you liked: whether you asked her to marry you; and what she said."

"I can tell you whether I found anyone I liked, and whether I asked her to marry me: but what she said is yet to be recorded in the book of Fate. For ten long years I roved about, living first in one capital, then another: sometimes in St. Petersburg; oftener in Paris; occasionally in Rome, Naples, and Florence. Provided with plenty of money and the passport of an old name, I could choose my own society: no circles were closed against me. I sought my ideal of a woman amongst English ladies, French countesses, Italian signoras, and German gräfinnen. I could not find her. Sometimes, for a fleeting moment, I thought I caught a glance, heard a tone, beheld a form, which announced the realisation of my dream: but I was presently undeceived. You are not to suppose that I desired perfection, either of mind or person. I longed only for what suited me – for the antipodes of the Creole: and I longed vainly. Amongst them all I found not one whom, had I been ever so free, I – warned as I was of the risks, the horrors, the loathings of incongruous unions – would have asked to marry me. Disappointment made me reckless. I tried dissipation – never debauchery: that I hated, and hate. That was my Indian Messalina's [29] attribute: rooted disgust at it and her restrained me much, even in pleasure. Any enjoyment that bordered on riot seemed to approach me to her and her vices, and I eschewed it.

"Yet I could not live alone; so I tried the companionship of mistresses. The first I chose was Céline Varens – another of those steps which make a man spurn himself when he recalls them. You already know what she was, and how my liaison with her terminated. She had two successors: an Italian, Giacinta, and a German, Clara; both considered singularly handsome. What was their beauty to me in a few weeks? Giacinta was unprincipled and violent: I tired of her in three months. Clara was honest and quiet; but heavy, mindless, and unimpressible: not one whit to my taste. I was glad to give her a sufficient sum to set her up in a good line of business, and so get decently rid of her. But, Jane, I see by your face you are not forming a very favourable opinion of me just now. You think me an unfeeling, loose-principled rake: don't you?"

"I don't like you so well as I have done sometimes, indeed, sir. Did it not seem to you in the least wrong to live in that way, first with one mistress and then another? You talk of it as a mere matter of course."

"It was with me; and I did not like it. It was a grovelling fashion of existence: I should never like to return to it. Hiring a mistress is the next worse thing to buying a slave: both are often by nature, and always by position, inferior: and to live familiarly with inferiors is degrading. I now hate the recollection of the time I passed with Céline, Giacinta, and Clara."

I felt the truth of these words; and I drew from them the certain inference, that if I were so far to forget myself and all the teaching that had ever been instilled into me, as – under any pretext – with any justification – through any temptation – to become the successor of these poor girls, he would one day regard me with the same feeling which now in his mind desecrated their memory. I did not give utterance to this conviction: it was enough to feel it. I impressed it on my heart, that it might remain there to serve me as aid in the time of trial.

"Now, Jane, why don't you say 'Well, sir?' I have not done. You are looking grave. You disapprove of me still, I see. But let me come to the point. Last January, rid of all mistresses – in a harsh, bitter frame of mind, the result of a useless, roving, lonely life – corroded with disappointment, sourly disposed against all men, and especially against all womankind (for I began to regard the notion of an intellectual, faithful, loving woman as a mere dream), recalled by business, I came back to England.

"On a frosty winter afternoon, I rode in sight of Thornfield Hall. Abhorred spot! I expected no peace – no pleasure there. On a stile in Hay Lane I saw a quiet little figure sitting by itself. I passed it as negligently as I did the pollard willow opposite to it: I had no presentiment of what it would be to me; no inward warning that the arbitress of my life – my genius for good or evil – waited there in humble guise. I did not know it, even when, on the occasion of Mesrour's accident, it came up and gravely offered me help. Childish and slender creature! It seemed as if a linnet had hopped to my foot and proposed to bear me on its tiny wing. I was surly; but the thing would not go: it stood by me with strange perseverance, and looked and spoke with a sort of authority. I must be aided, and by that hand: and aided I was.

"When once I had pressed the frail shoulder, something new – a fresh sap and sense – stole into my frame. It was well I had learnt that this elf must return to me – that it belonged to my house down below – or I could not have felt it pass away from under my hand, and seen it vanish behind the dim hedge, without singular regret. I heard you come home that night, Jane, though probably you were not aware that I thought of you or watched for you. The next day I observed you – myself unseen – for half an hour, while you played with Adèle in the gallery. It was a snowy day, I recollect, and you could not go out of doors. I was in my room; the door was ajar: I could both listen and watch. Adèle claimed your outward attention for a while; yet I fancied your thoughts were elsewhere: but you were very patient with her, my little Jane; you talked to her and amused her a long time. When at last she left you, you lapsed at once into deep reverie: you betook yourself slowly to pace the gallery. Now and then, in passing a casement, you glanced out at the thick-falling snow; you listened to the sobbing wind, and again you paced gently on and dreamed. I think those day visions were not dark: there was a pleasurable illumination in your eye occasionally, a soft excitement in your aspect, which told of no bitter, bilious, hypochondriac brooding: your look revealed rather the sweet musings of youth when its spirit follows on willing wings the flight of Hope up and on to an ideal heaven. The voice of Mrs. Fairfax, speaking to a servant in the hall, wakened you: and how curiously you smiled to and at yourself, Janet! There was much sense in your smile: it was very shrewd, and seemed to make light of your own abstraction. It seemed to say – 'My fine visions are all very well, but I must not forget they are absolutely unreal. I have a rosy sky and a green flowery Eden in my brain; but without, I am perfectly aware, lies at my feet a rough tract to travel, and around me gather black tempests to encounter.' You ran downstairs and demanded of Mrs. Fairfax some occupation: the weekly house accounts to make up, or something of that sort, I think it was. I was vexed with you for getting out of my sight.

"Impatiently I waited for evening, when I might summon you to my presence. An unusual – to me – a perfectly new character I suspected was yours: I desired to search it deeper and know it better. You entered the room with a look and air at once shy and independent: you were quaintly dressed – much as you are now. I made you talk: ere long I found you full of strange contrasts. Your garb and manner were restricted by rule; your air was often diffident, and altogether that of one refined by nature, but absolutely unused to society, and a good deal afraid of making herself disadvantageously conspicuous by some solecism or blunder; yet when addressed, you lifted a keen, a daring, and a glowing eye to your interlocutor's face: there was penetration and power in each glance you gave; when plied by close questions, you found ready and round answers. Very soon you seemed to get used to me: I believe you felt the existence of sympathy between you and your grim and cross master, Jane; for it was astonishing to see how quickly a certain pleasant ease tranquillised your manner: snarl as I would, you showed no surprise, fear, annoyance, or displeasure at my moroseness; you watched me, and now and then smiled at me with a simple yet sagacious grace I cannot describe. I was at once content and stimulated with what I saw: I liked what I had seen, and wished to see more. Yet, for a long time, I treated you distantly, and sought your company rarely. I was an intellectual epicure, and wished to prolong the gratification of making this novel and piquant acquaintance: besides, I was for a while troubled with a haunting fear that if I handled the flower freely its bloom would fade – the sweet charm of freshness would leave it. I did not then know that it was no transitory blossom, but rather the radiant resemblance of one, cut in an indestructible gem. Moreover, I wished to see whether you would seek me if I shunned you – but you did not; you kept in the schoolroom as still as your own desk and easel; if by chance I met you, you passed me as soon, and with as little token of recognition, as was consistent with respect. Your habitual expression in those days, Jane, was a thoughtful look; not despondent, for you were not sickly; but not buoyant, for you had little hope, and no actual pleasure. I wondered what you thought of me, or if you ever thought of me, and resolved to find this out.

"I resumed my notice of you. There was something glad in your glance, and genial in your manner, when you conversed: I saw you had a social heart; it was the silent schoolroom – it was the tedium of your life – that made you mournful. I permitted myself the delight of being kind to you; kindness stirred emotion soon: your face became soft in expression, your tones gentle; I liked my name pronounced by your lips in a grateful happy accent. I used to enjoy a chance meeting with you, Jane, at this time: there was a curious hesitation in your manner: you glanced at me with a slight trouble – a hovering doubt: you did not know what my caprice might be – whether I was going to play the master and be stern, or the friend and be benignant. I was now too fond of you often to simulate the first whim; and, when I stretched my hand out cordially, such bloom and light and bliss rose to your young, wistful features, I had much ado often to avoid straining you then and there to my heart."

"Don't talk any more of those days, sir," I interrupted, furtively dashing away some tears from my eyes; his language was torture to me; for I knew what I must do – and do soon – and all these reminiscences, and these revelations of his feelings only made my work more difficult.

"No, Jane," he returned: "what necessity is there to dwell on the Past, when the Present is so much surer – the Future so much brighter?"

I shuddered to hear the infatuated assertion.

"You see now how the case stands – do you not?" he continued. "After a youth and manhood passed half in unutterable misery and half in dreary solitude, I have for the first time found what I can truly love – I have found you. You are my sympathy – my better self – my good angel. I am bound to you with a strong attachment. I think you good, gifted, lovely: a fervent, a solemn passion is conceived in my heart; it leans to you, draws you to my centre and spring of life, wraps my existence about you, and, kindling in pure, powerful flame, fuses you and me in one.

"It was because I felt and knew this, that I resolved to marry you. To tell me that I had already a wife is empty mockery: you know now that I had but a hideous demon. I was wrong to attempt to deceive you; but I feared a stubbornness that exists in your character. I feared early instilled prejudice: I wanted to have you safe before hazarding confidences. This was cowardly: I should have appealed to your nobleness and magnanimity at first, as I do now – opened to you plainly my life of agony – described to you my hunger and thirst after a higher and worthier existence – shown to you, not my *resolution* (that word is weak), but my resistless *bent* to love faithfully and well, where I am faithfully and well loved in return. Then I should have asked you to accept my pledge of fidelity and to give me yours. Jane – give it me now."

A pause.

"Why are you silent, Jane?"

I was experiencing an ordeal: a hand of fiery iron grasped my vitals. Terrible moment: full of struggle, blackness, burning! Not a human being that ever lived could wish to be loved better than I was loved; and him who thus loved me I absolutely worshipped: and I must renounce love and idol. One drear word comprised my intolerable duty – "Depart!"

"Jane, you understand what I want of you? Just this promise – 'I will be yours, Mr. Rochester.'"

"Mr. Rochester, I will *not* be yours."

Another long silence.

"Jane!" recommenced he, with a gentleness that broke me down with grief, and turned me stone-cold with ominous terror – for this still voice was the pant of a lion rising – "Jane, do you mean to go one way in the world, and to let me go another?"

"I do."

"Jane" (bending towards and embracing me), "do you mean it now?"

"I do."

"And now?" softly kissing my forehead and cheek.

"I do," extricating myself from restraint rapidly and completely.

"Oh, Jane, this is bitter! This – this is wicked. It would not be wicked to love me."

"It would to obey you."

A wild look raised his brows – crossed his features: he rose; but he forebore yet. I laid my hand on the back of a chair for support: I shook, I feared – but I resolved.

"One instant, Jane. Give one glance to my horrible life when you are gone. All happiness will be torn away with you. What then is left? For a wife I have but the maniac upstairs: as well might you refer me to some corpse in yonder churchyard. What shall I do, Jane? Where turn for a companion and for some hope?"

"Do as I do: trust in God and yourself. Believe in heaven. Hope to meet again there."

"Then you will not yield?"

"No."

"Then you condemn me to live wretched and to die accursed?" His voice rose.

"I advise you to live sinless, and I wish you to die tranquil."

"Then you snatch love and innocence from me? You fling me back on lust for a passion – vice for an occupation?"

"Mr. Rochester, I no more assign this fate to you than I grasp it for myself. We were born to strive and endure – you as well as I: do so. You will forget me before I forget you."

"You make me a liar by such language: you sully my honour. I declared I could not change: you tell me to my face I shall change soon. And what a distortion in your judgment, what a perversity in your ideas, is proved by your conduct! Is it better to drive a fellow creature to despair than to transgress a mere human law, no man being injured by the breach? For you have neither relatives nor acquaintants whom you need fear to offend by living with me?"

This was true: and while he spoke my very conscience and reason turned traitors against me, and charged me with crime in resisting him. They spoke almost as loud as Feeling: and that clamoured wildly. "Oh, comply!" it said. "Think of his misery; think of his danger – look at his state when left alone; remember his headlong nature; consider the recklessness following on despair – soothe him; save him; love him; tell him you love him and will be his. Who in the world cares for *you*? Or who will be injured by what you do?"

Still indomitable was the reply – "*I* care for myself. The more solitary, the more friendless, the more unsustained I am, the more I will respect myself. I will keep the law given by God; sanctioned by man. I will hold to the principles received by me when I was sane, and not mad – as I am now. Laws and principles are not for the times when there is no temptation: they are for such moments as this, when body and soul rise in mutiny against their rigour; stringent are they; inviolate they shall be. If at my individual convenience I might break them, what would be their worth? They have a worth – so I have always believed; and if I cannot believe it now, it is because I am insane – quite insane: with my veins running fire, and my heart beating faster than I can count its throbs. Preconceived opinions, foregone determinations, are all I have at this hour to stand by: there I plant my foot."

I did. Mr. Rochester, reading my countenance, saw I had done so. His fury was wrought to the highest: he must yield to it for a moment, whatever followed; he crossed the floor and seized my arm and grasped my waist. He seemed to devour me with his flaming glance: physically, I felt, at the moment, powerless as stubble exposed to the draught and glow of a furnace: mentally, I still possessed my soul, and with it the certainty of ultimate safety. The soul, fortunately, has an interpreter – often an unconscious, but still a truthful interpreter – in the eye. My eye rose to his; and while I looked in his fierce face I gave an involuntary sigh; his gripe was painful, and my over-taxed strength almost exhausted.

"Never," said he, as he ground his teeth, "never was anything at once so frail and so indomitable. A mere reed she feels in my hand!" (And he shook me with the force of his hold.) "I could bend her with my finger and thumb: and what good would it do if I bent, if I uptore, if I crushed her? Consider that eye: consider the resolute, wild, free thing looking out of it, defying me, with more than courage – with a stern triumph. Whatever I do with its cage, I cannot get at it – the savage, beautiful creature! If I tear, if I rend the slight prison, my outrage will only let the captive loose. Conqueror I might be of the house; but the inmate would escape to heaven before I could call myself possessor of its clay dwelling-place. And it is you, spirit – with will and energy, and virtue and purity – that I want: not alone your brittle frame. Of yourself you could come with soft flight and nestle against my heart, if you would: seized against your will, you will elude the grasp like an essence – you will vanish ere I inhale your fragrance. Oh! Come, Jane, come!"

As he said this, he released me from his clutch, and only looked at me. The look was far worse to resist than the frantic strain: only an idiot, however, would have succumbed now. I had dared and baffled his fury; I must elude his sorrow: I retired to the door.

"You are going, Jane?"

"I am going, sir."

"You are leaving me?"

"Yes."

"You will not come? You will not be my comforter, my rescuer? My deep love, my wild woe, my frantic prayer, are all nothing to you?"

What unutterable pathos was in his voice! How hard it was to reiterate firmly, "I am going."

"Jane!"

"Mr. Rochester!"

"Withdraw, then, – I consent; but remember, you leave me here in anguish. Go up to your own room; think over all I have said, and, Jane, cast a glance on my sufferings – think of me."

He turned away; he threw himself on his face on the sofa. "Oh, Jane! My hope – my love – my life!" broke in anguish from his lips. Then came a deep, strong sob.

I had already gained the door; but, reader, I walked back – walked back as determinedly as I had retreated. I knelt down by him; I turned his face from the cushion to me; I kissed his cheek; I smoothed his hair with my hand.

"God bless you, my dear master!" I said. "God keep you from harm and wrong – direct you, solace you – reward you well for your past kindness to me."

"Little Jane's love would have been my best reward," he answered; "without it, my heart is broken. But Jane will give me her love: yes – nobly, generously."

Up the blood rushed to his face; forth flashed the fire from his eyes; erect he sprang; he held his arms out; but I evaded the embrace, and at once quitted the room.

"Farewell!" was the cry of my heart as I left him. Despair added, "Farewell for ever!"

* * *

That night I never thought to sleep; but a slumber fell on me as soon as I lay down in bed. I was transported in thought to the scenes of childhood: I dreamt I lay in the red-room at Gateshead; that the night was dark, and my mind impressed with strange fears. The light that long ago had struck me into syncope, recalled in this vision, seemed glidingly to mount the wall, and tremblingly to pause in the centre of the obscured ceiling. I lifted up my head to look: the roof resolved to clouds, high and dim; the gleam was such as the moon imparts to vapours she is about to sever. I watched her come – watched with the strangest anticipation; as though some word of doom were to be written on her disk. She broke forth as never moon yet burst from cloud: a hand first penetrated the sable folds and waved them away; then, not a moon, but a white human form shone in the azure, inclining a glorious brow earthward. It gazed and gazed on me. It spoke to my spirit: immeasurably distant was the tone, yet so near, it whispered in my heart:

"My daughter, flee temptation."

"Mother, I will."

So I answered after I had waked from the trance-like dream. It was yet night, but July nights are short: soon after midnight, dawn comes. "It cannot be too early to commence the task I have to fulfil," thought I. I rose: I was dressed; for I had taken off nothing but my shoes. I knew where to find in my drawers some linen, a locket, a ring. In seeking these articles, I encountered the beads of a pearl necklace Mr. Rochester had forced me to accept a few days ago. I left that; it was not mine: it was the visionary bride's who had melted in air. The other articles I made up in a parcel; my purse, containing twenty shillings (it was all I had), I put in my pocket: I tied on my straw bonnet, pinned my shawl, took the parcel and my slippers, which I would not put on yet, and stole from my room.

"Farewell, kind Mrs. Fairfax!" I whispered, as I glided past her door. "Farewell, my darling Adèle!" I said, as I glanced towards the nursery. No thought could be admitted of entering to embrace her. I had to deceive a fine ear: for aught I knew it might now be listening.

I would have got past Mr. Rochester's chamber without a pause; but my heart momentarily stopping its beat at that threshold, my foot was forced to stop also. No sleep was there: the inmate was walking restlessly from wall to wall; and again and again he sighed while I listened. There was a heaven – a temporary heaven – in this room for me, if I chose: I had but to go in and to say:

"Mr. Rochester, I will love you and live with you through life till death," and a fount of rapture would spring to my lips. I thought of this.

That kind master, who could not sleep now, was waiting with impatience for day. He would send for me in the morning; I should be gone. He would have me sought for: vainly. He would feel himself forsaken; his love rejected: he would suffer; perhaps grow desperate. I thought of this too. My hand moved towards the lock: I caught it back, and glided on.

Drearily I wound my way downstairs: I knew what I had to do, and I did it mechanically. I sought the key of the side-door in the kitchen; I sought, too, a phial of oil and a feather; I oiled the key and the lock. I got some water, I got some bread: for perhaps I should have to walk far; and my strength, sorely shaken of late, must not break down. All this I did without one sound. I opened the door, passed out, shut it softly. Dim dawn glimmered in the yard. The great gates were closed and locked; but a wicket in one of them was only latched. Through that I departed: it, too, I shut; and now I was out of Thornfield.

A mile off, beyond the fields, lay a road which stretched in the contrary direction to Millcote; a road I had never travelled, but often noticed, and wondered where it led: thither I bent my steps. No reflection was to be allowed now: not one glance was to be cast back; not even one forward. Not one thought was to be given either to the past or the future. The first was a page so heavenly sweet – so deadly sad – that to read one line of it would dissolve my courage and break down my energy. The last was an awful blank: something like the world when the deluge was gone by.

I skirted fields, and hedges, and lanes till after sunrise. I believe it was a lovely summer morning: I know my shoes, which I had put on when I left the house, were soon wet with dew. But I looked neither to rising sun, nor smiling sky, nor wakening nature. He who is taken out to pass through a fair scene to the scaffold, thinks not of the flowers that smile on his road, but of the block and axe-edge; of the disseverment of bone and vein; of the grave gaping at the end: and I thought of drear flight and homeless wandering – and oh! with agony I thought of what I left. I could not help it. I thought of him now – in his room – watching the sunrise; hoping I should soon come to say I would stay with him and be his. I longed to be his; I panted to return: it was not too late; I could yet spare him the bitter pang of bereavement. As yet my flight, I was sure, was undiscovered. I could go back and be his comforter – his pride; his redeemer from misery, perhaps from ruin. Oh, that fear of his self-abandonment – far worse than my abandonment – how it goaded me! It was a barbed arrow-head in my breast; it tore me when I tried to extract it; it sickened me when remembrance thrust it farther in. Birds began singing in brake and copse: birds were faithful to their mates; birds were emblems of love. What was I? In the midst of my pain of heart and frantic effort of principle, I abhorred myself. I had no solace from self-approbation: none even from self-respect. I had injured – wounded – left my master. I was hateful in my own eyes. Still I could not turn, nor retrace one step. God must have led me on. As to my own will or conscience, impassioned grief had trampled one and stifled the other. I was weeping wildly as I walked along my solitary way: fast, fast I went like one delirious. A weakness, beginning inwardly, extending to the limbs, seized me, and I fell: I lay on the ground some minutes, pressing my face to the wet turf. I had some fear – or hope – that here I should die: but I was soon up; crawling forwards on my hands and knees, and then again raised to my feet – as eager and as determined as ever to reach the road.

When I got there, I was forced to sit to rest me under the hedge; and while I sat, I heard wheels, and saw a coach come on. I stood up and lifted my hand; it stopped. I asked where it was going: the driver named a place a long way off, and where I was sure Mr. Rochester had no connections. I asked for what sum he would take me there; he said thirty shillings; I answered I had but twenty; well, he would try to make it do. He further gave me leave to get into the inside, as the vehicle was empty: I entered, was shut in, and it rolled on its way.

Gentle reader, may you never feel what I then felt! May your eyes never shed such stormy, scalding, heart-wrung tears as poured from mine. May you never appeal to Heaven in prayers so hopeless and so agonised as in that hour left my lips; for never may you, like me, dread to be the instrument of evil to what you wholly love.

Chapter Twenty-Eight

TWO DAYS ARE PASSED. It is a summer evening; the coachman has set me down at a place called Whitcross; he could take me no farther for the sum I had given, and I was not possessed of another shilling in the world. The coach is a mile off by this time; I am alone. At this moment I discover that I forgot to take my parcel out of the pocket of the coach, where I had placed it for safety; there it remains, there it must remain; and now, I am absolutely destitute.

Whitcross is no town, nor even a hamlet; it is but a stone pillar set up where four roads meet: whitewashed, I suppose, to be more obvious at a distance and in darkness. Four arms spring from its summit: the nearest town to which these point is, according to the inscription, distant ten miles; the farthest, above twenty. From the well-known names of these towns I learn in what county I have lighted; a north-midland shire, dusk with moorland, ridged with mountain: this I see. There are great moors behind and on each hand of me; there are waves of mountains far beyond that deep valley at my feet. The population here must be thin, and I see no passengers on these roads: they stretch out east, west, north, and south – white, broad, lonely; they are all cut in the moor, and the heather grows deep and wild to their very verge. Yet a chance traveller might pass by; and I wish no eye to see me now: strangers would wonder what I am doing, lingering here at the sign-post, evidently objectless and lost. I might be questioned: I could give no answer but what would sound incredible and excite suspicion. Not a tie holds me to human society at this moment – not a charm or hope calls me where my fellow creatures are – none that saw me would have a kind thought or a good wish for me. I have no relative but the universal mother, Nature: I will seek her breast and ask repose.

I struck straight into the heath; I held on to a hollow I saw deeply furrowing the brown moorside; I waded knee-deep in its dark growth; I turned with its turnings, and finding a moss-blackened granite crag in a hidden angle, I sat down under it. High banks of moor were about me; the crag protected my head: the sky was over that.

Some time passed before I felt tranquil even here: I had a vague dread that wild cattle might be near, or that some sportsman or poacher might discover me. If a gust of wind swept the waste, I looked up, fearing it was the rush of a bull; if a plover whistled, I imagined it a man. Finding my apprehensions unfounded, however, and calmed by the deep silence that reigned as evening declined at nightfall, I took confidence. As yet I had not thought; I had only listened, watched, dreaded; now I regained the faculty of reflection.

What was I to do? Where to go? Oh, intolerable questions, when I could do nothing and go nowhere! – When a long way must yet be measured by my weary, trembling limbs before I could reach human habitation – when cold charity must be entreated before I could get a lodging: reluctant sympathy importuned, almost certain repulse incurred, before my tale could be listened to, or one of my wants relieved!

I touched the heath: it was dry, and yet warm with the heat of the summer day. I looked at the sky; it was pure: a kindly star twinkled just above the chasm ridge. The dew fell, but with propitious softness; no breeze whispered. Nature seemed to me benign and good; I thought she loved me, outcast as I was; and I, who from man could anticipate only mistrust, rejection, insult, clung to her with filial fondness. Tonight, at least, I would be her guest, as I was her child: my mother would lodge me without money and without price. I had one morsel of bread yet: the remnant of a roll I had bought in a town we passed through at noon with a stray penny – my last coin. I saw ripe bilberries gleaming here and there, like jet beads in the heath: I gathered a handful and ate them with the bread. My hunger, sharp before, was, if not satisfied, appeased by this hermit's meal. I said my evening prayers at its conclusion, and then chose my couch.

Beside the crag the heath was very deep: when I lay down my feet were buried in it; rising high on each side, it left only a narrow space for the night-air to invade. I folded my shawl double, and spread it over me for a coverlet; a low, mossy swell was my pillow. Thus lodged, I was not, at least – at the commencement of the night, cold.

My rest might have been blissful enough, only a sad heart broke it. It plained of its gaping wounds, its inward bleeding, its riven chords. It trembled for Mr. Rochester and his doom; it bemoaned him with bitter pity; it demanded him with ceaseless longing; and, impotent as a bird with both wings broken, it still quivered its shattered pinions in vain attempts to seek him.

Worn out with this torture of thought, I rose to my knees. Night was come, and her planets were risen: a safe, still night: too serene for the companionship of fear. We know that God is everywhere; but certainly we feel His presence most when His works are on the grandest scale spread before us; and it is in the unclouded night sky, where His worlds wheel their silent course, that we read clearest His infinitude, His omnipotence, His omnipresence. I had risen to my knees to pray for Mr. Rochester. Looking up, I, with tear-dimmed eyes, saw the mighty Milky way. Remembering what it was – what countless systems there swept space like a soft trace of light – I felt the might and strength of God. Sure was I of His efficiency to save what He had made: convinced I grew that neither earth should perish, nor one of the souls it treasured. I turned my prayer to thanksgiving: the Source of Life was also the Saviour of spirits. Mr. Rochester was safe; he was God's, and by God would he be guarded. I again nestled to the breast of the hill; and ere long in sleep forgot sorrow.

But next day, Want came to me pale and bare. Long after the little birds had left their nests; long after bees had come in the sweet prime of day to gather the heath honey before the dew was dried – when the long morning shadows were curtailed, and the sun filled earth and sky – I got up, and I looked round me.

What a still, hot, perfect day! What a golden desert this spreading moor! Everywhere sunshine. I wished I could live in it and on it. I saw a lizard run over the crag; I saw a bee busy among the sweet bilberries. I would fain at the moment have become bee or lizard, that I might have found fitting nutriment, permanent shelter here. But I was a human being, and had a human being's wants: I must not linger where there was nothing to supply them. I rose; I looked back at the bed I had left. Hopeless of the future, I wished but this – that my Maker had that night thought good to require my soul of me while I slept; and that this weary frame, absolved by death from further conflict with fate, had now but to decay quietly, and mingle in peace with the soil of this wilderness. Life, however, was yet in my possession, with all its requirements, and pains, and responsibilities. The burden must be carried; the want provided for; the suffering endured; the responsibility fulfilled. I set out.

Whitcross regained, I followed a road which led from the sun, now fervent and high. By no other circumstance had I will to decide my choice. I walked a long time, and when I thought I had nearly done enough, and might conscientiously yield to the fatigue that almost overpowered me – might relax this forced action, and, sitting down on a stone I saw near, submit resistlessly to the apathy that clogged heart and limb – I heard a bell chime – a church bell.

I turned in the direction of the sound, and there, amongst the romantic hills, whose changes and aspect I had ceased to note an hour ago, I saw a hamlet and a spire. All the valley at my right hand was full of pasture-fields, and cornfields, and wood; and a glittering stream ran zig-zag through the varied shades of green, the mellowing grain, the sombre woodland, the clear and sunny lea. Recalled by the rumbling of wheels to the road before me, I saw a heavily-laden waggon labouring up the hill, and not far beyond were two cows and their drover. Human life and human labour were near. I must struggle on: strive to live and bend to toil like the rest.

About two o'clock p.m. I entered the village. At the bottom of its one street there was a little shop with some cakes of bread in the window. I coveted a cake of bread. With that refreshment I could perhaps regain a degree of energy: without it, it would be difficult to proceed. The wish to have some strength and some vigour returned to me as soon as I was amongst my fellow beings. I felt it would be degrading to faint with hunger on the causeway of a hamlet. Had I nothing about me I could offer in exchange for one of these rolls? I considered. I had a small silk handkerchief tied round my throat; I had my gloves. I could hardly tell how men and women in extremities of destitution proceeded. I did not know whether either of these articles would be accepted: probably they would not; but I must try.

I entered the shop: a woman was there. Seeing a respectably-dressed person, a lady as she supposed, she came forward with civility. How could she serve me? I was seized with shame: my tongue would not utter the request I had prepared. I dared not offer her the half-worn gloves, the creased handkerchief: besides, I felt it would be absurd. I only begged permission to sit down a moment, as I was tired. Disappointed in the expectation of a customer, she coolly acceded to my request. She pointed to a seat; I sank into it. I felt sorely urged to weep; but conscious how unseasonable such a manifestation would be, I restrained it. Soon I asked her "if there were any dressmaker or plain-workwoman in the village?"

"Yes; two or three. Quite as many as there was employment for."

I reflected. I was driven to the point now. I was brought face to face with Necessity. I stood in the position of one without a resource, without a friend, without a coin. I must do something. What? I must apply somewhere. Where?

"Did she know of any place in the neighbourhood where a servant was wanted?"

"Nay; she couldn't say."

"What was the chief trade in this place? What did most of the people do?"

"Some were farm labourers; a good deal worked at Mr. Oliver's needle-factory, and at the foundry."

"Did Mr. Oliver employ women?"

"Nay; it was men's work."

"And what do the women do?"

"I knawn't," was the answer. "Some does one thing, and some another. Poor folk mun get on as they can."

She seemed to be tired of my questions: and, indeed, what claim had I to importune her? A neighbour or two came in; my chair was evidently wanted. I took leave.

I passed up the street, looking as I went at all the houses to the right hand and to the left; but I could discover no pretext, nor see an inducement to enter any. I rambled round the hamlet, going sometimes to a little distance and returning again, for an hour or more. Much exhausted, and suffering greatly now for want of food, I turned aside into a lane and sat down under the hedge. Ere many minutes had elapsed, I was again on my feet, however, and again searching something – a resource, or at least an informant. A pretty little house stood at the top of the lane, with a garden before it, exquisitely neat and brilliantly blooming. I stopped at it. What business had I to approach the white door or touch the glittering knocker? In what way could it possibly be the interest of the inhabitants of that dwelling to serve me? Yet I drew near and knocked. A mild-looking, cleanly-attired young woman opened the door. In such a voice as might be expected from a hopeless heart and fainting frame – a voice wretchedly low and faltering – I asked if a servant was wanted here?

"No," said she; "we do not keep a servant."

"Can you tell me where I could get employment of any kind?" I continued. "I am a stranger, without acquaintance in this place. I want some work: no matter what."

But it was not her business to think for me, or to seek a place for me: besides, in her eyes, how doubtful must have appeared my character, position, tale. She shook her head, she "was sorry she could give me no information," and the white door closed, quite gently and civilly: but it shut me out. If she had held it open a little longer, I believe I should have begged a piece of bread; for I was now brought low.

I could not bear to return to the sordid village, where, besides, no prospect of aid was visible. I should have longed rather to deviate to a wood I saw not far off, which appeared in its thick shade to offer inviting shelter; but I was so sick, so weak, so gnawed with nature's cravings, instinct kept me roaming round abodes where there was a chance of food. Solitude would be no solitude – rest no rest – while the vulture, hunger, thus sank beak and talons in my side.

I drew near houses; I left them, and came back again, and again I wandered away: always repelled by the consciousness of having no claim to ask – no right to expect interest in my isolated lot. Meantime, the afternoon advanced, while I thus wandered about like a lost and starving dog. In crossing a field, I saw the church spire before me: I hastened towards it. Near the churchyard, and in the middle of a garden, stood a well-built though small house, which I had no doubt was the parsonage. I remembered that strangers who arrive at a place where they have no friends, and who want employment, sometimes apply to the clergyman for introduction and aid. It is the clergyman's function to help – at least with advice – those who wished to help themselves. I seemed to have something like a right to seek counsel here. Renewing then my courage, and gathering my feeble remains of strength, I pushed on. I reached the house, and knocked at the kitchen-door. An old woman opened: I asked was this the parsonage?

"Yes."

"Was the clergyman in?"

"No."

"Would he be in soon?"

"No, he was gone from home."

"To a distance?"

"Not so far – happen three mile. He had been called away by the sudden death of his father: he was at Marsh End now, and would very likely stay there a fortnight longer."

"Was there any lady of the house?"

"Nay, there was naught but her, and she was housekeeper;" and of her, reader, I could not bear to ask the relief for want of which I was sinking; I could not yet beg; and again I crawled away.

Once more I took off my handkerchief – once more I thought of the cakes of bread in the little shop. Oh, for but a crust! For but one mouthful to allay the pang of famine! Instinctively I turned my face again to the village; I found the shop again, and I went in; and though others were there besides the woman I ventured the request – "Would she give me a roll for this handkerchief?"

She looked at me with evident suspicion: "Nay, she never sold stuff i' that way."

Almost desperate, I asked for half a cake; she again refused. "How could she tell where I had got the handkerchief?" she said.

"Would she take my gloves?"

"No! What could she do with them?"

Reader, it is not pleasant to dwell on these details. Some say there is enjoyment in looking back to painful experience past; but at this day I can scarcely bear to review the times to which I allude: the moral degradation, blent with the physical suffering, form too distressing a recollection ever to be willingly dwelt on. I blamed none of those who repulsed me. I felt it was what was to be expected, and what could not be helped: an ordinary beggar is frequently an object of suspicion; a well-dressed beggar inevitably so. To be sure, what I begged was employment; but whose business was it to provide me with employment? Not, certainly, that of persons who saw me then for the first time, and who knew nothing about my character. And as to the woman who would not take my handkerchief in exchange for her bread, why, she was right, if the offer appeared to her sinister or the exchange unprofitable. Let me condense now. I am sick of the subject.

A little before dark I passed a farmhouse, at the open door of which the farmer was sitting, eating his supper of bread and cheese. I stopped and said:

"Will you give me a piece of bread? For I am very hungry." He cast on me a glance of surprise; but without answering, he cut a thick slice from his loaf, and gave it to me. I imagine he did not think I was a beggar, but only an eccentric sort of lady, who had taken a fancy to his brown loaf. As soon as I was out of sight of his house, I sat down and ate it.

I could not hope to get a lodging under a roof, and sought it in the wood I have before alluded to. But my night was wretched, my rest broken: the ground was damp, the air cold: besides, intruders passed near me more than once, and I had again and again to change my quarters; no sense of safety or tranquillity befriended me. Towards morning it rained; the whole of the following day was wet. Do not ask me, reader, to give a minute account of that day; as before, I sought work; as before, I was repulsed; as before, I starved; but once did food pass my lips. At the door of a cottage I saw a little girl about to throw a mess of cold porridge into a pig trough. "Will you give me that?" I asked.

She stared at me. "Mother!" she exclaimed, "there is a woman wants me to give her these porridge."

"Well lass," replied a voice within, "give it her if she's a beggar. T' pig doesn't want it."

The girl emptied the stiffened mould into my hand, and I devoured it ravenously.

As the wet twilight deepened, I stopped in a solitary bridle path, which I had been pursuing an hour or more.

"My strength is quite failing me," I said in a soliloquy. "I feel I cannot go much farther. Shall I be an outcast again this night? While the rain descends so, must I lay my head on the cold, drenched ground? I fear I cannot do otherwise: for who will receive me? But it will be very dreadful, with this feeling of hunger, faintness, chill, and this sense of desolation – this total prostration of hope. In all likelihood, though, I should die before morning. And why cannot I reconcile myself to the prospect of death? Why do I struggle to retain a valueless life? Because I know, or believe, Mr. Rochester is living: and then, to die of want and cold is a fate to which nature cannot submit passively. Oh, Providence! sustain me a little longer! Aid! – Direct me!"

My glazed eye wandered over the dim and misty landscape. I saw I had strayed far from the village: it was quite out of sight. The very cultivation surrounding it had disappeared. I had, by cross-ways and by-paths, once more drawn near the tract of moorland; and now, only a few fields, almost as wild and unproductive as the heath from which they were scarcely reclaimed, lay between me and the dusky hill.

"Well, I would rather die yonder than in a street or on a frequented road," I reflected. "And far better that crows and ravens – if any ravens there be in these regions – should pick my flesh from my bones, than that they should be prisoned in a workhouse coffin and moulder in a pauper's grave."

To the hill, then, I turned. I reached it. It remained now only to find a hollow where I could lie down, and feel at least hidden, if not secure. But all the surface of the waste looked level. It showed no variation but of tint: green, where rush and moss overgrew the marshes; black, where the dry soil bore only heath. Dark as it was getting, I could still see these changes, though but as mere alternations of light and shade; for colour had faded with the daylight.

My eye still roved over the sullen swell and along the moor-edge, vanishing amidst the wildest scenery, when at one dim point, far in among the marshes and the ridges, a light sprang up. "That is an *ignis fatuus*," was my first thought; and I expected it would soon vanish. It burnt on, however, quite steadily, neither receding nor advancing. "Is it, then, a bonfire just kindled?" I questioned. I watched to see whether it would spread: but no; as it did not diminish, so it did not enlarge. "It may be a candle in a house," I then conjectured; "but if so, I can never reach it. It is much too far away: and were it within a yard of me, what would it avail? I should but knock at the door to have it shut in my face."

And I sank down where I stood, and hid my face against the ground. I lay still a while: the night-wind swept over the hill and over me, and died moaning in the distance; the rain fell fast, wetting me afresh to the skin. Could I but have stiffened to the still frost – the friendly numbness of death – it might have pelted on; I should not have felt it; but my yet living flesh shuddered at its chilling influence. I rose ere long.

The light was yet there, shining dim but constant through the rain. I tried to walk again: I dragged my exhausted limbs slowly towards it. It led me aslant over the hill, through a wide bog, which would have been impassable in winter, and was splashy and shaking even now, in the height of summer. Here I fell twice; but as often I rose and rallied my faculties. This light was my forlorn hope: I must gain it.

Having crossed the marsh, I saw a trace of white over the moor. I approached it; it was a road or a track: it led straight up to the light, which now beamed from a sort of knoll, amidst a clump of trees – firs, apparently, from what I could distinguish of the character of their forms and foliage through the gloom. My star vanished as I drew near: some obstacle had intervened between me and it. I put out my hand to feel the dark mass before me: I discriminated the rough stones of a low wall – above it, something like palisades, and within, a high and prickly hedge. I groped on. Again a whitish object gleamed before me: it was a gate – a wicket; it moved on its hinges as I touched it. On each side stood a sable bush-holly or yew.

Entering the gate and passing the shrubs, the silhouette of a house rose to view, black, low, and rather long; but the guiding light shone nowhere. All was obscurity. Were the inmates retired to rest? I feared it must be so. In seeking the door, I turned an angle: there shot out the friendly gleam again, from the lozenged panes of a very small latticed window, within a foot of the ground, made still smaller by the growth of ivy or some other creeping plant, whose leaves clustered thick over the portion of the house wall in which it was set. The aperture was so screened and narrow, that curtain or shutter had been deemed unnecessary; and when I stooped down and put aside the spray of foliage shooting over it, I could see all within. I could see clearly a room with a sanded floor, clean scoured; a dresser of walnut, with pewter plates ranged in rows, reflecting the redness and radiance of a glowing peat-fire. I could see a clock, a white deal table, some chairs. The candle, whose ray had been my beacon, burnt on the table; and by its light an elderly woman, somewhat rough-looking, but scrupulously clean, like all about her, was knitting a stocking.

I noticed these objects cursorily only – in them there was nothing extraordinary. A group of more interest appeared near the hearth, sitting still amidst the rosy peace and warmth suffusing it. Two young, graceful women – ladies in every point – sat, one in a low rocking-chair, the other on a lower stool; both wore deep mourning of crape and bombazeen, which sombre garb singularly set off very fair necks and faces: a large old pointer dog rested its massive head on the knee of one girl – in the lap of the other was cushioned a black cat.

A strange place was this humble kitchen for such occupants! Who were they? They could not be the daughters of the elderly person at the table; for she looked like a rustic, and they were all delicacy and cultivation. I had nowhere seen such faces as theirs: and yet, as I gazed on them, I seemed intimate with every lineament. I cannot call them handsome – they were too pale and grave for the word: as they each bent over a book, they looked thoughtful almost to severity. A stand between them supported a second candle and two great volumes, to which they frequently referred, comparing them, seemingly, with the smaller books they held in their hands, like people consulting a dictionary to aid them in the task of translation. This scene was as silent as if all the figures had been shadows and the firelit apartment a picture: so hushed was it, I could hear the cinders fall from the grate, the clock tick in its obscure corner; and I even fancied I could distinguish the click-click of the woman's knitting-needles. When, therefore, a voice broke the strange stillness at last, it was audible enough to me.

"Listen, Diana," said one of the absorbed students; "Franz and old Daniel are together in the night-time, and Franz is telling a dream from which he has awakened in terror – listen!" And in a low voice she read something, of which not one word was intelligible to me; for it was in an unknown tongue – neither French nor Latin. Whether it were Greek or German I could not tell.

"That is strong," she said, when she had finished: "I relish it." The other girl, who had lifted her head to listen to her sister, repeated, while she gazed at the fire, a line of what had been read. At a later day, I knew the language and the book; therefore, I will here quote the line: though, when I first heard it, it was only like a stroke on sounding brass to me – conveying no meaning:

"'Da trat hervor Einer, anzusehen wie die Sternen Nacht.' Good! good!" she exclaimed, while her dark and deep eye sparkled. "There you have a dim and mighty archangel fitly set before you! The line is worth a hundred pages of fustian. 'Ich wäge die Gedanken in der Schale meines Zornes und die Werke mit dem Gewichte meines Grimms.' I like it!"

Both were again silent.

"Is there ony country where they talk i' that way?" asked the old woman, looking up from her knitting.

"Yes, Hannah – a far larger country than England, where they talk in no other way."

"Well, for sure case, I knawn't how they can understand t' one t'other: and if either o' ye went there, ye could tell what they said, I guess?"

"We could probably tell something of what they said, but not all – for we are not as clever as you think us, Hannah. We don't speak German, and we cannot read it without a dictionary to help us."

"And what good does it do you?"

"We mean to teach it some time – or at least the elements, as they say; and then we shall get more money than we do now."

"Varry like: but give ower studying; ye've done enough for tonight."

"I think we have: at least I'm tired. Mary, are you?"

"Mortally: after all, it's tough work fagging away at a language with no master but a lexicon."

"It is, especially such a language as this crabbed but glorious Deutsch. I wonder when St. John will come home."

"Surely he will not be long now: it is just ten (looking at a little gold watch she drew from her girdle). It rains fast, Hannah: will you have the goodness to look at the fire in the parlour?"

The woman rose: she opened a door, through which I dimly saw a passage: soon I heard her stir a fire in an inner room; she presently came back.

"Ah, childer!" said she, "it fair troubles me to go into yond' room now: it looks so lonesome wi' the chair empty and set back in a corner."

She wiped her eyes with her apron: the two girls, grave before, looked sad now.

"But he is in a better place," continued Hannah: "we shouldn't wish him here again. And then, nobody need to have a quieter death nor he had."

"You say he never mentioned us?" inquired one of the ladies.

"He hadn't time, bairn: he was gone in a minute, was your father. He had been a bit ailing like the day before, but naught to signify; and when Mr. St. John asked if he would like either o' ye to be sent for, he fair laughed at him. He began again with a bit of a heaviness in his head the next day – that is, a fortnight sin' – and he went to sleep and niver wakened: he wor a'most stark when your brother went into t' chamber and fand him. Ah, childer! That's t' last o' t' old stock – for ye and Mr. St. John is like of different soart to them 'at's gone; for all your mother wor mich i' your way, and a'most as book-learned. She wor the pictur' o' ye, Mary: Diana is more like your father."

I thought them so similar I could not tell where the old servant (for such I now concluded her to be) saw the difference. Both were fair complexioned and slenderly made; both possessed faces full of distinction and intelligence. One, to be sure, had hair a shade darker than the other, and there was a difference in their style of wearing it; Mary's pale brown locks were parted and braided smooth: Diana's duskier tresses covered her neck with thick curls. The clock struck ten.

"Ye'll want your supper, I am sure," observed Hannah; "and so will Mr. St. John when he comes in."

And she proceeded to prepare the meal. The ladies rose; they seemed about to withdraw to the parlour. Till this moment, I had been so intent on watching them, their appearance and conversation had excited in me so keen an interest, I had half-forgotten my own wretched position: now it recurred to me. More desolate, more desperate than ever, it seemed from contrast. And how impossible did it appear to touch the inmates of this house with concern on my behalf; to make them believe in the truth of my wants and woes – to induce them to vouchsafe a rest for my wanderings! As I groped out the door, and knocked at it hesitatingly, I felt that last idea to be a mere chimera. Hannah opened.

"What do you want?" she inquired, in a voice of surprise, as she surveyed me by the light of the candle she held.

"May I speak to your mistresses?" I said.

"You had better tell me what you have to say to them. Where do you come from?"

"I am a stranger."

"What is your business here at this hour?"

"I want a night's shelter in an out-house or anywhere, and a morsel of bread to eat."

Distrust, the very feeling I dreaded, appeared in Hannah's face. "I'll give you a piece of bread," she said, after a pause; "but we can't take in a vagrant to lodge. It isn't likely."

"Do let me speak to your mistresses."

"No, not I. What can they do for you? You should not be roving about now; it looks very ill."

"But where shall I go if you drive me away? What shall I do?"

"Oh, I'll warrant you know where to go and what to do. Mind you don't do wrong, that's all. Here is a penny; now go –"

"A penny cannot feed me, and I have no strength to go farther. Don't shut the door: – oh, don't, for God's sake!"

"I must; the rain is driving in –"

"Tell the young ladies. Let me see them –"

"Indeed, I will not. You are not what you ought to be, or you wouldn't make such a noise. Move off."

"But I must die if I am turned away."

"Not you. I'm fear'd you have some ill plans agate, that bring you about folk's houses at this time o' night. If you've any followers – housebreakers or such like – anywhere near, you may tell them we are not by ourselves in the house; we have a gentleman, and dogs, and guns." Here the honest but inflexible servant clapped the door to and bolted it within.

This was the climax. A pang of exquisite suffering – a throe of true despair – rent and heaved my heart. Worn out, indeed, I was; not another step could I stir. I sank on the wet doorstep: I groaned – I wrung my hands – I wept in utter anguish. Oh, this spectre of death! Oh, this last hour, approaching in such horror! Alas, this isolation – this banishment from my kind! Not only the anchor of hope, but the footing of fortitude was gone – at least for a moment; but the last I soon endeavoured to regain.

"I can but die," I said, "and I believe in God. Let me try to wait His will in silence."

These words I not only thought, but uttered; and thrusting back all my misery into my heart, I made an effort to compel it to remain there – dumb and still.

"All men must die," said a voice quite close at hand; "but all are not condemned to meet a lingering and premature doom, such as yours would be if you perished here of want."

"Who or what speaks?" I asked, terrified at the unexpected sound, and incapable now of deriving from any occurrence a hope of aid. A form was near – what form, the pitch-dark night and my enfeebled vision prevented me from distinguishing. With a loud long knock, the newcomer appealed to the door.

"Is it you, Mr. St. John?" cried Hannah.

"Yes – yes; open quickly."

"Well, how wet and cold you must be, such a wild night as it is! Come in – your sisters are quite uneasy about you, and I believe there are bad folks about. There has been a beggar-woman – I declare she is not gone yet! – laid down there. Get up! For shame! Move off, I say!"

"Hush, Hannah! I have a word to say to the woman. You have done your duty in excluding, now let me do mine in admitting her. I was near, and listened to both you and her. I think this is a peculiar case – I must at least examine into it. Young woman, rise, and pass before me into the house."

With difficulty I obeyed him. Presently I stood within that clean, bright kitchen – on the very hearth – trembling, sickening; conscious of an aspect in the last degree ghastly, wild, and weather-beaten. The two ladies, their brother, Mr. St. John, the old servant, were all gazing at me.

"St. John, who is it?" I heard one ask.

"I cannot tell: I found her at the door," was the reply.

"She does look white," said Hannah.

"As white as clay or death," was responded. "She will fall: let her sit."

And indeed my head swam: I dropped, but a chair received me. I still possessed my senses, though just now I could not speak.

"Perhaps a little water would restore her. Hannah, fetch some. But she is worn to nothing. How very thin, and how very bloodless!"

"A mere spectre!"

"Is she ill, or only famished?"

"Famished, I think. Hannah, is that milk? Give it me, and a piece of bread."

Diana (I knew her by the long curls which I saw drooping between me and the fire as she bent over me) broke some bread, dipped it in milk, and put it to my lips. Her face was near mine: I saw there was pity in it, and I felt sympathy in her hurried breathing. In her simple words, too, the same balm-like emotion spoke: "Try to eat."

"Yes – try," repeated Mary gently; and Mary's hand removed my sodden bonnet and lifted my head. I tasted what they offered me: feebly at first, eagerly soon.

"Not too much at first – restrain her," said the brother; "she has had enough." And he withdrew the cup of milk and the plate of bread.

"A little more, St. John – look at the avidity in her eyes."

"No more at present, sister. Try if she can speak now – ask her her name."

I felt I could speak, and I answered – "My name is Jane Elliott." Anxious as ever to avoid discovery, I had before resolved to assume an *alias*.

"And where do you live? Where are your friends?"

I was silent.

"Can we send for anyone you know?"

I shook my head.

"What account can you give of yourself?"

Somehow, now that I had once crossed the threshold of this house, and once was brought face to face with its owners, I felt no longer outcast, vagrant, and disowned by the wide world. I dared to put off the mendicant – to resume my natural manner and character. I began once more to know myself; and when Mr. St. John demanded an account – which at present I was far too weak to render – I said after a brief pause:

"Sir, I can give you no details tonight."

"But what, then," said he, "do you expect me to do for you?"

"Nothing," I replied. My strength sufficed for but short answers. Diana took the word:

"Do you mean," she asked, "that we have now given you what aid you require? And that we may dismiss you to the moor and the rainy night?"

I looked at her. She had, I thought, a remarkable countenance, instinct both with power and goodness. I took sudden courage. Answering her compassionate gaze with a smile, I said – "I will trust you. If I were a masterless and stray dog, I know that you would not turn me from your hearth tonight: as it is, I really have no fear. Do with me and for me as you like; but excuse me from much discourse – my breath is short – I feel a spasm when I speak." All three surveyed me, and all three were silent.

"Hannah," said Mr. St. John, at last, "let her sit there at present, and ask her no questions; in ten minutes more, give her the remainder of that milk and bread. Mary and Diana, let us go into the parlour and talk the matter over."

They withdrew. Very soon one of the ladies returned – I could not tell which. A kind of pleasant stupor was stealing over me as I sat by the genial fire. In an undertone she gave some directions to Hannah. Ere long, with the servant's aid, I contrived to mount a staircase; my dripping clothes were removed; soon a warm, dry bed received me. I thanked God – experienced amidst unutterable exhaustion a glow of grateful joy – and slept.

Chapter Twenty-Nine

THE RECOLLECTION OF about three days and nights succeeding this is very dim in my mind. I can recall some sensations felt in that interval; but few thoughts framed, and no actions performed. I knew I was in a small room and in a narrow bed. To that bed I seemed to have grown; I lay on it motionless as a stone; and to have torn me from it would have been almost to kill me. I took no note of the lapse of time – of the change from morning to noon, from noon to evening. I observed when anyone entered or left the apartment: I could even tell who they were; I could understand what was said when the speaker stood near to me; but I could not answer; to open my lips or move my limbs was equally impossible. Hannah, the servant, was my most frequent visitor. Her coming disturbed me. I had a feeling that she wished me away: that she did not understand me or my circumstances; that she was prejudiced against me. Diana and Mary appeared in the chamber once or twice a day. They would whisper sentences of this sort at my bedside:

"It is very well we took her in."

"Yes; she would certainly have been found dead at the door in the morning had she been left out all night. I wonder what she has gone through?"

"Strange hardships, I imagine – poor, emaciated, pallid wanderer?"

"She is not an uneducated person, I should think, by her manner of speaking; her accent was quite pure; and the clothes she took off, though splashed and wet, were little worn and fine."

"She has a peculiar face; fleshless and haggard as it is, I rather like it; and when in good health and animated, I can fancy her physiognomy would be agreeable."

Never once in their dialogues did I hear a syllable of regret at the hospitality they had extended to me, or of suspicion of, or aversion to, myself. I was comforted.

Mr. St. John came but once: he looked at me, and said my state of lethargy was the result of reaction from excessive and protracted fatigue. He pronounced it needless to send for a doctor: nature, he was sure, would manage best, left to herself. He said every nerve had been overstrained in some way, and the whole system must sleep torpid a while. There was no disease. He imagined my recovery would be rapid enough when once commenced. These opinions he delivered in a few words, in a quiet, low voice; and added, after a pause, in the tone of a man little accustomed to expansive comment, "Rather an unusual physiognomy; certainly, not indicative of vulgarity or degradation."

"Far otherwise," responded Diana. "To speak truth, St. John, my heart rather warms to the poor little soul. I wish we may be able to benefit her permanently."

"That is hardly likely," was the reply. "You will find she is some young lady who has had a misunderstanding with her friends, and has probably injudiciously left them. We may, perhaps, succeed in restoring her to them, if she is not obstinate: but I trace lines of force in her face which make me sceptical of her tractability." He stood considering me some minutes; then added, "She looks sensible, but not at all handsome."

"She is so ill, St. John."

"Ill or well, she would always be plain. The grace and harmony of beauty are quite wanting in those features."

On the third day I was better; on the fourth, I could speak, move, rise in bed, and turn. Hannah had brought me some gruel and dry toast, about, as I supposed, the dinner-hour. I had eaten with relish: the food was good – void of the feverish flavour which had hitherto poisoned what I had swallowed. When she left me, I felt comparatively strong and revived: ere long satiety of repose and desire for action stirred me. I wished to rise; but what could I put on? Only my damp and bemired apparel; in which I had slept on the ground and fallen in the marsh. I felt ashamed to appear before my benefactors so clad. I was spared the humiliation.

On a chair by the bedside were all my own things, clean and dry. My black silk frock hung against the wall. The traces of the bog were removed from it; the creases left by the wet smoothed out: it was quite decent. My very shoes and stockings were purified and rendered presentable. There were the means of washing in the room, and a comb and brush to smooth my hair. After a weary process, and resting every five minutes, I succeeded in dressing myself. My clothes hung loose on me; for I was much wasted, but I covered deficiencies with a shawl, and once more, clean and respectable looking – no speck of the dirt, no trace of the disorder I so hated, and which seemed so to degrade me, left – I crept down a stone staircase with the aid of the banisters, to a narrow low passage, and found my way presently to the kitchen.

It was full of the fragrance of new bread and the warmth of a generous fire. Hannah was baking. Prejudices, it is well known, are most difficult to eradicate from the heart whose soil has never been loosened or fertilised by education: they grow there, firm as weeds among stones. Hannah had been cold and stiff, indeed, at the first: latterly she had begun to relent a little; and when she saw me come in tidy and well dressed, she even smiled.

"What, you have got up!" she said. "You are better, then. You may sit you down in my chair on the hearthstone, if you will."

She pointed to the rocking chair: I took it. She bustled about, examining me every now and then with the corner of her eye. Turning to me, as she took some loaves from the oven, she asked bluntly:

"Did you ever go a-begging afore you came here?"

I was indignant for a moment; but remembering that anger was out of the question, and that I had indeed appeared as a beggar to her, I answered quietly, but still not without a certain marked firmness:

"You are mistaken in supposing me a beggar. I am no beggar; any more than yourself or your young ladies."

After a pause she said, "I dunnut understand that: you've like no house, nor no brass, I guess?"

"The want of house or brass (by which I suppose you mean money) does not make a beggar in your sense of the word."

"Are you book-learned?" she inquired presently.

"Yes, very."

"But you've never been to a boarding school?"

"I was at a boarding school eight years."

She opened her eyes wide. "Whatever cannot ye keep yourself for, then?"

"I have kept myself; and, I trust, shall keep myself again. What are you going to do with these gooseberries?" I inquired, as she brought out a basket of the fruit.

"Mak' 'em into pies."

"Give them to me and I'll pick them."

"Nay; I dunnut want ye to do nought."

"But I must do something. Let me have them."

She consented; and she even brought me a clean towel to spread over my dress, "lest," as she said, "I should mucky it."

"Ye've not been used to sarvant's wark, I see by your hands," she remarked. "Happen ye've been a dressmaker?"

"No, you are wrong. And now, never mind what I have been: don't trouble your head further about me; but tell me the name of the house where we are."

"Some calls it Marsh End, and some calls it Moor House."

"And the gentleman who lives here is called Mr. St. John?"

"Nay; he doesn't live here: he is only staying a while. When he is at home, he is in his own parish at Morton."

"That village a few miles off?

"Aye."

"And what is he?"

"He is a parson."

I remembered the answer of the old housekeeper at the parsonage, when I had asked to see the clergyman. "This, then, was his father's residence?"

"Aye; old Mr. Rivers lived here, and his father, and grandfather, and gurt (great) grandfather afore him."

"The name, then, of that gentleman, is Mr. St. John Rivers?"

"Aye; St. John is like his kirstened name."

"And his sisters are called Diana and Mary Rivers?"

"Yes."

"Their father is dead?"

"Dead three weeks sin' of a stroke."

"They have no mother?"

"The mistress has been dead this mony a year."

"Have you lived with the family long?"

"I've lived here thirty year. I nursed them all three."

"That proves you must have been an honest and faithful servant. I will say so much for you, though you have had the incivility to call me a beggar."

She again regarded me with a surprised stare. "I believe," she said, "I was quite mista'en in my thoughts of you: but there is so mony cheats goes about, you mun forgie me."

"And though," I continued, rather severely, "you wished to turn me from the door, on a night when you should not have shut out a dog."

"Well, it was hard: but what can a body do? I thought more o' th' childer nor of mysel: poor things! They've like nobody to tak' care on 'em but me. I'm like to look sharpish."

I maintained a grave silence for some minutes.

"You munnut think too hardly of me," she again remarked.

"But I do think hardly of you," I said; "and I'll tell you why – not so much because you refused to give me shelter, or regarded me as an impostor, as because you just now made it a species of reproach that I had no 'brass' and no house. Some of the best people that ever lived have been as destitute as I am; and if you are a Christian, you ought not to consider poverty a crime."

"No more I ought," said she: "Mr. St. John tells me so too; and I see I wor wrang – but I've clear a different notion on you now to what I had. You look a raight down dacent little crater."

"That will do – I forgive you now. Shake hands."

She put her floury and horny hand into mine; another and heartier smile illumined her rough face, and from that moment we were friends.

Hannah was evidently fond of talking. While I picked the fruit, and she made the paste for the pies, she proceeded to give me sundry details about her deceased master and mistress, and "the childer," as she called the young people.

Old Mr. Rivers, she said, was a plain man enough, but a gentleman, and of as ancient a family as could be found. Marsh End had belonged to the Rivers ever since it was a house: and it was, she affirmed, "aboon two hundred year old – for all it looked but a small, humble place, naught to compare wi' Mr. Oliver's grand hall down i' Morton Vale. But she could remember Bill Oliver's father a journeyman needlemaker; and th' Rivers wor gentry i' th' owd days o' th' Henrys, as anybody might see by looking into th' registers i' Morton Church vestry." Still, she allowed, "the owd maister was like other folk – naught mich out o' t' common way: stark mad o' shooting, and farming, and sich like." The mistress was different. She was a great reader, and studied a deal; and the "bairns" had taken after her. There was nothing like them in these parts, nor ever had been; they had liked learning, all three, almost from the time they could speak; and they had always been "of a mak' of their own." Mr. St. John, when he grew up, would go to college and be a parson; and the girls, as soon as they left school, would seek places as governesses: for they had told her their father had some years ago lost a great deal of money by a man he had trusted turning bankrupt; and as he was now not rich enough to give them fortunes, they must provide for themselves. They had lived very little at home for a long while, and were only come now to stay a few weeks on account of their father's death; but they did so like Marsh End and Morton, and all these moors and hills about. They had been in London, and many other grand towns; but they always said there was no place like home; and then they were so agreeable with each other – never fell out nor "threaped." She did not know where there was such a family for being united.

Having finished my task of gooseberry picking, I asked where the two ladies and their brother were now.

"Gone over to Morton for a walk; but they would be back in half an hour to tea."

They returned within the time Hannah had allotted them: they entered by the kitchen door. Mr. St. John, when he saw me, merely bowed and passed through; the two ladies stopped: Mary, in a few words, kindly and calmly expressed the pleasure she felt in seeing me well enough to be able to come down; Diana took my hand: she shook her head at me.

"You should have waited for my leave to descend," she said. "You still look very pale – and so thin! Poor child! – poor girl!"

Diana had a voice toned, to my ear, like the cooing of a dove. She possessed eyes whose gaze I delighted to encounter. Her whole face seemed to me full of charm. Mary's countenance was equally intelligent – her features equally pretty; but her expression was more reserved, and her manners, though gentle, more distant. Diana looked and spoke with a certain authority: she had a will, evidently. It was my nature to feel pleasure in yielding to an authority supported like hers, and to bend, where my conscience and self-respect permitted, to an active will.

"And what business have you here?" she continued. "It is not your place. Mary and I sit in the kitchen sometimes, because at home we like to be free, even to license – but you are a visitor, and must go into the parlour."

"I am very well here."

"Not at all, with Hannah bustling about and covering you with flour."

"Besides, the fire is too hot for you," interposed Mary.

"To be sure," added her sister. "Come, you must be obedient." And still holding my hand she made me rise, and led me into the inner room.

"Sit there," she said, placing me on the sofa, "while we take our things off and get the tea ready; it is another privilege we exercise in our little moorland home – to prepare our own meals when we are so inclined, or when Hannah is baking, brewing, washing, or ironing."

She closed the door, leaving me solus with Mr. St. John, who sat opposite, a book or newspaper in his hand. I examined first, the parlour, and then its occupant.

The parlour was rather a small room, very plainly furnished, yet comfortable, because clean and neat. The old-fashioned chairs were very bright, and the walnut-wood table was like a looking glass. A few strange, antique portraits of the men and women of other days decorated the stained walls; a cupboard with glass doors contained some books and an ancient set of china. There was no superfluous ornament in the room – not one modern piece of furniture, save a brace of workboxes and a lady's desk in rosewood, which stood on a side table: everything – including the carpet and curtains – looked at once well worn and well saved.

Mr. St. John – sitting as still as one of the dusty pictures on the walls, keeping his eyes fixed on the page he perused, and his lips mutely sealed – was easy enough to examine. Had he been a statue instead of a man, he could not have been easier. He was young – perhaps from twenty-eight to thirty – tall, slender; his face riveted the eye; it was like a Greek face, very pure in outline: quite a straight, classic nose; quite an Athenian mouth and chin. It is seldom, indeed, an English face comes so near the antique models as did his. He might well be a little shocked at the irregularity of my lineaments, his own being so harmonious. His eyes were large and blue, with brown lashes; his high forehead, colourless as ivory, was partially streaked over by careless locks of fair hair.

This is a gentle delineation, is it not, reader? Yet he whom it describes scarcely impressed one with the idea of a gentle, a yielding, an impressible, or even of a placid nature. Quiescent as he now sat, there was something about his nostril, his mouth, his brow, which, to my perceptions, indicated elements within either restless, or hard, or eager. He did not speak to me one word, nor even direct to me one glance, till his sisters returned. Diana, as she passed in and out, in the course of preparing tea, brought me a little cake, baked on the top of the oven.

"Eat that now," she said: "you must be hungry. Hannah says you have had nothing but some gruel since breakfast."

I did not refuse it, for my appetite was awakened and keen. Mr. Rivers now closed his book, approached the table, and, as he took a seat, fixed his blue pictorial-looking eyes full on me. There was an unceremonious directness, a searching, decided steadfastness in his gaze now, which told that intention, and not diffidence, had hitherto kept it averted from the stranger.

"You are very hungry," he said.

"I am, sir." It is my way – it always was my way, by instinct – ever to meet the brief with brevity, the direct with plainness.

"It is well for you that a low fever has forced you to abstain for the last three days: there would have been danger in yielding to the cravings of your appetite at first. Now you may eat, though still not immoderately."

"I trust I shall not eat long at your expense, sir," was my very clumsily-contrived, unpolished answer.

"No," he said coolly: "when you have indicated to us the residence of your friends, we can write to them, and you may be restored to home."

"That, I must plainly tell you, is out of my power to do; being absolutely without home and friends."

The three looked at me, but not distrustfully; I felt there was no suspicion in their glances: there was more of curiosity. I speak particularly of the young ladies. St. John's eyes, though clear enough in a literal sense, in a figurative one were difficult to fathom. He seemed to use them rather as instruments to search other people's thoughts, than as agents to reveal his own: the which combination of keenness and reserve was considerably more calculated to embarrass than to encourage.

"Do you mean to say," he asked, "that you are completely isolated from every connection?"

"I do. Not a tie links me to any living thing: not a claim do I possess to admittance under any roof in England."

"A most singular position at your age!"

Here I saw his glance directed to my hands, which were folded on the table before me. I wondered what he sought there: his words soon explained the quest.

"You have never been married? You are a spinster?"

Diana laughed. "Why, she can't be above seventeen or eighteen years old, St. John," said she.

"I am near nineteen: but I am not married. No."

I felt a burning glow mount to my face; for bitter and agitating recollections were awakened by the allusion to marriage. They all saw the embarrassment and the emotion. Diana and Mary relieved me by turning their eyes elsewhere than to my crimsoned visage; but the colder and sterner brother continued to gaze, till the trouble he had excited forced out tears as well as colour.

"Where did you last reside?" he now asked.

"You are too inquisitive, St. John," murmured Mary in a low voice; but he leaned over the table and required an answer by a second firm and piercing look.

"The name of the place where, and of the person with whom I lived, is my secret," I replied concisely.

"Which, if you like, you have, in my opinion, a right to keep, both from St. John and every other questioner," remarked Diana.

"Yet if I know nothing about you or your history, I cannot help you," he said. "And you need help, do you not?"

"I need it, and I seek it so far, sir, that some true philanthropist will put me in the way of getting work which I can do, and the remuneration for which will keep me, if but in the barest necessaries of life."

"I know not whether I am a true philanthropist; yet I am willing to aid you to the utmost of my power in a purpose so honest. First, then, tell me what you have been accustomed to do, and what you *can* do."

I had now swallowed my tea. I was mightily refreshed by the beverage; as much so as a giant with wine: it gave new tone to my unstrung nerves, and enabled me to address this penetrating young judge steadily.

"Mr. Rivers," I said, turning to him, and looking at him, as he looked at me, openly and without diffidence, "you and your sisters have done me a great service – the greatest man can do his fellow-being; you have rescued me, by your noble hospitality, from death. This benefit conferred gives you an unlimited claim on my gratitude, and a claim, to a certain extent, on my confidence. I will tell you as much of the history of the wanderer you have harboured, as I can tell without compromising my own peace of mind – my own security, moral and physical, and that of others.

"I am an orphan, the daughter of a clergyman. My parents died before I could know them. I was brought up a dependant; educated in a charitable institution. I will even tell you the name of the establishment, where I passed six years as a pupil, and two as a teacher – Lowood Orphan Asylum, —shire: you will have heard of it, Mr. Rivers? – the Rev. Robert Brocklehurst is the treasurer."

"I have heard of Mr. Brocklehurst, and I have seen the school."

"I left Lowood nearly a year since to become a private governess. I obtained a good situation, and was happy. This place I was obliged to leave four days before I came here. The reason of my departure I cannot and ought not to explain: it would be useless, dangerous, and would sound incredible. No blame attached to me: I am as free from culpability as any one of you three. Miserable I am, and must be for a time; for the catastrophe which drove me from a house I had found a paradise was of a strange and direful nature. I observed but two points in planning my departure – speed, secrecy: to secure these, I had to leave behind me everything I possessed except a small parcel; which, in my hurry and trouble of mind, I forgot to take out of the coach that brought me to Whitcross. To this neighbourhood, then, I came, quite destitute. I slept two nights in the open air, and wandered about two days without crossing a threshold: but twice in that space of time did I taste food; and it was when brought by hunger, exhaustion, and despair almost to the last gasp, that you, Mr. Rivers, forbade me to perish of want at your door, and took me under the shelter of your roof. I know all your sisters have done for me since – for I have not been insensible during my seeming torpor – and I owe to their spontaneous, genuine, genial compassion as large a debt as to your evangelical charity."

"Don't make her talk any more now, St. John," said Diana, as I paused; "she is evidently not yet fit for excitement. Come to the sofa and sit down now, Miss Elliott."

I gave an involuntary half start at hearing the *alias*: I had forgotten my new name. Mr. Rivers, whom nothing seemed to escape, noticed it at once.

"You said your name was Jane Elliott?" he observed.

"I did say so; and it is the name by which I think it expedient to be called at present, but it is not my real name, and when I hear it, it sounds strange to me."

"Your real name you will not give?"

"No: I fear discovery above all things; and whatever disclosure would lead to it, I avoid."

"You are quite right, I am sure," said Diana. "Now do, brother, let her be at peace a while."

But when St. John had mused a few moments he recommenced as imperturbably and with as much acumen as ever.

"You would not like to be long dependent on our hospitality – you would wish, I see, to dispense as soon as may be with my sisters' compassion, and, above all, with my *charity* (I am quite sensible of the distinction drawn, nor do I resent it – it is just): you desire to be independent of us?"

"I do: I have already said so. Show me how to work, or how to seek work: that is all I now ask; then let me go, if it be but to the meanest cottage; but till then, allow me to stay here: I dread another essay of the horrors of homeless destitution."

"Indeed you *shall* stay here," said Diana, putting her white hand on my head. "You *shall*," repeated Mary, in the tone of undemonstrative sincerity which seemed natural to her.

"My sisters, you see, have a pleasure in keeping you," said Mr. St. John, "as they would have a pleasure in keeping and cherishing a half-frozen bird, some wintry wind might have driven through their casement. I feel more inclination to put you in the way of keeping yourself, and shall endeavour to do so; but observe, my sphere is narrow. I am but the incumbent of a poor country parish: my aid must be of the humblest sort. And if you are inclined to despise the day of small things, seek some more efficient succour than such as I can offer."

"She has already said that she is willing to do anything honest she can do," answered Diana for me; "and you know, St. John, she has no choice of helpers: she is forced to put up with such crusty people as you."

"I will be a dressmaker; I will be a plain-workwoman; I will be a servant, a nurse-girl, if I can be no better," I answered.

"Right," said Mr. St. John, quite coolly. "If such is your spirit, I promise to aid you, in my own time and way."

He now resumed the book with which he had been occupied before tea. I soon withdrew, for I had talked as much, and sat up as long, as my present strength would permit.

Chapter Thirty

THE MORE I KNEW of the inmates of Moor House, the better I liked them. In a few days I had so far recovered my health that I could sit up all day, and walk out sometimes. I could join with Diana and Mary in all their occupations; converse with them as much as they wished, and aid them when and where they would allow me. There was a reviving pleasure in this intercourse, of a kind now tasted by me for the first time – the pleasure arising from perfect congeniality of tastes, sentiments, and principles.

I liked to read what they liked to read: what they enjoyed, delighted me; what they approved, I reverenced. They loved their sequestered home. I, too, in the grey, small, antique structure, with its low roof, its latticed casements, its mouldering walls, its avenue of aged firs – all grown aslant under the stress of mountain winds; its garden, dark with yew and holly – and where no flowers but of the hardiest species would bloom – found a charm both potent and permanent. They clung to the purple moors behind and around their dwelling – to the hollow vale into which the pebbly bridle path leading from their gate descended, and which wound between fern-banks first, and then amongst a few of the wildest little pasture-fields that ever bordered a wilderness of heath, or gave sustenance to a flock of grey moorland sheep, with their little mossy-faced lambs: – they clung to this scene, I say, with a perfect enthusiasm of attachment. I could comprehend the feeling, and share both its strength and truth. I saw the fascination of the locality. I felt the consecration of its loneliness: my eye feasted on the outline of swell and sweep – on the wild colouring communicated to ridge and dell by moss, by heath-bell, by flower-sprinkled turf, by brilliant bracken, and mellow granite crag. These details were just to me what they were to them – so many pure and sweet sources of pleasure. The strong blast and the soft breeze; the rough and the halcyon day; the hours of sunrise and sunset; the moonlight and the clouded night, developed for me, in these regions, the same attraction as for them – wound round my faculties the same spell that entranced theirs.

Indoors we agreed equally well. They were both more accomplished and better read than I was; but with eagerness I followed in the path of knowledge they had trodden before me. I devoured the books they lent me: then it was full satisfaction to discuss with them in the evening what I had perused during the day. Thought fitted thought; opinion met opinion: we coincided, in short, perfectly.

If in our trio there was a superior and a leader, it was Diana. Physically, she far excelled me: she was handsome; she was vigorous. In her animal spirits there was an affluence of life and certainty of flow, such as excited my wonder, while it baffled my comprehension. I could talk a while when the evening commenced, but the first gush of vivacity and fluency gone, I was fain to sit on a stool at Diana's feet, to rest my head on her knee, and listen alternately to her and Mary, while they sounded thoroughly the topic on which I had but touched. Diana offered to teach me German. I liked to learn of her: I saw the part of instructress pleased and suited her; that of scholar pleased and suited me no less. Our natures dovetailed: mutual affection – of the strongest kind – was the result. They discovered I could draw: their pencils and colour-boxes were immediately at my service. My skill, greater in this one point than theirs, surprised and charmed them. Mary would sit and watch me by the hour together: then she would take lessons; and a docile, intelligent, assiduous pupil she made. Thus occupied, and mutually entertained, days passed like hours, and weeks like days.

As to Mr. St John, the intimacy which had arisen so naturally and rapidly between me and his sisters did not extend to him. One reason of the distance yet observed between us was, that he was comparatively seldom at home: a large proportion of his time appeared devoted to visiting the sick and poor among the scattered population of his parish.

No weather seemed to hinder him in these pastoral excursions: rain or fair, he would, when his hours of morning study were over, take his hat, and, followed by his father's old pointer, Carlo, go out on his mission of love or duty – I scarcely know in which light he regarded it. Sometimes, when the day was very unfavourable, his sisters would expostulate. He would then say, with a peculiar smile, more solemn than cheerful:

"And if I let a gust of wind or a sprinkling of rain turn me aside from these easy tasks, what preparation would such sloth be for the future I propose to myself?"

Diana and Mary's general answer to this question was a sigh, and some minutes of apparently mournful meditation.

But besides his frequent absences, there was another barrier to friendship with him: he seemed of a reserved, an abstracted, and even of a brooding nature. Zealous in his ministerial labours, blameless in his life and habits, he yet did not appear to enjoy that mental serenity, that inward content, which should be the reward of every sincere Christian and practical philanthropist. Often, of an evening, when he sat at the window, his desk and papers before him, he would cease reading or writing, rest his chin on his hand, and deliver himself up to I know not what course of thought; but that it was perturbed and exciting might be seen in the frequent flash and changeful dilation of his eye.

I think, moreover, that Nature was not to him that treasury of delight it was to his sisters. He expressed once, and but once in my hearing, a strong sense of the rugged charm of the hills, and an inborn affection for the dark roof and hoary walls he called his home; but there was more of gloom than pleasure in the tone and words in which the sentiment was manifested; and never did he seem to roam the moors for the sake of their soothing silence – never seek out or dwell upon the thousand peaceful delights they could yield.

Incommunicative as he was, some time elapsed before I had an opportunity of gauging his mind. I first got an idea of its calibre when I heard him preach in his own church at Morton. I wish I could describe that sermon: but it is past my power. I cannot even render faithfully the effect it produced on me.

It began calm – and indeed, as far as delivery and pitch of voice went, it was calm to the end: an earnestly felt, yet strictly restrained zeal breathed soon in the distinct accents, and prompted the nervous language. This grew to force – compressed, condensed, controlled. The heart was thrilled, the mind astonished, by the power of the preacher: neither were softened. Throughout there was a strange bitterness; an absence of consolatory gentleness; stern allusions to Calvinistic doctrines – election, predestination, reprobation – were frequent; and each reference to these points sounded like a sentence pronounced for doom. When he had done, instead of feeling better, calmer, more enlightened by his discourse, I experienced an inexpressible sadness; for it seemed to me – I know not whether equally so to others – that the eloquence to which I had been listening had sprung from a depth where lay turbid dregs of disappointment – where moved troubling impulses of insatiate yearnings and disquieting aspirations. I was sure St. John Rivers – pure-lived, conscientious, zealous as he was – had not yet found that peace of God which passeth all understanding: he had no more found it, I thought, than had I with my concealed and racking regrets for my broken idol and lost elysium – regrets to which I have latterly avoided referring, but which possessed me and tyrannised over me ruthlessly.

Meantime a month was gone. Diana and Mary were soon to leave Moor House, and return to the far different life and scene which awaited them, as governesses in a large, fashionable, south-of-England city, where each held a situation in families by whose wealthy and haughty members they were regarded only as humble dependants, and who neither knew nor sought out their innate excellences, and appreciated only their acquired accomplishments as they appreciated the skill of their cook or the taste of their waiting-woman. Mr. St. John had said nothing to me yet about the employment he had promised to obtain for me; yet it became urgent that I should have a vocation of some kind. One morning, being left alone with him a few minutes in the parlour, I ventured to approach the window-recess – which his table, chair, and desk consecrated as a kind of study – and I was going to speak, though not very well knowing in what words to frame my inquiry – for it is at all times difficult to break the ice of reserve glassing over such natures as his – when he saved me the trouble by being the first to commence a dialogue.

Looking up as I drew near – "You have a question to ask of me?" he said.

"Yes; I wish to know whether you have heard of any service I can offer myself to undertake?"

"I found or devised something for you three weeks ago; but as you seemed both useful and happy here – as my sisters had evidently become attached to you, and your society gave them unusual pleasure – I deemed it inexpedient to break in on your mutual comfort till their approaching departure from Marsh End should render yours necessary."

"And they will go in three days now?" I said.

"Yes; and when they go, I shall return to the parsonage at Morton: Hannah will accompany me; and this old house will be shut up."

I waited a few moments, expecting he would go on with the subject first broached: but he seemed to have entered another train of reflection: his look denoted abstraction from me and my business. I was obliged to recall him to a theme which was of necessity one of close and anxious interest to me.

"What is the employment you had in view, Mr. Rivers? I hope this delay will not have increased the difficulty of securing it."

"Oh, no; since it is an employment which depends only on me to give, and you to accept."

He again paused: there seemed a reluctance to continue. I grew impatient: a restless movement or two, and an eager and exacting glance fastened on his face, conveyed the feeling to him as effectually as words could have done, and with less trouble.

"You need be in no hurry to hear," he said: "let me frankly tell you, I have nothing eligible or profitable to suggest. Before I explain, recall, if you please, my notice, clearly given, that if I helped you, it must be as the blind man would help the lame. I am poor; for I find that, when I have paid my father's debts, all the patrimony remaining to me will be this crumbling grange, the row of scathed firs behind, and the patch of moorish soil, with the yew-trees and holly-bushes in front. I am obscure: Rivers is an old name; but of the three sole descendants of the race, two earn the dependant's crust among strangers, and the third considers himself an alien from his native country – not only for life, but in death. Yes, and deems, and is bound to deem, himself honoured by the lot, and aspires but after the day when the cross of separation from fleshly ties shall be laid on his shoulders, and when the Head of that church-militant of whose humblest members he is one, shall give the word, 'Rise, follow Me!'"

St. John said these words as he pronounced his sermons, with a quiet, deep voice; with an unflushed cheek, and a coruscating radiance of glance. He resumed:

"And since I am myself poor and obscure, I can offer you but a service of poverty and obscurity. *You* may even think it degrading – for I see now your habits have been what the world calls refined: your tastes lean to the ideal, and your society has at least been amongst the educated; but *I* consider that no service degrades which can better our race. I hold that the more arid and unreclaimed the soil where the Christian labourer's task of tillage is appointed him – the scantier the meed his toil brings – the higher the honour. His, under such circumstances, is the destiny of the pioneer; and the first pioneers of the Gospel were the Apostles – their captain was Jesus, the Redeemer, Himself."

"Well?" I said, as he again paused – "proceed."

He looked at me before he proceeded: indeed, he seemed leisurely to read my face, as if its features and lines were characters on a page. The conclusions drawn from this scrutiny he partially expressed in his succeeding observations.

"I believe you will accept the post I offer you," said he, "and hold it for a while: not permanently, though: any more than I could permanently keep the narrow and narrowing – the tranquil, hidden office of English country incumbent; for in your nature is an alloy as detrimental to repose as that in mine, though of a different kind."

"Do explain," I urged, when he halted once more.

"I will; and you shall hear how poor the proposal is, – how trivial – how cramping. I shall not stay long at Morton, now that my father is dead, and that I am my own master. I shall leave the place probably in the course of a twelve-month; but while I do stay, I will exert myself to the utmost for its improvement. Morton, when I came to it two years ago, had no school: the children of the poor were excluded from every hope of progress. I established one for boys: I mean now to open a second school for girls. I have hired a building for the purpose, with a cottage of two rooms attached to it for the mistress's house. Her salary will be thirty pounds a year: her house is already furnished, very simply, but sufficiently, by the kindness of a lady, Miss Oliver; the only daughter of the sole rich man in my parish – Mr. Oliver, the proprietor of a needle factory and iron foundry in the valley. The same lady pays for the education and clothing of an orphan from the workhouse, on condition that she shall aid the mistress in such menial offices connected with her own house and the school as her occupation of teaching will prevent her having time to discharge in person. Will you be this mistress?"

He put the question rather hurriedly; he seemed half to expect an indignant, or at least a disdainful rejection of the offer: not knowing all my thoughts and feelings, though guessing some, he could not tell in what light the lot would appear to me. In truth it was humble – but then it was sheltered, and I wanted a safe asylum: it was plodding – but then, compared with that of a governess in a rich house, it was independent; and the fear of servitude with strangers entered my soul like iron: it was not ignoble – not unworthy – not mentally degrading, I made my decision.

"I thank you for the proposal, Mr. Rivers, and I accept it with all my heart."

"But you comprehend me?" he said. "It is a village school: your scholars will be only poor girls – cottagers' children – at the best, farmers' daughters. Knitting, sewing, reading, writing, ciphering, will be all you will have to teach. What will you do with your accomplishments? What, with the largest portion of your mind – sentiments – tastes?"

"Save them till they are wanted. They will keep."

"You know what you undertake, then?"

"I do."

He now smiled: and not a bitter or a sad smile, but one well pleased and deeply gratified.

"And when will you commence the exercise of your function?"

"I will go to my house tomorrow, and open the school, if you like, next week."

"Very well: so be it."

He rose and walked through the room. Standing still, he again looked at me. He shook his head.

"What do you disapprove of, Mr. Rivers?" I asked.

"You will not stay at Morton long: no, no!"

"Why? What is your reason for saying so?"

"I read it in your eye; it is not of that description which promises the maintenance of an even tenor in life."

"I am not ambitious."

He started at the word "ambitious." He repeated, "No. What made you think of ambition? Who is ambitious? I know I am: but how did you find it out?"

"I was speaking of myself."

"Well, if you are not ambitious, you are –" He paused.

"What?"

"I was going to say, impassioned: but perhaps you would have misunderstood the word, and been displeased. I mean, that human affections and sympathies have a most powerful hold on you. I am sure you cannot long be content to pass your leisure in solitude, and to devote your working hours to a monotonous labour wholly void of stimulus: any more than I can be content," he added, with emphasis, "to live here buried in morass, pent in with mountains – my nature, that God gave me, contravened; my faculties, heaven-bestowed, paralysed – made useless. You hear now how I contradict myself. I, who preached contentment with a humble lot, and justified the vocation even of hewers of wood and drawers of water in God's service – I, His ordained minister, almost rave in my restlessness. Well, propensities and principles must be reconciled by some means."

He left the room. In this brief hour I had learnt more of him than in the whole previous month: yet still he puzzled me.

Diana and Mary Rivers became more sad and silent as the day approached for leaving their brother and their home. They both tried to appear as usual; but the sorrow they had to struggle against was one that could not be entirely conquered or concealed. Diana intimated that this would be a different parting from any they had ever yet known. It would probably, as far as St. John was concerned, be a parting for years: it might be a parting for life.

"He will sacrifice all to his long-framed resolves," she said: "natural affection and feelings more potent still. St. John looks quiet, Jane; but he hides a fever in his vitals. You would think him gentle, yet in some things he is inexorable as death; and the worst of it is, my conscience will hardly permit me to dissuade him from his severe decision: certainly, I cannot for a moment blame him for it. It is right, noble, Christian: yet it breaks my heart!" And the tears gushed to her fine eyes. Mary bent her head low over her work.

"We are now without father: we shall soon be without home and brother," she murmured.

At that moment a little accident supervened, which seemed decreed by fate purposely to prove the truth of the adage, that 'misfortunes never come singly', and to add to their distresses the vexing one of the slip between the cup and the lip. St. John passed the window reading a letter. He entered.

"Our uncle John is dead," said he.

Both the sisters seemed struck: not shocked or appalled; the tidings appeared in their eyes rather momentous than afflicting.

"Dead?" repeated Diana.

"Yes."

She riveted a searching gaze on her brother's face. "And what then?" she demanded, in a low voice.

"What then, Die?" he replied, maintaining a marble immobility of feature. "What then? Why – nothing. Read."

He threw the letter into her lap. She glanced over it, and handed it to Mary. Mary perused it in silence, and returned it to her brother. All three looked at each other, and all three smiled – a dreary, pensive smile enough.

"Amen! We can yet live," said Diana at last.

"At any rate, it makes us no worse off than we were before," remarked Mary.

"Only it forces rather strongly on the mind the picture of what *might have been*," said Mr. Rivers, "and contrasts it somewhat too vividly with what *is*."

He folded the letter, locked it in his desk, and again went out.

For some minutes no one spoke. Diana then turned to me.

"Jane, you will wonder at us and our mysteries," she said, "and think us hard-hearted beings not to be more moved at the death of so near a relation as an uncle; but we have never seen him or known him. He was my mother's brother. My father and he quarrelled long ago. It was by his advice that my father risked most of his property in the speculation that ruined him. Mutual recrimination passed between them: they parted in anger, and were never reconciled. My uncle engaged afterwards in more prosperous undertakings: it appears he realised a fortune of twenty thousand pounds. He was never married, and had no near kindred but ourselves and one other person, not more closely related than we. My father always cherished the idea that he would atone for his error by leaving his possessions to us; that letter informs us that he has bequeathed every penny to the other relation, with the exception of thirty guineas, to be divided between St. John, Diana, and Mary Rivers, for the purchase of three mourning rings. He had a right, of course, to do as he pleased: and yet a momentary damp is cast on the spirits by the receipt of such news. Mary and I would have esteemed ourselves rich with a thousand pounds each; and to St. John such a sum would have been valuable, for the good it would have enabled him to do."

This explanation given, the subject was dropped, and no further reference made to it by either Mr. Rivers or his sisters. The next day I left Marsh End for Morton. The day after, Diana and Mary quitted it for distant B—. In a week, Mr. Rivers and Hannah repaired to the parsonage: and so the old grange was abandoned.

Chapter Thirty-One

MY HOME, THEN, when I at last find a home, – is a cottage; a little room with whitewashed walls and a sanded floor, containing four painted chairs and a table, a clock, a cupboard, with two or three plates and dishes, and a set of tea things in delf. Above, a chamber of the same dimensions as the kitchen, with a deal bedstead and chest of drawers; small, yet too large to be filled with my scanty wardrobe: though the kindness of my gentle and generous friends has increased that, by a modest stock of such things as are necessary.

It is evening. I have dismissed, with the fee of an orange, the little orphan who serves me as a handmaid. I am sitting alone on the hearth. This morning, the village school opened. I had twenty scholars. But three of the number can read: none write or cipher. Several knit, and a few sew a little. They speak with the broadest accent of the district. At present, they and I have a difficulty in understanding each other's language. Some of them are unmannered, rough, intractable, as well as ignorant; but others are docile, have a wish to learn, and evince a disposition that pleases me. I must not forget that these coarsely-clad little peasants are of flesh and blood as good as the scions of gentlest genealogy; and that the germs of native excellence, refinement, intelligence, kind feeling, are as likely to exist in their hearts as in those of the best-born. My duty will be to develop these germs: surely I shall find some happiness in discharging that office. Much enjoyment I do not expect in the life opening before me: yet it will, doubtless, if I regulate my mind, and exert my powers as I ought, yield me enough to live on from day to day.

Was I very gleeful, settled, content, during the hours I passed in yonder bare, humble schoolroom this morning and afternoon? Not to deceive myself, I must reply – No: I felt desolate to a degree. I felt – yes, idiot that I am – I felt degraded. I doubted I had taken a step which sank instead of raising me in the scale of social existence. I was weakly dismayed at the ignorance, the poverty, the coarseness of all I heard and saw round me. But let me not hate and despise myself too much for these feelings; I know them to be wrong – that is a great step gained; I shall strive to overcome them. Tomorrow, I trust, I shall get the better of them partially; and in a few weeks, perhaps, they will be quite subdued. In a few months, it is possible, the happiness of seeing progress, and a change for the better in my scholars may substitute gratification for disgust.

Meantime, let me ask myself one question – Which is better? – To have surrendered to temptation; listened to passion; made no painful effort – no struggle; – but to have sunk down in the silken snare; fallen asleep on the flowers covering it; wakened in a southern clime, amongst the luxuries of a pleasure villa: to have been now living in France, Mr. Rochester's mistress; delirious with his love half my time – for he would – oh, yes, he would have loved me well for a while. He *did* love me – no one will ever love me so again. I shall never more know the sweet homage given to beauty, youth, and grace – for never to anyone else shall I seem to possess these charms. He was fond and proud of me – it is what no man besides will ever be. – But where am I wandering, and what am I saying, and above all, feeling? Whether is it better, I ask, to be a slave in a fool's paradise at Marseilles – fevered with delusive bliss one hour – suffocating with the bitterest tears of remorse and shame the next – or to be a village-schoolmistress, free and honest, in a breezy mountain nook in the healthy heart of England?

Yes; I feel now that I was right when I adhered to principle and law, and scorned and crushed the insane promptings of a frenzied moment. God directed me to a correct choice: I thank His providence for the guidance!

Having brought my eventide musings to this point, I rose, went to my door, and looked at the sunset of the harvest-day, and at the quiet fields before my cottage, which, with the school, was distant half a mile from the village. The birds were singing their last strains:

"The air was mild, the dew was balm." [30]

While I looked, I thought myself happy, and was surprised to find myself ere long weeping – and why? For the doom which had reft me from adhesion to my master: for him I was no more to see; for the desperate grief and fatal fury – consequences of my departure – which might now, perhaps, be dragging him from the path of right, too far to leave hope of ultimate restoration thither. At this thought, I turned my face aside from the lovely sky of eve and lonely vale of Morton – I say *lonely*, for in that bend of it visible to me there was no building apparent save the church and the parsonage, half-hid in trees, and, quite at the extremity, the roof of Vale Hall, where the rich Mr. Oliver and his daughter lived. I hid my eyes, and leant my head against the stone frame of my door; but soon a slight noise near the wicket which shut in my tiny garden from the meadow beyond it made me look up. A dog – old Carlo, Mr. Rivers' pointer, as I saw in a moment – was pushing the gate with his nose, and St. John himself leant upon it with folded arms; his brow knit, his gaze, grave almost to displeasure, fixed on me. I asked him to come in.

"No, I cannot stay; I have only brought you a little parcel my sisters left for you. I think it contains a colour-box, pencils, and paper."

I approached to take it: a welcome gift it was. He examined my face, I thought, with austerity, as I came near: the traces of tears were doubtless very visible upon it.

"Have you found your first day's work harder than you expected?" he asked.

"Oh, no! On the contrary, I think in time I shall get on with my scholars very well."

"But perhaps your accommodations – your cottage – your furniture – have disappointed your expectations? They are, in truth, scanty enough; but –" I interrupted:

"My cottage is clean and weather-proof; my furniture sufficient and commodious. All I see has made me thankful, not despondent. I am not absolutely such a fool and sensualist as to regret the absence of a carpet, a sofa, and silver plate; besides, five weeks ago I had nothing – I was an outcast, a beggar, a vagrant; now I have acquaintance, a home, a business. I wonder at the goodness of God; the generosity of my friends; the bounty of my lot. I do not repine."

"But you feel solitude an oppression? The little house there behind you is dark and empty."

"I have hardly had time yet to enjoy a sense of tranquillity, much less to grow impatient under one of loneliness."

"Very well; I hope you feel the content you express: at any rate, your good sense will tell you that it is too soon yet to yield to the vacillating fears of Lot's wife. What you had left before I saw you, of course I do not know; but I counsel you to resist firmly every temptation which would incline you to look back: pursue your present career steadily, for some months at least."

"It is what I mean to do," I answered. St. John continued:

"It is hard work to control the workings of inclination and turn the bent of nature; but that it may be done, I know from experience. God has given us, in a measure, the power to make our own fate; and when our energies seem to demand a sustenance they cannot get – when our will strains after a path we may not follow – we need neither starve from inanition, nor stand still in despair: we have but to seek another nourishment for the mind, as strong as the forbidden food it longed to taste – and perhaps purer; and to hew out for the adventurous foot a road as direct and broad as the one Fortune has blocked up against us, if rougher than it.

"A year ago I was myself intensely miserable, because I thought I had made a mistake in entering the ministry: its uniform duties wearied me to death. I burnt for the more active life of the world – for the more exciting toils of a literary career – for the destiny of an artist, author, orator; anything rather than that of a priest: yes, the heart of a politician, of a soldier, of a votary of glory, a lover of renown, a luster after power, beat under my curate's surplice. I considered; my life was so wretched, it must be changed, or I must die. After a season of darkness and struggling, light broke and relief fell: my cramped existence all at once spread out to a plain without bounds – my powers heard a call from heaven to rise, gather their full strength, spread their wings, and mount beyond ken. God had an errand for me; to bear which afar, to deliver it well, skill and strength, courage and eloquence, the best qualifications of soldier, statesman, and orator, were all needed: for these all centre in the good missionary.

"A missionary I resolved to be. From that moment my state of mind changed; the fetters dissolved and dropped from every faculty, leaving nothing of bondage but its galling soreness – which time only can heal. My father, indeed, imposed the determination, but since his death, I have not a legitimate obstacle to contend with; some affairs settled, a successor for Morton provided, an entanglement or two of the feelings broken through or cut asunder – a last conflict with human weakness, in which I know I shall overcome, because I have vowed that I *will* overcome – and I leave Europe for the East."

He said this, in his peculiar, subdued, yet emphatic voice; looking, when he had ceased speaking, not at me, but at the setting sun, at which I looked too. Both he and I had our backs towards the path leading up the field to the wicket.

We had heard no step on that grass-grown track; the water running in the vale was the one lulling sound of the hour and scene; we might well then start when a gay voice, sweet as a silver bell, exclaimed:

"Good evening, Mr. Rivers. And good evening, old Carlo. Your dog is quicker to recognise his friends than you are, sir; he pricked his ears and wagged his tail when I was at the bottom of the field, and you have your back towards me now."

It was true. Though Mr. Rivers had started at the first of those musical accents, as if a thunderbolt had split a cloud over his head, he stood yet, at the close of the sentence, in the same attitude in which the speaker had surprised him – his arm resting on the gate, his face directed towards the west. He turned at last, with measured deliberation. A vision, as it seemed to me, had risen at his side. There appeared, within three feet of him, a form clad in pure white – a youthful, graceful form: full, yet fine in contour; and when, after bending to caress Carlo, it lifted up its head, and threw back a long veil, there bloomed under his glance a face of perfect beauty. Perfect beauty is a strong expression; but I do not retrace or qualify it: as sweet features as ever the temperate clime of Albion moulded; as pure hues of rose and lily as ever her humid gales and vapoury skies generated and screened, justified, in this instance, the term. No charm was wanting, no defect was perceptible; the young girl had regular and delicate lineaments; eyes shaped and coloured as we see them in lovely pictures, large, and dark, and full; the long and shadowy eyelash which encircles a fine eye with so soft a fascination; the pencilled brow which gives such clearness; the white smooth forehead, which adds such repose to the livelier beauties of tint and ray; the cheek oval, fresh, and smooth; the lips, fresh too, ruddy, healthy, sweetly formed; the even and gleaming teeth without flaw; the small dimpled chin; the ornament of rich, plenteous tresses – all advantages, in short, which, combined, realise the ideal of beauty, were fully hers. I wondered, as I looked at this fair creature: I admired her with my whole heart. Nature had surely formed her in a partial mood; and, forgetting her usual stinted stepmother dole of gifts, had endowed this, her darling, with a granddame's bounty.

What did St. John Rivers think of this earthly angel? I naturally asked myself that question as I saw him turn to her and look at her; and, as naturally, I sought the answer to the inquiry in his countenance. He had already withdrawn his eye from the Peri [31], and was looking at a humble tuft of daisies which grew by the wicket.

"A lovely evening, but late for you to be out alone," he said, as he crushed the snowy heads of the closed flowers with his foot.

"Oh, I only came home from S—" (she mentioned the name of a large town some twenty miles distant) "this afternoon. Papa told me you had opened your school, and that the new mistress was come; and so I put on my bonnet after tea, and ran up the valley to see her: this is she?" pointing to me.

"It is," said St. John.

"Do you think you shall like Morton?" she asked of me, with a direct and naive simplicity of tone and manner, pleasing, if child-like.

"I hope I shall. I have many inducements to do so."

"Did you find your scholars as attentive as you expected?"

"Quite."

"Do you like your house?"

"Very much."

"Have I furnished it nicely?"

"Very nicely, indeed."

"And made a good choice of an attendant for you in Alice Wood?"

"You have indeed. She is teachable and handy." (This then, I thought, is Miss Oliver, the heiress; favoured, it seems, in the gifts of fortune, as well as in those of nature! What happy combination of the planets presided over her birth, I wonder?)

"I shall come up and help you to teach sometimes," she added. "It will be a change for me to visit you now and then; and I like a change. Mr. Rivers, I have been *so* gay during my stay at S—. Last night, or rather this morning, I was dancing till two o'clock. The —th regiment are stationed there since the riots; and the officers are the most agreeable men in the world: they put all our young knife-grinders and scissor merchants to shame."

It seemed to me that Mr. St. John's under lip protruded, and his upper lip curled a moment. His mouth certainly looked a good deal compressed, and the lower part of his face unusually stern and square, as the laughing girl gave him this information. He lifted his gaze, too, from the daisies, and turned it on her. An unsmiling, a searching, a meaning gaze it was. She answered it with a second laugh, and laughter well became her youth, her roses, her dimples, her bright eyes.

As he stood, mute and grave, she again fell to caressing Carlo. "Poor Carlo loves me," said she. "*He* is not stern and distant to his friends; and if he could speak, he would not be silent."

As she patted the dog's head, bending with native grace before his young and austere master, I saw a glow rise to that master's face. I saw his solemn eye melt with sudden fire, and flicker with resistless emotion. Flushed and kindled thus, he looked nearly as beautiful for a man as she for a woman. His chest heaved once, as if his large heart, weary of despotic constriction, had expanded, despite the will, and made a vigorous bound for the attainment of liberty. But he curbed it, I think, as a resolute rider would curb a rearing steed. He responded neither by word nor movement to the gentle advances made him.

"Papa says you never come to see us now," continued Miss Oliver, looking up. "You are quite a stranger at Vale Hall. He is alone this evening, and not very well: will you return with me and visit him?"

"It is not a seasonable hour to intrude on Mr. Oliver," answered St. John.

"Not a seasonable hour! But I declare it is. It is just the hour when papa most wants company: when the works are closed and he has no business to occupy him. Now, Mr. Rivers, *do* come. Why are you so very shy, and so very sombre?" She filled up the hiatus his silence left by a reply of her own.

"I forgot!" she exclaimed, shaking her beautiful curled head, as if shocked at herself. "I am so giddy and thoughtless! *Do* excuse me. It had slipped my memory that you have good reasons to be indisposed for joining in my chatter. Diana and Mary have left you, and Moor House is shut up, and you are so lonely. I am sure I pity you. Do come and see papa."

"Not tonight, Miss Rosamond, not tonight."

Mr. St. John spoke almost like an automaton: himself only knew the effort it cost him thus to refuse.

"Well, if you are so obstinate, I will leave you; for I dare not stay any longer: the dew begins to fall. Good evening!"

She held out her hand. He just touched it. "Good evening!" he repeated, in a voice low and hollow as an echo. She turned, but in a moment returned.

"Are you well?" she asked. Well might she put the question: his face was blanched as her gown.

"Quite well," he enunciated; and, with a bow, he left the gate. She went one way; he another. She turned twice to gaze after him as she tripped fairy-like down the field; he, as he strode firmly across, never turned at all.

This spectacle of another's suffering and sacrifice rapt my thoughts from exclusive meditation on my own. Diana Rivers had designated her brother "inexorable as death." She had not exaggerated.

Chapter Thirty-Two

I CONTINUED THE labours of the village school as actively and faithfully as I could. It was truly hard work at first. Some time elapsed before, with all my efforts, I could comprehend my scholars and their nature. Wholly untaught, with faculties quite torpid, they seemed to me hopelessly dull; and, at first sight, all dull alike: but I soon found I was mistaken. There was a difference amongst them as amongst the educated; and when I got to know them, and they me, this difference rapidly developed itself. Their amazement at me, my language, my rules, and ways, once subsided, I found some of these heavy-looking, gaping rustics wake up into sharp-witted girls enough. Many showed themselves obliging, and amiable too; and I discovered amongst them not a few examples of natural politeness, and innate self-respect, as well as of excellent capacity, that won both my goodwill and my admiration. These soon took a pleasure in doing their work well, in keeping their persons neat, in learning their tasks regularly, in acquiring quiet and orderly manners. The rapidity of their progress, in some instances, was even surprising; and an honest and happy pride I took in it: besides, I began personally to like some of the best girls; and they liked me. I had amongst my scholars several farmers' daughters: young women grown, almost. These could already read, write, and sew; and to them I taught the elements of grammar, geography, history, and the finer kinds of needlework. I found estimable characters amongst them – characters desirous of information and disposed for improvement – with whom I passed many a pleasant evening hour in their own homes. Their parents then (the farmer and his wife) loaded me with attentions. There was an enjoyment in accepting their simple kindness, and in repaying it by a consideration – a scrupulous regard to their feelings – to which they were not, perhaps, at all times accustomed, and which both charmed and benefited them; because, while it elevated them in their own eyes, it made them emulous to merit the deferential treatment they received.

I felt I became a favourite in the neighbourhood. Whenever I went out, I heard on all sides cordial salutations, and was welcomed with friendly smiles. To live amidst general regard, though it be but the regard of working people, is like 'sitting in sunshine, calm and sweet'; serene inward feelings bud and bloom under the ray. At this period of my life, my heart far oftener swelled with thankfulness than sank with dejection: and yet, reader, to tell you all, in the midst of this calm, this useful existence – after a day passed in honourable exertion amongst my scholars, an evening spent in drawing or reading contentedly alone – I used to rush into strange dreams at night: dreams many-coloured, agitated, full of the ideal, the stirring, the stormy – dreams where, amidst unusual scenes, charged with adventure, with agitating risk and romantic chance, I still again and again met Mr. Rochester, always at some exciting crisis; and then the sense of being in his arms, hearing his voice, meeting his eye, touching his hand and cheek, loving him, being loved by him – the hope of passing a lifetime at his side, would be renewed, with all its first force and fire. Then I awoke. Then I recalled where I was, and how situated. Then I rose up on my curtainless bed, trembling and quivering; and then the still, dark night witnessed the convulsion of despair, and heard the burst of passion. By nine o'clock the next morning I was punctually opening the school; tranquil, settled, prepared for the steady duties of the day.

Rosamond Oliver kept her word in coming to visit me. Her call at the school was generally made in the course of her morning ride. She would canter up to the door on her pony, followed by a mounted livery servant. Anything more exquisite than her appearance, in her purple habit, with her Amazon's cap of black velvet placed gracefully above the long curls that kissed her cheek and floated to her shoulders, can scarcely be imagined: and it was thus she would enter the rustic building, and glide through the dazzled ranks of the village children. She generally came at the hour when Mr. Rivers was engaged in giving his daily catechising lesson. Keenly, I fear, did the eye of the visitress pierce the young pastor's heart. A sort of instinct seemed to warn him of her entrance, even when he did not see it; and when he was looking quite away from the door, if she appeared at it, his cheek would glow, and his marble-seeming features, though they refused to relax, changed indescribably, and in their very quiescence became expressive of a repressed fervour, stronger than working muscle or darting glance could indicate.

Of course, she knew her power: indeed, he did not, because he could not, conceal it from her. In spite of his Christian stoicism, when she went up and addressed him, and smiled gaily, encouragingly, even fondly in his face, his hand would tremble and his eye burn. He seemed to say, with his sad and resolute look, if he did not say it with his lips, "I love you, and I know you prefer me. It is not despair of success that keeps me dumb. If I offered my heart, I believe you would accept it. But that heart is already laid on a sacred altar: the fire is arranged round it. It will soon be no more than a sacrifice consumed."

And then she would pout like a disappointed child; a pensive cloud would soften her radiant vivacity; she would withdraw her hand hastily from his, and turn in transient petulance from his aspect, at once so heroic and so martyr-like. St. John, no doubt, would have given the world to follow, recall, retain her, when she thus left him; but he would not give one chance of heaven, nor relinquish, for the elysium of her love, one hope of the true, eternal Paradise. Besides, he could not bind all that he had in his nature – the rover, the aspirant, the poet, the priest – in the limits of a single passion. He could not – he would not – renounce his wild field of mission warfare for the parlours and the peace of Vale Hall. I learnt so much from himself in an inroad I once, despite his reserve, had the daring to make on his confidence.

Miss Oliver already honoured me with frequent visits to my cottage. I had learnt her whole character, which was without mystery or disguise: she was coquettish but not heartless; exacting, but not worthlessly selfish. She had been indulged from her birth, but was not absolutely spoilt. She was hasty, but good-humoured; vain (she could not help it, when every glance in the glass showed her such a flush of loveliness), but not affected; liberal-handed; innocent of the pride of wealth; ingenuous; sufficiently intelligent; gay, lively, and unthinking: she was very charming, in short, even to a cool observer of her own sex like me; but she was not profoundly interesting or thoroughly impressive. A very different sort of mind was hers from that, for instance, of the sisters of St. John. Still, I liked her almost as I liked my pupil Adèle; except that, for a child whom we have watched over and taught, a closer affection is engendered than we can give an equally attractive adult acquaintance.

She had taken an amiable caprice to me. She said I was like Mr. Rivers, only, certainly, she allowed, "not one-tenth so handsome, though I was a nice neat little soul enough, but he was an angel." I was, however, good, clever, composed, and firm, like him. I was a *lusus naturoe* [32], she affirmed, as a village schoolmistress: she was sure my previous history, if known, would make a delightful romance.

One evening, while, with her usual child-like activity, and thoughtless yet not offensive inquisitiveness, she was rummaging the cupboard and the table-drawer of my little kitchen, she discovered first two French books, a volume of Schiller, a German grammar and dictionary, and then my drawing-materials and some sketches, including a pencil-head of a pretty little cherub-like girl, one of my scholars, and sundry views from nature, taken in the Vale of Morton and on the surrounding moors. She was first transfixed with surprise, and then electrified with delight.

"Had I done these pictures? Did I know French and German? What a love – what a miracle I was! I drew better than her master in the first school in S—. Would I sketch a portrait of her, to show to papa?"

"With pleasure," I replied; and I felt a thrill of artist-delight at the idea of copying from so perfect and radiant a model. She had then on a dark-blue silk dress; her arms and her neck were bare; her only ornament was her chestnut tresses, which waved over her shoulders with all the wild grace of natural curls. I took a sheet of fine cardboard, and drew a careful outline. I promised myself the pleasure of colouring it; and, as it was getting late then, I told her she must come and sit another day.

She made such a report of me to her father, that Mr. Oliver himself accompanied her next evening – a tall, massive-featured, middle-aged, and grey-headed man, at whose side his lovely daughter looked like a bright flower near a hoary turret. He appeared a taciturn, and perhaps a proud personage; but he was very kind to me. The sketch of Rosamond's portrait pleased him highly: he said I must make a finished picture of it. He insisted, too, on my coming the next day to spend the evening at Vale Hall.

I went. I found it a large, handsome residence, showing abundant evidences of wealth in the proprietor. Rosamond was full of glee and pleasure all the time I stayed. Her father was affable; and when he entered into conversation with me after tea, he expressed in strong terms his approbation of what I had done in Morton school, and said he only feared, from what he saw and heard, I was too good for the place, and would soon quit it for one more suitable.

"Indeed," cried Rosamond, "she is clever enough to be a governess in a high family, papa."

I thought I would far rather be where I am than in any high family in the land. Mr. Oliver spoke of Mr. Rivers – of the Rivers family – with great respect. He said it was a very old name in that neighbourhood; that the ancestors of the house were wealthy; that all Morton had once belonged to them; that even now he considered the representative of that house might, if he liked, make an alliance with the best. He accounted it a pity that so fine and talented a young man should have formed the design of going out as a missionary; it was quite throwing a valuable life away. It appeared, then, that her father would throw no obstacle in the way of Rosamond's union with St. John. Mr. Oliver evidently regarded the young clergyman's good birth, old name, and sacred profession as sufficient compensation for the want of fortune.

It was the 5th of November, and a holiday. My little servant, after helping me to clean my house, was gone, well satisfied with the fee of a penny for her aid. All about me was spotless and bright – scoured floor, polished grate, and well-rubbed chairs. I had also made myself neat, and had now the afternoon before me to spend as I would.

The translation of a few pages of German occupied an hour; then I got my palette and pencils, and fell to the more soothing, because easier occupation, of completing Rosamond Oliver's miniature. The head was finished already: there was but the background to tint and the drapery to shade off; a touch of carmine, too, to add to the ripe lips – a soft curl here and there to the tresses – a deeper tinge to the shadow of the lash under the azured eyelid. I was absorbed in the execution of these nice details, when, after one rapid tap, my door unclosed, admitting St. John Rivers.

"I am come to see how you are spending your holiday," he said. "Not, I hope, in thought? No, that is well: while you draw you will not feel lonely. You see, I mistrust you still, though you have borne up wonderfully so far. I have brought you a book for evening solace," and he laid on the table a new publication – a poem: one of those genuine productions so often vouchsafed to the fortunate public of those days – the golden age of modern literature. Alas! The readers of our era are less favoured. But courage! I will not pause either to accuse or repine. I know poetry is not dead, nor genius lost; nor has Mammon gained power over either, to bind or slay: they will both assert their existence, their presence, their liberty and strength again one day. Powerful angels, safe in heaven! They smile when sordid souls triumph, and feeble ones weep over their destruction. Poetry destroyed? Genius banished? No! Mediocrity, no: do not let envy prompt you to the thought. No; they not only live, but reign and redeem: and without their divine influence spread everywhere, you would be in hell – the hell of your own meanness.

While I was eagerly glancing at the bright pages of *Marmion* (for *Marmion* it was), St. John stooped to examine my drawing. His tall figure sprang erect again with a start: he said nothing. I looked up at him: he shunned my eye. I knew his thoughts well, and could read his heart plainly; at the moment I felt calmer and cooler than he: I had then temporarily the advantage of him, and I conceived an inclination to do him some good, if I could.

"With all his firmness and self-control," thought I, "he tasks himself too far: locks every feeling and pang within – expresses, confesses, imparts nothing. I am sure it would benefit him to talk a little about this sweet Rosamond, whom he thinks he ought not to marry: I will make him talk."

I said first, "Take a chair, Mr. Rivers." But he answered, as he always did, that he could not stay. "Very well," I responded, mentally, "stand if you like; but you shall not go just yet, I am determined: solitude is at least as bad for you as it is for me. I'll try if I cannot discover the secret spring of your confidence, and find an aperture in that marble breast through which I can shed one drop of the balm of sympathy."

"Is this portrait like?" I asked bluntly.

"Like! Like whom? I did not observe it closely."

"You did, Mr. Rivers."

He almost started at my sudden and strange abruptness: he looked at me astonished. "Oh, that is nothing yet," I muttered within. "I don't mean to be baffled by a little stiffness on your part; I'm prepared to go to considerable lengths." I continued, "You observed it closely and distinctly; but I have no objection to your looking at it again," and I rose and placed it in his hand.

"A well-executed picture," he said; "very soft, clear colouring; very graceful and correct drawing."

"Yes, yes; I know all that. But what of the resemblance? Who is it like?"

Mastering some hesitation, he answered, "Miss Oliver, I presume."

"Of course. And now, sir, to reward you for the accurate guess, I will promise to paint you a careful and faithful duplicate of this very picture, provided you admit that the gift would be acceptable to you. I don't wish to throw away my time and trouble on an offering you would deem worthless."

He continued to gaze at the picture: the longer he looked, the firmer he held it, the more he seemed to covet it. "It is like!" he murmured; "the eye is well managed: the colour, light, expression, are perfect. It smiles!"

"Would it comfort, or would it wound you to have a similar painting? Tell me that. When you are at Madagascar, or at the Cape, or in India, would it be a consolation to have that memento in your possession? Or would the sight of it bring recollections calculated to enervate and distress?"

He now furtively raised his eyes: he glanced at me, irresolute, disturbed: he again surveyed the picture.

"That I should like to have it is certain: whether it would be judicious or wise is another question."

Since I had ascertained that Rosamond really preferred him, and that her father was not likely to oppose the match, I – less exalted in my views than St. John – had been strongly disposed in my own heart to advocate their union. It seemed to me that, should he become the possessor of Mr. Oliver's large fortune, he might do as much good with it as if he went and laid his genius out to wither, and his strength to waste, under a tropical sun. With this persuasion I now answered:

"As far as I can see, it would be wiser and more judicious if you were to take to yourself the original at once."

By this time he had sat down: he had laid the picture on the table before him, and with his brow supported on both hands, hung fondly over it. I discerned he was now neither angry nor shocked at my audacity. I saw even that to be thus frankly addressed on a subject he had deemed unapproachable – to hear it thus freely handled – was beginning to be felt by him as a new pleasure – an unhoped-for relief. Reserved people often really need the frank discussion of their sentiments and griefs more than the expansive. The sternest-seeming stoic is human after all; and to 'burst' with boldness and good will into 'the silent sea' of their souls is often to confer on them the first of obligations.

"She likes you, I am sure," said I, as I stood behind his chair, "and her father respects you. Moreover, she is a sweet girl – rather thoughtless; but you would have sufficient thought for both yourself and her. You ought to marry her."

"*Does* she like me?" he asked.

"Certainly; better than she likes anyone else. She talks of you continually: there is no subject she enjoys so much or touches upon so often."

"It is very pleasant to hear this," he said – "very: go on for another quarter of an hour." And he actually took out his watch and laid it upon the table to measure the time.

"But where is the use of going on," I asked, "when you are probably preparing some iron blow of contradiction, or forging a fresh chain to fetter your heart?"

"Don't imagine such hard things. Fancy me yielding and melting, as I am doing: human love rising like a freshly opened fountain in my mind and overflowing with sweet inundation all the field I have so carefully and with such labour prepared – so assiduously sown with the seeds of good intentions, of self-denying plans. And now it is deluged with a nectarous flood – the young germs swamped – delicious poison cankering them: now I see myself stretched on an ottoman in the drawing room at Vale Hall at my bride Rosamond Oliver's feet: she is talking to me with her sweet voice – gazing down on me with those eyes your skilful hand has copied so well – smiling at me with these coral lips. She is mine – I am hers – this present life and passing world suffice to me. Hush! say nothing – my heart is full of delight – my senses are entranced – let the time I marked pass in peace."

I humoured him: the watch ticked on: he breathed fast and low: I stood silent. Amidst this hush the quartet sped; he replaced the watch, laid the picture down, rose, and stood on the hearth.

"Now," said he, "that little space was given to delirium and delusion. I rested my temples on the breast of temptation, and put my neck voluntarily under her yoke of flowers. I tasted her cup. The pillow was burning: there is an asp in the garland: the wine has a bitter taste: her promises are hollow – her offers false: I see and know all this."

I gazed at him in wonder.

"It is strange," pursued he, "that while I love Rosamond Oliver so wildly – with all the intensity, indeed, of a first passion, the object of which is exquisitely beautiful, graceful, fascinating – I experience at the same time a calm, unwarped consciousness that she would not make me a good wife; that she is not the partner suited to me; that I should discover this within a year after marriage; and that to twelve months' rapture would succeed a lifetime of regret. This I know."

"Strange indeed!" I could not help ejaculating.

"While something in me," he went on, "is acutely sensible to her charms, something else is as deeply impressed with her defects: they are such that she could sympathise in nothing I aspired to – co-operate in nothing I undertook. Rosamond a sufferer, a labourer, a female apostle? Rosamond a missionary's wife? No!"

"But you need not be a missionary. You might relinquish that scheme."

"Relinquish! What! My vocation? My great work? My foundation laid on earth for a mansion in heaven? My hopes of being numbered in the band who have merged all ambitions in the glorious one of bettering their race – of carrying knowledge into the realms of ignorance – of substituting peace for war – freedom for bondage – religion for superstition – the hope of heaven for the fear of hell? Must I relinquish that? It is dearer than the blood in my veins. It is what I have to look forward to, and to live for."

After a considerable pause, I said – "And Miss Oliver? Are her disappointment and sorrow of no interest to you?"

"Miss Oliver is ever surrounded by suitors and flatterers: in less than a month, my image will be effaced from her heart. She will forget me; and will marry, probably, some one who will make her far happier than I should do."

"You speak coolly enough; but you suffer in the conflict. You are wasting away."

"No. If I get a little thin, it is with anxiety about my prospects, yet unsettled – my departure, continually procrastinated. Only this morning, I received intelligence that the successor, whose arrival I have been so long expecting, cannot be ready to replace me for three months to come yet; and perhaps the three months may extend to six."

"You tremble and become flushed whenever Miss Oliver enters the schoolroom."

Again the surprised expression crossed his face. He had not imagined that a woman would dare to speak so to a man. For me, I felt at home in this sort of discourse. I could never rest in communication with strong, discreet, and refined minds, whether male or female, till I had passed the outworks of conventional reserve, and crossed the threshold of confidence, and won a place by their heart's very hearthstone.

"You are original," said he, "and not timid. There is something brave in your spirit, as well as penetrating in your eye; but allow me to assure you that you partially misinterpret my emotions. You think them more profound and potent than they are. You give me a larger allowance of sympathy than I have a just claim to. When I colour, and when I shade before Miss Oliver, I do not pity myself. I scorn the weakness. I know it is ignoble: a mere fever of the flesh: not, I declare, the convulsion of the soul. *That* is just as fixed as a rock, firm set in the depths of a restless sea. Know me to be what I am – a cold hard man."

I smiled incredulously.

"You have taken my confidence by storm," he continued, "and now it is much at your service. I am simply, in my original state – stripped of that blood-bleached robe with which Christianity covers human deformity – a cold, hard, ambitious man. Natural affection only, of all the sentiments, has permanent power over me. Reason, and not feeling, is my guide; my ambition is unlimited: my desire to rise higher, to do more than others, insatiable. I honour endurance, perseverance, industry, talent; because these are the means by which men achieve great ends and mount to lofty eminence. I watch your career with interest, because I consider you a specimen of a diligent, orderly, energetic woman: not because I deeply compassionate what you have gone through, or what you still suffer."

"You would describe yourself as a mere pagan philosopher," I said.

"No. There is this difference between me and deistic philosophers: I believe; and I believe the Gospel. You missed your epithet. I am not a pagan, but a Christian philosopher – a follower of the sect of Jesus. As His disciple I adopt His pure, His merciful, His benignant doctrines. I advocate them: I am sworn to spread them. Won in youth to religion, she has cultivated my original qualities thus: – From the minute germ, natural affection, she has developed the overshadowing tree, philanthropy. From the wild stringy root of human uprightness, she has reared a due sense of the Divine justice. Of the ambition to win power and renown for my wretched self, she has formed the ambition to spread my Master's kingdom; to achieve victories for the standard of the cross. So much has religion done for me; turning the original materials to the best account; pruning and training nature. But she could not eradicate nature: nor will it be eradicated 'till this mortal shall put on immortality.'"

Having said this, he took his hat, which lay on the table beside my palette. Once more he looked at the portrait.

"She *is* lovely," he murmured. "She is well named the Rose of the World, indeed!"

"And may I not paint one like it for you?"

"*Cui bono*? No."

He drew over the picture the sheet of thin paper on which I was accustomed to rest my hand in painting, to prevent the cardboard from being sullied. What he suddenly saw on this blank paper, it was impossible for me to tell; but something had caught his eye. He took it up with a snatch; he looked at the edge; then shot a glance at me, inexpressibly peculiar, and quite incomprehensible: a glance that seemed to take and make note of every point in my shape, face, and dress; for it traversed all, quick, keen as lightning. His lips parted, as if to speak: but he checked the coming sentence, whatever it was.

"What is the matter?" I asked.

"Nothing in the world," was the reply; and, replacing the paper, I saw him dexterously tear a narrow slip from the margin. It disappeared in his glove; and, with one hasty nod and "good-afternoon," he vanished.

"Well!" I exclaimed, using an expression of the district, "that caps the globe, however!"

I, in my turn, scrutinised the paper; but saw nothing on it save a few dingy stains of paint where I had tried the tint in my pencil. I pondered the mystery a minute or two; but finding it insolvable, and being certain it could not be of much moment, I dismissed, and soon forgot it.

Chapter Thirty-Three

WHEN MR. ST. JOHN went, it was beginning to snow; the whirling storm continued all night. The next day a keen wind brought fresh and blinding falls; by twilight the valley was drifted up and almost impassable. I had closed my shutter, laid a mat to the door to prevent the snow from blowing in under it, trimmed my fire, and after sitting nearly an hour on the hearth listening to the muffled fury of the tempest, I lit a candle, took down *Marmion*, and beginning:

> *Day set on Norham's castled steep,*
> *And Tweed's fair river broad and deep,*
> *And Cheviot's mountains lone;*
> *The massive towers, the donjon keep,*
> *The flanking walls that round them sweep,*
> *In yellow lustre shone.*

I soon forgot storm in music.

I heard a noise: the wind, I thought, shook the door. No; it was St. John Rivers, who, lifting the latch, came in out of the frozen hurricane – the howling darkness – and stood before me: the cloak that covered his tall figure all white as a glacier. I was almost in consternation, so little had I expected any guest from the blocked-up vale that night.

"Any ill news?" I demanded. "Has anything happened?"

"No. How very easily alarmed you are!" he answered, removing his cloak and hanging it up against the door, towards which he again coolly pushed the mat which his entrance had deranged. He stamped the snow from his boots.

"I shall sully the purity of your floor," said he, "but you must excuse me for once." Then he approached the fire. "I have had hard work to get here, I assure you," he observed, as he warmed his hands over the flame. "One drift took me up to the waist; happily the snow is quite soft yet."

"But why are you come?" I could not forbear saying.

"Rather an inhospitable question to put to a visitor; but since you ask it, I answer simply to have a little talk with you; I got tired of my mute books and empty rooms. Besides, since yesterday I have experienced the excitement of a person to whom a tale has been half-told, and who is impatient to hear the sequel."

He sat down. I recalled his singular conduct of yesterday, and really I began to fear his wits were touched. If he were insane, however, his was a very cool and collected insanity: I had never seen that handsome-featured face of his look more like chiselled marble than it did just now, as he put aside his snow-wet hair from his forehead and let the firelight shine free on his pale brow and cheek as pale, where it grieved me to discover the hollow trace of care or sorrow now so plainly graved. I waited, expecting he would say something I could at least comprehend; but his hand was now at his chin, his finger on his lip: he was thinking. It struck me that his hand looked wasted like his face. A perhaps uncalled-for gush of pity came over my heart: I was moved to say:

"I wish Diana or Mary would come and live with you: it is too bad that you should be quite alone; and you are recklessly rash about your own health."

"Not at all," said he: "I care for myself when necessary. I am well now. What do you see amiss in me?"

This was said with a careless, abstracted indifference, which showed that my solicitude was, at least in his opinion, wholly superfluous. I was silenced.

He still slowly moved his finger over his upper lip, and still his eye dwelt dreamily on the glowing grate; thinking it urgent to say something, I asked him presently if he felt any cold draught from the door, which was behind him.

"No, no!" he responded shortly and somewhat testily.

"Well," I reflected, "if you won't talk, you may be still; I'll let you alone now, and return to my book."

So I snuffed the candle and resumed the perusal of *Marmion*. He soon stirred; my eye was instantly drawn to his movements; he only took out a morocco pocket book, thence produced a letter, which he read in silence, folded it, put it back, relapsed into meditation. It was vain to try to read with such an inscrutable fixture before me; nor could I, in impatience, consent to be dumb; he might rebuff me if he liked, but talk I would.

"Have you heard from Diana and Mary lately?"

"Not since the letter I showed you a week ago."

"There has not been any change made about your own arrangements? You will not be summoned to leave England sooner than you expected?"

"I fear not, indeed: such chance is too good to befall me." Baffled so far, I changed my ground. I bethought myself to talk about the school and my scholars.

"Mary Garrett's mother is better, and Mary came back to the school this morning, and I shall have four new girls next week from the Foundry Close – they would have come today but for the snow."

"Indeed!"

"Mr. Oliver pays for two."

"Does he?"

"He means to give the whole school a treat at Christmas."

"I know."

"Was it your suggestion?"

"No."

"Whose, then?"

"His daughter's, I think."

"It is like her: she is so good-natured."

"Yes."

Again came the blank of a pause: the clock struck eight strokes. It aroused him; he uncrossed his legs, sat erect, turned to me.

"Leave your book a moment, and come a little nearer the fire," he said.

Wondering, and of my wonder finding no end, I complied.

"Half an hour ago," he pursued, "I spoke of my impatience to hear the sequel of a tale: on reflection, I find the matter will be better managed by my assuming the narrator's part, and converting you into a listener. Before commencing, it is but fair to warn you that the story will sound somewhat hackneyed in your ears; but stale details often regain a degree of freshness when they pass through new lips. For the rest, whether trite or novel, it is short.

"Twenty years ago, a poor curate – never mind his name at this moment – fell in love with a rich man's daughter; she fell in love with him, and married him, against the advice of all her friends, who consequently disowned her immediately after the wedding. Before two years passed, the rash pair were both dead, and laid quietly side by side under one slab. (I have seen their grave; it formed part of the pavement of a huge churchyard surrounding the grim, soot-black old cathedral of an overgrown manufacturing town in —shire.) They left a daughter, which, at its very birth, Charity received in her lap – cold as that of the snow-drift I almost stuck fast in tonight. Charity carried the friendless thing to the house of its rich maternal relations; it was reared by an aunt-in-law, called (I come to names now) Mrs. Reed of Gateshead. You start – did you hear a noise? I daresay it is only a rat scrambling along the rafters of the adjoining schoolroom: it was a barn before I had it repaired and altered, and barns are generally haunted by rats. – To proceed. Mrs. Reed kept the orphan ten years: whether it was happy or not with her, I cannot say, never having been told; but at the end of that time she transferred it to a place you know – being no other than Lowood School, where you so long resided yourself. It seems her career there was very honourable: from a pupil, she became a teacher, like yourself – really it strikes me there are parallel points in her history and yours – she left it to be a governess: there, again, your fates were analogous; she undertook the education of the ward of a certain Mr. Rochester."

"Mr. Rivers!" I interrupted.

"I can guess your feelings," he said, "but restrain them for a while: I have nearly finished; hear me to the end. Of Mr. Rochester's character I know nothing, but the one fact that he professed to offer honourable marriage to this young girl, and that at the very altar she discovered he had a wife yet alive, though a lunatic. What his subsequent conduct and proposals were is a matter of pure conjecture; but when an event transpired which rendered inquiry after the governess necessary, it was discovered she was gone – no one could tell when, where, or how. She had left Thornfield Hall in the night; every research after her course had been vain: the country had been scoured far and wide; no vestige of information could be gathered respecting her. Yet that she should be found is become a matter of serious urgency: advertisements have been put in all the papers; I myself have received a letter from one Mr. Briggs, a solicitor, communicating the details I have just imparted. Is it not an odd tale?"

"Just tell me this," said I, "and since you know so much, you surely can tell it me – what of Mr. Rochester? How and where is he? What is he doing? Is he well?"

"I am ignorant of all concerning Mr. Rochester: the letter never mentions him but to narrate the fraudulent and illegal attempt I have adverted to. You should rather ask the name of the governess – the nature of the event which requires her appearance."

"Did no one go to Thornfield Hall, then? Did no one see Mr. Rochester?"

"I suppose not."

"But they wrote to him?"

"Of course."

"And what did he say? Who has his letters?"

"Mr. Briggs intimates that the answer to his application was not from Mr. Rochester, but from a lady: it is signed 'Alice Fairfax.'"

I felt cold and dismayed: my worst fears then were probably true: he had in all probability left England and rushed in reckless desperation to some former haunt on the Continent. And what opiate for his severe sufferings – what object for his strong passions – had he sought there? I dared not answer the question. Oh, my poor master – once almost my husband – whom I had often called "my dear Edward!"

"He must have been a bad man," observed Mr. Rivers.

"You don't know him – don't pronounce an opinion upon him," I said, with warmth.

"Very well," he answered quietly: "and indeed my head is otherwise occupied than with him: I have my tale to finish. Since you won't ask the governess's name, I must tell it of my own accord. Stay! I have it here – it is always more satisfactory to see important points written down, fairly committed to black and white."

And the pocket book was again deliberately produced, opened, sought through; from one of its compartments was extracted a shabby slip of paper, hastily torn off: I recognised in its texture and its stains of ultra-marine, and lake, and vermillion, the ravished margin of the portrait-cover. He got up, held it close to my eyes: and I read, traced in Indian ink, in my own handwriting, the words "Jane Eyre" – the work doubtless of some moment of abstraction.

"Briggs wrote to me of a Jane Eyre:" he said, "the advertisements demanded a Jane Eyre: I knew a Jane Elliott. – I confess I had my suspicions, but it was only yesterday afternoon they were at once resolved into certainty. You own the name and renounce the *alias*?"

"Yes – yes; but where is Mr. Briggs? He perhaps knows more of Mr. Rochester than you do."

"Briggs is in London. I should doubt his knowing anything at all about Mr. Rochester; it is not in Mr. Rochester he is interested. Meantime, you forget essential points in pursuing trifles: you do not inquire why Mr. Briggs sought after you – what he wanted with you."

"Well, what did he want?"

"Merely to tell you that your uncle, Mr. Eyre of Madeira, is dead; that he has left you all his property, and that you are now rich – merely that – nothing more."

"I! – Rich?"

"Yes, you, rich – quite an heiress."

Silence succeeded.

"You must prove your identity of course," resumed St. John presently: "a step which will offer no difficulties; you can then enter on immediate possession. Your fortune is vested in the English funds; Briggs has the will and the necessary documents."

Here was a new card turned up! It is a fine thing, reader, to be lifted in a moment from indigence to wealth – a very fine thing; but not a matter one can comprehend, or consequently enjoy, all at once. And then there are other chances in life far more thrilling and rapture-giving: *this* is solid, an affair of the actual world, nothing ideal about it: all its associations are solid and sober, and its manifestations are the same. One does not jump, and spring, and shout hurrah! at hearing one has got a fortune; one begins to consider responsibilities, and to ponder business; on a base of steady satisfaction rise certain grave cares, and we contain ourselves, and brood over our bliss with a solemn brow.

Besides, the words Legacy, Bequest, go side by side with the words, Death, Funeral. My uncle I had heard was dead – my only relative; ever since being made aware of his existence, I had cherished the hope of one day seeing him: now, I never should. And then this money came only to me: not to me and a rejoicing family, but to my isolated self. It was a grand boon doubtless; and independence would be glorious – yes, I felt that – that thought swelled my heart.

"You unbend your forehead at last," said Mr. Rivers. "I thought Medusa had looked at you, and that you were turning to stone. Perhaps now you will ask how much you are worth?"

"How much am I worth?"

"Oh, a trifle! Nothing of course to speak of – twenty thousand pounds, I think they say – but what is that?"

"Twenty thousand pounds?"

Here was a new stunner – I had been calculating on four or five thousand. This news actually took my breath for a moment: Mr. St. John, whom I had never heard laugh before, laughed now.

"Well," said he, "if you had committed a murder, and I had told you your crime was discovered, you could scarcely look more aghast."

"It is a large sum – don't you think there is a mistake?"

"No mistake at all."

"Perhaps you have read the figures wrong – it may be two thousand!"

"It is written in letters, not figures, – twenty thousand."

I again felt rather like an individual of but average gastronomical powers sitting down to feast alone at a table spread with provisions for a hundred. Mr. Rivers rose now and put his cloak on.

"If it were not such a very wild night," he said, "I would send Hannah down to keep you company: you look too desperately miserable to be left alone. But Hannah, poor woman!, could not stride the drifts so well as I: her legs are not quite so long: so I must e'en leave you to your sorrows. Goodnight."

He was lifting the latch: a sudden thought occurred to me. "Stop one minute!" I cried.

"Well?"

"It puzzles me to know why Mr. Briggs wrote to you about me; or how he knew you, or could fancy that you, living in such an out-of-the-way place, had the power to aid in my discovery."

"Oh! I am a clergyman," he said; "and the clergy are often appealed to about odd matters." Again the latch rattled.

"No; that does not satisfy me!" I exclaimed: and indeed there was something in the hasty and unexplanatory reply which, instead of allaying, piqued my curiosity more than ever.

"It is a very strange piece of business," I added; "I must know more about it."

"Another time."

"No; tonight! – Tonight!" and as he turned from the door, I placed myself between it and him. He looked rather embarrassed.

"You certainly shall not go till you have told me all," I said.

"I would rather not just now."

"You shall! – You must!"

"I would rather Diana or Mary informed you."

Of course these objections wrought my eagerness to a climax: gratified it must be, and that without delay; and I told him so.

"But I apprised you that I was a hard man," said he, "difficult to persuade."

"And I am a hard woman, – impossible to put off."

"And then," he pursued, "I am cold: no fervour infects me."

"Whereas I am hot, and fire dissolves ice. The blaze there has thawed all the snow from your cloak; by the same token, it has streamed on to my floor, and made it like a trampled street. As you hope ever to be forgiven, Mr. Rivers, the high crime and misdemeanour of spoiling a sanded kitchen, tell me what I wish to know."

"Well, then," he said, "I yield; if not to your earnestness, to your perseverance: as stone is worn by continual dropping. Besides, you must know some day, – as well now as later. Your name is Jane Eyre?"

"Of course: that was all settled before."

"You are not, perhaps, aware that I am your namesake? – that I was christened St. John Eyre Rivers?"

"No, indeed! I remember now seeing the letter E. comprised in your initials written in books you have at different times lent me; but I never asked for what name it stood. But what then? Surely –"

I stopped: I could not trust myself to entertain, much less to express, the thought that rushed upon me – that embodied itself, – that, in a second, stood out a strong, solid probability. Circumstances knit themselves, fitted themselves, shot into order: the chain that had been lying hitherto a formless lump of links was drawn out straight, – every ring was perfect, the connection complete. I knew, by instinct, how the matter stood, before St. John had said another word; but I cannot expect the reader to have the same intuitive perception, so I must repeat his explanation.

"My mother's name was Eyre; she had two brothers; one a clergyman, who married Miss Jane Reed, of Gateshead; the other, John Eyre, Esq., merchant, late of Funchal, Madeira. Mr. Briggs, being Mr. Eyre's solicitor, wrote to us last August to inform us of our uncle's death, and to say that he had left his property to his brother the clergyman's orphan daughter, overlooking us, in consequence of a quarrel, never forgiven, between him and my father. He wrote again a few weeks since, to intimate that the heiress was lost, and asking if we knew anything of her. A name casually written on a slip of paper has enabled me to find her out. You know the rest." Again he was going, but I set my back against the door.

"Do let me speak," I said; "let me have one moment to draw breath and reflect." I paused – he stood before me, hat in hand, looking composed enough. I resumed:

"Your mother was my father's sister?"

"Yes."

"My aunt, consequently?"

He bowed.

"My uncle John was your uncle John? You, Diana, and Mary are his sister's children, as I am his brother's child?"

"Undeniably."

"You three, then, are my cousins; half our blood on each side flows from the same source?"

"We are cousins; yes."

I surveyed him. It seemed I had found a brother: one I could be proud of, – one I could love; and two sisters, whose qualities were such, that, when I knew them but as mere strangers, they had inspired me with genuine affection and admiration. The two girls, on whom, kneeling down on the wet ground, and looking through the low, latticed window of Moor House kitchen, I had gazed with so bitter a mixture of interest and despair, were my near kinswomen; and the young and stately gentleman who had found me almost dying at his threshold was my blood relation. Glorious discovery to a lonely wretch! This was wealth indeed! – Wealth to the heart! – A mine of pure, genial affections. This was a blessing, bright, vivid, and exhilarating; – not like the ponderous gift of gold: rich and welcome enough in its way, but sobering from its weight. I now clapped my hands in sudden joy – my pulse bounded, my veins thrilled.

"Oh, I am glad! – I am glad!" I exclaimed.

St. John smiled. "Did I not say you neglected essential points to pursue trifles?" he asked. "You were serious when I told you you had got a fortune; and now, for a matter of no moment, you are excited."

"What can you mean? It may be of no moment to you; you have sisters and don't care for a cousin; but I had nobody; and now three relations, – or two, if you don't choose to be counted, – are born into my world full-grown. I say again, I am glad!"

I walked fast through the room: I stopped, half suffocated with the thoughts that rose faster than I could receive, comprehend, settle them: – thoughts of what might, could, would, and should be, and that ere long. I looked at the blank wall: it seemed a sky thick with ascending stars, – every one lit me to a purpose or delight. Those who had saved my life, whom, till this hour, I had loved barrenly, I could now benefit. They were under a yoke, – I could free them: they were scattered, – I could reunite them: the independence, the affluence which was mine, might be theirs too. Were we not four? Twenty thousand pounds shared equally would be five thousand each, justice – enough and to spare: justice would be done, – mutual happiness secured. Now the wealth did not weigh on me: now it was not a mere bequest of coin, – it was a legacy of life, hope, enjoyment.

How I looked while these ideas were taking my spirit by storm, I cannot tell; but I perceived soon that Mr. Rivers had placed a chair behind me, and was gently attempting to make me sit down on it. He also advised me to be composed; I scorned the insinuation of helplessness and distraction, shook off his hand, and began to walk about again.

"Write to Diana and Mary tomorrow," I said, "and tell them to come home directly. Diana said they would both consider themselves rich with a thousand pounds, so with five thousand they will do very well."

"Tell me where I can get you a glass of water," said St. John; "you must really make an effort to tranquillise your feelings."

"Nonsense! And what sort of an effect will the bequest have on you? Will it keep you in England, induce you to marry Miss Oliver, and settle down like an ordinary mortal?"

"You wander: your head becomes confused. I have been too abrupt in communicating the news; it has excited you beyond your strength."

"Mr. Rivers! You quite put me out of patience: I am rational enough; it is you who misunderstand, or rather who affect to misunderstand."

"Perhaps, if you explained yourself a little more fully, I should comprehend better."

"Explain! What is there to explain? You cannot fail to see that twenty thousand pounds, the sum in question, divided equally between the nephew and three nieces of our uncle, will give five thousand to each? What I want is, that you should write to your sisters and tell them of the fortune that has accrued to them."

"To you, you mean."

"I have intimated my view of the case: I am incapable of taking any other. I am not brutally selfish, blindly unjust, or fiendishly ungrateful. Besides, I am resolved I will have a home and connections. I like Moor House, and I will live at Moor House; I like Diana and Mary, and I will attach myself for life to Diana and Mary. It would please and benefit me to have five thousand pounds; it would torment and oppress me to have twenty thousand; which, moreover, could never be mine in justice, though it might in law. I abandon to you, then, what is absolutely superfluous to me. Let there be no opposition, and no discussion about it; let us agree amongst each other, and decide the point at once."

"This is acting on first impulses; you must take days to consider such a matter, ere your word can be regarded as valid."

"Oh! If all you doubt is my sincerity, I am easy: you see the justice of the case?"

"I *do* see a certain justice; but it is contrary to all custom. Besides, the entire fortune is your right: my uncle gained it by his own efforts; he was free to leave it to whom he would: he left it to you. After all, justice permits you to keep it: you may, with a clear conscience, consider it absolutely your own."

"With me," said I, "it is fully as much a matter of feeling as of conscience: I must indulge my feelings; I so seldom have had an opportunity of doing so. Were you to argue, object, and annoy me for a year, I could not forego the delicious pleasure of which I have caught a glimpse – that of repaying, in part, a mighty obligation, and winning to myself lifelong friends."

"You think so now," rejoined St. John, "because you do not know what it is to possess, nor consequently to enjoy wealth: you cannot form a notion of the importance twenty thousand pounds would give you; of the place it would enable you to take in society; of the prospects it would open to you: you cannot –"

"And you," I interrupted, "cannot at all imagine the craving I have for fraternal and sisterly love. I never had a home, I never had brothers or sisters; I must and will have them now: you are not reluctant to admit me and own me, are you?"

"Jane, I will be your brother – my sisters will be your sisters – without stipulating for this sacrifice of your just rights."

"Brother? Yes; at the distance of a thousand leagues! Sisters? Yes; slaving amongst strangers! I, wealthy – gorged with gold I never earned and do not merit! You, penniless! Famous equality and fraternisation! Close union! Intimate attachment!"

"But, Jane, your aspirations after family ties and domestic happiness may be realised otherwise than by the means you contemplate: you may marry."

"Nonsense, again! Marry! I don't want to marry, and never shall marry."

"That is saying too much: such hazardous affirmations are a proof of the excitement under which you labour."

"It is not saying too much: I know what I feel, and how averse are my inclinations to the bare thought of marriage. No one would take me for love; and I will not be regarded in the light of a mere money speculation. And I do not want a stranger – unsympathising, alien, different from me; I want my kindred: those with whom I have full fellow feeling. Say again you will be my brother: when you uttered the words I was satisfied, happy; repeat them, if you can, repeat them sincerely."

"I think I can. I know I have always loved my own sisters; and I know on what my affection for them is grounded, – respect for their worth and admiration of their talents. You too have principle and mind: your tastes and habits resemble Diana's and Mary's; your presence is always agreeable to me; in your conversation I have already for some time found a salutary solace. I feel I can easily and naturally make room in my heart for you, as my third and youngest sister."

"Thank you: that contents me for tonight. Now you had better go; for if you stay longer, you will perhaps irritate me afresh by some mistrustful scruple."

"And the school, Miss Eyre? It must now be shut up, I suppose?"

"No. I will retain my post of mistress till you get a substitute."

He smiled approbation: we shook hands, and he took leave.

I need not narrate in detail the further struggles I had, and arguments I used, to get matters regarding the legacy settled as I wished. My task was a very hard one; but, as I was absolutely resolved – as my cousins saw at length that my mind was really and immutably fixed on making a just division of the property – as they must in their own hearts have felt the equity of the intention; and must, besides, have been innately conscious that in my place they would have done precisely what I wished to do – they yielded at length so far as to consent to put the affair to arbitration. The judges chosen were Mr. Oliver and an able lawyer: both coincided in my opinion: I carried my point. The instruments of transfer were drawn out: St. John, Diana, Mary, and I, each became possessed of a competency.

Chapter Thirty-Four

IT WAS NEAR Christmas by the time all was settled: the season of general holiday approached. I now closed Morton school, taking care that the parting should not be barren on my side. Good fortune opens the hand as well as the heart wonderfully; and to give somewhat when we have largely received, is but to afford a vent to the unusual ebullition of the sensations. I had long felt with pleasure that many of my rustic scholars liked me, and when we parted, that consciousness was confirmed: they manifested their affection plainly and strongly. Deep was my gratification to find I had really a place in their unsophisticated hearts: I promised them that never a week should pass in future that I did not visit them, and give them an hour's teaching in their school.

Mr. Rivers came up as, having seen the classes, now numbering sixty girls, file out before me, and locked the door, I stood with the key in my hand, exchanging a few words of special farewell with some half-dozen of my best scholars: as decent, respectable, modest, and well-informed young women as could be found in the ranks of the British peasantry. And that is saying a great deal; for after all, the British peasantry are the best taught, best mannered, most self-respecting of any in Europe: since those days I have seen paysannes and Bäuerinnen; [33] and the best of them seemed to me ignorant, coarse, and besotted, compared with my Morton girls.

"Do you consider you have got your reward for a season of exertion?" asked Mr. Rivers, when they were gone. "Does not the consciousness of having done some real good in your day and generation give pleasure?"

"Doubtless."

"And you have only toiled a few months! Would not a life devoted to the task of regenerating your race be well spent?"

"Yes," I said; "but I could not go on for ever so: I want to enjoy my own faculties as well as to cultivate those of other people. I must enjoy them now; don't recall either my mind or body to the school; I am out of it and disposed for full holiday."

He looked grave. "What now? What sudden eagerness is this you evince? What are you going to do?"

"To be active: as active as I can. And first I must beg you to set Hannah at liberty, and get somebody else to wait on you."

"Do you want her?"

"Yes, to go with me to Moor House. Diana and Mary will be at home in a week, and I want to have everything in order against their arrival."

"I understand. I thought you were for flying off on some excursion. It is better so: Hannah shall go with you."

"Tell her to be ready by tomorrow then; and here is the schoolroom key: I will give you the key of my cottage in the morning."

He took it. "You give it up very gleefully," said he; "I don't quite understand your light-heartedness, because I cannot tell what employment you propose to yourself as a substitute for the one you are relinquishing. What aim, what purpose, what ambition in life have you now?"

"My first aim will be to *clean down* (do you comprehend the full force of the expression?) – to *clean down* Moor House from chamber to cellar; my next to rub it up with bees-wax, oil, and an indefinite number of cloths, till it glitters again; my third, to arrange every chair, table, bed, carpet, with mathematical precision; afterwards I shall go near to ruin you in coals and peat to keep up good fires in every room; and lastly, the two days preceding that on which your sisters are expected will be devoted by Hannah and me to such a beating of eggs, sorting of currants, grating of spices, compounding of Christmas cakes, chopping up of materials for mince-pies, and solemnising of other culinary rites, as words can convey but an inadequate notion of to the uninitiated like you. My purpose, in short, is to have all things in an absolutely perfect state of readiness for Diana and Mary before next Thursday; and my ambition is to give them a beau-ideal of a welcome when they come."

St. John smiled slightly: still he was dissatisfied.

"It is all very well for the present," said he; "but seriously, I trust that when the first flush of vivacity is over, you will look a little higher than domestic endearments and household joys."

"The best things the world has!" I interrupted.

"No, Jane, no: this world is not the scene of fruition; do not attempt to make it so: nor of rest; do not turn slothful."

"I mean, on the contrary, to be busy."

"Jane, I excuse you for the present: two months' grace I allow you for the full enjoyment of your new position, and for pleasing yourself with this late-found charm of relationship; but *then*, I hope you will begin to look beyond Moor House and Morton, and sisterly society, and the selfish calm and sensual comfort of civilised affluence. I hope your energies will then once more trouble you with their strength."

I looked at him with surprise. "St. John," I said, "I think you are almost wicked to talk so. I am disposed to be as content as a queen, and you try to stir me up to restlessness! To what end?"

"To the end of turning to profit the talents which God has committed to your keeping; and of which He will surely one day demand a strict account. Jane, I shall watch you closely and anxiously – I warn you of that. And try to restrain the disproportionate fervour with which you throw yourself into commonplace home pleasures. Don't cling so tenaciously to ties of the flesh; save your constancy and ardour for an adequate cause; forbear to waste them on trite transient objects. Do you hear, Jane?"

"Yes; just as if you were speaking Greek. I feel I have adequate cause to be happy, and I *will* be happy. Goodbye!"

Happy at Moor House I was, and hard I worked; and so did Hannah: she was charmed to see how jovial I could be amidst the bustle of a house turned topsy-turvy – how I could brush, and dust, and clean, and cook. And really, after a day or two of confusion worse confounded, it was delightful by degrees to invoke order from the chaos ourselves had made. I had previously taken a journey to S— to purchase some new furniture: my cousins having given me *carte blanche* to effect what alterations I pleased, and a sum having been set aside for that purpose. The ordinary sitting-room and bedrooms I left much as they were: for I knew Diana and Mary would derive more pleasure from seeing again the old homely tables, and chairs, and beds, than from the spectacle of the smartest innovations. Still some novelty was necessary, to give to their return the piquancy with which I wished it to be invested. Dark handsome new carpets and curtains, an arrangement of some carefully selected antique ornaments in porcelain and bronze, new coverings, and mirrors, and dressing-cases, for the toilet tables, answered the end: they looked fresh without being glaring. A spare parlour and bedroom I refurnished entirely, with old mahogany and crimson upholstery: I laid canvas on the passage, and carpets on the stairs. When all was finished, I thought Moor House as complete a model of bright modest snugness within, as it was, at this season, a specimen of wintry waste and desert dreariness without.

The eventful Thursday at length came. They were expected about dark, and ere dusk fires were lit upstairs and below; the kitchen was in perfect trim; Hannah and I were dressed, and all was in readiness.

St. John arrived first. I had entreated him to keep quite clear of the house till everything was arranged: and, indeed, the bare idea of the commotion, at once sordid and trivial, going on within its walls sufficed to scare him to estrangement. He found me in the kitchen, watching the progress of certain cakes for tea, then baking. Approaching the hearth, he asked, "If I was at last satisfied with housemaid's work?" I answered by inviting him to accompany me on a general inspection of the result of my labours. With some difficulty, I got him to make the tour of the house. He just looked in at the doors I opened; and when he had wandered upstairs and downstairs, he said I must have gone through a great deal of fatigue and trouble to have effected such considerable changes in so short a time: but not a syllable did he utter indicating pleasure in the improved aspect of his abode.

This silence damped me. I thought perhaps the alterations had disturbed some old associations he valued. I inquired whether this was the case: no doubt in a somewhat crestfallen tone.

"Not at all; he had, on the contrary, remarked that I had scrupulously respected every association: he feared, indeed, I must have bestowed more thought on the matter than it was worth. How many minutes, for instance, had I devoted to studying the arrangement of this very room? – By-the-bye, could I tell him where such a book was?"

I showed him the volume on the shelf: he took it down, and withdrawing to his accustomed window recess, he began to read it.

Now, I did not like this, reader. St. John was a good man; but I began to feel he had spoken truth of himself when he said he was hard and cold. The humanities and amenities of life had no attraction for him – its peaceful enjoyments no charm. Literally, he lived only to aspire – after what was good and great, certainly; but still he would never rest, nor approve of others resting round him. As I looked at his lofty forehead, still and pale as a white stone – at his fine lineaments fixed in study – I comprehended all at once that he would hardly make a good husband: that it would be a trying thing to be his wife. I understood, as by inspiration, the nature of his love for Miss Oliver; I agreed with him that it was but a love of the senses. I comprehended how he should despise himself for the feverish influence it exercised over him; how he should wish to stifle and destroy it; how he should mistrust its ever conducting permanently to his happiness or hers. I saw he was of the material from which nature hews her heroes – Christian and Pagan – her lawgivers, her statesmen, her conquerors: a steadfast bulwark for great interests to rest upon; but, at the fireside, too often a cold cumbrous column, gloomy and out of place.

"This parlour is not his sphere," I reflected: "the Himalayan ridge or Caffre bush, even the plague-cursed Guinea Coast swamp would suit him better. Well may he eschew the calm of domestic life; it is not his element: there his faculties stagnate – they cannot develop or appear to advantage. It is in scenes of strife and danger – where courage is proved, and energy exercised, and fortitude tasked – that he will speak and move, the leader and superior. A merry child would have the advantage of him on this hearth. He is right to choose a missionary's career – I see it now."

"They are coming! They are coming!" cried Hannah, throwing open the parlour door. At the same moment old Carlo barked joyfully. Out I ran. It was now dark; but a rumbling of wheels was audible. Hannah soon had a lantern lit. The vehicle had stopped at the wicket; the driver opened the door: first one well-known form, then another, stepped out. In a minute I had my face under their bonnets, in contact first with Mary's soft cheek, then with Diana's flowing curls. They laughed – kissed me – then Hannah: patted Carlo, who was half wild with delight; asked eagerly if all was well; and being assured in the affirmative, hastened into the house.

They were stiff with their long and jolting drive from Whitcross, and chilled with the frosty night air; but their pleasant countenances expanded to the cheerful firelight. While the driver and Hannah brought in the boxes, they demanded St. John. At this moment he advanced from the parlour. They both threw their arms round his neck at once. He gave each one quiet kiss, said in a low tone a few words of welcome, stood a while to be talked to, and then, intimating that he supposed they would soon rejoin him in the parlour, withdrew there as to a place of refuge.

I had lit their candles to go upstairs, but Diana had first to give hospitable orders respecting the driver; this done, both followed me. They were delighted with the renovation and decorations of their rooms; with the new drapery, and fresh carpets, and rich tinted china vases: they expressed their gratification ungrudgingly. I had the pleasure of feeling that my arrangements met their wishes exactly, and that what I had done added a vivid charm to their joyous return home.

Sweet was that evening. My cousins, full of exhilaration, were so eloquent in narrative and comment, that their fluency covered St. John's taciturnity: he was sincerely glad to see his sisters; but in their glow of fervour and flow of joy he could not sympathise. The event of the day – that is, the return of Diana and Mary – pleased him; but the accompaniments of that event, the glad tumult, the garrulous glee of reception irked him: I saw he wished the calmer morrow was come. In the very meridian of the night's enjoyment, about an hour after tea, a rap was heard at the door. Hannah entered with the intimation that "a poor lad was come, at that unlikely time, to fetch Mr. Rivers to see his mother, who was drawing away."

"Where does she live, Hannah?"

"Clear up at Whitcross Brow, almost four miles off, and moor and moss all the way."

"Tell him I will go."

"I'm sure, sir, you had better not. It's the worst road to travel after dark that can be: there's no track at all over the bog. And then it is such a bitter night – the keenest wind you ever felt. You had better send word, sir, that you will be there in the morning."

But he was already in the passage, putting on his cloak; and without one objection, one murmur, he departed. It was then nine o'clock: he did not return till midnight. Starved and tired enough he was: but he looked happier than when he set out. He had performed an act of duty; made an exertion; felt his own strength to do and deny, and was on better terms with himself.

I am afraid the whole of the ensuing week tried his patience. It was Christmas week: we took to no settled employment, but spent it in a sort of merry domestic dissipation. The air of the moors, the freedom of home, the dawn of prosperity, acted on Diana and Mary's spirits like some life-giving elixir: they were gay from morning till noon, and from noon till night. They could always talk; and their discourse, witty, pithy, original, had such charms for me, that I preferred listening to, and sharing in it, to doing anything else. St. John did not rebuke our vivacity; but he escaped from it: he was seldom in the house; his parish was large, the population scattered, and he found daily business in visiting the sick and poor in its different districts.

One morning at breakfast, Diana, after looking a little pensive for some minutes, asked him, "If his plans were yet unchanged."

"Unchanged and unchangeable," was the reply. And he proceeded to inform us that his departure from England was now definitively fixed for the ensuing year.

"And Rosamond Oliver?" suggested Mary, the words seeming to escape her lips involuntarily: for no sooner had she uttered them, than she made a gesture as if wishing to recall them. St. John had a book in his hand – it was his unsocial custom to read at meals – he closed it, and looked up.

"Rosamond Oliver," said he, "is about to be married to Mr. Granby, one of the best connected and most estimable residents in S—, grandson and heir to Sir Frederic Granby: I had the intelligence from her father yesterday."

His sisters looked at each other and at me; we all three looked at him: he was serene as glass.

"The match must have been got up hastily," said Diana: "they cannot have known each other long."

"But two months: they met in October at the county ball at S—. But where there are no obstacles to a union, as in the present case, where the connection is in every point desirable, delays are unnecessary: they will be married as soon as S— Place, which Sir Frederic gives up to them, can be refitted for their reception."

The first time I found St. John alone after this communication, I felt tempted to inquire if the event distressed him: but he seemed so little to need sympathy, that, so far from venturing to offer him more, I experienced some shame at the recollection of what I had already hazarded. Besides, I was out of practice in talking to him: his reserve was again frozen over, and my frankness was congealed beneath it. He had not kept his promise of treating me like his sisters; he continually made little chilling differences between us, which did not at all tend to the development of cordiality: in short, now that I was acknowledged his kinswoman, and lived under the same roof with him, I felt the distance between us to be far greater than when he had known me only as the village schoolmistress. When I remembered how far I had once been admitted to his confidence, I could hardly comprehend his present frigidity.

Such being the case, I felt not a little surprised when he raised his head suddenly from the desk over which he was stooping, and said:

"You see, Jane, the battle is fought and the victory won."

Startled at being thus addressed, I did not immediately reply: after a moment's hesitation I answered:

"But are you sure you are not in the position of those conquerors whose triumphs have cost them too dear? Would not such another ruin you?"

"I think not; and if I were, it does not much signify; I shall never be called upon to contend for such another. The event of the conflict is decisive: my way is now clear; I thank God for it!" So saying, he returned to his papers and his silence.

As our mutual happiness (*i.e.*, Diana's, Mary's, and mine) settled into a quieter character, and we resumed our usual habits and regular studies, St. John stayed more at home: he sat with us in the same room, sometimes for hours together. While Mary drew, Diana pursued a course of encyclopaedic reading she had (to my awe and amazement) undertaken, and I fagged away at German, he pondered a mystic lore of his own: that of some Eastern tongue, the acquisition of which he thought necessary to his plans.

Thus engaged, he appeared, sitting in his own recess, quiet and absorbed enough; but that blue eye of his had a habit of leaving the outlandish-looking grammar, and wandering over, and sometimes fixing upon us, his fellow-students, with a curious intensity of observation: if caught, it would be instantly withdrawn; yet ever and anon, it returned searchingly to our table. I wondered what it meant: I wondered, too, at the punctual satisfaction he never failed to exhibit on an occasion that seemed to me of small moment, namely, my weekly visit to Morton school; and still more was I puzzled when, if the day was unfavourable, if there was snow, or rain, or high wind, and his sisters urged me not to go, he would invariably make light of their solicitude, and encourage me to accomplish the task without regard to the elements.

"Jane is not such a weakling as you would make her," he would say: "she can bear a mountain blast, or a shower, or a few flakes of snow, as well as any of us. Her constitution is both sound and elastic; – better calculated to endure variations of climate than many more robust."

And when I returned, sometimes a good deal tired, and not a little weather-beaten, I never dared complain, because I saw that to murmur would be to vex him: on all occasions fortitude pleased him; the reverse was a special annoyance.

One afternoon, however, I got leave to stay at home, because I really had a cold. His sisters were gone to Morton in my stead: I sat reading Schiller; he, deciphering his crabbed Oriental scrolls. As I exchanged a translation for an exercise, I happened to look his way: there I found myself under the influence of the ever-watchful blue eye. How long it had been searching me through and through, and over and over, I cannot tell: so keen was it, and yet so cold, I felt for the moment superstitious – as if I were sitting in the room with something uncanny.

"Jane, what are you doing?"

"Learning German."

"I want you to give up German and learn Hindostanee."

"You are not in earnest?"

"In such earnest that I must have it so: and I will tell you why."

He then went on to explain that Hindostanee was the language he was himself at present studying; that, as he advanced, he was apt to forget the commencement; that it would assist him greatly to have a pupil with whom he might again and again go over the elements, and so fix them thoroughly in his mind; that his choice had hovered for some time between me and his sisters; but that he had fixed on me because he saw I could sit at a task the longest of the three. Would I do him this favour? I should not, perhaps, have to make the sacrifice long, as it wanted now barely three months to his departure.

St. John was not a man to be lightly refused: you felt that every impression made on him, either for pain or pleasure, was deep-graved and permanent. I consented. When Diana and Mary returned, the former found her scholar transferred from her to her brother: she laughed, and both she and Mary agreed that St. John should never have persuaded them to such a step. He answered quietly:

"I know it."

I found him a very patient, very forbearing, and yet an exacting master: he expected me to do a great deal; and when I fulfilled his expectations, he, in his own way, fully testified his approbation. By degrees, he acquired a certain influence over me that took away my liberty of mind: his praise and notice were more restraining than his indifference. I could no longer talk or laugh freely when he was by, because a tiresomely importunate instinct reminded me that vivacity (at least in me) was distasteful to him. I was so fully aware that only serious moods and occupations were acceptable, that in his presence every effort to sustain or follow any other became vain: I fell under a freezing spell. When he said "go," I went; "come," I came; "do this," I did it. But I did not love my servitude: I wished, many a time, he had continued to neglect me.

One evening when, at bedtime, his sisters and I stood round him, bidding him goodnight, he kissed each of them, as was his custom; and, as was equally his custom, he gave me his hand. Diana, who chanced to be in a frolicsome humour (*she* was not painfully controlled by his will; for hers, in another way, was as strong), exclaimed:

"St. John! You used to call Jane your third sister, but you don't treat her as such: you should kiss her too."

She pushed me towards him. I thought Diana very provoking, and felt uncomfortably confused; and while I was thus thinking and feeling, St. John bent his head; his Greek face was brought to a level with mine, his eyes questioned my eyes piercingly – he kissed me. There are no such things as marble kisses or ice kisses, or I should say my ecclesiastical cousin's salute belonged to one of these classes; but there may be experiment kisses, and his was an experiment kiss. When given, he viewed me to learn the result; it was not striking: I am sure I did not blush; perhaps I might have turned a little pale, for I felt as if this kiss were a seal affixed to my fetters. He never omitted the ceremony afterwards, and the gravity and quiescence with which I underwent it, seemed to invest it for him with a certain charm.

As for me, I daily wished more to please him; but to do so, I felt daily more and more that I must disown half my nature, stifle half my faculties, wrest my tastes from their original bent, force myself to the adoption of pursuits for which I had no natural vocation. He wanted to train me to an elevation I could never reach; it racked me hourly to aspire to the standard he uplifted. The thing was as impossible as to mould my irregular features to his correct and classic pattern, to give to my changeable green eyes the sea-blue tint and solemn lustre of his own.

Not his ascendancy alone, however, held me in thrall at present. Of late it had been easy enough for me to look sad: a cankering evil sat at my heart and drained my happiness at its source – the evil of suspense.

Perhaps you think I had forgotten Mr. Rochester, reader, amidst these changes of place and fortune. Not for a moment. His idea was still with me, because it was not a vapour sunshine could disperse, nor a sand-traced effigy storms could wash away; it was a name graven on a tablet, fated to last as long as the marble it inscribed. The craving to know what had become of him followed me everywhere; when I was at Morton, I re-entered my cottage every evening to think of that; and now at Moor House, I sought my bedroom each night to brood over it.

In the course of my necessary correspondence with Mr. Briggs about the will, I had inquired if he knew anything of Mr. Rochester's present residence and state of health; but, as St. John had conjectured, he was quite ignorant of all concerning him. I then wrote to Mrs. Fairfax, entreating information on the subject. I had calculated with certainty on this step answering my end: I felt sure it would elicit an early answer. I was astonished when a fortnight passed without reply; but when two months wore away, and day after day the post arrived and brought nothing for me, I fell a prey to the keenest anxiety.

I wrote again: there was a chance of my first letter having missed. Renewed hope followed renewed effort: it shone like the former for some weeks, then, like it, it faded, flickered: not a line, not a word reached me. When half a year wasted in vain expectancy, my hope died out, and then I felt dark indeed.

A fine spring shone round me, which I could not enjoy. Summer approached; Diana tried to cheer me: she said I looked ill, and wished to accompany me to the sea-side. This St. John opposed; he said I did not want dissipation, I wanted employment; my present life was too purposeless, I required an aim; and, I suppose, by way of supplying deficiencies, he prolonged still further my lessons in Hindostanee, and grew more urgent in requiring their accomplishment: and I, like a fool, never thought of resisting him – I could not resist him.

One day I had come to my studies in lower spirits than usual; the ebb was occasioned by a poignantly felt disappointment. Hannah had told me in the morning there was a letter for me, and when I went down to take it, almost certain that the long-looked for tidings were vouchsafed me at last, I found only an unimportant note from Mr. Briggs on business. The bitter check had wrung from me some tears; and now, as I sat poring over the crabbed characters and flourishing tropes of an Indian scribe, my eyes filled again.

St. John called me to his side to read; in attempting to do this my voice failed me: words were lost in sobs. He and I were the only occupants of the parlour: Diana was practising her music in the drawing room, Mary was gardening – it was a very fine May day, clear, sunny, and breezy. My companion expressed no surprise at this emotion, nor did he question me as to its cause; he only said:

"We will wait a few minutes, Jane, till you are more composed." And while I smothered the paroxysm with all haste, he sat calm and patient, leaning on his desk, and looking like a physician watching with the eye of science an expected and fully understood crisis in a patient's malady. Having stifled my sobs, wiped my eyes, and muttered something about not being very well that morning, I resumed my task, and succeeded in completing it. St. John put away my books and his, locked his desk, and said:

"Now, Jane, you shall take a walk; and with me."

"I will call Diana and Mary."

"No; I want only one companion this morning, and that must be you. Put on your things; go out by the kitchen door: take the road towards the head of Marsh Glen: I will join you in a moment."

I know no medium: I never in my life have known any medium in my dealings with positive, hard characters, antagonistic to my own, between absolute submission and determined revolt. I have always faithfully observed the one, up to the very moment of bursting, sometimes with volcanic vehemence, into the other; and as neither present circumstances warranted, nor my present mood inclined me to mutiny, I observed careful obedience to St. John's directions; and in ten minutes I was treading the wild track of the glen, side by side with him.

The breeze was from the west: it came over the hills, sweet with scents of heath and rush; the sky was of stainless blue; the stream descending the ravine, swelled with past spring rains, poured along plentiful and clear, catching golden gleams from the sun, and sapphire tints from the firmament. As we advanced and left the track, we trod a soft turf, mossy fine and emerald green, minutely enamelled with a tiny white flower, and spangled with a star-like yellow blossom: the hills, meantime, shut us quite in; for the glen, towards its head, wound to their very core.

"Let us rest here," said St. John, as we reached the first stragglers of a battalion of rocks, guarding a sort of pass, beyond which the beck rushed down a waterfall; and where, still a little farther, the mountain shook off turf and flower, had only heath for raiment and crag for gem – where it exaggerated the wild to the savage, and exchanged the fresh for the frowning – where it guarded the forlorn hope of solitude, and a last refuge for silence.

I took a seat: St. John stood near me. He looked up the pass and down the hollow; his glance wandered away with the stream, and returned to traverse the unclouded heaven which coloured it: he removed his hat, let the breeze stir his hair and kiss his brow. He seemed in communion with the genius of the haunt: with his eye he bade farewell to something.

"And I shall see it again," he said aloud, "in dreams when I sleep by the Ganges: and again in a more remote hour – when another slumber overcomes me – on the shore of a darker stream!"

Strange words of a strange love! An austere patriot's passion for his fatherland! He sat down; for half an hour we never spoke; neither he to me nor I to him: that interval past, he recommenced:

"Jane, I go in six weeks; I have taken my berth in an East Indiaman which sails on the 20th of June."

"God will protect you; for you have undertaken His work," I answered.

"Yes," said he, "there is my glory and joy. I am the servant of an infallible Master. I am not going out under human guidance, subject to the defective laws and erring control of my feeble fellow-worms: my king, my lawgiver, my captain, is the All-perfect. It seems strange to me that all round me do not burn to enlist under the same banner, – to join in the same enterprise."

"All have not your powers, and it would be folly for the feeble to wish to march with the strong."

"I do not speak to the feeble, or think of them: I address only such as are worthy of the work, and competent to accomplish it."

"Those are few in number, and difficult to discover."

"You say truly; but when found, it is right to stir them up – to urge and exhort them to the effort – to show them what their gifts are, and why they were given – to speak Heaven's message in their ear, – to offer them, direct from God, a place in the ranks of His chosen."

"If they are really qualified for the task, will not their own hearts be the first to inform them of it?"

I felt as if an awful charm was framing round and gathering over me: I trembled to hear some fatal word spoken which would at once declare and rivet the spell.

"And what does *your* heart say?" demanded St. John.

"My heart is mute, – my heart is mute," I answered, struck and thrilled.

"Then I must speak for it," continued the deep, relentless voice. "Jane, come with me to India: come as my helpmeet and fellow-labourer."

The glen and sky spun round: the hills heaved! It was as if I had heard a summons from Heaven – as if a visionary messenger, like him of Macedonia, had enounced, "Come over and help us!" But I was no apostle, – I could not behold the herald, – I could not receive his call.

"Oh, St. John!" I cried, "have some mercy!"

I appealed to one who, in the discharge of what he believed his duty, knew neither mercy nor remorse. He continued:

"God and nature intended you for a missionary's wife. It is not personal, but mental endowments they have given you: you are formed for labour, not for love. A missionary's wife you must – shall be. You shall be mine: I claim you – not for my pleasure, but for my Sovereign's service."

"I am not fit for it: I have no vocation," I said.

He had calculated on these first objections: he was not irritated by them. Indeed, as he leaned back against the crag behind him, folded his arms on his chest, and fixed his countenance, I saw he was prepared for a long and trying opposition, and had taken in a stock of patience to last him to its close – resolved, however, that that close should be conquest for him.

"Humility, Jane," said he, "is the groundwork of Christian virtues: you say right that you are not fit for the work. Who is fit for it? Or who, that ever was truly called, believed himself worthy of the summons? I, for instance, am but dust and ashes. With St. Paul, I acknowledge myself the chiefest of sinners; but I do not suffer this sense of my personal vileness to daunt me. I know my Leader: that He is just as well as mighty; and while He has chosen a feeble instrument to perform a great task, He will, from the boundless stores of His providence, supply the inadequacy of the means to the end. Think like me, Jane – trust like me. It is the Rock of Ages I ask you to lean on: do not doubt but it will bear the weight of your human weakness."

"I do not understand a missionary life: I have never studied missionary labours."

"There I, humble as I am, can give you the aid you want: I can set you your task from hour to hour; stand by you always; help you from moment to moment. This I could do in the beginning: soon (for I know your powers) you would be as strong and apt as myself, and would not require my help."

"But my powers – where are they for this undertaking? I do not feel them. Nothing speaks or stirs in me while you talk. I am sensible of no light kindling – no life quickening – no voice counselling or cheering. Oh, I wish I could make you see how much my mind is at this moment like a rayless dungeon, with one shrinking fear fettered in its depths – the fear of being persuaded by you to attempt what I cannot accomplish!"

"I have an answer for you – hear it. I have watched you ever since we first met: I have made you my study for ten months. I have proved you in that time by sundry tests: and what have I seen and elicited? In the village school I found you could perform well, punctually, uprightly, labour uncongenial to your habits and inclinations; I saw you could perform it with capacity and tact: you could win while you controlled. In the calm with which you learnt you had become suddenly rich, I read a mind clear of the vice of Demas: – lucre had no undue power over you. In the resolute readiness with which you cut your wealth into four shares, keeping but one to yourself, and relinquishing the three others to the claim of abstract justice, I recognised a soul that revelled in the flame and excitement of sacrifice. In the tractability with which, at my wish, you forsook a study in which you were interested, and adopted another because it interested me; in the untiring assiduity with which you have since persevered in it – in the unflagging energy and unshaken temper with which you have met its difficulties – I acknowledge the complement of the qualities I seek. Jane, you are docile, diligent, disinterested, faithful, constant, and courageous; very gentle, and very heroic: cease to mistrust yourself – I can trust you unreservedly. As a conductress of Indian schools, and a helper amongst Indian women, your assistance will be to me invaluable."

My iron shroud contracted round me; persuasion advanced with slow sure step. Shut my eyes as I would, these last words of his succeeded in making the way, which had seemed blocked up, comparatively clear. My work, which had appeared so vague, so hopelessly diffuse, condensed itself as he proceeded, and assumed a definite form under his shaping hand. He waited for an answer. I demanded a quarter of an hour to think, before I again hazarded a reply.

"Very willingly," he rejoined; and rising, he strode a little distance up the pass, threw himself down on a swell of heath, and there lay still.

"I *can* do what he wants me to do: I am forced to see and acknowledge that," I meditated, – "that is, if life be spared me. But I feel mine is not the existence to be long protracted under an Indian sun. What then? He does not care for that: when my time came to die, he would resign me, in all serenity and sanctity, to the God who gave me. The case is very plain before me. In leaving England, I should leave a loved but empty land – Mr. Rochester is not there; and if he were, what is, what can that ever be to me? My business is to live without him now: nothing so absurd, so weak as to drag on from day to day, as if I were waiting some impossible change in circumstances, which might reunite me to him. Of course (as St. John once said) I must seek another interest in life to replace the one lost: is not the occupation he now offers me truly the most glorious man can adopt or God assign? Is it not, by its noble cares and sublime results, the one best calculated to fill the void left by uptorn affections and demolished hopes? I believe I must say, Yes – and yet I shudder. Alas! If I join St. John, I abandon half myself: if I go to India, I go to premature death. And how will the interval between leaving England for India, and India for the grave, be filled? Oh, I know well! That, too, is very clear to my vision. By straining to satisfy St. John till my sinews ache, I *shall* satisfy him – to the finest central point and farthest outward circle of his expectations. If I *do* go with him – if I *do* make the sacrifice he urges, I will make it absolutely: I will throw all on the altar – heart, vitals, the entire victim. He will never love me; but he shall approve me; I will show him energies he has not yet seen, resources he has never suspected. Yes, I can work as hard as he can, and with as little grudging.

"Consent, then, to his demand is possible: but for one item – one dreadful item. It is – that he asks me to be his wife, and has no more of a husband's heart for me than that frowning giant of a rock, down which the stream is foaming in yonder gorge. He prizes me as a soldier would a good weapon; and that is all. Unmarried to him, this would never grieve me; but can I let him complete his calculations – coolly put into practice his plans – go through the wedding ceremony? Can I receive from him the bridal ring, endure all the forms of love (which I doubt not he would scrupulously observe) and know that the spirit was quite absent? Can I bear the consciousness that every endearment he bestows is a sacrifice made on principle? No: such a martyrdom would be monstrous. I will never undergo it. As his sister, I might accompany him – not as his wife: I will tell him so."

I looked towards the knoll: there he lay, still as a prostrate column; his face turned to me: his eye beaming watchful and keen. He started to his feet and approached me.

"I am ready to go to India, if I may go free."

"Your answer requires a commentary," he said; "it is not clear."

"You have hitherto been my adopted brother – I, your adopted sister: let us continue as such: you and I had better not marry."

He shook his head. "Adopted fraternity will not do in this case. If you were my real sister it would be different: I should take you, and seek no wife. But as it is, either our union must be consecrated and sealed by marriage, or it cannot exist: practical obstacles oppose themselves to any other plan. Do you not see it, Jane? Consider a moment – your strong sense will guide you."

I did consider; and still my sense, such as it was, directed me only to the fact that we did not love each other as man and wife should: and therefore it inferred we ought not to marry. I said so. "St. John," I returned, "I regard you as a brother – you, me as a sister: so let us continue."

"We cannot – we cannot," he answered, with short, sharp determination: "it would not do. You have said you will go with me to India: remember – you have said that."

"Conditionally."

"Well – well. To the main point – the departure with me from England, the co-operation with me in my future labours – you do not object. You have already as good as put your hand to the plough: you are too consistent to withdraw it. You have but one end to keep in view – how the work you have undertaken can best be done. Simplify your complicated interests, feelings, thoughts, wishes, aims; merge all considerations in one purpose: that of fulfilling with effect – with power – the mission of your great Master. To do so, you must have a coadjutor: not a brother – that is a loose tie – but a husband. I, too, do not want a sister: a sister might any day be taken from me. I want a wife: the sole helpmeet I can influence efficiently in life, and retain absolutely till death."

I shuddered as he spoke: I felt his influence in my marrow – his hold on my limbs.

"Seek one elsewhere than in me, St. John: seek one fitted to you."

"One fitted to my purpose, you mean – fitted to my vocation. Again I tell you it is not the insignificant private individual – the mere man, with the man's selfish senses – I wish to mate: it is the missionary."

"And I will give the missionary my energies – it is all he wants – but not myself: that would be only adding the husk and shell to the kernel. For them he has no use: I retain them."

"You cannot – you ought not. Do you think God will be satisfied with half an oblation? Will He accept a mutilated sacrifice? It is the cause of God I advocate: it is under His standard I enlist you. I cannot accept on His behalf a divided allegiance: it must be entire."

"Oh! I will give my heart to God," I said. "*You* do not want it."

I will not swear, reader, that there was not something of repressed sarcasm both in the tone in which I uttered this sentence, and in the feeling that accompanied it. I had silently feared St. John till now, because I had not understood him. He had held me in awe, because he had held me in doubt. How much of him was saint, how much mortal, I could not heretofore tell: but revelations were being made in this conference: the analysis of his nature was proceeding before my eyes. I saw his fallibilities: I comprehended them. I understood that, sitting there where I did, on the bank of heath, and with that handsome form before me, I sat at the feet of a man, caring as I. The veil fell from his hardness and despotism. Having felt in him the presence of these qualities, I felt his imperfection and took courage. I was with an equal – one with whom I might argue – one whom, if I saw good, I might resist.

He was silent after I had uttered the last sentence, and I presently risked an upward glance at his countenance.

His eye, bent on me, expressed at once stern surprise and keen inquiry. "Is she sarcastic, and sarcastic to *me*!" it seemed to say. "What does this signify?"

"Do not let us forget that this is a solemn matter," he said ere long; "one of which we may neither think nor talk lightly without sin. I trust, Jane, you are in earnest when you say you will serve your heart to God: it is all I want. Once wrench your heart from man, and fix it on your Maker, the advancement of that Maker's spiritual kingdom on earth will be your chief delight and endeavour; you will be ready to do at once whatever furthers that end. You will see what impetus would be given to your efforts and mine by our physical and mental union in marriage: the only union that gives a character of permanent conformity to the destinies and designs of human beings; and, passing over all minor caprices – all trivial difficulties and delicacies of feeling – all scruple about the degree, kind, strength or tenderness of mere personal inclination – you will hasten to enter into that union at once."

"Shall I?" I said briefly; and I looked at his features, beautiful in their harmony, but strangely formidable in their still severity; at his brow, commanding but not open; at his eyes, bright and deep and searching, but never soft; at his tall imposing figure; and fancied myself in idea *his wife*. Oh! It would never do! As his curate, his comrade, all would be right: I would cross oceans with him in that capacity; toil under Eastern suns, in Asian deserts with him in that office; admire and emulate his courage and devotion and vigour; accommodate quietly to his masterhood; smile undisturbed at his ineradicable ambition; discriminate the Christian from the man: profoundly esteem the one, and freely forgive the other. I should suffer often, no doubt, attached to him only in this capacity: my body would be under rather a stringent yoke, but my heart and mind would be free. I should still have my unblighted self to turn to: my natural unenslaved feelings with which to communicate in moments of loneliness. There would be recesses in my mind which would be only mine, to which he never came, and sentiments growing there fresh and sheltered which his austerity could never blight, nor his measured warrior-march trample down: but as his wife – at his side always, and always restrained, and always checked – forced to keep the fire of my nature continually low, to compel it to burn inwardly and never utter a cry, though the imprisoned flame consumed vital after vital – *this* would be unendurable.

"St. John!" I exclaimed, when I had got so far in my meditation.

"Well?" he answered icily.

"I repeat I freely consent to go with you as your fellow-missionary, but not as your wife; I cannot marry you and become part of you."

"A part of me you must become," he answered steadily; "otherwise the whole bargain is void. How can I, a man not yet thirty, take out with me to India a girl of nineteen, unless she be married to me? How can we be for ever together – sometimes in solitudes, sometimes amidst savage tribes – and unwed?"

"Very well," I said shortly; "under the circumstances, quite as well as if I were either your real sister, or a man and a clergyman like yourself."

"It is known that you are not my sister; I cannot introduce you as such: to attempt it would be to fasten injurious suspicions on us both. And for the rest, though you have a man's vigorous brain, you have a woman's heart and – it would not do."

"It would do," I affirmed with some disdain, "perfectly well. I have a woman's heart, but not where you are concerned; for you I have only a comrade's constancy; a fellow-soldier's frankness, fidelity, fraternity, if you like; a neophyte's respect and submission to his hierophant: nothing more – don't fear."

"It is what I want," he said, speaking to himself; "it is just what I want. And there are obstacles in the way: they must be hewn down. Jane, you would not repent marrying me – be certain of that; we *must* be married. I repeat it: there is no other way; and undoubtedly enough of love would follow upon marriage to render the union right even in your eyes."

"I scorn your idea of love," I could not help saying, as I rose up and stood before him, leaning my back against the rock. "I scorn the counterfeit sentiment you offer: yes, St. John, and I scorn you when you offer it."

He looked at me fixedly, compressing his well-cut lips while he did so. Whether he was incensed or surprised, or what, it was not easy to tell: he could command his countenance thoroughly.

"I scarcely expected to hear that expression from you," he said: "I think I have done and uttered nothing to deserve scorn."

I was touched by his gentle tone, and overawed by his high, calm mien.

"Forgive me the words, St. John; but it is your own fault that I have been roused to speak so unguardedly. You have introduced a topic on which our natures are at variance – a topic we should never discuss: the very name of love is an apple of discord between us. If the reality were required, what should we do? How should we feel? My dear cousin, abandon your scheme of marriage – forget it."

"No," said he; "it is a long-cherished scheme, and the only one which can secure my great end: but I shall urge you no further at present. Tomorrow, I leave home for Cambridge: I have many friends there to whom I should wish to say farewell. I shall be absent a fortnight – take that space of time to consider my offer: and do not forget that if you reject it, it is not me you deny, but God. Through my means, He opens to you a noble career; as my wife only can you enter upon it. Refuse to be my wife, and you limit yourself for ever to a track of selfish ease and barren obscurity. Tremble lest in that case you should be numbered with those who have denied the faith, and are worse than infidels!"

He had done. Turning from me, he once more:

Looked to river, looked to hill. [34]

But this time his feelings were all pent in his heart: I was not worthy to hear them uttered. As I walked by his side homeward, I read well in his iron silence all he felt towards me: the disappointment of an austere and despotic nature, which has met resistance where it expected submission – the disapprobation of a cool, inflexible judgment, which has detected in another feelings and views in which it has no power to sympathise: in short, as a man, he would have wished to coerce me into obedience: it was only as a sincere Christian he bore so patiently with my perversity, and allowed so long a space for reflection and repentance.

That night, after he had kissed his sisters, he thought proper to forget even to shake hands with me, but left the room in silence. I – who, though I had no love, had much friendship for him – was hurt by the marked omission: so much hurt that tears started to my eyes.

"I see you and St. John have been quarrelling, Jane," said Diana, "during your walk on the moor. But go after him; he is now lingering in the passage expecting you – he will make it up."

I have not much pride under such circumstances: I would always rather be happy than dignified; and I ran after him – he stood at the foot of the stairs.

"Goodnight, St. John," said I.

"Goodnight, Jane," he replied calmly.

"Then shake hands," I added.

What a cold, loose touch, he impressed on my fingers! He was deeply displeased by what had occurred that day; cordiality would not warm, nor tears move him. No happy reconciliation was to be had with him – no cheering smile or generous word: but still the Christian was patient and placid; and when I asked him if he forgave me, he answered that he was not in the habit of cherishing the remembrance of vexation; that he had nothing to forgive, not having been offended.

And with that answer he left me. I would much rather he had knocked me down.

Chapter Thirty-Five

HE DID NOT LEAVE for Cambridge the next day, as he had said he would. He deferred his departure a whole week, and during that time he made me feel what severe punishment a good yet stern, a conscientious yet implacable man can inflict on one who has offended him. Without one overt act of hostility, one upbraiding word, he contrived to impress me momently with the conviction that I was put beyond the pale of his favour.

Not that St. John harboured a spirit of unchristian vindictiveness – not that he would have injured a hair of my head, if it had been fully in his power to do so. Both by nature and principle, he was superior to the mean gratification of vengeance: he had forgiven me for saying I scorned him and his love, but he had not forgotten the words; and as long as he and I lived he never would forget them. I saw by his look, when he turned to me, that they were always written on the air between me and him; whenever I spoke, they sounded in my voice to his ear, and their echo toned every answer he gave me.

He did not abstain from conversing with me: he even called me as usual each morning to join him at his desk; and I fear the corrupt man within him had a pleasure unimparted to, and unshared by, the pure Christian, in evincing with what skill he could, while acting and speaking apparently just as usual, extract from every deed and every phrase the spirit of interest and approval which had formerly communicated a certain austere charm to his language and manner. To me, he was in reality become no longer flesh, but marble; his eye was a cold, bright, blue gem; his tongue a speaking instrument – nothing more.

All this was torture to me – refined, lingering torture. It kept up a slow fire of indignation and a trembling trouble of grief, which harassed and crushed me altogether. I felt how – if I were his wife, this good man, pure as the deep sunless source, could soon kill me, without drawing from my veins a single drop of blood, or receiving on his own crystal conscience the faintest stain of crime. Especially I felt this when I made any attempt to propitiate him. No ruth met my ruth. *He* experienced no suffering from estrangement – no yearning after reconciliation; and though, more than once, my fast falling tears blistered the page over which we both bent, they produced no more effect on him than if his heart had been really a matter of stone or metal. To his sisters, meantime, he was somewhat kinder than usual: as if afraid that mere coldness would not sufficiently convince me how completely I was banished and banned, he added the force of contrast; and this I am sure he did not by force, but on principle.

The night before he left home, happening to see him walking in the garden about sunset, and remembering, as I looked at him, that this man, alienated as he now was, had once saved my life, and that we were near relations, I was moved to make a last attempt to regain his friendship. I went out and approached him as he stood leaning over the little gate; I spoke to the point at once.

"St. John, I am unhappy because you are still angry with me. Let us be friends."

"I hope we are friends," was the unmoved reply; while he still watched the rising of the moon, which he had been contemplating as I approached.

"No, St. John, we are not friends as we were. You know that."

"Are we not? That is wrong. For my part, I wish you no ill and all good."

"I believe you, St. John; for I am sure you are incapable of wishing anyone ill; but, as I am your kinswoman, I should desire somewhat more of affection than that sort of general philanthropy you extend to mere strangers."

"Of course," he said. "Your wish is reasonable, and I am far from regarding you as a stranger."

This, spoken in a cool, tranquil tone, was mortifying and baffling enough. Had I attended to the suggestions of pride and ire, I should immediately have left him; but something worked within me more strongly than those feelings could. I deeply venerated my cousin's talent and principle. His friendship was of value to me: to lose it tried me severely. I would not so soon relinquish the attempt to reconquer it.

"Must we part in this way, St. John? And when you go to India, will you leave me so, without a kinder word than you have yet spoken?"

He now turned quite from the moon and faced me.

"When I go to India, Jane, will I leave you! What! Do you not go to India?"

"You said I could not unless I married you."

"And you will not marry me! You adhere to that resolution?"

Reader, do you know, as I do, what terror those cold people can put into the ice of their questions? How much of the fall of the avalanche is in their anger? Of the breaking up of the frozen sea in their displeasure?

"No. St. John, I will not marry you. I adhere to my resolution."

The avalanche had shaken and slid a little forward, but it did not yet crash down.

"Once more, why this refusal?" he asked.

"Formerly," I answered, "because you did not love me; now, I reply, because you almost hate me. If I were to marry you, you would kill me. You are killing me now."

His lips and cheeks turned white – quite white.

"*I should kill you – I am killing you*? Your words are such as ought not to be used: violent, unfeminine, and untrue. They betray an unfortunate state of mind: they merit severe reproof: they would seem inexcusable, but that it is the duty of man to forgive his fellow even until seventy-and-seven times."

I had finished the business now. While earnestly wishing to erase from his mind the trace of my former offence, I had stamped on that tenacious surface another and far deeper impression, I had burnt it in.

"Now you will indeed hate me," I said. "It is useless to attempt to conciliate you: I see I have made an eternal enemy of you."

A fresh wrong did these words inflict: the worse, because they touched on the truth. That bloodless lip quivered to a temporary spasm. I knew the steely ire I had whetted. I was heart-wrung.

"You utterly misinterpret my words," I said, at once seizing his hand: "I have no intention to grieve or pain you – indeed, I have not."

Most bitterly he smiled – most decidedly he withdrew his hand from mine. "And now you recall your promise, and will not go to India at all, I presume?" said he, after a considerable pause.

"Yes, I will, as your assistant," I answered.

A very long silence succeeded. What struggle there was in him between Nature and Grace in this interval, I cannot tell: only singular gleams scintillated in his eyes, and strange shadows passed over his face. He spoke at last.

"I before proved to you the absurdity of a single woman of your age proposing to accompany abroad a single man of mine. I proved it to you in such terms as, I should have thought, would have prevented your ever again alluding to the plan. That you have done so, I regret – for your sake."

I interrupted him. Anything like a tangible reproach gave me courage at once. "Keep to common sense, St. John: you are verging on nonsense. You pretend to be shocked by what I have said. You are not really shocked: for, with your superior mind, you cannot be either so dull or so conceited as to misunderstand my meaning. I say again, I will be your curate, if you like, but never your wife."

Again he turned lividly pale; but, as before, controlled his passion perfectly. He answered emphatically but calmly:

"A female curate, who is not my wife, would never suit me. With me, then, it seems, you cannot go: but if you are sincere in your offer, I will, while in town, speak to a married missionary, whose wife needs a coadjutor. Your own fortune will make you independent of the Society's aid; and thus you may still be spared the dishonour of breaking your promise and deserting the band you engaged to join."

Now I never had, as the reader knows, either given any formal promise or entered into any engagement; and this language was all much too hard and much too despotic for the occasion. I replied:

"There is no dishonour, no breach of promise, no desertion in the case. I am not under the slightest obligation to go to India, especially with strangers. With you I would have ventured much, because I admire, confide in, and, as a sister, I love you; but I am convinced that, go when and with whom I would, I should not live long in that climate."

"Ah! You are afraid of yourself," he said, curling his lip.

"I am. God did not give me my life to throw away; and to do as you wish me would, I begin to think, be almost equivalent to committing suicide. Moreover, before I definitively resolve on quitting England, I will know for certain whether I cannot be of greater use by remaining in it than by leaving it."

"What do you mean?"

"It would be fruitless to attempt to explain; but there is a point on which I have long endured painful doubt, and I can go nowhere till by some means that doubt is removed."

"I know where your heart turns and to what it clings. The interest you cherish is lawless and unconsecrated. Long since you ought to have crushed it: now you should blush to allude to it. You think of Mr. Rochester?"

It was true. I confessed it by silence.

"Are you going to seek Mr. Rochester?"

"I must find out what is become of him."

"It remains for me, then," he said, "to remember you in my prayers, and to entreat God for you, in all earnestness, that you may not indeed become a castaway. I had thought I recognised in you one of the chosen. But God sees not as man sees: *His* will be done –"

He opened the gate, passed through it, and strayed away down the glen. He was soon out of sight.

On re-entering the parlour, I found Diana standing at the window, looking very thoughtful. Diana was a great deal taller than I: she put her hand on my shoulder, and, stooping, examined my face.

"Jane," she said, "you are always agitated and pale now. I am sure there is something the matter. Tell me what business St. John and you have on hands. I have watched you this half hour from the window; you must forgive my being such a spy, but for a long time I have fancied I hardly know what. St. John is a strange being –"

She paused – I did not speak: soon she resumed:

"That brother of mine cherishes peculiar views of some sort respecting you, I am sure: he has long distinguished you by a notice and interest he never showed to anyone else – to what end? I wish he loved you – does he, Jane?"

I put her cool hand to my hot forehead; "No, Die, not one whit."

"Then why does he follow you so with his eyes, and get you so frequently alone with him, and keep you so continually at his side? Mary and I had both concluded he wished you to marry him."

"He does – he has asked me to be his wife."

Diana clapped her hands. "That is just what we hoped and thought! And you will marry him, Jane, won't you? And then he will stay in England."

"Far from that, Diana; his sole idea in proposing to me is to procure a fitting fellow-labourer in his Indian toils."

"What! He wishes you to go to India?"

"Yes."

"Madness!" she exclaimed. "You would not live three months there, I am certain. You never shall go: you have not consented, have you, Jane?"

"I have refused to marry him –"

"And have consequently displeased him?" she suggested.

"Deeply: he will never forgive me, I fear: yet I offered to accompany him as his sister."

"It was frantic folly to do so, Jane. Think of the task you undertook – one of incessant fatigue, where fatigue kills even the strong, and you are weak. St. John – you know him – would urge you to impossibilities: with him there would be no permission to rest during the hot hours; and unfortunately, I have noticed, whatever he exacts, you force yourself to perform. I am astonished you found courage to refuse his hand. You do not love him then, Jane?"

"Not as a husband."

"Yet he is a handsome fellow."

"And I am so plain, you see, Die. We should never suit."

"Plain! You? Not at all. You are much too pretty, as well as too good, to be grilled alive in Calcutta." And again she earnestly conjured me to give up all thoughts of going out with her brother.

"I must indeed," I said; "for when just now I repeated the offer of serving him for a deacon, he expressed himself shocked at my want of decency. He seemed to think I had committed an impropriety in proposing to accompany him unmarried: as if I had not from the first hoped to find in him a brother, and habitually regarded him as such."

"What makes you say he does not love you, Jane?"

"You should hear himself on the subject. He has again and again explained that it is not himself, but his office he wishes to mate. He has told me I am formed for labour – not for love: which is true, no doubt. But, in my opinion, if I am not formed for love, it follows that I am not formed for marriage. Would it not be strange, Die, to be chained for life to a man who regarded one but as a useful tool?"

"Insupportable – unnatural – out of the question!"

"And then," I continued, "though I have only sisterly affection for him now, yet, if forced to be his wife, I can imagine the possibility of conceiving an inevitable, strange, torturing kind of love for him, because he is so talented; and there is often a certain heroic grandeur in his look, manner, and conversation. In that case, my lot would become unspeakably wretched. He would not want me to love him; and if I showed the feeling, he would make me sensible that it was a superfluity, unrequired by him, unbecoming in me. I know he would."

"And yet St. John is a good man," said Diana.

"He is a good and a great man; but he forgets, pitilessly, the feelings and claims of little people, in pursuing his own large views. It is better, therefore, for the insignificant to keep out of his way, lest, in his progress, he should trample them down. Here he comes! I will leave you, Diana." And I hastened upstairs as I saw him entering the garden.

But I was forced to meet him again at supper. During that meal he appeared just as composed as usual. I had thought he would hardly speak to me, and I was certain he had given up the pursuit of his matrimonial scheme: the sequel showed I was mistaken on both points. He addressed me precisely in his ordinary manner, or what had, of late, been his ordinary manner – one scrupulously polite. No doubt he had invoked the help of the Holy Spirit to subdue the anger I had roused in him, and now believed he had forgiven me once more.

For the evening reading before prayers, he selected the twenty-first chapter of Revelation. It was at all times pleasant to listen while from his lips fell the words of the Bible: never did his fine voice sound at once so sweet and full – never did his manner become so impressive in its noble simplicity, as when he delivered the oracles of God: and tonight that voice took a more solemn tone – that manner a more thrilling meaning – as he sat in the midst of his household circle (the May moon shining in through the uncurtained window, and rendering almost unnecessary the light of the candle on the table): as he sat there, bending over the great old Bible, and described from its page the vision of the new heaven and the new earth – told how God would come to dwell with men, how He would wipe away all tears from their eyes, and promised that there should be no more death, neither sorrow nor crying, nor any more pain, because the former things were passed away.

The succeeding words thrilled me strangely as he spoke them: especially as I felt, by the slight, indescribable alteration in sound, that in uttering them, his eye had turned on me.

"He that overcometh shall inherit all things; and I will be his God, and he shall be my son. But," was slowly, distinctly read, "the fearful, the unbelieving, etc., shall have their part in the lake which burneth with fire and brimstone, which is the second death."

Henceforward, I knew what fate St. John feared for me.

A calm, subdued triumph, blent with a longing earnestness, marked his enunciation of the last glorious verses of that chapter. The reader believed his name was already written in the Lamb's book of life, and he yearned after the hour which should admit him to the city to which the kings of the earth bring their glory and honour; which has no need of sun or moon to shine in it, because the glory of God lightens it, and the Lamb is the light thereof.

In the prayer following the chapter, all his energy gathered – all his stern zeal woke: he was in deep earnest, wrestling with God, and resolved on a conquest. He supplicated strength for the weak-hearted; guidance for wanderers from the fold: a return, even at the eleventh hour, for those whom the temptations of the world and the flesh were luring from the narrow path. He asked, he urged, he claimed the boon of a brand snatched from the burning. Earnestness is ever deeply solemn: first, as I listened to that prayer, I wondered at his; then, when it continued and rose, I was touched by it, and at last awed. He felt the greatness and goodness of his purpose so sincerely: others who heard him plead for it, could not but feel it too.

The prayer over, we took leave of him: he was to go at a very early hour in the morning. Diana and Mary having kissed him, left the room – in compliance, I think, with a whispered hint from him: I tendered my hand, and wished him a pleasant journey.

"Thank you, Jane. As I said, I shall return from Cambridge in a fortnight: that space, then, is yet left you for reflection. If I listened to human pride, I should say no more to you of marriage with me; but I listen to my duty, and keep steadily in view my first aim – to do all things to the glory of God. My Master was long-suffering: so will I be. I cannot give you up to perdition as a vessel of wrath: repent – resolve, while there is yet time. Remember, we are bid to work while it is day – warned that 'the night cometh when no man shall work.' Remember the fate of Dives, who had his good things in this life. God give you strength to choose that better part which shall not be taken from you!"

He laid his hand on my head as he uttered the last words. He had spoken earnestly, mildly: his look was not, indeed, that of a lover beholding his mistress, but it was that of a pastor recalling his wandering sheep – or better, of a guardian angel watching the soul for which he is responsible. All men of talent, whether they be men of feeling or not; whether they be zealots, or aspirants, or despots – provided only they be sincere – have their sublime moments, when they subdue and rule. I felt veneration for St. John – veneration so strong that its impetus thrust me at once to the point I had so long shunned. I was tempted to cease struggling with him – to rush down the torrent of his will into the gulf of his existence, and there lose my own. I was almost as hard beset by him now as I had been once before, in a different way, by another. I was a fool both times. To have yielded then would have been an error of principle; to have yielded now would have been an error of judgment. So I think at this hour, when I look back to the crisis through the quiet medium of time: I was unconscious of folly at the instant.

I stood motionless under my hierophant's touch. My refusals were forgotten – my fears overcome – my wrestlings paralysed. The Impossible – *i.e.*, my marriage with St. John – was fast becoming the Possible. All was changing utterly with a sudden sweep. Religion called – Angels beckoned – God commanded – life rolled together like a scroll – death's gates opening, showed eternity beyond: it seemed, that for safety and bliss there, all here might be sacrificed in a second. The dim room was full of visions.

"Could you decide now?" asked the missionary. The inquiry was put in gentle tones: he drew me to him as gently. Oh, that gentleness! How far more potent is it than force! I could resist St. John's wrath: I grew pliant as a reed under his kindness. Yet I knew all the time, if I yielded now, I should not the less be made to repent, some day, of my former rebellion. His nature was not changed by one hour of solemn prayer: it was only elevated.

"I could decide if I were but certain," I answered: "were I but convinced that it is God's will I should marry you, I could vow to marry you here and now – come afterwards what would!"

"My prayers are heard!" ejaculated St. John. He pressed his hand firmer on my head, as if he claimed me: he surrounded me with his arm, *almost* as if he loved me (I say *almost* – I knew the difference – for I had felt what it was to be loved; but, like him, I had now put love out of the question, and thought only of duty). I contended with my inward dimness of vision, before which clouds yet rolled. I sincerely, deeply, fervently longed to do what was right; and only that. "Show me, show me the path!" I entreated of Heaven. I was excited more than I had ever been; and whether what followed was the effect of excitement the reader shall judge.

All the house was still; for I believe all, except St. John and myself, were now retired to rest. The one candle was dying out: the room was full of moonlight. My heart beat fast and thick: I heard its throb. Suddenly it stood still to an inexpressible feeling that thrilled it through, and passed at once to my head and extremities. The feeling was not like an electric shock, but it was quite as sharp, as strange, as startling: it acted on my senses as if their utmost activity hitherto had been but torpor, from which they were now summoned and forced to wake. They rose expectant: eye and ear waited while the flesh quivered on my bones.

"What have you heard? What do you see?" asked St. John. I saw nothing, but I heard a voice somewhere cry:

"Jane! Jane! Jane!" – nothing more.

"O God! What is it?" I gasped.

I might have said, "Where is it?" for it did not seem in the room – nor in the house – nor in the garden; it did not come out of the air – nor from under the earth – nor from overhead. I had heard it – where, or whence, for ever impossible to know! And it was the voice of a human being – a known, loved, well-remembered voice – that of Edward Fairfax Rochester; and it spoke in pain and woe, wildly, eerily, urgently.

"I am coming!" I cried. "Wait for me! Oh, I will come!" I flew to the door and looked into the passage: it was dark. I ran out into the garden: it was void.

"Where are you?" I exclaimed.

The hills beyond Marsh Glen sent the answer faintly back – "Where are you?" I listened. The wind sighed low in the firs: all was moorland loneliness and midnight hush.

"Down superstition!" I commented, as that spectre rose up black by the black yew at the gate. "This is not thy deception, nor thy witchcraft: it is the work of nature. She was roused, and did – no miracle – but her best."

I broke from St. John, who had followed, and would have detained me. It was *my* time to assume ascendency. *My* powers were in play and in force. I told him to forbear question or remark; I desired him to leave me: I must and would be alone. He obeyed at once. Where there is energy to command well enough, obedience never fails. I mounted to my chamber; locked myself in; fell on my knees; and prayed in my way – a different way to St. John's, but effective in its own fashion. I seemed to penetrate very near a Mighty Spirit; and my soul rushed out in gratitude at His feet. I rose from the thanksgiving – took a resolve – and lay down, unscared, enlightened – eager but for the daylight.

Chapter Thirty-Six

THE DAYLIGHT CAME. I rose at dawn. I busied myself for an hour or two with arranging my things in my chamber, drawers, and wardrobe, in the order wherein I should wish to leave them during a brief absence. Meantime, I heard St. John quit his room. He stopped at my door: I feared he would knock – no, but a slip of paper was passed under the door. I took it up. It bore these words:

"You left me too suddenly last night. Had you stayed but a little longer, you would have laid your hand on the Christian's cross and the angel's crown. I shall expect your clear decision when I return this day fortnight. Meantime, watch and pray that you enter not into temptation: the spirit, I trust, is willing, but the flesh, I see, is weak. I shall pray for you hourly. – Yours, St. John."

"My spirit," I answered mentally, "is willing to do what is right; and my flesh, I hope, is strong enough to accomplish the will of Heaven, when once that will is distinctly known to me. At any rate, it shall be strong enough to search – inquire – to grope an outlet from this cloud of doubt, and find the open day of certainty."

It was the first of June; yet the morning was overcast and chilly: rain beat fast on my casement. I heard the front-door open, and St. John pass out. Looking through the window, I saw him traverse the garden. He took the way over the misty moors in the direction of Whitcross – there he would meet the coach.

"In a few more hours I shall succeed you in that track, cousin," thought I: "I too have a coach to meet at Whitcross. I too have some to see and ask after in England, before I depart for ever."

It wanted yet two hours of breakfast time. I filled the interval in walking softly about my room, and pondering the visitation which had given my plans their present bent. I recalled that inward sensation I had experienced: for I could recall it, with all its unspeakable strangeness. I recalled the voice I had heard; again I questioned whence it came, as vainly as before: it seemed in *me* – not in the external world. I asked was it a mere nervous impression – a delusion? I could not conceive or believe: it was more like an inspiration. The wondrous shock of feeling had come like the earthquake which shook the foundations of Paul and Silas's prison; it had opened the doors of the soul's cell and loosed its bands – it had wakened it out of its sleep, whence it sprang trembling, listening, aghast; then vibrated thrice a cry on my startled ear, and in my quaking heart and through my spirit, which neither feared nor shook, but exulted as if in joy over the success of one effort it had been privileged to make, independent of the cumbrous body.

"Ere many days," I said, as I terminated my musings, "I will know something of him whose voice seemed last night to summon me. Letters have proved of no avail – personal inquiry shall replace them."

At breakfast I announced to Diana and Mary that I was going a journey, and should be absent at least four days.

"Alone, Jane?" they asked.

"Yes; it was to see or hear news of a friend about whom I had for some time been uneasy."

They might have said, as I have no doubt they thought, that they had believed me to be without any friends save them: for, indeed, I had often said so; but, with their true natural delicacy, they abstained from comment, except that Diana asked me if I was sure I was well enough to travel. I looked very pale, she observed. I replied, that nothing ailed me save anxiety of mind, which I hoped soon to alleviate.

It was easy to make my further arrangements; for I was troubled with no inquiries – no surmises. Having once explained to them that I could not now be explicit about my plans, they kindly and wisely acquiesced in the silence with which I pursued them, according to me the privilege of free action I should under similar circumstances have accorded them.

I left Moor House at three o'clock p.m., and soon after four I stood at the foot of the signpost of Whitcross, waiting the arrival of the coach which was to take me to distant Thornfield. Amidst the silence of those solitary roads and desert hills, I heard it approach from a great distance. It was the same vehicle whence, a year ago, I had alighted one summer evening on this very spot – how desolate, and hopeless, and objectless! It stopped as I beckoned. I entered – not now obliged to part with my whole fortune as the price of its accommodation. Once more on the road to Thornfield, I felt like the messenger-pigeon flying home.

It was a journey of six-and-thirty hours. I had set out from Whitcross on a Tuesday afternoon, and early on the succeeding Thursday morning the coach stopped to water the horses at a wayside inn, situated in the midst of scenery whose green hedges and large fields and low pastoral hills (how mild of feature and verdant of hue compared with the stern North-Midland moors of Morton!) met my eye like the lineaments of a once familiar face. Yes, I knew the character of this landscape: I was sure we were near my bourne.

"How far is Thornfield Hall from here?" I asked of the ostler.

"Just two miles, ma'am, across the fields."

"My journey is closed," I thought to myself. I got out of the coach, gave a box I had into the ostler's charge, to be kept till I called for it; paid my fare; satisfied the coachman, and was going: the brightening day gleamed on the sign of the inn, and I read in gilt letters, 'The Rochester Arms'. My heart leapt up: I was already on my master's very lands. It fell again: the thought struck it:

"Your master himself may be beyond the British Channel, for aught you know: and then, if he is at Thornfield Hall, towards which you hasten, who besides him is there? His lunatic wife: and you have nothing to do with him: you dare not speak to him or seek his presence. You have lost your labour – you had better go no farther," urged the monitor. "Ask information of the people at the inn; they can give you all you seek: they can solve your doubts at once. Go up to that man, and inquire if Mr. Rochester be at home."

The suggestion was sensible, and yet I could not force myself to act on it. I so dreaded a reply that would crush me with despair. To prolong doubt was to prolong hope. I might yet once more see the Hall under the ray of her star. There was the stile before me – the very fields through which I had hurried, blind, deaf, distracted with a revengeful fury tracking and scourging me, on the morning I fled from Thornfield: ere I well knew what course I had resolved to take, I was in the midst of them. How fast I walked! How I ran sometimes! How I looked forward to catch the first view of the well-known woods! With what feelings I welcomed single trees I knew, and familiar glimpses of meadow and hill between them!

At last the woods rose; the rookery clustered dark; a loud cawing broke the morning stillness. Strange delight inspired me: on I hastened. Another field crossed – a lane threaded – and there were the courtyard walls – the back offices: the house itself, the rookery still hid. "My first view of it shall be in front," I determined, "where its bold battlements will strike the eye nobly at once, and where I can single out my master's very window: perhaps he will be standing at it – he rises early: perhaps he is now walking in the orchard, or on the pavement in front. Could I but see him! – but a moment! Surely, in that case, I should not be so mad as to run to him? I cannot tell – I am not certain. And if I did – what then? God bless him! What then? Who would be hurt by my once more tasting the life his glance can give me? I rave: perhaps at this moment he is watching the sun rise over the Pyrenees, or on the tideless sea of the south."

I had coasted along the lower wall of the orchard – turned its angle: there was a gate just there, opening into the meadow, between two stone pillars crowned by stone balls. From behind one pillar I could peep round quietly at the full front of the mansion. I advanced my head with precaution, desirous to ascertain if any bedroom window-blinds were yet drawn up: battlements, windows, long front – all from this sheltered station were at my command.

The crows sailing overhead perhaps watched me while I took this survey. I wonder what they thought. They must have considered I was very careful and timid at first, and that gradually I grew very bold and reckless. A peep, and then a long stare; and then a departure from my niche and a straying out into the meadow; and a sudden stop full in front of the great mansion, and a protracted, hardy gaze towards it. "What affectation of diffidence was this at first?" they might have demanded; "what stupid regardlessness now?"

Hear an illustration, reader.

A lover finds his mistress asleep on a mossy bank; he wishes to catch a glimpse of her fair face without waking her. He steals softly over the grass, careful to make no sound; he pauses – fancying she has stirred: he withdraws: not for worlds would he be seen. All is still: he again advances: he bends above her; a light veil rests on her features: he lifts it, bends lower; now his eyes anticipate the vision of beauty – warm, and blooming, and lovely, in rest. How hurried was their first glance! But how they fix! How he starts! How he suddenly and vehemently clasps in both arms the form he dared not, a moment since, touch with his finger! How he calls aloud a name, and drops his burden, and gazes on it wildly! He thus grasps and cries, and gazes, because he no longer fears to waken by any sound he can utter – by any movement he can make. He thought his love slept sweetly: he finds she is stone dead.

I looked with timorous joy towards a stately house: I saw a blackened ruin.

No need to cower behind a gate-post, indeed! – To peep up at chamber lattices, fearing life was astir behind them! No need to listen for doors opening – to fancy steps on the pavement or the gravel-walk! The lawn, the grounds were trodden and waste: the portal yawned void. The front was, as I had once seen it in a dream, but a well-like wall, very high and very fragile-looking, perforated with paneless windows: no roof, no battlements, no chimneys – all had crashed in.

And there was the silence of death about it: the solitude of a lonesome wild. No wonder that letters addressed to people here had never received an answer: as well despatch epistles to a vault in a church aisle. The grim blackness of the stones told by what fate the Hall had fallen – by conflagration: but how kindled? What story belonged to this disaster? What loss, besides mortar and marble and woodwork had followed upon it? Had life been wrecked as well as property? If so, whose? Dreadful question: there was no one here to answer it – not even dumb sign, mute token.

In wandering round the shattered walls and through the devastated interior, I gathered evidence that the calamity was not of late occurrence. Winter snows, I thought, had drifted through that void arch, winter rains beaten in at those hollow casements; for, amidst the drenched piles of rubbish, spring had cherished vegetation: grass and weed grew here and there between the stones and fallen rafters. And oh! where meantime was the hapless owner of this wreck? In what land? Under what auspices? My eye involuntarily wandered to the grey church tower near the gates, and I asked, "Is he with Damer de Rochester, sharing the shelter of his narrow marble house?"

Some answer must be had to these questions. I could find it nowhere but at the inn, and thither, ere long, I returned. The host himself brought my breakfast into the parlour. I requested him to shut the door and sit down: I had some questions to ask him. But when he complied, I scarcely knew how to begin; such horror had I of the possible answers. And yet the spectacle of desolation I had just left prepared me in a measure for a tale of misery. The host was a respectable-looking, middle-aged man.

"You know Thornfield Hall, of course?" I managed to say at last.

"Yes, ma'am; I lived there once."

"Did you?" Not in my time, I thought: you are a stranger to me.

"I was the late Mr. Rochester's butler," he added.

The late! I seem to have received, with full force, the blow I had been trying to evade.

"The late!" I gasped. "Is he dead?"

"I mean the present gentleman, Mr. Edward's father," he explained. I breathed again: my blood resumed its flow. Fully assured by these words that Mr. Edward – *my* Mr. Rochester (God bless him, wherever he was!) – was at least alive: was, in short, "the present gentleman." Gladdening words! It seemed I could hear all that was to come – whatever the disclosures might be – with comparative tranquillity. Since he was not in the grave, I could bear, I thought, to learn that he was at the Antipodes.

"Is Mr. Rochester living at Thornfield Hall now?" I asked, knowing, of course, what the answer would be, but yet desirous of deferring the direct question as to where he really was.

"No, ma'am – oh, no! No one is living there. I suppose you are a stranger in these parts, or you would have heard what happened last autumn, – Thornfield Hall is quite a ruin: it was burnt down just about harvest-time. A dreadful calamity! Such an immense quantity of valuable property destroyed: hardly any of the furniture could be saved. The fire broke out at dead of night, and before the engines arrived from Millcote, the building was one mass of flame. It was a terrible spectacle: I witnessed it myself."

"At dead of night!" I muttered. Yes, that was ever the hour of fatality at Thornfield. "Was it known how it originated?" I demanded.

"They guessed, ma'am: they guessed. Indeed, I should say it was ascertained beyond a doubt. You are not perhaps aware," he continued, edging his chair a little nearer the table, and speaking low, "that there was a lady – a – a lunatic, kept in the house?"

"I have heard something of it."

"She was kept in very close confinement, ma'am: people even for some years was not absolutely certain of her existence. No one saw her: they only knew by rumour that such a person was at the Hall; and who or what she was it was difficult to conjecture. They said Mr. Edward had brought her from abroad, and some believed she had been his mistress. But a queer thing happened a year since – a very queer thing."

I feared now to hear my own story. I endeavoured to recall him to the main fact.

"And this lady?"

"This lady, ma'am," he answered, "turned out to be Mr. Rochester's wife! The discovery was brought about in the strangest way. There was a young lady, a governess at the Hall, that Mr. Rochester fell in –"

"But the fire," I suggested.

"I'm coming to that, ma'am – that Mr. Edward fell in love with. The servants say they never saw anybody so much in love as he was: he was after her continually. They used to watch him – servants will, you know, ma'am – and he set store on her past everything: for all, nobody but him thought her so very handsome. She was a little small thing, they say, almost like a child. I never saw her myself; but I've heard Leah, the house maid, tell of her. Leah liked her well enough. Mr. Rochester was about forty, and this governess not twenty; and you see, when gentlemen of his age fall in love with girls, they are often like as if they were bewitched. Well, he would marry her."

"You shall tell me this part of the story another time," I said; "but now I have a particular reason for wishing to hear all about the fire. Was it suspected that this lunatic, Mrs. Rochester, had any hand in it?"

"You've hit it, ma'am: it's quite certain that it was her, and nobody but her, that set it going. She had a woman to take care of her called Mrs. Poole – an able woman in her line, and very trustworthy, but for one fault – a fault common to a deal of them nurses and matrons – she *kept a private bottle of gin by her*, and now and then took a drop over-much. It is excusable, for she had a hard life of it: but still it was dangerous; for when Mrs. Poole was fast asleep after the gin and water, the mad lady, who was as cunning as a witch, would take the keys out of her pocket, let herself out of her chamber, and go roaming about the house, doing any wild mischief that came into her head. They say she had nearly burnt her husband in his bed once: but I don't know about that. However, on this night, she set fire first to the hangings of the room next her own, and then she got down to a lower storey, and made her way to the chamber that had been the governess's – (she was like as if she knew somehow how matters had gone on, and had a spite at her) – and she kindled the bed there; but there was nobody sleeping in it, fortunately. The governess had run away two months before; and for all Mr. Rochester sought her as if she had been the most precious thing he had in the world, he never could hear a word of her; and he grew savage – quite savage on his disappointment: he never was a wild man, but he got dangerous after he lost her. He would be alone, too. He sent Mrs. Fairfax, the housekeeper, away to her friends at a distance; but he did it handsomely, for he settled an annuity on her for life: and she deserved it – she was a very good woman. Miss Adèle, a ward he had, was put to school. He broke off acquaintance with all the gentry, and shut himself up like a hermit at the Hall."

"What! Did he not leave England?"

"Leave England? Bless you, no! He would not cross the door-stones of the house, except at night, when he walked just like a ghost about the grounds and in the orchard as if he had lost his senses – which it is my opinion he had; for a more spirited, bolder, keener gentleman than he was before that midge of a governess crossed him, you never saw, ma'am. He was not a man given to wine, or cards, or racing, as some are, and he was not so very handsome; but he had a courage and a will of his own, if ever man had. I knew him from a boy, you see: and for my part, I have often wished that Miss Eyre had been sunk in the sea before she came to Thornfield Hall."

"Then Mr. Rochester was at home when the fire broke out?"

"Yes, indeed was he; and he went up to the attics when all was burning above and below, and got the servants out of their beds and helped them down himself, and went back to get his mad wife out of her cell. And then they called out to him that she was on the roof, where she was standing, waving her arms, above the battlements, and shouting out till they could hear her a mile off: I saw her and heard her with my own eyes. She was a big woman, and had long black hair: we could see it streaming against the flames as she stood. I witnessed, and several more witnessed, Mr. Rochester ascend through the sky-light on to the roof; we heard him call 'Bertha!' We saw him approach her; and then, ma'am, she yelled and gave a spring, and the next minute she lay smashed on the pavement."

"Dead?"

"Dead! Ay, dead as the stones on which her brains and blood were scattered."

"Good God!"

"You may well say so, ma'am: it was frightful!"

He shuddered.

"And afterwards?" I urged.

"Well, ma'am, afterwards the house was burnt to the ground: there are only some bits of walls standing now."

"Were any other lives lost?"

"No – perhaps it would have been better if there had."

"What do you mean?"

"Poor Mr. Edward!" he ejaculated, "I little thought ever to have seen it! Some say it was a just judgment on him for keeping his first marriage secret, and wanting to take another wife while he had one living: but I pity him, for my part."

"You said he was alive?" I exclaimed.

"Yes, yes: he is alive; but many think he had better be dead."

"Why? How?" My blood was again running cold. "Where is he?" I demanded. "Is he in England?"

"Ay – ay – he's in England; he can't get out of England, I fancy – he's a fixture now."

What agony was this! And the man seemed resolved to protract it.

"He is stone-blind," he said at last. "Yes, he is stone-blind, is Mr. Edward."

I had dreaded worse. I had dreaded he was mad. I summoned strength to ask what had caused this calamity.

"It was all his own courage, and a body may say, his kindness, in a way, ma'am: he wouldn't leave the house till every one else was out before him. As he came down the great staircase at last, after Mrs. Rochester had flung herself from the battlements, there was a great crash – all fell. He was taken out from under the ruins, alive, but sadly hurt: a beam had fallen in such a way as to protect him partly; but one eye was knocked out, and one hand so crushed that Mr. Carter, the surgeon, had to amputate it directly. The other eye inflamed: he lost the sight of that also. He is now helpless, indeed – blind and a cripple."

"Where is he? Where does he now live?"

"At Ferndean, a manor-house on a farm he has, about thirty miles off: quite a desolate spot."

"Who is with him?"

"Old John and his wife: he would have none else. He is quite broken down, they say."

"Have you any sort of conveyance?"

"We have a chaise, ma'am, a very handsome chaise."

"Let it be got ready instantly; and if your post-boy can drive me to Ferndean before dark this day, I'll pay both you and him twice the hire you usually demand."

Chapter Thirty-Seven

THE MANOR-HOUSE of Ferndean was a building of considerable antiquity, moderate size, and no architectural pretensions, deep buried in a wood. I had heard of it before. Mr. Rochester often spoke of it, and sometimes went there. His father had purchased the estate for the sake of the game covers. He would have let the house, but could find no tenant, in consequence of its ineligible and insalubrious site. Ferndean then remained uninhabited and unfurnished, with the exception of some two or three rooms fitted up for the accommodation of the squire when he went there in the season to shoot.

To this house I came just ere dark on an evening marked by the characteristics of sad sky, cold gale, and continued small penetrating rain. The last mile I performed on foot, having dismissed the chaise and driver with the double remuneration I had promised. Even when within a very short distance of the manor-house, you could see nothing of it, so thick and dark grew the timber of the gloomy wood about it. Iron gates between granite pillars showed me where to enter, and passing through them, I found myself at once in the twilight of close-ranked trees. There was a grass-grown track descending the forest aisle between hoar and knotty shafts and under branched arches. I followed it, expecting soon to reach the dwelling; but it stretched on and on, it wound far and farther: no sign of habitation or grounds was visible.

I thought I had taken a wrong direction and lost my way. The darkness of natural as well as of sylvan dusk gathered over me. I looked round in search of another road. There was none: all was interwoven stem, columnar trunk, dense summer foliage – no opening anywhere.

I proceeded: at last my way opened, the trees thinned a little; presently I beheld a railing, then the house – scarce, by this dim light, distinguishable from the trees; so dank and green were its decaying walls. Entering a portal, fastened only by a latch, I stood amidst a space of enclosed ground, from which the wood swept away in a semicircle. There were no flowers, no garden-beds; only a broad gravel-walk girdling a grass-plat, and this set in the heavy frame of the forest. The house presented two pointed gables in its front; the windows were latticed and narrow: the front door was narrow too, one step led up to it. The whole looked, as the host of the Rochester Arms had said, "quite a desolate spot." It was as still as a church on a weekday: the pattering rain on the forest leaves was the only sound audible in its vicinage.

"Can there be life here?" I asked.

Yes, life of some kind there was; for I heard a movement – that narrow front door was unclosing, and some shape was about to issue from the grange.

It opened slowly: a figure came out into the twilight and stood on the step; a man without a hat: he stretched forth his hand as if to feel whether it rained. Dusk as it was, I had recognised him – it was my master, Edward Fairfax Rochester, and no other.

I stayed my step, almost my breath, and stood to watch him – to examine him, myself unseen, and alas! to him invisible. It was a sudden meeting, and one in which rapture was kept well in check by pain. I had no difficulty in restraining my voice from exclamation, my step from hasty advance.

His form was of the same strong and stalwart contour as ever: his port was still erect, his hair was still raven black; nor were his features altered or sunk: not in one year's space, by any sorrow, could his athletic strength be quelled or his vigorous prime blighted. But in his countenance I saw a change: that looked desperate and brooding – that reminded me of some wronged and fettered wild beast or bird, dangerous to approach in his sullen woe. The caged eagle, whose gold-ringed eyes cruelty has extinguished, might look as looked that sightless Samson.

And, reader, do you think I feared him in his blind ferocity? – if you do, you little know me. A soft hope blest with my sorrow that soon I should dare to drop a kiss on that brow of rock, and on those lips so sternly sealed beneath it: but not yet. I would not accost him yet.

He descended the one step, and advanced slowly and gropingly towards the grass-plat. Where was his daring stride now? Then he paused, as if he knew not which way to turn. He lifted his hand and opened his eyelids; gazed blank, and with a straining effort, on the sky, and toward the amphitheatre of trees: one saw that all to him was void darkness. He stretched his right hand (the left arm, the mutilated one, he kept hidden in his bosom); he seemed to wish by touch to gain an idea of what lay around him: he met but vacancy still; for the trees were some yards off where he stood. He relinquished the endeavour, folded his arms, and stood quiet and mute in the rain, now falling fast on his uncovered head. At this moment John approached him from some quarter.

"Will you take my arm, sir?" he said; "there is a heavy shower coming on: had you not better go in?"

"Let me alone," was the answer.

John withdrew without having observed me. Mr. Rochester now tried to walk about: vainly, – all was too uncertain. He groped his way back to the house, and, re-entering it, closed the door.

I now drew near and knocked: John's wife opened for me. "Mary," I said, "how are you?"

She started as if she had seen a ghost: I calmed her. To her hurried "Is it really you, miss, come at this late hour to this lonely place?" I answered by taking her hand; and then I followed her into the kitchen, where John now sat by a good fire. I explained to them, in few words, that I had heard all which had happened since I left Thornfield, and that I was come to see Mr. Rochester. I asked John to go down to the turn-pike-house, where I had dismissed the chaise, and bring my trunk, which I had left there: and then, while I removed my bonnet and shawl, I questioned Mary as to whether I could be accommodated at the Manor House for the night; and finding that arrangements to that effect, though difficult, would not be impossible, I informed her I should stay. Just at this moment the parlour bell rang.

"When you go in," said I, "tell your master that a person wishes to speak to him, but do not give my name."

"I don't think he will see you," she answered; "he refuses everybody."

When she returned, I inquired what he had said. "You are to send in your name and your business," she replied. She then proceeded to fill a glass with water, and place it on a tray, together with candles.

"Is that what he rang for?" I asked.

"Yes: he always has candles brought in at dark, though he is blind."

"Give the tray to me; I will carry it in."

I took it from her hand: she pointed me out the parlour door. The tray shook as I held it; the water spilt from the glass; my heart struck my ribs loud and fast. Mary opened the door for me, and shut it behind me.

This parlour looked gloomy: a neglected handful of fire burnt low in the grate; and, leaning over it, with his head supported against the high, old-fashioned mantelpiece, appeared the blind tenant of the room. His old dog, Pilot, lay on one side, removed out of the way, and coiled up as if afraid of being inadvertently trodden upon. Pilot pricked up his ears when I came in: then he jumped up with a yelp and a whine, and bounded towards me: he almost knocked the tray from my hands. I set it on the table; then patted him, and said softly, "Lie down!" Mr. Rochester turned mechanically to *see* what the commotion was: but as he *saw* nothing, he returned and sighed.

"Give me the water, Mary," he said.

I approached him with the now only half-filled glass; Pilot followed me, still excited.

"What is the matter?" he inquired.

"Down, Pilot!" I again said. He checked the water on its way to his lips, and seemed to listen: he drank, and put the glass down. "This is you, Mary, is it not?"

"Mary is in the kitchen," I answered.

He put out his hand with a quick gesture, but not seeing where I stood, he did not touch me. "Who is this? Who is this?" he demanded, trying, as it seemed, to *see* with those sightless eyes – unavailing and distressing attempt! "Answer me – speak again!" he ordered, imperiously and aloud.

"Will you have a little more water, sir? I spilt half of what was in the glass," I said.

"*Who* is it? *What* is it? Who speaks?"

"Pilot knows me, and John and Mary know I am here. I came only this evening," I answered.

"Great God! – What delusion has come over me? What sweet madness has seized me?"

"No delusion – no madness: your mind, sir, is too strong for delusion, your health too sound for frenzy."

"And where is the speaker? Is it only a voice? Oh! I *cannot* see, but I must feel, or my heart will stop and my brain burst. Whatever – whoever you are – be perceptible to the touch or I cannot live!"

He groped; I arrested his wandering hand, and prisoned it in both mine.

"Her very fingers!" he cried; "her small, slight fingers! If so there must be more of her."

The muscular hand broke from my custody; my arm was seized, my shoulder – neck – waist – I was entwined and gathered to him.

"Is it Jane? *What* is it? This is her shape – this is her size –"

"And this her voice," I added. "She is all here: her heart, too. God bless you, sir! I am glad to be so near you again."

"Jane Eyre! – Jane Eyre," was all he said.

"My dear master," I answered, "I am Jane Eyre: I have found you out – I am come back to you."

"In truth? – In the flesh? My living Jane?"

"You touch me, sir, – you hold me, and fast enough: I am not cold like a corpse, nor vacant like air, am I?"

"My living darling! These are certainly her limbs, and these her features; but I cannot be so blest, after all my misery. It is a dream; such dreams as I have had at night when I have clasped her once more to my heart, as I do now; and kissed her, as thus – and felt that she loved me, and trusted that she would not leave me."

"Which I never will, sir, from this day."

"Never will, says the vision? But I always woke and found it an empty mockery; and I was desolate and abandoned – my life dark, lonely, hopeless – my soul athirst and forbidden to drink – my heart famished and never to be fed. Gentle, soft dream, nestling in my arms now, you will fly, too, as your sisters have all fled before you: but kiss me before you go – embrace me, Jane."

"There, sir – and there!'"

I pressed my lips to his once brilliant and now rayless eyes – I swept his hair from his brow, and kissed that too. He suddenly seemed to arouse himself: the conviction of the reality of all this seized him.

"It is you – is it, Jane? You are come back to me then?"

"I am."

"And you do not lie dead in some ditch under some stream? And you are not a pining outcast amongst strangers?"

"No, sir! I am an independent woman now."

"Independent! What do you mean, Jane?"

"My uncle in Madeira is dead, and he left me five thousand pounds."

"Ah! This is practical – this is real!" he cried: "I should never dream that. Besides, there is that peculiar voice of hers, so animating and piquant, as well as soft: it cheers my withered heart; it puts life into it. – What, Janet! Are you an independent woman? A rich woman?"

"If you won't let me live with you, I can build a house of my own close up to your door, and you may come and sit in my parlour when you want company of an evening."

"But as you are rich, Jane, you have now, no doubt, friends who will look after you, and not suffer you to devote yourself to a blind lameter like me?"

"I told you I am independent, sir, as well as rich: I am my own mistress."

"And you will stay with me?"

"Certainly – unless you object. I will be your neighbour, your nurse, your housekeeper. I find you lonely: I will be your companion – to read to you, to walk with you, to sit with you, to wait on you, to be eyes and hands to you. Cease to look so melancholy, my dear master; you shall not be left desolate, so long as I live."

He replied not: he seemed serious – abstracted; he sighed; he half-opened his lips as if to speak: he closed them again. I felt a little embarrassed. Perhaps I had too rashly over-leaped conventionalities; and he, like St. John, saw impropriety in my inconsiderateness. I had indeed made my proposal from the idea that he wished and would ask me to be his wife: an expectation, not the less certain because unexpressed, had buoyed me up, that he would claim me at once as his own. But no hint to that effect escaping him and his countenance becoming more overcast, I suddenly remembered that I might have been all wrong, and was perhaps playing the fool unwittingly; and I began gently to withdraw myself from his arms – but he eagerly snatched me closer.

"No – no – Jane; you must not go. No – I have touched you, heard you, felt the comfort of your presence – the sweetness of your consolation: I cannot give up these joys. I have little left in myself – I must have you. The world may laugh – may call me absurd, selfish – but it does not signify. My very soul demands you: it will be satisfied, or it will take deadly vengeance on its frame."

"Well, sir, I will stay with you: I have said so."

"Yes – but you understand one thing by staying with me; and I understand another. You, perhaps, could make up your mind to be about my hand and chair – to wait on me as a kind little nurse (for you have an affectionate heart and a generous spirit, which prompt you to make sacrifices for those you pity), and that ought to suffice for me no doubt. I suppose I should now entertain none but fatherly feelings for you: do you think so? Come – tell me."

"I will think what you like, sir: I am content to be only your nurse, if you think it better."

"But you cannot always be my nurse, Janet: you are young – you must marry one day."

"I don't care about being married."

"You should care, Janet: if I were what I once was, I would try to make you care – but – a sightless block!"

He relapsed again into gloom. I, on the contrary, became more cheerful, and took fresh courage: these last words gave me an insight as to where the difficulty lay; and as it was no difficulty with me, I felt quite relieved from my previous embarrassment. I resumed a livelier vein of conversation.

"It is time some one undertook to rehumanise you," said I, parting his thick and long uncut locks; "for I see you are being metamorphosed into a lion, or something of that sort. You have a 'faux air' of Nebuchadnezzar in the fields about you, that is certain: your hair reminds me of eagles' feathers; whether your nails are grown like birds' claws or not, I have not yet noticed."

"On this arm, I have neither hand nor nails," he said, drawing the mutilated limb from his breast, and showing it to me. "It is a mere stump – a ghastly sight! Don't you think so, Jane?"

"It is a pity to see it; and a pity to see your eyes – and the scar of fire on your forehead: and the worst of it is, one is in danger of loving you too well for all this; and making too much of you."

"I thought you would be revolted, Jane, when you saw my arm, and my cicatrised visage."

"Did you? Don't tell me so – lest I should say something disparaging to your judgment. Now, let me leave you an instant, to make a better fire, and have the hearth swept up. Can you tell when there is a good fire?"

"Yes; with the right eye I see a glow – a ruddy haze."

"And you see the candles?"

"Very dimly – each is a luminous cloud."

"Can you see me?"

"No, my fairy: but I am only too thankful to hear and feel you."

"When do you take supper?"

"I never take supper."

"But you shall have some tonight. I am hungry: so are you, I daresay, only you forget."

Summoning Mary, I soon had the room in more cheerful order: I prepared him, likewise, a comfortable repast. My spirits were excited, and with pleasure and ease I talked to him during supper, and for a long time after. There was no harassing restraint, no repressing of glee and vivacity with him; for with him I was at perfect ease, because I knew I suited him; all I said or did seemed either to console or revive him. Delightful consciousness! It brought to life and light my whole nature: in his presence I thoroughly lived; and he lived in mine. Blind as he was, smiles played over his face, joy dawned on his forehead: his lineaments softened and warmed.

After supper, he began to ask me many questions, of where I had been, what I had been doing, how I had found him out; but I gave him only very partial replies: it was too late to enter into particulars that night. Besides, I wished to touch no deep-thrilling chord – to open no fresh well of emotion in his heart: my sole present aim was to cheer him. Cheered, as I have said, he was: and yet but by fits. If a moment's silence broke the conversation, he would turn restless, touch me, then say, "Jane."

"You are altogether a human being, Jane? You are certain of that?"

"I conscientiously believe so, Mr. Rochester."

"Yet how, on this dark and doleful evening, could you so suddenly rise on my lone hearth? I stretched my hand to take a glass of water from a hireling, and it was given me by you: I asked a question, expecting John's wife to answer me, and your voice spoke at my ear."

"Because I had come in, in Mary's stead, with the tray."

"And there is enchantment in the very hour I am now spending with you. Who can tell what a dark, dreary, hopeless life I have dragged on for months past? Doing nothing, expecting nothing; merging night in day; feeling but the sensation of cold when I let the fire go out, of hunger when I forgot to eat: and then a ceaseless sorrow, and, at times, a very delirium of desire to behold my Jane again. Yes: for her restoration I longed, far more than for that of my lost sight. How can it be that Jane is with me, and says she loves me? Will she not depart as suddenly as she came? Tomorrow, I fear I shall find her no more."

A commonplace, practical reply, out of the train of his own disturbed ideas, was, I was sure, the best and most reassuring for him in this frame of mind. I passed my finger over his eyebrows, and remarked that they were scorched, and that I would apply something which would make them grow as broad and black as ever.

"Where is the use of doing me good in any way, beneficent spirit, when, at some fatal moment, you will again desert me – passing like a shadow, whither and how to me unknown, and for me remaining afterwards undiscoverable?"

"Have you a pocket-comb about you, sir?"

"What for, Jane?"

"Just to comb out this shaggy black mane. I find you rather alarming, when I examine you close at hand: you talk of my being a fairy, but I am sure, you are more like a brownie."

"Am I hideous, Jane?"

"Very, sir: you always were, you know."

"Humph! The wickedness has not been taken out of you, wherever you have sojourned."

"Yet I have been with good people; far better than you: a hundred times better people; possessed of ideas and views you never entertained in your life: quite more refined and exalted."

"Who the deuce have you been with?"

"If you twist in that way you will make me pull the hair out of your head; and then I think you will cease to entertain doubts of my substantiality."

"Who have you been with, Jane?"

"You shall not get it out of me tonight, sir; you must wait till tomorrow; to leave my tale half told, will, you know, be a sort of security that I shall appear at your breakfast table to finish it. By the bye, I must mind not to rise on your hearth with only a glass of water then: I must bring an egg at the least, to say nothing of fried ham."

"You mocking changeling – fairy-born and human-bred! You make me feel as I have not felt these twelve months. If Saul could have had you for his David, the evil spirit would have been exorcised without the aid of the harp."

"There, sir, you are redd up and made decent. Now I'll leave you: I have been travelling these last three days, and I believe I am tired. Goodnight."

"Just one word, Jane: were there only ladies in the house where you have been?"

I laughed and made my escape, still laughing as I ran upstairs. "A good idea!" I thought with glee. "I see I have the means of fretting him out of his melancholy for some time to come."

Very early the next morning I heard him up and astir, wandering from one room to another. As soon as Mary came down I heard the question: "Is Miss Eyre here?" Then: "Which room did you put her into? Was it dry? Is she up? Go and ask if she wants anything; and when she will come down."

I came down as soon as I thought there was a prospect of breakfast. Entering the room very softly, I had a view of him before he discovered my presence. It was mournful, indeed, to witness the subjugation of that vigorous spirit to a corporeal infirmity. He sat in his chair – still, but not at rest: expectant evidently; the lines of now habitual sadness marking his strong features. His countenance reminded one of a lamp quenched, waiting to be re-lit – and alas! it was not himself that could now kindle the lustre of animated expression: he was dependent on another for that office! I had meant to be gay and careless, but the powerlessness of the strong man touched my heart to the quick: still I accosted him with what vivacity I could.

"It is a bright, sunny morning, sir," I said. "The rain is over and gone, and there is a tender shining after it: you shall have a walk soon."

I had wakened the glow: his features beamed.

"Oh, you are indeed there, my skylark! Come to me. You are not gone: not vanished? I heard one of your kind an hour ago, singing high over the wood: but its song had no music for me, any more than the rising sun had rays. All the melody on earth is concentrated in my Jane's tongue to my ear (I am glad it is not naturally a silent one): all the sunshine I can feel is in her presence."

The water stood in my eyes to hear this avowal of his dependence; just as if a royal eagle, chained to a perch, should be forced to entreat a sparrow to become its purveyor. But I would not be lachrymose: I dashed off the salt drops, and busied myself with preparing breakfast.

Most of the morning was spent in the open air. I led him out of the wet and wild wood into some cheerful fields: I described to him how brilliantly green they were; how the flowers and hedges looked refreshed; how sparklingly blue was the sky. I sought a seat for him in a hidden and lovely spot, a dry stump of a tree; nor did I refuse to let him, when seated, place me on his knee. Why should I, when both he and I were happier near than apart? Pilot lay beside us: all was quiet. He broke out suddenly while clasping me in his arms:

"Cruel, cruel deserter! Oh, Jane, what did I feel when I discovered you had fled from Thornfield, and when I could nowhere find you; and, after examining your apartment, ascertained that you had taken no money, nor anything which could serve as an equivalent! A pearl necklace I had given you lay untouched in its little casket; your trunks were left corded and locked as they had been prepared for the bridal tour. What could my darling do, I asked, left destitute and penniless? And what did she do? Let me hear now."

Thus urged, I began the narrative of my experience for the last year. I softened considerably what related to the three days of wandering and starvation, because to have told him all would have been to inflict unnecessary pain: the little I did say lacerated his faithful heart deeper than I wished.

I should not have left him thus, he said, without any means of making my way: I should have told him my intention. I should have confided in him: he would never have forced me to be his mistress. Violent as he had seemed in his despair, he, in truth, loved me far too well and too tenderly to constitute himself my tyrant: he would have given me half his fortune, without demanding so much as a kiss in return, rather than I should have flung myself friendless on the wide world. I had endured, he was certain, more than I had confessed to him.

"Well, whatever my sufferings had been, they were very short," I answered: and then I proceeded to tell him how I had been received at Moor House; how I had obtained the office of schoolmistress, etc. The accession of fortune, the discovery of my relations, followed in due order. Of course, St. John Rivers' name came in frequently in the progress of my tale. When I had done, that name was immediately taken up.

"This St. John, then, is your cousin?"

"Yes."

"You have spoken of him often: do you like him?"

"He was a very good man, sir; I could not help liking him."

"A good man. Does that mean a respectable well-conducted man of fifty? Or what does it mean?"

"St John was only twenty-nine, sir."

"'*Jeune encore*', [35] as the French say. Is he a person of low stature, phlegmatic, and plain. A person whose goodness consists rather in his guiltlessness of vice, than in his prowess in virtue."

"He is untiringly active. Great and exalted deeds are what he lives to perform."

"But his brain? That is probably rather soft? He means well: but you shrug your shoulders to hear him talk?"

"He talks little, sir: what he does say is ever to the point. His brain is first-rate, I should think not impressible, but vigorous."

"Is he an able man, then?"

"Truly able."

"A thoroughly educated man?"

"St. John is an accomplished and profound scholar."

"His manners, I think, you said are not to your taste? – Priggish and parsonic?"

"I never mentioned his manners; but, unless I had a very bad taste, they must suit it; they are polished, calm, and gentlemanlike."

"His appearance, – I forget what description you gave of his appearance; – a sort of raw curate, half strangled with his white neckcloth, and stilted up on his thick-soled high-lows, eh?"

"St. John dresses well. He is a handsome man: tall, fair, with blue eyes, and a Grecian profile."

(Aside.) "Damn him!" – (To me.) "Did you like him, Jane?"

"Yes, Mr. Rochester, I liked him: but you asked me that before."

I perceived, of course, the drift of my interlocutor. Jealousy had got hold of him: she stung him; but the sting was salutary: it gave him respite from the gnawing fang of melancholy. I would not, therefore, immediately charm the snake.

"Perhaps you would rather not sit any longer on my knee, Miss Eyre?" was the next somewhat unexpected observation.

"Why not, Mr. Rochester?"

"The picture you have just drawn is suggestive of a rather too overwhelming contrast. Your words have delineated very prettily a graceful Apollo: he is present to your imagination, – tall, fair, blue-eyed, and with a Grecian profile. Your eyes dwell on a Vulcan, – a real blacksmith, brown, broad-shouldered: and blind and lame into the bargain."

"I never thought of it, before; but you certainly are rather like Vulcan, sir."

"Well, you can leave me, ma'am: but before you go" (and he retained me by a firmer grasp than ever), "you will be pleased just to answer me a question or two." He paused.

"What questions, Mr. Rochester?"

Then followed this cross-examination.

"St. John made you schoolmistress of Morton before he knew you were his cousin?"

"Yes."

"You would often see him? He would visit the school sometimes?"

"Daily."

"He would approve of your plans, Jane? I know they would be clever, for you are a talented creature!"

"He approved of them – yes."

"He would discover many things in you he could not have expected to find? Some of your accomplishments are not ordinary."

"I don't know about that."

"You had a little cottage near the school, you say: did he ever come there to see you?"

"Now and then?"

"Of an evening?"

"Once or twice."

A pause.

"How long did you reside with him and his sisters after the cousinship was discovered?"

"Five months."

"Did Rivers spend much time with the ladies of his family?"

"Yes; the back parlour was both his study and ours: he sat near the window, and we by the table."

"Did he study much?"

"A good deal."

"What?"

"Hindostanee."

"And what did you do meantime?"

"I learnt German, at first."

"Did he teach you?"

"He did not understand German."

"Did he teach you nothing?"

"A little Hindostanee."

"Rivers taught you Hindostanee?"

"Yes, sir."

"And his sisters also?"

"No."

"Only you?"

"Only me."

"Did you ask to learn?"

"No."

"He wished to teach you?"

"Yes."

A second pause.

"Why did he wish it? Of what use could Hindostanee be to you?"

"He intended me to go with him to India."

"Ah! Here I reach the root of the matter. He wanted you to marry him?"

"He asked me to marry him."

"That is a fiction – an impudent invention to vex me."

"I beg your pardon, it is the literal truth: he asked me more than once, and was as stiff about urging his point as ever you could be."

"Miss Eyre, I repeat it, you can leave me. How often am I to say the same thing? Why do you remain pertinaciously perched on my knee, when I have given you notice to quit?"

"Because I am comfortable there."

"No, Jane, you are not comfortable there, because your heart is not with me: it is with this cousin – this St. John. Oh, till this moment, I thought my little Jane was all mine! I had a belief she loved me even when she left me: that was an atom of sweet in much bitter. Long as we have been parted, hot tears as I have wept over our separation, I never thought that while I was mourning her, she was loving another! But it is useless grieving. Jane, leave me: go and marry Rivers."

"Shake me off, then, sir, – push me away, for I'll not leave you of my own accord."

"Jane, I ever like your tone of voice: it still renews hope, it sounds so truthful. When I hear it, it carries me back a year. I forget that you have formed a new tie. But I am not a fool – go –"

"Where must I go, sir?"

"Your own way – with the husband you have chosen."

"Who is that?"

"You know – this St. John Rivers."

"He is not my husband, nor ever will be. He does not love me: I do not love him. He loves (as he *can* love, and that is not as you love) a beautiful young lady called Rosamond. He wanted to marry me only because he thought I should make a suitable missionary's wife, which she would not have done. He is good and great, but severe; and, for me, cold as an iceberg. He is not like you, sir: I am not happy at his side, nor near him, nor with him. He has no indulgence for me – no fondness. He sees nothing attractive in me; not even youth – only a few useful mental points. – Then I must leave you, sir, to go to him?"

I shuddered involuntarily, and clung instinctively closer to my blind but beloved master. He smiled.

"What, Jane! Is this true? Is such really the state of matters between you and Rivers?"

"Absolutely, sir! Oh, you need not be jealous! I wanted to tease you a little to make you less sad: I thought anger would be better than grief. But if you wish me to love you, could you but see how much I *do* love you, you would be proud and content. All my heart is yours, sir: it belongs to you; and with you it would remain, were fate to exile the rest of me from your presence for ever."

Again, as he kissed me, painful thoughts darkened his aspect.

"My seared vision! My crippled strength!" he murmured regretfully.

I caressed, in order to soothe him. I knew of what he was thinking, and wanted to speak for him, but dared not. As he turned aside his face a minute, I saw a tear slide from under the sealed eyelid, and trickle down the manly cheek. My heart swelled.

"I am no better than the old lightning-struck chestnut-tree in Thornfield orchard," he remarked ere long. "And what right would that ruin have to bid a budding woodbine cover its decay with freshness?"

"You are no ruin, sir – no lightning-struck tree: you are green and vigorous. Plants will grow about your roots, whether you ask them or not, because they take delight in your bountiful shadow; and as they grow they will lean towards you, and wind round you, because your strength offers them so safe a prop."

Again he smiled: I gave him comfort.

"You speak of friends, Jane?" he asked.

"Yes, of friends," I answered rather hesitatingly: for I knew I meant more than friends, but could not tell what other word to employ. He helped me.

"Ah! Jane. But I want a wife."

"Do you, sir?"

"Yes: is it news to you?"

"Of course: you said nothing about it before."

"Is it unwelcome news?"

"That depends on circumstances, sir – on your choice."

"Which you shall make for me, Jane. I will abide by your decision."

"Choose then, sir – *her who loves you best*."

"I will at least choose – *her I love best*. Jane, will you marry me?"

"Yes, sir."

"A poor blind man, whom you will have to lead about by the hand?"

"Yes, sir."

"A crippled man, twenty years older than you, whom you will have to wait on?"

"Yes, sir."

"Truly, Jane?"

"Most truly, sir."

"Oh! My darling! God bless you and reward you!"

"Mr. Rochester, if ever I did a good deed in my life – if ever I thought a good thought – if ever I prayed a sincere and blameless prayer – if ever I wished a righteous wish, – I am rewarded now. To be your wife is, for me, to be as happy as I can be on earth."

"Because you delight in sacrifice."

"Sacrifice! What do I sacrifice? Famine for food, expectation for content. To be privileged to put my arms round what I value – to press my lips to what I love – to repose on what I trust: is that to make a sacrifice? If so, then certainly I delight in sacrifice."

"And to bear with my infirmities, Jane: to overlook my deficiencies."

"Which are none, sir, to me. I love you better now, when I can really be useful to you, than I did in your state of proud independence, when you disdained every part but that of the giver and protector."

"Hitherto I have hated to be helped – to be led: henceforth, I feel I shall hate it no more. I did not like to put my hand into a hireling's, but it is pleasant to feel it circled by Jane's little fingers. I preferred utter loneliness to the constant attendance of servants; but Jane's soft ministry will be a perpetual joy. Jane suits me: do I suit her?"

"To the finest fibre of my nature, sir."

"The case being so, we have nothing in the world to wait for: we must be married instantly."

He looked and spoke with eagerness: his old impetuosity was rising.

"We must become one flesh without any delay, Jane: there is but the licence to get – then we marry."

"Mr. Rochester, I have just discovered the sun is far declined from its meridian, and Pilot is actually gone home to his dinner. Let me look at your watch."

"Fasten it into your girdle, Janet, and keep it henceforward: I have no use for it."

"It is nearly four o'clock in the afternoon, sir. Don't you feel hungry?"

"The third day from this must be our wedding day, Jane. Never mind fine clothes and jewels, now: all that is not worth a fillip."

"The sun has dried up all the raindrops, sir. The breeze is still: it is quite hot."

"Do you know, Jane, I have your little pearl necklace at this moment fastened round my bronze scrag under my cravat? I have worn it since the day I lost my only treasure, as a memento of her."

"We will go home through the wood: that will be the shadiest way."

He pursued his own thoughts without heeding me.

"Jane! You think me, I daresay, an irreligious dog: but my heart swells with gratitude to the beneficent God of this earth just now. He sees not as man sees, but far clearer: judges not as man judges, but far more wisely. I did wrong: I would have sullied my innocent flower – breathed guilt on its purity: the Omnipotent snatched it from me. I, in my stiff-necked rebellion, almost cursed the dispensation: instead of bending to the decree, I defied it. Divine justice pursued its course;

disasters came thick on me: I was forced to pass through the valley of the shadow of death. *His* chastisements are mighty; and one smote me which has humbled me for ever. You know I was proud of my strength: but what is it now, when I must give it over to foreign guidance, as a child does its weakness? Of late, Jane – only – only of late – I began to see and acknowledge the hand of God in my doom. I began to experience remorse, repentance; the wish for reconcilement to my Maker. I began sometimes to pray: very brief prayers they were, but very sincere.

"Some days since: nay, I can number them – four; it was last Monday night, a singular mood came over me: one in which grief replaced frenzy – sorrow, sullenness. I had long had the impression that since I could nowhere find you, you must be dead. Late that night – perhaps it might be between eleven and twelve o'clock – ere I retired to my dreary rest, I supplicated God, that, if it seemed good to Him, I might soon be taken from this life, and admitted to that world to come, where there was still hope of rejoining Jane.

"I was in my own room, and sitting by the window, which was open: it soothed me to feel the balmy night-air; though I could see no stars and only by a vague, luminous haze, knew the presence of a moon. I longed for thee, Janet! Oh, I longed for thee both with soul and flesh! I asked of God, at once in anguish and humility, if I had not been long enough desolate, afflicted, tormented; and might not soon taste bliss and peace once more. That I merited all I endured, I acknowledged – that I could scarcely endure more, I pleaded; and the alpha and omega of my heart's wishes broke involuntarily from my lips in the words – 'Jane! Jane! Jane!'"

"Did you speak these words aloud?"

"I did, Jane. If any listener had heard me, he would have thought me mad: I pronounced them with such frantic energy."

"And it was last Monday night, somewhere near midnight?"

"Yes; but the time is of no consequence: what followed is the strange point. You will think me superstitious, – some superstition I have in my blood, and always had: nevertheless, this is true – true at least it is that I heard what I now relate.

"As I exclaimed 'Jane! Jane! Jane!' a voice – I cannot tell whence the voice came, but I know whose voice it was – replied, 'I am coming: wait for me;' and a moment after, went whispering on the wind the words – 'Where are you?'

"I'll tell you, if I can, the idea, the picture these words opened to my mind: yet it is difficult to express what I want to express. Ferndean is buried, as you see, in a heavy wood, where sound falls dull, and dies unreverberating. 'Where are you?' seemed spoken amongst mountains; for I heard a hill-sent echo repeat the words. Cooler and fresher at the moment the gale seemed to visit my brow: I could have deemed that in some wild, lone scene, I and Jane were meeting. In spirit, I believe we must have met. You no doubt were, at that hour, in unconscious sleep, Jane: perhaps your soul wandered from its cell to comfort mine; for those were your accents – as certain as I live – they were yours!"

Reader, it was on Monday night – near midnight – that I too had received the mysterious summons: those were the very words by which I replied to it. I listened to Mr. Rochester's narrative, but made no disclosure in return. The coincidence struck me as too awful and inexplicable to be communicated or discussed. If I told anything, my tale would be such as must necessarily make a profound impression on the mind of my hearer: and that mind, yet from its sufferings too prone to gloom, needed not the deeper shade of the supernatural. I kept these things then, and pondered them in my heart.

"You cannot now wonder," continued my master, "that when you rose upon me so unexpectedly last night, I had difficulty in believing you any other than a mere voice and vision, something that would melt to silence and annihilation, as the midnight whisper and mountain echo had melted before. Now, I thank God! I know it to be otherwise. Yes, I thank God!"

He put me off his knee, rose, and reverently lifting his hat from his brow, and bending his sightless eyes to the earth, he stood in mute devotion. Only the last words of the worship were audible.

"I thank my Maker, that, in the midst of judgment, he has remembered mercy. I humbly entreat my Redeemer to give me strength to lead henceforth a purer life than I have done hitherto!"

Then he stretched his hand out to be led. I took that dear hand, held it a moment to my lips, then let it pass round my shoulder: being so much lower of stature than he, I served both for his prop and guide. We entered the wood, and wended homeward.

Chapter Thirty-Eight

Conclusion

READER, I MARRIED HIM. A quiet wedding we had: he and I, the parson and clerk, were alone present. When we got back from church, I went into the kitchen of the manor house, where Mary was cooking the dinner and John cleaning the knives, and I said:

"Mary, I have been married to Mr. Rochester this morning." The housekeeper and her husband were both of that decent phlegmatic order of people, to whom one may at any time safely communicate a remarkable piece of news without incurring the danger of having one's ears pierced by some shrill ejaculation, and subsequently stunned by a torrent of wordy wonderment. Mary did look up, and she did stare at me: the ladle with which she was basting a pair of chickens roasting at the fire, did for some three minutes hang suspended in air; and for the same space of time John's knives also had rest from the polishing process: but Mary, bending again over the roast, said only:

"Have you, Miss? Well, for sure!"

A short time after she pursued – "I seed you go out with the master, but I didn't know you were gone to church to be wed;" and she basted away. John, when I turned to him, was grinning from ear to ear.

"I told Mary how it would be," he said: "I knew what Mr. Edward" (John was an old servant, and had known his master when he was the cadet of the house, therefore, he often gave him his Christian name) – "I knew what Mr. Edward would do; and I was certain he would not wait long neither: and he's done right, for aught I know. I wish you joy, Miss!" and he politely pulled his forelock.

"Thank you, John. Mr. Rochester told me to give you and Mary this." I put into his hand a five-pound note. Without waiting to hear more, I left the kitchen. In passing the door of that sanctum some time after, I caught the words:

"She'll happen do better for him nor ony o't' grand ladies." And again, "If she ben't one o' th' handsomest, she's noan faâl and varry good-natured; and i' his een she's fair beautiful, onybody may see that."

I wrote to Moor House and to Cambridge immediately, to say what I had done: fully explaining also why I had thus acted. Diana and Mary approved the step unreservedly. Diana announced that she would just give me time to get over the honeymoon, and then she would come and see me.

"She had better not wait till then, Jane," said Mr. Rochester, when I read her letter to him; "if she does, she will be too late, for our honeymoon will shine our life long: its beams will only fade over your grave or mine."

How St. John received the news, I don't know: he never answered the letter in which I communicated it: yet six months after he wrote to me, without, however, mentioning Mr. Rochester's name or alluding to my marriage. His letter was then calm, and, though very serious, kind. He has maintained a regular, though not frequent, correspondence ever since: he hopes I am happy, and trusts I am not of those who live without God in the world, and only mind earthly things.

You have not quite forgotten little Adèle, have you, reader? I had not; I soon asked and obtained leave of Mr. Rochester, to go and see her at the school where he had placed her. Her frantic joy at beholding me again moved me much. She looked pale and thin: she said she was not happy. I found the rules of the establishment were too strict, its course of study too severe for a child of her age: I took her home with me. I meant to become her governess once more, but I soon found this impracticable; my time and cares were now required by another – my husband needed them all. So I sought out a school conducted on a more indulgent system, and near enough to permit of my visiting her often, and bringing her home sometimes. I took care she should never want for anything that could contribute to her comfort: she soon settled in her new abode, became very happy there, and made fair progress in her studies. As she grew up, a sound English education corrected in a great measure her French defects; and when she left school, I found in her a pleasing and obliging companion: docile, good-tempered, and well-principled. By her grateful attention to me and mine, she has long since well repaid any little kindness I ever had it in my power to offer her.

My tale draws to its close: one word respecting my experience of married life, and one brief glance at the fortunes of those whose names have most frequently recurred in this narrative, and I have done.

I have now been married ten years. I know what it is to live entirely for and with what I love best on earth. I hold myself supremely blest – blest beyond what language can express; because I am my husband's life as fully as he is mine. No woman was ever nearer to her mate than I am: ever more absolutely bone of his bone and flesh of his flesh. I know no weariness of my Edward's society: he knows none of mine, any more than we each do of the pulsation of the heart that beats in our separate bosoms; consequently, we are ever together. To be together is for us to be at once as free as in solitude, as gay as in company. We talk, I believe, all day long: to talk to each other is but a more animated and an audible thinking. All my confidence is bestowed on him, all his confidence is devoted to me; we are precisely suited in character – perfect concord is the result.

Mr. Rochester continued blind the first two years of our union; perhaps it was that circumstance that drew us so very near – that knit us so very close: for I was then his vision, as I am still his right hand. Literally, I was (what he often called me) the apple of his eye. He saw nature – he saw books through me; and never did I weary of gazing for his behalf, and of putting into words the effect of field, tree, town, river, cloud, sunbeam – of the landscape before us; of the weather round us – and impressing by sound on his ear what light could no longer stamp on his eye. Never did I weary of reading to him; never did I weary of conducting him where he wished to go: of doing for him what he wished to be done. And there was a pleasure in my services, most full, most exquisite, even though sad – because he claimed these services without painful shame or damping humiliation. He loved me so truly, that he knew no reluctance in profiting by my attendance: he felt I loved him so fondly, that to yield that attendance was to indulge my sweetest wishes.

One morning at the end of the two years, as I was writing a letter to his dictation, he came and bent over me, and said – "Jane, have you a glittering ornament round your neck?"

I had a gold watch-chain: I answered "Yes."

"And have you a pale blue dress on?"

I had. He informed me then, that for some time he had fancied the obscurity clouding one eye was becoming less dense; and that now he was sure of it.

He and I went up to London. He had the advice of an eminent oculist; and he eventually recovered the sight of that one eye. He cannot now see very distinctly: he cannot read or write much; but he can find his way without being led by the hand: the sky is no longer a blank to him – the earth no longer a void. When his first-born was put into his arms, he could see that the boy had inherited his own eyes, as they once were – large, brilliant, and black. On that occasion, he again, with a full heart, acknowledged that God had tempered judgment with mercy.

My Edward and I, then, are happy: and the more so, because those we most love are happy likewise. Diana and Mary Rivers are both married: alternately, once every year, they come to see us, and we go to see them. Diana's husband is a captain in the navy, a gallant officer and a good man. Mary's is a clergyman, a college friend of her brother's, and, from his attainments and principles, worthy of the connection. Both Captain Fitzjames and Mr. Wharton love their wives, and are loved by them.

As to St. John Rivers, he left England: he went to India. He entered on the path he had marked for himself; he pursues it still. A more resolute, indefatigable pioneer never wrought amidst rocks and dangers. Firm, faithful, and devoted, full of energy, and zeal, and truth, he labours for his race; he clears their painful way to improvement; he hews down like a giant the prejudices of creed and caste that encumber it. He may be stern; he may be exacting; he may be ambitious yet; but his is the sternness of the warrior Greatheart, who guards his pilgrim convoy from the onslaught of Apollyon. His is the exaction of the apostle, who speaks but for Christ, when he says – "Whosoever will come after me, let him deny himself, and take up his cross and follow me." His is the ambition of the high master-spirit, which aims to fill a place in the first rank of those who are redeemed from the earth – who stand without fault before the throne of God, who share the last mighty victories of the Lamb, who are called, and chosen, and faithful.

St. John is unmarried: he never will marry now. Himself has hitherto sufficed to the toil, and the toil draws near its close: his glorious sun hastens to its setting. The last letter I received from him drew from my eyes human tears, and yet filled my heart with divine joy: he anticipated his sure reward, his incorruptible crown. I know that a stranger's hand will write to me next, to say that the good and faithful servant has been called at length into the joy of his Lord. And why weep for this? No fear of death will darken St. John's last hour: his mind will be unclouded, his heart will be undaunted, his hope will be sure, his faith steadfast. His own words are a pledge of this:

"My Master," he says, "has forewarned me. Daily He announces more distinctly, – 'Surely I come quickly!' and hourly I more eagerly respond, – 'Amen; even so come, Lord Jesus!'"

Footnotes for *Jane Eyre*

1: 'onding on snaw': 'pelting with snow', from Walter Scott's *The Heart of Mid-Lothian* (ch. 8).

2: 'stony street': from Byron's *Childe Harold's Pilgrimage*, III.xxii.2.

3: 'irids': a rare plural of 'iris'.

4: 'Barmecide supper': an imaginary meal, named after a rich man in *The Arabian Nights* who serves an illusory banquet to a starving beggar.

5: '"ing" and holm': waterside meadow and flatland.

6: *La Ligue des Rats*: an 'Aesopian' animal fable by Jean de la Fontaine (1621–95).

7: 'after life's fitful fever …': from *Macbeth*, III.ii.23.

8: *Like heath… away*: from Thomas Moore's 'Fallen is Thy Throne', lines 19–20.

9: 'prenomens': Brontë may have coined this term herself from the Latin.

10: 'The likeness …' and '… shape had none': from Milton's *Paradise Lost*, II.673 & 666.

11: *nonnette*: from the French, 'little nun'.

12: *et j'y tiens*: 'and I firmly believe it'.

13: Adèle is delighted with her outfit, and she asks Rochester to confirm that she is performing just like her mother, to which he agrees. Also: "and, 'comme cela'": "and, 'like that'".

14: 'hotel': town house.

15: 'dentelles': lacework.

16: 'spoony': someone foolishly head over heels in love.

17: 'a very pleasant refuge…': Brontë refers to Psalm XLVI.i.

18: 'Some natural tears…': *Paradise Lost*, XII.645.

19: Adèle explains that, when she lived with her mother, when there were parties, she would follow the guests around and would watch the chambermaids dress the ladies and style their hair, and in that way she would learn.

20: *minois chiffoné*: quirkily attractive.

21: 'She hasted…': referring to Genesis XXIV.19, where Rebecca reveals herself as worthy of being Isaac's wife.

22: 'le cas': the thing to do.

23: '"nichered" a laugh': laughed in a soft whinnying neigh-like way.

24: 'blackaviced': dark-complexioned.

25: 'quiz': an odd or eccentric person.

26: *ignis fatuus*: will-o'-the-wisp.

27: "prête à croquer sa petite maman Anglaise": 'ready to eat her little English mother.'

28: 'a blue-piled thunderloft': quoted from *Blackwood's Magazine*, issue 28 (1830), p813 – likening his face to towering storm clouds.

29: 'Indian Messalina': Valeria Messalina (c. 17/20–48) was the wife of the Roman Emperor Claudius, and became notorious for her promiscuity.

30: *The air … balm*: Scott, *The Lay of the Last Minstrel*, III.xiv.3–4.

31: Peri: a winged fairy-like spirit from Persian mythology.

32: *lusus naturoe*: a freak of nature.

33: paysannes and Bäuerinnen: French and German terms for peasant women.

34: *Looked … hill*: Scott, *The Lay of the Last Minstrel*, V.xxvi.1.

35: *Jeune encore*: still young.

Anne Brontë

The Tenant of Wildfell Hall

Volume One

Chapter One

YOU MUST GO back with me to the autumn of 1827.

My father, as you know, was a sort of gentleman farmer in —shire; and I, by his express desire, succeeded him in the same quiet occupation, not very willingly, for ambition urged me to higher aims, and self-conceit assured me that, in disregarding its voice, I was burying my talent in the earth, and hiding my light under a bushel. My mother had done her utmost to persuade me that I was capable of great achievements; but my father, who thought ambition was the surest road to ruin, and change but another word for destruction, would listen to no scheme for bettering either my own condition, or that of my fellow mortals. He assured me it was all rubbish, and exhorted me, with his dying breath, to continue in the good old way, to follow his steps, and those of his father before him, and let my highest ambition be to walk honestly through the world, looking neither to the right hand nor to the left, and to transmit the paternal acres to my children in, at least, as flourishing a condition as he left them to me.

"Well! – An honest and industrious farmer is one of the most useful members of society; and if I devote my talents to the cultivation of my farm, and the improvement of agriculture in general, I shall thereby benefit, not only my own immediate connections and dependants, but, in some degree, mankind at large: – hence I shall not have lived in vain." With such reflections as these I was endeavouring to console myself, as I plodded home from the fields, one cold, damp, cloudy evening towards the close of October. But the gleam of a bright red fire through the parlour window had more effect in cheering my spirits, and rebuking my thankless repinings, than all the sage reflections and good resolutions I had forced my mind to frame; – for I was young then, remember – only four-and-twenty – and had not acquired half the rule over my own spirit that I now possess – trifling as that may be.

However, that haven of bliss must not be entered till I had exchanged my miry boots for a clean pair of shoes, and my rough surtout for a respectable coat, and made myself generally presentable before decent society; for my mother, with all her kindness, was vastly particular on certain points.

In ascending to my room I was met upon the stairs by a smart, pretty girl of nineteen, with a tidy, dumpy figure, a round face, bright, blooming cheeks, glossy, clustering curls, and little merry brown eyes. I need not tell you this was my sister Rose. She is, I know, a comely matron still, and, doubtless, no less lovely – in your eyes – than on the happy day you first beheld her. Nothing told me then that she, a few years hence, would be the wife of one entirely unknown to me as yet, but destined hereafter to become a closer friend than even herself, more intimate than that unmannerly lad of seventeen, by whom I was collared in the passage, on coming down, and well-nigh jerked off my equilibrium, and who, in correction for his impudence, received a resounding whack over the sconce, which, however, sustained no serious injury from the infliction; as, besides being more than commonly thick, it was protected by a redundant shock of short, reddish curls, that my mother called auburn.

On entering the parlour we found that honoured lady seated in her arm-chair at the fireside, working away at her knitting, according to her usual custom, when she had nothing else to do. She had swept the hearth, and made a bright blazing fire for our reception; the servant had just brought in the tea-tray; and Rose was producing the sugar-basin and tea-caddy from the cupboard in the black oak side-board, that shone like polished ebony, in the cheerful parlour twilight.

"Well! Here they both are," cried my mother, looking round upon us without retarding the motion of her nimble fingers and glittering needles. "Now shut the door, and come to the fire, while Rose gets the tea ready; I'm sure you must be starved; – and tell me what you've been about all day; – I like to know what my children have been about."

"I've been breaking in the grey colt – no easy business that – directing the ploughing of the last wheat stubble – for the ploughboy has not the sense to direct himself – and carrying out a plan for the extensive and efficient draining of the low meadowlands."

"That's my brave boy! – And Fergus, what have you been doing?"

"Badger-baiting."

And here he proceeded to give a particular account of his sport, and the respective traits of prowess evinced by the badger and the dogs; my mother pretending to listen with deep attention, and watching his animated countenance with a degree of maternal admiration I thought highly disproportioned to its object.

"It's time you should be doing something else, Fergus," said I, as soon as a momentary pause in his narration allowed me to get in a word.

"What can I do?" replied he; "my mother won't let me go to sea or enter the army; and I'm determined to do nothing else – except make myself such a nuisance to you all, that you will be thankful to get rid of me on any terms."

Our parent soothingly stroked his stiff, short curls. He growled, and tried to look sulky, and then we all took our seats at the table, in obedience to the thrice-repeated summons of Rose.

"Now take your tea," said she; "and I'll tell you what I've been doing. I've been to call on the Wilsons; and it's a thousand pities you didn't go with me, Gilbert, for Eliza Millward was there!"

"Well! What of her?"

"Oh, nothing! – I'm not going to tell you about her; – only that she's a nice, amusing little thing, when she is in a merry humour, and I shouldn't mind calling her –"

"Hush, hush, my dear! Your brother has no such idea!" whispered my mother earnestly, holding up her finger.

"Well," resumed Rose; "I was going to tell you an important piece of news I heard there – I have been bursting with it ever since. You know it was reported a month ago, that somebody was going to take Wildfell Hall – and – what do you think? It has actually been inhabited above a week! – And we never knew!"

"Impossible!" cried my mother.

"Preposterous!!!" shrieked Fergus.

"It has indeed! – And by a single lady!"

"Good gracious, my dear! The place is in ruins!"

"She has had two or three rooms made habitable; and there she lives, all alone – except an old woman for a servant!"

"Oh, dear! That spoils it – I'd hoped she was a witch," observed Fergus, while carving his inch-thick slice of bread and butter. "Nonsense, Fergus! But isn't it strange, mamma?"

"Strange! I can hardly believe it."

"But you may believe it; for Jane Wilson has seen her. She went with her mother, who, of course, when she heard of a stranger being in the neighbourhood, would be on pins and needles till she had seen her and got all she could out of her. She is called Mrs. Graham, and she is in mourning – not widow's weeds, but slightish mourning – and she is quite young, they say, – not above five or six and twenty, – but so reserved! They tried all they could to find out who she was and where she came from, and, all about her, but neither Mrs. Wilson, with her pertinacious and impertinent home-thrusts, nor Miss Wilson, with her skilful manoeuvring, could manage to elicit a single satisfactory answer, or even a casual remark, or chance expression calculated to allay their curiosity, or throw the faintest ray of light upon her history, circumstances, or connections. Moreover, she was barely civil to them, and evidently better pleased to say 'goodbye,' than 'how do you do.' But Eliza Millward says her father intends to call upon her soon, to offer some pastoral advice, which he fears she needs, as, though she is known to have entered the neighbourhood early last week, she did not make her appearance at church on Sunday; and she – Eliza, that is – will beg to accompany him, and is sure she can succeed in wheedling something out of her – you know, Gilbert, she can do anything. And we should call some time, mamma; it's only proper, you know."

"Of course, my dear. Poor thing! How lonely she must feel!"

"And pray, be quick about it; and mind you bring me word how much sugar she puts in her tea, and what sort of caps and aprons she wears, and all about it; for I don't know how I can live till I know," said Fergus, very gravely.

But if he intended the speech to be hailed as a master-stroke of wit, he signally failed, for nobody laughed. However, he was not much disconcerted at that; for when he had taken a mouthful of bread and butter and was about to swallow a gulp of tea, the humour of the thing burst upon him with such irresistible force, that he was obliged to jump up from the table, and rush snorting and choking from the room; and a minute after, was heard screaming in fearful agony in the garden.

As for me, I was hungry, and contented myself with silently demolishing the tea, ham, and toast, while my mother and sister went on talking, and continued to discuss the apparent or non-apparent circumstances, and probable or improbable history of the mysterious lady; but I must confess that, after my brother's misadventure, I once or twice raised the cup to my lips, and put it down again without daring to taste the contents, lest I should injure my dignity by a similar explosion.

The next day my mother and Rose hastened to pay their compliments to the fair recluse; and came back but little wiser than they went; though my mother declared she did not regret the journey, for if she had not gained much good, she flattered herself she had imparted some, and that was better: she had given some useful advice, which, she hoped, would not be thrown away; for Mrs. Graham, though she said little to any purpose, and appeared somewhat self-opinionated, seemed not incapable of reflection, – though she did not know where she had been all her life, poor thing, for she betrayed a lamentable ignorance on certain points, and had not even the sense to be ashamed of it.

"On what points, mother?" asked I.

"On household matters, and all the little niceties of cookery, and such things, that every lady ought to be familiar with, whether she be required to make a practical use of her knowledge or not. I gave her some useful pieces of information, however, and several excellent receipts, the value of which she evidently could not appreciate, for she begged I would not trouble myself, as she lived in such a plain, quiet way, that she was sure she should never make use of them. 'No matter, my dear,' said I; 'it is what every respectable female ought to know; – and besides, though you are alone now, you will not be always so; you have been married, and probably – I might say almost certainly – will be again.' 'You are mistaken there, ma'am,' said she, almost haughtily; 'I am certain I never shall.' – But I told her I knew better."

"Some romantic young widow, I suppose," said I, "come there to end her days in solitude, and mourn in secret for the dear departed – but it won't last long."

"No, I think not," observed Rose; "for she didn't seem very disconsolate after all; and she's excessively pretty – handsome rather – you must see her, Gilbert; you will call her a perfect beauty, though you could hardly pretend to discover a resemblance between her and Eliza Millward."

"Well, I can imagine many faces more beautiful than Eliza's, though not more charming. I allow she has small claims to perfection; but then, I maintain that, if she were more perfect, she would be less interesting."

"And so you prefer her faults to other people's perfections?"

"Just so – saving my mother's presence."

"Oh, my dear Gilbert, what nonsense you talk! – I know you don't mean it; it's quite out of the question," said my mother, getting up, and bustling out of the room, under pretence of household business, in order to escape the contradiction that was trembling on my tongue.

After that Rose favoured me with further particulars respecting Mrs. Graham. Her appearance, manners, and dress, and the very furniture of the room she inhabited, were all set before me, with rather more clearness and precision than I cared to see them; but, as I was not a very attentive listener, I could not repeat the description if I would.

The next day was Saturday; and, on Sunday, everybody wondered whether or not the fair unknown would profit by the vicar's remonstrance, and come to church. I confess I looked with some interest myself towards the old family pew, appertaining to Wildfell Hall, where the faded crimson cushions and lining had been unpressed and unrenewed so many years, and the grim escutcheons, with their lugubrious borders of rusty black cloth, frowned so sternly from the wall above.

And there I beheld a tall, lady-like figure, clad in black. Her face was towards me, and there was something in it which, once seen, invited me to look again. Her hair was raven black, and disposed in long glossy ringlets, a style of coiffure rather unusual in those days, but always graceful and becoming; her complexion was clear and pale; her eyes I could not see, for, being bent upon her prayer-book, they were concealed by their drooping lids and long black lashes, but the brows above were expressive and well defined; the forehead was lofty and intellectual, the nose, a perfect aquiline and the features, in general, unexceptionable – only there was a slight hollowness about the cheeks and eyes, and the lips, though finely formed, were a little too thin, a little too firmly compressed, and had something about them that betokened, I thought, no very soft or amiable temper; and I said in my heart – "I would rather admire you from this distance, fair lady, than be the partner of your home."

Just then she happened to raise her eyes, and they met mine; I did not choose to withdraw my gaze, and she turned again to her book, but with a momentary, indefinable expression of quiet scorn, that was inexpressibly provoking to me.

"She thinks me an impudent puppy," thought I. "Humph! – She shall change her mind before long, if I think it worth while."

But then it flashed upon me that these were very improper thoughts for a place of worship, and that my behaviour, on the present occasion, was anything but what it ought to be. Previous, however, to directing my mind to the service,

I glanced round the church to see if any one had been observing me; – but no, – all, who were not attending to their prayer-books, were attending to the strange lady, – my good mother and sister among the rest, and Mrs. Wilson and her daughter; and even Eliza Millward was slily glancing from the corners of her eyes towards the object of general attraction. Then she glanced at me, simpered a little, and blushed, modestly looked at her prayer-book, and endeavoured to compose her features.

Here I was transgressing again; and this time I was made sensible of it by a sudden dig in the ribs, from the elbow of my pert brother. For the present, I could only resent the insult by pressing my foot upon his toes, deferring further vengeance till we got out of church.

Now, Halford, before I close this letter, I'll tell you who Eliza Millward was: she was the vicar's younger daughter, and a very engaging little creature, for whom I felt no small degree of partiality; – and she knew it, though I had never come to any direct explanation, and had no definite intention of so doing, for my mother, who maintained there was no one good enough for me within twenty miles round, could not bear the thoughts of my marrying that insignificant little thing, who, in addition to her numerous other disqualifications, had not twenty pounds to call her own. Eliza's figure was at once slight and plump, her face small, and nearly as round as my sister's, – complexion, something similar to hers, but more delicate and less decidedly blooming, – nose, *retroussé*, – features, generally irregular; and, altogether, she was rather charming than pretty. But her eyes – I must not forget those remarkable features, for therein her chief attraction lay – in outward aspect at least; – they were long and narrow in shape, the irids black, or very dark brown, the expression various, and ever changing, but always either preternaturally – I had almost said diabolically – wicked, or irresistibly bewitching – often both. Her voice was gentle and childish, her tread light and soft as that of a cat: – but her manners more frequently resembled those of a pretty playful kitten, that is now pert and roguish, now timid and demure, according to its own sweet will.

Her sister, Mary, was several years older, several inches taller, and of a larger, coarser build – a plain, quiet, sensible girl, who had patiently nursed their mother, through her last long, tedious illness, and been the housekeeper, and family drudge, from thence to the present time. She was trusted and valued by her father, loved and courted by all dogs, cats, children, and poor people, and slighted and neglected by everybody else.

The Reverend Michael Millward himself was a tall, ponderous elderly gentleman, who placed a shovel hat above his large, square, massive-featured face, carried a stout walking-stick in his hand, and incased his still powerful limbs in knee-breeches and gaiters, – or black silk stockings on state occasions. He was a man of fixed principles, strong prejudices, and regular habits, intolerant of dissent in any shape, acting under a firm conviction that his opinions were always right, and whoever differed from them must be either most deplorably ignorant, or wilfully blind.

In childhood, I had always been accustomed to regard him with a feeling of reverential awe – but lately, even now, surmounted, for, though he had a fatherly kindness for the well-behaved, he was a strict disciplinarian, and had often sternly reproved our juvenile failings and peccadilloes; and moreover, in those days, whenever he called upon our parents, we had to stand up before him, and say our catechism, or repeat, "How doth the little busy bee," or some other hymn, or – worse than all – be questioned about his last text, and the heads of the discourse, which we never could remember. Sometimes, the worthy gentleman would reprove my mother for being over-indulgent to her sons, with a reference to old Eli, or David and Absalom, which was particularly galling to her feelings; and, very highly as she respected him, and all his sayings, I once heard her exclaim, "I wish to goodness he had a son himself! He wouldn't be so ready with his advice to other people then; – he'd see what it is to have a couple of boys to keep in order."

He had a laudable care for his own bodily health – kept very early hours, regularly took a walk before breakfast, was vastly particular about warm and dry clothing, had never been known to preach a sermon without previously swallowing a raw egg – albeit he was gifted with good lungs and a powerful voice, – and was, generally, extremely particular about what he ate and drank, though by no means abstemious, and having a mode of dietary peculiar to himself, – being a great despiser of tea and such slops, and a patron of malt liquors, bacon and eggs, ham, hung beef, and other strong meats, which agreed well enough with his digestive organs, and therefore were maintained by him to be good and wholesome for everybody, and confidently recommended to the most delicate convalescents or dyspeptics, who, if they failed to derive the promised benefit from his prescriptions, were told it was because they had not persevered, and if they complained of inconvenient results therefrom, were assured it was all fancy.

I will just touch upon two other persons whom I have mentioned, and then bring this long letter to a close. These are Mrs. Wilson and her daughter. The former was the widow of a substantial farmer, a narrow-minded, tattling old gossip, whose character is not worth describing. She had two sons, Robert, a rough countrified farmer, and Richard, a retiring, studious young man, who was studying the classics with the vicar's assistance, preparing for college, with a view to enter the church.

Their sister Jane was a young lady of some talents, and more ambition. She had, at her own desire, received a regular boarding-school education, superior to what any member of the family had obtained before. She had taken the polish well, acquired considerable elegance of manners, quite lost her provincial accent, and could boast of more accomplishments than the vicar's daughters. She was considered a beauty besides; but never for a moment could she number me amongst her admirers. She was about six and twenty, rather tall and very slender, her hair was neither chestnut nor auburn, but a most decided bright, light red; her complexion was remarkably fair and brilliant, her head small, neck long, chin well turned, but very short, lips thin and red, eyes clear hazel, quick, and penetrating, but entirely destitute of poetry or feeling. She had, or might have had, many suitors in her own rank of life, but scornfully repulsed or rejected them all; for none but a gentleman could please her refined taste, and none but a rich one could satisfy her soaring ambition. One gentleman there was, from whom she had lately received some rather pointed attentions, and upon whose heart, name, and fortune, it was whispered, she had serious designs. This was Mr. Lawrence, the young squire, whose family had formerly occupied Wildfell Hall, but had deserted it, some fifteen years ago, for a more modern and commodious mansion in the neighbouring parish.

Now, Halford, I bid you adieu for the present. This is the first instalment of my debt. If the coin suits you, tell me so, and I'll send you the rest at my leisure: if you would rather remain my creditor than stuff your purse with such ungainly, heavy pieces, – tell me still, and I'll pardon your bad taste, and willingly keep the treasure to myself.

Yours immutably,
Gilbert Markham

Chapter Two

I PERCEIVE, with joy, my most valued friend, that the cloud of your displeasure has passed away; the light of your countenance blesses me once more, and you desire the continuation of my story: therefore, without more ado, you shall have it.

I think the day I last mentioned was a certain Sunday, the latest in the October of 1827. On the following Tuesday I was out with my dog and gun, in pursuit of such game as I could find within the territory of Linden-Car; but finding none at all, I turned my arms against the hawks and carrion crows, whose depredations, as I suspected, had deprived me of better prey. To this end I left the more frequented regions, the wooded valleys, the corn-fields, and the meadow-lands, and proceeded to mount the steep acclivity of Wildfell, the wildest and the loftiest eminence in our neighbourhood, where, as you ascend, the hedges, as well as the trees, become scanty and stunted, the former, at length, giving place to rough stone fences, partly greened over with ivy and moss, the latter to larches and Scotch fir-trees, or isolated blackthorns. The fields, being rough and stony, and wholly unfit for the plough, were mostly devoted to the posturing of sheep and cattle; the soil was thin and poor: bits of grey rock here and there peeped out from the grassy hillocks; bilberry-plants and heather – relics of more savage wildness – grew under the walls; and in many of the enclosures, ragweeds and rushes usurped supremacy over the scanty herbage; but these were not my property.

Near the top of this hill, about two miles from Linden-Car, stood Wildfell Hall, a superannuated mansion of the Elizabethan era, built of dark grey stone, venerable and picturesque to look at, but doubtless, cold and gloomy enough to inhabit, with its thick stone mullions and little latticed panes, its time-eaten air-holes, and its too lonely, too unsheltered situation, – only shielded from the war of wind and weather by a group of Scotch firs, themselves half blighted with storms, and looking as stern and gloomy as the Hall itself. Behind it lay a few desolate fields, and then the brown heath-clad summit of the hill; before it (enclosed by stone walls, and entered by an iron gate, with large balls of grey granite – similar to those which decorated the roof and gables – surmounting the gate-posts) was a garden, – once stocked with such hard plants and flowers as could best brook the soil and climate, and such trees and shrubs as could best endure the gardener's torturing shears, and most readily assume the shapes he chose to give them, – now, having been left so many years untilled and untrimmed, abandoned to the weeds and the grass, to the frost and the wind, the rain and the drought, it presented a very singular appearance indeed. The close green walls of privet, that had bordered the principal walk, were two-thirds withered away, and the rest grown beyond all reasonable bounds; the old boxwood swan, that sat beside the scraper, had lost its neck and half its body: the castellated towers of laurel in the middle of the garden, the gigantic warrior that stood on one side of the gateway, and the lion that guarded the other, were sprouted into such fantastic shapes as resembled nothing either in heaven or earth, or in the waters under the earth; but, to my young imagination, they presented all of them a goblinish appearance, that harmonised well with the ghostly legions and dark traditions our old nurse had told us respecting the haunted hall and its departed occupants.

I had succeeded in killing a hawk and two crows when I came within sight of the mansion; and then, relinquishing further depredations, I sauntered on, to have a look at the old place, and see what changes had been wrought in it by its new inhabitant. I did not like to go quite to the front and stare in at the gate; but I paused beside the garden wall, and looked, and saw no change – except in one wing, where the broken windows and dilapidated roof had evidently been repaired, and where a thin wreath of smoke was curling up from the stack of chimneys.

While I thus stood, leaning on my gun, and looking up at the dark gables, sunk in an idle reverie, weaving a tissue of wayward fancies, in which old associations and the fair young hermit, now within those walls, bore a nearly equal part, I heard a slight rustling and scrambling just within the garden; and, glancing in the direction whence the sound proceeded, I beheld a tiny hand elevated above the wall: it clung to the topmost stone, and then another little hand was raised to take a firmer hold, and then appeared a small white forehead, surmounted with wreaths of light brown hair, with a pair of deep blue eyes beneath, and the upper portion of a diminutive ivory nose.

The eyes did not notice me, but sparkled with glee on beholding Sancho, my beautiful black and white setter, that was coursing about the field with its muzzle to the ground. The little creature raised its face and called aloud to the dog. The good-natured animal paused, looked up, and wagged his tail, but made no further advances. The child (a little boy, apparently about five years old) scrambled up to the top of the wall, and called again and again; but finding this of no avail, apparently made up his mind, like Mahomet, to go to the mountain, since the mountain would not come to him, and attempted to get over; but a crabbed old cherry-tree, that grew hard by, caught him by the frock in one of its crooked scraggy arms that stretched over the wall. In attempting to disengage himself his foot slipped, and down he tumbled – but not to the earth; – the tree still kept him suspended. There was a silent struggle, and then a piercing shriek; – but, in an instant, I had dropped my gun on the grass, and caught the little fellow in my arms.

I wiped his eyes with his frock, told him he was all right and called Sancho to pacify him. He was just putting little hand on the dog's neck and beginning to smile through his tears, when I heard behind me a click of the iron gate, and a rustle of female garments, and lo! Mrs. Graham darted upon me – her neck uncovered, her black locks streaming in the wind.

"Give me the child!" she said, in a voice scarce louder than a whisper, but with a tone of startling vehemence, and, seizing the boy, she snatched him from me, as if some dire contamination were in my touch, and then stood with one hand firmly clasping his, the other on his shoulder, fixing upon me her large, luminous dark eyes – pale, breathless, quivering with agitation.

"I was not harming the child, madam," said I, scarce knowing whether to be most astonished or displeased; "he was tumbling off the wall there; and I was so fortunate as to catch him, while he hung suspended headlong from that tree, and prevent I know not what catastrophe."

"I beg your pardon, sir," stammered she; – suddenly calming down, – the light of reason seeming to break upon her beclouded spirit, and a faint blush mantling on her cheek – "I did not know you; – and I thought –"

She stooped to kiss the child, and fondly clasped her arm round his neck.

"You thought I was going to kidnap your son, I suppose?"

She stroked his head with a half-embarrassed laugh, and replied, – "I did not know he had attempted to climb the wall. – I have the pleasure of addressing Mr. Markham, I believe?" she added, somewhat abruptly.

I bowed, but ventured to ask how she knew me.

"Your sister called here, a few days ago, with Mrs. Markham."

"Is the resemblance so strong then?" I asked, in some surprise, and not so greatly flattered at the idea as I ought to have been.

"There is a likeness about the eyes and complexion I think," replied she, somewhat dubiously surveying my face; – "and I think I saw you at church on Sunday."

I smiled. – There was something either in that smile or the recollections it awakened that was particularly displeasing to her, for she suddenly assumed again that proud, chilly look that had so unspeakably roused my aversion at church – a look of repellent scorn, so easily assumed, and so entirely without the least distortion of a single feature, that, while there, it seemed like the natural expression of the face, and was the more provoking to me, because I could not think it affected.

"Good morning, Mr. Markham," said she; and without another word or glance, she withdrew, with her child, into the garden; and I returned home, angry and dissatisfied – I could scarcely tell you why, and therefore will not attempt it.

I only stayed to put away my gun and powder-horn, and give some requisite directions to one of the farming-men, and then repaired to the vicarage, to solace my spirit and soothe my ruffled temper with the company and conversation of Eliza Millward.

I found her, as usual, busy with some piece of soft embroidery (the mania for Berlin wools had not yet commenced), while her sister was seated at the chimney-corner, with the cat on her knee, mending a heap of stockings.

"Mary – Mary! Put them away!" Eliza was hastily saying, just as I entered the room.

"Not I, indeed!" was the phlegmatic reply; and my appearance prevented further discussion.

"You're so unfortunate, Mr. Markham!" observed the younger sister, with one of her arch, sidelong glances. "Papa's just gone out into the parish, and not likely to be back for an hour!"

"Never mind; I can manage to spend a few minutes with his daughters, if they'll allow me," said I, bringing a chair to the fire, and seating myself therein, without waiting to be asked.

"Well, if you'll be very good and amusing, we shall not object."

"Let your permission be unconditional, pray; for I came not to give pleasure, but to seek it," I answered.

However, I thought it but reasonable to make some slight exertion to render my company agreeable; and what little effort I made, was apparently pretty successful, for Miss Eliza was never in a better humour. We seemed, indeed, to be mutually pleased with each other, and managed to maintain between us a cheerful and animated though not very profound conversation. It was little better than a *tête-à-tête*, for Miss Millward never opened her lips, except occasionally to correct some random assertion or exaggerated expression of her sister's, and once to ask her to pick up the ball of cotton that had rolled under the table. I did this myself, however, as in duty bound.

"Thank you, Mr. Markham," said she, as I presented it to her. "I would have picked it up myself; only I did not want to disturb the cat."

"Mary, dear, that won't excuse you in Mr. Markham's eyes," said Eliza; "he hates cats, I daresay, as cordially as he does old maids – like all other gentlemen. Don't you, Mr. Markham?"

"I believe it is natural for our unamiable sex to dislike the creatures," replied I; "for you ladies lavish so many caresses upon them."

"Bless them – little darlings!" cried she, in a sudden burst of enthusiasm, turning round and overwhelming her sister's pet with a shower of kisses.

"Don't, Eliza!" said Miss Millward, somewhat gruffly, as she impatiently pushed her away.

But it was time for me to be going: make what haste I would, I should still be too late for tea; and my mother was the soul of order and punctuality.

My fair friend was evidently unwilling to bid me adieu. I tenderly squeezed her little hand at parting; and she repaid me with one of her softest smiles and most bewitching glances. I went home very happy, with a heart brimful of complacency for myself, and overflowing with love for Eliza.

Chapter Three

TWO DAYS AFTER, Mrs. Graham called at Linden-Car, contrary to the expectation of Rose, who entertained an idea that the mysterious occupant of Wildfell Hall would wholly disregard the common observances of civilized life, – in which opinion she was supported by the Wilsons, who testified that neither their call nor the Millwards' had been returned as yet. Now, however, the cause of that omission was explained, though not entirely to the satisfaction of Rose. Mrs. Graham had brought her child with her, and on my mother's expressing surprise that he could walk so far, she replied, – "It is a long walk for him; but I must have either taken him with me, or relinquished the visit altogether; for I never leave him alone; and I think, Mrs. Markham, I must beg you to make my excuses to the Millwards and Mrs. Wilson, when you see them, as I fear I cannot do myself the pleasure of calling upon them till my little Arthur is able to accompany me."

"But you have a servant," said Rose; "could you not leave him with her?"

"She has her own occupations to attend to; and besides, she is too old to run after a child, and he is too mercurial to be tied to an elderly woman."

"But you left him to come to church."

"Yes, once; but I would not have left him for any other purpose; and I think, in future, I must contrive to bring him with me, or stay at home."

"Is he so mischievous?" asked my mother, considerably shocked.

"No," replied the lady, sadly smiling, as she stroked the wavy locks of her son, who was seated on a low stool at her feet; "but he is my only treasure, and I am his only friend: so we don't like to be separated."

"But, my dear, I call that doting," said my plain-spoken parent. "You should try to suppress such foolish fondness, as well to save your son from ruin as yourself from ridicule."

"Ruin! Mrs. Markham!"

"Yes; it is spoiling the child. Even at his age, he ought not to be always tied to his mother's apron-string; he should learn to be ashamed of it."

"Mrs. Markham, I beg you will not say such things, in his presence, at least. I trust my son will never be ashamed to love his mother!" said Mrs. Graham, with a serious energy that startled the company.

My mother attempted to appease her by an explanation; but she seemed to think enough had been said on the subject, and abruptly turned the conversation.

"Just as I thought," said I to myself: "the lady's temper is none of the mildest, notwithstanding her sweet, pale face and lofty brow, where thought and suffering seem equally to have stamped their impress."

All this time I was seated at a table on the other side of the room, apparently immersed in the perusal of a volume of the *Farmer's Magazine*, which I happened to have been reading at the moment of our visitor's arrival; and, not choosing to be over civil, I had merely bowed as she entered, and continued my occupation as before.

In a little while, however, I was sensible that some one was approaching me, with a light, but slow and hesitating tread. It was little Arthur, irresistibly attracted by my dog Sancho, that was lying at my feet. On looking up I beheld him standing about two yards off, with his clear blue eyes wistfully gazing on the dog, transfixed to the spot, not by fear of the animal, but by a timid disinclination to approach its master. A little encouragement, however, induced him to come forward. The child, though shy, was not sullen. In a minute he was kneeling on the carpet, with his arms round Sancho's neck, and, in a minute or two more, the little fellow was seated on my knee, surveying with eager interest the various specimens of horses, cattle, pigs, and model farms portrayed in the volume before me. I glanced at his mother now and then to see how she relished the new-sprung intimacy; and I saw, by the unquiet aspect of her eye, that for some reason or other she was uneasy at the child's position.

"Arthur," said she, at length, "come here. You are troublesome to Mr. Markham: he wishes to read."

"By no means, Mrs. Graham; pray let him stay. I am as much amused as he is," pleaded I. But still, with hand and eye, she silently called him to her side.

"No, mamma," said the child; "let me look at these pictures first; and then I'll come, and tell you all about them."

"We are going to have a small party on Monday, the fifth of November," said my mother; "and I hope you will not refuse to make one, Mrs. Graham. You can bring your little boy with you, you know – I daresay we shall be able to amuse him; – and then you can make your own apologies to the Millwards and Wilsons – they will all be here, I expect."

"Thank you, I never go to parties."

"Oh! But this will be quite a family concern – early hours, and nobody here but ourselves, and just the Millwards and Wilsons, most of whom you already know, and Mr. Lawrence, your landlord, with whom you ought to make acquaintance."

"I do know something of him – but you must excuse me this time; for the evenings, now, are dark and damp, and Arthur, I fear, is too delicate to risk exposure to their influence with impunity. We must defer the enjoyment of your hospitality till the return of longer days and warmer nights."

Rose, now, at a hint from my mother, produced a decanter of wine, with accompaniments of glasses and cake, from the cupboard and the oak sideboard, and the refreshment was duly presented to the guests. They both partook of the cake, but obstinately refused the wine, in spite of their hostess's hospitable attempts to force it upon them. Arthur, especially shrank from the ruby nectar as if in terror and disgust, and was ready to cry when urged to take it.

"Never mind, Arthur," said his mamma; "Mrs. Markham thinks it will do you good, as you were tired with your walk; but she will not oblige you to take it! – I daresay you will do very well without. He detests the very sight of wine," she added, "and the smell of it almost makes him sick. I have been accustomed to make him swallow a little wine or weak spirits-and-water, by way of medicine, when he was sick, and, in fact, I have done what I could to make him hate them."

Everybody laughed, except the young widow and her son.

"Well, Mrs. Graham," said my mother, wiping the tears of merriment from her bright blue eyes – "well, you surprise me! I really gave you credit for having more sense. – The poor child will be the veriest milksop that ever was sopped! Only think what a man you will make of him, if you persist in –"

"I think it a very excellent plan," interrupted Mrs. Graham, with imperturbable gravity. "By that means I hope to save him from one degrading vice at least. I wish I could render the incentives to every other equally innoxious in his case."

"But by such means," said I, "you will never render him virtuous. – What is it that constitutes virtue, Mrs. Graham? Is it the circumstance of being able and willing to resist temptation; or that of having no temptations to resist? – Is he a strong man that overcomes great obstacles and performs surprising achievements, though by dint of great muscular exertion, and at the risk of some subsequent fatigue, or he that sits in his chair all day, with nothing to do more laborious than stirring the fire, and carrying his food to his mouth? If you would have your son to walk honourably through the world, you must not attempt to clear the stones from his path, but teach him to walk firmly over them – not insist upon leading him by the hand, but let him learn to go alone."

"I will lead him by the hand, Mr. Markham, till he has strength to go alone; and I will clear as many stones from his path as I can, and teach him to avoid the rest – or walk firmly over them, as you say; – for when I have done my utmost, in the way of clearance, there will still be plenty left to exercise all the agility, steadiness, and circumspection he will ever have. – It is all very well to talk about noble resistance, and trials of virtue; but for fifty – or five hundred men that have yielded to temptation, show me one that has had virtue to resist. And why should I take it for granted that my son will be one in a thousand? – And not rather prepare for the worst, and suppose he will be like his – like the rest of mankind, unless I take care to prevent it?"

"You are very complimentary to us all," I observed.

"I know nothing about you – I speak of those I do know – and when I see the whole race of mankind (with a few rare exceptions) stumbling and blundering along the path of life, sinking into every pitfall, and breaking their shins over every impediment that lies in their way, shall I not use all the means in my power to insure for him a smoother and a safer passage?"

"Yes, but the surest means will be to endeavour to fortify him against temptation, not to remove it out of his way."

"I will do both, Mr. Markham. God knows he will have temptations enough to assail him, both from within and without, when I have done all I can to render vice as uninviting to him, as it is abominable in its own nature – I myself have had, indeed, but few incentives to what the world calls vice, but yet I have experienced temptations and trials of another kind, that have required, on many occasions, more watchfulness and firmness to resist than I have hitherto been able to muster against them. And this, I believe, is what most others would acknowledge who are accustomed to reflection, and wishful to strive against their natural corruptions."

"Yes," said my mother, but half apprehending her drift; "but you would not judge of a boy by yourself – and, my dear Mrs. Graham, let me warn you in good time against the error – the fatal error, I may call it – of taking that boy's education upon yourself. Because you are clever in some things and well informed, you may fancy yourself equal to the task; but indeed you are not; and if you persist in the attempt, believe me you will bitterly repent it when the mischief is done."

"I am to send him to school, I suppose, to learn to despise his mother's authority and affection!" said the lady, with rather a bitter smile.

"Oh, no! – But if you would have a boy to despise his mother, let her keep him at home, and spend her life in petting him up, and slaving to indulge his follies and caprices."

"I perfectly agree with you, Mrs. Markham; but nothing can be further from my principles and practice than such criminal weakness as that."

"Well, but you will treat him like a girl – you'll spoil his spirit, and make a mere Miss Nancy of him – you will, indeed, Mrs. Graham, whatever you may think. But I'll get Mr. Millward to talk to you about it: – he'll tell you the consequences; – he'll set it before you as plain as the day; – and tell you what you ought to do, and all about it; – and, I don't doubt, he'll be able to convince you in a minute."

"No occasion to trouble the vicar," said Mrs. Graham, glancing at me – I suppose I was smiling at my mother's unbounded confidence in that worthy gentleman – "Mr. Markham here thinks his powers of conviction at least equal to Mr. Millward's. If I hear not him, neither should I be convinced though one rose from the dead, he would tell you. Well, Mr. Markham, you that maintain that a boy should not be shielded from evil, but sent out to battle against it, alone and unassisted – not taught to avoid the snares of life, but boldly to rush into them, or over them, as he may – to seek danger, rather than shun it, and feed his virtue by temptation, – would you –?"

"I beg your pardon, Mrs. Graham – but you get on too fast. I have not yet said that a boy should be taught to rush into the snares of life, – or even wilfully to seek temptation for the sake of exercising his virtue by overcoming it; – I only say that it is better to arm and strengthen your hero, than to disarm and enfeeble the foe; – and if you were to rear an oak sapling in a hothouse, tending it carefully night and day, and shielding it from every breath of wind, you could not expect it to become a hardy tree, like that which has grown up on the mountain-side, exposed to all the action of the elements, and not even sheltered from the shock of the tempest."

"Granted; – but would you use the same argument with regard to a girl?"

"Certainly not."

"No; you would have her to be tenderly and delicately nurtured, like a hot-house plant – taught to cling to others for direction and support, and guarded, as much as possible, from the very knowledge of evil. But will you be so good as to inform me why you make this distinction? Is it that you think she has no virtue?"

"Assuredly not."

"Well, but you affirm that virtue is only elicited by temptation; – and you think that a woman cannot be too little exposed to temptation, or too little acquainted with vice, or anything connected therewith. It must be either that you think she is essentially so vicious, or so feeble-minded, that she cannot withstand temptation, – and though she may be pure and innocent as long as she is kept in ignorance and restraint, yet, being destitute of real virtue, to teach her how to sin is at once to make her a sinner, and the greater her knowledge, the wider her liberty, the deeper will be her depravity, – whereas, in the nobler sex, there is a natural tendency to goodness, guarded by a superior fortitude, which, the more it is exercised by trials and dangers, is only the further developed –"

"Heaven forbid that I should think so!" I interrupted her at last.

"Well, then, it must be that you think they are both weak and prone to err, and the slightest error, the merest shadow of pollution, will ruin the one, while the character of the other will be strengthened and embellished his education properly finished by a little practical acquaintance with forbidden things. Such experience, to him (to use a trite simile), will be like the storm to the oak, which, though it may scatter the leaves, and snap the smaller branches, serves but to rivet the roots, and to harden and condense the fibres of the tree. You would have us encourage our sons to prove all things by their own experience, while our daughters must not even profit by the experience of others. Now I would have both so to benefit by the experience of others, and the precepts of a higher authority, that they should know beforehand to refuse the evil and choose the good, and require no experimental proofs to teach them the evil of transgression. I would not send a poor girl into the world, unarmed against her foes, and ignorant of the snares that beset her path; nor would

I watch and guard her, till, deprived of self-respect and self-reliance, she lost the power or the will to watch and guard herself; – and as for my son – if I thought he would grow up to be what you call a man of the world – one that has 'seen life,' and glories in his experience, even though he should so far profit by it as to sober down, at length, into a useful and respected member of society – I would rather that he died tomorrow! – Rather a thousand times!" she earnestly repeated, pressing her darling to her side and kissing his forehead with intense affection. He had already left his new companion, and been standing for some time beside his mother's knee, looking up into her face, and listening in silent wonder to her incomprehensible discourse.

"Well! You ladies must always have the last word, I suppose," said I, observing her rise, and begin to take leave of my mother.

"You may have as many words as you please, – only I can't stay to hear them."

"No; that is the way: you hear just as much of an argument as you please; and the rest may be spoken to the wind."

"If you are anxious to say anything more on the subject," replied she, as she shook hands with Rose, "you must bring your sister to see me some fine day, and I'll listen, as patiently as you could wish, to whatever you please to say. I would rather be lectured by you than the vicar, because I should have less remorse in telling you, at the end of the discourse, that I preserve my own opinion precisely the same as at the beginning – as would be the case, I am persuaded, with regard to either logician."

"Yes, of course," replied I, determined to be as provoking as herself; "for when a lady does consent to listen to an argument against her own opinions, she is always predetermined to withstand it – to listen only with her bodily ears, keeping the mental organs resolutely closed against the strongest reasoning."

"Good morning, Mr. Markham," said my fair antagonist, with a pitying smile; and deigning no further rejoinder, she slightly bowed, and was about to withdraw; but her son, with childish impertinence, arrested her by exclaiming, – "Mamma, you have not shaken hands with Mr. Markham!"

She laughingly turned round and held out her hand. I gave it a spiteful squeeze, for I was annoyed at the continual injustice she had done me from the very dawn of our acquaintance. Without knowing anything about my real disposition and principles, she was evidently prejudiced against me, and seemed bent upon showing me that her opinions respecting me, on every particular, fell far below those I entertained of myself. I was naturally touchy, or it would not have vexed me so much. Perhaps, too, I was a little bit spoiled by my mother and sister, and some other ladies of my acquaintance; – and yet I was by no means a fop – of that I am fully convinced, whether you are or not.

Chapter Four

OUR PARTY, on the 5th of November, passed off very well, in spite of Mrs. Graham's refusal to grace it with her presence. Indeed, it is probable that, had she been there, there would have been less cordiality, freedom, and frolic amongst us than there was without her.

My mother, as usual, was cheerful and chatty, full of activity and good-nature, and only faulty in being too anxious to make her guests happy, thereby forcing several of them to do what their soul abhorred in the way of eating or drinking, sitting opposite the blazing fire, or talking when they would be silent. Nevertheless, they bore it very well, being all in their holiday humours.

Mr. Millward was mighty in important dogmas and sententious jokes, pompous anecdotes and oracular discourses, dealt out for the edification of the whole assembly in general, and of the admiring Mrs. Markham, the polite Mr. Lawrence, the sedate Mary Millward, the quiet Richard Wilson, and the matter-of-fact Robert in particular, – as being the most attentive listeners.

Mrs. Wilson was more brilliant than ever, with her budgets of fresh news and old scandal, strung together with trivial questions and remarks, and oft-repeated observations, uttered apparently for the sole purpose of denying a moment's rest to her inexhaustible organs of speech. She had brought her knitting with her, and it seemed as if her tongue had laid a wager with her fingers, to outdo them in swift and ceaseless motion.

Her daughter Jane was, of course, as graceful and elegant, as witty and seductive, as she could possibly manage to be; for here were all the ladies to outshine, and all the gentlemen to charm, – and Mr. Lawrence, especially, to capture and subdue. Her little arts to effect his subjugation were too subtle and impalpable to attract my observation; but I thought there was a certain refined affectation of superiority, and an ungenial self-consciousness about her, that negatived all her advantages; and after she was gone, Rose interpreted to me her various looks, words, and actions with a mingled acuteness and asperity that made me wonder, equally, at the lady's artifice and my sister's penetration, and ask myself if she too had an eye to the squire – but never mind, Halford; she had not.

Richard Wilson, Jane's younger brother, sat in a corner, apparently good-tempered, but silent and shy, desirous to escape observation, but willing enough to listen and observe: and, although somewhat out of his element, he would have been happy enough in his own quiet way, if my mother could only have let him alone; but in her mistaken kindness, she would keep persecuting him with her attentions – pressing upon him all manner of viands, under the notion that he was too bashful to help himself, and obliging him to shout across the room his monosyllabic replies to the numerous questions and observations by which she vainly attempted to draw him into conversation.

Rose informed me that he never would have favoured us with his company but for the importunities of his sister Jane, who was most anxious to show Mr. Lawrence that she had at least one brother more gentlemanly and refined than Robert. That worthy individual she had been equally solicitous to keep away; but he affirmed that he saw no reason why he should not enjoy a crack with Markham and the old lady (my mother was not old, really), and bonny Miss Rose and the parson, as well as the best; – and he was in the right of it too. So he talked common-place with my mother and Rose, and discussed parish affairs with the vicar, farming matters with me, and politics with us both.

Mary Millward was another mute, – not so much tormented with cruel kindness as Dick Wilson, because she had a certain short, decided way of answering and refusing, and was supposed to be rather sullen than diffident. However that might be, she certainly did not give much pleasure to the company; – nor did she appear to derive much from it. Eliza told me she had only come because her father insisted upon it, having taken it into his head that she devoted herself too exclusively to her household duties, to the neglect of such relaxations and innocent enjoyments as were proper to her age and sex. She seemed to me to be good-humoured enough on the whole. Once or twice she was provoked to laughter by the wit or the merriment of some favoured individual amongst us; and then I observed she sought the eye of Richard Wilson, who sat over against her. As he studied with her father, she had some acquaintance with him, in spite of the retiring habits of both, and I suppose there was a kind of fellow-feeling established between them.

My Eliza was charming beyond description, coquettish without affectation, and evidently more desirous to engage my attention than that of all the room besides. Her delight in having me near her, seated or standing by her side, whispering in her ear, or pressing her hand in the dance, was plainly legible in her glowing face and heaving bosom, however belied by saucy words and gestures. But I had better hold my tongue: if I boast of these things now, I shall have to blush hereafter.

To proceed, then, with the various individuals of our party; Rose was simple and natural as usual, and full of mirth and vivacity.

Fergus was impertinent and absurd; but his impertinence and folly served to make others laugh, if they did not raise himself in their estimation.

And finally (for I omit myself), Mr. Lawrence was gentlemanly and inoffensive to all, and polite to the vicar and the ladies, especially his hostess and her daughter, and Miss Wilson – misguided man; he had not the taste to prefer Eliza Millward. Mr. Lawrence and I were on tolerably intimate terms. Essentially of reserved habits, and but seldom quitting the secluded place of his birth, where he had lived in solitary state since the death of his father, he had neither the opportunity nor the inclination for forming many acquaintances; and, of all he had ever known, I (judging by the results) was the companion most agreeable to his taste. I liked the man well enough, but he was too cold, and shy, and self-contained, to obtain my cordial sympathies. A spirit of candour and frankness, when wholly unaccompanied with coarseness, he admired in others, but he could not acquire it himself. His excessive reserve upon all his own concerns was, indeed, provoking and chilly enough; but I forgave it, from a conviction that it originated less in pride and want of confidence in his friends, than in a certain morbid feeling of delicacy, and a peculiar diffidence, that he was sensible of, but wanted energy to overcome. His heart was like a sensitive plant, that opens for a moment in the sunshine, but curls up and shrinks into itself at the slightest touch of the finger, or the lightest breath of wind. And, upon the whole, our intimacy was rather a mutual predilection than a deep and solid friendship, such as has since arisen between myself and you, Halford, whom, in spite of your occasional crustiness, I can liken to nothing so well as an old coat, unimpeachable in texture, but easy and loose – that has conformed itself to the shape of the wearer, and which he may use as he pleases, without being bothered with the fear of spoiling it; – whereas Mr. Lawrence was like a new garment, all very neat and trim to look at, but so tight in the elbows, that you would fear to split the seams by the unrestricted motion of your arms, and so smooth and fine in surface that you scruple to expose it to a single drop of rain.

Soon after the arrival of the guests, my mother mentioned Mrs. Graham, regretted she was not there to meet them, and explained to the Millwards and Wilsons the reasons she had given for neglecting to return their calls, hoping they would excuse her, as she was sure she did not mean to be uncivil, and would be glad to see them at any time. – "But she is a very singular lady, Mr. Lawrence," added she; "we don't know what to make of her – but I daresay you can tell us something about her, for she is your tenant, you know, – and she said she knew you a little."

All eyes were turned to Mr. Lawrence. I thought he looked unnecessarily confused at being so appealed to.

"I, Mrs. Markham!" said he; "you are mistaken – I don't – that is – I have seen her, certainly; but I am the last person you should apply to for information respecting Mrs. Graham."

He then immediately turned to Rose, and asked her to favour the company with a song, or a tune on the piano.

"No," said she, "you must ask Miss Wilson: she outshines us all in singing, and music too."

Miss Wilson demurred.

"She'll sing readily enough," said Fergus, "if you'll undertake to stand by her, Mr. Lawrence, and turn over the leaves for her."

"I shall be most happy to do so, Miss Wilson; will you allow me?"

She bridled her long neck and smiled, and suffered him to lead her to the instrument, where she played and sang, in her very best style, one piece after another; while he stood patiently by, leaning one hand on the back of her chair, and turning over the leaves of her book with the other. Perhaps he was as much charmed with her performance as she was. It was all very fine in its way; but I cannot say that it moved me very deeply. There was plenty of skill and execution, but precious little feeling.

But we had not done with Mrs. Graham yet.

"I don't take wine, Mrs. Markham," said Mr. Millward, upon the introduction of that beverage; "I'll take a little of your home-brewed ale. I always prefer your home-brewed to anything else."

Flattered at this compliment, my mother rang the bell, and a china jug of our best ale was presently brought and set before the worthy gentleman who so well knew how to appreciate its excellences.

"Now *this* is the thing!" cried he, pouring out a glass of the same in a long stream, skilfully directed from the jug to the tumbler, so as to produce much foam without spilling a drop; and, having surveyed it for a moment opposite the candle, he took a deep draught, and then smacked his lips, drew a long breath, and refilled his glass, my mother looking on with the greatest satisfaction.

"There's nothing like this, Mrs. Markham!" said he. "I always maintain that there's nothing to compare with your home-brewed ale."

"I'm sure I'm glad you like it, sir. I always look after the brewing myself, as well as the cheese and the butter – I like to have things well done, while we're about it."

"Quite right, Mrs. Markham!"

"But then, Mr. Millward, you don't think it wrong to take a little wine now and then – or a little spirits either!" said my mother, as she handed a smoking tumbler of gin-and-water to Mrs. Wilson, who affirmed that wine sat heavy on her stomach, and whose son Robert was at that moment helping himself to a pretty stiff glass of the same.

"By no means!" replied the oracle, with a Jove-like nod; "these things are all blessings and mercies, if we only knew how to make use of them."

"But Mrs. Graham doesn't think so. You shall just hear now what she told us the other day – I told her I'd tell you."

And my mother favoured the company with a particular account of that lady's mistaken ideas and conduct regarding the matter in hand, concluding with, "Now, don't you think it is wrong?"

"Wrong!" repeated the vicar, with more than common solemnity – "criminal, I should say – criminal! Not only is it making a fool of the boy, but it is despising the gifts of Providence, and teaching him to trample them under his feet."

He then entered more fully into the question, and explained at large the folly and impiety of such a proceeding. My mother heard him with profoundest reverence; and even Mrs. Wilson vouchsafed to rest her tongue for a moment, and listen in silence, while she complacently sipped her gin-and-water. Mr. Lawrence sat with his elbow on the table, carelessly playing with his half-empty wine-glass, and covertly smiling to himself.

"But don't you think, Mr. Millward," suggested he, when at length that gentleman paused in his discourse, "that when a child may be naturally prone to intemperance – by the fault of its parents or ancestors, for instance – some precautions are advisable?" (Now it was generally believed that Mr. Lawrence's father had shortened his days by intemperance.)

"Some precautions, it may be; but temperance, sir, is one thing, and abstinence another."

"But I have heard that, with some persons, temperance – that is, moderation – is almost impossible; and if abstinence be an evil (which some have doubted), no one will deny that excess is a greater. Some parents have entirely prohibited their children from tasting intoxicating liquors; but a parent's authority cannot last for ever; children are naturally prone to hanker after forbidden things; and a child, in such a case, would be likely to have a strong curiosity to taste, and try the effect of what has been so lauded and enjoyed by others, so strictly forbidden to himself – which curiosity would generally be gratified on the first convenient opportunity; and the restraint once broken, serious consequences might ensue. I don't pretend to be a judge of such matters, but it seems to me, that this plan of Mrs. Graham's, as you describe it, Mrs. Markham, extraordinary as it may be, is not without its advantages; for here you see the child is delivered at once from temptation; he has no secret curiosity, no hankering desire; he is as well acquainted with the tempting liquors as he ever wishes to be; and is thoroughly disgusted with them, without having suffered from their effects."

"And is that right, sir? Have I not proven to you how wrong it is – how contrary to Scripture and to reason, to teach a child to look with contempt and disgust upon the blessings of Providence, instead of to use them aright?"

"You may consider laudanum a blessing of Providence, sir," replied Mr. Lawrence, smiling; "and yet, you will allow that most of us had better abstain from it, even in moderation; but," added he, "I would not desire you to follow out my simile too closely – in witness whereof I finish my glass."

"And take another, I hope, Mr. Lawrence," said my mother, pushing the bottle towards him.

He politely declined, and pushing his chair a little away from the table, leant back towards me – I was seated a trifle behind, on the sofa beside Eliza Millward – and carelessly asked me if I knew Mrs. Graham.

"I have met her once or twice," I replied.

"What do you think of her?"

"I cannot say that I like her much. She is handsome – or rather I should say distinguished and interesting – in her appearance, but by no means amiable – a woman liable to take strong prejudices, I should fancy, and stick to them through thick and thin, twisting everything into conformity with her own preconceived opinions – too hard, too sharp, too bitter for my taste."

He made no reply, but looked down and bit his lip, and shortly after rose and sauntered up to Miss Wilson, as much repelled by me, I fancy, as attracted by her. I scarcely noticed it at the time, but afterwards I was led to recall this and other trifling facts, of a similar nature, to my remembrance, when – but I must not anticipate.

We wound up the evening with dancing – our worthy pastor thinking it no scandal to be present on the occasion, though one of the village musicians was engaged to direct our evolutions with his violin. But Mary Millward obstinately refused to join us; and so did Richard Wilson, though my mother earnestly entreated him to do so, and even offered to be his partner.

We managed very well without them, however. With a single set of quadrilles, and several country dances, we carried it on to a pretty late hour; and at length, having called upon our musician to strike up a waltz, I was just about to whirl Eliza round in that delightful dance, accompanied by Lawrence and Jane Wilson, and Fergus and Rose, when Mr. Millward interposed with: – "No, no; I don't allow that! Come, it's time to be going now."

"Oh, no, papa!" pleaded Eliza.

"High time, my girl – high time! Moderation in all things, remember! That's the plan – 'Let your moderation be known unto all men!'"

But in revenge I followed Eliza into the dimly-lighted passage, where, under pretence of helping her on with her shawl, I fear I must plead guilty to snatching a kiss behind her father's back, while he was enveloping his throat and chin in the folds of a mighty comforter. But alas! In turning round, there was my mother close beside me. The consequence was, that no sooner were the guests departed, than I was doomed to a very serious remonstrance, which unpleasantly checked the galloping course of my spirits, and made a disagreeable close to the evening.

"My dear Gilbert," said she, "I wish you wouldn't do so! You know how deeply I have your advantage at heart, how I love you and prize you above everything else in the world, and how much I long to see you well settled in life – and how bitterly it would grieve me to see you married to that girl – or any other in the neighbourhood. What you see in her I don't know. It isn't only the want of money that I think about – nothing of the kind – but there's neither beauty, nor cleverness, nor goodness, nor anything else that's desirable. If you knew your own value, as I do, you wouldn't dream of it. Do wait awhile and see! If you bind yourself to her, you'll repent it all your lifetime when you look round and see how many better there are. Take my word for it, you will."

"Well, mother, do be quiet! – I hate to be lectured! – I'm not going to marry yet, I tell you; but – dear me! Mayn't I enjoy myself at all?"

"Yes, my dear boy, but not in that way. Indeed, you shouldn't do such things. You would be wronging the girl, if she were what she ought to be; but I assure you she is as artful a little hussy as anybody need wish to see; and you'll got entangled in her snares before you know where you are. And if you marry her, Gilbert, you'll break my heart – so there's an end of it."

"Well, don't cry about it, mother," said I, for the tears were gushing from her eyes; "there, let that kiss efface the one I gave Eliza; don't abuse her any more, and set your mind at rest; for I'll promise never – that is, I'll promise to think twice before I take any important step you seriously disapprove of."

So saying, I lighted my candle, and went to bed, considerably quenched in spirit.

Chapter Five

IT WAS ABOUT the close of the month, that, yielding at length to the urgent importunities of Rose, I accompanied her in a visit to Wildfell Hall. To our surprise, we were ushered into a room where the first object that met the eye was a painter's easel, with a table beside it covered with rolls of canvas, bottles of oil and varnish, palette, brushes, paints, etc. Leaning against the wall were several sketches in various stages of progression, and a few finished paintings – mostly of landscapes and figures.

"I must make you welcome to my studio," said Mrs. Graham; "there is no fire in the sitting-room today, and it is rather too cold to show you into a place with an empty grate."

And disengaging a couple of chairs from the artistical lumber that usurped them, she bid us be seated, and resumed her place beside the easel – not facing it exactly, but now and then glancing at the picture upon it while she conversed, and giving it an occasional touch with her brush, as if she found it impossible to wean her attention entirely from her occupation to fix it upon her guests. It was a view of Wildfell Hall, as seen at early morning from the field below, rising in dark relief against a sky of clear silvery blue, with a few red streaks on the horizon, faithfully drawn and coloured, and very elegantly and artistically handled.

"I see your heart is in your work, Mrs. Graham," observed I: "I must beg you to go on with it; for if you suffer our presence to interrupt you, we shall be constrained to regard ourselves as unwelcome intruders."

"Oh, no!" replied she, throwing her brush on to the table, as if startled into politeness. "I am not so beset with visitors but that I can readily spare a few minutes to the few that do favour me with their company."

"You have almost completed your painting," said I, approaching to observe it more closely, and surveying it with a greater degree of admiration and delight than I cared to express. "A few more touches in the foreground will finish it, I should think. But why have you called it Fernley Manor, Cumberland, instead of Wildfell Hall, —shire?" I asked, alluding to the name she had traced in small characters at the bottom of the canvas.

But immediately I was sensible of having committed an act of impertinence in so doing; for she coloured and hesitated; but after a moment's pause, with a kind of desperate frankness, she replied:

"Because I have friends – acquaintances at least – in the world, from whom I desire my present abode to be concealed; and as they might see the picture, and might possibly recognise the style in spite of the false initials I have put in the corner, I take the precaution to give a false name to the place also, in order to put them on a wrong scent, if they should attempt to trace me out by it."

"Then you don't intend to keep the picture?" said I, anxious to say anything to change the subject.

"No; I cannot afford to paint for my own amusement."

"Mamma sends all her pictures to London," said Arthur; "and somebody sells them for her there, and sends us the money."

In looking round upon the other pieces, I remarked a pretty sketch of Linden-hope from the top of the hill; another view of the old hall basking in the sunny haze of a quiet summer afternoon; and a simple but striking little picture of a child brooding, with looks of silent but deep and sorrowful regret, over a handful of withered flowers, with glimpses of dark low hills and autumnal fields behind it, and a dull beclouded sky above.

"You see there is a sad dearth of subjects," observed the fair artist. "I took the old hall once on a moonlight night, and I suppose I must take it again on a snowy winter's day, and then again on a dark cloudy evening; for I really have nothing else to paint. I have been told that you have a fine view of the sea somewhere in the neighbourhood. Is it true? – And is it within walking distance?"

"Yes, if you don't object to walking four miles – or nearly so – little short of eight miles, there and back – and over a somewhat rough, fatiguing road."

"In what direction does it lie?"

I described the situation as well as I could, and was entering upon an explanation of the various roads, lanes, and fields to be traversed in order to reach it, the goings straight on, and turnings to the right and the left, when she checked me with, –

"Oh, stop! Don't tell me now: I shall forget every word of your directions before I require them. I shall not think about going till next spring; and then, perhaps, I may trouble you. At present we have the winter before us, and –"

She suddenly paused, with a suppressed exclamation, started up from her seat, and saying, "Excuse me one moment," hurried from the room, and shut the door behind her.

Curious to see what had startled her so, I looked towards the window – for her eyes had been carelessly fixed upon it the moment before – and just beheld the skirts of a man's coat vanishing behind a large holly-bush that stood between the window and the porch.

"It's mamma's friend," said Arthur.

Rose and I looked at each other.

"I don't know what to make of her at all," whispered Rose.

The child looked at her in grave surprise. She straightway began to talk to him on indifferent matters, while I amused myself with looking at the pictures. There was one in an obscure corner that I had not before observed. It was a little child, seated on the grass with its lap full of flowers. The tiny features and large blue eyes, smiling through a shock of light brown curls, shaken over the forehead as it bent above its treasure, bore sufficient resemblance to those of the young gentleman before me to proclaim it a portrait of Arthur Graham in his early infancy.

In taking this up to bring it to the light, I discovered another behind it, with its face to the wall. I ventured to take that up too. It was the portrait of a gentleman in the full prime of youthful manhood – handsome enough, and not badly executed; but if done by the same hand as the others, it was evidently some years before; for there was far more careful minuteness of detail, and less of that freshness of colouring and freedom of handling that delighted and surprised me in them. Nevertheless, I surveyed it with considerable interest. There was a certain individuality in the features and expression that stamped it, at once, a successful likeness. The bright blue eyes regarded the spectator with a kind of lurking drollery – you almost expected to see them wink; the lips – a little too voluptuously full – seemed ready to break into a smile; the warmly-tinted cheeks were embellished with a luxuriant growth of reddish whiskers; while the bright chestnut hair, clustering in abundant, wavy curls, trespassed too much upon the forehead, and seemed to intimate that the owner thereof was prouder of his beauty than his intellect – as, perhaps, he had reason to be; and yet he looked no fool.

I had not had the portrait in my hands two minutes before the fair artist returned.

"Only some one come about the pictures," said she, in apology for her abrupt departure: "I told him to wait."

"I fear it will be considered an act of impertinence," said "to presume to look at a picture that the artist has turned to the wall; but may I ask –"

"It is an act of very great impertinence, sir; and therefore I beg you will ask nothing about it, for your curiosity will not be gratified," replied she, attempting to cover the tartness of her rebuke with a smile; but I could see, by her flushed cheek and kindling eye, that she was seriously annoyed.

"I was only going to ask if you had painted it yourself," said I, sulkily resigning the picture into her hands; for without a grain of ceremony she took it from me; and quickly restoring it to the dark corner, with its face to the wall, placed the other against it as before, and then turned to me and laughed.

But I was in no humour for jesting. I carelessly turned to the window, and stood looking out upon the desolate garden, leaving her to talk to Rose for a minute or two; and then, telling my sister it was time to go, shook hands with the little gentleman, coolly bowed to the lady, and moved towards the door. But, having bid adieu to Rose, Mrs. Graham presented her hand to me, saying, with a soft voice, and by no means a disagreeable smile, – "Let not the sun go down upon your wrath, Mr. Markham. I'm sorry I offended you by my abruptness."

When a lady condescends to apologise, there is no keeping one's anger, of course; so we parted good friends for once; and this time I squeezed her hand with a cordial, not a spiteful pressure.

Chapter Six

DURING THE NEXT four months I did not enter Mrs. Graham's house, nor she mine; but still the ladies continued to talk about her, and still our acquaintance continued, though slowly, to advance. As for their talk, I paid but little attention to that (when it related to the fair hermit, I mean), and the only information I derived from it was, that one fine frosty day she had ventured to take her little boy as far as the vicarage, and that, unfortunately, nobody was at home but Miss Millward; nevertheless, she had sat a long time, and, by all accounts, they had found a good deal to say to each other, and parted with a mutual desire to meet again. But Mary liked children, and fond mammas like those who can duly appreciate their treasures.

But sometimes I saw her myself, not only when she came to church, but when she was out on the hills with her son, whether taking a long, purpose-like walk, or – on special fine days – leisurely rambling over the moor or the bleak pasture-lands, surrounding the old hall, herself with a book in her hand, her son gambolling about her; and, on any of these occasions, when I caught sight of her in my solitary walks or rides, or while following my agricultural pursuits, I generally contrived to meet or overtake her, for I rather liked to see Mrs. Graham, and to talk to her, and I decidedly liked to talk to her little companion, whom, when once the ice of his shyness was fairly broken, I found to be a very amiable, intelligent, and entertaining little fellow; and we soon became excellent friends – how much to the gratification of his mamma I cannot undertake to say. I suspected at first that she was desirous of throwing cold water on this growing intimacy – to quench, as it were, the kindling flame of our friendship – but discovering, at length, in spite of her prejudice against me, that I was perfectly harmless, and even well-intentioned, and that, between myself and my dog, her son derived a great deal of pleasure from the acquaintance that he would not otherwise have known, she ceased to object, and even welcomed my coming with a smile.

As for Arthur, he would shout his welcome from afar, and run to meet me fifty yards from his mother's side. If I happened to be on horseback he was sure to get a canter or a gallop; or, if there was one of the draught horses within an available distance, he was treated to a steady ride upon that, which served his turn almost as well; but his mother would always follow and trudge beside him – not so much, I believe, to ensure his safe conduct, as to see that I instilled no objectionable notions into his infant mind, for she was ever on the watch, and never would allow him to be taken out of her sight. What pleased her best of all was to see him romping and racing with Sancho, while I walked by her side – not, I fear, for love of my company (though I sometimes deluded myself with that idea), so much as for the delight she took in seeing her son thus happily engaged in the enjoyment of those active sports so invigorating to his tender frame, yet so seldom exercised for want of playmates suited to his years: and, perhaps, her pleasure was sweetened not a little by the fact of my being with her instead of with him, and therefore incapable of doing him any injury directly or indirectly, designedly or otherwise, small thanks to her for that same.

But sometimes, I believe, she really had some little gratification in conversing with me; and one bright February morning, during twenty minutes' stroll along the moor, she laid aside her usual asperity and reserve, and fairly entered into conversation with me, discoursing with so much eloquence and depth of thought and feeling on a subject happily coinciding with my own ideas, and looking so beautiful withal, that I went home enchanted; and on the way (morally) started to find myself thinking that, after all, it would, perhaps, be better to spend one's days with such a woman than with Eliza Millward; and then I (figuratively) blushed for my inconstancy.

On entering the parlour I found Eliza there with Rose, and no one else. The surprise was not altogether so agreeable as it ought to have been. We chatted together a long time, but I found her rather frivolous, and even a little insipid, compared with the more mature and earnest Mrs. Graham. Alas, for human constancy!

"However," thought I, "I ought not to marry Eliza, since my mother so strongly objects to it, and I ought not to delude the girl with the idea that I intended to do so. Now, if this mood continue, I shall have less difficulty in emancipating my affections from her soft yet unrelenting sway; and, though Mrs. Graham might be equally objectionable, I may be permitted, like the doctors, to cure a greater evil by a less, for I shall not fall seriously in love with the young widow, I think, nor she with me – that's certain – but if I find a little pleasure in her society I may surely be allowed to seek it; and if the star of her divinity be bright enough to dim the lustre of Eliza's, so much the better, but I scarcely can think it."

And thereafter I seldom suffered a fine day to pass without paying a visit to Wildfell about the time my new acquaintance usually left her hermitage; but so frequently was I baulked in my expectations of another interview, so changeable was she in her times of coming forth and in her places of resort, so transient were the occasional glimpses I was able to obtain, that I felt half inclined to think she took as much pains to avoid my company as I to seek hers; but this was too disagreeable a supposition to be entertained a moment after it could conveniently be dismissed.

One calm, clear afternoon, however, in March, as I was superintending the rolling of the meadow-land, and the repairing of a hedge in the valley, I saw Mrs. Graham down by the brook, with a sketch-book in her hand, absorbed in the exercise of her favourite art, while Arthur was putting on the time with constructing dams and breakwaters in the shallow, stony stream. I was rather in want of amusement, and so rare an opportunity was not to be neglected; so, leaving both meadow and hedge, I quickly repaired to the spot, but not before Sancho, who, immediately upon perceiving his young friend, scoured at full gallop the intervening space, and pounced upon him with an impetuous mirth that precipitated the child almost into the middle of the beck; but, happily, the stones preserved him from any serious wetting, while their smoothness prevented his being too much hurt to laugh at the untoward event.

Mrs. Graham was studying the distinctive characters of the different varieties of trees in their winter nakedness, and copying, with a spirited, though delicate touch, their various ramifications. She did not talk much, but I stood and watched the progress of her pencil: it was a pleasure to behold it so dexterously guided by those fair and graceful fingers. But ere long their dexterity became impaired, they began to hesitate, to tremble slightly, and make false strokes, and then suddenly came to a pause, while their owner laughingly raised her face to mine, and told me that her sketch did not profit by my superintendence.

"Then," said I, "I'll talk to Arthur till you've done."

"I should like to have a ride, Mr. Markham, if mamma will let me," said the child.

"What on, my boy?"

"I think there's a horse in that field," replied he, pointing to where the strong black mare was pulling the roller.

"No, no, Arthur; it's too far," objected his mother.

But I promised to bring him safe back after a turn or two up and down the meadow; and when she looked at his eager face she smiled and let him go. It was the first time she had even allowed me to take him so much as half a field's length from her side.

Enthroned upon his monstrous steed, and solemnly proceeding up and down the wide, steep field, he looked the very incarnation of quiet, gleeful satisfaction and delight. The rolling, however, was soon completed; but when I dismounted the gallant horseman, and restored him to his mother, she seemed rather displeased at my keeping him so long. She had shut up her sketch-book, and been, probably, for some minutes impatiently waiting his return.

It was now high time to go home, she said, and would have bid me good evening, but I was not going to leave her yet: I accompanied her half-way up the hill. She became more sociable, and I was beginning to be very happy; but, on coming within sight of the grim old hall, she stood still, and turned towards me while she spoke, as if expecting I should go no further, that the conversation would end here, and I should now take leave and depart – as, indeed, it was time to do, for 'the clear, cold eve' was fast 'declining,' the sun had set, and the gibbous moon was visibly brightening in the pale grey sky; but a feeling almost of compassion riveted me to the spot. It seemed hard to leave her to such a lonely, comfortless home. I looked up at it. Silent and grim it frowned; before us. A faint, red light was gleaming from the lower windows of one wing, but all the other windows were in darkness, and many exhibited their black, cavernous gulfs, entirely destitute of glazing or framework.

"Do you not find it a desolate place to live in?" said I, after a moment of silent contemplation.

"I do, sometimes," replied she. "On winter evenings, when Arthur is in bed, and I am sitting there alone, hearing the bleak wind moaning round me and howling through the ruinous old chambers, no books or occupations can repress the dismal thoughts and apprehensions that come crowding in – but it is folly to give way to such weakness, I know. If Rachel is satisfied with such a life, why should not I? – Indeed, I cannot be too thankful for such an asylum, while it is left me."

The closing sentence was uttered in an under-tone, as if spoken rather to herself than to me. She then bid me good evening and withdrew.

I had not proceeded many steps on my way homewards when I perceived Mr. Lawrence, on his pretty grey pony, coming up the rugged lane that crossed over the hill-top. I went a little out of my way to speak to him; for we had not met for some time.

"Was that Mrs. Graham you were speaking to just now?" said he, after the first few words of greeting had passed between us.

"Yes."

"Humph! I thought so." He looked contemplatively at his horse's mane, as if he had some serious cause of dissatisfaction with it, or something else.

"Well! What then?"

"Oh, nothing!" replied he. "Only I thought you disliked her," he quietly added, curling his classic lip with a slightly sarcastic smile.

"Suppose I did; mayn't a man change his mind on further acquaintance?"

"Yes, of course," returned he, nicely reducing an entanglement in the pony's redundant hoary mane. Then suddenly turning to me, and fixing his shy, hazel eyes upon me with a steady penetrating gaze, he added, "Then you have changed your mind?"

"I can't say that I have exactly. No; I think I hold the same opinion respecting her as before – but slightly ameliorated."

"Oh!" He looked round for something else to talk about; and glancing up at the moon, made some remark upon the beauty of the evening, which I did not answer, as being irrelevant to the subject.

"Lawrence," said I, calmly looking him in the face, "are you in love with Mrs. Graham?"

Instead of his being deeply offended at this, as I more than half expected he would, the first start of surprise, at the audacious question, was followed by a tittering laugh, as if he was highly amused at the idea.

"I in love with her!" repeated he. "What makes you dream of such a thing?"

"From the interest you take in the progress of my acquaintance with the lady, and the changes of my opinion concerning her, I thought you might be jealous."

He laughed again. "Jealous! No. But I thought you were going to marry Eliza Millward."

"You thought wrong, then; I am not going to marry either one or the other – that I know of –"

"Then I think you'd better let them alone."

"Are you going to marry Jane Wilson?"

He coloured, and played with the mane again, but answered – "No, I think not."

"Then you had better let her alone."

"She won't let me alone," he might have said; but he only looked silly and said nothing for the space of half a minute, and then made another attempt to turn the conversation; and this time I let it pass; for he had borne enough: another word on the subject would have been like the last atom that breaks the camel's back.

I was too late for tea; but my mother had kindly kept the teapot and muffin warm upon the hobs, and, though she scolded me a little, readily admitted my excuses; and when I complained of the flavour of the overdrawn tea, she poured the remainder into the slop-basin, and bade Rose put some fresh into the pot, and reboil the kettle, which offices were performed with great commotion, and certain remarkable comments.

"Well! – If it had been me now, I should have had no tea at all – if it had been Fergus, even, he would have to put up with such as there was, and been told to be thankful, for it was far too good for him; but you – we can't do too much for you. It's always so – if there's anything particularly nice at table, mamma winks and nods at me to abstain from it, and if I don't attend to that, she whispers, 'Don't eat so much of that, Rose; Gilbert will like it for his supper.' – I'm nothing at all. In the parlour, it's 'Come, Rose, put away your things, and let's have the room nice and tidy against they come in; and keep up a good fire; Gilbert likes a cheerful fire.' In the kitchen – 'Make that pie a large one, Rose; I daresay the boys'll be hungry; and don't put so much pepper in, they'll not like it, I'm sure' – or, 'Rose, don't put so many spices in the pudding, Gilbert likes it plain,' – or, 'Mind you put plenty of currants in the cake, Fergus liked plenty.' If I say, 'Well, mamma, I don't,' I'm told I ought not to think of myself. 'You know, Rose, in all household matters, we have only two things to consider, first, what's proper to be done; and, secondly, what's most agreeable to the gentlemen of the house – anything will do for the ladies.'"

"And very good doctrine too," said my mother. "Gilbert thinks so, I'm sure."

"Very convenient doctrine, for us, at all events," said I; "but if you would really study my pleasure, mother, you must consider your own comfort and convenience a little more than you do – as for Rose, I have no doubt she'll take care of herself; and whenever she does make a sacrifice or perform a remarkable act of devotedness, she'll take good care to let me know the extent of it. But for you I might sink into the grossest condition of self-indulgence and carelessness about the wants of others, from the mere habit of being constantly cared for myself, and having all my wants anticipated or immediately supplied, while left in total ignorance of what is done for me, – if Rose did not enlighten me now and then; and I should receive all your kindness as a matter of course, and never know how much I owe you."

"Ah! And you never will know, Gilbert, till you're married. Then, when you've got some trifling, self-conceited girl like Eliza Millward, careless of everything but her own immediate pleasure and advantage, or some misguided, obstinate woman, like Mrs. Graham, ignorant of her principal duties, and clever only in what concerns her least to know – then you'll find the difference."

"It will do me good, mother; I was not sent into the world merely to exercise the good capacities and good feelings of others – was I? – but to exert my own towards them; and when I marry, I shall expect to find more pleasure in making my wife happy and comfortable, than in being made so by her: I would rather give than receive."

"Oh! That's all nonsense, my dear. It's mere boy's talk that! You'll soon tire of petting and humouring your wife, be she ever so charming, and then comes the trial."

"Well, then, we must bear one another's burdens."

"Then you must fall each into your proper place. You'll do your business, and she, if she's worthy of you, will do hers; but it's your business to please yourself, and hers to please you. I'm sure your poor, dear father was as good a husband as ever lived, and after the first six months or so were over, I should as soon have expected him to fly, as to put himself out of his way to pleasure me. He always said I was a good wife, and did my duty; and he always did his – bless him! – he was steady and punctual, seldom found fault without a reason, always did justice to my good dinners, and hardly ever spoiled my cookery by delay – and that's as much as any woman can expect of any man."

Is it so, Halford? Is that the extent of your domestic virtues; and does your happy wife exact no more?

Chapter Seven

NOT MANY DAYS after this, on a mild sunny morning – rather soft under foot; for the last fall of snow was only just wasted away, leaving yet a thin ridge, here and there, lingering on the fresh green grass beneath the hedges; but beside them already, the young primroses were peeping from among their moist, dark foliage, and the lark above was singing of summer, and hope, and love, and every heavenly thing – I was out on the hill-side, enjoying these delights, and looking after the well-being of my young lambs and their mothers, when, on glancing round me, I beheld three persons ascending from the vale below. They were Eliza Millward, Fergus, and Rose; so I crossed the field to meet them; and, being told they were going to Wildfell Hall, I declared myself willing to go with them, and offering my arm to Eliza, who readily accepted it in lieu of my brother's, told the latter he might go back, for I would accompany the ladies.

"I beg your pardon!" exclaimed he. "It's the ladies that are accompanying me, not I them. You had all had a peep at this wonderful stranger but me, and I could endure my wretched ignorance no longer – come what would, I must be satisfied; so I begged Rose to go with me to the Hall, and introduce me to her at once. She swore she would not, unless Miss Eliza would go too; so I ran to the vicarage and fetched her; and we've come hooked all the way, as fond as a pair of lovers – and now you've taken her from me; and you want to deprive me of my walk and my visit besides. Go back to your fields and your cattle, you lubberly fellow; you're not fit to associate with ladies and gentlemen like us, that have nothing to do but to run snooking about to our neighbours' houses, peeping into their private corners, and scenting out their secrets, and picking holes in their coats, when we don't find them ready made to our hands – you don't understand such refined sources of enjoyment."

"Can't you both go?" suggested Eliza, disregarding the latter half of the speech.

"Yes, both, to be sure!" cried Rose; "the more the merrier – and I'm sure we shall want all the cheerfulness we can carry with us to that great, dark, gloomy room, with its narrow latticed windows, and its dismal old furniture – unless she shows us into her studio again."

So we went all in a body; and the meagre old maid-servant, that opened the door, ushered us into an apartment such as Rose had described to me as the scene of her first introduction to Mrs. Graham, a tolerably spacious and lofty room, but obscurely lighted by the old-fashioned windows, the ceiling, panels, and chimney-piece of grim black oak – the latter elaborately but not very tastefully carved, – with tables and chairs to match, an old bookcase on one side of the fire-place, stocked with a motley assemblage of books, and an elderly cabinet piano on the other.

The lady was seated in a stiff, high-backed arm-chair, with a small round table, containing a desk and a work-basket on one side of her, and her little boy on the other, who stood leaning his elbow on her knee, and reading to her, with wonderful fluency, from a small volume that lay in her lap; while she rested her hand on his shoulder, and abstractedly played with the long, wavy curls that fell on his ivory neck. They struck me as forming a pleasing contrast to all the surrounding objects; but of course their position was immediately changed on our entrance. I could only observe the picture during the few brief seconds that Rachel held the door for our admittance.

I do not think Mrs. Graham was particularly delighted to see us: there was something indescribably chilly in her quiet, calm civility; but I did not talk much to her. Seating myself near the window, a little back from the circle, I called Arthur to me, and he and I and Sancho amused ourselves very pleasantly together, while the two young ladies baited his mother with small talk, and Fergus sat opposite with his legs crossed and his hands in his breeches-pockets, leaning back in his chair, and staring now up at the ceiling, now straight forward at his hostess (in a manner that made me strongly inclined to kick him out of the room), now whistling sotto voce to himself a snatch of a favourite air, now interrupting the conversation, or filling up a pause (as the case might be) with some most impertinent question or remark. At one time it was, – "It, amazes me, Mrs. Graham, how you could choose such a dilapidated, rickety old place as this to live in. If you couldn't afford to occupy the whole house, and have it mended up, why couldn't you take a neat little cottage?"

"Perhaps I was too proud, Mr. Fergus," replied she, smiling; "perhaps I took a particular fancy for this romantic, old-fashioned place – but, indeed, it has many advantages over a cottage – in the first place, you see, the rooms are larger and more airy; in the second place, the unoccupied apartments, which I don't pay for, may serve as lumber-rooms, if I have anything to put in them; and they are very useful for my little boy to run about in on rainy days when he can't go out; and then there is the garden for him to play in, and for me to work in. You see I have effected some little improvement already," continued she, turning to the window. "There is a bed of young vegetables in that corner, and here are some snowdrops and primroses already in bloom – and there, too, is a yellow crocus just opening in the sunshine."

"But then how can you bear such a situation – your nearest neighbours two miles distant, and nobody looking in or passing by? Rose would go stark mad in such a place. She can't put on life unless she sees half a dozen fresh gowns and bonnets a day – not to speak of the faces within; but you might sit watching at these windows all day long, and never see so much as an old woman carrying her eggs to market."

"I am not sure the loneliness of the place was not one of its chief recommendations. I take no pleasure in watching people pass the windows; and I like to be quiet."

"Oh! As good as to say you wish we would all of us mind our own business, and let you alone."

"No, I dislike an extensive acquaintance; but if I have a few friends, of course I am glad to see them occasionally. No one can be happy in eternal solitude. Therefore, Mr. Fergus, if you choose to enter my house as a friend, I will make you welcome; if not, I must confess, I would rather you kept away." She then turned and addressed some observation to Rose or Eliza.

"And, Mrs. Graham," said he again, five minutes after, "we were disputing, as we came along, a question that you can readily decide for us, as it mainly regarded yourself – and, indeed, we often hold discussions about you; for some of us have nothing better to do than to talk about our neighbours' concerns, and we, the indigenous plants of the soil, have known each other so long, and talked each other over so often, that we are quite sick of that game; so that a stranger coming amongst us makes an invaluable addition to our exhausted sources of amusement. Well, the question, or questions, you are requested to solve –"

"Hold your tongue, Fergus!" cried Rose, in a fever of apprehension and wrath.

"I won't, I tell you. The questions you are requested to solve are these: First, concerning your birth, extraction, and previous residence. Some will have it that you are a foreigner, and some an Englishwoman; some a native of the north country, and some of the south; some say –"

"Well, Mr. Fergus, I'll tell you. I'm an Englishwoman – and I don't see why any one should doubt it – and I was born in the country, neither in the extreme north nor south of our happy isle; and in the country I have chiefly passed my life, and now I hope you are satisfied; for I am not disposed to answer any more questions at present."

"Except this –"

"No, not one more!" laughed she, and, instantly quitting her seat, she sought refuge at the window by which I was seated, and, in very desperation, to escape my brother's persecutions, endeavoured to draw me into conversation.

"Mr. Markham," said she, her rapid utterance and heightened colour too plainly evincing her disquietude, "have you forgotten the fine sea-view we were speaking of some time ago? I think I must trouble you, now, to tell me the nearest way to it; for if this beautiful weather continue, I shall, perhaps, be able to walk there, and take my sketch; I have exhausted every other subject for painting; and I long to see it."

I was about to comply with her request, but Rose would not suffer me to proceed.

"Oh, don't tell her, Gilbert!" cried she; "she shall go with us. It's —Bay you are thinking about, I suppose, Mrs. Graham? It is a very long walk, too far for you, and out of the question for Arthur. But we were thinking about making a picnic to see it some fine day; and, if you will wait till the settled fine weather comes, I'm sure we shall all be delighted to have you amongst us."

Poor Mrs. Graham looked dismayed, and attempted to make excuses, but Rose, either compassionating her lonely life, or anxious to cultivate her acquaintance, was determined to have her; and every objection was overruled. She was told it would only be a small party, and all friends, and that the best view of all was from —Cliffs, full five miles distant.

"Just a nice walk for the gentlemen," continued Rose; "but the ladies will drive and walk by turns; for we shall have our pony-carriage, which will be plenty large enough to contain little Arthur and three ladies, together with your sketching apparatus, and our provisions."

So the proposal was finally acceded to; and, after some further discussion respecting the time and manner of the projected excursion, we rose, and took our leave.

But this was only March: a cold, wet April, and two weeks of May passed over before we could venture forth on our expedition with the reasonable hope of obtaining that pleasure we sought in pleasant prospects, cheerful society, fresh air, good cheer and exercise, without the alloy of bad roads, cold winds, or threatening clouds. Then, on a glorious morning, we gathered our forces and set forth. The company consisted of Mrs. and Master Graham, Mary and Eliza Millward, Jane and Richard Wilson, and Rose, Fergus, and Gilbert Markham.

Mr. Lawrence had been invited to join us, but, for some reason best known to himself, had refused to give us his company. I had solicited the favour myself. When I did so, he hesitated, and asked who were going. Upon my naming Miss Wilson among the rest, he seemed half inclined to go, but when I mentioned Mrs. Graham, thinking it might be a further inducement, it appeared to have a contrary effect, and he declined it altogether, and, to confess the truth, the decision was not displeasing to me, though I could scarcely tell you why.

It was about midday when we reached the place of our destination. Mrs. Graham walked all the way to the cliffs; and little Arthur walked the greater part of it too; for he was now much more hardy and active than when he first entered the neighbourhood, and he did not like being in the carriage with strangers, while all his four friends, mamma, and Sancho, and Mr. Markham, and Miss Millward, were on foot, journeying far behind, or passing through distant fields and lanes.

I have a very pleasant recollection of that walk, along the hard, white, sunny road, shaded here and there with bright green trees, and adorned with flowery banks and blossoming hedges of delicious fragrance; or through pleasant fields and lanes, all glorious in the sweet flowers and brilliant verdure of delightful May. It was true, Eliza was not beside me; but she was with her friends in the pony-carriage, as happy, I trusted, as I was; and even when we pedestrians, having forsaken the highway for a short cut across the fields, beheld the little carriage far away, disappearing amid the green, embowering trees, I did not hate those trees for snatching the dear little bonnet and shawl from my sight, nor did I feel that all those intervening objects lay between my happiness and me; for, to confess the truth, I was too happy in the company of Mrs. Graham to regret the absence of Eliza Millward.

The former, it is true, was most provokingly unsociable at first – seemingly bent upon talking to no one but Mary Millward and Arthur. She and Mary journeyed along together, generally with the child between them; – but where the road permitted, I always walked on the other side of her, Richard Wilson taking the other side of Miss Millward, and Fergus roving here and there according to his fancy; and, after a while, she became more friendly, and at length I succeeded in securing her attention almost entirely to myself – and then I was happy indeed; for whenever she did condescend to converse, I liked to listen. Where her opinions and sentiments tallied with mine, it was her extreme good sense, her exquisite taste and feeling, that delighted me; where they differed, it was still her uncompromising boldness in the avowal or defence of that difference, her earnestness and keenness, that piqued my fancy: and even when she angered me by her unkind words or looks, and her uncharitable conclusions respecting me, it only made me the more dissatisfied with myself for having so unfavourably impressed her, and the more desirous to vindicate my character and disposition in her eyes, and, if possible, to win her esteem.

At length our walk was ended. The increasing height and boldness of the hills had for some time intercepted the prospect; but, on gaining the summit of a steep acclivity, and looking downward, an opening lay before us – and the blue sea burst upon our sight! – Deep violet blue – not deadly calm, but covered with glinting breakers – diminutive white specks twinkling on its bosom, and scarcely to be distinguished, by the keenest vision, from the little seamews that sported above, their white wings glittering in the sunshine: only one or two vessels were visible, and those were far away.

I looked at my companion to see what she thought of this glorious scene. She said nothing: but she stood still, and fixed her eyes upon it with a gaze that assured me she was not disappointed. She had very fine eyes, by-the-by – I don't know whether I have told you before, but they were full of soul, large, clear, and nearly black – not brown, but very dark grey. A cool, reviving breeze blew from the sea – soft, pure, salubrious: it waved her drooping ringlets, and imparted a livelier colour to her usually too pallid lip and cheek. She felt its exhilarating influence, and so did I – I felt it tingling through my frame, but dared not give way to it while she remained so quiet. There was an aspect of subdued exhilaration in her face, that kindled into almost a smile of exalted, glad intelligence as her eye met mine. Never had she looked so lovely: never had my heart so warmly cleaved to her as now. Had we been left two minutes longer standing there alone, I cannot answer for the consequences. Happily for my discretion, perhaps for my enjoyment during the remainder of the day, we were speedily summoned to the repast – a very respectable collation, which Rose, assisted by Miss Wilson and

Eliza, who, having shared her seat in the carriage, had arrived with her a little before the rest, had set out upon an elevated platform overlooking the sea, and sheltered from the hot sun by a shelving rock and overhanging trees.

Mrs. Graham seated herself at a distance from me. Eliza was my nearest neighbour. She exerted herself to be agreeable, in her gentle, unobtrusive way, and was, no doubt, as fascinating and charming as ever, if I could only have felt it. But soon my heart began to warm towards her once again; and we were all very merry and happy together – as far as I could see – throughout the protracted social meal.

When that was over, Rose summoned Fergus to help her to gather up the fragments, and the knives, dishes, etc., and restore them to the baskets; and Mrs. Graham took her camp-stool and drawing materials; and having begged Miss Millward to take charge of her precious son, and strictly enjoined him not to wander from his new guardian's side, she left us and proceeded along the steep, stony hill, to a loftier, more precipitous eminence at some distance, whence a still finer prospect was to be had, where she preferred taking her sketch, though some of the ladies told her it was a frightful place, and advised her not to attempt it.

When she was gone, I felt as if there was to be no more fun – though it is difficult to say what she had contributed to the hilarity of the party. No jests, and little laughter, had escaped her lips; but her smile had animated my mirth; a keen observation or a cheerful word from her had insensibly sharpened my wits, and thrown an interest over all that was done and said by the rest. Even my conversation with Eliza had been enlivened by her presence, though I knew it not; and now that she was gone, Eliza's playful nonsense ceased to amuse me – nay, grew wearisome to my soul, and I grew weary of amusing her: I felt myself drawn by an irresistible attraction to that distant point where the fair artist sat and plied her solitary task – and not long did I attempt to resist it: while my little neighbour was exchanging a few words with Miss Wilson, I rose and cannily slipped away. A few rapid strides, and a little active clambering, soon brought me to the place where she was seated – a narrow ledge of rock at the very verge of the cliff, which descended with a steep, precipitous slant, quite down to the rocky shore.

She did not hear me coming: the falling of my shadow across her paper gave her an electric start; and she looked hastily round – any other lady of my acquaintance would have screamed under such a sudden alarm.

"Oh! I didn't know it was you. – Why did you startle me so?" said she, somewhat testily. "I hate anybody to come upon me so unexpectedly."

"Why, what did you take me for?" said I: "if I had known you were so nervous, I would have been more cautious; but –"

"Well, never mind. What did you come for? Are they all coming?"

"No; this little ledge could scarcely contain them all."

"I'm glad, for I'm tired of talking."

"Well, then, I won't talk. I'll only sit and watch your drawing."

"Oh, but you know I don't like that."

"Then I'll content myself with admiring this magnificent prospect."

She made no objection to this; and, for some time, sketched away in silence. But I could not help stealing a glance, now and then, from the splendid view at our feet to the elegant white hand that held the pencil, and the graceful neck and glossy raven curls that drooped over the paper.

"Now," thought I, "if I had but a pencil and a morsel of paper, I could make a lovelier sketch than hers, admitting I had the power to delineate faithfully what is before me."

But, though this satisfaction was denied me, I was very well content to sit beside her there, and say nothing.

"Are you there still, Mr. Markham?" said she at length, looking round upon me – for I was seated a little behind on a mossy projection of the cliff. – "Why don't you go and amuse yourself with your friends?"

"Because I am tired of them, like you; and I shall have enough of them tomorrow – or at any time hence; but you I may not have the pleasure of seeing again for I know not how long."

"What was Arthur doing when you came away?"

"He was with Miss Millward, where you left him – all right, but hoping mamma would not be long away. You didn't intrust him to me, by-the-by," I grumbled, "though I had the honour of a much longer acquaintance; but Miss Millward has the art of conciliating and amusing children," I carelessly added, "if she is good for nothing else."

"Miss Millward has many estimable qualities, which such as you cannot be expected to perceive or appreciate. Will you tell Arthur that I shall come in a few minutes?"

"If that be the case, I will wait, with your permission, till those few minutes are past; and then I can assist you to descend this difficult path."

"Thank you – I always manage best, on such occasions, without assistance."

"But, at least, I can carry your stool and sketch-book."

She did not deny me this favour; but I was rather offended at her evident desire to be rid of me, and was beginning to repent of my pertinacity, when she somewhat appeased me by consulting my taste and judgment about some doubtful matter in her drawing. My opinion, happily, met her approbation, and the improvement I suggested was adopted without hesitation.

"I have often wished in vain," said she, "for another's judgment to appeal to when I could scarcely trust the direction of my own eye and head, they having been so long occupied with the contemplation of a single object as to become almost incapable of forming a proper idea respecting it."

"That," replied I, "is only one of many evils to which a solitary life exposes us."

"True," said she; and again we relapsed into silence.

About two minutes after, however, she declared her sketch completed, and closed the book.

On returning to the scene of our repast we found all the company had deserted it, with the exception of three – Mary Millward, Richard Wilson, and Arthur Graham. The younger gentleman lay fast asleep with his head pillowed on the lady's lap; the other was seated beside her with a pocket edition of some classic author in his hand. He never went anywhere without such a companion wherewith to improve his leisure moments: all time seemed lost that was not devoted to study, or exacted, by his physical nature, for the bare support of life. Even now he could not abandon himself to the enjoyment of that pure air and balmy sunshine – that splendid prospect, and those soothing sounds, the music of the waves and of the soft wind in the sheltering trees above him – not even with a lady by his side (though not a very charming one, I will allow) – he must pull out his book, and make the most of his time while digesting his temperate meal, and reposing his weary limbs, unused to so much exercise.

Perhaps, however, he spared a moment to exchange a word or a glance with his companion now and then – at any rate, she did not appear at all resentful of his conduct; for her homely features wore an expression of unusual cheerfulness and serenity, and she was studying his pale, thoughtful face with great complacency when we arrived.

The journey homeward was by no means so agreeable to me as the former part of the day: for now Mrs. Graham was in the carriage, and Eliza Millward was the companion of my walk. She had observed my preference for the young widow, and evidently felt herself neglected. She did not manifest her chagrin by keen reproaches, bitter sarcasms, or pouting sullen silence – any or all of these I could easily have endured, or lightly laughed away; but she showed it by a kind of gentle melancholy, a mild, reproachful sadness that cut me to the heart. I tried to cheer her up, and apparently succeeded in some degree, before the walk was over; but in the very act my conscience reproved me, knowing, as I did, that, sooner or later, the tie must be broken, and this was only nourishing false hopes and putting off the evil day.

When the pony-carriage had approached as near Wildfell Hall as the road would permit – unless, indeed, it proceeded up the long rough lane, which Mrs. Graham would not allow – the young widow and her son alighted, relinquishing the driver's seat to Rose; and I persuaded Eliza to take the latter's place. Having put her comfortably in, bid her take care of the evening air, and wished her a kind goodnight, I felt considerably relieved, and hastened to offer my services to Mrs. Graham to carry her apparatus up the fields, but she had already hung her camp-stool on her arm and taken her sketch-book in her hand, and insisted upon bidding me adieu then and there, with the rest of the company. But this time she declined my proffered aid in so kind and friendly a manner that I almost forgave her.

Chapter Eight

SIX WEEKS had passed away. It was a splendid morning about the close of June. Most of the hay was cut, but the last week had been very unfavourable; and now that fine weather was come at last, being determined to make the most of it, I had gathered all hands together into the hay-field, and was working away myself, in the midst of them, in my shirt-sleeves, with a light, shady straw hat on my head, catching up armfuls of moist, reeking grass, and shaking it out to the four winds of heaven, at the head of a goodly file of servants and hirelings – intending so to labour, from morning till night, with as much zeal and assiduity as I could look for from any of them, as well to prosper the work by my own exertion as to animate the workers by my example – when lo! My resolutions were overthrown in a moment, by the simple fact of my brother's running up to me and putting into my hand a small parcel, just arrived from London, which I had been for some time expecting. I tore off the cover, and disclosed an elegant and portable edition of *Marmion*.

"I guess I know who that's for," said Fergus, who stood looking on while I complacently examined the volume. "That's for Miss Eliza, now."

He pronounced this with a tone and look so prodigiously knowing, that I was glad to contradict him.

"You're wrong, my lad," said I; and, taking up my coat, I deposited the book in one of its pockets, and then put it on (i.e. the coat). "Now come here, you idle dog, and make yourself useful for once," I continued. "Pull off your coat, and take my place in the field till I come back."

"Till you come back? – And where are you going, pray? 'No matter where – the when is all that concerns you; – and I shall be back by dinner, at least."

"Oh – oh! And I'm to labour away till then, am I? – And to keep all these fellows hard at it besides? Well, well! I'll submit – for once in a way. – Come, my lads, you must look sharp: I'm come to help you now: – and woe be to that man, or woman either, that pauses for a moment amongst you – whether to stare about him, to scratch his head, or blow his nose – no pretext will serve – nothing but work, work, work in the sweat of your face," etc., etc.

Leaving him thus haranguing the people, more to their amusement than edification, I returned to the house, and, having made some alteration in my toilet, hastened away to Wildfell Hall, with the book in my pocket; for it was destined for the shelves of Mrs. Graham.

"What! Then had she and you got on so well together as to come to the giving and receiving of presents?" – Not precisely, old buck; this was my first experiment in that line; and I was very anxious to see the result of it.

We had met several times since the —Bay excursion, and I had found she was not averse to my company, provided I confined my conversation to the discussion of abstract matters, or topics of common interest; – the moment I touched upon the sentimental or the complimentary, or made the slightest approach to tenderness in word or look, I was not only punished by an immediate change in her manner at the time, but doomed to find her more cold and distant, if not entirely inaccessible, when next I sought her company. This circumstance did not greatly disconcert me, however, because I attributed it, not so much to any dislike of my person, as to some absolute resolution against a second marriage formed prior to the time of our acquaintance, whether from excess of affection for her late husband, or because she had had enough of him and the matrimonial state together. At first, indeed, she had seemed to take a pleasure in mortifying my vanity and crushing my presumption – relentlessly nipping off bud by bud as they ventured to appear; and then, I confess, I was deeply wounded, though, at the same time, stimulated to seek revenge; – but latterly finding, beyond a doubt, that I was not that empty-headed coxcomb she had first supposed me, she had repulsed my modest advances in quite a different spirit. It was a kind of serious, almost sorrowful displeasure, which I soon learnt carefully to avoid awakening.

"Let me first establish my position as a friend," thought I – "the patron and playfellow of her son, the sober, solid, plain-dealing friend of herself, and then, when I have made myself fairly necessary to her comfort and enjoyment in life (as I believe I can), we'll see what next may be effected."

So we talked about painting, poetry, and music, theology, geology, and philosophy: once or twice I lent her a book, and once she lent me one in return: I met her in her walks as often as I could; I came to her house as often as I dared.

My first pretext for invading the sanctum was to bring Arthur a little waddling puppy of which Sancho was the father, and which delighted the child beyond expression, and, consequently, could not fail to please his mamma. My second was to bring him a book, which, knowing his mother's particularity, I had carefully selected, and which I submitted for her approbation before presenting it to him. Then, I brought her some plants for her garden, in my sister's name – having previously persuaded Rose to send them. Each of these times I inquired after the picture she was painting from the sketch taken on the cliff, and was admitted into the studio, and asked my opinion or advice respecting its progress.

My last visit had been to return the book she had lent me; and then it was that, in casually discussing the poetry of Sir Walter Scott, she had expressed a wish to see *Marmion*, and I had conceived the presumptuous idea of making her a present of it, and, on my return home, instantly sent for the smart little volume I had this morning received. But an apology for invading the hermitage was still necessary; so I had furnished myself with a blue morocco collar for Arthur's little dog; and that being given and received, with much more joy and gratitude, on the part of the receiver, than the worth of the gift or the selfish motive of the giver deserved, I ventured to ask Mrs. Graham for one more look at the picture, if it was still there.

"Oh, yes! Come in," said she (for I had met them in the garden). "It is finished and framed, all ready for sending away; but give me your last opinion, and if you can suggest any further improvement, it shall be – duly considered, at least."

The picture was strikingly beautiful; it was the very scene itself, transferred as if by magic to the canvas; but I expressed my approbation in guarded terms, and few words, for fear of displeasing her. She, however, attentively watched my looks, and her artist's pride was gratified, no doubt, to read my heartfelt admiration in my eyes. But, while I gazed, I thought upon the book, and wondered how it was to be presented. My heart failed me; but I determined not to be such a fool as to come away without having made the attempt. It was useless waiting for an opportunity, and useless trying to concoct a speech for the occasion. The more plainly and naturally the thing was done, the better, I thought; so I just looked out of the window to screw up my courage, and then pulled out the book, turned round, and put it into her hand, with this short explanation:

"You were wishing to see *Marmion*, Mrs. Graham; and here it is, if you will be so kind as to take it."

A momentary blush suffused her face – perhaps, a blush of sympathetic shame for such an awkward style of presentation: she gravely examined the volume on both sides; then silently turned over the leaves, knitting her brows the while, in serious cogitation; then closed the book, and turning from it to me, quietly asked the price of it – I felt the hot blood rush to my face.

"I'm sorry to offend you, Mr. Markham," said she, "but unless I pay for the book, I cannot take it." And she laid it on the table.

"Why cannot you?"

"Because," – she paused, and looked at the carpet.

"Why cannot you?" I repeated, with a degree of irascibility that roused her to lift her eyes and look me steadily in the face.

"Because I don't like to put myself under obligations that I can never repay – I am obliged to you already for your kindness to my son; but his grateful affection and your own good feelings must reward you for that."

"Nonsense!" ejaculated I.

She turned her eyes on me again, with a look of quiet, grave surprise, that had the effect of a rebuke, whether intended for such or not.

"Then you won't take the book?" I asked, more mildly than I had yet spoken.

"I will gladly take it, if you will let me pay for it." I told her the exact price, and the cost of the carriage besides, in as calm a tone as I could command – for, in fact, I was ready to weep with disappointment and vexation.

She produced her purse, and coolly counted out the money, but hesitated to put it into my hand. Attentively regarding me, in a tone of soothing softness, she observed, – "You think yourself insulted, Mr Markham – I wish I could make you understand that – that I –"

"I do understand you, perfectly," I said. "You think that if you were to accept that trifle from me now, I should presume upon it hereafter; but you are mistaken: – if you will only oblige me by taking it, believe me, I shall build no hopes upon it, and consider this no precedent for future favours: – and it is nonsense to talk about putting yourself under obligations to me when you must know that in such a case the obligation is entirely on my side, – the favour on yours."

"Well, then, I'll take you at your word," she answered, with a most angelic smile, returning the odious money to her purse – "but remember!"

"I will remember – what I have said; – but do not you punish my presumption by withdrawing your friendship entirely from me, – or expect me to atone for it by being more distant than before," said I, extending my hand to take leave, for I was too much excited to remain.

"Well, then! Let us be as we were," replied she, frankly placing her hand in mine; and while I held it there, I had much difficulty to refrain from pressing it to my lips; – but that would be suicidal madness: I had been bold enough already, and this premature offering had well-nigh given the death-blow to my hopes.

It was with an agitated, burning heart and brain that I hurried homewards, regardless of that scorching noonday sun – forgetful of everything but her I had just left – regretting nothing but her impenetrability, and my own precipitancy and want of tact – fearing nothing but her hateful resolution, and my inability to overcome it – hoping nothing – but halt, – I will not bore you with my conflicting hopes and fears – my serious cogitations and resolves.

Chapter Nine

THOUGH MY AFFECTIONS might now be said to be fairly weaned from Eliza Millward, I did not yet entirely relinquish my visits to the vicarage, because I wanted, as it were, to let her down easy; without raising much sorrow, or incurring much resentment, – or making myself the talk of the parish; and besides, if I had wholly kept away, the vicar, who looked upon my visits as paid chiefly, if not entirely, to himself, would have felt himself decidedly affronted by the neglect. But when I called there the day after my interview with Mrs. Graham, he happened to be from home – a circumstance by no means so agreeable to me now as it had been on former occasions. Miss Millward was there, it is true, but she, of course, would be little better than a nonentity. However, I resolved to make my visit a short one, and to talk to Eliza in a brotherly, friendly sort of way, such as our long acquaintance might warrant me in assuming, and which, I thought, could neither give offence nor serve to encourage false hopes.

It was never my custom to talk about Mrs. Graham either to her or any one else; but I had not been seated three minutes before she brought that lady on to the carpet herself in a rather remarkable manner.

"Oh, Mr. Markham!" said she, with a shocked expression and voice subdued almost to a whisper, "what do you think of these shocking reports about Mrs. Graham? – Can you encourage us to disbelieve them?"

"What reports?"

"Ah, now! You know!" she slily smiled and shook her head.

"I know nothing about them. What in the world do you mean, Eliza?"

"Oh, don't ask me! *I* can't explain it." She took up the cambric handkerchief which she had been beautifying with a deep lace border, and began to be very busy.

"What is it, Miss Millward? What does she mean?" said I, appealing to her sister, who seemed to be absorbed in the hemming of a large, coarse sheet.

"I don't know," replied she. "Some idle slander somebody has been inventing, I suppose. I never heard it till Eliza told me the other day, – but if all the parish dinned it in my ears, I shouldn't believe a word of it – I know Mrs. Graham too well!"

"Quite right, Miss Millward! – And so do I – whatever it may be."

"Well," observed Eliza, with a gentle sigh, "it's well to have such a comfortable assurance regarding the worth of those we love. I only wish you may not find your confidence misplaced."

And she raised her face, and gave me such a look of sorrowful tenderness as might have melted my heart, but within those eyes there lurked a something that I did not like; and I wondered how I ever could have admired them – her sister's honest face and small grey optics appeared far more agreeable. But I was out of temper with Eliza at that moment for her insinuations against Mrs. Graham, which were false, I was certain, whether she knew it or not.

I said nothing more on the subject, however, at the time, and but little on any other; for, finding I could not well recover my equanimity, I presently rose and took leave, excusing myself under the plea of business at the farm; and to the farm I went, not troubling my mind one whit about the possible truth of these mysterious reports, but only wondering what they were, by whom originated, and on what foundations raised, and how they could the most effectually be silenced or disproved.

A few days after this we had another of our quiet little parties, to which the usual company of friends and neighbours had been invited, and Mrs. Graham among the number. She could not now absent herself under the plea of dark evenings or inclement weather, and, greatly to my relief, she came. Without her I should have found the whole affair an intolerable bore; but the moment of her arrival brought new life to the house, and though I might not neglect the other guests for her, or expect to engross much of her attention and conversation to myself alone, I anticipated an evening of no common enjoyment.

Mr. Lawrence came too. He did not arrive till some time after the rest were assembled. I was curious to see how he would comport himself to Mrs. Graham. A slight bow was all that passed between them on his entrance; and having politely greeted the other members of the company, he seated himself quite aloof from the young widow, between my mother and Rose.

"Did you ever see such art?" whispered Eliza, who was my nearest neighbour. "Would you not say they were perfect strangers?"

"Almost; but what then?"

"What then; why, you can't pretend to be ignorant?"

"Ignorant of what?" demanded I, so sharply that she started and replied, –

"Oh, hush! Don't speak so loud."

"Well, tell me then," I answered in a lower tone, "what is it you mean? I hate enigmas."

"Well, you know, I don't vouch for the truth of it – indeed, far from it – but haven't you heard?"

"I've heard nothing, except from you."

"You must be wilfully deaf then, for anyone will tell you that; but I shall only anger you by repeating it, I see, so I had better hold my tongue."

She closed her lips and folded her hands before her, with an air of injured meekness.

"If you had wished not to anger me, you should have held your tongue from the beginning, or else spoken out plainly and honestly all you had to say."

She turned aside her face, pulled out her handkerchief, rose, and went to the window, where she stood for some time, evidently dissolved in tears. I was astounded, provoked, ashamed – not so much of my harshness as for her childish weakness. However, no one seemed to notice her, and shortly after we were summoned to the tea-table: in those parts it was customary to sit to the table at tea-time on all occasions, and make a meal of it, for we dined early. On taking my seat, I had Rose on one side of me and an empty chair on the other.

"May I sit by you?" said a soft voice at my elbow.

"If you like," was the reply; and Eliza slipped into the vacant chair; then, looking up in my face with a half-sad, half-playful smile, she whispered, – "You're so stern, Gilbert."

I handed down her tea with a slightly contemptuous smile, and said nothing, for I had nothing to say.

"What have I done to offend you?" said she, more plaintively. "I wish I knew."

"Come, take your tea, Eliza, and don't be foolish," responded I, handing her the sugar and cream.

Just then there arose a slight commotion on the other side of me, occasioned by Miss Wilson's coming to negotiate an exchange of seats with Rose.

"Will you be so good as to exchange places with me, Miss Markham?" said she; "for I don't like to sit by Mrs. Graham. If your mamma thinks proper to invite such persons to her house, she cannot object to her daughter's keeping company with them."

This latter clause was added in a sort of soliloquy when Rose was gone; but I was not polite enough to let it pass.

"Will you be so good as to tell me what you mean, Miss Wilson?" said I.

The question startled her a little, but not much.

"Why, Mr. Markham," replied she, coolly, having quickly recovered her self-possession, "it surprises me rather that Mrs. Markham should invite such a person as Mrs. Graham to her house; but, perhaps, she is not aware that the lady's character is considered scarcely respectable."

"She is not, nor am I; and therefore you would oblige me by explaining your meaning a little further."

"This is scarcely the time or the place for such explanations; but I think you can hardly be so ignorant as you pretend – you must know her as well as I do."

"I think I do, perhaps a little better; and therefore, if you will inform me what you have heard or imagined against her, I shall, perhaps, be able to set you right."

"Can you tell me, then, who was her husband, or if she ever had any?"

Indignation kept me silent. At such a time and place I could not trust myself to answer.

"Have you never observed," said Eliza, "what a striking likeness there is between that child of hers and –"

"And whom?" demanded Miss Wilson, with an air of cold, but keen severity.

Eliza was startled; the timidly spoken suggestion had been intended for my ear alone.

"Oh, I beg your pardon!" pleaded she; "I may be mistaken – perhaps I was mistaken." But she accompanied the words with a sly glance of derision directed to me from the corner of her disingenuous eye.

"There's no need to ask my pardon," replied her friend, "but I see no one here that at all resembles that child, except his mother, and when you hear ill-natured reports, Miss Eliza, I will thank you, that is, I think you will do well, to refrain from repeating them. I presume the person you allude to is Mr. Lawrence; but I think I can assure you that your suspicions, in that respect, are utterly misplaced; and if he has any particular connection with the lady at all (which no one has a right to assert), at least he has (what cannot be said of some others) sufficient sense of propriety to withhold him from acknowledging anything more than a bowing acquaintance in the presence of respectable persons; he was evidently both surprised and annoyed to find her here."

"Go it!" cried Fergus, who sat on the other side of Eliza, and was the only individual who shared that side of the table with us. "Go it like bricks! Mind you don't leave her one stone upon another."

Miss Wilson drew herself up with a look of freezing scorn, but said nothing. Eliza would have replied, but I interrupted her by saying as calmly as I could, though in a tone which betrayed, no doubt, some little of what I felt within, – "We have had enough of this subject; if we can only speak to slander our betters, let us hold our tongues."

"I think you'd better," observed Fergus, "and so does our good parson; he has been addressing the company in his richest vein all the while, and eyeing you, from time to time, with looks of stern distaste, while you sat there, irreverently whispering and muttering together; and once he paused in the middle of a story or a sermon, I don't know which, and fixed his eyes upon you, Gilbert, as much as to say, 'When Mr. Markham has done flirting with those two ladies I will proceed.'"

What more was said at the tea-table I cannot tell, nor how I found patience to sit till the meal was over. I remember, however, that I swallowed with difficulty the remainder of the tea that was in my cup, and ate nothing; and that the first thing I did was to stare at Arthur Graham, who sat beside his mother on the opposite side of the table, and the second to stare at Mr. Lawrence, who sat below; and, first, it struck me that there was a likeness; but, on further contemplation, I concluded it was only in imagination.

Both, it is true, had more delicate features and smaller bones than commonly fall to the lot of individuals of the rougher sex, and Lawrence's complexion was pale and clear, and Arthur's delicately fair; but Arthur's tiny, somewhat snubby nose could never become so long and straight as Mr. Lawrence's; and the outline of his face, though not full enough to be round, and too finely converging to the small, dimpled chin to be square, could never be drawn out to the long oval of the other's, while the child's hair was evidently of a lighter, warmer tint than the elder gentleman's had ever been, and his large, clear blue eyes, though prematurely serious at times, were utterly dissimilar to the shy hazel eyes of Mr. Lawrence, whence the sensitive soul looked so distrustfully forth, as ever ready to retire within, from the offences of a too rude, too uncongenial world. Wretch that I was to harbour that detestable idea for a moment! Did I not know Mrs. Graham? Had I not seen her, conversed with her time after time? Was I not certain that she, in intellect, in purity and elevation of soul, was immeasurably superior to any of her detractors; that she was, in fact, the noblest, the most adorable, of her sex I had ever beheld, or even imagined to exist? Yes, and I would say with Mary Millward (sensible girl as she was), that if all the parish, ay, or all the world, should din these horrible lies in my ears, I would not believe them, for I knew her better than they.

Meantime, my brain was on fire with indignation, and my heart seemed ready to burst from its prison with conflicting passions. I regarded my two fair neighbours with a feeling of abhorrence and loathing I scarcely endeavoured to conceal. I was rallied from several quarters for my abstraction and ungallant neglect of the ladies; but I cared little for that: all I cared about, besides that one grand subject of my thoughts, was to see the cups travel up to the tea-tray, and not come down again. I thought Mr. Millward never would cease telling us that he was no tea-drinker, and that it was highly injurious to keep loading the stomach with slops to the exclusion of more wholesome sustenance, and so give himself time to finish his fourth cup.

At length it was over; and I rose and left the table and the guests without a word of apology – I could endure their company no longer. I rushed out to cool my brain in the balmy evening air, and to compose my mind or indulge my passionate thoughts in the solitude of the garden.

To avoid being seen from the windows I went down a quiet little avenue that skirted one side of the inclosure, at the bottom of which was a seat embowered in roses and honeysuckles. Here I sat down to think over the virtues and wrongs of the lady of Wildfell Hall; but I had not been so occupied two minutes, before voices and laughter, and glimpses of moving objects through the trees, informed me that the whole company had turned out to take an airing in the garden too. However, I nestled up in a corner of the bower, and hoped to retain possession of it, secure alike from observation and intrusion. But no – confound it – there was some one coming down the avenue! Why couldn't they enjoy the flowers and sunshine of the open garden, and leave that sunless nook to me, and the gnats and midges?

But, peeping through my fragrant screen of the interwoven branches to discover who the intruders were (for a murmur of voices told me it was more than one), my vexation instantly subsided, and far other feelings agitated my still unquiet soul; for there was Mrs. Graham, slowly moving down the walk with Arthur by her side, and no one else. Why were they alone? Had the poison of detracting tongues already spread through all; and had they all turned their backs upon her? I now recollected having seen Mrs. Wilson, in the early part of the evening, edging her chair close up to my mother, and bending forward, evidently in the delivery of some important confidential intelligence; and from the incessant wagging of her head, the frequent distortions of her wrinkled physiognomy, and the winking and malicious twinkle of her little ugly eyes, I judged it was some spicy piece of scandal that engaged her powers; and from the cautious privacy of the communication I supposed some person then present was the luckless object of her calumnies: and from all these tokens, together with my mother's looks and gestures of mingled horror and incredulity, I now concluded that object to have been Mrs. Graham. I did not emerge from my place of concealment till she had nearly reached the bottom of the walk, lest my appearance should drive her away; and when I did step forward she stood still and seemed inclined to turn back as it was.

"Oh, don't let us disturb you, Mr. Markham!" said she. "We came here to seek retirement ourselves, not to intrude on your seclusion."

"I am no hermit, Mrs. Graham – though I own it looks rather like it to absent myself in this uncourteous fashion from my guests."

"I feared you were unwell," said she, with a look of real concern.

"I was rather, but it's over now. Do sit here a little and rest, and tell me how you like this arbour," said I, and, lifting Arthur by the shoulders, I planted him in the middle of the seat by way of securing his mamma, who, acknowledging it to be a tempting place of refuge, threw herself back in one corner, while I took possession of the other.

But that word refuge disturbed me. Had their unkindness then really driven her to seek for peace in solitude?

"Why have they left you alone?" I asked.

"It is I who have left them," was the smiling rejoinder. "I was wearied to death with small talk – nothing wears me out like that. I cannot imagine how they can go on as they do."

I could not help smiling at the serious depth of her wonderment.

"Is it that they think it a duty to be continually talking," pursued she: "and so never pause to think, but fill up with aimless trifles and vain repetitions when subjects of real interest fail to present themselves, or do they really take a pleasure in such discourse?"

"Very likely they do," said I; "their shallow minds can hold no great ideas, and their light heads are carried away by trivialities that would not move a better-furnished skull; and their only alternative to such discourse is to plunge over head and ears into the slough of scandal – which is their chief delight."

"Not all of them, surely?" cried the lady, astonished at the bitterness of my remark.

"No, certainly; I exonerate my sister from such degraded tastes, and my mother too, if you included her in your animadversions."

"I meant no animadversions against any one, and certainly intended no disrespectful allusions to your mother. I have known some sensible persons great adepts in that style of conversation when circumstances impelled them to it; but it is a gift I cannot boast the possession of. I kept up my attention on this occasion as long as I could, but when my powers were exhausted I stole away to seek a few minutes' repose in this quiet walk. I hate talking where there is no exchange of ideas or sentiments, and no good given or received."

"Well," said I, "if ever I trouble you with my loquacity, tell me so at once, and I promise not to be offended; for I possess the faculty of enjoying the company of those I – of my friends as well in silence as in conversation."

"I don't quite believe you; but if it were so you would exactly suit me for a companion."

"I am all you wish, then, in other respects?"

"No, I don't mean that. How beautiful those little clusters of foliage look, where the sun comes through behind them!" said she, on purpose to change the subject.

And they did look beautiful, where at intervals the level rays of the sun penetrating the thickness of trees and shrubs on the opposite side of the path before us, relieved their dusky verdure by displaying patches of semi-transparent leaves of resplendent golden green.

"I almost wish I were not a painter," observed my companion.

"Why so? One would think at such a time you would most exult in your privilege of being able to imitate the various brilliant and delightful touches of nature."

"No; for instead of delivering myself up to the full enjoyment of them as others do, I am always troubling my head about how I could produce the same effect upon canvas; and as that can never be done, it is more vanity and vexation of spirit."

"Perhaps you cannot do it to satisfy yourself, but you may and do succeed in delighting others with the result of your endeavours."

"Well, after all, I should not complain: perhaps few people gain their livelihood with so much pleasure in their toil as I do. Here is some one coming."

She seemed vexed at the interruption.

"It is only Mr. Lawrence and Miss Wilson," said I, "coming to enjoy a quiet stroll. They will not disturb us."

I could not quite decipher the expression of her face; but I was satisfied there was no jealousy therein. What business had I to look for it?

"What sort of a person is Miss Wilson?" she asked.

"She is elegant and accomplished above the generality of her birth and station; and some say she is ladylike and agreeable."

"I thought her somewhat frigid and rather supercilious in her manner today."

"Very likely she might be so to you. She has possibly taken a prejudice against you, for I think she regards you in the light of a rival."

"Me! Impossible, Mr. Markham!" said she, evidently astonished and annoyed.

"Well, I know nothing about it," returned I, rather doggedly; for I thought her annoyance was chiefly against myself.

The pair had now approached within a few paces of us. Our arbour was set snugly back in a corner, before which the avenue at its termination turned off into the more airy walk along the bottom of the garden. As they approached this, I saw, by the aspect of Jane Wilson, that she was directing her companion's attention to us; and, as well by her cold, sarcastic smile as by the few isolated words of her discourse that reached me, I knew full well that she was impressing him with the idea, that we were strongly attached to each other. I noticed that he coloured up to the temples, gave us one furtive glance in passing, and walked on, looking grave, but seemingly offering no reply to her remarks.

It was true, then, that he had some designs upon Mrs. Graham; and, were they honourable, he would not be so anxious to conceal them. She was blameless, of course, but he was detestable beyond all count.

While these thoughts flashed through my mind, my companion abruptly rose, and calling her son, said they would now go in quest of the company, and departed up the avenue. Doubtless she had heard or guessed something of Miss Wilson's remarks, and therefore it was natural enough she should choose to continue the *tête-à-tête* no longer, especially as at that moment my cheeks were burning with indignation against my former friend, the token of which she might mistake for a blush of stupid embarrassment. For this I owed Miss Wilson yet another grudge; and still the more I thought upon her conduct the more I hated her.

It was late in the evening before I joined the company. I found Mrs. Graham already equipped for departure, and taking leave of the rest, who were now returned to the house. I offered, nay, begged to accompany her home. Mr. Lawrence was standing by at the time conversing with some one else. He did not look at us, but, on hearing my earnest request, he paused in the middle of a sentence to listen for her reply, and went on, with a look of quiet satisfaction, the moment he found it was to be a denial.

A denial it was, decided, though not unkind. She could not be persuaded to think there was danger for herself or her child in traversing those lonely lanes and fields without attendance. It was daylight still, and she should meet no one; or if she did, the people were quiet and harmless she was well assured. In fact, she would not hear of any one's putting himself out of the way to accompany her, though Fergus vouchsafed to offer his services in case they should be more acceptable than mine, and my mother begged she might send one of the farming-men to escort her.

When she was gone the rest was all a blank or worse. Lawrence attempted to draw me into conversation, but I snubbed him and went to another part of the room. Shortly after the party broke up and he himself took leave. When he came to me I was blind to his extended hand, and deaf to his goodnight till he repeated it a second time; and then, to get rid of him, I muttered an inarticulate reply, accompanied by a sulky nod.

"What is the matter, Markham?" whispered he.

I replied by a wrathful and contemptuous stare.

"Are you angry because Mrs. Graham would not let you go home with her?" he asked, with a faint smile that nearly exasperated me beyond control.

But, swallowing down all fiercer answers, I merely demanded, – "What business is it of yours?"

"Why, none," replied he with provoking quietness; "only," – and he raised his eyes to my face, and spoke with unusual solemnity, – "only let me tell you, Markham, that if you have any designs in that quarter, they will certainly fail; and it grieves me to see you cherishing false hopes, and wasting your strength in useless efforts, for –"

"Hypocrite!" I exclaimed; and he held his breath, and looked very blank, turned white about the gills, and went away without another word.

I had wounded him to the quick; and I was glad of it.

Chapter Ten

WHEN ALL were gone, I learnt that the vile slander had indeed been circulated throughout the company, in the very presence of the victim. Rose, however, vowed she did not and would not believe it, and my mother made the same declaration, though not, I fear, with the same amount of real, unwavering incredulity. It seemed to dwell continually on her mind, and she kept irritating me from time to time by such expressions as – "Dear, dear, who would have thought it! – Well! I always thought there was something odd about her. – You see what it is for women to affect to be different to other people." And once it was, – "I misdoubted that appearance of mystery from the very first – I thought there would no good come of it; but this is a sad, sad business, to be sure!"

"Why, mother, you said you didn't believe these tales," said Fergus.

"No more I do, my dear; but then, you know, there must be some foundation."

"The foundation is in the wickedness and falsehood of the world," said I, "and in the fact that Mr. Lawrence has been seen to go that way once or twice of an evening – and the village gossips say he goes to pay his addresses to the strange lady, and the scandal-mongers have greedily seized the rumour, to make it the basis of their own infernal structure."

"Well, but, Gilbert, there must be something in her manner to countenance such reports."

"Did you see anything in her manner?"

"No, certainly; but then, you know, I always said there was something strange about her."

I believe it was on that very evening that I ventured on another invasion of Wildfell Hall. From the time of our party, which was upwards of a week ago, I had been making daily efforts to meet its mistress in her walks; and always disappointed (she must have managed it so on purpose), had nightly kept revolving in my mind some pretext for another call. At length I concluded that the separation could be endured no longer (by this time, you will see, I was pretty far gone); and, taking from the book-case an old volume that I thought she might be interested in, though, from its unsightly and somewhat dilapidated condition, I had not yet ventured to offer it for perusal, I hastened away, – but not without sundry misgivings as to how she would receive me, or how I could summon courage to present myself with so slight an excuse. But, perhaps, I might see her in the field or the garden, and then there would be no great difficulty: it was the formal knocking at the door, with the prospect of being gravely ushered in by Rachel, to the presence of a surprised, uncordial mistress, that so greatly disturbed me.

My wish, however, was not gratified. Mrs. Graham herself was not to be seen; but there was Arthur playing with his frolicsome little dog in the garden. I looked over the gate and called him to me. He wanted me to come in; but I told him I could not without his mother's leave.

"I'll go and ask her," said the child.

"No, no, Arthur, you mustn't do that; but if she's not engaged, just ask her to come here a minute. Tell her I want to speak to her."

He ran to perform my bidding, and quickly returned with his mother. How lovely she looked with her dark ringlets streaming in the light summer breeze, her fair cheek slightly flushed, and her countenance radiant with smiles. Dear Arthur! What did I not owe to you for this and every other happy meeting? Through him I was at once delivered from all formality, and terror, and constraint. In love affairs, there is no mediator like a merry, simple-hearted child – ever ready to cement divided hearts, to span the unfriendly gulf of custom, to melt the ice of cold reserve, and overthrow the separating walls of dread formality and pride.

"Well, Mr. Markham, what is it?" said the young mother, accosting me with a pleasant smile.

"I want you to look at this book, and, if you please, to take it, and peruse it at your leisure. I make no apology for calling you out on such a lovely evening, though it be for a matter of no greater importance."

"Tell him to come in, mamma," said Arthur.

"Would you like to come in?" asked the lady.

"Yes; I should like to see your improvements in the garden."

"And how your sister's roots have prospered in my charge," added she, as she opened the gate.

And we sauntered through the garden, and talked of the flowers, the trees, and the book, and then of other things. The evening was kind and genial, and so was my companion. By degrees I waxed more warm and tender than, perhaps, I had ever been before; but still I said nothing tangible, and she attempted no repulse, until, in passing a moss rose-tree that I had brought her some weeks since, in my sister's name, she plucked a beautiful half-open bud and bade me give it to Rose.

"May I not keep it myself?" I asked.

"No; but here is another for you."

Instead of taking it quietly, I likewise took the hand that offered it, and looked into her face. She let me hold it for a moment, and I saw a flash of ecstatic brilliance in her eye, a glow of glad excitement on her face – I thought my hour of victory was come – but instantly a painful recollection seemed to flash upon her; a cloud of anguish darkened her brow, a marble paleness blanched her cheek and lip; there seemed a moment of inward conflict, and, with a sudden effort, she withdrew her hand, and retreated a step or two back.

"Now, Mr. Markham," said she, with a kind of desperate calmness, "I must tell you plainly that I cannot do with this. I like your company, because I am alone here, and your conversation pleases me more than that of any other person; but if you cannot be content to regard me as a friend – a plain, cold, motherly, or sisterly friend – I must beg you to leave me now, and let me alone hereafter: in fact, we must be strangers for the future."

"I will, then – be your friend, or brother, or anything you wish, if you will only let me continue to see you; but tell me why I cannot be anything more?"

There was a perplexed and thoughtful pause.

"Is it in consequence of some rash vow?"

"It is something of the kind," she answered. "Some day I may tell you, but at present you had better leave me; and never, Gilbert, put me to the painful necessity of repeating what I have just now said to you," she earnestly added, giving me her hand in serious kindness. How sweet, how musical my own name sounded in her mouth!

"I will not," I replied. "But you pardon this offence?"

"On condition that you never repeat it."

"And may I come to see you now and then?"

"Perhaps – occasionally; provided you never abuse the privilege."

"I make no empty promises, but you shall see."

"The moment you do our intimacy is at an end, that's all."

"And will you always call me Gilbert? It sounds more sisterly, and it will serve to remind me of our contract."

She smiled, and once more bid me go; and at length I judged it prudent to obey, and she re-entered the house and I went down the hill. But as I went the tramp of horses' hoofs fell on my ear, and broke the stillness of the dewy evening; and, looking towards the lane, I saw a solitary equestrian coming up. Inclining to dusk as it was, I knew him at a glance: it was Mr. Lawrence on his grey pony. I flew across the field, leaped the stone fence, and then walked down the lane to meet him. On seeing me, he suddenly drew in his little steed, and seemed inclined to turn back, but on second thought apparently judged it better to continue his course as before. He accosted me with a slight bow, and, edging close to the wall, endeavoured to pass on; but I was not so minded. Seizing his horse by the bridle, I exclaimed, – "Now, Lawrence, I will have this mystery explained! Tell me where you are going, and what you mean to do – at once, and distinctly!"

"Will you take your hand off the bridle?" said he, quietly – "you're hurting my pony's mouth."

"You and your pony be –"

"What makes you so coarse and brutal, Markham? I'm quite ashamed of you."

"You answer my questions – before you leave this spot I will know what you mean by this perfidious duplicity!"

"I shall answer no questions till you let go the bridle, – if you stand till morning."

"Now then," said I, unclosing my hand, but still standing before him.

"Ask me some other time, when you can speak like a gentleman," returned he, and he made an effort to pass me again; but I quickly re-captured the pony, scarce less astonished than its master at such uncivil usage.

"Really, Mr. Markham, this is too much!" said the latter. "Can I not go to see my tenant on matters of business, without being assaulted in this manner by –?"

"This is no time for business, sir! – I'll tell you, now, what I think of your conduct."

"You'd better defer your opinion to a more convenient season," interrupted he in a low tone – "here's the vicar." And, in truth, the vicar was just behind me, plodding homeward from some remote corner of his parish. I immediately released the squire; and he went on his way, saluting Mr. Millward as he passed.

"What! Quarrelling, Markham?" cried the latter, addressing himself to me, – "and about that young widow, I doubt?" he added, reproachfully shaking his head. "But let me tell you, young man" (here he put his face into mine with an important, confidential air), "she's not worth it!" and he confirmed the assertion by a solemn nod.

"Mr. Millward," I exclaimed, in a tone of wrathful menace that made the reverend gentleman look round – aghast – astounded at such unwonted insolence, and stare me in the face, with a look that plainly said, "What, this to me!" But I was too indignant to apologise, or to speak another word to him: I turned away, and hastened homewards, descending with rapid strides the steep, rough lane, and leaving him to follow as he pleased.

Chapter Eleven

YOU MUST SUPPOSE about three weeks passed over. Mrs. Graham and I were now established friends – or brother and sister, as we rather chose to consider ourselves. She called me Gilbert, by my express desire, and I called her Helen, for I had seen that name written in her books. I seldom attempted to see her above twice a week; and still I made our meetings appear the result of accident as often as I could – for I found it necessary to be extremely careful – and, altogether, I behaved with such exceeding propriety that she never had occasion to reprove me once. Yet I could not but perceive that she was at times unhappy and dissatisfied with herself or her position, and truly I myself was not quite contented with the latter: this assumption of brotherly nonchalance was very hard to sustain, and I often felt myself a most confounded hypocrite with it all; I saw too, or rather I felt, that, in spite of herself, "I was not indifferent to her," as the novel heroes modestly express it, and while I thankfully enjoyed my present good fortune, I could not fail to wish and hope for something better in future; but, of course, I kept such dreams entirely to myself.

"Where are you going, Gilbert?" said Rose, one evening, shortly after tea, when I had been busy with the farm all day.

"To take a walk," was the reply.

"Do you always brush your hat so carefully, and do your hair so nicely, and put on such smart new gloves when you take a walk?"

"Not always."

"You're going to Wildfell Hall, aren't you?"

"What makes you think so?"

"Because you look as if you were – but I wish you wouldn't go so often."

"Nonsense, child! I don't go once in six weeks – what do you mean?"

"Well, but if I were you, I wouldn't have so much to do with Mrs. Graham."

"Why, Rose, are you, too, giving in to the prevailing opinion?"

"No," returned she, hesitatingly – "but I've heard so much about her lately, both at the Wilsons' and the vicarage; – and besides, mamma says, if she were a proper person she would not be living there by herself – and don't you remember last winter, Gilbert, all that about the false name to the picture; and how she explained it – saying she had friends or acquaintances from whom she wished her present residence to be concealed, and that she was afraid of their tracing her out; – and then, how suddenly she started up and left the room when that person came – whom she took good care not to let us catch a glimpse of, and who Arthur, with such an air of mystery, told us was his mamma's friend?"

"Yes, Rose, I remember it all; and I can forgive your uncharitable conclusions; for, perhaps, if I did not know her myself, I should put all these things together, and believe the same as you do; but thank God, I do know her; and I should be unworthy the name of a man, if I could believe anything that was said against her, unless I heard it from her own lips. – I should as soon believe such things of you, Rose."

"Oh, Gilbert!"

"Well, do you think I could believe anything of the kind, – whatever the Wilsons and Millwards dared to whisper?"

"I should hope not indeed!"

"And why not? – Because I know you – Well, and I know her just as well."

"Oh, no! You know nothing of her former life; and last year, at this time, you did not know that such a person existed."

"No matter. There is such a thing as looking through a person's eyes into the heart, and learning more of the height, and breadth, and depth of another's soul in one hour than it might take you a lifetime to discover, if he or she were not disposed to reveal it, or if you had not the sense to understand it."

"Then you are going to see her this evening?"

"To be sure I am!"

"But what would mamma say, Gilbert!"

"Mamma needn't know."

"But she must know some time, if you go on."

"Go on! – There's no going on in the matter. Mrs. Graham and I are two friends – and will be; and no man breathing shall hinder it, – or has a right to interfere between us."

"But if you knew how they talk you would be more careful, for her sake as well as for your own. Jane Wilson thinks your visits to the old hall but another proof of her depravity –"

"Confound Jane Wilson!"

"And Eliza Millward is quite grieved about you."

"I hope she is."

"But I wouldn't, if I were you."

"Wouldn't what? – How do they know that I go there?"

"There's nothing hid from them: they spy out everything."

"Oh, I never thought of this! – And so they dare to turn my friendship into food for further scandal against her! – That proves the falsehood of their other lies, at all events, if any proof were wanting. – Mind you contradict them, Rose, whenever you can."

"But they don't speak openly to me about such things: it is only by hints and innuendoes, and by what I hear others say, that I knew what they think."

"Well, then, I won't go today, as it's getting latish. But oh, deuce take their cursed, envenomed tongues!" I muttered, in the bitterness of my soul.

And just at that moment the vicar entered the room: we had been too much absorbed in our conversation to observe his knock. After his customary cheerful and fatherly greeting of Rose, who was rather a favourite with the old gentleman, he turned somewhat sternly to me:

"Well, sir!" said he, "you're quite a stranger. It is – let – me – see," he continued, slowly, as he deposited his ponderous bulk in the arm-chair that Rose officiously brought towards him; "it is just – six-weeks – by my reckoning, since you darkened – my – door!" He spoke it with emphasis, and struck his stick on the floor.

"Is it, sir?" said I.

"Ay! It is so!" He added an affirmatory nod, and continued to gaze upon me with a kind of irate solemnity, holding his substantial stick between his knees, with his hands clasped upon its head.

"I have been busy," I said, for an apology was evidently demanded.

"Busy!" repeated he, derisively.

"Yes, you know I've been getting in my hay; and now the harvest is beginning."

"Humph!"

Just then my mother came in, and created a diversion in my favour by her loquacious and animated welcome of the reverend guest. She regretted deeply that he had not come a little earlier, in time for tea, but offered to have some immediately prepared, if he would do her the favour to partake of it.

"Not any for me, I thank you," replied he; "I shall be at home in a few minutes."

"Oh, but do stay and take a little! It will be ready in five minutes."

But he rejected the offer with a majestic wave of the hand.

"I'll tell you what I'll take, Mrs. Markham," said he: "I'll take a glass of your excellent ale."

"With pleasure!" cried my mother, proceeding with alacrity to pull the bell and order the favoured beverage.

"I thought," continued he, "I'd just look in upon you as I passed, and taste your home-brewed ale. I've been to call on Mrs. Graham."

"Have you, indeed?"

He nodded gravely, and added with awful emphasis – "I thought it incumbent upon me to do so."

"Really!" ejaculated my mother.

"Why so, Mr. Millward?" asked I.

He looked at me with some severity, and turning again to my mother, repeated, – "I thought it incumbent upon me!" and struck his stick on the floor again. My mother sat opposite, an awe-struck but admiring auditor.

"'Mrs. Graham,' said I," he continued, shaking his head as he spoke, "'these are terrible reports!' 'What, sir?' says she, affecting to be ignorant of my meaning. 'It is my – duty – as – your pastor,' said I, 'to tell you both everything that I myself see reprehensible in your conduct, and all I have reason to suspect, and what others tell me concerning you.' – So I told her!"

"You did, sir?" cried I, starting from my seat and striking my fist on the table. He merely glanced towards me, and continued – addressing his hostess:

"It was a painful duty, Mrs. Markham – but I told her!"

"And how did she take it?" asked my mother.

"Hardened, I fear – hardened!" he replied, with a despondent shake of the head; "and, at the same time, there was a strong display of unchastened, misdirected passions. She turned white in the face, and drew her breath through her teeth in a savage sort of way; – but she offered no extenuation or defence; and with a kind of shameless calmness – shocking indeed to witness in one so young – as good as told me that my remonstrance was unavailing, and my pastoral advice quite thrown away upon her – nay, that my very presence was displeasing while I spoke such things. And I withdrew at length, too plainly seeing that nothing could be done – and sadly grieved to find her case so hopeless. But I am fully determined, Mrs. Markham, that my daughters – shall – not – consort with her. Do you adopt the same resolution with regard to yours! – As for your sons – as for you, young man," he continued, sternly turning to me –

"As for *me*, sir," I began, but checked by some impediment in my utterance, and finding that my whole frame trembled with fury, I said no more, but took the wiser part of snatching up my hat and bolting from the room, slamming the door behind me, with a bang that shook the house to its foundations, and made my mother scream, and gave a momentary relief to my excited feelings.

The next minute saw me hurrying with rapid strides in the direction of Wildfell Hall – to what intent or purpose I could scarcely tell, but I must be moving somewhere, and no other goal would do – I must see her too, and speak to her – that was certain; but what to say, or how to act, I had no definite idea. Such stormy thoughts – so many different resolutions crowded in upon me, that my mind was little better than a chaos of conflicting passions.

Chapter Twelve

IN LITTLE MORE than twenty minutes the journey was accomplished. I paused at the gate to wipe my streaming forehead, and recover my breath and some degree of composure. Already the rapid walking had somewhat mitigated my excitement; and with a firm and steady tread I paced the garden-walk. In passing the inhabited wing of the building, I caught a sight of Mrs. Graham, through the open window, slowly pacing up and down her lonely room.

She seemed agitated and even dismayed at my arrival, as if she thought I too was coming to accuse her. I had entered her presence intending to condole with her upon the wickedness of the world, and help her to abuse the vicar and his vile informants, but now I felt positively ashamed to mention the subject, and determined not to refer to it, unless she led the way.

"I am come at an unseasonable hour," said I, assuming a cheerfulness I did not feel, in order to reassure her; "but I won't stay many minutes."

She smiled upon me, faintly it is true, but most kindly – I had almost said thankfully, as her apprehensions were removed.

"How dismal you are, Helen! Why have you no fire?" I said, looking round on the gloomy apartment.

"It is summer yet," she replied.

"But we always have a fire in the evenings, if we can bear it; and you especially require one in this cold house and dreary room."

"You should have come a little sooner, and I would have had one lighted for you: but it is not worth while now – you won't stay many minutes, you say, and Arthur is gone to bed."

"But I have a fancy for a fire, nevertheless. Will you order one, if I ring?"

"Why, Gilbert, you don't look cold!" said she, smilingly regarding my face, which no doubt seemed warm enough.

"No," replied I, "but I want to see you comfortable before I go."

"Me comfortable!" repeated she, with a bitter laugh, as if there were something amusingly absurd in the idea. "It suits me better as it is," she added, in a tone of mournful resignation.

But determined to have my own way, I pulled the bell.

"There now, Helen!" I said, as the approaching steps of Rachel were heard in answer to the summons. There was nothing for it but to turn round and desire the maid to light the fire.

I owe Rachel a grudge to this day for the look she cast upon me ere she departed on her mission, the sour, suspicious, inquisitorial look that plainly demanded, "What are you here for, I wonder?" Her mistress did not fail to notice it, and a shade of uneasiness darkened her brow.

"You must not stay long, Gilbert," said she, when the door was closed upon us.

"I'm not going to," said I, somewhat testily, though without a grain of anger in my heart against any one but the meddling old woman. "But, Helen, I've something to say to you before I go."

"What is it?"

"No, not now – I don't know yet precisely what it is, or how to say it," replied I, with more truth than wisdom; and then, fearing lest she should turn me out of the house, I began talking about indifferent matters in order to gain time. Meanwhile Rachel came in to kindle the fire, which was soon effected by thrusting a red-hot poker between the bars of the grate, where the fuel was already disposed for ignition. She honoured me with another of her hard, inhospitable looks in departing, but, little moved thereby, I went on talking; and setting a chair for Mrs. Graham on one side of the hearth, and one for myself on the other, I ventured to sit down, though half suspecting she would rather see me go.

In a little while we both relapsed into silence, and continued for several minutes gazing abstractedly into the fire – she intent upon her own sad thoughts, and I reflecting how delightful it would be to be seated thus beside her with no other presence to restrain our intercourse – not even that of Arthur, our mutual friend, without whom we had never met before – if only I could venture to speak my mind, and disburden my full heart of the feelings that had so long oppressed it, and which it now struggled to retain, with an effort that it seemed impossible to continue much longer, – and revolving the pros and cons for opening my heart to her there and then, and imploring a return of affection, the permission to regard her thenceforth as my own, and the right and the power to defend her from the calumnies of malicious tongues. On the one hand, I felt a new-born confidence in my powers of persuasion – a strong conviction that my own fervour of spirit would grant me eloquence – that my very determination – the absolute necessity for succeeding, that I felt must win me what I sought; while, on the other, I feared to lose the ground I had already gained with so much toil and skill, and destroy all future hope by one rash effort, when time and patience might have won success. It was like setting my life upon the cast of a die; and yet I was ready to resolve upon the attempt. At any rate, I would entreat the explanation she had half promised to give me before; I would demand the reason of this hateful barrier, this mysterious impediment to my happiness, and, as I trusted, to her own.

But while I considered in what manner I could best frame my request, my companion, wakened from her reverie with a scarcely audible sigh, and looking towards the window, where the blood-red harvest moon, just rising over one of the grim, fantastic evergreens, was shining in upon us, said, – "Gilbert, it is getting late."

"I see," said I. "You want me to go, I suppose?"

"I think you ought. If my kind neighbours get to know of this visit – as no doubt they will – they will not turn it much to my advantage." It was with what the vicar would doubtless have called a savage sort of smile that she said this.

"Let them turn it as they will," said I. "What are their thoughts to you or me, so long as we are satisfied with ourselves – and each other. Let them go to the deuce with their vile constructions and their lying inventions!"

This outburst brought a flush of colour to her face.

"You have heard, then, what they say of me?"

"I heard some detestable falsehoods; but none but fools would credit them for a moment, Helen, so don't let them trouble you."

"I did not think Mr. Millward a fool, and he believes it all; but however little you may value the opinions of those about you – however little you may esteem them as individuals, it is not pleasant to be looked upon as a liar and a hypocrite, to be thought to practise what you abhor, and to encourage the vices you would discountenance, to find your good intentions frustrated, and your hands crippled by your supposed unworthiness, and to bring disgrace on the principles you profess."

"True; and if I, by my thoughtlessness and selfish disregard to appearances, have at all assisted to expose you to these evils, let me entreat you not only to pardon me, but to enable me to make reparation; authorise me to clear your name from every imputation: give me the right to identify your honour with my own, and to defend your reputation as more precious than my life!"

"Are you hero enough to unite yourself to one whom you know to be suspected and despised by all around you, and identify your interests and your honour with hers? Think! It is a serious thing."

"I should be proud to do it, Helen! – Most happy – delighted beyond expression! – And if that be all the obstacle to our union, it is demolished, and you must – you shall be mine!"

And starting from my seat in a frenzy of ardour, I seized her hand and would have pressed it to my lips, but she as suddenly caught it away, exclaiming in the bitterness of intense affliction, – "No, no, it is not all!"

"What is it, then? You promised I should know some time, and –"

"You shall know some time – but not now – my head aches terribly," she said, pressing her hand to her forehead, "and I must have some repose – and surely I have had misery enough today!" she added, almost wildly.

"But it could not harm you to tell it," I persisted: "it would ease your mind; and I should then know how to comfort you."

She shook her head despondingly. "If you knew all, you, too, would blame me – perhaps even more than I deserve – though I have cruelly wronged you," she added in a low murmur, as if she mused aloud.

"You, Helen? Impossible?"

"Yes, not willingly; for I did not know the strength and depth of your attachment. I thought – at least I endeavoured to think your regard for me was as cold and fraternal as you professed it to be."

"Or as yours?"

"Or as mine – ought to have been – of such a light and selfish, superficial nature, that –"

"There, indeed, you wronged me."

"I know I did; and, sometimes, I suspected it then; but I thought, upon the whole, there could be no great harm in leaving your fancies and your hopes to dream themselves to nothing – or flutter away to some more fitting object, while your friendly sympathies remained with me; but if I had known the depth of your regard, the generous, disinterested affection you seem to feel –"

"Seem, Helen?"

"That you do feel, then, I would have acted differently."

"How? You could not have given me less encouragement, or treated me with greater severity than you did! And if you think you have wronged me by giving me your friendship, and occasionally admitting me to the enjoyment of your company and conversation, when all hopes of closer intimacy were vain – as indeed you always gave me to understand – if you think you have wronged me by this, you are mistaken; for such favours, in themselves alone, are not only delightful to my heart, but purifying, exalting, ennobling to my soul; and I would rather have your friendship than the love of any other woman in the world!"

Little comforted by this, she clasped her hands upon her knee, and glancing upward, seemed, in silent anguish, to implore divine assistance; then, turning to me, she calmly said, – "Tomorrow, if you meet me on the moor about mid-day, I will tell you all you seek to know; and perhaps you will then see the necessity of discontinuing our intimacy – if, indeed, you do not willingly resign me as one no longer worthy of regard."

"I can safely answer no to that: you cannot have such grave confessions to make – you must be trying my faith, Helen."

"No, no, no," she earnestly repeated – "I wish it were so! Thank heaven!" she added, "I have no great crime to confess; but I have more than you will like to hear, or, perhaps, can readily excuse, – and more than I can tell you now; so let me entreat you to leave me!"

"I will; but answer me this one question first; – do you love me?"

"I will not answer it!"

"Then I will conclude you do; and so goodnight."

She turned from me to hide the emotion she could not quite control; but I took her hand and fervently kissed it.

"Gilbert, do leave me!" she cried, in a tone of such thrilling anguish that I felt it would be cruel to disobey.

But I gave one look back before I closed the door, and saw her leaning forward on the table, with her hands pressed against her eyes, sobbing convulsively; yet I withdrew in silence. I felt that to obtrude my consolations on her then would only serve to aggravate her sufferings.

To tell you all the questionings and conjectures – the fears, and hopes, and wild emotions that jostled and chased each other through my mind as I descended the hill, would almost fill a volume in itself. But before I was half-way down, a sentiment of strong sympathy for her I had left behind me had displaced all other feelings, and seemed imperatively to draw me back: I began to think, "Why am I hurrying so fast in this direction? Can I find comfort or consolation – peace, certainty, contentment, all – or anything that I want at home? And can I leave all perturbation, sorrow, and anxiety behind me there?"

And I turned round to look at the old Hall. There was little besides the chimneys visible above my contracted horizon. I walked back to get a better view of it. When it rose in sight, I stood still a moment to look, and then continued moving towards the gloomy object of attraction. Something called me nearer – nearer still – and why not, pray? Might I not find more benefit in the contemplation of that venerable pile with the full moon in the cloudless heaven shining so calmly above it – with that warm yellow lustre peculiar to an August night – and the mistress of my soul within, than in returning to my home, where all comparatively was light, and life, and cheerfulness, and therefore inimical to me in my present frame of mind, – and the more so that its inmates all were more or less imbued with that detestable belief, the very thought of which made my blood boil in my veins – and how could I endure to hear it openly declared, or cautiously insinuated – which was worse? – I had had trouble enough already, with some babbling fiend that would keep whispering in my ear, "It may be true," till I had shouted aloud, "It is false! I defy you to make me suppose it!"

I could see the red firelight dimly gleaming from her parlour window. I went up to the garden wall, and stood leaning over it, with my eyes fixed upon the lattice, wondering what she was doing, thinking, or suffering now, and wishing I could speak to her but one word, or even catch one glimpse of her, before I went.

I had not thus looked, and wished, and wondered long, before I vaulted over the barrier, unable to resist the temptation of taking one glance through the window, just to see if she were more composed than when we parted; – and if I found her still in deep distress, perhaps I might venture attempt a word of comfort – to utter one of the many things I should have said before, instead of aggravating her sufferings by my stupid impetuosity. I looked. Her chair was vacant: so was the room. But at that moment some one opened the outer door, and a voice – her voice – said, – "Come out – I want to see the moon, and breathe the evening air: they will do me good – if anything will."

Here, then, were she and Rachel coming to take a walk in the garden. I wished myself safe back over the wall. I stood, however, in the shadow of the tall holly-bush, which, standing between the window and the porch, at present screened me from observation, but did not prevent me from seeing two figures come forth into the moonlight: Mrs. Graham followed by another – not Rachel, but a young man, slender and rather tall. O heavens, how my temples throbbed! Intense anxiety darkened my sight; but I thought – yes, and the voice confirmed it – it was Mr. Lawrence!

"You should not let it worry you so much, Helen," said he; "I will be more careful in future; and in time –"

I did not hear the rest of the sentence; for he walked close beside her and spoke so gently that I could not catch the words. My heart was splitting with hatred; but I listened intently for her reply. I heard it plainly enough.

"But I must leave this place, Frederick," she said – "I never can be happy here, – nor anywhere else, indeed," she added, with a mirthless laugh, – "but I cannot rest here."

"But where could you find a better place?" replied he, "so secluded – so near me, if you think anything of that."

"Yes," interrupted she, "it is all I could wish, if they could only have left me alone."

"But wherever you go, Helen, there will be the same sources of annoyance. I cannot consent to lose you: I must go with you, or come to you; and there are meddling fools elsewhere, as well as here."

While thus conversing they had sauntered slowly past me, down the walk, and I heard no more of their discourse; but I saw him put his arm round her waist, while she lovingly rested her hand on his shoulder; – and then, a tremulous darkness obscured my sight, my heart sickened and my head burned like fire: I half rushed, half staggered from the spot, where horror had kept me rooted, and leaped or tumbled over the wall – I hardly know which – but I know that, afterwards, like a passionate child, I dashed myself on the ground and lay there in a paroxysm of anger and despair – how long, I cannot undertake to say; but it must have been a considerable time; for when, having partially relieved myself by a torment of tears, and looked up at the moon, shining so calmly and carelessly on, as little influenced by my misery as I was by its peaceful radiance, and earnestly prayed for death or forgetfulness, I had risen and journeyed homewards – little regarding the way, but carried instinctively by my feet to the door, I found it bolted against me, and every one in bed except my mother, who hastened to answer my impatient knocking, and received me with a shower of questions and rebukes.

"Oh, Gilbert! How could you do so? Where have you been? Do come in and take your supper. I've got it all ready, though you don't deserve it, for keeping me in such a fright, after the strange manner you left the house this evening. Mr. Millward was quite – Bless the boy! How ill he looks. Oh, gracious! What is the matter?"

"Nothing, nothing – give me a candle."

"But won't you take some supper?"

"No; I want to go to bed," said I, taking a candle and lighting it at the one she held in her hand.

"Oh, Gilbert, how you tremble!" exclaimed my anxious parent. "How white you look! Do tell me what it is? Has anything happened?"

"It's nothing," cried I, ready to stamp with vexation because the candle would not light. Then, suppressing my irritation, I added, "I've been walking too fast, that's all. Goodnight," and marched off to bed, regardless of the "Walking too fast! Where have you been?" that was called after me from below.

My mother followed me to the very door of my room with her questionings and advice concerning my health and my conduct; but I implored her to let me alone till morning; and she withdrew, and at length I had the satisfaction to hear her close her own door. There was no sleep for me, however, that night as I thought; and instead of attempting to solicit it, I employed myself in rapidly pacing the chamber, having first removed my boots, lest my mother should hear me. But the boards creaked, and she was watchful. I had not walked above a quarter of an hour before she was at the door again.

"Gilbert, why are you not in bed – you said you wanted to go?"

"Confound it! I'm going," said I.

"But why are you so long about it? You must have something on your mind –"

"For heaven's sake, let me alone, and get to bed yourself."

"Can it be that Mrs. Graham that distresses you so?"

"No, no, I tell you – it's nothing."

"I wish to goodness it mayn't," murmured she, with a sigh, as she returned to her own apartment, while I threw myself on the bed, feeling most undutifully disaffected towards her for having deprived me of what seemed the only shadow of a consolation that remained, and chained me to that wretched couch of thorns.

Never did I endure so long, so miserable a night as that. And yet it was not wholly sleepless. Towards morning my distracting thoughts began to lose all pretensions to coherency, and shape themselves into confused and feverish dreams, and, at length, there followed an interval of unconscious slumber. But then the dawn of bitter recollection that succeeded – the waking to find life a blank, and worse than a blank, teeming with torment and misery – not a mere barren wilderness, but full of thorns and briers – to find myself deceived, duped, hopeless, my affections trampled upon, my angel not an angel, and my friend a fiend incarnate – it was worse than if I had not slept at all.

It was a dull, gloomy morning; the weather had changed like my prospects, and the rain was pattering against the window. I rose, nevertheless, and went out; not to look after the farm, though that would serve as my excuse, but to cool my brain, and regain, if possible, a sufficient degree of composure to meet the family at the morning meal without exciting inconvenient remarks. If I got a wetting, that, in conjunction with a pretended over-exertion before breakfast, might excuse my sudden loss of appetite; and if a cold ensued, the severer the better – it would help to account for the sullen moods and moping melancholy likely to cloud my brow for long enough.

Chapter Thirteen

"MY DEAR Gilbert, I wish you would try to be a little more amiable," said my mother one morning after some display of unjustifiable ill-humour on my part. "You say there is nothing the matter with you, and nothing has happened to grieve you, and yet I never saw anyone so altered as you within these last few days. You haven't a good word for anybody – friends and strangers, equals and inferiors – it's all the same. I do wish you'd try to check it."

"Check what?"

"Why, your strange temper. You don't know how it spoils you. I'm sure a finer disposition than yours by nature could not be, if you'd let it have fair play: so you've no excuse that way."

While she thus remonstrated, I took up a book, and laying it open on the table before me, pretended to be deeply absorbed in its perusal, for I was equally unable to justify myself and unwilling to acknowledge my errors; and I wished to have nothing to say on the matter. But my excellent parent went on lecturing, and then came to coaxing, and began to stroke my hair; and I was getting to feel quite a good boy, but my mischievous brother, who was idling about the room, revived my corruption by suddenly calling out, – "Don't touch him, mother! He'll bite! He's a very tiger in human form. I've given him up for my part – fairly disowned him – cast him off, root and branch. It's as much as my life is worth to come within six yards of him. The other day he nearly fractured my skull for singing a pretty, inoffensive love-song, on purpose to amuse him."

"Oh, Gilbert! How could you?" exclaimed my mother.

"I told you to hold your noise first, you know, Fergus," said I.

"Yes, but when I assured you it was no trouble and went on with the next verse, thinking you might like it better, you clutched me by the shoulder and dashed me away, right against the wall there, with such force that I thought I had bitten my tongue in two, and expected to see the place plastered with my brains; and when I put my hand to my head, and found my skull not broken, I thought it was a miracle, and no mistake. But, poor fellow!" added he, with a sentimental sigh – "his heart's broken – that's the truth of it – and his head's –"

"Will you be silent *now*?" cried I, starting up, and eyeing the fellow so fiercely that my mother, thinking I meant to inflict some grievous bodily injury, laid her hand on my arm, and besought me to let him alone, and he walked leisurely out, with his hands in his pockets, singing provokingly – "Shall I, because a woman's fair," etc.

"I'm not going to defile my fingers with him," said I, in answer to the maternal intercession. "I wouldn't touch him with the tongs."

I now recollected that I had business with Robert Wilson, concerning the purchase of a certain field adjoining my farm – a business I had been putting off from day to day; for I had no interest in anything now; and besides, I was misanthropically inclined, and, moreover, had a particular objection to meeting Jane Wilson or her mother; for though I had too good reason, now, to credit their reports concerning Mrs. Graham, I did not like them a bit the better for it – or Eliza Millward either – and the thought of meeting them was the more repugnant to me that I could not, now, defy their seeming calumnies and triumph in my own convictions as before. But today I determined to make an effort to return to my duty. Though I found no pleasure in it, it would be less irksome than idleness – at all events it would be more profitable. If life promised no enjoyment within my vocation, at least it offered no allurements out of it; and henceforth I would put my shoulder to the wheel and toil away, like any poor drudge of a cart-horse that was fairly broken in to its labour, and plod through life, not wholly useless if not agreeable, and uncomplaining if not contented with my lot.

Thus resolving, with a kind of sullen resignation, if such a term may be allowed, I wended my way to Ryecote Farm, scarcely expecting to find its owner within at this time of day, but hoping to learn in what part of the premises he was most likely to be found.

Absent he was, but expected home in a few minutes; and I was desired to step into the parlour and wait. Mrs. Wilson was busy in the kitchen, but the room was not empty; and I scarcely checked an involuntary recoil as I entered it; for there sat Miss Wilson chattering with Eliza Millward. However, I determined to be cool and civil. Eliza seemed to have made the same resolution on her part. We had not met since the evening of the tea-party; but there was no visible emotion either of pleasure or pain, no attempt at pathos, no display of injured pride: she was cool in temper, civil in demeanour. There was even an ease and cheerfulness about her air and manner that I made no pretension to; but there was a depth of malice in her too expressive eye that plainly told me I was not forgiven; for, though she no longer hoped to win me to herself, she still hated her rival, and evidently delighted to wreak her spite on me. On the other hand, Miss Wilson was as affable and courteous as heart could wish, and though I was in no very conversable humour myself, the two ladies between them managed to keep up a pretty continuous fire of small talk. But Eliza took advantage of the first convenient pause to ask if I had lately seen Mrs. Graham, in a tone of merely casual inquiry, but with a sidelong glance – intended to be playfully mischievous – really, brimful and running over with malice.

"Not lately," I replied, in a careless tone, but sternly repelling her odious glances with my eyes; for I was vexed to feel the colour mounting to my forehead, despite my strenuous efforts to appear unmoved.

"What! Are you beginning to tire already? I thought so noble a creature would have power to attach you for a year at least!"

"I would rather not speak of her now."

"Ah! Then you are convinced, at last, of your mistake – you have at length discovered that your divinity is not quite the immaculate –"

"I desired you not to speak of her, Miss Eliza."

"Oh, I beg your pardon! I perceive Cupid's arrows have been too sharp for you: the wounds, being more than skin-deep, are not yet healed, and bleed afresh at every mention of the loved one's name."

"Say, rather," interposed Miss Wilson, "that Mr. Markham feels that name is unworthy to be mentioned in the presence of right-minded females. I wonder, Eliza, you should think of referring to that unfortunate person – you might know the mention of her would be anything but agreeable to any one here present."

How could this be borne? I rose and was about to clap my hat upon my head and burst away, in wrathful indignation from the house; but recollecting – just in time to save my dignity – the folly of such a proceeding, and how it would only give my fair tormentors a merry laugh at my expense, for the sake of one I acknowledged in my own heart to be unworthy of the slightest sacrifice – though the ghost of my former reverence and love so hung about me still, that I could not bear to hear her name aspersed by others – I merely walked to the window, and having spent a few seconds in vengibly biting my lips and sternly repressing the passionate heavings of my chest, I observed to Miss Wilson, that I could see nothing of her brother, and added that, as my time was precious, it would perhaps be better to call again tomorrow, at some time when I should be sure to find him at home.

"Oh, no!" said she; "if you wait a minute, he will be sure to come; for he has business at L—" (that was our market-town), "and will require a little refreshment before he goes."

I submitted accordingly, with the best grace I could; and, happily, I had not long to wait. Mr. Wilson soon arrived, and, indisposed for business as I was at that moment, and little as I cared for the field or its owner, I forced my attention to the matter in hand, with very creditable determination, and quickly concluded the bargain – perhaps more to the thrifty farmer's satisfaction than he cared to acknowledge. Then, leaving him to the discussion of his substantial 'refreshment,' I gladly quitted the house, and went to look after my reapers.

Leaving them busy at work on the side of the valley, I ascended the hill, intending to visit a corn-field in the more elevated regions, and see when it would be ripe for the sickle. But I did not visit it that day; for, as I approached, I beheld, at no great distance, Mrs. Graham and her son coming down in the opposite direction. They saw me; and Arthur already was running to meet me; but I immediately turned back and walked steadily homeward; for I had fully determined never to encounter his mother again; and regardless of the shrill voice in my ear, calling upon me to "wait a moment," I pursued the even tenor of my way; and he soon relinquished the pursuit as hopeless, or was called away by his mother. At all events, when I looked back, five minutes after, not a trace of either was to be seen.

This incident agitated and disturbed me most unaccountably – unless you would account for it by saying that Cupid's arrows not only had been too sharp for me, but they were barbed and deeply rooted, and I had not yet been able to wrench them from my heart. However that be, I was rendered doubly miserable for the remainder of the day.

Chapter Fourteen

NEXT MORNING, I bethought me, I, too, had business at L—; so I mounted my horse, and set forth on the expedition soon after breakfast. It was a dull, drizzly day; but that was no matter: it was all the more suitable to my frame of mind. It was likely to be a lonely journey; for it was no market-day, and the road I traversed was little frequented at any other time; but that suited me all the better too.

As I trotted along, however, chewing the cud of – bitter fancies, I heard another horse at no great distance behind me; but I never conjectured who the rider might be, or troubled my head about him, till, on slackening my pace to ascend a gentle acclivity, or rather, suffering my horse to slacken his pace into a lazy walk – for, rapt in my own reflections, I was letting it jog on as leisurely as it thought proper – I lost ground, and my fellow-traveller overtook me. He accosted me by name, for it was no stranger – it was Mr. Lawrence! Instinctively the fingers of my whip-hand tingled, and grasped their charge with convulsive energy; but I restrained the impulse, and answering his salutation with a nod, attempted to push on; but he pushed on beside me, and began to talk about the weather and the crops. I gave the briefest possible answers to his queries and observations, and fell back. He fell back too, and asked if my horse was lame. I replied with a look, at which he placidly smiled.

I was as much astonished as exasperated at this singular pertinacity and imperturbable assurance on his part. I had thought the circumstances of our last meeting would have left such an impression on his mind as to render him cold and distant ever after: instead of that, he appeared not only to have forgotten all former offences, but to be impenetrable to all present incivilities. Formerly, the slightest hint, or mere fancied coldness in tone or glance, had sufficed to repulse him: now, positive rudeness could not drive him away. Had he heard of my disappointment; and was he come to witness the result, and triumph in my despair? I grasped my whip with more determined energy than before – but still forbore to raise it, and rode on in silence, waiting for some more tangible cause of offence, before I opened the floodgates of my soul and poured out the dammed-up fury that was foaming and swelling within.

"Markham," said he, in his usual quiet tone, "why do you quarrel with your friends, because you have been disappointed in one quarter? You have found your hopes defeated; but how am I to blame for it? I warned you beforehand, you know, but you would not –"

He said no more; for, impelled by some fiend at my elbow, I had seized my whip by the small end, and – swift and sudden as a flash of lightning – brought the other down upon his head. It was not without a feeling of savage satisfaction that I beheld the instant, deadly pallor that overspread his face, and the few red drops that trickled down his forehead, while he reeled a moment in his saddle, and then fell backward to the ground. The pony, surprised to be so strangely relieved of its burden, started and capered, and kicked a little, and then made use of its freedom to go and crop the grass of the hedge-bank: while its master lay as still and silent as a corpse. Had I killed him? – An icy hand seemed to grasp my heart and check its pulsation, as I bent over him, gazing with breathless intensity upon the ghastly, upturned face. But no; he moved his eyelids and uttered a slight groan. I breathed again – he was only stunned by the fall. It served him right – it would teach him better manners in future. Should I help him to his horse? No. For any other combination of offences I would; but his were too unpardonable. He might mount it himself, if he liked – in a while: already he was beginning to stir and look about him – and there it was for him, quietly browsing on the road-side.

So with a muttered execration I left the fellow to his fate, and clapping spurs to my own horse, galloped away, excited by a combination of feelings it would not be easy to analyse; and perhaps, if I did so, the result would not be very creditable to my disposition; for I am not sure that a species of exultation in what I had done was not one principal concomitant.

Shortly, however, the effervescence began to abate, and not many minutes elapsed before I had turned and gone back to look after the fate of my victim. It was no generous impulse – no kind relentings that led me to this – nor even the fear of what might be the consequences to myself, if I finished my assault upon the squire by leaving him thus neglected, and exposed to further injury; it was, simply, the voice of conscience; and I took great credit to myself for attending so promptly to its dictates – and judging the merit of the deed by the sacrifice it cost, I was not far wrong.

Mr. Lawrence and his pony had both altered their positions in some degree. The pony had wandered eight or ten yards further away; and he had managed, somehow, to remove himself from the middle of the road: I found him seated in a recumbent position on the bank, – looking very white and sickly still, and holding his cambric handkerchief (now more red than white) to his head. It must have been a powerful blow; but half the credit – or the blame of it (which you please) must be attributed to the whip, which was garnished with a massive horse's head of plated metal. The grass, being sodden with rain, afforded the young gentleman a rather inhospitable couch; his clothes were considerably bemired; and his hat was rolling in the mud on the other side of the road. But his thoughts seemed chiefly bent upon his pony, on which he was wistfully gazing – half in helpless anxiety, and half in hopeless abandonment to his fate.

I dismounted, however, and having fastened my own animal to the nearest tree, first picked up his hat, intending to clap it on his head; but either he considered his head unfit for a hat, or the hat, in its present condition, unfit for his head; for shrinking away the one, he took the other from my hand, and scornfully cast it aside.

"It's good enough for you," I muttered.

My next good office was to catch his pony and bring it to him, which was soon accomplished; for the beast was quiet enough in the main, and only winced and flirted a trifle till I got hold of the bridle – but then, I must see him in the saddle.

"Here, you fellow – scoundrel – dog – give me your hand, and I'll help you to mount."

No; he turned from me in disgust. I attempted to take him by the arm. He shrank away as if there had been contamination in my touch.

"What, you won't! Well! You may sit there till doomsday, for what I care. But I suppose you don't want to lose all the blood in your body – I'll just condescend to bind that up for you."

"Let me alone, if you please."

"Humph; with all my heart. You may go to the d—l, if you choose – and say I sent you."

But before I abandoned him to his fate I flung his pony's bridle over a stake in the hedge, and threw him my handkerchief, as his own was now saturated with blood. He took it and cast it back to me in abhorrence and contempt, with all the strength he could muster. It wanted but this to fill the measure of his offences. With execrations not loud but deep I left him to live or die as he could, well satisfied that I had done my duty in attempting to save him – but forgetting how I had erred in bringing him into such a condition, and how insultingly my after-services had been offered – and sullenly prepared to meet the consequences if he should choose to say I had attempted to murder him – which I thought not unlikely, as it seemed probable he was actuated by such spiteful motives in so perseveringly refusing my assistance.

Having remounted my horse, I just looked back to see how he was getting on, before I rode away. He had risen from the ground, and grasping his pony's mane, was attempting to resume his seat in the saddle; but scarcely had he put his foot in the stirrup, when a sickness or dizziness seemed to overpower him: he leant forward a moment, with his head drooped on the animal's back, and then made one more effort, which proving ineffectual, he sank back on the bank, where I left him, reposing his head on the oozy turf, and to all appearance, as calmly reclining as if he had been taking his rest on his sofa at home.

I ought to have helped him in spite of himself – to have bound up the wound he was unable to staunch, and insisted upon getting him on his horse and seeing him safe home; but, besides my bitter indignation against himself, there was the question what to say to his servants – and what to my own family. Either I should have to acknowledge the deed, which would set me down as a madman, unless I acknowledged the motive too – and that seemed impossible – or I must get up a lie, which seemed equally out of the question – especially as Mr. Lawrence would probably reveal the whole truth, and thereby bring me to tenfold disgrace – unless I were villain enough, presuming on the absence of witnesses, to persist in my own version of the case, and make him out a still greater scoundrel than he was. No; he had only received a cut above the temple, and perhaps a few bruises from the fall, or the hoofs of his own pony: that could not kill him if he lay there half the day; and, if he could not help himself, surely some one would be coming by: it would be impossible that a whole day should pass and no one traverse the road but ourselves. As for what he might choose to say hereafter, I would take my chance about it: if he told lies, I would contradict him; if he told the truth, I would bear it as best I could. I was not obliged to enter into explanations further than I thought proper. Perhaps he might choose to be silent on the subject, for fear of raising inquiries as to the cause of the quarrel, and drawing the public attention to his connection with Mrs. Graham, which, whether for her sake or his own, he seemed so very desirous to conceal.

Thus reasoning, I trotted away to the town, where I duly transacted my business, and performed various little commissions for my mother and Rose, with very laudable exactitude, considering the different circumstances of the case. In returning home,

I was troubled with sundry misgivings about the unfortunate Lawrence. The question, What if I should find him lying still on the damp earth, fairly dying of cold and exhaustion – or already stark and chill? Thrust itself most unpleasantly upon my mind, and the appalling possibility pictured itself with painful vividness to my imagination as I approached the spot where I had left him. But no, thank heaven, both man and horse were gone, and nothing was left to witness against me but two objects – unpleasant enough in themselves to be sure, and presenting a very ugly, not to say murderous appearance – in one place, the hat saturated with rain and coated with mud, indented and broken above the brim by that villainous whip-handle; in another, the crimson handkerchief, soaking in a deeply tinctured pool of water – for much rain had fallen in the interim.

Bad news flies fast: it was hardly four o'clock when I got home, but my mother gravely accosted me with – "Oh, Gilbert! – Such an accident! Rose has been shopping in the village, and she's heard that Mr. Lawrence has been thrown from his horse and brought home dying!"

This shocked me a trifle, as you may suppose; but I was comforted to hear that he had frightfully fractured his skull and broken a leg; for, assured of the falsehood of this, I trusted the rest of the story was equally exaggerated; and when I heard my mother and sister so feelingly deploring his condition, I had considerable difficulty in preventing myself from telling them the real extent of the injuries, as far as I knew them.

"You must go and see him tomorrow," said my mother.

"Or today," suggested Rose: "there's plenty of time; and you can have the pony, as your horse is tired. Won't you, Gilbert – as soon as you've had something to eat?"

"No, no – how can we tell that it isn't all a false report? It's highly im—"

"Oh, I'm sure it isn't; for the village is all alive about it; and I saw two people that had seen others that had seen the man that found him. That sounds far-fetched; but it isn't so when you think of it."

"Well, but Lawrence is a good rider; it is not likely he would fall from his horse at all; and if he did, it is highly improbable he would break his bones in that way. It must be a gross exaggeration at least."

"No; but the horse kicked him – or something."

"What, his quiet little pony?"

"How do you know it was that?"

"He seldom rides any other."

"At any rate," said my mother, "you will call tomorrow. Whether it be true or false, exaggerated or otherwise, we shall like to know how he is."

"Fergus may go."

"Why not you?"

"He has more time. I am busy just now."

"Oh! But, Gilbert, how can you be so composed about it? You won't mind business for an hour or two in a case of this sort, when your friend is at the point of death."

"He is not, I tell you."

"For anything you know, he may be: you can't tell till you have seen him. At all events, he must have met with some terrible accident, and you ought to see him: he'll take it very unkind if you don't."

"Confound it! I can't. He and I have not been on good terms of late."

"Oh, my dear boy! Surely, surely you are not so unforgiving as to carry your little differences to such a length as –"

"Little differences, indeed!" I muttered.

"Well, but only remember the occasion. Think how –"

"Well, well, don't bother me now – I'll see about it," I replied.

And my seeing about it was to send Fergus next morning, with my mother's compliments, to make the requisite inquiries; for, of course, my going was out of the question – or sending a message either. He brought back intelligence that the young squire was laid up with the complicated evils of a broken head and certain contusions (occasioned by a fall – of which he did not trouble himself to relate the particulars – and the subsequent misconduct of his horse), and a severe cold, the consequence of lying on the wet ground in the rain; but there were no broken bones, and no immediate prospects of dissolution.

It was evident, then, that for Mrs. Graham's sake it was not his intention to criminate me.

Chapter Fifteen

THAT DAY was rainy like its predecessor; but towards evening it began to clear up a little, and the next morning was fair and promising. I was out on the hill with the reapers. A light wind swept over the corn, and all nature laughed in the sunshine. The lark was rejoicing among the silvery floating clouds. The late rain had so sweetly freshened and cleared the air, and washed the sky, and left such glittering gems on branch and blade, that not even the farmers could have the heart to blame it. But no ray of sunshine could reach my heart, no breeze could freshen it; nothing could fill the void my faith, and hope, and joy in Helen Graham had left, or drive away the keen regrets and bitter dregs of lingering love that still oppressed it.

While I stood with folded arms abstractedly gazing on the undulating swell of the corn, not yet disturbed by the reapers, something gently pulled my skirts, and a small voice, no longer welcome to my ears, aroused me with the startling words, – "Mr. Markham, mamma wants you."

"Wants me, Arthur?"

"Yes. Why do you look so queer?" said he, half laughing, half frightened at the unexpected aspect of my face in suddenly turning towards him, – "and why have you kept so long away? Come! Won't you come?"

"I'm busy just now," I replied, scarce knowing what to answer.

He looked up in childish bewilderment; but before I could speak again the lady herself was at my side.

"Gilbert, I must speak with you!" said she, in a tone of suppressed vehemence.

I looked at her pale cheek and glittering eye, but answered nothing.

"Only for a moment," pleaded she. "Just step aside into this other field." She glanced at the reapers, some of whom were directing looks of impertinent curiosity towards her. "I won't keep you a minute."

I accompanied her through the gap.

"Arthur, darling, run and gather those bluebells," said she, pointing to some that were gleaming at some distance under the hedge along which we walked. The child hesitated, as if unwilling to quit my side. "Go, love!" repeated she more urgently, and in a tone which, though not unkind, demanded prompt obedience, and obtained it.

"Well, Mrs. Graham?" said I, calmly and coldly; for, though I saw she was miserable, and pitied her, I felt glad to have it in my power to torment her.

She fixed her eyes upon me with a look that pierced me to the heart; and yet it made me smile.

"I don't ask the reason of this change, Gilbert," said she, with bitter calmness: "I know it too well; but though I could see myself suspected and condemned by every one else, and bear it with calmness, I cannot endure it from you. – Why did you not come to hear my explanation on the day I appointed to give it?"

"Because I happened, in the interim, to learn all you would have told me – and a trifle more, I imagine."

"Impossible, for I would have told you all!" cried she, passionately – "but I won't now, for I see you are not worthy of it!"

And her pale lips quivered with agitation.

"Why not, may I ask?"

She repelled my mocking smile with a glance of scornful indignation.

"Because you never understood me, or you would not soon have listened to my traducers – my confidence would be misplaced in you – you are not the man I thought you. Go! I won't care what you think of me."

She turned away, and I went; for I thought that would torment her as much as anything; and I believe I was right; for, looking back a minute after, I saw her turn half round, as if hoping or expecting to find me still beside her; and then she stood still, and cast one look behind. It was a look less expressive of anger than of bitter anguish and despair; but I immediately assumed an aspect of indifference, and affected to be gazing carelessly around me, and I suppose she went on; for after lingering awhile to see if she would come back or call, I ventured one more glance, and saw her a good way off, moving rapidly up the field, with little Arthur running by her side and apparently talking as he went; but she kept her face averted from him, as if to hide some uncontrollable emotion. And I returned to my business.

But I soon began to regret my precipitancy in leaving her so soon. It was evident she loved me – probably she was tired of Mr. Lawrence, and wished to exchange him for me; and if I had loved and reverenced her less to begin with, the preference might have gratified and amused me; but now the contrast between her outward seeming and her inward mind, as I supposed, – between my former and my present opinion of her, was so harrowing – so distressing to my feelings, that it swallowed up every lighter consideration.

But still I was curious to know what sort of an explanation she would have given me – or would give now, if I pressed her for it – how much she would confess, and how she would endeavour to excuse herself. I longed to know what to despise, and what to admire in her; how much to pity, and how much to hate; – and, what was more, I would know. I would see her once more, and fairly satisfy myself in what light to regard her, before we parted. Lost to me she was, for ever, of course; but still I could not bear to think that we had parted, for the last time, with so much unkindness and misery on both sides. That last look of hers had sunk into my heart; I could not forget it. But what a fool I was! Had she not deceived me, injured me – blighted my happiness for life? "Well, I'll see her, however," was my concluding resolve, "but not today: today and tonight she may think upon her sins, and be as miserable as she will: tomorrow I will see her once again, and know something more about her. The interview may be serviceable to her, or it may not. At any rate, it will give a breath of excitement to the life she has doomed to stagnation, and may calm with certainty some agitating thoughts."

I did go on the morrow, but not till towards evening, after the business of the day was concluded, that is, between six and seven; and the westering sun was gleaming redly on the old Hall, and flaming in the latticed windows, as I reached it, imparting to the place a cheerfulness not its own. I need not dilate upon the feelings with which I approached the shrine of my former divinity – that spot teeming with a thousand delightful recollections and glorious dreams – all darkened now by one disastrous truth.

Rachel admitted me into the parlour, and went to call her mistress, for she was not there: but there was her desk left open on the little round table beside the high-backed chair, with a book laid upon it. Her limited but choice collection of books was almost as familiar to me as my own; but this volume I had not seen before. I took it up. It was Sir Humphry Davy's *Last Days of a Philosopher*, and on the first leaf was written, 'Frederick Lawrence.' I closed the book, but kept it in my hand, and stood facing the door, with my back to the fire-place, calmly waiting her arrival; for I did not doubt she would come. And soon I heard her step in the hall. My heart was beginning to throb, but I checked it with an internal rebuke, and maintained my composure – outwardly at least. She entered, calm, pale, collected.

"To what am I indebted for this favour, Mr. Markham?" said she, with such severe but quiet dignity as almost disconcerted me; but I answered with a smile, and impudently enough, –

"Well, I am come to hear your explanation."

"I told you I would not give it," said she. "I said you were unworthy of my confidence."

"Oh, very well," replied I, moving to the door.

"Stay a moment," said she. "This is the last time I shall see you: don't go just yet."

I remained, awaiting her further commands.

"Tell me," resumed she, "on what grounds you believe these things against me; who told you; and what did they say?"

I paused a moment. She met my eye as unflinchingly as if her bosom had been steeled with conscious innocence. She was resolved to know the worst, and determined to dare it too. "I can crush that bold spirit," thought I. But while I secretly exulted in my power, I felt disposed to dally with my victim like a cat. Showing her the book that I still held, in my hand, and pointing to the name on the fly-leaf, but fixing my eye upon her face, I asked, – "Do you know that gentleman?"

"Of course I do," replied she; and a sudden flush suffused her features – whether of shame or anger I could not tell: it rather resembled the latter. "What next, sir?"

"How long is it since you saw him?"

"Who gave you the right to catechize me on this or any other subject?"

"Oh, no one! – It's quite at your option whether to answer or not. And now, let me ask – have you heard what has lately befallen this friend of yours? – Because, if you have not –"

"I will not be insulted, Mr. Markham!" cried she, almost infuriated at my manner. "So you had better leave the house at once, if you came only for that."

"I did not come to insult you: I came to hear your explanation."

"And I tell you I won't give it!" retorted she, pacing the room in a state of strong excitement, with her hands clasped tightly together, breathing short, and flashing fires of indignation from her eyes. "I will not condescend to explain myself to one that can make a jest of such horrible suspicions, and be so easily led to entertain them."

"I do not make a jest of them, Mrs. Graham," returned I, dropping at once my tone of taunting sarcasm. "I heartily wish I could find them a jesting matter. And as to being easily led to suspect, God only knows what a blind, incredulous fool I have hitherto been, perseveringly shutting my eyes and stopping my ears against everything that threatened to shake my confidence in you, till proof itself confounded my infatuation!"

"What proof, sir?"

"Well, I'll tell you. You remember that evening when I was here last?"

"I do."

"Even then you dropped some hints that might have opened the eyes of a wiser man; but they had no such effect upon me: I went on trusting and believing, hoping against hope, and adoring where I could not comprehend. It so happened, however, that after I left you I turned back – drawn by pure depth of sympathy and ardour of affection – not daring to intrude my presence openly upon you, but unable to resist the temptation of catching one glimpse through the window, just to see how you were: for I had left you apparently in great affliction, and I partly blamed my own want of forbearance and discretion as the cause of it. If I did wrong, love alone was my incentive, and the punishment was severe enough; for it was just as I had reached that tree, that you came out into the garden with your friend. Not choosing to show myself, under the circumstances, I stood still, in the shadow, till you had both passed by."

"And how much of our conversation did you hear?"

"I heard quite enough, Helen. And it was well for me that I did hear it; for nothing less could have cured my infatuation. I always said and thought, that I would never believe a word against you, unless I heard it from your own lips. All the hints and affirmations of others I treated as malignant, baseless slanders; your own self-accusations I believed to be overstrained; and all that seemed unaccountable in your position I trusted that you could account for if you chose."

Mrs. Graham had discontinued her walk. She leant against one end of the chimney-piece, opposite that near which I was standing, with her chin resting on her closed hand, her eyes – no longer burning with anger, but gleaming with restless excitement – sometimes glancing at me while I spoke, then coursing the opposite wall, or fixed upon the carpet.

"You should have come to me after all," said she, "and heard what I had to say in my own justification. It was ungenerous and wrong to withdraw yourself so secretly and suddenly, immediately after such ardent protestations of attachment, without ever assigning a reason for the change. You should have told me all–no matter how bitterly. It would have been better than this silence."

"To what end should I have done so? You could not have enlightened me further, on the subject which alone concerned me; nor could you have made me discredit the evidence of my senses. I desired our intimacy to be discontinued at once, as you yourself had acknowledged would probably be the case if I knew all; but I did not wish to upbraid you, – though (as you also acknowledged) you had deeply wronged me. Yes, you have done me an injury you can never repair – or any other either – you have blighted the freshness and promise of youth, and made my life a wilderness! I might live a hundred years, but I could never recover from the effects of this withering blow – and never forget it! Hereafter – You smile, Mrs. Graham," said I, suddenly stopping short, checked in my passionate declamation by unutterable feelings to behold her actually smiling at the picture of the ruin she had wrought.

"Did I?" replied she, looking seriously up; "I was not aware of it. If I did, it was not for pleasure at the thoughts of the harm I had done you. Heaven knows I have had torment enough at the bare possibility of that; it was for joy to find that you had some depth of soul and feeling after all, and to hope that I had not been utterly mistaken in your worth. But smiles and tears are so alike with me, they are neither of them confined to any particular feelings: I often cry when I am happy, and smile when I am sad."

She looked at me again, and seemed to expect a reply; but I continued silent.

"Would you be very glad," resumed she, "to find that you were mistaken in your conclusions?"

"How can you ask it, Helen?"

"I don't say I can clear myself altogether," said she, speaking low and fast, while her heart beat visibly and her bosom heaved with excitement, – "but would you be glad to discover I was better than you think me?"

"Anything that could in the least degree tend to restore my former opinion of you, to excuse the regard I still feel for you, and alleviate the pangs of unutterable regret that accompany it, would be only too gladly, too eagerly received!" Her cheeks burned, and her whole frame trembled, now, with excess of agitation. She did not speak, but flew to her desk, and snatching thence what seemed a thick album or manuscript volume, hastily tore away a few leaves from the end, and thrust the rest into my hand, saying, "You needn't read it all; but take it home with you," and hurried from the room. But when I had left the house, and was proceeding down the walk, she opened the window and called me back. It was only to say, – "Bring it back when you have read it; and don't breathe a word of what it tells you to any living being. I trust to your honour."

Before I could answer she had closed the casement and turned away. I saw her cast herself back in the old oak chair, and cover her face with her hands. Her feelings had been wrought to a pitch that rendered it necessary to seek relief in tears.

Panting with eagerness, and struggling to suppress my hopes, I hurried home, and rushed up-stairs to my room, having first provided myself with a candle, though it was scarcely twilight yet – then, shut and bolted the door, determined to tolerate no interruption; and sitting down before the table, opened out my prize and delivered myself up to its perusal – first hastily turning over the leaves and snatching a sentence here and there, and then setting myself steadily to read it through.

I have it now before me; and though you could not, of course, peruse it with half the interest that I did, I know you would not be satisfied with an abbreviation of its contents, and you shall have the whole, save, perhaps, a few passages here and there of merely temporary interest to the writer, or such as would serve to encumber the story rather than elucidate it. It begins somewhat abruptly, thus – but we will reserve its commencement for another chapter.

Chapter Sixteen

❧

JUNE 1ST, 1821. – We have just returned to Staningley – that is, we returned some days ago, and I am not yet settled, and feel as if I never should be. We left town sooner than was intended, in consequence of my uncle's indisposition; – I wonder what would have been the result if we had stayed the full time. I am quite ashamed of my new-sprung distaste for country life. All my former occupations seem so tedious and dull, my former amusements so insipid and unprofitable. I cannot enjoy my music, because there is no one to hear it. I cannot enjoy my walks, because there is no one to meet. I cannot enjoy my books, because they have not power to arrest my attention: my head is so haunted with the recollections of the last few weeks, that I cannot attend to them. My drawing suits me best, for I can draw and think at the same time; and if my productions cannot now be seen by any one but myself, and those who do not care about them, they, possibly, may be, hereafter. But, then, there is one face I am always trying to paint or to sketch, and always without success; and that vexes me. As for the owner of that face, I cannot get him out of my mind – and, indeed, I never try. I wonder whether he ever thinks of me; and I wonder whether I shall ever see him again. And then might follow a train of other wonderments – questions for time and fate to answer – concluding with – Supposing all the rest be answered in the affirmative, I wonder whether I shall ever repent it? As my aunt would tell me I should, if she knew what I was thinking about.

How distinctly I remember our conversation that evening before our departure for town, when we were sitting together over the fire, my uncle having gone to bed with a slight attack of the gout.

"Helen," said she, after a thoughtful silence, "do you ever think about marriage?"

"Yes, aunt, often."

"And do you ever contemplate the possibility of being married yourself, or engaged, before the season is over?"

"Sometimes; but I don't think it at all likely that I ever shall."

"Why so?"

"Because, I imagine, there must be only a very, very few men in the world that I should like to marry; and of those few, it is ten to one I may never be acquainted with one; or if I should, it is twenty to one he may not happen to be single, or to take a fancy to me."

"That is no argument at all. It may be very true – and I hope is true, that there are very few men whom you would choose to marry, of yourself. It is not, indeed, to be supposed that you would wish to marry any one till you were asked: a girl's affections should never be won unsought. But when they are sought – when the citadel of the heart is fairly besieged – it is apt to surrender sooner than the owner is aware of, and often against her better judgment, and in opposition to all her preconceived ideas of what she could have loved, unless she be extremely careful and discreet. Now, I want to warn you, Helen, of these things, and to exhort you to be watchful and circumspect from the very commencement of your career, and not to suffer your heart to be stolen from you by the first foolish or unprincipled person that covets the possession of it. – You know, my dear, you are only just eighteen; there is plenty of time before you, and neither your uncle nor I are in any hurry to get you off our hands, and I may venture to say, there will be no lack of suitors; for you can boast a good family, a pretty considerable fortune and expectations, and, I may as well tell you likewise – for, if I don't, others will – that you have a fair share of beauty besides – and I hope you may never have cause to regret it!"

"I hope not, aunt; but why should you fear it?"

"Because, my dear, beauty is that quality which, next to money, is generally the most attractive to the worst kinds of men; and, therefore, it is likely to entail a great deal of trouble on the possessor."

"Have you been troubled in that way, aunt?"

"No, Helen," said she, with reproachful gravity, "but I know many that have; and some, through carelessness, have been the wretched victims of deceit; and some, through weakness, have fallen into snares and temptations terrible to relate."

"Well, I shall be neither careless nor weak."

"Remember Peter, Helen! Don't boast, but watch. Keep a guard over your eyes and ears as the inlets of your heart, and over your lips as the outlet, lest they betray you in a moment of unwariness. Receive, coldly and dispassionately, every attention, till you have ascertained and duly considered the worth of the aspirant; and let your affections be consequent upon approbation alone. First study; then approve; then love. Let your eyes be blind to all external attractions, your ears deaf to all the fascinations of flattery and light discourse. – These are nothing – and worse than nothing – snares and wiles of the tempter, to lure the thoughtless to their own destruction. Principle is the first thing, after all; and next to that, good sense, respectability, and moderate wealth. If you should marry the handsomest, and most accomplished and superficially agreeable man in the world, you little know the misery that would overwhelm you if, after all, you should find him to be a worthless reprobate, or even an impracticable fool."

"But what are all the poor fools and reprobates to do, aunt? If everybody followed your advice, the world would soon come to an end."

"Never fear, my dear! The male fools and reprobates will never want for partners, while there are so many of the other sex to match them; but do you follow my advice. And this is no subject for jesting, Helen – I am sorry to see you treat the matter in that light way. Believe me, matrimony is a serious thing." And she spoke it so seriously, that one might have fancied she had known it to her cost; but I asked no more impertinent questions, and merely answered, – "I know it is; and I know there is truth and sense in what you say; but you need not fear me, for I not only should think it wrong to marry a man that was deficient in sense or in principle, but I should never be tempted to do it; for I could not like him, if he were ever so handsome, and ever so charming, in other respects; I should hate him – despise him – pity him – anything but love him. My affections not only ought to be founded on approbation, but they will and must be so: for, without approving, I cannot love. It is needless to say, I ought to be able to respect and honour the man I marry, as well as love him, for I cannot love him without. So set your mind at rest."

"I hope it may be so," answered she.

"I know it is so," persisted I.

"You have not been tried yet, Helen – we can but hope," said she in her cold, cautious way.

I was vexed at her incredulity; but I am not sure her doubts were entirely without sagacity; I fear I have found it much easier to remember her advice than to profit by it; – indeed, I have sometimes been led to question the soundness of her doctrines on those subjects. Her counsels may be good, as far as they go – in the main points at least; – but there are some things she has overlooked in her calculations. I wonder if she was ever in love.

I commenced my career – or my first campaign, as my uncle calls it – kindling with bright hopes and fancies – chiefly raised by this conversation – and full of confidence in my own discretion. At first, I was delighted with the novelty and excitement of our London life; but soon I began to weary of its mingled turbulence and constraint, and sigh for the freshness and freedom of home. My new acquaintances, both male and female, disappointed my expectations, and vexed and depressed me by turns; for I soon grew tired of studying their peculiarities, and laughing at their foibles – particularly as I was obliged to keep my criticisms to myself, for my aunt would not hear them – and they – the ladies especially – appeared so provokingly mindless, and heartless, and artificial. The gentlemen seemed better, but, perhaps, it was because I knew them less – perhaps, because they flattered me; but I did not fall in love with any of them; and, if their attentions pleased me one moment, they provoked me the next, because they put me out of humour with myself, by revealing my vanity and making me fear I was becoming like some of the ladies I so heartily despised.

There was one elderly gentleman that annoyed me very much; a rich old friend of my uncle's, who, I believe, thought I could not do better than marry him; but, besides being old, he was ugly and disagreeable, – and wicked, I am sure, though my aunt scolded me for saying so; but she allowed he was no saint. And there was another, less hateful, but still more tiresome, because she favoured him, and was always thrusting him upon me, and sounding his praises in my ears – Mr. Boarham by name, Bore'em, as I prefer spelling it, for a terrible bore he was: I shudder still at the remembrance of his voice – drone, drone, drone, in my ear – while he sat beside me, prosing away by the half-hour together, and beguiling himself with the notion that he was improving my mind by useful information, or impressing his dogmas upon me and reforming my errors of judgment, or perhaps that he was talking down to my level, and amusing me with entertaining discourse. Yet he was a decent man enough in the main, I daresay; and if he had kept his distance, I never would have hated him. As it was, it was almost impossible to help it, for he not only bothered me with the infliction of his own presence, but he kept me from the enjoyment of more agreeable society.

One night, however, at a ball, he had been more than usually tormenting, and my patience was quite exhausted. It appeared as if the whole evening was fated to be insupportable: I had just had one dance with an empty-headed coxcomb, and then Mr. Boarham had come upon me and seemed determined to cling to me for the rest of the night. He never danced himself, and there he sat, poking his head in my face, and impressing all beholders with the idea that he was a confirmed, acknowledged lover; my aunt looking complacently on all the time, and wishing him God-speed. In vain I attempted to drive him away by giving a loose to my exasperated feelings, even to positive rudeness: nothing could convince him that his presence was disagreeable. Sullen silence was taken for rapt attention, and gave him greater room to talk; sharp answers were received as smart sallies of girlish vivacity, that only required an indulgent rebuke; and flat contradictions were but as oil to the flames, calling forth new strains of argument to support his dogmas, and bringing down upon me endless floods of reasoning to overwhelm me with conviction.

But there was one present who seemed to have a better appreciation of my frame of mind. A gentleman stood by, who had been watching our conference for some time, evidently much amused at my companion's remorseless pertinacity and my manifest annoyance, and laughing to himself at the asperity and uncompromising spirit of my replies. At length, however, he withdrew, and went to the lady of the house, apparently for the purpose of asking an introduction to me, for, shortly after, they both came up, and she introduced him as Mr. Huntingdon, the son of a late friend of my uncle's. He asked me to dance. I gladly consented, of course; and he was my companion during the remainder of my stay, which was not long, for my aunt, as usual, insisted upon an early departure.

I was sorry to go, for I had found my new acquaintance a very lively and entertaining companion. There was a certain graceful ease and freedom about all he said and did, that gave a sense of repose and expansion to the mind, after so much constraint and formality as I had been doomed to suffer. There might be, it is true, a little too much careless boldness in his manner and address, but I was in so good a humour, and so grateful for my late deliverance from Mr. Boarham, that it did not anger me.

"Well, Helen, how do you like Mr. Boarham now?" said my aunt, as we took our seats in the carriage and drove away.

"Worse than ever," I replied.

She looked displeased, but said no more on that subject.

"Who was the gentleman you danced with last," resumed she, after a pause – "that was so officious in helping you on with your shawl?"

"He was not officious at all, aunt: he never attempted to help me till he saw Mr. Boarham coming to do so; and then he stepped laughingly forward and said, 'Come, I'll preserve you from that infliction.'"

"Who was it, I ask?" said she, with frigid gravity.

"It was Mr. Huntingdon, the son of uncle's old friend."

"I have heard your uncle speak of young Mr. Huntingdon. I've heard him say, 'He's a fine lad, that young Huntingdon, but a bit wildish, I fancy.' So I'd have you beware."

"What does 'a bit wildish' mean?" I inquired.

"It means destitute of principle, and prone to every vice that is common to youth."

"But I've heard uncle say he was a sad wild fellow himself, when he was young."

She sternly shook her head.

"He was jesting then, I suppose," said I, "and here he was speaking at random – at least, I cannot believe there is any harm in those laughing blue eyes."

"False reasoning, Helen!" said she, with a sigh.

"Well, we ought to be charitable, you know, aunt – besides, I don't think it is false: I am an excellent physiognomist, and I always judge of people's characters by their looks – not by whether they are handsome or ugly, but by the general cast of the countenance. For instance, I should know by your countenance that you were not of a cheerful, sanguine disposition; and I should know by Mr. Wilmot's, that he was a worthless old reprobate; and by Mr. Boarham's, that he was not an agreeable companion; and by Mr. Huntingdon's, that he was neither a fool nor a knave, though, possibly, neither a sage nor a saint – but that is no matter to me, as I am not likely to meet him again – unless as an occasional partner in the ball-room."

It was not so, however, for I met him again next morning. He came to call upon my uncle, apologising for not having done so before, by saying he was only lately returned from the Continent, and had not heard, till the previous night, of my uncle's arrival in town; and after that I often met him; sometimes in public, sometimes at home; for he was very assiduous in paying his respects to his old friend, who did not, however, consider himself greatly obliged by the attention.

"I wonder what the deuce the lad means by coming so often," he would say, – "can you tell, Helen? – Hey? He wants none o' my company, nor I his – that's certain."

"I wish you'd tell him so, then," said my aunt.

"Why, what for? If I don't want him, somebody does, mayhap" (winking at me). "Besides, he's a pretty tidy fortune, Peggy, you know – not such a catch as Wilmot; but then Helen won't hear of that match: for, somehow, these old chaps don't go down with the girls – with all their money, and their experience to boot. I'll bet anything she'd rather have this young fellow without a penny, than Wilmot with his house full of gold. Wouldn't you, Nell?"

"Yes, uncle; but that's not saying much for Mr. Huntingdon; for I'd rather be an old maid and a pauper than Mrs. Wilmot."

"And Mrs. Huntingdon? What would you rather be than Mrs. Huntingdon – eh?"

"I'll tell you when I've considered the matter."

"Ah! It needs consideration, then? But come, now – would you rather be an old maid – let alone the pauper?"

"I can't tell till I'm asked."

And I left the room immediately, to escape further examination. But five minutes after, in looking from my window, I beheld Mr. Boarham coming up to the door. I waited nearly half-an-hour in uncomfortable suspense, expecting every minute to be called, and vainly longing to hear him go. Then footsteps were heard on the stairs, and my aunt entered the room with a solemn countenance, and closed the door behind her.

"Here is Mr. Boarham, Helen," said she. "He wishes to see you."

"Oh, aunt! – Can't you tell him I'm indisposed? – I'm sure I am – to see him."

"Nonsense, my dear! This is no trifling matter. He is come on a very important errand – to ask your hand in marriage of your uncle and me."

"I hope my uncle and you told him it was not in your power to give it. What right had he to ask any one before me?"

"Helen!"

"What did my uncle say?"

"He said he would not interfere in the matter; if you liked to accept Mr. Boarham's obliging offer, you –"

"Did he say obliging offer?"

"No; he said if you liked to take him you might; and if not, you might please yourself."

"He said right; and what did you say?"

"It is no matter what I said. What will you say? – That is the question. He is now waiting to ask you himself; but consider well before you go; and if you intend to refuse him, give me your reasons."

"I shall refuse him, of course; but you must tell me how, for I want to be civil and yet decided – and when I've got rid of him, I'll give you my reasons afterwards."

"But stay, Helen; sit down a little and compose yourself. Mr. Boarham is in no particular hurry, for he has little doubt of your acceptance; and I want to speak with you. Tell me, my dear, what are your objections to him? Do you deny that he is an upright, honourable man?"

"No."

"Do you deny that he is sensible, sober, respectable?"

"No; he may be all this, but –"

"But, Helen! How many such men do you expect to meet with in the world? Upright, honourable, sensible, sober, respectable! Is this such an every-day character that you should reject the possessor of such noble qualities without a moment's hesitation? Yes, noble I may call them; for think of the full meaning of each, and how many inestimable virtues they include (and I might add many more to the list), and consider that all this is laid at your feet. It is in your power to secure this inestimable blessing for life – a worthy and excellent husband, who loves you tenderly, but not too fondly so as to blind him to your faults, and will be your guide throughout life's pilgrimage, and your partner in eternal bliss. Think how –"

"But I hate him, aunt," said I, interrupting this unusual flow of eloquence.

"Hate him, Helen! Is this a Christian spirit? – You hate him? And he so good a man!"

"I don't hate him as a man, but as a husband. As a man, I love him so much that I wish him a better wife than I – one as good as himself, or better – if you think that possible – provided she could like him; but I never could, and therefore –"

"But why not? What objection do you find?"

"Firstly, he is at least forty years old – considerably more, I should think – and I am but eighteen; secondly, he is narrow-minded and bigoted in the extreme; thirdly, his tastes and feelings are wholly dissimilar to mine; fourthly, his looks, voice, and manner are particularly displeasing to me; and, finally, I have an aversion to his whole person that I never can surmount."

"Then you ought to surmount it. And please to compare him for a moment with Mr. Huntingdon, and, good looks apart (which contribute nothing to the merit of the man, or to the happiness of married life, and which you have so often professed to hold in light esteem), tell me which is the better man."

"I have no doubt Mr. Huntingdon is a much better man than you think him; but we are not talking about him now, but about Mr. Boarham; and as I would rather grow, live, and die in single blessedness – than be his wife, it is but right that I should tell him so at once, and put him out of suspense – so let me go."

"But don't give him a flat denial; he has no idea of such a thing, and it would offend him greatly: say you have no thoughts of matrimony at present –"

"But I have thoughts of it."

"Or that you desire a further acquaintance."

"But I don't desire a further acquaintance – quite the contrary."

And without waiting for further admonitions I left the room and went to seek Mr. Boarham. He was walking up and down the drawing room, humming snatches of tunes and nibbling the end of his cane.

"My dear young lady," said he, bowing and smirking with great complacency, "I have your kind guardian's permission –"

"I know, sir," said I, wishing to shorten the scene as much as possible, "and I am greatly obliged for your preference, but must beg to decline the honour you wish to confer, for I think we were not made for each other, as you yourself would shortly discover if the experiment were tried."

My aunt was right. It was quite evident he had had little doubt of my acceptance, and no idea of a positive denial. He was amazed, astounded at such an answer, but too incredulous to be much offended; and after a little humming and hawing, he returned to the attack.

"I know, my dear, that there exists a considerable disparity between us in years, in temperament, and perhaps some other things; but let me assure you, I shall not be severe to mark the faults and foibles of a young and ardent nature such as yours, and while I acknowledge them to myself, and even rebuke them with all a father's care, believe me, no youthful lover could be more tenderly indulgent towards the object of his affections than I to you; and, on the other hand, let me hope that my more experienced years and graver habits of reflection will be no disparagement in your eyes, as I shall endeavour to make them all conducive to your happiness. Come, now! What do you say? Let us have no young lady's affectations and caprices, but speak out at once."

"I will, but only to repeat what I said before, that I am certain we were not made for each other."

"You really think so?"

"I do."

"But you don't know me – you wish for a further acquaintance – a longer time to –"

"No, I don't. I know you as well as I ever shall, and better than you know me, or you would never dream of uniting yourself to one so incongruous – so utterly unsuitable to you in every way."

"But, my dear young lady, I don't look for perfection; I can excuse –"

"Thank you, Mr. Boarham, but I won't trespass upon your goodness. You may save your indulgence and consideration for some more worthy object, that won't tax them so heavily."

"But let me beg you to consult your aunt; that excellent lady, I am sure, will –"

"I have consulted her; and I know her wishes coincide with yours; but in such important matters, I take the liberty of judging for myself; and no persuasion can alter my inclinations, or induce me to believe that such a step would be conducive to my happiness or yours – and I wonder that a man of your experience and discretion should think of choosing such a wife."

"Ah, well!" said he, "I have sometimes wondered at that myself. I have sometimes said to myself, 'Now Boarham, what is this you're after? Take care, man – look before you leap! This is a sweet, bewitching creature, but remember, the brightest attractions to the lover too often prove the husband's greatest torments!' I assure you my choice has not been made without much reasoning and reflection. The seeming imprudence of the match has cost me many an anxious thought by day, and many a sleepless hour by night; but at length I satisfied myself that it was not, in very deed, imprudent. I saw my sweet girl was not without her faults, but of these her youth, I trusted, was not one, but rather an earnest of virtues yet unblown – a strong ground of presumption that her little defects of temper and errors of judgment, opinion, or manner were not irremediable, but might easily be removed or mitigated by the patient efforts of a watchful and judicious adviser, and where I failed to enlighten and control, I thought I might safely undertake to pardon, for the sake of her many excellences. Therefore, my dearest girl, since I am satisfied, why should you object – on my account, at least?"

"But to tell you the truth, Mr. Boarham, it is on my own account I principally object; so let us – drop the subject," I would have said, "for it is worse than useless to pursue it any further," but he pertinaciously interrupted me with, – "But why so? I would love you, cherish you, protect you," etc., etc.

I shall not trouble myself to put down all that passed between us. Suffice it to say, that I found him very troublesome, and very hard to convince that I really meant what I said, and really was so obstinate and blind to my own interests, that there was no shadow of a chance that either he or my aunt would ever be able to overcome my objections. Indeed, I am not sure that I succeeded after all; though wearied with his so pertinaciously returning to the same point and repeating the same arguments over and over again, forcing me to reiterate the same replies, I at length turned short and sharp upon him, and my last words were, – "I tell you plainly, that it cannot be. No consideration can induce me to marry against my inclinations. I respect you – at least, I would respect you, if you would behave like a sensible man – but I cannot love you, and never could – and the more you talk the further you repel me; so pray don't say any more about it."

Whereupon he wished me a good morning, and withdrew, disconcerted and offended, no doubt; but surely it was not my fault.

Chapter Seventeen

THE NEXT DAY I accompanied my uncle and aunt to a dinner-party at Mr. Wilmot's. He had two ladies staying with him: his niece Annabella, a fine dashing girl, or rather young woman, – of some five-and-twenty, too great a flirt to be married, according to her own assertion, but greatly admired by the gentlemen, who universally pronounced her a splendid woman; and her gentle cousin, Milicent Hargrave, who had taken a violent fancy to me, mistaking me for something vastly better than I was. And I, in return, was very fond of her. I should entirely exclude poor Milicent in my general animadversions against the ladies of my acquaintance. But it was not on her account, or her cousin's, that I have mentioned the party: it was for the sake of another of Mr. Wilmot's guests, to wit Mr. Huntingdon. I have good reason to remember his presence there, for this was the last time I saw him.

He did not sit near me at dinner; for it was his fate to hand in a capacious old dowager, and mine to be handed in by Mr. Grimsby, a friend of his, but a man I very greatly disliked: there was a sinister cast in his countenance, and a mixture of lurking ferocity and fulsome insincerity in his demeanour, that I could not away with. What a tiresome custom that is, by-the-by – one among the many sources of factitious annoyance of this ultra-civilised life. If the gentlemen must lead the ladies into the dining room, why cannot they take those they like best?

I am not sure, however, that Mr. Huntingdon would have taken me, if he had been at liberty to make his own selection. It is quite possible he might have chosen Miss Wilmot; for she seemed bent upon engrossing his attention to herself, and he seemed nothing loth to pay the homage she demanded. I thought so, at least, when I saw how they talked and laughed, and glanced across the table, to the neglect and evident umbrage of their respective neighbours – and afterwards, as the gentlemen joined us in the drawing room, when she, immediately upon his entrance, loudly called upon him to be the arbiter of a dispute between herself and another lady, and he answered the summons with alacrity, and decided the question without a moment's hesitation in her favour – though, to my thinking, she was obviously in the wrong – and then stood chatting familiarly with her and a group of other ladies; while I sat with Milicent Hargrave at the opposite end of the room, looking over the latter's drawings, and aiding her with my critical observations and advice, at her particular desire. But in spite of my efforts to remain composed, my attention wandered from the drawings to the merry group, and against my better judgment my wrath rose, and doubtless my countenance lowered; for Milicent, observing that I must be tired of her daubs and scratches, begged I would join the company now, and defer the examination of the remainder to another opportunity. But while I was assuring her that I had no wish to join them, and was not tired, Mr. Huntingdon himself came up to the little round table at which we sat.

"Are these yours?" said he, carelessly taking up one of the drawings.

"No, they are Miss Hargrave's."

"Oh! Well, let's have a look at them."

And, regardless of Miss Hargrave's protestations that they were not worth looking at, he drew a chair to my side, and receiving the drawings, one by one from my hand, successively scanned them over, and threw them on the table, but said not a word about them, though he was talking all the time. I don't know what Milicent Hargrave thought of such conduct, but I found his conversation extremely interesting; though, as I afterwards discovered, when I came to analyse it, it was chiefly confined to quizzing the different members of the company present; and albeit he made some clever remarks, and some excessively droll ones, I do not think the whole would appear anything very particular, if written here, without the adventitious aids of look, and tone, and gesture, and that ineffable but indefinite charm, which cast a halo over all he did and said, and which would have made it a delight to look in his face, and hear the music of his voice, if he had been talking positive nonsense – and which, moreover, made me feel so bitter against my aunt when she put a stop to this enjoyment, by coming composedly forward, under pretence of wishing to see the drawings, that she cared and knew nothing about, and while making believe to examine them, addressing herself to Mr. Huntingdon, with one of her coldest and most repellent aspects, and beginning a series of the most common-place and formidably formal questions and observations, on purpose to wrest his attention from me – on purpose to vex me, as I thought: and having now looked through the portfolio, I left them to their *tête-à-tête*, and seated myself on a sofa, quite apart from the company – never thinking how strange such conduct would appear, but merely to indulge, at first, the vexation of the moment, and subsequently to enjoy my private thoughts.

But I was not left long alone, for Mr. Wilmot, of all men the least welcome, took advantage of my isolated position to come and plant himself beside me. I had flattered myself that I had so effectually repulsed his advances on all former occasions, that I had nothing more to apprehend from his unfortunate predilection; but it seems I was mistaken: so great was his confidence, either in his wealth or his remaining powers of attraction, and so firm his conviction of feminine weakness, that he thought himself warranted to return to the siege, which he did with renovated ardour, enkindled by the quantity of wine he had drunk – a circumstance that rendered him infinitely the more disgusting; but greatly as I abhorred him at that moment, I did not like to treat him with rudeness, as I was now his guest, and had just been enjoying his hospitality; and I was no hand at a polite but determined rejection, nor would it have greatly availed me if I had, for he was too coarse-minded to take any repulse that was not as plain and positive as his own effrontery. The consequence was, that he waxed more fulsomely tender, and more repulsively warm, and I was driven to the very verge of desperation, and about to say I know not what, when I felt my hand, that hung over the arm of the sofa, suddenly taken by another and gently but fervently pressed. Instinctively, I guessed who it was, and, on looking up, was less surprised than delighted to see Mr. Huntingdon smiling upon me. It was like turning from some purgatorial fiend to an angel of light, come to announce that the season of torment was past.

"Helen," said he (he frequently called me Helen, and I never resented the freedom), "I want you to look at this picture. Mr. Wilmot will excuse you a moment, I'm sure."

I rose with alacrity. He drew my arm within his, and led me across the room to a splendid painting of Vandyke's that I had noticed before, but not sufficiently examined. After a moment of silent contemplation, I was beginning to comment on its beauties and peculiarities, when, playfully pressing the hand he still retained within his arm, he interrupted me with, – "Never mind the picture: it was not for that I brought you here; it was to get you away from that scoundrelly old profligate yonder, who is looking as if he would like to challenge me for the affront."

"I am very much obliged to you," said I. "This is twice you have delivered me from such unpleasant companionship."

"Don't be too thankful," he answered: "it is not all kindness to you; it is partly from a feeling of spite to your tormentors that makes me delighted to do the old fellows a bad turn, though I don't think I have any great reason to dread them as rivals. Have I, Helen?"

"You know I detest them both."

"And me?"

"I have no reason to detest you."

"But what are your sentiments towards me? Helen – Speak! How do you regard me?"

And again he pressed my hand; but I feared there was more of conscious power than tenderness in his demeanour, and I felt he had no right to extort a confession of attachment from me when he had made no correspondent avowal himself, and knew not what to answer. At last I said, – "How do you regard me?"

"Sweet angel, I adore you! I –"

"Helen, I want you a moment," said the distinct, low voice of my aunt, close beside us. And I left him, muttering maledictions against his evil angel.

"Well, aunt, what is it? What do you want?" said I, following her to the embrasure of the window.

"I want you to join the company, when you are fit to be seen," returned she, severely regarding me; "but please to stay here a little, till that shocking colour is somewhat abated, and your eyes have recovered something of their natural expression. I should be ashamed for anyone to see you in your present state."

Of course, such a remark had no effect in reducing the 'shocking colour'; on the contrary, I felt my face glow with redoubled fires kindled by a complication of emotions, of which indignant, swelling anger was the chief. I offered no reply, however, but pushed aside the curtain and looked into the night – or rather into the lamp-lit square.

"Was Mr. Huntingdon proposing to you, Helen?" inquired my too watchful relative.

"No."

"What was he saying then? I heard something very like it."

"I don't know what he would have said, if you hadn't interrupted him."

"And would you have accepted him, Helen, if he had proposed?"

"Of course not – without consulting uncle and you."

"Oh! I'm glad, my dear, you have so much prudence left. Well, now," she added, after a moment's pause, "you have made yourself conspicuous enough for one evening. The ladies are directing inquiring glances towards us at this moment, I see: I shall join them. Do you come too, when you are sufficiently composed to appear as usual."

"I am so now."

"Speak gently then, and don't look so malicious," said my calm, but provoking aunt. "We shall return home shortly, and then," she added with solemn significance, "I have much to say to you."

So I went home prepared for a formidable lecture. Little was said by either party in the carriage during our short transit homewards; but when I had entered my room and thrown myself into an easy-chair, to reflect on the events of the day, my aunt followed me thither, and having dismissed Rachel, who was carefully stowing away my ornaments, closed the door; and placing a chair beside me, or rather at right angles with mine, sat down. With due deference I offered her my more commodious seat. She declined it, and thus opened the conference: "Do you remember, Helen, our conversation the night but one before we left Staningley?"

"Yes, aunt."

"And do you remember how I warned you against letting your heart be stolen from you by those unworthy of its possession, and fixing your affections where approbation did not go before, and where reason and judgment withheld their sanction?"

"Yes; but my reason –"

"Pardon me – and do you remember assuring me that there was no occasion for uneasiness on your account; for you should never be tempted to marry a man who was deficient in sense or principle, however handsome or charming in other respects he might be, for you could not love him; you should hate – despise – pity – anything but love him – were not those your words?"

"Yes; but –"

"And did you not say that your affection must be founded on approbation; and that, unless you could approve and honour and respect, you could not love?"

"Yes; but I do approve, and honour, and respect –"

"How so, my dear? Is Mr. Huntingdon a good man?"

"He is a much better man than you think him."

"That is nothing to the purpose. Is he a good man?"

"Yes – in some respects. He has a good disposition."

"Is he a man of principle?"

"Perhaps not, exactly; but it is only for want of thought. If he had some one to advise him, and remind him of what is right –"

"He would soon learn, you think – and you yourself would willingly undertake to be his teacher? But, my dear, he is, I believe, full ten years older than you – how is it that you are so beforehand in moral acquirements?"

"Thanks to you, aunt, I have been well brought up, and had good examples always before me, which he, most likely, has not; and, besides, he is of a sanguine temperament, and a gay, thoughtless temper, and I am naturally inclined to reflection."

"Well, now you have made him out to be deficient in both sense and principle, by your own confession –"

"Then, my sense and my principle are at his service."

"That sounds presumptuous, Helen. Do you think you have enough for both; and do you imagine your merry, thoughtless profligate would allow himself to be guided by a young girl like you?"

"No; I should not wish to guide him; but I think I might have influence sufficient to save him from some errors, and I should think my life well spent in the effort to preserve so noble a nature from destruction. He always listens attentively now when I speak seriously to him (and I often venture to reprove his random way of talking), and sometimes he says that if he had me always by his side he should never do or say a wicked thing, and that a little daily talk with me would make him quite a saint. It may be partly jest and partly flattery, but still –"

"But still you think it may be truth?"

"If I do think there is any mixture of truth in it, it is not from confidence in my own powers, but in his natural goodness. And you have no right to call him a profligate, aunt; he is nothing of the kind."

"Who told you so, my dear? What was that story about his intrigue with a married lady – Lady who was it? – Miss Wilmot herself was telling you the other day?"

"It was false – false!" I cried. "I don't believe a word of it."

"You think, then, that he is a virtuous, well-conducted young man?"

"I know nothing positive respecting his character. I only know that I have heard nothing definite against it – nothing that could be proved, at least; and till people can prove their slanderous accusations, I will not believe them. And I know this, that if he has committed errors, they are only such as are common to youth, and such as nobody thinks anything about; for I see that everybody likes him, and all the mammas smile upon him, and their daughters – and Miss Wilmot herself – are only too glad to attract his attention."

"Helen, the world may look upon such offences as venial; a few unprincipled mothers may be anxious to catch a young man of fortune without reference to his character; and thoughtless girls may be glad to win the smiles of so handsome a gentleman, without seeking to penetrate beyond the surface; but you, I trusted, were better informed than to see with their eyes, and judge with their perverted judgment. I did not think you would call these venial errors!"

"Nor do I, aunt; but if I hate the sins, I love the sinner, and would do much for his salvation, even supposing your suspicions to be mainly true, which I do not and will not believe."

"Well, my dear, ask your uncle what sort of company he keeps, and if he is not banded with a set of loose, profligate young men, whom he calls his friends, his jolly companions, and whose chief delight is to wallow in vice, and vie with each other who can run fastest and furthest down the headlong road to the place prepared for the devil and his angels."

"Then I will save him from them."

"Oh, Helen, Helen! You little know the misery of uniting your fortunes to such a man!"

"I have such confidence in him, aunt, notwithstanding all you say, that I would willingly risk my happiness for the chance of securing his. I will leave better men to those who only consider their own advantage. If he has done amiss, I shall consider my life well spent in saving him from the consequences of his early errors, and striving to recall him to the path of virtue. God grant me success!"

Here the conversation ended, for at this juncture my uncle's voice was heard from his chamber, loudly calling upon my aunt to come to bed. He was in a bad humour that night; for his gout was worse. It had been gradually increasing upon him ever since we came to town; and my aunt took advantage of the circumstance next morning to persuade him to return to the country immediately, without waiting for the close of the season. His physician supported and enforced her arguments; and contrary to her usual habits, she so hurried the preparations for removal (as much for my sake as my uncle's, I think), that in a very few days we departed; and I saw no more of Mr. Huntingdon. My aunt flatters herself I shall soon forget him – perhaps she thinks I have forgotten him already, for I never mention his name; and she may continue to think so, till we meet again – if ever that should be. I wonder if it will?

Chapter Eighteen

AUGUST 25TH. – I am now quite settled down to my usual routine of steady occupations and quiet amusements – tolerably contented and cheerful, but still looking forward to spring with the hope of returning to town, not for its gaieties and dissipations, but for the chance of meeting Mr. Huntingdon once again; for still he is always in my thoughts and in my dreams. In all my employments, whatever I do, or see, or hear, has an ultimate reference to him; whatever skill or knowledge I acquire is some day to be turned to his advantage or amusement; whatever new beauties in nature or art I discover are to be depicted to meet his eye, or stored in my memory to be told him at some future period. This, at least, is the hope that I cherish, the fancy that lights me on my lonely way. It may be only an ignis fatuus, after all, but it can do no harm to follow it with my eyes and rejoice in its lustre, as long as it does not lure me from the path I ought to keep; and I think it will not, for I have thought deeply on my aunt's advice, and I see clearly, now, the folly of throwing myself away on one that is unworthy of all the love I have to give, and incapable of responding to the best and deepest feelings of my inmost heart – so clearly, that even if I should see him again, and if he should remember me and love me still (which, alas! is too little probable, considering how he is situated, and by whom surrounded), and if he should ask me to marry him – I am determined not to consent until I know for certain whether my aunt's opinion of him or mine is nearest the truth; for if mine is altogether wrong, it is not he that I love; it is a creature of my own imagination. But I think it is not wrong – no, no – there is a secret something – an inward instinct that assures me I am right. There is essential goodness in him; – and what delight to unfold it! If he has wandered, what bliss to recall him! If he is now exposed to the baneful influence of corrupting and wicked companions, what glory to deliver him from them! Oh! If I could but believe that Heaven has designed me for this!

* * *

Today is the first of September; but my uncle has ordered the gamekeeper to spare the partridges till the gentlemen come. "What gentlemen?" I asked when I heard it. A small party he had invited to shoot. His friend Mr. Wilmot was one, and my aunt's friend, Mr. Boarham, another. This struck me as terrible news at the moment; but all regret and apprehension vanished like a dream when I heard that Mr. Huntingdon was actually to be a third! My aunt is greatly against his coming, of course: she earnestly endeavoured to dissuade my uncle from asking him; but he, laughing at her objections, told her it was no use talking, for the mischief was already done: he had invited Huntingdon and his friend Lord Lowborough before we left London, and nothing now remained but to fix the day for their coming. So he is safe, and I am sure of seeing him. I cannot express my joy. I find it very difficult to conceal it from my aunt; but I don't wish to trouble her with my feelings till I know whether I ought to indulge them or not. If I find it my absolute duty to suppress them, they shall trouble no one but myself; and if I can really feel myself justified in indulging this attachment, I can dare anything, even the anger and grief of my best friend, for its object – surely, I shall soon know. But they are not coming till about the middle of the month.

We are to have two lady visitors also: Mr. Wilmot is to bring his niece and her cousin Milicent. I suppose my aunt thinks the latter will benefit me by her society, and the salutary example of her gentle deportment and lowly and tractable spirit; and the former I suspect she intends as a species of counter-attraction to win Mr. Huntingdon's attention from me. I don't thank her for this; but I shall be glad of Milicent's company: she is a sweet, good girl, and I wish I were like her – more like her, at least, than I am.

* * *

19th. – They are come. They came the day before yesterday. The gentlemen are all gone out to shoot, and the ladies are with my aunt, at work in the drawing room. I have retired to the library, for I am very unhappy, and I want to be alone.

Books cannot divert me; so having opened my desk, I will try what may be done by detailing the cause of my uneasiness. This paper will serve instead of a confidential friend into whose ear I might pour forth the overflowings of my heart. It will not sympathise with my distresses, but then it will not laugh at them, and, if I keep it close, it cannot tell again; so it is, perhaps, the best friend I could have for the purpose.

First, let me speak of his arrival – how I sat at my window, and watched for nearly two hours, before his carriage entered the park-gates – for they all came before him, – and how deeply I was disappointed at every arrival, because it was not his. First came Mr. Wilmot and the ladies. When Milicent had got into her room, I quitted my post a few minutes to look in upon her and have a little private conversation, for she was now my intimate friend, several long epistles having passed between us since our parting. On returning to my window, I beheld another carriage at the door. Was it his? No; it was Mr. Boarham's plain dark chariot; and there stood he upon the steps, carefully superintending the dislodging of his various boxes and packages. What a collection! One would have thought he projected a visit of six months at least. A considerable time after, came Lord Lowborough in his barouche. Is he one of the profligate friends, I wonder? I should think not; for no one could call him a jolly companion, I'm sure, – and, besides, he appears too sober and gentlemanly in his demeanour to merit such suspicions. He is a tall, thin, gloomy-looking man, apparently between thirty and forty, and of a somewhat sickly, careworn aspect.

At last, Mr. Huntingdon's light phaeton came bowling merrily up the lawn. I had but a transient glimpse of him: for the moment it stopped, he sprang out over the side on to the portico steps, and disappeared into the house.

I now submitted to be dressed for dinner – a duty which Rachel had been urging upon me for the last twenty minutes; and when that important business was completed, I repaired to the drawing room, where I found Mr. and Miss Wilmot and Milicent Hargrave already assembled. Shortly after, Lord Lowborough entered, and then Mr. Boarham, who seemed quite willing to forget and forgive my former conduct, and to hope that a little conciliation and steady perseverance on his part might yet succeed in bringing me to reason. While I stood at the window, conversing with Milicent, he came up to me, and was beginning to talk in nearly his usual strain, when Mr. Huntingdon entered the room.

"How will he greet me, I wonder?" said my bounding heart; and, instead of advancing to meet him, I turned to the window to hide or subdue my emotion. But having saluted his host and hostess, and the rest of the company, he came to me, ardently squeezed my hand, and murmured he was glad to see me once again. At that moment dinner was announced: my aunt desired him to take Miss Hargrave into the dining room, and odious Mr. Wilmot, with unspeakable grimaces, offered his arm to me; and I was condemned to sit between himself and Mr. Boarham. But afterwards, when we were all again assembled in the drawing room, I was indemnified for so much suffering by a few delightful minutes of conversation with Mr. Huntingdon.

In the course of the evening, Miss Wilmot was called upon to sing and play for the amusement of the company, and I to exhibit my drawings, and, though he likes music, and she is an accomplished musician, I think I am right in affirming, that he paid more attention to my drawings than to her music.

So far so good; – but hearing him pronounce, sotto voce, but with peculiar emphasis, concerning one of the pieces, "This is better than all!" – I looked up, curious to see which it was, and, to my horror, beheld him complacently gazing at the back of the picture: – it was his own face that I had sketched there and forgotten to rub out! To make matters worse, in the agony of the moment, I attempted to snatch it from his hand; but he prevented me, and exclaiming, "No – by George, I'll keep it!" placed it against his waistcoat and buttoned his coat upon it with a delighted chuckle.

Then, drawing a candle close to his elbow, he gathered all the drawings to himself, as well what he had seen as the others, and muttering, "I must look at both sides now," he eagerly commenced an examination, which I watched, at first, with tolerable composure, in the confidence that his vanity would not be gratified by any further discoveries; for, though I must plead guilty to having disfigured the backs of several with abortive attempts to delineate that too fascinating physiognomy, I was sure that, with that one unfortunate exception, I had carefully obliterated all such witnesses of my infatuation. But the pencil frequently leaves an impression upon cardboard that no amount of rubbing can efface. Such, it seems, was the case with most of these; and, I confess, I trembled when I saw him holding them so close to the candle, and poring so intently over the seeming blanks; but still, I trusted, he would not be able to make out these dim traces to his own satisfaction. I was mistaken, however. Having ended his scrutiny, he quietly remarked, – "I perceive the backs of young ladies' drawings, like the postscripts of their letters, are the most important and interesting part of the concern."

Then, leaning back in his chair, he reflected a few minutes in silence, complacently smiling to himself, and while I was concocting some cutting speech wherewith to check his gratification, he rose, and passing over to where Annabella Wilmot sat vehemently coquetting with Lord Lowborough, seated himself on the sofa beside her, and attached himself to her for the rest of the evening.

"So then," thought I, "he despises me, because he knows I love him."

And the reflection made me so miserable I knew not what to do. Milicent came and began to admire my drawings, and make remarks upon them; but I could not talk to her – I could talk to no one, and, upon the introduction of tea, I took advantage of the open door and the slight diversion caused by its entrance to slip out – for I was sure I could not take any – and take refuge in the library. My aunt sent Thomas in quest of me, to ask if I were not coming to tea; but I bade him say I should not take any tonight, and, happily, she was too much occupied with her guests to make any further inquiries at the time.

As most of the company had travelled far that day, they retired early to rest; and having heard them all, as I thought, go up-stairs, I ventured out, to get my candlestick from the drawing room sideboard. But Mr. Huntingdon had lingered behind the rest. He was just at the foot of the stairs when I opened the door, and hearing my step in the hall – though I could hardly hear it myself – he instantly turned back.

"Helen, is that you?" said he. "Why did you run away from us?"

"Goodnight, Mr. Huntingdon," said I, coldly, not choosing to answer the question. And I turned away to enter the drawing room.

"But you'll shake hands, won't you?" said he, placing himself in the doorway before me. And he seized my hand and held it, much against my will.

"Let me go, Mr. Huntingdon," said I. "I want to get a candle."

"The candle will keep," returned he.

I made a desperate effort to free my hand from his grasp.

"Why are you in such a hurry to leave me, Helen?" he said, with a smile of the most provoking self-sufficiency. "You don't hate me, you know."

"Yes, I do – at this moment."

"Not you. It is Annabella Wilmot you hate, not me."

"I have nothing to do with Annabella Wilmot," said I, burning with indignation.

"But I have, you know," returned he, with peculiar emphasis.

"That is nothing to me, sir," I retorted.

"Is it nothing to you, Helen? Will you swear it? Will you?"

"No I won't, Mr. Huntingdon! And I will go," cried I, not knowing whether to laugh, or to cry, or to break out into a tempest of fury.

"Go, then, you vixen!" he said; but the instant he released my hand he had the audacity to put his arm round my neck, and kiss me.

Trembling with anger and agitation, and I don't know what besides, I broke away, and got my candle, and rushed up-stairs to my room. He would not have done so but for that hateful picture. And there he had it still in his possession, an eternal monument to his pride and my humiliation.

It was but little sleep I got that night, and in the morning I rose perplexed and troubled with the thoughts of meeting him at breakfast. I knew not how it was to be done. An assumption of dignified, cold indifference would hardly do, after what he knew of my devotion – to his face, at least. Yet something must be done to check his presumption – I would not submit to be tyrannised over by those bright, laughing eyes. And, accordingly, I received his cheerful morning salutation as calmly and coldly as my aunt could have wished, and defeated with brief answers his one or two attempts to draw me into conversation, while I comported myself with unusual cheerfulness and complaisance towards every other member of the party, especially Annabella Wilmot, and even her uncle and Mr. Boarham were treated with an extra amount of civility on the occasion, not from any motives of coquetry, but just to show him that my particular coolness and reserve arose from no general ill-humour or depression of spirits.

He was not, however, to be repelled by such acting as this. He did not talk much to me, but when he did speak it was with a degree of freedom and openness, and kindliness too, that plainly seemed to intimate he knew his words were music to my ears; and when his looks met mine it was with a smile – presumptuous, it might be – but oh! So sweet, so bright, so genial, that I could not possibly retain my anger; every vestige of displeasure soon melted away beneath it like morning clouds before the summer sun.

Soon after breakfast all the gentlemen save one, with boyish eagerness, set out on their expedition against the hapless partridges; my uncle and Mr. Wilmot on their shooting ponies, Mr. Huntingdon and Lord Lowborough on their legs: the one exception being Mr. Boarham, who, in consideration of the rain that had fallen during the night, thought it prudent to remain behind a little and join them in a while when the sun had dried the grass. And he favoured us all with a long and minute disquisition upon the evils and dangers attendant upon damp feet, delivered with the most imperturbable gravity, amid the jeers and laughter of Mr. Huntingdon and my uncle, who, leaving the prudent sportsman to entertain the ladies with his medical discussions, sallied forth with their guns, bending their steps to the stables first, to have a look at the horses and let out the dogs.

Not desirous of sharing Mr. Boarham's company for the whole of the morning, I betook myself to the library, and there brought forth my easel and began to paint. The easel and the painting apparatus would serve as an excuse for abandoning the drawing room if my aunt should come to complain of the desertion, and besides I wanted to finish the picture. It was one I had taken great pains with, and I intended it to be my masterpiece, though it was somewhat presumptuous in the design. By the bright azure of the sky, and by the warm and brilliant lights and deep long shadows, I had endeavoured to convey the idea of a sunny morning. I had ventured to give more of the bright verdure of spring or early summer to the grass and foliage than is commonly attempted in painting. The scene represented was an open glade in a wood. A group of dark Scotch firs was introduced in the middle distance to relieve the prevailing freshness of the rest; but in the foreground was part of the gnarled trunk and of the spreading boughs of a large forest-tree, whose foliage was of a brilliant golden green – not golden from autumnal mellowness, but from the sunshine and the very immaturity of the scarce expanded leaves. Upon this bough, that stood out in bold relief against the sombre firs, were seated an amorous pair of turtle doves, whose soft sad-coloured plumage afforded a contrast of another nature; and beneath it a young girl was kneeling on the daisy-spangled turf, with head thrown back and masses of fair hair falling on her shoulders, her hands clasped, lips parted, and eyes intently gazing upward in pleased yet earnest contemplation of those feathered lovers – too deeply absorbed in each other to notice her.

I had scarcely settled to my work, which, however, wanted but a few touches to the finishing, when the sportsmen passed the window on their return from the stables. It was partly open, and Mr. Huntingdon must have seen me as he went by, for in half a minute he came back, and setting his gun against the wall, threw up the sash and sprang in, and set himself before my picture.

"Very pretty, i'faith," said he, after attentively regarding it for a few seconds; "and a very fitting study for a young lady. Spring just opening into summer – morning just approaching noon – girlhood just ripening into womanhood, and hope just verging on fruition. She's a sweet creature! But why didn't you make her black hair?"

"I thought light hair would suit her better. You see I have made her blue-eyed and plump, and fair and rosy."

"Upon my word – a very Hebe! I should fall in love with her if I hadn't the artist before me. Sweet innocent! She's thinking there will come a time when she will be wooed and won like that pretty hen-dove by as fond and fervent a lover; and she's thinking how pleasant it will be, and how tender and faithful he will find her."

"And perhaps," suggested I, "how tender and faithful she shall find him."

"Perhaps, for there is no limit to the wild extravagance of Hope's imaginings at such an age."

"Do you call that, then, one of her wild, extravagant delusions?"

"No; my heart tells me it is not. I might have thought so once, but now, I say, give me the girl I love, and I will swear eternal constancy to her and her alone, through summer and winter, through youth and age, and life and death! If age and death must come."

He spoke this in such serious earnest that my heart bounded with delight; but the minute after he changed his tone, and asked, with a significant smile, if I had "any more portraits."

"No," replied I, reddening with confusion and wrath.

But my portfolio was on the table: he took it up, and coolly sat down to examine its contents.

"Mr. Huntingdon, those are my unfinished sketches," cried I, "and I never let any one see them."

And I placed my hand on the portfolio to wrest it from him, but he maintained his hold, assuring me that he "liked unfinished sketches of all things."

"But I hate them to be seen," returned I. "I can't let you have it, indeed!"

"Let me have its bowels then," said he; and just as I wrenched the portfolio from his hand, he deftly abstracted the greater part of its contents, and after turning them over a moment he cried out, – "Bless my stars, here's another;" and slipped a small oval of ivory paper into his waistcoat pocket – a complete miniature portrait that I had sketched with such tolerable success as to be induced to colour it with great pains and care. But I was determined he should not keep it.

"Mr. Huntingdon," cried I, "I insist upon having that back! It is mine, and you have no right to take it. Give it me directly – I'll never forgive you if you don't!"

But the more vehemently I insisted, the more he aggravated my distress by his insulting, gleeful laugh. At length, however, he restored it to me, saying, – "Well, well, since you value it so much, I'll not deprive you of it."

To show him how I valued it, I tore it in two and threw it into the fire. He was not prepared for this. His merriment suddenly ceasing, he stared in mute amazement at the consuming treasure; and then, with a careless "Humph! I'll go and shoot now," he turned on his heel and vacated the apartment by the window as he came, and setting on his hat with an air, took up his gun and walked away, whistling as he went – and leaving me not too much agitated to finish my picture, for I was glad, at the moment, that I had vexed him.

When I returned to the drawing room, I found Mr. Boarham had ventured to follow his comrades to the field; and shortly after lunch, to which they did not think of returning, I volunteered to accompany the ladies in a walk, and show Annabella and Milicent the beauties of the country. We took a long ramble, and re-entered the park just as the sportsmen were returning from their expedition. Toil-spent and travel-stained, the main body of them crossed over the grass to avoid us, but Mr. Huntingdon, all spattered and splashed as he was, and stained with the blood of his prey – to the no small offence of my aunt's strict sense of propriety – came out of his way to meet us, with cheerful smiles and words for all but me, and placing himself between Annabella Wilmot and myself, walked up the road and began to relate the various exploits and disasters of the day, in a manner that would have convulsed me with laughter if I had been on good terms with him; but he addressed himself entirely to Annabella, and I, of course, left all the laughter and all the badinage to her, and affecting the utmost indifference to whatever passed between them, walked along a few paces apart, and looking every way but theirs, while my aunt and Milicent went before, linked arm in arm and gravely discoursing together. At length Mr. Huntingdon turned to me, and addressing me in a confidential whisper, said, – "Helen, why did you burn my picture?"

"Because I wished to destroy it," I answered, with an asperity it is useless now to lament.

"Oh, very good!" was the reply; "if you don't value me, I must turn to somebody that will."

I thought it was partly in jest – a half-playful mixture of mock resignation and pretended indifference: but immediately he resumed his place beside Miss Wilmot, and from that hour to this – during all that evening, and all the next day, and the next, and the next, and all this morning (the 22nd), he has never given me one kind word or one pleasant look – never spoken to me, but from pure necessity – never glanced towards me but with a cold, unfriendly look I thought him quite incapable of assuming.

My aunt observes the change, and though she has not inquired the cause or made any remark to me on the subject, I see it gives her pleasure. Miss Wilmot observes it, too, and triumphantly ascribes it to her own superior charms and blandishments; but I am truly miserable – more so than I like to acknowledge to myself. Pride refuses to aid me. It has brought me into the scrape, and will not help me out of it.

He meant no harm – it was only his joyous, playful spirit; and I, by my acrimonious resentment – so serious, so disproportioned to the offence – have so wounded his feelings, so deeply offended him, that I fear he will never forgive me – and all for a mere jest! He thinks I dislike him, and he must continue to think so. I must lose him for ever, and Annabella may win him, and triumph as she will.

But it is not my loss nor her triumph that I deplore so greatly as the wreck of my fond hopes for his advantage, and her unworthiness of his affection, and the injury he will do himself by trusting his happiness to her. She does not love him: she thinks only of herself. She cannot appreciate the good that is in him: she will neither see it, nor value it, nor cherish it. She will neither deplore his faults nor attempt their amendment, but rather aggravate them by her own. And I doubt whether she will not deceive him after all. I see she is playing double between him and Lord Lowborough, and while she amuses herself with the lively Huntingdon, she tries her utmost to enslave his moody friend; and should she succeed in bringing both to her feet, the fascinating commoner will have but little chance against the lordly peer. If he observes her artful by-play, it gives him no uneasiness, but rather adds new zest to his diversion by opposing a stimulating check to his otherwise too easy conquest.

Messrs. Wilmot and Boarham have severally taken occasion by his neglect of me to renew their advances; and if I were like Annabella and some others I should take advantage of their perseverance to endeavour to pique him into a revival of affection; but, justice and honesty apart, I could not bear to do it. I am annoyed enough by their present persecutions without encouraging them further; and even if I did it would have precious little effect upon him. He sees me suffering under the condescending attentions and prosaic discourses of the one, and the repulsive obtrusions of the other, without so much as a shadow of commiseration for me, or resentment against my tormentors. He never could have loved me, or he would not have resigned me so willingly, and he would not go on talking to everybody else so cheerfully as he does – laughing and jesting with Lord Lowborough and my uncle, teasing Milicent Hargrave, and flirting with Annabella Wilmot – as if nothing were on his mind. Oh! Why can't I hate him? I must be infatuated, or I should scorn to regret him as I do. But I must rally all the powers I have remaining, and try to tear him from my heart. There goes the dinner-bell, and here comes my aunt to scold me for sitting here at my desk all day, instead of staying with the company: wish the company were – gone.

Chapter Nineteen

TWENTY SECOND: Night. – What have I done? And what will be the end of it? I cannot calmly reflect upon it; I cannot sleep. I must have recourse to my diary again; I will commit it to paper tonight, and see what I shall think of it tomorrow.

I went down to dinner resolving to be cheerful and well-conducted, and kept my resolution very creditably, considering how my head ached and how internally wretched I felt. I don't know what is come over me of late; my very energies, both mental and physical, must be strangely impaired, or I should not have acted so weakly in many respects as I have done; but I have not been well this last day or two. I suppose it is with sleeping and eating so little, and thinking so much, and being so continually out of humour. But to return. I was exerting myself to sing and play for the amusement, and at the request, of my aunt and Milicent, before the gentlemen came into the drawing room (Miss Wilmot never likes to waste her musical efforts on ladies' ears alone). Milicent had asked for a little Scotch song, and I was just in the middle of it when they entered. The first thing Mr. Huntingdon did was to walk up to Annabella.

"Now, Miss Wilmot, won't you give us some music tonight?" said he. "Do now! I know you will, when I tell you that I have been hungering and thirsting all day for the sound of your voice. Come! The piano's vacant."

It was, for I had quitted it immediately upon hearing his petition. Had I been endowed with a proper degree of self-possession, I should have turned to the lady myself, and cheerfully joined my entreaties to his, whereby I should have disappointed his expectations, if the affront had been purposely given, or made him sensible of the wrong, if it had only arisen from thoughtlessness; but I felt it too deeply to do anything but rise from the music-stool, and throw myself back on the sofa, suppressing with difficulty the audible expression of the bitterness I felt within. I knew Annabella's musical talents were superior to mine, but that was no reason why I should be treated as a perfect nonentity. The time and the manner of his asking her appeared like a gratuitous insult to me; and I could have wept with pure vexation.

Meantime, she exultingly seated herself at the piano, and favoured him with two of his favourite songs, in such superior style that even I soon lost my anger in admiration, and listened with a sort of gloomy pleasure to the skilful modulations of her full-toned and powerful voice, so judiciously aided by her rounded and spirited touch; and while my ears drank in the sound, my eyes rested on the face of her principal auditor, and derived an equal or superior delight from the contemplation of his speaking countenance, as he stood beside her – that eye and brow lighted up with keen enthusiasm, and that sweet smile passing and appearing like gleams of sunshine on an April day. No wonder he should hunger and thirst to hear her sing. I now forgave him from my heart his reckless slight of me, and I felt ashamed at my pettish resentment of such a trifle – ashamed too of those bitter envious pangs that gnawed my inmost heart, in spite of all this admiration and delight.

"There now," said she, playfully running her fingers over the keys when she had concluded the second song. "What shall I give you next?"

But in saying this she looked back at Lord Lowborough, who was standing a little behind, leaning against the back of a chair, an attentive listener, too, experiencing, to judge by his countenance, much the same feelings of mingled pleasure and sadness as I did. But the look she gave him plainly said, "Do you choose for me now: I have done enough for him, and will gladly exert myself to gratify you;" and thus encouraged, his lordship came forward, and turning over the music, presently set before her a little song that I had noticed before, and read more than once, with an interest arising from the circumstance of my connecting it in my mind with the reigning tyrant of my thoughts. And now, with my nerves already excited and half unstrung, I could not hear those words so sweetly warbled forth without some symptoms of emotion I was not able to suppress. Tears rose unbidden to my eyes, and I buried my face in the sofa-pillow that they might flow unseen while I listened. The air was simple, sweet, and sad. It is still running in my head, and so are the words:

> *Farewell to thee! But not farewell*
> *To all my fondest thoughts of thee:*
> *Within my heart they still shall dwell;*
> *And they shall cheer and comfort me.*

O beautiful, and full of grace!
If thou hadst never met mine eye,
I had not dreamed a living face
Could fancied charms so far outvie.
If I may ne'er behold again
That form and face so dear to me,
Nor hear thy voice, still would I fain
Preserve, for aye, their memory.
That voice, the magic of whose tone
Can wake an echo in my breast,
Creating feelings that, alone,
Can make my tranced spirit blest.
That laughing eye, whose sunny beam
My memory would not cherish less; –
And oh, that smile! I whose joyous gleam
No mortal languish can express.
Adieu! but let me cherish, still,
The hope with which I cannot part.
Contempt may wound, and coldness chill,
But still it lingers in my heart.
And who can tell but Heaven, at last,
May answer all my thousand prayers,
And bid the future pay the past
With joy for anguish, smiles for tears.

When it ceased, I longed for nothing so much as to be out of the room. The sofa was not far from the door, but I did not dare to raise my head, for I knew Mr. Huntingdon was standing near me, and I knew by the sound of his voice, as he spoke in answer to some remark of Lord Lowborough's, that his face was turned towards me. Perhaps a half-suppressed sob had caught his ear, and caused him to look round – heaven forbid! But with a violent effort, I checked all further signs of weakness, dried my tears, and, when I thought he had turned away again, rose, and instantly left the apartment, taking refuge in my favourite resort, the library.

There was no light there but the faint red glow of the neglected fire; – but I did not want a light; I only wanted to indulge my thoughts, unnoticed and undisturbed; and sitting down on a low stool before the easy-chair, I sunk my head upon its cushioned seat, and thought, and thought, until the tears gushed out again, and I wept like any child. Presently, however, the door was gently opened and someone entered the room. I trusted it was only a servant, and did not stir. The door was closed again – but I was not alone; a hand gently touched my shoulder, and a voice said, softly, – "Helen, what is the matter?"

I could not answer at the moment.

"You must, and shall tell me," was added, more vehemently, and the speaker threw himself on his knees beside me on the rug, and forcibly possessed himself of my hand; but I hastily caught it away, and replied, – "It is nothing to you, Mr. Huntingdon."

"Are you sure it is nothing to me?" he returned; "can you swear that you were not thinking of me while you wept?" This was unendurable. I made an effort to rise, but he was kneeling on my dress.

"Tell me," continued he – "I want to know, – because if you were, I have something to say to you, – and if not, I'll go."

"Go then!" I cried; but, fearing he would obey too well, and never come again, I hastily added – "Or say what you have to say, and have done with it!"

"But which?" said he – "for I shall only say it if you really were thinking of me. So tell me, Helen."

"You're excessively impertinent, Mr. Huntingdon!"

"Not at all – too pertinent, you mean. So you won't tell me? – Well, I'll spare your woman's pride, and, construing your silence into 'Yes,' I'll take it for granted that I was the subject of your thoughts, and the cause of your affliction –"

"Indeed, sir –"

"If you deny it, I won't tell you my secret," threatened he; and I did not interrupt him again, or even attempt to repulse him: though he had taken my hand once more, and half embraced me with his other arm, I was scarcely conscious of it at the time.

"It is this," resumed he: "that Annabella Wilmot, in comparison with you, is like a flaunting peony compared with a sweet, wild rosebud gemmed with dew – and I love you to distraction! – Now, tell me if that intelligence gives you any pleasure. Silence again? That means yes. Then let me add, that I cannot live without you, and if you answer No to this last question, you will drive me mad. – Will you bestow yourself upon me? – You will!" he cried, nearly squeezing me to death in his arms.

"No, no!" I exclaimed, struggling to free myself from him – "you must ask my uncle and aunt."

"They won't refuse me, if you don't."

"I'm not so sure of that – my aunt dislikes you."

"But you don't, Helen – say you love me, and I'll go."

"I wish you would go!" I replied.

"I will, this instant, – if you'll only say you love me."

"You know I do," I answered. And again he caught me in his arms, and smothered me with kisses.

At that moment my aunt opened wide the door, and stood before us, candle in hand, in shocked and horrified amazement, gazing alternately at Mr. Huntingdon and me – for we had both started up, and now stood wide enough asunder. But his confusion was only for a moment. Rallying in an instant, with the most enviable assurance, he began, – "I beg ten thousand pardons, Mrs. Maxwell! Don't be too severe upon me. I've been asking your sweet niece to take me for better, for worse; and she, like a good girl, informs me she cannot think of it without her uncle's and aunt's consent. So let me implore you not to condemn me to eternal wretchedness: if you favour my cause, I am safe; for Mr. Maxwell, I am certain, can refuse you nothing."

"We will talk of this tomorrow, sir," said my aunt, coldly. "It is a subject that demands mature and serious deliberation. At present, you had better return to the drawing room."

"But meantime," pleaded he, "let me commend my cause to your most indulgent –"

"No indulgence for you, Mr. Huntingdon, must come between me and the consideration of my niece's happiness."

"Ah, true! I know she is an angel, and I am a presumptuous dog to dream of possessing such a treasure; but, nevertheless, I would sooner die than relinquish her in favour of the best man that ever went to heaven – and as for her happiness, I would sacrifice my body and soul –"

"Body and soul, Mr. Huntingdon – sacrifice your soul?"

"Well, I would lay down life –"

"You would not be required to lay it down."

"I would spend it, then – devote my life – and all its powers to the promotion and preservation –"

"Another time, sir, we will talk of this – and I should have felt disposed to judge more favourably of your pretensions, if you too had chosen another time and place, and let me add – another manner for your declaration."

"Why, you see, Mrs. Maxwell," he began –

"Pardon me, sir," said she, with dignity – "The company are inquiring for you in the other room." And she turned to me.

"Then you must plead for me, Helen," said he, and at length withdrew.

"You had better retire to your room, Helen," said my aunt, gravely. "I will discuss this matter with you, too, tomorrow."

"Don't be angry, aunt," said I.

"My dear, I am not angry," she replied: "I am surprised. If it is true that you told him you could not accept his offer without our consent –"

"It is true," interrupted I.

"Then how could you permit –?"

"I couldn't help it, aunt," I cried, bursting into tears. They were not altogether the tears of sorrow, or of fear for her displeasure, but rather the outbreak of the general tumultuous excitement of my feelings. But my good aunt was touched at my agitation. In a softer tone, she repeated her recommendation to retire, and, gently kissing my forehead, bade me goodnight, and put her candle in my hand; and I went; but my brain worked so, I could not think of sleeping. I feel calmer now that I have written all this; and I will go to bed, and try to win tired nature's sweet restorer.

Volume Two

Chapter Twenty

SEPTEMBER 24TH. – In the morning I rose, light and cheerful – nay, intensely happy. The hovering cloud cast over me by my aunt's views, and by the fear of not obtaining her consent, was lost in the bright effulgence of my own hopes, and the too delightful consciousness of requited love. It was a splendid morning; and I went out to enjoy it, in a quiet ramble, in company with my own blissful thoughts. The dew was on the grass, and ten thousand gossamers were waving in the breeze; the happy red-breast was pouring out its little soul in song, and my heart overflowed with silent hymns of gratitude and praise to heaven.

But I had not wandered far before my solitude was interrupted by the only person that could have disturbed my musings, at that moment, without being looked upon as an unwelcome intruder: Mr. Huntingdon came suddenly upon me. So unexpected was the apparition, that I might have thought it the creation of an over-excited imagination, had the sense of sight alone borne witness to his presence; but immediately I felt his strong arm round my waist and his warm kiss on my cheek, while his keen and gleeful salutation, "My own Helen!" was ringing in my ear.

"Not yours yet!" said I, hastily swerving aside from this too presumptuous greeting. "Remember my guardians. You will not easily obtain my aunt's consent. Don't you see she is prejudiced against you?"

"I do, dearest; and you must tell me why, that I may best know how to combat her objections. I suppose she thinks I am a prodigal," pursued he, observing that I was unwilling to reply, "and concludes that I shall have but little worldly goods wherewith to endow my better half? If so, you must tell her that my property is mostly entailed, and I cannot get rid of it. There may be a few mortgages on the rest – a few trifling debts and incumbrances here and there, but nothing to speak of; and though I acknowledge I am not so rich as I might be – or have been – still, I think, we could manage pretty comfortably on what's left. My father, you know, was something of a miser, and in his latter days especially saw no pleasure in life but to amass riches; and so it is no wonder that his son should make it his chief delight to spend them, which was accordingly the case, until my acquaintance with you, dear Helen, taught me other views and nobler aims. And the very idea of having you to care for under my roof would force me to moderate my expenses and live like a Christian – not to speak of all the prudence and virtue you would instil into my mind by your wise counsels and sweet, attractive goodness."

"But it is not that," said I; "it is not money my aunt thinks about. She knows better than to value worldly wealth above its price."

"What is it, then?"

"She wishes me to – to marry none but a really good man."

"What, a man of 'decided piety'? – Ahem! – Well, come, I'll manage that too! It's Sunday today, isn't it? I'll go to church morning, afternoon, and evening, and comport myself in such a godly sort that she shall regard me with admiration and sisterly love, as a brand plucked from the burning. I'll come home sighing like a furnace, and full of the savour and unction of dear Mr. Blatant's discourse –"

"Mr. Leighton," said I, dryly.

"Is Mr. Leighton a 'sweet preacher,' Helen – a 'dear, delightful, heavenly-minded man'?"

"He is a good man, Mr. Huntingdon. I wish I could say half as much for you."

"Oh, I forgot, you are a saint, too. I crave your pardon, dearest – but don't call me Mr. Huntingdon; my name is Arthur."

"I'll call you nothing – for I'll have nothing at all to do with you if you talk in that way any more. If you really mean to deceive my aunt as you say, you are very wicked; and if not, you are very wrong to jest on such a subject."

"I stand corrected," said he, concluding his laugh with a sorrowful sigh. "Now," resumed he, after a momentary pause, "let us talk about something else. And come nearer to me, Helen, and take my arm; and then I'll let you alone. I can't be quiet while I see you walking there."

I complied; but said we must soon return to the house.

"No one will be down to breakfast yet, for long enough," he answered. "You spoke of your guardians just now, Helen, but is not your father still living?"

"Yes, but I always look upon my uncle and aunt as my guardians, for they are so in deed, though not in name. My father has entirely given me up to their care. I have never seen him since dear mamma died, when I was a very little girl, and my aunt, at her request, offered to take charge of me, and took me away to Staningley, where I have remained ever since; and I don't think he would object to anything for me that she thought proper to sanction."

"But would he sanction anything to which she thought proper to object?"

"No, I don't think he cares enough about me."

"He is very much to blame – but he doesn't know what an angel he has for his daughter – which is all the better for me, as, if he did, he would not be willing to part with such a treasure."

"And Mr. Huntingdon," said I, "I suppose you know I am not an heiress?"

He protested he had never given it a thought, and begged I would not disturb his present enjoyment by the mention of such uninteresting subjects. I was glad of this proof of disinterested affection; for Annabella Wilmot is the probable heiress to all her uncle's wealth, in addition to her late father's property, which she has already in possession.

I now insisted upon retracing our steps to the house; but we walked slowly, and went on talking as we proceeded. I need not repeat all we said: let me rather refer to what passed between my aunt and me, after breakfast, when Mr. Huntingdon called my uncle aside, no doubt to make his proposals, and she beckoned me into another room, where she once more commenced a solemn remonstrance, which, however, entirely failed to convince me that her view of the case was preferable to my own.

"You judge him uncharitably, aunt, I know," said I. "His very friends are not half so bad as you represent them. There is Walter Hargrave, Milicent's brother, for one: he is but a little lower than the angels, if half she says of him is true. She is continually talking to me about him, and lauding his many virtues to the skies."

"You will form a very inadequate estimate of a man's character," replied she, "if you judge by what a fond sister says of him. The worst of them generally know how to hide their misdeeds from their sisters' eyes, and their mother's, too."

"And there is Lord Lowborough," continued I, "quite a decent man."

"Who told you so? Lord Lowborough is a desperate man. He has dissipated his fortune in gambling and other things, and is now seeking an heiress to retrieve it. I told Miss Wilmot so; but you're all alike: she haughtily answered she was very much obliged to me, but she believed she knew when a man was seeking her for her fortune, and when for herself; she flattered herself she had had experience enough in those matters to be justified in trusting to her own judgment – and as for his lordship's lack of fortune, she cared nothing about that, as she hoped her own would suffice for both; and as for his wildness, she supposed he was no worse than others – besides, he was reformed now. Yes, they can all play the hypocrite when they want to take in a fond, misguided woman!"

"Well, I think he's about as good as she is," said I. "But when Mr. Huntingdon is married, he won't have many opportunities of consorting with his bachelor friends; – and the worse they are, the more I long to deliver him from them."

"To be sure, my dear; and the worse he is, I suppose, the more you long to deliver him from himself."

"Yes, provided he is not incorrigible – that is, the more I long to deliver him from his faults – to give him an opportunity of shaking off the adventitious evil got from contact with others worse than himself, and shining out in the unclouded light of his own genuine goodness – to do my utmost to help his better self against his worse, and make him what he would have been if he had not, from the beginning, had a bad, selfish, miserly father, who, to gratify his own sordid passions, restricted him in the most innocent enjoyments of childhood and youth, and so disgusted him with every kind of restraint; – and a foolish mother who indulged him to the top of his bent, deceiving her husband for him, and doing her utmost to encourage those germs of folly and vice it was her duty to suppress, – and then, such a set of companions as you represent his friends to be –"

"Poor man!" said she, sarcastically, "his kind have greatly wronged him!"

"They have!" cried I – "and they shall wrong him no more – his wife shall undo what his mother did!"

"Well," said she, after a short pause, "I must say, Helen, I thought better of your judgment than this – and your taste too. How you can love such a man I cannot tell, or what pleasure you can find in his company; for 'what fellowship hath light with darkness; or he that believeth with an infidel?'"

"He is not an infidel; – and I am not light, and he is not darkness; his worst and only vice is thoughtlessness."

"And thoughtlessness," pursued my aunt, "may lead to every crime, and will but poorly excuse our errors in the sight of God. Mr. Huntingdon, I suppose, is not without the common faculties of men: he is not so light-headed as to be irresponsible: his Maker has endowed him with reason and conscience as well as the rest of us; the Scriptures are open to him as well as to others; – and 'if he hear not them, neither will he hear though one rose from the dead.' And remember, Helen," continued she, solemnly, "'the wicked shall be turned into hell, and they that forget God!' And suppose, even, that he should continue to love you, and you him, and that you should pass through life together with tolerable comfort – how will it be in the end, when you see yourselves parted for ever; you, perhaps, taken into eternal bliss, and he cast into the lake that burneth with unquenchable fire – there for ever to –"

"Not for ever," I exclaimed, "'only till he has paid the uttermost farthing;' for 'if any man's work abide not the fire, he shall suffer loss, yet himself shall be saved, but so as by fire;' and He that 'is able to subdue all things to Himself will have all men to be saved,' and 'will, in the fulness of time, gather together in one all things in Christ Jesus, who tasted death for every man, and in whom God will reconcile all things to Himself, whether they be things in earth or things in heaven.'"

"Oh, Helen! Where did you learn all this?"

"In the Bible, aunt. I have searched it through, and found nearly thirty passages, all tending to support the same theory."

"And is that the use you make of your Bible? And did you find no passages tending to prove the danger and the falsity of such a belief?"

"No: I found, indeed, some passages that, taken by themselves, might seem to contradict that opinion; but they will all bear a different construction to that which is commonly given, and in most the only difficulty is in the word which we translate 'everlasting' or 'eternal.' I don't know the Greek, but I believe it strictly means for ages, and might signify either endless or long-enduring. And as for the danger of the belief, I would not publish it abroad if I thought any poor wretch would be likely to presume upon it to his own destruction, but it is a glorious thought to cherish in one's own heart, and I would not part with it for all the world can give!"

Here our conference ended, for it was now high time to prepare for church. Every one attended the morning service, except my uncle, who hardly ever goes, and Mr. Wilmot, who stayed at home with him to enjoy a quiet game of cribbage. In the afternoon Miss Wilmot and Lord Lowborough likewise excused themselves from attending; but Mr. Huntingdon vouchsafed to accompany us again. Whether it was to ingratiate himself with my aunt I cannot tell, but, if so, he certainly should have behaved better. I must confess, I did not like his conduct during service at all. Holding his prayer-book upside down, or open at any place but the right, he did nothing but stare about him, unless he happened to catch my aunt's eye or mine, and then he would drop his own on his book, with a puritanical air of mock solemnity that would have been ludicrous, if it had not been too provoking. Once, during the sermon, after attentively regarding Mr. Leighton for a few minutes, he suddenly produced his gold pencil-case and snatched up a Bible. Perceiving that I observed the movement, he whispered that he was going to make a note of the sermon; but instead of that, as I sat next him, I could not help seeing that he was making a caricature of the preacher, giving to the respectable, pious, elderly gentleman, the air and aspect of a most absurd old hypocrite. And yet, upon his return, he talked to my aunt about the sermon with a degree of modest, serious discrimination that tempted me to believe he had really attended to and profited by the discourse.

Just before dinner my uncle called me into the library for the discussion of a very important matter, which was dismissed in few words.

"Now, Nell," said he, "this young Huntingdon has been asking for you: what must I say about it? Your aunt would answer 'no' – but what say you?"

"I say yes, uncle," replied I, without a moment's hesitation; for I had thoroughly made up my mind on the subject.

"Very good!" cried he. "Now that's a good honest answer – wonderful for a girl! – Well, I'll write to your father tomorrow. He's sure to give his consent; so you may look on the matter as settled. You'd have done a deal better if you'd taken Wilmot, I can tell you; but that you won't believe. At your time of life, it's love that rules the roast: at mine, it's solid, serviceable gold. I suppose now, you'd never dream of looking into the state of your husband's finances, or troubling your head about settlements, or anything of that sort?"

"I don't think I should."

"Well, be thankful, then, that you've wiser heads to think for you. I haven't had time, yet, to examine thoroughly into this young rascal's affairs, but I see that a great part of his father's fine property has been squandered away; – but still, I think, there's a pretty fair share of it left, and a little careful nursing may make a handsome thing of it yet; and then we must persuade your father to give you a decent fortune, as he has only one besides yourself to care for; – and, if you behave well, who knows but what I may be induced to remember you in my will!" continued he, putting his fingers to his nose, with a knowing wink.

"Thanks, uncle, for that and all your kindness," replied I.

"Well, and I questioned this young spark on the matter of settlements," continued he; "and he seemed disposed to be generous enough on that point –"

"I knew he would!" said I. "But pray don't trouble your head – or his, or mine about that; for all I have will be his, and all he has will be mine; and what more could either of us require?" And I was about to make my exit, but he called me back.

"Stop, stop!" cried he; "we haven't mentioned the time yet. When must it be? Your aunt would put it off till the Lord knows when, but he is anxious to be bound as soon as may be: he won't hear of waiting beyond next month; and you, I guess, will be of the same mind, so –"

"Not at all, uncle; on the contrary, I should like to wait till after Christmas, at least."

"Oh! Pooh, pooh! Never tell me that tale – I know better," cried he; and he persisted in his incredulity. Nevertheless, it is quite true. I am in no hurry at all. How can I be, when I think of the momentous change that awaits me, and of all I have to leave? It is happiness enough to know that we are to be united; and that he really loves me, and I may love him as devotedly, and think of him as often as I please. However, I insisted upon consulting my aunt about the time of the wedding, for I determined her counsels should not be utterly disregarded; and no conclusions on that particular are come to yet.

Chapter Twenty-One

OCTOBER 1ST. – All is settled now. My father has given his consent, and the time is fixed for Christmas, by a sort of compromise between the respective advocates for hurry and delay. Milicent Hargrave is to be one bridesmaid and Annabella Wilmot the other – not that I am particularly fond of the latter, but she is an intimate of the family, and I have not another friend.

When I told Milicent of my engagement, she rather provoked me by her manner of taking it. After staring a moment in mute surprise, she said, – "Well, Helen, I suppose I ought to congratulate you – and I am glad to see you so happy; but I did not think you would take him; and I can't help feeling surprised that you should like him so much."

"Why so?"

"Because you are so superior to him in every way, and there's something so bold and reckless about him – so, I don't know how – but I always feel a wish to get out of his way when I see him approach."

"You are timid, Milicent; but that's no fault of his."

"And then his look," continued she. "People say he's handsome, and of course he is; but I don't like that kind of beauty, and I wonder that you should."

"Why so, pray?"

"Well, you know, I think there's nothing noble or lofty in his appearance."

"In fact, you wonder that I can like any one so unlike the stilted heroes of romance. Well, give me my flesh and blood lover, and I'll leave all the Sir Herberts and Valentines to you – if you can find them."

"I don't want them," said she. "I'll be satisfied with flesh and blood too – only the spirit must shine through and predominate. But don't you think Mr. Huntingdon's face is too red?"

"No!" cried I, indignantly. "It is not red at all. There is just a pleasant glow, a healthy freshness in his complexion – the warm, pinky tint of the whole harmonising with the deeper colour of the cheeks, exactly as it ought to do. I hate a man to be red and white, like a painted doll, or all sickly white, or smoky black, or cadaverous yellow."

"Well, tastes differ – but I like pale or dark," replied she. "But, to tell you the truth, Helen, I had been deluding myself with the hope that you would one day be my sister. I expected Walter would be introduced to you next season; and I thought you would like him, and was certain he would like you; and I flattered myself I should thus have the felicity of seeing the two persons I like best in the world – except mamma – united in one. He mayn't be exactly what you would call handsome, but he's far more distinguished-looking, and nicer and better than Mr. Huntingdon; – and I'm sure you would say so, if you knew him."

"Impossible, Milicent! You think so, because you're his sister; and, on that account, I'll forgive you; but nobody else should so disparage Arthur Huntingdon to me with impunity."

Miss Wilmot expressed her feelings on the subject almost as openly.

"And so, Helen," said she, coming up to me with a smile of no amiable import, "you are to be Mrs. Huntingdon, I suppose?"

"Yes," replied I. "Don't you envy me?"

"Oh, dear, no!" she exclaimed. "I shall probably be Lady Lowborough some day, and then you know, dear, I shall be in a capacity to inquire, 'Don't you envy me?'"

"Henceforth I shall envy no one," returned I.

"Indeed! Are you so happy then?" said she, thoughtfully; and something very like a cloud of disappointment shadowed her face. "And does he love you – I mean, does he idolise you as much as you do him?" she added, fixing her eyes upon me with ill-disguised anxiety for the reply.

"I don't want to be idolised," I answered; "but I am well assured that he loves me more than anybody else in the world – as I do him."

"Exactly," said she, with a nod. "I wish –" she paused.

"What do you wish?" asked I, annoyed at the vindictive expression of her countenance.

"I wish," returned, she, with a short laugh, "that all the attractive points and desirable qualifications of the two gentlemen were united in one – that Lord Lowborough had Huntingdon's handsome face and good temper, and all his wit, and mirth and charm, or else that Huntingdon had Lowborough's pedigree, and title, and delightful old family seat, and I had him; and you might have the other and welcome."

"Thank you, dear Annabella: I am better satisfied with things as they are, for my own part; and for you, I wish you were as well content with your intended as I am with mine," said I; and it was true enough; for, though vexed at first at her unamiable spirit, her frankness touched me, and the contrast between our situations was such, that I could well afford to pity her and wish her well.

Mr. Huntingdon's acquaintances appear to be no better pleased with our approaching union than mine. This morning's post brought him letters from several of his friends, during the perusal of which, at the breakfast-table, he excited the attention of the company by the singular variety of his grimaces. But he crushed them all into his pocket, with a private laugh, and said nothing till the meal was concluded. Then, while the company were hanging over the fire or loitering through the room, previous to settling to their various morning avocations, he came and leant over the back of my chair, with his face in contact with my curls, and commencing with a quiet little kiss, poured forth the following complaints into my ear:

"Helen, you witch, do you know that you've entailed upon me the curses of all my friends? I wrote to them the other day, to tell them of my happy prospects, and now, instead of a bundle of congratulations, I've got a pocketful of bitter execrations and reproaches. There's not one kind wish for me, or one good word for you, among them all. They say there'll be no more fun now, no more merry days and glorious nights – and all my fault – I am the first to break up the jovial band, and others, in pure despair, will follow my example. I was the very life and prop of the community, they do me the honour to say, and I have shamefully betrayed my trust –"

"You may join them again, if you like," said I, somewhat piqued at the sorrowful tone of his discourse. "I should be sorry to stand between any man – or body of men, and so much happiness; and perhaps I can manage to do without you, as well as your poor deserted friends."

"Bless you, no," murmured he. "It's 'all for love or the world well lost,' with me. Let them go to – where they belong, to speak politely. But if you saw how they abuse me, Helen, you would love me all the more for having ventured so much for your sake."

He pulled out his crumpled letters. I thought he was going to show them to me, and told him I did not wish to see them.

"I'm not going to show them to you, love," said he. "They're hardly fit for a lady's eyes – the most part of them. But look here. This is Grimsby's scrawl – only three lines, the sulky dog! He doesn't say much, to be sure, but his very silence implies more than all the others' words, and the less he says, the more he thinks – and this is Hargrave's missive. He is particularly grieved at me, because, forsooth he had fallen in love with you from his sister's reports, and meant to have married you himself, as soon as he had sown his wild oats."

"I'm vastly obliged to him," observed I.

"And so am I," said he. "And look at this. This is Hattersley's – every page stuffed full of railing accusations, bitter curses, and lamentable complaints, ending up with swearing that he'll get married himself in revenge: he'll throw himself away on the first old maid that chooses to set her cap at him, – as if I cared what he did with himself."

"Well," said I, "if you do give up your intimacy with these men, I don't think you will have much cause to regret the loss of their society; for it's my belief they never did you much good."

"Maybe not; but we'd a merry time of it, too, though mingled with sorrow and pain, as Lowborough knows to his cost – ha, ha!" and while he was laughing at the recollection of Lowborough's troubles, my uncle came and slapped him on the shoulder.

"Come, my lad!" said he. "Are you too busy making love to my niece to make war with the pheasants? – First of October, remember! Sun shines out – rain ceased – even Boarham's not afraid to venture in his waterproof boots; and Wilmot and I are going to beat you all. I declare, we old 'uns are the keenest sportsmen of the lot!"

"I'll show you what I can do today, however," said my companion. "I'll murder your birds by wholesale, just for keeping me away from better company than either you or them."

And so saying he departed; and I saw no more of him till dinner. It seemed a weary time; I wonder what I shall do without him.

It is very true that the three elder gentlemen have proved themselves much keener sportsmen than the two younger ones; for both Lord Lowborough and Arthur Huntingdon have of late almost daily neglected the shooting excursions to accompany us in our various rides and rambles. But these merry times are fast drawing to a close. In less than a fortnight the party break up, much to my sorrow, for every day I enjoy it more and more – now that Messrs. Boarham and Wilmot have ceased to tease me, and my aunt has ceased to lecture me, and I have ceased to be jealous of Annabella – and even to dislike her – and now that Mr. Huntingdon is become my Arthur, and I may enjoy his society without restraint. What shall I do without him, I repeat?

Chapter Twenty-Two

OCTOBER 5TH. – My cup of sweets is not unmingled: it is dashed with a bitterness that I cannot hide from myself, disguise it as I will. I may try to persuade myself that the sweetness overpowers it; I may call it a pleasant aromatic flavour; but say what I will, it is still there, and I cannot but taste it. I cannot shut my eyes to Arthur's faults; and the more I love him the more they trouble me. His very heart, that I trusted so, is, I fear, less warm and generous than I thought it. At least, he gave me a specimen of his character today that seemed to merit a harder name than thoughtlessness. He and Lord Lowborough were accompanying Annabella and me in a long, delightful ride; he was riding by my side, as usual, and Annabella and Lord Lowborough were a little before us, the latter bending towards his companion as if in tender and confidential discourse.

"Those two will get the start of us, Helen, if we don't look sharp," observed Huntingdon. "They'll make a match of it, as sure as can be. That Lowborough's fairly besotted. But he'll find himself in a fix when he's got her, I doubt."

"And she'll find herself in a fix when she's got him," said I, "if what I've heard of him is true."

"Not a bit of it. She knows what she's about; but he, poor fool, deludes himself with the notion that she'll make him a good wife, and because she has amused him with some rodomontade about despising rank and wealth in matters of love and marriage, he flatters himself that she's devotedly attached to him; that she will not refuse him for his poverty, and does not court him for his rank, but loves him for himself alone."

"But is not he courting her for her fortune?"

"No, not he. That was the first attraction, certainly; but now he has quite lost sight of it: it never enters his calculations, except merely as an essential without which, for the lady's own sake, he could not think of marrying her. No; he's fairly in love. He thought he never could be again, but he's in for it once more. He was to have been married before, some two or three years ago; but he lost his bride by losing his fortune. He got into a bad way among us in London: he had an unfortunate taste for gambling; and surely the fellow was born under an unlucky star, for he always lost thrice where he gained once. That's a mode of self-torment I never was much addicted to. When I spend my money I like to enjoy the full value of it: I see no fun in wasting it on thieves and blacklegs; and as for gaining money, hitherto I have always had sufficient; it's time enough to be clutching for more, I think, when you begin to see the end of what you have. But I have sometimes frequented the gaming-houses just to watch the on-goings of those mad votaries of chance – a very interesting study, I assure you, Helen, and sometimes very diverting: I've had many a laugh at the boobies and bedlamites. Lowborough was quite infatuated – not willingly, but of necessity, – he was always resolving to give it up, and always breaking his resolutions. Every venture was the 'just once more:' if he gained a little, he hoped to gain a little more next time, and if he lost, it would not do to leave off at that juncture; he must go on till he had retrieved that last misfortune, at least: bad luck could not last for ever; and every lucky hit was looked upon as the dawn of better times, till experience proved the contrary. At length he grew desperate, and we were daily on the look-out for a case of *felo-de-se* – no great matter, some of us whispered, as his existence had ceased to be an acquisition to our club. At last, however, he came to a check. He made a large stake, which he determined should be the last, whether he lost or won. He had often so determined before, to be sure, and as often broken his determination; and so it was this time. He lost; and while his antagonist smilingly swept away the stakes, he turned chalky white, drew back in silence, and wiped his forehead. I was present at the time; and while he stood with folded arms and eyes fixed on the ground, I knew well enough what was passing in his mind.

"'Is it to be the last, Lowborough?' said I, stepping up to him.

"'The last but one,' he answered, with a grim smile; and then, rushing back to the table, he struck his hand upon it, and, raising his voice high above all the confusion of jingling coins and muttered oaths and curses in the room, he swore a deep and solemn oath that, come what would, this trial should be the last, and imprecated unspeakable curses on his head if ever he should shuffle a card or rattle a dice-box again. He then doubled his former stake, and challenged any one present to play against him. Grimsby instantly presented himself. Lowborough glared fiercely at him, for Grimsby was almost as celebrated for his luck as he was for his ill-fortune. However, they fell to work. But Grimsby had much skill and little scruple, and whether he took advantage of the other's trembling, blinded eagerness to deal unfairly by him, I cannot undertake to say; but Lowborough lost again, and fell dead sick.

"'You'd better try once more,' said Grimsby, leaning across the table. And then he winked at me.

"'I've nothing to try with,' said the poor devil, with a ghastly smile.

"'Oh, Huntingdon will lend you what you want,' said the other.

"'No; you heard my oath,' answered Lowborough, turning away in quiet despair. And I took him by the arm and led him out.

"'Is it to be the last, Lowborough?' I asked, when I got him into the street.

"'The last,' he answered, somewhat against my expectation. And I took him home – that is, to our club – for he was as submissive as a child – and plied him with brandy-and-water till he began to look rather brighter – rather more alive, at least.

"'Huntingdon, I'm ruined!' said he, taking the third glass from my hand – he had drunk the others in dead silence.

"'Not you,' said I. 'You'll find a man can live without his money as merrily as a tortoise without its head, or a wasp without its body.'

"'But I'm in debt,' said he – 'deep in debt. And I can never, never get out of it.'

"'Well, what of that? Many a better man than you has lived and died in debt; and they can't put you in prison, you know, because you're a peer.' And I handed him his fourth tumbler.

"'But I hate to be in debt!' he shouted. 'I wasn't born for it, and I cannot bear it.'

"'What can't be cured must be endured,' said I, beginning to mix the fifth.

"'And then, I've lost my Caroline.' And he began to snivel then, for the brandy had softened his heart.

"'No matter,' I answered, 'there are more Carolines in the world than one.'

"'There's only one for me,' he replied, with a dolorous sigh. 'And if there were fifty more, who's to get them, I wonder, without money?'

"'Oh, somebody will take you for your title; and then you've your family estate yet; that's entailed, you know.'

"'I wish to God I could sell it to pay my debts,' he muttered.

"'And then,' said Grimsby, who had just come in, 'you can try again, you know. I would have more than one chance, if I were you. I'd never stop here.'

"'I won't, I tell you!' shouted he. And he started up, and left the room – walking rather unsteadily, for the liquor had got into his head. He was not so much used to it then, but after that he took to it kindly to solace his cares.

"He kept his oath about gambling (not a little to the surprise of us all), though Grimsby did his utmost to tempt him to break it, but now he had got hold of another habit that bothered him nearly as much, for he soon discovered that the demon of drink was as black as the demon of play, and nearly as hard to get rid of – especially as his kind friends did all they could to second the promptings of his own insatiable cravings."

"Then, they were demons themselves," cried I, unable to contain my indignation. "And you, Mr. Huntingdon, it seems, were the first to tempt him."

"Well, what could we do?" replied he, deprecatingly. – "We meant it in kindness – we couldn't bear to see the poor fellow so miserable: – and besides, he was such a damper upon us, sitting there silent and glum, when he was under the threefold influence – of the loss of his sweetheart, the loss of his fortune, and the reaction of the lost night's debauch; whereas, when he had something in him, if he was not merry himself, he was an unfailing source of merriment to us. Even Grimsby could chuckle over his odd sayings: they delighted him far more than my merry jests, or Hattersley's riotous mirth. But one evening, when we were sitting over our wine, after one of our club dinners, and all had been hearty together, – Lowborough giving us mad toasts, and hearing our wild songs, and bearing a hand in the applause, if he did not help us to sing them himself, – he suddenly relapsed into silence, sinking his head on his hand, and never lifting his glass to his lips; – but this was nothing new; so we let him alone, and went on with our jollification, till, suddenly raising his head, he interrupted us in the middle of a roar of laughter by exclaiming, – 'Gentlemen, where is all this to end? – Will you just tell me that now? – Where is it all to end?' He rose.

"'A speech, a speech!' shouted we. 'Hear, hear! Lowborough's going to give us a speech!'

"He waited calmly till the thunders of applause and jingling of glasses had ceased, and then proceeded, – 'It's only this, gentlemen, – that I think we'd better go no further. We'd better stop while we can.'

"'Just so!' cried Hattersley –

'Stop, poor sinner, stop and think
Before you further go,
No longer sport upon the brink
Of everlasting woe.'

"'Exactly!' replied his lordship, with the utmost gravity. 'And if you choose to visit the bottomless pit, I won't go with you – we must part company, for I swear I'll not move another step towards it! – What's this?' he said, taking up his glass of wine.

"'Taste it,' suggested I.

"'This is hell broth!' he exclaimed. 'I renounce it for ever!' And he threw it out into the middle of the table.

"'Fill again!' said I, handing him the bottle – 'and let us drink to your renunciation.'

"'It's rank poison,' said he, grasping the bottle by the neck, 'and I forswear it! I've given up gambling, and I'll give up this too.' He was on the point of deliberately pouring the whole contents of the bottle on to the table, but Hargrave wrested it from him. 'On you be the curse, then!' said he. And, backing from the room, he shouted, 'Farewell, ye tempters!' and vanished amid shouts of laughter and applause.

"We expected him back among us the next day; but, to our surprise, the place remained vacant: we saw nothing of him for a whole week; and we really began to think he was going to keep his word. At last, one evening, when we were most of us assembled together again, he entered, silent and grim as a ghost, and would have quietly slipped into his usual seat at my elbow, but we all rose to welcome him, and several voices were raised to ask what he would have, and several hands were busy with bottle and glass to serve him; but I knew a smoking tumbler of brandy-and-water would comfort him best, and had nearly prepared it, when he peevishly pushed it away, saying, –

"'Do let me alone, Huntingdon! Do be quiet, all of you! I'm not come to join you: I'm only come to be with you awhile, because I can't bear my own thoughts.' And he folded his arms, and leant back in his chair; so we let him be. But I left the glass by him; and, after awhile, Grimsby directed my attention towards it, by a significant wink; and, on turning my head, I saw it was drained to the bottom. He made me a sign to replenish, and quietly pushed up the bottle. I willingly complied; but Lowborough detected the pantomime, and, nettled at the intelligent grins that were passing between us, snatched the glass from my hand, dashed the contents of it in Grimsby's face, threw the empty tumbler at me, and then bolted from the room."

"I hope he broke your head," said I.

"No, love," replied he, laughing immoderately at the recollection of the whole affair; "he would have done so, – and perhaps, spoilt my face, too, but, providentially, this forest of curls" (taking off his hat, and showing his luxuriant chestnut locks) "saved my skull, and prevented the glass from breaking, till it reached the table."

"After that," he continued, "Lowborough kept aloof from us a week or two longer. I used to meet him occasionally in the town; and then, as I was too good-natured to resent his unmannerly conduct, and he bore no malice against me, – he was never unwilling to talk to me; on the contrary, he would cling to me, and follow me anywhere but to the club, and the gaming-houses, and such-like dangerous places of resort – he was so weary of his own moping, melancholy mind. At last, I got him to come in with me to the club, on condition that I would not tempt him to drink; and, for some time, he continued to look in upon us pretty regularly of an evening, – still abstaining, with wonderful perseverance, from the 'rank poison' he had so bravely forsworn. But some of our members protested against this conduct. They did not like to have him sitting there like a skeleton at a feast, instead of contributing his quota to the general amusement, casting a cloud over all, and watching, with greedy eyes, every drop they carried to their lips – they vowed it was not fair; and some of them maintained that he should either be compelled to do as others did, or expelled from the society; and swore that, next time he showed himself, they would tell him as much, and, if he did not take the warning, proceed to active measures. However, I befriended him on this occasion, and recommended them to let him be for a while, intimating that, with a little patience on our parts, he would soon come round again. But, to be sure, it was rather provoking; for, though he refused to drink like an honest Christian, it was well known to me that he kept a private bottle of laudanum about him, which he was continually soaking at – or rather, holding off and on with, abstaining one day and exceeding the next – just like the spirits.

"One night, however, during one of our orgies – one of our high festivals, I mean – he glided in, like the ghost in 'Macbeth,' and seated himself, as usual, a little back from the table, in the chair we always placed for 'the spectre,' whether it chose to fill it or not. I saw by his face that he was suffering from the effects of an overdose of his insidious comforter; but nobody spoke to him, and he spoke to nobody. A few sidelong glances, and a whispered observation, that 'the ghost was come,' was all the notice he drew by his appearance, and we went on with our merry carousals as before, till he startled us all by suddenly drawing in his chair, and leaning forward with his elbows on the table, and exclaiming with portentous solemnity, – 'Well! it puzzles me what you can find to be so merry about. What you see in life I don't know – I see only the blackness of darkness, and a fearful looking for of judgment and fiery indignation!'

"All the company simultaneously pushed up their glasses to him, and I set them before him in a semicircle, and, tenderly patting him on the back, bid him drink, and he would soon see as bright a prospect as any of us; but he pushed them back, muttering, –

"'Take them away! I won't taste it, I tell you. I won't – I won't!' So I handed them down again to the owners; but I saw that he followed them with a glare of hungry regret as they departed. Then he clasped his hands before his eyes to shut out the sight, and two minutes after lifted his head again, and said, in a hoarse but vehement whisper, –

"'And yet I must! Huntingdon, get me a glass!'

"'Take the bottle, man!' said I, thrusting the brandy-bottle into his hand – but stop, I'm telling too much," muttered the narrator, startled at the look I turned upon him. "But no matter," he recklessly added, and thus continued his relation: "In his desperate eagerness, he seized the bottle and sucked away, till he suddenly dropped from his chair, disappearing under the table amid a tempest of applause. The consequence of this imprudence was something like an apoplectic fit, followed by a rather severe brain fever –"

"And what did you think of yourself, sir?" said I, quickly.

"Of course, I was very penitent," he replied. "I went to see him once or twice – nay, twice or thrice – or by'r lady, some four times – and when he got better, I tenderly brought him back to the fold."

"What do you mean?"

"I mean, I restored him to the bosom of the club, and compassionating the feebleness of his health and extreme lowness of his spirits, I recommended him to 'take a little wine for his stomach's sake,' and, when he was sufficiently re-established, to embrace the media-via, ni-jamais-ni-toujours plan – not to kill himself like a fool, and not to abstain like a ninny – in a word, to enjoy himself like a rational creature, and do as I did; for, don't think, Helen, that I'm a tippler; I'm nothing at all of the kind, and never was, and never shall be. I value my comfort far too much. I see that a man cannot give himself up to drinking without being miserable one-half his days and mad the other; besides, I like to enjoy my life at all sides and ends, which cannot be done by one that suffers himself to be the slave of a single propensity – and, moreover, drinking spoils one's good looks," he concluded, with a most conceited smile that ought to have provoked me more than it did.

"And did Lord Lowborough profit by your advice?" I asked.

"Why, yes, in a manner. For a while he managed very well; indeed, he was a model of moderation and prudence – something too much so for the tastes of our wild community; but, somehow, Lowborough had not the gift of moderation: if he stumbled a little to one side, he must go down before he could right himself: if he overshot the mark one night, the effects of it rendered him so miserable the next day that he must repeat the offence to mend it; and so on from day to day, till his clamorous conscience brought him to a stand. And then, in his sober moments, he so bothered his friends with his remorse, and his terrors and woes, that they were obliged, in self-defence, to get him to drown his sorrows in wine, or any more potent beverage that came to hand; and when his first scruples of conscience were overcome, he would need no more persuading, he would often grow desperate, and be as great a blackguard as any of them could desire – but only to lament his own unutterable wickedness and degradation the more when the fit was over.

"At last, one day when he and I were alone together, after pondering awhile in one of his gloomy, abstracted moods, with his arms folded and his head sunk on his breast, he suddenly woke up, and vehemently grasping my arm, said, –

"'Huntingdon, this won't do! I'm resolved to have done with it.'

"'What, are you going to shoot yourself?' said I.

"'No; I'm going to reform.'

"'Oh, that's nothing new! You've been going to reform these twelve months and more.'

"'Yes, but you wouldn't let me; and I was such a fool I couldn't live without you. But now I see what it is that keeps me back, and what's wanted to save me; and I'd compass sea and land to get it – only I'm afraid there's no chance.' And he sighed as if his heart would break.

"'What is it, Lowborough?' said I, thinking he was fairly cracked at last.

"'A wife,' he answered; 'for I can't live alone, because my own mind distracts me, and I can't live with you, because you take the devil's part against me.'

"'Who – I?'

"'Yes – all of you do – and you more than any of them, you know. But if I could get a wife, with fortune enough to pay off my debts and set me straight in the world –'

"'To be sure,' said I.

"'And sweetness and goodness enough,' he continued, 'to make home tolerable, and to reconcile me to myself, I think I should do yet. I shall never be in love again, that's certain; but perhaps that would be no great matter, it would enable me to choose with my eyes open – and I should make a good husband in spite of it; but could any one be in love with me? – that's the question. With your good looks and powers of fascination' (he was pleased to say), 'I might hope; but as it is, Huntingdon, do you think anybody would take me – ruined and wretched as I am?'

"'Yes, certainly.'

"'Who?'

"'Why, any neglected old maid, fast sinking in despair, would be delighted to –'

"'No, no,' said he – 'it must be somebody that I can love.'

"'Why, you just said you never could be in love again!'

"'Well, love is not the word – but somebody that I can like. I'll search all England through, at all events!' he cried, with a sudden burst of hope, or desperation. 'Succeed or fail, it will be better than rushing headlong to destruction at that d—d club: so farewell to it and you. Whenever I meet you on honest ground or under a Christian roof, I shall be glad to see you; but never more shall you entice me to that devil's den!'

"This was shameful language, but I shook hands with him, and we parted. He kept his word; and from that time forward he has been a pattern of propriety, as far as I can tell; but till lately I have not had very much to do with him. He occasionally sought my company, but as frequently shrunk from it, fearing lest I should wile him back to destruction, and I found his not very entertaining, especially as he sometimes attempted to awaken my conscience and draw me from the perdition he considered himself to have escaped; but when I did happen to meet him, I seldom failed to ask after the progress of his matrimonial efforts and researches, and, in general, he could give me but a poor account. The mothers were repelled by his empty coffers and his reputation for gambling, and the daughters by his cloudy brow and melancholy temper – besides, he didn't understand them; he wanted the spirit and assurance to carry his point.

"I left him at it when I went to the continent; and on my return, at the year's end, I found him still a disconsolate bachelor – though, certainly, looking somewhat less like an unblest exile from the tomb than before. The young ladies had ceased to be afraid of him, and were beginning to think him quite interesting; but the mammas were still unrelenting. It was about this time, Helen, that my good angel brought me into conjunction with you; and then I had eyes and ears for nobody else. But, meantime, Lowborough became acquainted with our charming friend, Miss Wilmot – through the intervention of his good angel, no doubt he would tell you, though he did not dare to fix his hopes on one so courted and admired, till after they were brought into closer contact here at Staningley, and she, in the absence of her other admirers, indubitably courted his notice and held out every encouragement to his timid advances. Then, indeed, he began to hope for a dawn of brighter days; and if, for a while, I darkened his prospects by standing between him and his sun – and so nearly plunged him again into the abyss of despair – it only intensified his ardour and strengthened his hopes when I chose to abandon the field in the pursuit of a brighter treasure. In a word, as I told you, he is fairly besotted. At first, he could dimly perceive her faults, and they gave him considerable uneasiness; but now his passion and her art together have blinded him to everything but her perfections and his amazing good fortune. Last night he came to me brimful of his new-found felicity:

"'Huntingdon, I am not a castaway!' said he, seizing my hand and squeezing it like a vice. 'There is happiness in store for me yet – even in this life – she loves me!'

"'Indeed!' said I. 'Has she told you so?'

"'No, but I can no longer doubt it. Do you not see how pointedly kind and affectionate she is? And she knows the utmost extent of my poverty, and cares nothing about it! She knows all the folly and all the wickedness of my former life, and is not afraid to trust me – and my rank and title are no allurements to her; for them she utterly disregards. She is the most generous, high-minded being that can be conceived of. She will save me, body and soul, from destruction. Already, she has ennobled me in my own estimation, and made me three times better, wiser, greater than I was. Oh! If I had but known her before, how much degradation and misery I should have been spared! But what have I done to deserve so magnificent a creature?'

"And the cream of the jest," continued Mr. Huntingdon, laughing, "is, that the artful minx loves nothing about him but his title and pedigree, and 'that delightful old family seat.'"

"How do you know?" said I.

"She told me so herself; she said, 'As for the man himself, I thoroughly despise him; but then, I suppose, it is time to be making my choice, and if I waited for some one capable of eliciting my esteem and affection, I should have to pass my life in single blessedness, for I detest you all!' Ha, ha! I suspect she was wrong there; but, however, it is evident she has no love for him, poor fellow."

"Then you ought to tell him so."

"What! And spoil all her plans and prospects, poor girl? No, no: that would be a breach of confidence, wouldn't it, Helen? Ha, ha! Besides, it would break his heart." And he laughed again.

"Well, Mr. Huntingdon, I don't know what you see so amazingly diverting in the matter; I see nothing to laugh at."

"I'm laughing at you, just now, love," said he, redoubling his machinations.

And leaving him to enjoy his merriment alone, I touched Ruby with the whip, and cantered on to rejoin our companions; for we had been walking our horses all this time, and were consequently a long way behind. Arthur was soon at my side again; but not disposed to talk to him, I broke into a gallop. He did the same; and we did not slacken our pace till we came up with Miss Wilmot and Lord Lowborough, which was within half a mile of the park-gates. I avoided all further conversation with him till we came to the end of our ride, when I meant to jump off my horse and vanish into the house, before he could offer his assistance; but while I was disengaging my habit from the crutch, he lifted me off, and held me by both hands, asserting that he would not let me go till I had forgiven him.

"I have nothing to forgive," said I. "You have not injured me."

"No, darling – God forbid that I should! But you are angry because it was to me that Annabella confessed her lack of esteem for her lover."

"No, Arthur, it is not that that displeases me: it is the whole system of your conduct towards your friend, and if you wish me to forget it, go now, and tell him what sort of a woman it is that he adores so madly, and on whom he has hung his hopes of future happiness."

"I tell you, Helen, it would break his heart – it would be the death of him – besides being a scandalous trick to poor Annabella. There is no help for him now; he is past praying for. Besides, she may keep up the deception to the end of the chapter; and then he will be just as happy in the illusion as if it were reality; or perhaps he will only discover his mistake when he has ceased to love her; and if not, it is much better that the truth should dawn gradually upon him. So now, my angel, I hope I have made out a clear case, and fully convinced you that I cannot make the atonement you require. What other requisition have you to make? Speak, and I will gladly obey."

"I have none but this," said I, as gravely as before: "that, in future, you will never make a jest of the sufferings of others, and always use your influence with your friends for their own advantage against their evil propensities, instead of seconding their evil propensities against themselves."

"I will do my utmost," said he, "to remember and perform the injunctions of my angel monitress;" and after kissing both my gloved hands, he let me go.

When I entered my room, I was surprised to see Annabella Wilmot standing before my toilet-table, composedly surveying her features in the glass, with one hand flirting her gold-mounted whip, and the other holding up her long habit.

"She certainly is a magnificent creature!" thought I, as I beheld that tall, finely developed figure, and the reflection of the handsome face in the mirror before me, with the glossy dark hair, slightly and not ungracefully disordered by the breezy ride, the rich brown complexion glowing with exercise, and the black eyes sparkling with unwonted brilliance. On perceiving me, she turned round, exclaiming, with a laugh that savoured more of malice than of mirth, – "Why, Helen! What have you been doing so long? I came to tell you my good fortune," she continued, regardless of Rachel's presence. "Lord Lowborough has proposed, and I have been graciously pleased to accept him. Don't you envy me, dear?"

"No, love," said I – "or him either," I mentally added. "And do you like him, Annabella?"

"Like him! Yes, to be sure – over head and ears in love!"

"Well, I hope you'll make him a good wife."

"Thank you, my dear! And what besides do you hope?"

"I hope you will both love each other, and both be happy."

"Thanks; and I hope you will make a very good wife to Mr. Huntingdon!" said she, with a queenly bow, and retired.

"Oh, Miss! How could you say so to her!" cried Rachel.

"Say what?" replied I.

"Why, that you hoped she would make him a good wife. I never heard such a thing!"

"Because I do hope it, or rather, I wish it; she's almost past hope."

"Well," said she, "I'm sure I hope he'll make her a good husband. They tell queer things about him downstairs. They were saying –"

"I know, Rachel. I've heard all about him; but he's reformed now. And they have no business to tell tales about their masters."

"No, mum – or else, they have said some things about Mr. Huntingdon too."

"I won't hear them, Rachel; they tell lies."

"Yes, mum," said she, quietly, as she went on arranging my hair.

"Do you believe them, Rachel?" I asked, after a short pause.

"No, Miss, not all. You know when a lot of servants gets together they like to talk about their betters; and some, for a bit of swagger, likes to make it appear as though they knew more than they do, and to throw out hints and things just to astonish the others. But I think, if I was you, Miss Helen, I'd look very well before I leaped. I do believe a young lady can't be too careful who she marries."

"Of course not," said I; "but be quick, will you, Rachel? I want to be dressed."

And, indeed, I was anxious to be rid of the good woman, for I was in such a melancholy frame I could hardly keep the tears out of my eyes while she dressed me. It was not for Lord Lowborough – it was not for Annabella – it was not for myself – it was for Arthur Huntingdon that they rose.

* * *

13th. – They are gone, and he is gone. We are to be parted for more than two months, above ten weeks! A long, long time to live and not to see him. But he has promised to write often, and made me promise to write still oftener, because he will be busy settling his affairs, and I shall have nothing better to do. Well, I think I shall always have plenty to say. But oh! For the time when we shall be always together, and can exchange our thoughts without the intervention of these cold go-betweens, pen, ink, and paper!

* * *

22nd. – I have had several letters from Arthur already. They are not long, but passing sweet, and just like himself, full of ardent affection, and playful lively humour; but there is always a 'but' in this imperfect world, and I do wish he would sometimes be serious. I cannot get him to write or speak in real, solid earnest. I don't much mind it now, but if it be always so, what shall I do with the serious part of myself?

Chapter Twenty-Three

FEB. 18, 1822. – Early this morning Arthur mounted his hunter and set off in high glee to meet the hounds. He will be away all day, and so I will amuse myself with my neglected diary, if I can give that name to such an irregular composition. It is exactly four months since I opened it last.

I am married now, and settled down as Mrs. Huntingdon of Grassdale Manor. I have had eight weeks' experience of matrimony. And do I regret the step I have taken? No, though I must confess, in my secret heart, that Arthur is not what I thought him at first, and if I had known him in the beginning as thoroughly as I do now, I probably never should have loved him, and if I loved him first, and then made the discovery, I fear I should have thought it my duty not to have married him. To be sure I might have known him, for every one was willing enough to tell me about him, and he himself was no accomplished hypocrite, but I was wilfully blind; and now, instead of regretting that I did not discern his full character before I was indissolubly bound to him, I am glad, for it has saved me a great deal of battling with my conscience, and a great deal of consequent trouble and pain; and, whatever I ought to have done, my duty now is plainly to love him and to cleave to him, and this just tallies with my inclination.

He is very fond of me, almost too fond. I could do with less caressing and more rationality. I should like to be less of a pet and more of a friend, if I might choose; but I won't complain of that: I am only afraid his affection loses in depth where it gains in ardour. I sometimes liken it to a fire of dry twigs and branches compared with one of solid coal, very bright and hot; but if it should burn itself out and leave nothing but ashes behind, what shall I do? But it won't, it sha'n't, I am determined; and surely I have power to keep it alive. So let me dismiss that thought at once. But Arthur is selfish; I am constrained to acknowledge that; and, indeed, the admission gives me less pain than might be expected, for, since I love him so much, I can easily forgive him for loving himself: he likes to be pleased, and it is my delight to please him; and when I regret this tendency of his, it is for his own sake, not for mine.

The first instance he gave was on the occasion of our bridal tour. He wanted to hurry it over, for all the continental scenes were already familiar to him: many had lost their interest in his eyes, and others had never had anything to lose. The consequence was, that after a flying transit through part of France and part of Italy, I came back nearly as ignorant as I went, having made no acquaintance with persons and manners, and very little with things, my head swarming with a motley confusion of objects and scenes; some, it is true, leaving a deeper and more pleasing impression than others, but these embittered by the recollection that my emotions had not been shared by my companion, but that, on the contrary, when I had expressed a particular interest in anything that I saw or desired to see, it had been displeasing to him, inasmuch as it proved that I could take delight in anything disconnected with himself.

As for Paris, we only just touched at that, and he would not give me time to see one-tenth of the beauties and interesting objects of Rome. He wanted to get me home, he said, to have me all to himself, and to see me safely installed as the mistress of Grassdale Manor, just as single-minded, as naïve, and piquante as I was; and as if I had been some frail butterfly, he expressed himself fearful of rubbing the silver off my wings by bringing me into contact with society, especially that of Paris and Rome; and, more-over, he did not scruple to tell me that there were ladies in both places that would tear his eyes out if they happened to meet him with me.

Of course I was vexed at all this; but still it was less the disappointment to myself that annoyed me, than the disappointment in him, and the trouble I was at to frame excuses to my friends for having seen and observed so little, without imputing one particle of blame to my companion. But when we got home – to my new, delightful home – I was so happy and he was so kind that I freely forgave him all; and I was beginning to think my lot too happy, and my husband actually too good for me, if not too good for this world, when, on the second Sunday after our arrival, he shocked and horrified me by another instance of his unreasonable exaction. We were walking home from the morning service, for it was a fine frosty day, and as we are so near the church, I had requested the carriage should not be used.

"Helen," said he, with unusual gravity, "I am not quite satisfied with you."

I desired to know what was wrong.

"But will you promise to reform if I tell you?"

"Yes, if I can, and without offending a higher authority."

"Ah! There it is, you see: you don't love me with all your heart."

"I don't understand you, Arthur (at least I hope I don't): pray tell me what I have done or said amiss."

"It is nothing you have done or said; it is something that you are – you are too religious. Now I like a woman to be religious, and I think your piety one of your greatest charms; but then, like all other good things, it may be carried too far. To my thinking, a woman's religion ought not to lessen her devotion to her earthly lord. She should have enough to purify and etherealise her soul, but not enough to refine away her heart, and raise her above all human sympathies."

"And am I above all human sympathies?" said I.

"No, darling; but you are making more progress towards that saintly condition than I like; for all these two hours I have been thinking of you and wanting to catch your eye, and you were so absorbed in your devotions that you had not even a glance to spare for me – I declare it is enough to make one jealous of one's Maker – which is very wrong, you know; so don't excite such wicked passions again, for my soul's sake."

"I will give my whole heart and soul to my Maker if I can," I answered, "and not one atom more of it to you than He allows. What are you, sir, that you should set yourself up as a god, and presume to dispute possession of my heart with Him to whom I owe all I have and all I am, every blessing I ever did or ever can enjoy – and yourself among the rest – if you are a blessing, which I am half inclined to doubt."

"Don't be so hard upon me, Helen; and don't pinch my arm so: you are squeezing your fingers into the bone."

"Arthur," continued I, relaxing my hold of his arm, "you don't love me half as much as I do you; and yet, if you loved me far less than you do, I would not complain, provided you loved your Maker more. I should rejoice to see you at any time so deeply absorbed in your devotions that you had not a single thought to spare for me. But, indeed, I should lose nothing by the change, for the more you loved your God the more deep and pure and true would be your love to me."

At this he only laughed and kissed my hand, calling me a sweet enthusiast. Then taking off his hat, he added: "But look here, Helen – what can a man do with such a head as this?"

The head looked right enough, but when he placed my hand on the top of it, it sunk in a bed of curls, rather alarmingly low, especially in the middle.

"You see I was not made to be a saint," said he, laughing, "If God meant me to be religious, why didn't He give me a proper organ of veneration?"

"You are like the servant," I replied, "who, instead of employing his one talent in his master's service, restored it to him unimproved, alleging, as an excuse, that he knew him 'to be a hard man, reaping where he had not sown, and gathering where he had not strawed.' Of him to whom less is given, less will be required, but our utmost exertions are required of us all. You are not without the capacity of veneration, and faith and hope, and conscience and reason, and every other requisite to a Christian's character, if you choose to employ them; but all our talents increase in the using, and every faculty, both good and bad, strengthens by exercise: therefore, if you choose to use the bad, or those which tend to evil, till they become your masters, and neglect the good till they dwindle away, you have only yourself to blame. But you have talents, Arthur – natural endowments both of heart and mind and temper, such as many a better Christian would be glad to possess, if you would only employ them in God's service. I should never expect to see you a devotee, but it is quite possible to be a good Christian without ceasing to be a happy, merry-hearted man."

"You speak like an oracle, Helen, and all you say is indisputably true; but listen here: I am hungry, and I see before me a good substantial dinner; I am told that if I abstain from this today I shall have a sumptuous feast tomorrow, consisting of all manner of dainties and delicacies. Now, in the first place, I should be loth to wait till tomorrow when I have the means of appeasing my hunger already before me: in the second place, the solid viands of today are more to my taste than the dainties that are promised me; in the third place, I don't see tomorrow's banquet, and how can I tell that it is not all a fable, got up by the greasy-faced fellow that is advising me to abstain in order that he may have all the good victuals to himself? In the fourth place, this table must be spread for somebody, and, as Solomon says, 'Who can eat, or who else can hasten hereunto more than I?' and finally, with your leave, I'll sit down and satisfy my cravings of today, and leave tomorrow to shift for itself – who knows but what I may secure both this and that?"

"But you are not required to abstain from the substantial dinner of today: you are only advised to partake of these coarser viands in such moderation as not to incapacitate you from enjoying the choicer banquet of tomorrow. If, regardless of that counsel, you choose to make a beast of yourself now, and over-eat and over-drink yourself till you turn the good victuals into poison, who is to blame if, hereafter, while you are suffering the torments of yesterday's gluttony and drunkenness, you see more temperate men sitting down to enjoy themselves at that splendid entertainment which you are unable to taste?"

"Most true, my patron saint; but again, our friend Solomon says, 'There is nothing better for a man than to eat and to drink, and to be merry.'"

"And again," returned I, "he says, 'Rejoice, O young man, in thy youth; and walk in the ways of thine heart, and in the sight of thine eyes: but know thou, that for all these things God will bring thee into judgment.'"

"Well, but, Helen, I'm sure I've been very good these last few weeks. What have you seen amiss in me, and what would you have me to do?"

"Nothing more than you do, Arthur: your actions are all right so far; but I would have your thoughts changed; I would have you to fortify yourself against temptation, and not to call evil good, and good evil; I should wish you to think more deeply, to look further, and aim higher than you do."

Chapter Twenty-Four

MARCH 25TH. – Arthur is getting tired – not of me, I trust, but of the idle, quiet life he leads – and no wonder, for he has so few sources of amusement: he never reads anything but newspapers and sporting magazines; and when he sees me occupied with a book, he won't let me rest till I close it. In fine weather he generally manages to get through the time pretty well, but on rainy days, of which we have had a good many of late, it is quite painful to witness his ennui. I do all I can to amuse him, but it is impossible to get him to feel interested in what I most like to talk about, while, on the other hand, he likes to talk about things that cannot interest me – or even that annoy me – and these please him – the most of all: for his favourite amusement is to sit or loll beside me on the sofa, and tell me stories of his former amours, always turning upon the ruin of some confiding girl or the cozening of some unsuspecting husband; and when I express my horror and indignation, he lays it all to the charge of jealousy, and laughs till the tears run down his cheeks. I used to fly into passions or melt into tears at first, but seeing that his delight increased in proportion to my anger and agitation, I have since endeavoured to suppress my feelings and receive his revelations in the silence of calm contempt; but still he reads the inward struggle in my face, and misconstrues my bitterness of soul for his unworthiness into the pangs of wounded jealousy; and when he has sufficiently diverted himself with that, or fears my displeasure will become too serious for his comfort, he tries to kiss and soothe me into smiles again – never were his caresses so little welcome as then! This is double selfishness displayed to me and to the victims of his former love. There are times when, with a momentary pang – a flash of wild dismay, I ask myself, "Helen, what have you done?" But I rebuke the inward questioner, and repel the obtrusive thoughts that crowd upon me; for were he ten times as sensual and impenetrable to good and lofty thoughts, I well know I have no right to complain. And I don't and won't complain. I do and will love him still; and I do not and will not regret that I have linked my fate with his.

April 4th. – We have had a downright quarrel. The particulars are as follows: Arthur had told me, at different intervals, the whole story of his intrigue with Lady F—, which I would not believe before. It was some consolation, however, to find that in this instance the lady had been more to blame than he, for he was very young at the time, and she had decidedly made the first advances, if what he said was true. I hated her for it, for it seemed as if she had chiefly contributed to his corruption; and when he was beginning to talk about her the other day, I begged he would not mention her, for I detested the very sound of her name.

"Not because you loved her, Arthur, mind, but because she injured you and deceived her husband, and was altogether a very abominable woman, whom you ought to be ashamed to mention."

But he defended her by saying that she had a doting old husband, whom it was impossible to love.

"Then why did she marry him?" said I.

"For his money," was the reply.

"Then that was another crime, and her solemn promise to love and honour him was another, that only increased the enormity of the last."

"You are too severe upon the poor lady," laughed he. "But never mind, Helen, I don't care for her now; and I never loved any of them half as much as I do you, so you needn't fear to be forsaken like them."

"If you had told me these things before, Arthur, I never should have given you the chance."

"Wouldn't you, my darling?"

"Most certainly not!"

He laughed incredulously.

"I wish I could convince you of it now!" cried I, starting up from beside him: and for the first time in my life, and I hope the last, I wished I had not married him.

"Helen," said he, more gravely, "do you know that if I believed you now I should be very angry? But thank heaven I don't. Though you stand there with your white face and flashing eyes, looking at me like a very tigress, I know the heart within you perhaps a trifle better than you know it yourself."

Without another word I left the room and locked myself up in my own chamber. In about half an hour he came to the door, and first he tried the handle, then he knocked.

"Won't you let me in, Helen?" said he. "No; you have displeased me," I replied, "and I don't want to see your face or hear your voice again till the morning."

He paused a moment as if dumfounded or uncertain how to answer such a speech, and then turned and walked away. This was only an hour after dinner: I knew he would find it very dull to sit alone all the evening; and this considerably softened my resentment, though it did not make me relent. I was determined to show him that my heart was not his slave, and I could live without him if I chose; and I sat down and wrote a long letter to my aunt, of course telling her nothing of all this. Soon after ten o'clock I heard him come up again, but he passed my door and went straight to his own dressing room, where he shut himself in for the night.

I was rather anxious to see how he would meet me in the morning, and not a little disappointed to behold him enter the breakfast-room with a careless smile.

"Are you cross still, Helen?" said he, approaching as if to salute me. I coldly turned to the table, and began to pour out the coffee, observing that he was rather late.

He uttered a low whistle and sauntered away to the window, where he stood for some minutes looking out upon the pleasing prospect of sullen grey clouds, streaming rain, soaking lawn, and dripping leafless trees, and muttering execrations on the weather, and then sat down to breakfast. While taking his coffee he muttered it was "d—d cold."

"You should not have left it so long," said I.

He made no answer, and the meal was concluded in silence. It was a relief to both when the letter-bag was brought in. It contained upon examination a newspaper and one or two letters for him, and a couple of letters for me, which he tossed across the table without a remark. One was from my brother, the other from Milicent Hargrave, who is now in London with her mother. His, I think, were business letters, and apparently not much to his mind, for he crushed them into his pocket with some muttered expletives that I should have reproved him for at any other time. The paper he set before him, and pretended to be deeply absorbed in its contents during the remainder of breakfast, and a considerable time after.

The reading and answering of my letters, and the direction of household concerns, afforded me ample employment for the morning: after lunch I got my drawing, and from dinner till bed-time I read. Meanwhile, poor Arthur was sadly at a loss for something to amuse him or to occupy his time. He wanted to appear as busy and as unconcerned as I did. Had the weather at all permitted, he would doubtless have ordered his horse and set off to some distant region, no matter where, immediately after breakfast, and not returned till night: had there been a lady anywhere within reach, of any age between fifteen and forty-five, he would have sought revenge and found employment in getting up, or trying to get up, a desperate flirtation with her; but being, to my private satisfaction, entirely cut off from both these sources of diversion, his sufferings were truly deplorable. When he had done yawning over his paper and scribbling short answers to his shorter letters, he spent the remainder of the morning and the whole of the afternoon in fidgeting about from room to room, watching the clouds, cursing the rain, alternately petting and teasing and abusing his dogs, sometimes lounging on the sofa with a book that he could not force himself to read, and very often fixedly gazing at me when he thought I did not perceive it, with the vain hope of detecting some traces of tears, or some tokens of remorseful anguish in my face. But I managed to preserve an undisturbed though grave serenity throughout the day. I was not really angry: I felt for him all the time, and longed to be reconciled; but I determined he should make the first advances, or at least show some signs of an humble and contrite spirit first; for, if I began, it would only minister to his self-conceit, increase his arrogance, and quite destroy the lesson I wanted to give him.

He made a long stay in the dining room after dinner, and, I fear, took an unusual quantity of wine, but not enough to loosen his tongue: for when he came in and found me quietly occupied with my book, too busy to lift my head on his entrance, he merely murmured an expression of suppressed disapprobation, and, shutting the door with a bang, went and stretched himself at full length on the sofa, and composed himself to sleep. But his favourite cocker, Dash, that had been lying at my feet, took the liberty of jumping upon him and beginning to lick his face. He struck it off with a smart blow, and the poor dog squeaked and ran cowering back to me. When he woke up, about half an hour after, he called it to him again, but Dash only looked sheepish and wagged the tip of his tail. He called again more sharply, but Dash only clung the closer to me, and licked my hand, as if imploring protection. Enraged at this, his master snatched up a heavy book and hurled it at his head. The poor dog set up a piteous outcry, and ran to the door. I let him out, and then quietly took up the book.

"Give that book to me," said Arthur, in no very courteous tone. I gave it to him.

"Why did you let the dog out?" he asked; "you knew I wanted him."

"By what token?" I replied; "by your throwing the book at him? But perhaps it was intended for me?"

"No; but I see you've got a taste of it," said he, looking at my hand, that had also been struck, and was rather severely grazed.

I returned to my reading, and he endeavoured to occupy himself in the same manner; but in a little while, after several portentous yawns, he pronounced his book to be "cursed trash," and threw it on the table. Then followed eight or ten minutes of silence, during the greater part of which, I believe, he was staring at me. At last his patience was tired out.

"What is that book, Helen?" he exclaimed.

I told him.

"Is it interesting?"

"Yes, very."

I went on reading, or pretending to read, at least – I cannot say there was much communication between my eyes and my brain; for, while the former ran over the pages, the latter was earnestly wondering when Arthur would speak next, and what he would say, and what I should answer. But he did not speak again till I rose to make the tea, and then it was only to say he should not take any. He continued lounging on the sofa, and alternately closing his eyes and looking at his watch and at me, till bed-time, when I rose, and took my candle and retired.

"Helen!" cried he, the moment I had left the room. I turned back, and stood awaiting his commands.

"What do you want, Arthur?" I said at length.

"Nothing," replied he. "Go!"

I went, but hearing him mutter something as I was closing the door, I turned again. It sounded very like 'confounded slut,' but I was quite willing it should be something else.

"Were you speaking, Arthur?" I asked.

"No," was the answer, and I shut the door and departed. I saw nothing more of him till the following morning at breakfast, when he came down a full hour after the usual time.

"You're very late," was my morning's salutation.

"You needn't have waited for me," was his; and he walked up to the window again. It was just such weather as yesterday.

"Oh, this confounded rain!" he muttered. But, after studiously regarding it for a minute or two, a bright idea, seemed to strike him, for he suddenly exclaimed, "But I know what I'll do!" and then returned and took his seat at the table. The letter-bag was already there, waiting to be opened. He unlocked it and examined the contents, but said nothing about them.

"Is there anything for me?" I asked.

"No."

He opened the newspaper and began to read.

"You'd better take your coffee," suggested I; "it will be cold again."

"You may go," said he, "if you've done; I don't want you."

I rose and withdrew to the next room, wondering if we were to have another such miserable day as yesterday, and wishing intensely for an end of these mutually inflicted torments. Shortly after I heard him ring the bell and give some orders about his wardrobe that sounded as if he meditated a long journey. He then sent for the coachman, and I heard something about the carriage and the horses, and London, and seven o'clock tomorrow morning, that startled and disturbed me not a little.

"I must not let him go to London, whatever comes of it," said I to myself; "he will run into all kinds of mischief, and I shall be the cause of it. But the question is, How am I to alter his purpose? Well, I will wait awhile, and see if he mentions it."

I waited most anxiously, from hour to hour; but not a word was spoken, on that or any other subject, to me. He whistled and talked to his dogs, and wandered from room to room, much the same as on the previous day. At last I began to think I must introduce the subject myself, and was pondering how to bring it about, when John unwittingly came to my relief with the following message from the coachman:

"Please, sir, Richard says one of the horses has got a very bad cold, and he thinks, sir, if you could make it convenient to go the day after tomorrow, instead of tomorrow, he could physic it today, so as –"

"Confound his impudence!" interjected the master.

"Please, sir, he says it would be a deal better if you could," persisted John, "for he hopes there'll be a change in the weather shortly, and he says it's not likely, when a horse is so bad with a cold, and physicked and all –"

"Devil take the horse!" cried the gentleman. "Well, tell him I'll think about it," he added, after a moment's reflection. He cast a searching glance at me, as the servant withdrew, expecting to see some token of deep astonishment and alarm; but, being previously prepared, I preserved an aspect of stoical indifference. His countenance fell as he met my steady gaze, and he turned away in very obvious disappointment, and walked up to the fire-place, where he stood in an attitude of undisguised dejection, leaning against the chimney-piece with his forehead sunk upon his arm.

"Where do you want to go, Arthur?" said I.

"To London," replied he, gravely.

"What for?" I asked.

"Because I cannot be happy here."

"Why not?"

"Because my wife doesn't love me."

"She would love you with all her heart, if you deserved it."

"What must I do to deserve it?"

This seemed humble and earnest enough; and I was so much affected, between sorrow and joy, that I was obliged to pause a few seconds before I could steady my voice to reply.

"If she gives you her heart," said I, "you must take it, thankfully, and use it well, and not pull it in pieces, and laugh in her face, because she cannot snatch it away."

He now turned round, and stood facing me, with his back to the fire. "Come, then, Helen, are you going to be a good girl?" said he.

This sounded rather too arrogant, and the smile that accompanied it did not please me. I therefore hesitated to reply. Perhaps my former answer had implied too much: he had heard my voice falter, and might have seen me brush away a tear.

"Are you going to forgive me, Helen?" he resumed, more humbly.

"Are you penitent?" I replied, stepping up to him and smiling in his face.

"Heart-broken!" he answered, with a rueful countenance, yet with a merry smile just lurking within his eyes and about the corners of his mouth; but this could not repulse me, and I flew into his arms. He fervently embraced me, and though I shed a torrent of tears, I think I never was happier in my life than at that moment.

"Then you won't go to London, Arthur?" I said, when the first transport of tears and kisses had subsided.

"No, love, – unless you will go with me."

"I will, gladly," I answered, "if you think the change will amuse you, and if you will put off the journey till next week."

He readily consented, but said there was no need of much preparation, as he should not be for staying long, for he did not wish me to be Londonized, and to lose my country freshness and originality by too much intercourse with the ladies of the world. I thought this folly; but I did not wish to contradict him now: I merely said that I was of very domestic habits, as he well knew, and had no particular wish to mingle with the world.

So we are to go to London on Monday, the day after tomorrow. It is now four days since the termination of our quarrel, and I am sure it has done us both good: it has made me like Arthur a great deal better, and made him behave a great deal better to me. He has never once attempted to annoy me since, by the most distant allusion to Lady F—, or any of those disagreeable reminiscences of his former life. I wish I could blot them from my memory, or else get him to regard such matters in the same light as I do. Well! It is something, however, to have made him see that they are not fit subjects for a conjugal jest. He may see further some time. I will put no limits to my hopes; and, in spite of my aunt's forebodings and my own unspoken fears, I trust we shall be happy yet.

Chapter Twenty-Five

ON THE EIGHTH OF APRIL we went to London, on the eighth of May I returned, in obedience to Arthur's wish; very much against my own, because I left him behind. If he had come with me, I should have been very glad to get home again, for he led me such a round of restless dissipation while there, that, in that short space of time, I was quite tired out. He seemed bent upon displaying me to his friends and acquaintances in particular, and the public in general, on every possible occasion, and to the greatest possible advantage. It was something to feel that he considered me a worthy object of pride; but I paid dear for the gratification: for, in the first place, to please him I had to violate my cherished predilections, my almost rooted principles in favour of a plain, dark, sober style of dress – I must sparkle in costly jewels and deck myself out like a painted butterfly, just as I had, long since, determined I would never do – and this was no trifling sacrifice; in the second place, I was continually straining to satisfy his sanguine expectations and do honour to his choice by my general conduct and deportment, and fearing to disappoint him by some awkward misdemeanour, or some trait of inexperienced ignorance about the customs of society, especially when I acted the part of hostess, which I was not unfrequently called upon to do; and, in the third place, as I intimated before, I was wearied of the throng and bustle, the restless hurry and ceaseless change of a life so alien to all my previous habits. At last, he suddenly discovered that the London air did not agree with me, and I was languishing for my country home, and must immediately return to Grassdale.

I laughingly assured him that the case was not so urgent as he appeared to think it, but I was quite willing to go home if he was. He replied that he should be obliged to remain a week or two longer, as he had business that required his presence.

"Then I will stay with you," said I.

"But I can't do with you, Helen," was his answer: "as long as you stay I shall attend to you and neglect my business."

"But I won't let you," I returned; "now that I know you have business to attend to, I shall insist upon your attending to it, and letting me alone; and, to tell the truth, I shall be glad of a little rest. I can take my rides and walks in the Park as usual; and your business cannot occupy all your time: I shall see you at meal-times, and in the evenings at least, and that will be better than being leagues away and never seeing you at all."

"But, my love, I cannot let you stay. How can I settle my affairs when I know that you are here, neglected – ?"

"I shall not feel myself neglected: while you are doing your duty, Arthur, I shall never complain of neglect. If you had told me before, that you had anything to do, it would have been half done before this; and now you must make up for lost time by redoubled exertions. Tell me what it is; and I will be your taskmaster, instead of being a hindrance."

"No, no," persisted the impracticable creature; "you must go home, Helen; I must have the satisfaction of knowing that you are safe and well, though far away. Your bright eyes are faded, and that tender, delicate bloom has quite deserted your cheek."

"That is only with too much gaiety and fatigue."

"It is not, I tell you; it is the London air: you are pining for the fresh breezes of your country home, and you shall feel them before you are two days older. And remember your situation, dearest Helen; on your health, you know, depends the health, if not the life, of our future hope."

"Then you really wish to get rid of me?"

"Positively, I do; and I will take you down myself to Grassdale, and then return. I shall not be absent above a week or fortnight at most."

"But if I must go, I will go alone: if you must stay, it is needless to waste your time in the journey there and back."

But he did not like the idea of sending me alone.

"Why, what helpless creature do you take me for," I replied, "that you cannot trust me to go a hundred miles in our own carriage, with our own footman and a maid to attend me? If you come with me I shall assuredly keep you. But tell me, Arthur, what is this tiresome business; and why did you never mention it before?"

"It is only a little business with my lawyer," said he; and he told me something about a piece of property he wanted to sell, in order to pay off a part of the incumbrances on his estate; but either the account was a little confused, or I was rather dull of comprehension, for I could not clearly understand how that should keep him in town a fortnight after me. Still less can I now comprehend how it should keep him a month, for it is nearly that time since I left him, and no signs of his return as yet. In every letter he promises to be with me in a few days, and every time deceives me, or deceives himself. His excuses are vague and insufficient. I cannot doubt that he has got among his former companions again. Oh, why did I leave him! I wish – I do intensely wish he would return!

June 29th. – No Arthur yet; and for many days I have been looking and longing in vain for a letter. His letters, when they come, are kind, if fair words and endearing epithets can give them a claim to the title – but very short, and full of trivial excuses and promises that I cannot trust; and yet how anxiously I look forward to them! How eagerly I open and devour one of those little, hastily-scribbled returns for the three or four long letters, hitherto unanswered, he has had from me!

Oh, it is cruel to leave me so long alone! He knows I have no one but Rachel to speak to, for we have no neighbours here, except the Hargraves, whose residence I can dimly descry from these upper windows embosomed among those low, woody hills beyond the Dale. I was glad when I learnt that Milicent was so near us; and her company would be a soothing solace to me now; but she is still in town with her mother; there is no one at the Grove but little Esther and her French governess, for Walter is always away. I saw that paragon of manly perfections in London: he seemed scarcely to merit the eulogiums of his mother and sister, though he certainly appeared more conversable and agreeable than Lord Lowborough, more candid and high-minded than Mr. Grimsby, and more polished and gentlemanly than Mr. Hattersley, Arthur's only other friend whom he judged fit to introduce to me. – Oh, Arthur, why won't you come? Why won't you write to me at least? You talked about my health: how can you expect me to gather bloom and vigour here, pining in solitude and restless anxiety from day to day? – It would serve you right to come back and find my good looks entirely wasted away. I would beg my uncle and aunt, or my brother, to come and see me, but I do not like to complain of my loneliness to them, and indeed loneliness is the least of my sufferings. But what is he, doing – what is it that keeps him away? It is this ever-recurring question, and the horrible suggestions it raises, that distract me.

July 3rd. – My last bitter letter has wrung from him an answer at last, and a rather longer one than usual; but still I don't know what to make of it. He playfully abuses me for the gall and vinegar of my latest effusion, tells me I can have no conception of the multitudinous engagements that keep him away, but avers that, in spite of them all, he will assuredly be with me before the close of next week; though it is impossible for a man so circumstanced as he is to fix the precise day of his return: meantime he exhorts me to the exercise of patience, 'that first of woman's virtues,' and desires me to remember the saying, 'Absence makes the heart grow fonder,' and comfort myself with the assurance that the longer he stays away the better he shall love me when he returns; and till he does return, he begs I will continue to write to him constantly, for, though he is sometimes too idle and often too busy to answer my letters as they come, he likes to receive them daily; and if I fulfil my threat of punishing his seeming neglect by ceasing to write, he shall be so angry that he will do his utmost to forget me. He adds this piece of intelligence respecting poor Milicent Hargrave:

"Your little friend Milicent is likely, before long, to follow your example, and take upon her the yoke of matrimony in conjunction with a friend of mine. Hattersley, you know, has not yet fulfilled his direful threat of throwing his precious person away on the first old maid that chose to evince a tenderness for him; but he still preserves a resolute determination to see himself a married man before the year is out. 'Only,' said he to me, 'I must have somebody that will let me have my own way in everything – not like your wife, Huntingdon: she is a charming creature, but she looks as if she had a will of her own, and could play the vixen upon occasion' (I thought 'you're right there, man,' but I didn't say so). 'I must have some good, quiet soul that will let me just do what I like and go where I like, keep at home or stay away, without a word of reproach or complaint; for I can't do with being bothered.' 'Well,' said I, 'I know somebody that will suit you to a tee, if you don't care for money, and that's Hargrave's sister, Milicent.' He desired to be introduced to her forthwith, for he said he had plenty of the needful himself, or should have when his old governor chose to quit the stage. So you see, Helen, I have managed pretty well, both for your friend and mine."

Poor Milicent! But I cannot imagine she will ever be led to accept such a suitor – one so repugnant to all her ideas of a man to be honoured and loved.

July 5th. – Alas! I was mistaken. I have got a long letter from her this morning, telling me she is already engaged, and expects to be married before the close of the month.

"I hardly know what to say about it," she writes, "or what to think. To tell you the truth, Helen, I don't like the thoughts of it at all. If I am to be Mr. Hattersley's wife, I must try to love him; and I do try with all my might; but I have made very little progress yet; and the worst symptom of the case is, that the further he is from me the better I like him: he frightens me with his abrupt manners and strange hectoring ways, and I dread the thoughts of marrying him. 'Then why have you accepted him?' you will ask; and I didn't know I had accepted him; but mamma tells me I have, and he seems to think so too. I certainly didn't mean to do so; but I did not like to give him a flat refusal, for fear mamma should be grieved and angry (for I knew she wished me to marry him), and I wanted to talk to her first about it: so I gave him what I thought was an evasive, half negative answer; but she says it was as good as an acceptance, and he would think me very capricious if I were to attempt to draw back – and indeed I was so confused and frightened at the moment, I can hardly tell what I said. And next time I saw him, he accosted me in all confidence as his affianced bride, and immediately began to settle matters with mamma. I had not courage to contradict them then, and how can I do it now? I cannot; they would think me mad. Besides, mamma is so delighted with the idea of the match; she thinks she has managed so well for me; and I cannot bear to disappoint her. I do object sometimes, and tell her what I feel, but you don't know how she talks. Mr. Hattersley, you know, is the son of a rich banker, and as Esther and I have no fortunes, and Walter very little, our dear mamma is very anxious to see us all well married, that is, united to rich partners. It is not my idea of being well married, but she means it all for the best. She says when I am safe off her hands it will be such a relief to her mind; and she assures me it will be a good thing for the family as well as for me. Even Walter is pleased at the prospect, and when I confessed my reluctance to him, he said it was all childish nonsense. Do you think it nonsense, Helen? I should not care if I could see any prospect of being able to love and admire him, but I can't. There is nothing about him to hang one's esteem and affection upon; he is so diametrically opposite to what I imagined my husband should be. Do write to me, and say all you can to encourage me. Don't attempt to dissuade me, for my fate is fixed: preparations for the important event are already going on around me; and don't say a word against Mr. Hattersley, for I want to think well of him; and though I have spoken against him myself, it is for the last time: hereafter, I shall never permit myself to utter a word in his dispraise, however he may seem to deserve it; and whoever ventures to speak slightingly of the man I have promised to love, to honour, and obey, must expect my serious displeasure. After all, I think he is quite as good as Mr. Huntingdon, if not better; and yet you love him, and seem to be happy and contented; and perhaps I may manage as well. You must tell me, if you can, that Mr. Hattersley is better than he seems – that he is upright, honourable, and open-hearted – in fact, a perfect diamond in the rough. He may be all this, but I don't know him. I know only the exterior, and what, I trust, is the worst part of him."

She concludes with "Goodbye, dear Helen. I am waiting anxiously for your advice – but mind you let it be all on the right side."

Alas! Poor Milicent, what encouragement can I give you? Or what advice – except that it is better to make a bold stand now, though at the expense of disappointing and angering both mother and brother and lover, than to devote your whole life, hereafter, to misery and vain regret?

Saturday, 13th. – The week is over, and he is not come. All the sweet summer is passing away without one breath of pleasure to me or benefit to him. And I had all along been looking forward to this season with the fond, delusive hope that we should enjoy it so sweetly together; and that, with God's help and my exertions, it would be the means of elevating his mind, and refining his taste to a due appreciation of the salutary and pure delights of nature, and peace, and holy love. But now – at evening, when I see the round red sun sink quietly down behind those woody hills, leaving them sleeping in a warm, red, golden haze, I only think another lovely day is lost to him and me; and at morning, when roused by the flutter and chirp of the sparrows, and the gleeful twitter of the swallows – all intent upon feeding their young, and full of life and joy in their own little frames – I open the window to inhale the balmy, soul-reviving air, and look out upon the lovely landscape, laughing in dew and sunshine – I too often shame that glorious scene with tears of thankless misery, because he cannot feel its freshening influence; and when I wander in the ancient woods, and meet the little wild flowers smiling in my path, or sit in the shadow of our noble ash-trees by the water-side, with their branches gently swaying in the light summer breeze that murmurs through their feathery foliage – my ears full of that low music mingled with the dreamy hum of insects, my eyes abstractedly gazing on the glassy surface of the little lake before me, with the trees that crowd about its bank, some gracefully bending to kiss its waters, some rearing their stately heads high above, but stretching their wide arms over its margin, all faithfully mirrored far, far down in its glassy depth – though sometimes the images are partially broken by the sport of aquatic insects, and sometimes, for a moment, the whole is shivered into trembling fragments by a transient breeze that sweeps the surface too roughly – still I have no pleasure; for the greater the happiness that nature sets before me, the more I lament that he is not here to taste it: the greater the bliss we might enjoy together, the more I feel our present wretchedness apart (yes, ours; he must be wretched, though he may not know it); and the more my senses are pleased, the more my heart is oppressed; for he keeps it with him confined amid the dust and smoke of London – perhaps shut up within the walls of his own abominable club.

But most of all, at night, when I enter my lonely chamber, and look out upon the summer moon, 'sweet regent of the sky,' floating above me in the 'black blue vault of heaven,' shedding a flood of silver radiance over park, and wood, and water, so pure, so peaceful, so divine – and think, Where is he now? – What is he doing at this moment? Wholly unconscious of this heavenly scene – perhaps revelling with his boon companions, perhaps – God help me, it is too – too much!

23rd. – Thank heaven, he is come at last! But how altered! Flushed and feverish, listless and languid, his beauty strangely diminished, his vigour and vivacity quite departed. I have not upbraided him by word or look; I have not even asked him what he has been doing. I have not the heart to do it, for I think he is ashamed of himself-he must be so indeed, and such inquiries could not fail to be painful to both. My forbearance pleases him – touches him even, I am inclined to think. He says he is glad to be home again, and God knows how glad I am to get him back, even as he is. He lies on the sofa, nearly all day long; and I play and sing to him for hours together. I write his letters for him, and get him everything he wants; and sometimes I read to him, and sometimes I talk, and sometimes only sit by him and soothe him with silent caresses. I know he does not deserve it; and I fear I am spoiling him; but this once, I will forgive him, freely and entirely. I will shame him into virtue if I can, and I will never let him leave me again.

He is pleased with my attentions – it may be, grateful for them. He likes to have me near him: and though he is peevish and testy with his servants and his dogs, he is gentle and kind to me. What he would be, if I did not so watchfully anticipate his wants, and so carefully avoid, or immediately desist from doing anything that has a tendency to irritate or disturb him, with however little reason, I cannot tell. How intensely I wish he were worthy of all this care! Last night, as I sat beside him, with his head in my lap, passing my fingers through his beautiful curls, this thought made my eyes overflow with sorrowful tears – as it often does; but this time, a tear fell on his face and made him look up. He smiled, but not insultingly.

"Dear Helen!" he said – "why do you cry? You know that I love you" (and he pressed my hand to his feverish lips), "and what more could you desire?"

"Only, Arthur, that you would love yourself as truly and as faithfully as you are loved by me."

"That would be hard, indeed!" he replied, tenderly squeezing my hand.

August 24th. – Arthur is himself again, as lusty and reckless, as light of heart and head as ever, and as restless and hard to amuse as a spoilt child, and almost as full of mischief too, especially when wet weather keeps him within doors. I wish he had something to do, some useful trade, or profession, or employment – anything to occupy his head or his hands for a few hours a day, and give him something besides his own pleasure to think about. If he would play the country gentleman and attend to the farm – but that he knows nothing about, and won't give his mind to consider, – or if he would take up with some literary study, or learn to draw or to play – as he is so fond of music, I often try to persuade him to learn the piano, but he is far too idle for such an undertaking: he has no more idea of exerting himself to overcome obstacles than he has of restraining his natural appetites; and these two things are the ruin of him. I lay them both to the charge of his harsh yet careless father, and his madly indulgent mother. – If ever I am a mother I will zealously strive against this crime of over-indulgence. I can hardly give it a milder name when I think of the evils it brings.

Happily, it will soon be the shooting season, and then, if the weather permit, he will find occupation enough in the pursuit and destruction of the partridges and pheasants: we have no grouse, or he might have been similarly occupied at this moment, instead of lying under the acacia-tree pulling poor Dash's ears. But he says it is dull work shooting alone; he must have a friend or two to help him.

"Let them be tolerably decent then, Arthur," said I. The word 'friend' in his mouth makes me shudder: I know it was some of his 'friends' that induced him to stay behind me in London, and kept him away so long: indeed, from what he has unguardedly told me, or hinted from time to time, I cannot doubt that he frequently showed them my letters, to let them see how fondly his wife watched over his interests, and how keenly she regretted his absence; and that they induced him to remain week after week, and to plunge into all manner of excesses, to avoid being laughed at for a wife-ridden fool, and, perhaps, to show how far he could venture to go without danger of shaking the fond creature's devoted attachment. It is a hateful idea, but I cannot believe it is a false one.

"Well," replied he, "I thought of Lord Lowborough for one; but there is no possibility of getting him without his better half, our mutual friend, Annabella; so we must ask them both. You're not afraid of her, are you, Helen?" he asked, with a mischievous twinkle in his eyes.

"Of course not," I answered: "why should I? And who besides?"

"Hargrave for one. He will be glad to come, though his own place is so near, for he has little enough land of his own to shoot over, and we can extend our depredations into it, if we like; and he is thoroughly respectable, you know, Helen – quite a lady's man: and I think, Grimsby for another: he's a decent, quiet fellow enough. You'll not object to Grimsby?"

"I hate him: but, however, if you wish it, I'll try to endure his presence for a while."

"All a prejudice, Helen, a mere woman's antipathy."

"No; I have solid grounds for my dislike. And is that all?"

"Why, yes, I think so. Hattersley will be too busy billing and cooing, with his bride to have much time to spare for guns and dogs at present," he replied. And that reminds me, that I have had several letters from Milicent since her marriage, and that she either is, or pretends to be, quite reconciled to her lot. She professes to have discovered numberless virtues and perfections in her husband, some of which, I fear, less partial eyes would fail to distinguish, though they sought them carefully with tears; and now that she is accustomed to his loud voice, and abrupt, uncourteous manners, she affirms she finds no difficulty in loving him as a wife should do, and begs I will burn that letter wherein she spoke so unadvisedly against him. So that I trust she may yet be happy; but, if she is, it will be entirely the reward of her own goodness of heart; for had she chosen to consider herself the victim of fate, or of her mother's worldly wisdom, she might have been thoroughly miserable; and if, for duty's sake, she had not made every effort to love her husband, she would, doubtless, have hated him to the end of her days.

Chapter Twenty-Six

SEPT. 23RD. – Our guests arrived about three weeks ago. Lord and Lady Lowborough have now been married above eight months; and I will do the lady the credit to say that her husband is quite an altered man; his looks, his spirits, and his temper, are all perceptibly changed for the better since I last saw him. But there is room for improvement still. He is not always cheerful, nor always contented, and she often complains of his ill-humour, which, however, of all persons, she ought to be the last to accuse him of, as he never displays it against her, except for such conduct as would provoke a saint. He adores her still, and would go to the world's end to please her. She knows her power, and she uses it too; but well knowing that to wheedle and coax is safer than to command, she judiciously tempers her despotism with flattery and blandishments enough to make him deem himself a favoured and a happy man.

But she has a way of tormenting him, in which I am a fellow-sufferer, or might be, if I chose to regard myself as such. This is by openly, but not too glaringly, coquetting with Mr. Huntingdon, who is quite willing to be her partner in the game; but I don't care for it, because, with him, I know there is nothing but personal vanity, and a mischievous desire to excite my jealousy, and, perhaps, to torment his friend; and she, no doubt, is actuated by much the same motives; only, there is more of malice and less of playfulness in her manoeuvres. It is obviously, therefore, my interest to disappoint them both, as far as I am concerned, by preserving a cheerful, undisturbed serenity throughout; and, accordingly, I endeavour to show the fullest confidence in my husband, and the greatest indifference to the arts of my attractive guest. I have never reproached the former but once, and that was for laughing at Lord Lowborough's depressed and anxious countenance one evening, when they had both been particularly provoking; and then, indeed, I said a good deal on the subject, and rebuked him sternly enough; but he only laughed, and said, – "You can feel for him, Helen, can't you?"

"I can feel for anyone that is unjustly treated," I replied, "and I can feel for those that injure them too."

"Why, Helen, you are as jealous as he is!" cried he, laughing still more; and I found it impossible to convince him of his mistake. So, from that time, I have carefully refrained from any notice of the subject whatever, and left Lord Lowborough to take care of himself. He either has not the sense or the power to follow my example, though he does try to conceal his uneasiness as well as he can; but still, it will appear in his face, and his ill-humour will peep out at intervals, though not in the expression of open resentment – they never go far enough for that. But I confess I do feel jealous at times, most painfully, bitterly so; when she sings and plays to him, and he hangs over the instrument, and dwells upon her voice with no affected interest; for then I know he is really delighted, and I have no power to awaken similar fervour. I can amuse and please him with my simple songs, but not delight him thus.

28th. – Yesterday, we all went to the Grove, Mr. Hargrave's much-neglected home. His mother frequently asks us over, that she may have the pleasure of her dear Walter's company; and this time she had invited us to a dinner-party, and got together as many of the country gentry as were within reach to meet us. The entertainment was very well got up; but I could not help thinking about the cost of it all the time. I don't like Mrs. Hargrave; she is a hard, pretentious, worldly-minded woman. She has money enough to live very comfortably, if she only knew how to use it judiciously, and had taught her son to do the same; but she is ever straining to keep up appearances, with that despicable pride that shuns the semblance of poverty as of a shameful crime. She grinds her dependents, pinches her servants, and deprives even her daughters and herself of the real comforts of life, because she will not consent to yield the palm in outward show to those who have three times her wealth; and, above all, because she is determined her cherished son shall be enabled to 'hold up his head with the highest gentlemen in the land.' This same son, I imagine, is a man of expensive habits, no reckless spendthrift and no abandoned sensualist, but one who likes to have 'everything handsome about him,' and to go to a certain length in youthful indulgences, not so much to gratify his own tastes as to maintain his reputation as a man of fashion in the world, and a respectable fellow among his own lawless companions; while he is too selfish to consider how many comforts might be obtained for his fond mother and sisters with the money he thus wastes upon himself: as long as they can contrive to make a respectable appearance once a year, when they come to town, he gives himself little concern about their private stintings and struggles at home. This is a harsh judgment to form of 'dear, noble-minded, generous-hearted Walter,' but I fear it is too just.

Mrs. Hargrave's anxiety to make good matches for her daughters is partly the cause, and partly the result, of these errors: by making a figure in the world, and showing them off to advantage, she hopes to obtain better chances for them; and by thus living beyond her legitimate means, and lavishing so much on their brother, she renders them portionless, and makes them burdens on her hands. Poor Milicent, I fear, has already fallen a sacrifice to the manoeuvrings of this mistaken mother, who congratulates herself on having so satisfactorily discharged her maternal duty, and hopes to do as well for Esther. But Esther is a child as yet, a little merry romp of fourteen: as honest-hearted, and as guileless and simple as her sister, but with a fearless spirit of her own, that I fancy her mother will find some difficulty in bending to her purposes.

Chapter Twenty-Seven

OCTOBER 9TH. – It was on the night of the 4th, a little after tea, that Annabella had been singing and playing, with Arthur as usual at her side: she had ended her song, but still she sat at the instrument; and he stood leaning on the back of her chair, conversing in scarcely audible tones, with his face in very close proximity with hers. I looked at Lord Lowborough. He was at the other end of the room, talking with Messrs. Hargrave and Grimsby; but I saw him dart towards his lady and his host a quick, impatient glance, expressive of intense disquietude, at which Grimsby smiled. Determined to interrupt the *tête-à-tête*, I rose, and, selecting a piece of music from the music stand, stepped up to the piano, intending to ask the lady to play it; but I stood transfixed and speechless on seeing her seated there, listening, with what seemed an exultant smile on her flushed face to his soft murmurings, with her hand quietly surrendered to his clasp. The blood rushed first to my heart, and then to my head; for there was more than this: almost at the moment of my approach, he cast a hurried glance over his shoulder towards the other occupants of the room, and then ardently pressed the unresisting hand to his lips. On raising his eyes, he beheld me, and dropped them again, confounded and dismayed. She saw me too, and confronted me with a look of hard defiance. I laid the music on the piano, and retired. I felt ill; but I did not leave the room: happily, it was getting late, and could not be long before the company dispersed.

I went to the fire, and leant my head against the chimney-piece. In a minute or two, some one asked me if I felt unwell. I did not answer; indeed, at the time, I knew not what was said; but I mechanically looked up, and saw Mr. Hargrave standing beside me on the rug.

"Shall I get you a glass of wine?" said he.

"No, thank you," I replied; and, turning from him, I looked round. Lady Lowborough was beside her husband, bending over him as he sat, with her hand on his shoulder, softly talking and smiling in his face; and Arthur was at the table, turning over a book of engravings. I seated myself in the nearest chair; and Mr. Hargrave, finding his services were not desired, judiciously withdrew. Shortly after, the company broke up, and, as the guests were retiring to their rooms, Arthur approached me, smiling with the utmost assurance.

"Are you very angry, Helen?" murmured he.

"This is no jest, Arthur," said I, seriously, but as calmly as I could – "unless you think it a jest to lose my affection for ever."

"What! So bitter?" he exclaimed, laughingly, clasping my hand between both his; but I snatched it away, in indignation – almost in disgust, for he was obviously affected with wine.

"Then I must go down on my knees," said he; and kneeling before me, with clasped hands, uplifted in mock humiliation, he continued imploringly – "Forgive me, Helen – dear Helen, forgive me, and I'll never do it again!" and, burying his face in his handkerchief, he affected to sob aloud.

Leaving him thus employed, I took my candle, and, slipping quietly from the room, hastened up-stairs as fast as I could. But he soon discovered that I had left him, and, rushing up after me, caught me in his arms, just as I had entered the chamber, and was about to shut the door in his face.

"No, no, by heaven, you sha'n't escape me so!" he cried. Then, alarmed at my agitation, he begged me not to put myself in such a passion, telling me I was white in the face, and should kill myself if I did so.

"Let me go, then," I murmured; and immediately he released me – and it was well he did, for I was really in a passion. I sank into the easy-chair and endeavoured to compose myself, for I wanted to speak to him calmly. He stood beside me, but did not venture to touch me or to speak for a few seconds; then, approaching a little nearer, he dropped on one knee – not in mock humility, but to bring himself nearer my level, and leaning his hand on the arm of the chair, he began in a low voice: "It is all nonsense, Helen – a jest, a mere nothing – not worth a thought. Will you never learn," he continued more boldly, "that you have nothing to fear from me? That I love you wholly and entirely? – Or if," he added with a lurking smile, "I ever give a thought to another, you may well spare it, for those fancies are here and gone like a flash of lightning, while my love for you burns on steadily, and for ever, like the sun. You little exorbitant tyrant, will not that – ?"

"Be quiet a moment, will you, Arthur?" said I, "and listen to me – and don't think I'm in a jealous fury: I am perfectly calm. Feel my hand." And I gravely extended it towards him – but closed it upon his with an energy that seemed to disprove the assertion, and made him smile. "You needn't smile, sir," said I, still tightening my grasp, and looking steadfastly on him till he almost quailed before me. "You may think it all very fine, Mr. Huntingdon, to amuse yourself with rousing my jealousy; but take care you don't rouse my hate instead. And when you have once extinguished my love, you will find it no easy matter to kindle it again."

"Well, Helen, I won't repeat the offence. But I meant nothing by it, I assure you. I had taken too much wine, and I was scarcely myself at the time."

"You often take too much; and that is another practice I detest." He looked up astonished at my warmth. "Yes," I continued; "I never mentioned it before, because I was ashamed to do so; but now I'll tell you that it distresses me, and may disgust me, if you go on and suffer the habit to grow upon you, as it will if you don't check it in time. But the whole system of your conduct to Lady Lowborough is not referable to wine; and this night you knew perfectly well what you were doing."

"Well, I'm sorry for it," replied he, with more of sulkiness than contrition: "what more would you have?"

"You are sorry that I saw you, no doubt," I answered coldly.

"If you had not seen me," he muttered, fixing his eyes on the carpet, "it would have done no harm."

My heart felt ready to burst; but I resolutely swallowed back my emotion, and answered calmly, "You think not?"

"No," replied he, boldly. "After all, what have I done? It's nothing – except as you choose to make it a subject of accusation and distress."

"What would Lord Lowborough, your friend, think, if he knew all? Or what would you yourself think, if he or any other had acted the same part to me, throughout, as you have to Annabella?"

"I would blow his brains out."

"Well, then, Arthur, how can you call it nothing – an offence for which you would think yourself justified in blowing another man's brains out? Is it nothing to trifle with your friend's feelings and mine – to endeavour to steal a woman's affections from her husband – what he values more than his gold, and therefore what it is more dishonest to take? Are the marriage vows a jest; and is it nothing to make it your sport to break them, and to tempt another to do the same? Can I love a man that does such things, and coolly maintains it is nothing?"

"You are breaking your marriage vows yourself," said he, indignantly rising and pacing to and fro. "You promised to honour and obey me, and now you attempt to hector over me, and threaten and accuse me, and call me worse than a highwayman. If it were not for your situation, Helen, I would not submit to it so tamely. I won't be dictated to by a woman, though she be my wife."

"What will you do then? Will you go on till I hate you, and then accuse me of breaking my vows?"

He was silent a moment, and then replied: "You never will hate me." Returning and resuming his former position at my feet, he repeated more vehemently – "You cannot hate me as long as I love you."

"But how can I believe that you love me, if you continue to act in this way? Just imagine yourself in my place: would you think I loved you, if I did so? Would you believe my protestations, and honour and trust me under such circumstances?"

"The cases are different," he replied. "It is a woman's nature to be constant – to love one and one only, blindly, tenderly, and for ever – bless them, dear creatures! And you above them all; but you must have some commiseration for us, Helen; you must give us a little more licence, for, as Shakespeare has it –

> However we do praise ourselves,
> Our fancies are more giddy and unfirm,
> More longing, wavering, sooner lost and won
> Than women's are."

"Do you mean by that, that your fancies are lost to me, and won by Lady Lowborough?"

"No! Heaven is my witness that I think her mere dust and ashes in comparison with you, and shall continue to think so, unless you drive me from you by too much severity. She is a daughter of earth; you are an angel of heaven; only be not too austere in your divinity, and remember that I am a poor, fallible mortal. Come now, Helen; won't you forgive me?" he said, gently taking my hand, and looking up with an innocent smile.

"If I do, you will repeat the offence."

"I swear by –"

"Don't swear; I'll believe your word as well as your oath. I wish I could have confidence in either."

"Try me, then, Helen: only trust and pardon me this once, and you shall see! Come, I am in hell's torments till you speak the word."

I did not speak it, but I put my hand on his shoulder and kissed his forehead, and then burst into tears. He embraced me tenderly; and we have been good friends ever since. He has been decently temperate at table, and well-conducted towards Lady Lowborough. The first day he held himself aloof from her, as far as he could without any flagrant breach of hospitality: since that he has been friendly and civil, but nothing more – in my presence, at least, nor, I think, at any other time; for she seems haughty and displeased, and Lord Lowborough is manifestly more cheerful, and more cordial towards his host than before. But I shall be glad when they are gone, for I have so little love for Annabella that it is quite a task to be civil to her, and as she is the only woman here besides myself, we are necessarily thrown so much together. Next time Mrs. Hargrave calls I shall hail her advent as quite a relief. I have a good mind to ask Arthur's leave to invite the old lady to stay with us till our guests depart. I think I will. She will take it as a kind attention, and, though I have little relish for her society, she will be truly welcome as a third to stand between Lady Lowborough and me.

The first time the latter and I were alone together, after that unhappy evening, was an hour or two after breakfast on the following day, when the gentlemen were gone out, after the usual time spent in the writing of letters, the reading of newspapers, and desultory conversation. We sat silent for two or three minutes. She was busy with her work, and I was running over the columns of a paper from which I had extracted all the pith some twenty minutes before. It was a moment of painful embarrassment to me, and I thought it must be infinitely more so to her; but it seems I was mistaken. She was the first to speak; and, smiling with the coolest assurance, she began, –

"Your husband was merry last night, Helen: is he often so?"

My blood boiled in my face; but it was better she should seem to attribute his conduct to this than to anything else.

"No," replied I, "and never will be so again, I trust."

"You gave him a curtain lecture, did you?"

"No! But I told him I disliked such conduct, and he promised me not to repeat it."

"I thought he looked rather subdued this morning," she continued; "and you, Helen? You've been weeping, I see – that's our grand resource, you know. But doesn't it make your eyes smart? And do you always find it to answer?"

"I never cry for effect; nor can I conceive how any one can."

"Well, I don't know: I never had occasion to try it; but I think if Lowborough were to commit such improprieties, I'd make him cry. I don't wonder at your being angry, for I'm sure I'd give my husband a lesson he would not soon forget for a lighter offence than that. But then he never will do anything of the kind; for I keep him in too good order for that."

"Are you sure you don't arrogate too much of the credit to yourself. Lord Lowborough was quite as remarkable for his abstemiousness for some time before you married him, as he is now, I have heard."

"Oh, about the wine you mean – yes, he's safe enough for that. And as to looking askance to another woman, he's safe enough for that too, while I live, for he worships the very ground I tread on."

"Indeed! And are you sure you deserve it?"

"Why, as to that, I can't say: you know we're all fallible creatures, Helen; we none of us deserve to be worshipped. But are you sure your darling Huntingdon deserves all the love you give to him?"

I knew not what to answer to this. I was burning with anger; but I suppressed all outward manifestations of it, and only bit my lip and pretended to arrange my work.

"At any rate," resumed she, pursuing her advantage, "you can console yourself with the assurance that you are worthy of all the love he gives to you."

"You flatter me," said I; "but, at least, I can try to be worthy of it." And then I turned the conversation.

Chapter Twenty-Eight

DECEMBER 25TH. – Last Christmas I was a bride, with a heart overflowing with present bliss, and full of ardent hopes for the future, though not unmingled with foreboding fears. Now I am a wife: my bliss is sobered, but not destroyed; my hopes diminished, but not departed; my fears increased, but not yet thoroughly confirmed; and, thank heaven, I am a mother too. God has sent me a soul to educate for heaven, and give me a new and calmer bliss, and stronger hopes to comfort me.

Dec. 25th, 1823. – Another year is gone. My little Arthur lives and thrives. He is healthy, but not robust, full of gentle playfulness and vivacity, already affectionate, and susceptible of passions and emotions it will be long ere he can find words to express. He has won his father's heart at last; and now my constant terror is, lest he should be ruined by that father's thoughtless indulgence. But I must beware of my own weakness too, for I never knew till now how strong are a parent's temptations to spoil an only child.

I have need of consolation in my son, for (to this silent paper I may confess it) I have but little in my husband. I love him still; and he loves me, in his own way – but oh, how different from the love I could have given, and once had hoped to receive! How little real sympathy there exists between us; how many of my thoughts and feelings are gloomily cloistered within my own mind; how much of my higher and better self is indeed unmarried – doomed either to harden and sour in the sunless shade of solitude, or to quite degenerate and fall away for lack of nutriment in this unwholesome soil! But, I repeat, I have no right to complain; only let me state the truth – some of the truth, at least, – and see hereafter if any darker truths will blot these pages. We have now been full two years united; the 'romance' of our attachment must be worn away. Surely I have now got down to the lowest gradation in Arthur's affection, and discovered all the evils of his nature: if there be any further change, it must be for the better, as we become still more accustomed to each other; surely we shall find no lower depth than this. And, if so, I can bear it well – as well, at least, as I have borne it hitherto.

Arthur is not what is commonly called a bad man: he has many good qualities; but he is a man without self-restraint or lofty aspirations, a lover of pleasure, given up to animal enjoyments: he is not a bad husband, but his notions of matrimonial duties and comforts are not my notions. Judging from appearances, his idea of a wife is a thing to love one devotedly, and to stay at home to wait upon her husband, and amuse him and minister to his comfort in every possible way, while he chooses to stay with her; and, when he is absent, to attend to his interests, domestic or otherwise, and patiently wait his return, no matter how he may be occupied in the meantime.

Early in spring he announced his intention of going to London: his affairs there demanded his attendance, he said, and he could refuse it no longer. He expressed his regret at having to leave me, but hoped I would amuse myself with the baby till he returned.

"But why leave me?" I said. "I can go with you: I can be ready at any time."

"You would not take that child to town?"

"Yes; why not?"

The thing was absurd: the air of the town would be certain to disagree with him, and with me as a nurse; the late hours and London habits would not suit me under such circumstances; and altogether he assured me that it would be excessively troublesome, injurious, and unsafe. I over-ruled his objections as well as I could, for I trembled at the thoughts of his going alone, and would sacrifice almost anything for myself, much even for my child, to prevent it; but at length he told me, plainly, and somewhat testily, that he could not do with me: he was worn out with the baby's restless nights, and must have some repose. I proposed separate apartments; but it would not do.

"The truth is, Arthur," I said at last, "you are weary of my company, and determined not to have me with you. You might as well have said so at once."

He denied it; but I immediately left the room, and flew to the nursery, to hide my feelings, if I could not soothe them, there.

I was too much hurt to express any further dissatisfaction with his plans, or at all to refer to the subject again, except for the necessary arrangements concerning his departure and the conduct of affairs during his absence, till the day before he went, when I earnestly exhorted him to take care of himself and keep out of the way of temptation. He laughed at my anxiety, but assured me there was no cause for it, and promised to attend to my advice.

"I suppose it is no use asking you to fix a day for your return?" said I.

"Why, no; I hardly can, under the circumstances; but be assured, love, I shall not be long away."

"I don't wish to keep you a prisoner at home," I replied; "I should not grumble at your staying whole months away – if you can be happy so long without me – provided I knew you were safe; but I don't like the idea of your being there among your friends, as you call them."

"Pooh, pooh, you silly girl! Do you think I can't take care of myself?"

"You didn't last time. But *this* time, Arthur," I added, earnestly, "show me that you can, and teach me that I need not fear to trust you!"

He promised fair, but in such a manner as we seek to soothe a child. And did he keep his promise? No; and henceforth I can never trust his word. Bitter, bitter confession! Tears blind me while I write. It was early in March that he went, and he did not return till July. This time he did not trouble himself to make excuses as before, and his letters were less frequent, and shorter and less affectionate, especially after the first few weeks: they came slower and slower, and more terse and careless every time. But still, when I omitted writing, he complained of my neglect. When I wrote sternly and coldly, as I confess I frequently did at the last, he blamed my harshness, and said it was enough to scare him from his home: when I tried mild persuasion, he was a little more gentle in his replies, and promised to return; but I had learnt, at last, to disregard his promises.

Chapter Twenty-Nine

THOSE WERE FOUR miserable months, alternating between intense anxiety, despair, and indignation, pity for him and pity for myself. And yet, through all, I was not wholly comfortless: I had my darling, sinless, inoffensive little one to console me; but even this consolation was embittered by the constantly-recurring thought, 'How shall I teach him hereafter to respect his father, and yet to avoid his example?'

But I remembered that I had brought all these afflictions, in a manner wilfully, upon myself; and I determined to bear them without a murmur. At the same time I resolved not to give myself up to misery for the transgressions of another, and endeavoured to divert myself as much as I could; and besides the companionship of my child, and my dear, faithful Rachel, who evidently guessed my sorrows and felt for them, though she was too discreet to allude to them, I had my books and pencil, my domestic affairs, and the welfare and comfort of Arthur's poor tenants and labourers to attend to: and I sometimes sought and obtained amusement in the company of my young friend Esther Hargrave: occasionally I rode over to see her, and once or twice I had her to spend the day with me at the Manor. Mrs. Hargrave did not visit London that season: having no daughter to marry, she thought it as well to stay at home and economise; and, for a wonder, Walter came down to join her in the beginning of June, and stayed till near the close of August.

The first time I saw him was on a sweet, warm evening, when I was sauntering in the park with little Arthur and Rachel, who is head-nurse and lady's-maid in one – for, with my secluded life and tolerably active habits, I require but little attendance, and as she had nursed me and coveted to nurse my child, and was moreover so very trustworthy, I preferred committing the important charge to her, with a young nursery-maid under her directions, to engaging any one else: besides, it saves money; and since I have made acquaintance with Arthur's affairs, I have learnt to regard that as no trifling recommendation; for, by my own desire, nearly the whole of the income of my fortune is devoted, for years to come, to the paying off of his debts, and the money he contrives to squander away in London is incomprehensible. But to return to Mr. Hargrave. I was standing with Rachel beside the water, amusing the laughing baby in her arms with a twig of willow laden with golden catkins, when, greatly to my surprise, he entered the park, mounted on his costly black hunter, and crossed over the grass to meet me. He saluted me with a very fine compliment, delicately worded, and modestly delivered withal, which he had doubtless concocted as he rode along. He told me he had brought a message from his mother, who, as he was riding that way, had desired him to call at the Manor and beg the pleasure of my company to a friendly family dinner tomorrow.

"There is no one to meet but ourselves," said he; "but Esther is very anxious to see you; and my mother fears you will feel solitary in this great house so much alone, and wishes she could persuade you to give her the pleasure of your company more frequently, and make yourself at home in our more humble dwelling, till Mr. Huntingdon's return shall render this a little more conducive to your comfort."

"She is very kind," I answered, "but I am not alone, you see; – and those whose time is fully occupied seldom complain of solitude."

"Will you not come tomorrow, then? She will be sadly disappointed if you refuse."

I did not relish being thus compassionated for my loneliness; but, however, I promised to come.

"What a sweet evening this is!" observed he, looking round upon the sunny park, with its imposing swell and slope, its placid water, and majestic clumps of trees. "And what a paradise you live in!"

"It is a lovely evening," answered I; and I sighed to think how little I had felt its loveliness, and how little of a paradise sweet Grassdale was to me – how still less to the voluntary exile from its scenes. Whether Mr. Hargrave divined my thoughts, I cannot tell, but, with a half-hesitating, sympathising seriousness of tone and manner, he asked if I had lately heard from Mr. Huntingdon.

"Not lately," I replied.

"I thought not," he muttered, as if to himself, looking thoughtfully on the ground.

"Are you not lately returned from London?" I asked.

"Only yesterday."

"And did you see him there?"

"Yes – I saw him."

"Was he well?"

"Yes – that is," said he, with increasing hesitation and an appearance of suppressed indignation, "he was as well as – as he deserved to be, but under circumstances I should have deemed incredible for a man so favoured as he is." He here looked up and pointed the sentence with a serious bow to me. I suppose my face was crimson.

"Pardon me, Mrs. Huntingdon," he continued, "but I cannot suppress my indignation when I behold such infatuated blindness and perversion of taste; – but, perhaps, you are not aware –" He paused.

"I am aware of nothing, sir – except that he delays his coming longer than I expected; and if, at present, he prefers the society of his friends to that of his wife, and the dissipations of the town to the quiet of country life, I suppose I have those friends to thank for it. Their tastes and occupations are similar to his, and I don't see why his conduct should awaken either their indignation or surprise."

"You wrong me cruelly," answered he. "I have shared but little of Mr. Huntingdon's society for the last few weeks; and as for his tastes and occupations, they are quite beyond me – lonely wanderer as I am. Where I have but sipped and tasted, he drains the cup to the dregs; and if ever for a moment I have sought to drown the voice of reflection in madness and folly, or if I have wasted too much of my time and talents among reckless and dissipated companions, God knows I would gladly renounce them entirely and for ever, if I had but half the blessings that man so thanklessly casts behind his back – but half the inducements to virtue and domestic, orderly habits that he despises – but such a home, and such a partner to share it! It is infamous!" he muttered, between his teeth. "And don't think, Mrs. Huntingdon," he added aloud, "that I could be guilty of inciting him to persevere in his present pursuits: on the contrary, I have remonstrated with him again and again; I have frequently expressed my surprise at his conduct, and reminded him of his duties and his privileges – but to no purpose; he only –"

"Enough, Mr. Hargrave; you ought to be aware that whatever my husband's faults may be, it can only aggravate the evil for me to hear them from a stranger's lips."

"Am I then a stranger?" said he in a sorrowful tone. "I am your nearest neighbour, your son's godfather, and your husband's friend; may I not be yours also?"

"Intimate acquaintance must precede real friendship; I know but little of you, Mr. Hargrave, except from report."

"Have you then forgotten the six or seven weeks I spent under your roof last autumn? I have not forgotten them. And I know enough of you, Mrs. Huntingdon, to think that your husband is the most enviable man in the world, and I should be the next if you would deem me worthy of your friendship."

"If you knew more of me, you would not think it, or if you did you would not say it, and expect me to be flattered by the compliment."

I stepped backward as I spoke. He saw that I wished the conversation to end; and immediately taking the hint, he gravely bowed, wished me good evening, and turned his horse towards the road. He appeared grieved and hurt at my unkind reception of his sympathising overtures. I was not sure that I had done right in speaking so harshly to him; but, at the time, I had felt irritated – almost insulted by his conduct; it seemed as if he was presuming upon the absence and neglect of my husband, and insinuating even more than the truth against him.

Rachel had moved on, during our conversation, to some yards' distance. He rode up to her, and asked to see the child. He took it carefully into his arms, looked upon it with an almost paternal smile, and I heard him say, as I approached, –

"And this, too, he has forsaken!"

He then tenderly kissed it, and restored it to the gratified nurse.

"Are you fond of children, Mr. Hargrave?" said I, a little softened towards him.

"Not in general," he replied, "but that is such a sweet child, and so like its mother," he added in a lower tone.

"You are mistaken there; it is its father it resembles."

"Am I not right, nurse?" said he, appealing to Rachel.

"I think, sir, there's a bit of both," she replied.

He departed; and Rachel pronounced him a very nice gentleman. I had still my doubts on the subject.

In the course of the following six weeks I met him several times, but always, save once, in company with his mother, or his sister, or both. When I called on them, he always happened to be at home, and, when they called on me, it was always he that drove them over in the phaeton. His mother, evidently, was quite delighted with his dutiful attentions and newly-acquired domestic habits.

The time that I met him alone was on a bright, but not oppressively hot day, in the beginning of July: I had taken little Arthur into the wood that skirts the park, and there seated him on the moss-cushioned roots of an old oak; and, having gathered a handful of bluebells and wild-roses, I was kneeling before him, and presenting them, one by one, to the grasp of his tiny fingers; enjoying the heavenly beauty of the flowers, through the medium of his smiling eyes: forgetting, for the moment, all my cares, laughing at his gleeful laughter, and delighting myself with his delight, – when a shadow suddenly eclipsed the little space of sunshine on the grass before us; and looking up, I beheld Walter Hargrave standing and gazing upon us.

"Excuse me, Mrs. Huntingdon," said he, "but I was spell-bound; I had neither the power to come forward and interrupt you, nor to withdraw from the contemplation of such a scene. How vigorous my little godson grows! And how merry he is this morning!" He approached the child, and stooped to take his hand; but, on seeing that his caresses were likely to produce tears and lamentations, instead of a reciprocation of friendly demonstrations, he prudently drew back.

"What a pleasure and comfort that little creature must be to you, Mrs. Huntingdon!" he observed, with a touch of sadness in his intonation, as he admiringly contemplated the infant.

"It is," replied I; and then I asked after his mother and sister.

He politely answered my inquiries, and then returned again to the subject I wished to avoid; though with a degree of timidity that witnessed his fear to offend.

"You have not heard from Huntingdon lately?" he said.

"Not this week," I replied. Not these three weeks, I might have said.

"I had a letter from him this morning. I wish it were such a one as I could show to his lady." He half drew from his waistcoat-pocket a letter with Arthur's still beloved hand on the address, scowled at it, and put it back again, adding – "But he tells me he is about to return next week."

"He tells me so every time he writes."

"Indeed! Well, it is like him. But to me he always avowed it his intention to stay till the present month."

It struck me like a blow, this proof of premeditated transgression and systematic disregard of truth.

"It is only of a piece with the rest of his conduct," observed Mr. Hargrave, thoughtfully regarding me, and reading, I suppose, my feelings in my face.

"Then he is really coming next week?" said I, after a pause.

"You may rely upon it, if the assurance can give you any pleasure. And is it possible, Mrs. Huntingdon, that you can rejoice at his return?" he exclaimed, attentively perusing my features again.

"Of course, Mr. Hargrave; is he not my husband?"

"Oh, Huntingdon; you know not what you slight!" he passionately murmured.

I took up my baby, and, wishing him good morning, departed, to indulge my thoughts unscrutinized, within the sanctum of my home.

And was I glad? Yes, delighted; though I was angered by Arthur's conduct, and though I felt that he had wronged me, and was determined he should feel it too.

Chapter Thirty

ON THE FOLLOWING morning I received a few lines from him myself, confirming Hargrave's intimations respecting his approaching return. And he did come next week, but in a condition of body and mind even worse than before. I did not, however, intend to pass over his derelictions this time without a remark; I found it would not do. But the first day he was weary with his journey, and I was glad to get him back: I would not upbraid him then; I would wait till tomorrow. Next morning he was weary still: I would wait a little longer. But at dinner, when, after breakfasting at twelve o'clock on a bottle of soda-water and a cup of strong coffee, and lunching at two on another bottle of soda-water mingled with brandy, he was finding fault with everything on the table, and declaring we must change our cook, I thought the time was come.

"It is the same cook as we had before you went, Arthur," said I. "You were generally pretty well satisfied with her then."

"You must have been letting her get into slovenly habits, then, while I was away. It is enough to poison one, eating such a disgusting mess!" And he pettishly pushed away his plate, and leant back despairingly in his chair.

"I think it is you that are changed, not she," said I, but with the utmost gentleness, for I did not wish to irritate him.

"It may be so," he replied carelessly, as he seized a tumbler of wine and water, adding, when he had tossed it off, "for I have an infernal fire in my veins, that all the waters of the ocean cannot quench!"

"What kindled it?" I was about to ask, but at that moment the butler entered and began to take away the things.

"Be quick, Benson; do have done with that infernal clatter!" cried his master. "And don't bring the cheese, unless you want to make me sick outright!"

Benson, in some surprise, removed the cheese, and did his best to effect a quiet and speedy clearance of the rest; but, unfortunately, there was a rumple in the carpet, caused by the hasty pushing back of his master's chair, at which he tripped and stumbled, causing a rather alarming concussion with the trayful of crockery in his hands, but no positive damage, save the fall and breaking of a sauce tureen; but, to my unspeakable shame and dismay, Arthur turned furiously around upon him, and swore at him with savage coarseness. The poor man turned pale, and visibly trembled as he stooped to pick up the fragments.

"He couldn't help it, Arthur," said I; "the carpet caught his foot, and there's no great harm done. Never mind the pieces now, Benson; you can clear them away afterwards."

Glad to be released, Benson expeditiously set out the dessert and withdrew.

"What could you mean, Helen, by taking the servant's part against me," said Arthur, as soon as the door was closed, "when you knew I was distracted?"

"I did not know you were distracted, Arthur: and the poor man was quite frightened and hurt at your sudden explosion."

"Poor man, indeed! And do you think I could stop to consider the feelings of an insensate brute like that, when my own nerves were racked and torn to pieces by his confounded blunders?"

"I never heard you complain of your nerves before."

"And why shouldn't I have nerves as well as you?"

"Oh, I don't dispute your claim to their possession, but I never complain of mine."

"No, how should you, when you never do anything to try them?"

"Then why do you try yours, Arthur?"

"Do you think I have nothing to do but to stay at home and take care of myself like a woman?"

"Is it impossible, then, to take care of yourself like a man when you go abroad? You told me that you could, and would too; and you promised –"

"Come, come, Helen, don't begin with that nonsense now; I can't bear it."

"Can't bear what? – To be reminded of the promises you have broken?"

"Helen, you are cruel. If you knew how my heart throbbed, and how every nerve thrilled through me while you spoke, you would spare me. You can pity a dolt of a servant for breaking a dish; but you have no compassion for me when my head is split in two and all on fire with this consuming fever."

He leant his head on his hand, and sighed. I went to him and put my hand on his forehead. It was burning indeed.

"Then come with me into the drawing room, Arthur; and don't take any more wine: you have taken several glasses since dinner, and eaten next to nothing all the day. How can that make you better?"

With some coaxing and persuasion, I got him to leave the table. When the baby was brought I tried to amuse him with that; but poor little Arthur was cutting his teeth, and his father could not bear his complaints: sentence of immediate banishment was passed upon him on the first indication of fretfulness; and because, in the course of the evening, I went to share his exile for a little while, I was reproached, on my return, for preferring my child to my husband. I found the latter reclining on the sofa just as I had left him.

"Well!" exclaimed the injured man, in a tone of pseudo-resignation. "I thought I wouldn't send for you; I thought I'd just see how long it would please you to leave me alone."

"I have not been very long, have I, Arthur? I have not been an hour, I'm sure."

"Oh, of course, an hour is nothing to you, so pleasantly employed; but to me –"

"It has not been pleasantly employed," interrupted I. "I have been nursing our poor little baby, who is very far from well, and I could not leave him till I got him to sleep."

"Oh, to be sure, you're overflowing with kindness and pity for everything but me."

"And why should I pity you? What is the matter with you?"

"Well! That passes everything! After all the wear and tear that I've had, when I come home sick and weary, longing for comfort, and expecting to find attention and kindness, at least from my wife, she calmly asks what is the matter with me!"

"There is nothing the matter with you," returned I, "except what you have wilfully brought upon yourself, against my earnest exhortation and entreaty."

"Now, Helen," said he emphatically, half rising from his recumbent posture, "if you bother me with another word, I'll ring the bell and order six bottles of wine, and, by heaven, I'll drink them dry before I stir from this place!"

I said no more, but sat down before the table and drew a book towards me.

"Do let me have quietness at least!" continued he, "if you deny me every other comfort;" and sinking back into his former position, with an impatient expiration between a sigh and a groan, he languidly closed his eyes, as if to sleep.

What the book was that lay open on the table before me, I cannot tell, for I never looked at it. With an elbow on each side of it, and my hands clasped before my eyes, I delivered myself up to silent weeping. But Arthur was not asleep: at the first slight sob, he raised his head and looked round, impatiently exclaiming, "What are you crying for, Helen? What the deuce is the matter now?"

"I'm crying for you, Arthur," I replied, speedily drying my tears; and starting up, I threw myself on my knees before him, and clasping his nerveless hand between my own, continued: "Don't you know that you are a part of myself? And do you think you can injure and degrade yourself, and I not feel it?"

"Degrade myself, Helen?"

"Yes, degrade! What have you been doing all this time?"

"You'd better not ask," said he, with a faint smile.

"And you had better not tell; but you cannot deny that you have degraded yourself miserably. You have shamefully wronged yourself, body and soul, and me too; and I can't endure it quietly, and I won't!"

"Well, don't squeeze my hand so frantically, and don't agitate me so, for heaven's sake! Oh, Hattersley! You were right: this woman will be the death of me, with her keen feelings and her interesting force of character. There, there, do spare me a little."

"Arthur, you must repent!" cried I, in a frenzy of desperation, throwing my arms around him and burying my face in his bosom. "You shall say you are sorry for what you have done!"

"Well, well, I am."

"You are not! You'll do it again."

"I shall never live to do it again if you treat me so savagely," replied he, pushing me from him. "You've nearly squeezed the breath out of my body." He pressed his hand to his heart, and looked really agitated and ill.

"Now get me a glass of wine," said he, "to remedy what you've done, you she tiger! I'm almost ready to faint."

I flew to get the required remedy. It seemed to revive him considerably.

"What a shame it is," said I, as I took the empty glass from his hand, "for a strong young man like you to reduce yourself to such a state!"

"If you knew all, my girl, you'd say rather, 'What a wonder it is you can bear it so well as you do!' I've lived more in these four months, Helen, than you have in the whole course of your existence, or will to the end of your days, if they numbered a hundred years; so I must expect to pay for it in some shape."

"You will have to pay a higher price than you anticipate, if you don't take care: there will be the total loss of your own health, and of my affection too, if that is of any value to you."

"What! You're at that game of threatening me with the loss of your affection again, are you? I think it couldn't have been very genuine stuff to begin with, if it's so easily demolished. If you don't mind, my pretty tyrant, you'll make me regret my choice in good earnest, and envy my friend Hattersley his meek little wife: she's quite a pattern to her sex, Helen. He had her with him in London all the season, and she was no trouble at all. He might amuse himself just as he pleased, in regular bachelor style, and she never complained of neglect; he might come home at any hour of the night or morning, or not come home at all; be sullen, sober, or glorious drunk; and play the fool or the madman to his own heart's desire, without any fear or botheration. She never gives him a word of reproach or complaint, do what he will. He says there's not such a jewel in all England, and swears he wouldn't take a kingdom for her."

"But he makes her life a curse to her."

"Not he! She has no will but his, and is always contented and happy as long as he is enjoying himself."

"In that case she is as great a fool as he is; but it is not so. I have several letters from her, expressing the greatest anxiety about his proceedings, and complaining that you incite him to commit those extravagances – one especially, in which she implores me to use my influence with you to get you away from London, and affirms that her husband never did such things before you came, and would certainly discontinue them as soon as you departed and left him to the guidance of his own good sense."

"The detestable little traitor! Give me the letter, and he shall see it as sure as I'm a living man."

"No, he shall not see it without her consent; but if he did, there is nothing there to anger him, nor in any of the others. She never speaks a word against him: it is only anxiety for him that she expresses. She only alludes to his conduct in the most delicate terms, and makes every excuse for him that she can possibly think of; and as for her own misery, I rather feel it than see it expressed in her letters."

"But she abuses me; and no doubt you helped her."

"No; I told her she over-rated my influence with you, that I would gladly draw you away from the temptations of the town if I could, but had little hope of success, and that I thought she was wrong in supposing that you enticed Mr. Hattersley or any one else into error. I had myself held the contrary opinion at one time, but I now believed that you mutually corrupted each other; and, perhaps, if she used a little gentle but serious remonstrance with her husband, it might be of some service; as, though he was more rough-hewn than mine, I believed he was of a less impenetrable material."

"And so that is the way you go on – heartening each other up to mutiny, and abusing each other's partners, and throwing out implications against your own, to the mutual gratification of both!"

"According to your own account," said I, "my evil counsel has had but little effect upon her. And as to abuse and aspersions, we are both of us far too deeply ashamed of the errors and vices of our other halves, to make them the common subject of our correspondence. Friends as we are, we would willingly keep your failings to ourselves – even from ourselves if we could, unless by knowing them we could deliver you from them."

"Well, well! Don't worry me about them: you'll never effect any good by that. Have patience with me, and bear with my languor and crossness a little while, till I get this cursed low fever out of my veins, and then you'll find me cheerful and kind as ever. Why can't you be gentle and good, as you were last time? – I'm sure I was very grateful for it."

"And what good did your gratitude do? I deluded myself with the idea that you were ashamed of your transgressions, and hoped you would never repeat them again; but now you have left me nothing to hope!"

"My case is quite desperate, is it? A very blessed consideration, if it will only secure me from the pain and worry of my dear anxious wife's efforts to convert me, and her from the toil and trouble of such exertions, and her sweet face and silver accents from the ruinous effects of the same. A burst of passion is a fine rousing thing upon occasion, Helen, and a flood of tears is marvellously affecting, but, when indulged too often, they are both deuced plaguy things for spoiling one's beauty and tiring out one's friends."

Thenceforth I restrained my tears and passions as much as I could. I spared him my exhortations and fruitless efforts at conversion too, for I saw it was all in vain: God might awaken that heart, supine and stupefied with self-indulgence, and remove the film of sensual darkness from his eyes, but I could not. His injustice and ill-humour towards his inferiors, who could not defend themselves, I still resented and withstood; but when I alone was their object, as was frequently the case, I endured it with calm forbearance, except at times, when my temper, worn out by repeated annoyances, or stung to distraction by some new instance of irrationality, gave way in spite of myself, and exposed me to the imputations of fierceness, cruelty, and impatience. I attended carefully to his wants and amusements, but not, I own, with the same devoted fondness as before, because I could not feel it; besides, I had now another claimant on my time and care – my ailing infant, for whose sake I frequently braved and suffered the reproaches and complaints of his unreasonably exacting father.

But Arthur is not naturally a peevish or irritable man; so far from it, that there was something almost ludicrous in the incongruity of this adventitious fretfulness and nervous irritability, rather calculated to excite laughter than anger, if it were not for the intensely painful considerations attendant upon those symptoms of a disordered frame, and his temper gradually improved as his bodily health was restored, which was much sooner than would have been the case but for my strenuous exertions; for there was still one thing about him that I did not give up in despair, and one effort for his preservation that I would not remit. His appetite for the stimulus of wine had increased upon him, as I had too well foreseen. It was now something more to him than an accessory to social enjoyment: it was an important source of enjoyment in itself. In this time of weakness and depression he would have made it his medicine and support, his comforter, his recreation, and his friend, and thereby sunk deeper and deeper, and bound himself down for ever in the bathos whereinto he had fallen. But I determined this should never be, as long as I had any influence left; and though I could not prevent him from taking more than was good for him, still, by incessant perseverance, by kindness, and firmness, and vigilance, by coaxing, and daring, and determination, I succeeded in preserving him from absolute bondage to that detestable propensity, so insidious in its advances, so inexorable in its tyranny, so disastrous in its effects.

And here I must not forget that I am not a little indebted to his friend Mr. Hargrave. About that time he frequently called at Grassdale, and often dined with us, on which occasions I fear Arthur would willingly have cast prudence and decorum to the winds, and made 'a night of it,' as often as his friend would have consented to join him in that exalted pastime; and if the latter had chosen to comply, he might, in a night or two, have ruined the labour of weeks, and overthrown with a touch the frail bulwark it had cost me such trouble and toil to construct. I was so fearful of this at first, that I humbled myself to intimate to him, in private, my apprehensions of Arthur's proneness to these excesses, and to express a hope that he would not encourage it. He was pleased with this mark of confidence, and certainly did not betray it. On that and every subsequent occasion his presence served rather as a check upon his host, than an incitement to further acts of intemperance; and he always succeeded in bringing him from the dining room in good time, and in tolerably good condition; for if Arthur disregarded such intimations as "Well, I must not detain you from your lady," or "We must not forget that Mrs. Huntingdon is alone," he would insist upon leaving the table himself, to join me, and his host, however unwillingly, was obliged to follow.

Hence I learned to welcome Mr. Hargrave as a real friend to the family, a harmless companion for Arthur, to cheer his spirits and preserve him from the tedium of absolute idleness and a total isolation from all society but mine, and a useful ally to me. I could not but feel grateful to him under such circumstances; and I did not scruple to acknowledge my obligation on the first convenient opportunity; yet, as I did so, my heart whispered all was not right, and brought a glow to my face, which he heightened by his steady, serious gaze, while, by his manner of receiving those acknowledgments, he more than doubled my misgivings. His high delight at being able to serve me was chastened by sympathy for me and commiseration for himself – about, I know not what, for I would not stay to inquire, or suffer him to unburden his sorrows to me. His sighs and intimations of suppressed affliction seemed to come from a full heart; but either he must contrive to retain them within it, or breathe them forth in other ears than mine: there was enough of confidence between us already. It seemed wrong that there should exist a secret understanding between my husband's friend and me, unknown to him, of which he was the object. But my after-thought was, "If it is wrong, surely Arthur's is the fault, not mine."

And indeed I know not whether, at the time, it was not for him rather than myself that I blushed; for, since he and I are one, I so identify myself with him, that I feel his degradation, his failings, and transgressions as my own: I blush for him, I fear for him; I repent for him, weep, pray, and feel for him as for myself; but I cannot act for him; and hence I must be, and I am, debased, contaminated by the union, both in my own eyes and in the actual truth. I am so determined to love him, so intensely anxious to excuse his errors, that I am continually dwelling upon them, and labouring to extenuate the loosest of his principles and the worst of his practices, till I am familiarised with vice, and almost a partaker in his sins. Things that formerly shocked and disgusted me, now seem only natural. I know them to be wrong, because reason and God's word declare them to be so; but I am gradually losing that instinctive horror and repulsion which were given me by nature, or instilled into me by the precepts and example of my aunt. Perhaps then I was too severe in my judgments, for I abhorred the sinner as well as the sin; now I flatter myself I am more charitable and considerate; but am I not becoming more indifferent and insensate too? Fool that I was, to dream that I had strength and purity enough to save myself and him! Such vain presumption would be rightly served, if I should perish with him in the gulf from which I sought to save him! Yet, God preserve me from it, and him too! Yes, poor Arthur, I will still hope and pray for you; and though I write as if you were some abandoned wretch, past hope and past reprieve, it is only my anxious fears, my strong desires that make me do so; one who loved you less would be less bitter, less dissatisfied.

His conduct has, of late, been what the world calls irreproachable; but then I know his heart is still unchanged; and I know that spring is approaching, and deeply dread the consequences.

As he began to recover the tone and vigour of his exhausted frame, and with it something of his former impatience of retirement and repose, I suggested a short residence by the sea-side, for his recreation and further restoration, and for the benefit of our little one as well. But no: watering-places were so intolerably dull; besides, he had been invited by one of his friends to spend a month or two in Scotland for the better recreation of grouse-shooting and deer-stalking, and had promise to go.

"Then you will leave me again, Arthur?" said I.

"Yes, dearest, but only to love you the better when I come back, and make up for all past offences and short-comings; and you needn't fear me this time: there are no temptations on the mountains. And during my absence you may pay a visit to Staningley, if you like: your uncle and aunt have long been wanting us to go there, you know; but somehow there's such a repulsion between the good lady and me, that I never could bring myself up to the scratch."

About the third week in August, Arthur set out for Scotland, and Mr. Hargrave accompanied him thither, to my private satisfaction. Shortly after, I, with little Arthur and Rachel, went to Staningley, my dear old home, which, as well as my dear old friends its inhabitants, I saw again with mingled feelings of pleasure and pain so intimately blended that I could scarcely distinguish the one from the other, or tell to which to attribute the various tears, and smiles, and sighs awakened by those old familiar scenes, and tones, and faces.

Arthur did not come home till several weeks after my return to Grassdale; but I did not feel so anxious about him now; to think of him engaged in active sports among the wild hills of Scotland, was very different from knowing him to be immersed amid the corruptions and temptations of London. His letters now; though neither long nor loverlike, were more regular than ever they had been before; and when he did return, to my great joy, instead of being worse than when he went, he was more cheerful and vigorous, and better in every respect. Since that time I have had little cause to complain. He still has an unfortunate predilection for the pleasures of the table, against which I have to struggle and watch; but he has begun to notice his boy, and that is an increasing source of amusement to him within-doors, while his fox-hunting and coursing are a sufficient occupation for him without, when the ground is not hardened by frost; so that he is not wholly dependent on me for entertainment. But it is now January; spring is approaching; and, I repeat, I dread the consequences of its arrival. That sweet season, I once so joyously welcomed as the time of hope and gladness, awakens now far other anticipations by its return.

Chapter Thirty-One

MARCH 20TH, 1824. The dreaded time is come, and Arthur is gone, as I expected. This time he announced it his intention to make but a short stay in London, and pass over to the Continent, where he should probably stay a few weeks; but I shall not expect him till after the lapse of many weeks: I now know that, with him, days signify weeks, and weeks months.

July 30th. – He returned about three weeks ago, rather better in health, certainly, than before, but still worse in temper. And yet, perhaps, I am wrong: it is I that am less patient and forbearing. I am tired out with his injustice, his selfishness and hopeless depravity. I wish a milder word would do; I am no angel, and my corruption rises against it. My poor father died last week: Arthur was vexed to hear of it, because he saw that I was shocked and grieved, and he feared the circumstance would mar his comfort. When I spoke of ordering my mourning, he exclaimed, – "Oh, I hate black! But, however, I suppose you must wear it awhile, for form's sake; but I hope, Helen, you won't think it your bounden duty to compose your face and manners into conformity with your funereal garb. Why should you sigh and groan, and I be made uncomfortable, because an old gentleman in —shire, a perfect stranger to us both, has thought proper to drink himself to death? There, now, I declare you're crying! Well, it must be affectation."

He would not hear of my attending the funeral, or going for a day or two, to cheer poor Frederick's solitude. It was quite unnecessary, he said, and I was unreasonable to wish it. What was my father to me? I had never seen him but once since I was a baby, and I well knew he had never cared a stiver about me; and my brother, too, was little better than a stranger. "Besides, dear Helen," said he, embracing me with flattering fondness, "I cannot spare you for a single day."

"Then how have you managed without me these many days?" said I.

"Ah! Then I was knocking about the world, now I am at home, and home without you, my household deity, would be intolerable."

"Yes, as long as I am necessary to your comfort; but you did not say so before, when you urged me to leave you, in order that you might get away from your home without me," retorted I; but before the words were well out of my mouth, I regretted having uttered them. It seemed so heavy a charge: if false, too gross an insult; if true, too humiliating a fact to be thus openly cast in his teeth. But I might have spared myself that momentary pang of self-reproach. The accusation awoke neither shame nor indignation in him: he attempted neither denial nor excuse, but only answered with a long, low, chuckling laugh, as if he viewed the whole transaction as a clever, merry jest from beginning to end. Surely that man will make me dislike him at last!

Sine as ye brew, my maiden fair,
Keep mind that ye maun drink the yill.

Yes; and I will drink it to the very dregs: and none but myself shall know how bitter I find it!

August 20th. – We are shaken down again to about our usual position. Arthur has returned to nearly his former condition and habits; and I have found it my wisest plan to shut my eyes against the past and future, as far as he, at least, is concerned, and live only for the present: to love him when I can; to smile (if possible) when he smiles, be cheerful when he is cheerful, and pleased when he is agreeable; and when he is not, to try to make him so; and if that won't answer, to bear with him, to excuse him, and forgive him as well as I can, and restrain my own evil passions from aggravating his; and yet, while I thus yield and minister to his more harmless propensities to self-indulgence, to do all in my power to save him from the worse.

But we shall not be long alone together. I shall shortly be called upon to entertain the same select body of friends as we had the autumn before last, with the addition of Mr. Hattersley and, at my special request, his wife and child. I long to see Milicent, and her little girl too. The latter is now above a year old; she will be a charming playmate for my little Arthur.

September 30th. – Our guests have been here a week or two; but I have had no leisure to pass any comments upon them till now. I cannot get over my dislike to Lady Lowborough. It is not founded on mere personal pique; it is the woman herself that I dislike, because I so thoroughly disapprove of her. I always avoid her company as much as I can without violating the laws of hospitality; but when we do speak or converse together, it is with the utmost civility, even apparent cordiality on her part; but preserve me from such cordiality! It is like handling brier-roses and may-blossoms, bright enough to the eye, and outwardly soft to the touch, but you know there are thorns beneath, and every now and then you feel them too; and perhaps resent the injury by crushing them in till you have destroyed their power, though somewhat to the detriment of your own fingers.

Of late, however, I have seen nothing in her conduct towards Arthur to anger or alarm me. During the first few days I thought she seemed very solicitous to win his admiration. Her efforts were not unnoticed by him: I frequently saw him smiling to himself at her artful manoeuvres: but, to his praise be it spoken, her shafts fell powerless by his side. Her most bewitching smiles, her haughtiest frowns were ever received with the same immutable, careless good-humour; till, finding he was indeed impenetrable, she suddenly remitted her efforts, and became, to all appearance, as perfectly indifferent as himself. Nor have I since witnessed any symptom of pique on his part, or renewed attempts at conquest upon hers.

This is as it should be; but Arthur never will let me be satisfied with him. I have never, for a single hour since I married him, known what it is to realise that sweet idea, 'In quietness and confidence shall be your rest.' Those two detestable men, Grimsby and Hattersley, have destroyed all my labour against his love of wine. They encourage him daily to overstep the bounds of moderation, and not unfrequently to disgrace himself by positive excess. I shall not soon forget the second night after their arrival. Just as I had retired from the dining room with the ladies, before the door was closed upon us, Arthur exclaimed, – "Now then, my lads, what say you to a regular jollification?"

Milicent glanced at me with a half-reproachful look, as if I could hinder it; but her countenance changed when she heard Hattersley's voice, shouting through door and wall, – "I'm your man! Send for more wine: here isn't half enough!"

We had scarcely entered the drawing room before we were joined by Lord Lowborough.

"What can induce you to come so soon?" exclaimed his lady, with a most ungracious air of dissatisfaction.

"You know I never drink, Annabella," replied he seriously.

"Well, but you might stay with them a little: it looks so silly to be always dangling after the women; I wonder you can!"

He reproached her with a look of mingled bitterness and surprise, and, sinking into a chair, suppressed a heavy sigh, bit his pale lips, and fixed his eyes upon the floor.

"You did right to leave them, Lord Lowborough," said I. "I trust you will always continue to honour us so early with your company. And if Annabella knew the value of true wisdom, and the misery of folly and – and intemperance, she would not talk such nonsense – even in jest."

He raised his eyes while I spoke, and gravely turned them upon me, with a half-surprised, half-abstracted look, and then bent them on his wife.

"At least," said she, "I know the value of a warm heart and a bold, manly spirit."

"Well, Annabella," said he, in a deep and hollow tone, "since my presence is disagreeable to you, I will relieve you of it."

"Are you going back to them, then?" said she, carelessly.

"No," exclaimed he, with harsh and startling emphasis. "I will not go back to them! And I will never stay with them one moment longer than I think right, for you or any other tempter! But you needn't mind that; I shall never trouble you again by intruding my company upon you so unseasonably."

He left the room: I heard the hall-door open and shut, and immediately after, on putting aside the curtain, I saw him pacing down the park, in the comfortless gloom of the damp, cloudy twilight.

"It would serve you right, Annabella," said I, at length, "if Lord Lowborough were to return to his old habits, which had so nearly effected his ruin, and which it cost him such an effort to break: you would then see cause to repent such conduct as this."

"Not at all, my dear! I should not mind if his lordship were to see fit to intoxicate himself every day: I should only the sooner be rid of him."

"Oh, Annabella!" cried Milicent. "How can you say such wicked things! It would, indeed, be a just punishment, as far as you are concerned, if Providence should take you at your word, and make you feel what others feel, that –" She paused as a sudden burst of loud talking and laughter reached us from the dining room, in which the voice of Hattersley was pre-eminently conspicuous, even to my unpractised ear.

"What you feel at this moment, I suppose?" said Lady Lowborough, with a malicious smile, fixing her eyes upon her cousin's distressed countenance.

The latter offered no reply, but averted her face and brushed away a tear. At that moment the door opened and admitted Mr. Hargrave, just a little flushed, his dark eyes sparkling with unwonted vivacity.

"Oh, I'm so glad you're come, Walter?" cried his sister. "But I wish you could have got Ralph to come too."

"Utterly impossible, dear Milicent," replied he, gaily. "I had much ado to get away myself. Ralph attempted to keep me by violence; Huntingdon threatened me with the eternal loss of his friendship; and Grimsby, worse than all, endeavoured to make me ashamed of my virtue, by such galling sarcasms and innuendoes as he knew would wound me the most. So you see, ladies, you ought to make me welcome when I have braved and suffered so much for the favour of your sweet society." He smilingly turned to me and bowed as he finished the sentence.

"Isn't he handsome now, Helen!" whispered Milicent, her sisterly pride overcoming, for the moment, all other considerations.

"He would be," I returned, "if that brilliance of eye, and lip, and cheek were natural to him; but look again, a few hours hence."

Here the gentleman took a seat near me at the table, and petitioned for a cup of coffee.

"I consider this an apt illustration of heaven taken by storm," said he, as I handed one to him. "I am in paradise, now; but I have fought my way through flood and fire to win it. Ralph Hattersley's last resource was to set his back against the door, and swear I should find no passage but through his body (a pretty substantial one too). Happily, however, that was not the only door, and I effected my escape by the side entrance through the butler's pantry, to the infinite amazement of Benson, who was cleaning the plate."

Mr. Hargrave laughed, and so did his cousin; but his sister and I remained silent and grave.

"Pardon my levity, Mrs. Huntingdon," murmured he, more seriously, as he raised his eyes to my face. "You are not used to these things: you suffer them to affect your delicate mind too sensibly. But I thought of you in the midst of those lawless roysterers; and I endeavoured to persuade Mr. Huntingdon to think of you too; but to no purpose: I fear he is fully determined to enjoy himself this night; and it will be no use keeping the coffee waiting for him or his companions; it will be much if they join us at tea. Meantime, I earnestly wish I could banish the thoughts of them from your mind – and my own too, for I hate to think of them – yes – even of my dear friend Huntingdon, when I consider the power he possesses over the happiness of one so immeasurably superior to himself, and the use he makes of it – I positively detest the man!"

"You had better not say so to me, then," said I; "for, bad as he is, he is part of myself, and you cannot abuse him without offending me."

"Pardon me, then, for I would sooner die than offend you. But let us say no more of him for the present, if you please."

At last they came; but not till after ten, when tea, which had been delayed for more than half an hour, was nearly over. Much as I had longed for their coming, my heart failed me at the riotous uproar of their approach; and Milicent turned pale, and almost started from her seat, as Mr. Hattersley burst into the room with a clamorous volley of oaths in his mouth, which Hargrave endeavoured to check by entreating him to remember the ladies.

"Ah! You do well to remind me of the ladies, you dastardly deserter," cried he, shaking his formidable fist at his brother-in-law. "If it were not for them, you well know, I'd demolish you in the twinkling of an eye, and give your body to the fowls of heaven and the lilies of the fields!" Then, planting a chair by Lady Lowborough's side, he stationed himself in it, and began to talk to her with a mixture of absurdity and impudence that seemed rather to amuse than to offend her; though she affected to resent his insolence, and to keep him at bay with sallies of smart and spirited repartee.

Meantime Mr. Grimsby seated himself by me, in the chair vacated by Hargrave as they entered, and gravely stated that he would thank me for a cup of tea: and Arthur placed himself beside poor Milicent, confidentially pushing his head into her face, and drawing in closer to her as she shrank away from him. He was not so noisy as Hattersley, but his face was exceedingly flushed: he laughed incessantly, and while I blushed for all I saw and heard of him, I was glad that he chose to talk to his companion in so low a tone that no one could hear what he said but herself.

"What fools they are!" drawled Mr. Grimsby, who had been talking away, at my elbow, with sententious gravity all the time; but I had been too much absorbed in contemplating the deplorable state of the other two – especially Arthur – to attend to him.

"Did you ever hear such nonsense as they talk, Mrs. Huntingdon?" he continued. "I'm quite ashamed of them for my part: they can't take so much as a bottle between them without its getting into their heads –"

"You are pouring the cream into your saucer, Mr. Grimsby."

"Ah! Yes, I see, but we're almost in darkness here. Hargrave, snuff those candles, will you?"

"They're wax; they don't require snuffing," said I.

"'The light of the body is the eye,'" observed Hargrave, with a sarcastic smile. "'If thine eye be single, thy whole body shall be full of light.'"

Grimsby repulsed him with a solemn wave of the hand, and then turning to me, continued, with the same drawling tones and strange uncertainty of utterance and heavy gravity of aspect as before: "But as I was saying, Mrs. Huntingdon, they have no head at all: they can't take half a bottle without being affected some way; whereas I – well, I've taken three times as much as they have tonight, and you see I'm perfectly steady. Now that may strike you as very singular, but I think I can explain it: you see their brains – I mention no names, but you'll understand to whom I allude – their brains are light to begin with, and the fumes of the fermented liquor render them lighter still, and produce an entire light-headedness, or giddiness, resulting in intoxication; whereas my brains, being composed of more solid materials, will absorb a considerable quantity of this alcoholic vapour without the production of any sensible result –"

"I think you will find a sensible result produced on that tea," interrupted Mr. Hargrave, "by the quantity of sugar you have put into it. Instead of your usual complement of one lump, you have put in six."

"Have I so?" replied the philosopher, diving with his spoon into the cup, and bringing up several half-dissolved pieces in confirmation of the assertion. "Hum! I perceive. Thus, Madam, you see the evil of absence of mind – of thinking too much while engaged in the common concerns of life. Now, if I had had my wits about me, like ordinary men, instead of within me like a philosopher, I should not have spoiled this cup of tea, and been constrained to trouble you for another."

"That is the sugar-basin, Mr. Grimsby. Now you have spoiled the sugar too; and I'll thank you to ring for some more, for here is Lord Lowborough at last; and I hope his lordship will condescend to sit down with us, such as we are, and allow me to give him some tea."

His lordship gravely bowed in answer to my appeal, but said nothing. Meantime, Hargrave volunteered to ring for the sugar, while Grimsby lamented his mistake, and attempted to prove that it was owing to the shadow of the urn and the badness of the lights.

Lord Lowborough had entered a minute or two before, unobserved by anyone but me, and had been standing before the door, grimly surveying the company. He now stepped up to Annabella, who sat with her back towards him, with Hattersley still beside her, though not now attending to her, being occupied in vociferously abusing and bullying his host.

"Well, Annabella," said her husband, as he leant over the back of her chair, "which of these three 'bold, manly spirits' would you have me to resemble?"

"By heaven and earth, you shall resemble us all!" cried Hattersley, starting up and rudely seizing him by the arm. "Hallo, Huntingdon!" he shouted – "I've got him! Come, man, and help me! And d—n me, if I don't make him drunk before I let him go! He shall make up for all past delinquencies as sure as I'm a living soul!"

There followed a disgraceful contest: Lord Lowborough, in desperate earnest, and pale with anger, silently struggling to release himself from the powerful madman that was striving to drag him from the room. I attempted to urge Arthur to interfere in behalf of his outraged guest, but he could do nothing but laugh.

"Huntingdon, you fool, come and help me, can't you!" cried Hattersley, himself somewhat weakened by his excesses.

"I'm wishing you God-speed, Hattersley," cried Arthur, "and aiding you with my prayers: I can't do anything else if my life depended on it! I'm quite used up. Oh – oh!" and leaning back in his seat, he clapped his hands on his sides and groaned aloud.

"Annabella, give me a candle!" said Lowborough, whose antagonist had now got him round the waist and was endeavouring to root him from the door-post, to which he madly clung with all the energy of desperation.

"I shall take no part in your rude sports!" replied the lady coldly drawing back. "I wonder you can expect it." But I snatched up a candle and brought it to him. He took it and held the flame to Hattersley's hands, till, roaring like a wild beast, the latter unclasped them and let him go. He vanished, I suppose to his own apartment, for nothing more was seen of him till the morning. Swearing and cursing like a maniac, Hattersley threw himself on to the ottoman beside the window. The door being now free, Milicent attempted to make her escape from the scene of her husband's disgrace; but he called her back, and insisted upon her coming to him.

"What do you want, Ralph?" murmured she, reluctantly approaching him.

"I want to know what's the matter with you," said he, pulling her on to his knee like a child. "What are you crying for, Milicent? – Tell me!"

"I'm not crying."

"You are," persisted he, rudely pulling her hands from her face. "How dare you tell such a lie!"

"I'm not crying now," pleaded she.

"But you have been, and just this minute too; and I will know what for. Come, now, you shall tell me!"

"Do let me alone, Ralph! Remember, we are not at home."

"No matter: you shall answer my question!" exclaimed her tormentor; and he attempted to extort the confession by shaking her, and remorselessly crushing her slight arms in the gripe of his powerful fingers.

"Don't let him treat your sister in that way," said I to Mr. Hargrave.

"Come now, Hattersley, I can't allow that," said that gentleman, stepping up to the ill-assorted couple. "Let my sister alone, if you please."

And he made an effort to unclasp the ruffian's fingers from her arm, but was suddenly driven backward, and nearly laid upon the floor by a violent blow on the chest, accompanied with the admonition, "Take that for your insolence! And learn to interfere between me and mine again."

"If you were not drunk, I'd have satisfaction for that!" gasped Hargrave, white and breathless as much from passion as from the immediate effects of the blow.

"Go to the devil!" responded his brother-in-law. "Now, Milicent, tell me what you were crying for."

"I'll tell you some other time," murmured she, "when we are alone."

"Tell me now!" said he, with another shake and a squeeze that made her draw in her breath and bite her lip to suppress a cry of pain.

"I'll tell you, Mr. Hattersley," said I. "She was crying from pure shame and humiliation for you; because she could not bear to see you conduct yourself so disgracefully."

"Confound you, Madam!" muttered he, with a stare of stupid amazement at my 'impudence.' "It was not that – was it, Milicent?"

She was silent.

"Come, speak up, child!"

"I can't tell now," sobbed she.

"But you can say 'yes' or 'no' as well as 'I can't tell.' – Come!"

"Yes," she whispered, hanging her head, and blushing at the awful acknowledgment.

"Curse you for an impertinent hussy, then!" cried he, throwing her from him with such violence that she fell on her side; but she was up again before either I or her brother could come to her assistance, and made the best of her way out of the room, and, I suppose, up-stairs, without loss of time.

The next object of assault was Arthur, who sat opposite, and had, no doubt, richly enjoyed the whole scene.

"Now, Huntingdon," exclaimed his irascible friend, "I will not have you sitting there and laughing like an idiot!"

"Oh, Hattersley," cried he, wiping his swimming eyes – "you'll be the death of me."

"Yes, I will, but not as you suppose: I'll have the heart out of your body, man, if you irritate me with any more of that imbecile laughter! – What! Are you at it yet? – There! See if that'll settle you!" cried Hattersley, snatching up a footstool and hurting it at the head of his host; but he as well as missed his aim, and the latter still sat collapsed and quaking with feeble laughter, with tears running down his face: a deplorable spectacle indeed.

Hattersley tried cursing and swearing, but it would not do: he then took a number of books from the table beside him, and threw them, one by one, at the object of his wrath; but Arthur only laughed the more; and, finally, Hattersley rushed upon him in a frenzy and seizing him by the shoulders, gave him a violent shaking, under which he laughed and shrieked alarmingly. But I saw no more: I thought I had witnessed enough of my husband's degradation; and leaving Annabella and the rest to follow when they pleased, I withdrew, but not to bed. Dismissing Rachel to her rest, I walked up and down my room, in an agony of misery for what had been done, and suspense, not knowing what might further happen, or how or when that unhappy creature would come up to bed.

At last he came, slowly and stumblingly ascending the stairs, supported by Grimsby and Hattersley, who neither of them walked quite steadily themselves, but were both laughing and joking at him, and making noise enough for all the servants to hear. He himself was no longer laughing now, but sick and stupid. I will write no more about that.

Such disgraceful scenes (or nearly such) have been repeated more than once. I don't say much to Arthur about it, for, if I did, it would do more harm than good; but I let him know that I intensely dislike such exhibitions; and each time he has promised they should never again be repeated. But I fear he is losing the little self-command and self-respect he once possessed: formerly, he would have been ashamed to act thus – at least, before any other witnesses than his boon companions, or such as they. His friend Hargrave, with a prudence and self-government that I envy for him, never disgraces himself by taking more than sufficient to render him a little 'elevated,' and is always the first to leave the table after Lord Lowborough, who, wiser still, perseveres in vacating the dining room immediately after us: but never once, since Annabella offended him so deeply, has he entered the drawing room before the rest; always spending the interim in the library, which I take care to have lighted for his accommodation; or, on fine moonlight nights, in roaming about the grounds. But I think she regrets her misconduct, for she has never repeated it since, and of late she has comported herself with wonderful propriety towards him, treating him with more uniform kindness and consideration than ever I have observed her to do before. I date the time of this improvement from the period when she ceased to hope and strive for Arthur's admiration.

Chapter Thirty-Two

OCTOBER 5TH. – Esther Hargrave is getting a fine girl. She is not out of the school-room yet, but her mother frequently brings her over to call in the mornings when the gentlemen are out, and sometimes she spends an hour or two in company with her sister and me, and the children; and when we go to the Grove, I always contrive to see her, and talk more to her than to any one else, for I am very much attached to my little friend, and so is she to me. I wonder what she can see to like in me though, for I am no longer the happy, lively girl I used to be; but she has no other society, save that of her uncongenial mother, and her governess (as artificial and conventional a person as that prudent mother could procure to rectify the pupil's natural qualities), and, now and then, her subdued, quiet sister. I often wonder what will be her lot in life, and so does she; but her speculations on the future are full of buoyant hope; so were mine once. I shudder to think of her being awakened, like me, to a sense of their delusive vanity. It seems as if I should feel her disappointment, even more deeply than my own. I feel almost as if I were born for such a fate, but she is so joyous and fresh, so light of heart and free of spirit, and so guileless and unsuspecting too. Oh, it would be cruel to make her feel as I feel now, and know what I have known!

Her sister trembles for her too. Yesterday morning, one of October's brightest, loveliest days, Milicent and I were in the garden enjoying a brief half-hour together with our children, while Annabella was lying on the drawing room sofa, deep in the last new novel. We had been romping with the little creatures, almost as merry and wild as themselves, and now paused in the shade of the tall copper beech, to recover breath and rectify our hair, disordered by the rough play and the frolicsome breeze, while they toddled together along the broad, sunny walk; my Arthur supporting the feebler steps of her little Helen, and sagaciously pointing out to her the brightest beauties of the border as they passed, with semi-articulate prattle, that did as well for her as any other mode of discourse. From laughing at the pretty sight, we began to talk of the children's future life; and that made us thoughtful. We both relapsed into silent musing as we slowly proceeded up the walk; and I suppose Milicent, by a train of associations, was led to think of her sister.

"Helen," said she, "you often see Esther, don't you?"

"Not very often."

"But you have more frequent opportunities of meeting her than I have; and she loves you, I know, and reverences you too: there is nobody's opinion she thinks so much of; and she says you have more sense than mamma."

"That is because she is self-willed, and my opinions more generally coincide with her own than your mamma's. But what then, Milicent?"

"Well, since you have so much influence with her, I wish you would seriously impress it upon her, never, on any account, or for anybody's persuasion, to marry for the sake of money, or rank, or establishment, or any earthly thing, but true affection and well-grounded esteem."

"There is no necessity for that," said I, "for we have had some discourse on that subject already, and I assure you her ideas of love and matrimony are as romantic as any one could desire."

"But romantic notions will not do: I want her to have true notions."

"Very right: but in my judgment, what the world stigmatises as romantic, is often more nearly allied to the truth than is commonly supposed; for, if the generous ideas of youth are too often over-clouded by the sordid views of after-life, that scarcely proves them to be false."

"Well, but if you think her ideas are what they ought to be, strengthen them, will you? And confirm them, as far as you can; for I had romantic notions once, and – I don't mean to say that I regret my lot, for I am quite sure I don't, but –"

"I understand you," said I; "you are contented for yourself, but you would not have your sister to suffer the same as you."

"No – or worse. She might have far worse to suffer than I, for I am really contented, Helen, though you mayn't think it: I speak the solemn truth in saying that I would not exchange my husband for any man on earth, if I might do it by the plucking of this leaf."

"Well, I believe you: now that you have him, you would not exchange him for another; but then you would gladly exchange some of his qualities for those of better men."

"Yes: just as I would gladly exchange some of my own qualities for those of better women; for neither he nor I are perfect, and I desire his improvement as earnestly as my own. And he will improve, don't you think so, Helen? He's only six-and-twenty yet."

"He may," I answered.

"He will, he *will*!" repeated she.

"Excuse the faintness of my acquiescence, Milicent, I would not discourage your hopes for the world, but mine have been so often disappointed, that I am become as cold and doubtful in my expectations as the flattest of octogenarians."

"And yet you do hope, still, even for Mr. Huntingdon?"

"I do, I confess, 'even' for him; for it seems as if life and hope must cease together. And is he so much worse, Milicent, than Mr. Hattersley?"

"Well, to give you my candid opinion, I think there is no comparison between them. But you mustn't be offended, Helen, for you know I always speak my mind, and you may speak yours too. I sha'n't care."

"I am not offended, love; and my opinion is, that if there be a comparison made between the two, the difference, for the most part, is certainly in Hattersley's favour."

Milicent's own heart told her how much it cost me to make this acknowledgment; and, with a childlike impulse, she expressed her sympathy by suddenly kissing my cheek, without a word of reply, and then turning quickly away, caught up her baby, and hid her face in its frock. How odd it is that we so often weep for each other's distresses, when we shed not a tear for our own! Her heart had been full enough of her own sorrows, but it overflowed at the idea of mine; and I, too, shed tears at the sight of her sympathetic emotion, though I had not wept for myself for many a week.

It was one rainy day last week; most of the company were killing time in the billiard-room, but Milicent and I were with little Arthur and Helen in the library, and between our books, our children, and each other, we expected to make out a very agreeable morning. We had not been thus secluded above two hours, however, when Mr. Hattersley came in, attracted, I suppose, by the voice of his child, as he was crossing the hall, for he is prodigiously fond of her, and she of him.

He was redolent of the stables, where he had been regaling himself with the company of his fellow-creatures the horses ever since breakfast. But that was no matter to my little namesake; as soon as the colossal person of her father darkened the door, she uttered a shrill scream of delight, and, quitting her mother's side, ran crowing towards him, balancing her course with outstretched arms, and embracing his knee, threw back her head and laughed in his face. He might well look smilingly down upon those small, fair features, radiant with innocent mirth, those clear blue shining eyes, and that soft flaxen hair cast back upon the little ivory neck and shoulders. Did he not think how unworthy he was of such a possession? I fear no such idea crossed his mind. He caught her up, and there followed some minutes of very rough play, during which it is difficult to say whether the father or the daughter laughed and shouted the loudest. At length, however, the boisterous pastime terminated, suddenly, as might be expected: the little one was hurt, and began to cry; and the ungentle play-fellow tossed it into its mother's lap, bidding her 'make all straight.' As happy to return to that gentle comforter as it had been to leave her, the child nestled in her arms, and hushed its cries in a moment; and sinking its little weary head on her bosom, soon dropped asleep.

Meantime Mr. Hattersley strode up to the fire, and interposing his height and breadth between us and it, stood with arms akimbo, expanding his chest, and gazing round him as if the house and all its appurtenances and contents were his own undisputed possessions.

"Deuced bad weather this!" he began. "There'll be no shooting today, I guess." Then, suddenly lifting up his voice, he regaled us with a few bars of a rollicking song, which abruptly ceasing, he finished the tune with a whistle, and then continued: – "I say, Mrs. Huntingdon, what a fine stud your husband has! Not large, but good. I've been looking at them a bit this morning; and upon my word, Black Boss, and Grey Tom, and that young Nimrod are the finest animals I've seen for many a day!" Then followed a particular discussion of their various merits, succeeded by a sketch of the great things he intended to do in the horse-jockey line, when his old governor thought proper to quit the stage. "Not that I wish him to close his accounts," added he: "the old Trojan is welcome to keep his books open as long as he pleases for me."

"I hope so, indeed, Mr. Hattersley."

"Oh, yes! It's only my way of talking. The event must come some time, and so I look to the bright side of it: that's the right plan – isn't it, Mrs. H.? What are you two doing here? By-the-by, where's Lady Lowborough?"

"In the billiard-room."

"What a splendid creature she is!" continued he, fixing his eyes on his wife, who changed colour, and looked more and more disconcerted as he proceeded. "What a noble figure she has; and what magnificent black eyes; and what a fine spirit of her own; and what a tongue of her own, too, when she likes to use it. I perfectly adore her! But never mind, Milicent: I wouldn't have her for my wife, not if she'd a kingdom for her dowry! I'm better satisfied with the one I have. Now then! What do you look so sulky for? Don't you believe me?"

"Yes, I believe you," murmured she, in a tone of half sad, half sullen resignation, as she turned away to stroke the hair of her sleeping infant, that she had laid on the sofa beside her.

"Well, then, what makes you so cross? Come here, Milly, and tell me why you can't be satisfied with my assurance."

She went, and putting her little hand within his arm, looked up in his face, and said softly, –

"What does it amount to, Ralph? Only to this, that though you admire Annabella so much, and for qualities that I don't possess, you would still rather have me than her for your wife, which merely proves that you don't think it necessary to love your wife; you are satisfied if she can keep your house, and take care of your child. But I'm not cross; I'm only sorry; for," added she, in a low, tremulous accent, withdrawing her hand from his arm, and bending her looks on the rug, "if you don't love me, you don't, and it can't be helped."

"Very true; but who told you I didn't? Did I say I loved Annabella?"

"You said you adored her."

"True, but adoration isn't love. I adore Annabella, but I don't love her; and I love thee, Milicent, but I don't adore thee." In proof of his affection, he clutched a handful of her light brown ringlets, and appeared to twist them unmercifully.

"Do you really, Ralph?" murmured she, with a faint smile beaming through her tears, just putting up her hand to his, in token that he pulled rather too hard.

"To be sure I do," responded he: "only you bother me rather, sometimes."

"I bother you!" cried she, in very natural surprise.

"Yes, you – but only by your exceeding goodness. When a boy has been eating raisins and sugar-plums all day, he longs for a squeeze of sour orange by way of a change. And did you never, Milly, observe the sands on the sea-shore; how nice and smooth they look, and how soft and easy they feel to the foot? But if you plod along, for half an hour, over this soft, easy carpet – giving way at every step, yielding the more the harder you press, – you'll find it rather wearisome work, and be glad enough to come to a bit of good, firm rock, that won't budge an inch whether you stand, walk, or stamp upon it; and, though it be hard as the nether millstone, you'll find it the easier footing after all."

"I know what you mean, Ralph," said she, nervously playing with her watchguard and tracing the figure on the rug with the point of her tiny foot – "I know what you mean: but I thought you always liked to be yielded to, and I can't alter now."

"I do like it," replied he, bringing her to him by another tug at her hair. "You mustn't mind my talk, Milly. A man must have something to grumble about; and if he can't complain that his wife harries him to death with her perversity and ill-humour, he must complain that she wears him out with her kindness and gentleness."

"But why complain at all, unless because you are tired and dissatisfied?"

"To excuse my own failings, to be sure. Do you think I'll bear all the burden of my sins on my own shoulders, as long as there's another ready to help me, with none of her own to carry?"

"There is no such one on earth," said she seriously; and then, taking his hand from her head, she kissed it with an air of genuine devotion, and tripped away to the door.

"What now?" said he. "Where are you going?"

"To tidy my hair," she answered, smiling through her disordered locks; "you've made it all come down."

"Off with you then! – An excellent little woman," he remarked when she was gone, "but a thought too soft – she almost melts in one's hands. I positively think I ill-use her sometimes, when I've taken too much – but I can't help it, for she never complains, either at the time or after. I suppose she doesn't mind it."

"I can enlighten you on that subject, Mr. Hattersley," said I: "she does mind it; and some other things she minds still more, which yet you may never hear her complain of."

"How do you know? – Does she complain to you?" demanded he, with a sudden spark of fury ready to burst into a flame if I should answer 'yes.'

"No," I replied; "but I have known her longer and studied her more closely than you have done. – And I can tell you, Mr. Hattersley, that Milicent loves you more than you deserve, and that you have it in your power to make her very happy, instead of which you are her evil genius, and, I will venture to say, there is not a single day passes in which you do not inflict upon her some pang that you might spare her if you would."

"Well – it's not my fault," said he, gazing carelessly up at the ceiling and plunging his hands into his pockets: "if my ongoings don't suit her, she should tell me so."

"Is she not exactly the wife you wanted? Did you not tell Mr. Huntingdon you must have one that would submit to anything without a murmur, and never blame you, whatever you did?"

"True, but we shouldn't always have what we want: it spoils the best of us, doesn't it? How can I help playing the deuce when I see it's all one to her whether I behave like a Christian or like a scoundrel, such as nature made me? And how can I help teasing her when she's so invitingly meek and mim, when she lies down like a spaniel at my feet and never so much as squeaks to tell me that's enough?"

"If you are a tyrant by nature, the temptation is strong, I allow; but no generous mind delights to oppress the weak, but rather to cherish and protect."

"I don't oppress her; but it's so confounded flat to be always cherishing and protecting; and then, how can I tell that I am oppressing her when she 'melts away and makes no sign'? I sometimes think she has no feeling at all; and then I go on till she cries, and that satisfies me."

"Then you do delight to oppress her?"

"I don't, I tell you! Only when I'm in a bad humour, or a particularly good one, and want to afflict for the pleasure of comforting; or when she looks flat and wants shaking up a bit. And sometimes she provokes me by crying for nothing, and won't tell me what it's for; and then, I allow, it enrages me past bearing, especially when I'm not my own man."

"As is no doubt generally the case on such occasions," said I. "But in future, Mr. Hattersley, when you see her looking flat, or crying for 'nothing' (as you call it), ascribe it all to yourself: be assured it is something you have done amiss, or your general misconduct, that distresses her."

"I don't believe it. If it were, she should tell me so: I don't like that way of moping and fretting in silence, and saying nothing: it's not honest. How can she expect me to mend my ways at that rate?"

"Perhaps she gives you credit for having more sense than you possess, and deludes herself with the hope that you will one day see your own errors and repair them, if left to your own reflection."

"None of your sneers, Mrs. Huntingdon. I have the sense to see that I'm not always quite correct, but sometimes I think that's no great matter, as long as I injure nobody but myself –"

"It is a great matter," interrupted I, "both to yourself (as you will hereafter find to your cost) and to all connected with you, most especially your wife. But, indeed, it is nonsense to talk about injuring no one but yourself: it is impossible to injure yourself, especially by such acts as we allude to, without injuring hundreds, if not thousands, besides, in a greater or less, degree, either by the evil you do or the good you leave undone." "And as I was saying," continued he, "or would have said if you hadn't taken me up so short, I sometimes think I should do better if I were joined to one that would always remind me when I was wrong, and give me a motive for doing good and eschewing evil, by decidedly showing her approval of the one and disapproval of the other."

"If you had no higher motive than the approval of your fellow-mortal, it would do you little good."

"Well, but if I had a mate that would not always be yielding, and always equally kind, but that would have the spirit to stand at bay now and then, and honestly tell me her mind at all times, such a one as yourself for instance. Now, if I went on with you as I do with her when I'm in London, you'd make the house too hot to hold me at times, I'll be sworn."

"You mistake me: I'm no termagant."

"Well, all the better for that, for I can't stand contradiction, in a general way, and I'm as fond of my own will as another; only I think too much of it doesn't answer for any man."

"Well, I would never contradict you without a cause, but certainly I would always let you know what I thought of your conduct; and if you oppressed me, in body, mind, or estate, you should at least have no reason to suppose 'I didn't mind it.'"

"I know that, my lady; and I think if my little wife were to follow the same plan, it would be better for us both."

"I'll tell her."

"No, no, let her be; there's much to be said on both sides, and, now I think upon it, Huntingdon often regrets that you are not more like her, scoundrelly dog that he is, and you see, after all, you can't reform him: he's ten times worse than I. He's afraid of you, to be sure; that is, he's always on his best behaviour in your presence – but –"

"I wonder what his worst behaviour is like, then?" I could not forbear observing.

"Why, to tell you the truth, it's very bad indeed – isn't it, Hargrave?" said he, addressing that gentleman, who had entered the room unperceived by me, for I was now standing near the fire, with my back to the door. "Isn't Huntingdon," he continued, "as great a reprobate as ever was d—d?"

"His lady will not hear him censured with impunity," replied Mr. Hargrave, coming forward; "but I must say, I thank God I am not such another."

"Perhaps it would become you better," said I, "to look at what you are, and say, 'God be merciful to me a sinner.'"

"You are severe," returned he, bowing slightly and drawing himself up with a proud yet injured air. Hattersley laughed, and clapped him on the shoulder. Moving from under his hand with a gesture of insulted dignity, Mr. Hargrave took himself away to the other end of the rug.

"Isn't it a shame, Mrs. Huntingdon?" cried his brother-in-law; "I struck Walter Hargrave when I was drunk, the second night after we came, and he's turned a cold shoulder on me ever since; though I asked his pardon the very morning after it was done!"

"Your manner of asking it," returned the other, "and the clearness with which you remembered the whole transaction, showed you were not too drunk to be fully conscious of what you were about, and quite responsible for the deed."

"You wanted to interfere between me and my wife," grumbled Hattersley, "and that is enough to provoke any man."

"You justify it, then?" said his opponent, darting upon him a most vindictive glance.

"No, I tell you I wouldn't have done it if I hadn't been under excitement; and if you choose to bear malice for it after all the handsome things I've said, do so and be d—d!"

"I would refrain from such language in a lady's presence, at least," said Mr. Hargrave, hiding his anger under a mask of disgust.

"What have I said?" returned Hattersley: "nothing but heaven's truth. He will be damned, won't he, Mrs. Huntingdon, if he doesn't forgive his brother's trespasses?"

"You ought to forgive him, Mr. Hargrave, since he asks you," said I.

"Do you say so? Then I will!" And, smiling almost frankly, he stepped forward and offered his hand. It was immediately clasped in that of his relative, and the reconciliation was apparently cordial on both sides.

"The affront," continued Hargrave, turning to me, "owed half its bitterness to the fact of its being offered in your presence; and since you bid me forgive it, I will, and forget it too."

"I guess the best return I can make will be to take myself off," muttered Hattersley, with a broad grin. His companion smiled, and he left the room. This put me on my guard. Mr. Hargrave turned seriously to me, and earnestly began, –

"Dear Mrs. Huntingdon, how I have longed for, yet dreaded, this hour! Do not be alarmed," he added, for my face was crimson with anger: "I am not about to offend you with any useless entreaties or complaints. I am not going to presume to trouble you with the mention of my own feelings or your perfections, but I have something to reveal to you which you ought to know, and which, yet, it pains me inexpressibly –"

"Then don't trouble yourself to reveal it!"

"But it is of importance –"

"If so I shall hear it soon enough, especially if it is bad news, as you seem to consider it. At present I am going to take the children to the nursery."

"But can't you ring and send them?"

"No; I want the exercise of a run to the top of the house. Come, Arthur."

"But you will return?"

"Not yet; don't wait."

"Then when may I see you again?"

"At lunch," said I, departing with little Helen in one arm and leading Arthur by the hand.

He turned away, muttering some sentence of impatient censure or complaint, in which 'heartless' was the only distinguishable word.

"What nonsense is this, Mr. Hargrave?" said I, pausing in the doorway. "What do you mean?"

"Oh, nothing; I did not intend you should hear my soliloquy. But the fact is, Mrs. Huntingdon, I have a disclosure to make, painful for me to offer as for you to hear; and I want you to give me a few minutes of your attention in private at any time and place you like to appoint. It is from no selfish motive that I ask it, and not for any cause that could alarm your superhuman purity: therefore you need not kill me with that look of cold and pitiless disdain. I know too well the feelings with which the bearers of bad tidings are commonly regarded not to –"

"What is this wonderful piece of intelligence?" said I, impatiently interrupting him. "If it is anything of real importance, speak it in three words before I go."

"In three words I cannot. Send those children away and stay with me."

"No; keep your bad tidings to yourself. I know it is something I don't want to hear, and something you would displease me by telling."

"You have divined too truly, I fear; but still, since I know it, I feel it my duty to disclose it to you."

"Oh, spare us both the infliction, and I will exonerate you from the duty. You have offered to tell; I have refused to hear: my ignorance will not be charged on you."

"Be it so: you shall not hear it from me. But if the blow fall too suddenly upon you when it comes, remember I wished to soften it!"

I left him. I was determined his words should not alarm me. What could he, of all men, have to reveal that was of importance for me to hear? It was no doubt some exaggerated tale about my unfortunate husband that he wished to make the most of to serve his own bad purposes.

6th. – He has not alluded to this momentous mystery since, and I have seen no reason to repent of my unwillingness to hear it. The threatened blow has not been struck yet, and I do not greatly fear it. At present I am pleased with Arthur: he has not positively disgraced himself for upwards of a fortnight, and all this last week has been so very moderate in his indulgence at table that I can perceive a marked difference in his general temper and appearance. Dare I hope this will continue?

Chapter Thirty-Three

SEVENTH. – Yes, I will hope! Tonight I heard Grimsby and Hattersley grumbling together about the inhospitality of their host. They did not know I was near, for I happened to be standing behind the curtain in the bow of the window, watching the moon rising over the clump of tall dark elm-trees below the lawn, and wondering why Arthur was so sentimental as to stand without, leaning against the outer pillar of the portico, apparently watching it too.

"So, I suppose we've seen the last of our merry carousals in this house," said Mr. Hattersley; "I thought his good-fellowship wouldn't last long. But," added he, laughing, "I didn't expect it would meet its end this way. I rather thought our pretty hostess would be setting up her porcupine quills, and threatening to turn us out of the house if we didn't mind our manners."

"You didn't foresee this, then?" answered Grimsby, with a guttural chuckle. "But he'll change again when he's sick of her. If we come here a year or two hence, we shall have all our own way, you'll see."

"I don't know," replied the other: "she's not the style of woman you soon tire of. But be that as it may, it's devilish provoking now that we can't be jolly, because he chooses to be on his good behaviour."

"It's all these cursed women!" muttered Grimsby: "they're the very bane of the world! They bring trouble and discomfort wherever they come, with their false, fair faces and their deceitful tongues."

At this juncture I issued from my retreat, and smiling on Mr. Grimsby as I passed, left the room and went out in search of Arthur. Having seen him bend his course towards the shrubbery, I followed him thither, and found him just entering the shadowy walk. I was so light of heart, so overflowing with affection, that I sprang upon him and clasped him in my arms. This startling conduct had a singular effect upon him: first, he murmured, "Bless you, darling!" and returned my close embrace with a fervour like old times, and then he started, and, in a tone of absolute terror, exclaimed, "Helen! what the devil is this?" and I saw, by the faint light gleaming through the overshadowing tree, that he was positively pale with the shock.

How strange that the instinctive impulse of affection should come first, and then the shock of the surprise! It shows, at least, that the affection is genuine: he is not sick of me yet.

"I startled you, Arthur," said I, laughing in my glee. "How nervous you are!"

"What the deuce did you do it for?" cried he, quite testily, extricating himself from my arms, and wiping his forehead with his handkerchief. "Go back, Helen – go back directly! You'll get your death of cold!"

"I won't, till I've told you what I came for. They are blaming you, Arthur, for your temperance and sobriety, and I'm come to thank you for it. They say it is all 'these cursed women,' and that we are the bane of the world; but don't let them laugh or grumble you out of your good resolutions, or your affection for me."

He laughed. I squeezed him in my arms again, and cried in tearful earnest, "Do, do persevere! And I'll love you better than ever I did before!"

"Well, well, I will!" said he, hastily kissing me. "There, now, go. You mad creature, how could you come out in your light evening dress this chill autumn night?"

"It is a glorious night," said I.

"It is a night that will give you your death, in another minute. Run away, do!"

"Do you see my death among those trees, Arthur?" said I, for he was gazing intently at the shrubs, as if he saw it coming, and I was reluctant to leave him, in my new-found happiness and revival of hope and love. But he grew angry at my delay, so I kissed him and ran back to the house.

I was in such a good humour that night: Milicent told me I was the life of the party, and whispered she had never seen me so brilliant. Certainly, I talked enough for twenty, and smiled upon them all. Grimsby, Hattersley, Hargrave, Lady Lowborough, all shared my sisterly kindness. Grimsby stared and wondered; Hattersley laughed and jested (in spite of the little wine he had been suffered to imbibe), but still behaved as well as he knew how. Hargrave and Annabella, from different motives and in different ways, emulated me, and doubtless both surpassed me, the former in his discursive versatility and eloquence, the latter in boldness and animation at least. Milicent, delighted to see her husband, her brother, and her over-estimated friend acquitting themselves so well, was lively and gay too, in her quiet way. Even Lord Lowborough caught the general contagion: his dark greenish eyes were lighted up beneath their moody brows; his sombre countenance was beautified by smiles; all traces of gloom and proud or cold reserve had vanished for the time; and he astonished us all, not only by his general cheerfulness and animation, but by the positive flashes of true force and brilliance he emitted from time to time. Arthur did not talk much, but he laughed, and listened to the rest, and was in perfect good-humour, though not excited by wine. So that, altogether, we made a very merry, innocent, and entertaining party.

9th. – Yesterday, when Rachel came to dress me for dinner, I saw that she had been crying. I wanted to know the cause of it, but she seemed reluctant to tell. Was she unwell? No. Had she heard bad news from her friends? No. Had any of the servants vexed her?

"Oh, no, ma'am!" she answered; "it's not for myself."

"What then, Rachel? Have you been reading novels?"

"Bless you, no!" said she, with a sorrowful shake of the head; and then she sighed and continued: "But to tell you the truth, ma'am, I don't like master's ways of going on."

"What do you mean, Rachel? He's going on very properly at present."

"Well, ma'am, if you think so, it's right."

And she went on dressing my hair, in a hurried way, quite unlike her usual calm, collected manner, murmuring, half to herself, she was sure it was beautiful hair: she 'could like to see 'em match it.' When it was done, she fondly stroked it, and gently patted my head.

"Is that affectionate ebullition intended for my hair, or myself, nurse?" said I, laughingly turning round upon her; but a tear was even now in her eye.

"What do you mean, Rachel?" I exclaimed.

"Well, ma'am, I don't know; but if –"

"If what?"

"Well, if I was you, I wouldn't have that Lady Lowborough in the house another minute – not another minute I wouldn't!"

I was thunderstruck; but before I could recover from the shock sufficiently to demand an explanation, Milicent entered my room, as she frequently does when she is dressed before me; and she stayed with me till it was time to go down. She must have found me a very unsociable companion this time, for Rachel's last words rang in my ears. But still I hoped, I trusted they had no foundation but in some idle rumour of the servants from what they had seen in Lady Lowborough's manner last month; or perhaps from something that had passed between their master and her during her former visit. At dinner I narrowly observed both her and Arthur, and saw nothing extraordinary in the conduct of either, nothing calculated to excite suspicion, except in distrustful minds, which mine was not, and therefore I would not suspect.

Almost immediately after dinner Annabella went out with her husband to share his moonlight ramble, for it was a splendid evening like the last. Mr. Hargrave entered the drawing room a little before the others, and challenged me to a game of chess. He did it without any of that sad but proud humility he usually assumes in addressing me, unless he is excited with wine. I looked at his face to see if that was the case now. His eye met mine keenly, but steadily: there was something about him I did not understand, but he seemed sober enough. Not choosing to engage with him, I referred him to Milicent.

"She plays badly," said he, "I want to match my skill with yours. Come now! You can't pretend you are reluctant to lay down your work. I know you never take it up except to pass an idle hour, when there is nothing better you can do."

"But chess-players are so unsociable," I objected; "they are no company for any but themselves."

"There is no one here but Milicent, and she –"

"Oh, I shall be delighted to watch you!" cried our mutual friend. "Two such players – it will be quite a treat! I wonder which will conquer."

I consented.

"Now, Mrs. Huntingdon," said Hargrave, as he arranged the men on the board, speaking distinctly, and with a peculiar emphasis, as if he had a double meaning to all his words, "you are a good player, but I am a better: we shall have a long game, and you will give me some trouble; but I can be as patient as you, and in the end I shall certainly win." He fixed his eyes upon me with a glance I did not like, keen, crafty, bold, and almost impudent; – already half triumphant in his anticipated success.

"I hope not, Mr. Hargrave!" returned I, with vehemence that must have startled Milicent at least; but he only smiled and murmured, "Time will show."

We set to work: he sufficiently interested in the game, but calm and fearless in the consciousness of superior skill: I, intensely eager to disappoint his expectations, for I considered this the type of a more serious contest, as I imagined he did, and I felt an almost superstitious dread of being beaten: at all events, I could ill endure that present success should add one tittle to his conscious power (his insolent self-confidence I ought to say), or encourage for a moment his dream of future conquest. His play was cautious and deep, but I struggled hard against him. For some time the combat was doubtful: at length, to my joy, the victory seemed inclining to my side: I had taken several of his best pieces, and manifestly baffled his projects. He put his hand to his brow and paused, in evident perplexity. I rejoiced in my advantage, but dared not glory in it yet. At length, he lifted his head, and quietly making his move, looked at me and said, calmly, "Now you think you will win, don't you?"

"I hope so," replied I, taking his pawn that he had pushed into the way of my bishop with so careless an air that I thought it was an oversight, but was not generous enough, under the circumstances, to direct his attention to it, and too heedless, at the moment, to foresee the after-consequences of my move. "It is those bishops that trouble me," said he; "but the bold knight can overleap the reverend gentlemen," taking my last bishop with his knight; "and now, those sacred persons once removed, I shall carry all before me." ·

"Oh, Walter, how you talk!" cried Milicent; "she has far more pieces than you still."

"I intend to give you some trouble yet," said I; "and perhaps, sir, you will find yourself checkmated before you are aware. Look to your queen."

The combat deepened. The game was a long one, and I did give him some trouble: but he was a better player than I.

"What keen gamesters you are!" said Mr. Hattersley, who had now entered, and been watching us for some time. "Why, Mrs. Huntingdon, your hand trembles as if you had staked your all upon it! And, Walter, you dog, you look as deep and cool as if you were certain of success, and as keen and cruel as if you would drain her heart's blood! But if I were you, I wouldn't beat her, for very fear: she'll hate you if you do – she will, by heaven! I see it in her eye."

"Hold your tongue, will you?" said I: his talk distracted me, for I was driven to extremities. A few more moves, and I was inextricably entangled in the snare of my antagonist.

"Check," cried he: I sought in agony some means of escape. "Mate!" he added, quietly, but with evident delight. He had suspended the utterance of that last fatal syllable the better to enjoy my dismay. I was foolishly disconcerted by the event. Hattersley laughed; Milicent was troubled to see me so disturbed. Hargrave placed his hand on mine that rested on the table, and squeezing it with a firm but gentle pressure, murmured, "Beaten, beaten!" and gazed into my face with a look where exultation was blended with an expression of ardour and tenderness yet more insulting.

"No, never, Mr. Hargrave!" exclaimed I, quickly withdrawing my hand.

"Do you deny?" replied he, smilingly pointing to the board. "No, no," I answered, recollecting how strange my conduct must appear: "you have beaten me in that game."

"Will you try another, then?"

"No."

"You acknowledge my superiority?"

"Yes, as a chess-player."

I rose to resume my work.

"Where is Annabella?" said Hargrave, gravely, after glancing round the room.

"Gone out with Lord Lowborough," answered I, for he looked at me for a reply.

"And not yet returned!" he said, seriously.

"I suppose not."

"Where is Huntingdon?" looking round again.

"Gone out with Grimsby, as you know," said Hattersley, suppressing a laugh, which broke forth as he concluded the sentence. Why did he laugh? Why did Hargrave connect them thus together? Was it true, then? And was this the dreadful secret he had wished to reveal to me? I must know, and that quickly. I instantly rose and left the room to go in search of Rachel and demand an explanation of her words; but Mr. Hargrave followed me into the anteroom, and before I could open its outer door, gently laid his hand upon the lock. "May I tell you something, Mrs. Huntingdon?" said he, in a subdued tone, with serious, downcast eyes.

"If it be anything worth hearing," replied I, struggling to be composed, for I trembled in every limb.

He quietly pushed a chair towards me. I merely leant my hand upon it, and bid him go on.

"Do not be alarmed," said he: "what I wish to say is nothing in itself; and I will leave you to draw your own inferences from it. You say that Annabella is not yet returned?"

"Yes, yes – go on!" said I, impatiently; for I feared my forced calmness would leave me before the end of his disclosure, whatever it might be.

"And you hear," continued he, "that Huntingdon is gone out with Grimsby?"

"Well?"

"I heard the latter say to your husband – or the man who calls himself so –"

"Go on, sir!"

He bowed submissively, and continued: "I heard him say, – 'I shall manage it, you'll see! They're gone down by the water; I shall meet them there, and tell him I want a bit of talk with him about some things that we needn't trouble the lady with; and she'll say she can be walking back to the house; and then I shall apologise, you know, and all that, and tip her a wink to take the way of the shrubbery. I'll keep him talking there, about those matters I mentioned, and anything else I can think of, as long as I can, and then bring him round the other way, stopping to look at the trees, the fields, and anything else I can find to discourse of.'" Mr. Hargrave paused, and looked at me.

Without a word of comment or further questioning, I rose, and darted from the room and out of the house. The torment of suspense was not to be endured: I would not suspect my husband falsely, on this man's accusation, and I would not trust him unworthily – I must know the truth at once. I flew to the shrubbery. Scarcely had I reached it, when a sound of voices arrested my breathless speed.

"We have lingered too long; he will be back," said Lady Lowborough's voice.

"Surely not, dearest!" was his reply; "but you can run across the lawn, and get in as quietly as you can; I'll follow in a while."

My knees trembled under me; my brain swam round. I was ready to faint. She must not see me thus. I shrunk among the bushes, and leant against the trunk of a tree to let her pass.

"Ah, Huntingdon!" said she reproachfully, pausing where I had stood with him the night before – "it was here you kissed that woman!" she looked back into the leafy shade. Advancing thence, he answered, with a careless laugh, –

"Well, dearest, I couldn't help it. You know I must keep straight with her as long as I can. Haven't I seen you kiss your dolt of a husband scores of times? – And do I ever complain?"

"But tell me, don't you love her still – a little?" said she, placing her hand on his arm, looking earnestly in his face – for I could see them, plainly, the moon shining full upon them from between the branches of the tree that sheltered me.

"Not one bit, by all that's sacred!" he replied, kissing her glowing cheek.

"Good heavens, I must be gone!" cried she, suddenly breaking from him, and away she flew.

There he stood before me; but I had not strength to confront him now: my tongue cleaved to the roof of my mouth; I was well-nigh sinking to the earth, and I almost wondered he did not hear the beating of my heart above the low sighing of the wind and the fitful rustle of the falling leaves. My senses seemed to fail me, but still I saw his shadowy form pass before me, and through the rushing sound in my ears I distinctly heard him say, as he stood looking up the lawn, – "There goes the fool! Run, Annabella, run! There – in with you! Ah, – he didn't see! That's right, Grimsby, keep him back!" And even his low laugh reached me as he walked away.

"God help me now!" I murmured, sinking on my knees among the damp weeds and brushwood that surrounded me, and looking up at the moonlit sky, through the scant foliage above. It seemed all dim and quivering now to my darkened sight. My burning, bursting heart strove to pour forth its agony to God, but could not frame its anguish into prayer; until a gust of wind swept over me, which, while it scattered the dead leaves, like blighted hopes, around, cooled my forehead, and seemed a little to revive my sinking frame. Then, while I lifted up my soul in speechless, earnest supplication, some heavenly influence seemed to strengthen me within: I breathed more freely; my vision cleared; I saw distinctly the pure moon shining on, and the light clouds skimming the clear, dark sky; and then I saw the eternal stars twinkling down upon me; I knew their God was mine, and He was strong to save and swift to hear. "I will never leave thee, nor forsake thee," seemed whispered from above their myriad orbs. No, no; I felt He would not leave me comfortless: in spite of earth and hell I should have strength for all my trials, and win a glorious rest at last!

Refreshed, invigorated, if not composed, I rose and returned to the house. Much of my new-born strength and courage forsook me, I confess, as I entered it, and shut out the fresh wind and the glorious sky: everything I saw and heard seemed to sicken my heart – the hall, the lamp, the staircase, the doors of the different apartments, the social sound of talk and laughter from the drawing room. How could I bear my future life! In this house, among those people – oh, how could I endure to live! John just then entered the hall, and seeing me, told me he had been sent in search of me, adding that he had taken in the tea, and master wished to know if I were coming.

"Ask Mrs. Hattersley to be so kind as to make the tea, John," said I. "Say I am not well tonight, and wish to be excused."

I retired into the large, empty dining room, where all was silence and darkness, but for the soft sighing of the wind without, and the faint gleam of moonlight that pierced the blinds and curtains; and there I walked rapidly up and down, thinking of my bitter thoughts alone. How different was this from the evening of yesterday! That, it seems, was the last expiring flash of my life's happiness. Poor, blinded fool that I was to be so happy! I could now see the reason of Arthur's strange reception of me in the shrubbery; the burst of kindness was for his paramour, the start of horror for his wife. Now, too, I could better understand the conversation between Hattersley and Grimsby; it was doubtless of his love for her they spoke, not for me.

I heard the drawing room door open: a light quick step came out of the ante-room, crossed the hall, and ascended the stairs. It was Milicent, poor Milicent, gone to see how I was – no one else cared for me; but she still was kind. I shed no tears before, but now they came, fast and free. Thus she did me good, without approaching me. Disappointed in her search, I heard her come down, more slowly than she had ascended. Would she come in there, and find me out? No, she turned in the opposite direction and re-entered the drawing room. I was glad, for I knew not how to meet her, or what to say. I wanted no confidante in my distress. I deserved none, and I wanted none. I had taken the burden upon myself; let me bear it alone.

As the usual hour of retirement approached I dried my eyes, and tried to clear my voice and calm my mind. I must see Arthur tonight, and speak to him; but I would do it calmly: there should be no scene – nothing to complain or to boast of to his companions – nothing to laugh at with his lady-love. When the company were retiring to their chambers I gently opened the door, and just as he passed, beckoned him in.

"What's to do with you, Helen?" said he. "Why couldn't you come to make tea for us? And what the deuce are you here for, in the dark? What ails you, young woman: you look like a ghost!" he continued, surveying me by the light of his candle.

"No matter," I answered, "to you; you have no longer any regard for me it appears; and I have no longer any for you."

"Hal-lo! What the devil is this?" he muttered. "I would leave you tomorrow," continued I, "and never again come under this roof, but for my child" – I paused a moment to steady, my voice.

"What in the devil's name is this, Helen?" cried he. "What can you be driving at?"

"You know perfectly well. Let us waste no time in useless explanation, but tell me, will you – ?"

He vehemently swore he knew nothing about it, and insisted upon hearing what poisonous old woman had been blackening his name, and what infamous lies I had been fool enough to believe.

"Spare yourself the trouble of forswearing yourself and racking your brains to stifle truth with falsehood," I coldly replied. "I have trusted to the testimony of no third person. I was in the shrubbery this evening, and I saw and heard for myself."

This was enough. He uttered a suppressed exclamation of consternation and dismay, and muttering, "I shall catch it now!" set down his candle on the nearest chair, and rearing his back against the wall, stood confronting me with folded arms.

"Well, what then?" said he, with the calm insolence of mingled shamelessness and desperation.

"Only this," returned I; "will you let me take our child and what remains of my fortune, and go?"

"Go where?"

"Anywhere, where he will be safe from your contaminating influence, and I shall be delivered from your presence, and you from mine."

"No."

"Will you let me have the child then, without the money?"

"No, nor yourself without the child. Do you think I'm going to be made the talk of the country for your fastidious caprices?"

"Then I must stay here, to be hated and despised. But henceforth we are husband and wife only in the name."

"Very good."

"I am your child's mother, and your housekeeper, nothing more. So you need not trouble yourself any longer to feign the love you cannot feel: I will exact no more heartless caresses from you, nor offer nor endure them either. I will not be mocked with the empty husk of conjugal endearments, when you have given the substance to another!"

"Very good, if you please. We shall see who will tire first, my lady."

"If I tire, it will be of living in the world with you: not of living without your mockery of love. When you tire of your sinful ways, and show yourself truly repentant, I will forgive you, and, perhaps, try to love you again, though that will be hard indeed."

"Humph! And meantime you will go and talk me over to Mrs. Hargrave, and write long letters to aunt Maxwell to complain of the wicked wretch you have married?"

"I shall complain to no one. Hitherto I have struggled hard to hide your vices from every eye, and invest you with virtues you never possessed; but now you must look to yourself."

I left him muttering bad language to himself, and went up-stairs.

"You are poorly, ma'am," said Rachel, surveying me with deep anxiety.

"It is too true, Rachel," said I, answering her sad looks rather than her words.

"I knew it, or I wouldn't have mentioned such a thing."

"But don't you trouble yourself about it," said I, kissing her pale, time-wasted cheek. "I can bear it better than you imagine."

"Yes, you were always for 'bearing.' But if I was you I wouldn't bear it; I'd give way to it, and cry right hard! And I'd talk too, I just would – I'd let him know what it was to –"

"I have talked," said I; "I've said enough."

"Then I'd cry," persisted she. "I wouldn't look so white and so calm, and burst my heart with keeping it in."

"I have cried," said I, smiling, in spite of my misery; "and I am calm now, really: so don't discompose me again, nurse: let us say no more about it, and don't mention it to the servants. There, you may go now. Goodnight; and don't disturb your rest for me: I shall sleep well – if I can."

Notwithstanding this resolution, I found my bed so intolerable that, before two o'clock, I rose, and lighting my candle by the rushlight that was still burning, I got my desk and sat down in my dressing-gown to recount the events of the past evening. It was better to be so occupied than to be lying in bed torturing my brain with recollections of the far past and anticipations of the dreadful future. I have found relief in describing the very circumstances that have destroyed my peace, as well as the little trivial details attendant upon their discovery. No sleep I could have got this night would have done so much towards composing my mind, and preparing me to meet the trials of the day. I fancy so, at least; and yet, when I cease writing, I find my head aches terribly; and when I look into the glass, I am startled at my haggard, worn appearance.

Rachel has been to dress me, and says I have had a sad night of it, she can see. Milicent has just looked in to ask me how I was. I told her I was better, but to excuse my appearance admitted I had had a restless night. I wish this day were over! I shudder at the thoughts of going down to breakfast. How shall I encounter them all? Yet let me remember it is not I that am guilty: I have no cause to fear; and if they scorn me as a victim of their guilt, I can pity their folly and despise their scorn.

Chapter Thirty-Four

EVENING. – Breakfast passed well over: I was calm and cool throughout. I answered composedly all inquiries respecting my health; and whatever was unusual in my look or manner was generally attributed to the trifling indisposition that had occasioned my early retirement last night. But how am I to get over the ten or twelve days that must yet elapse before they go? Yet why so long for their departure? When they are gone, how shall I get through the months or years of my future life in company with that man – my greatest enemy? For none could injure me as he has done. Oh! When I think how fondly, how foolishly I have loved him, how madly I have trusted him, how constantly I have laboured, and studied, and prayed, and struggled for his advantage; and how cruelly he has trampled on my love, betrayed my trust, scorned my prayers and tears, and efforts for his preservation, crushed my hopes, destroyed my youth's best feelings, and doomed me to a life of hopeless misery, as far as man can do it, it is not enough to say that I no longer love my husband – I *hate* him! The word stares me in the face like a guilty confession, but it is true: I hate him – I hate him! But God have mercy on his miserable soul! And make him see and feel his guilt – I ask no other vengeance! If he could but fully know and truly feel my wrongs I should be well avenged, and I could freely pardon all; but he is so lost, so hardened in his heartless depravity, that in this life I believe he never will. But it is useless dwelling on this theme: let me seek once more to dissipate reflection in the minor details of passing events.

Mr. Hargrave has annoyed me all day long with his serious, sympathising, and (as he thinks) unobtrusive politeness. If it were more obtrusive it would trouble me less, for then I could snub him; but, as it is, he contrives to appear so really kind and thoughtful that I cannot do so without rudeness and seeming ingratitude. I sometimes think I ought to give him credit for the good feeling he simulates so well; and then again, I think it is my duty to suspect him under the peculiar circumstances in which I am placed. His kindness may not all be feigned; but still, let not the purest impulse of gratitude to him induce me to forget myself: let me remember the game of chess, the expressions he used on the occasion, and those indescribable looks of his, that so justly roused my indignation, and I think I shall be safe enough. I have done well to record them so minutely.

I think he wishes to find an opportunity of speaking to me alone: he has seemed to be on the watch all day; but I have taken care to disappoint him – not that I fear anything he could say, but I have trouble enough without the addition of his insulting consolations, condolences, or whatever else he might attempt; and, for Milicent's sake, I do not wish to quarrel with him. He excused himself from going out to shoot with the other gentlemen in the morning, under the pretext of having letters to write; and instead of retiring for that purpose into the library, he sent for his desk into the morning room, where I was seated with Milicent and Lady Lowborough. They had betaken themselves to their work; I, less to divert my mind than to deprecate conversation, had provided myself with a book. Milicent saw that I wished to be quiet, and accordingly let me alone. Annabella, doubtless, saw it too: but that was no reason why she should restrain her tongue, or curb her cheerful spirits: she accordingly chatted away, addressing herself almost exclusively to me, and with the utmost assurance and familiarity, growing the more animated and friendly the colder and briefer my answers became. Mr. Hargrave saw that I could ill endure it, and, looking up from his desk, he answered her questions and observations for me, as far as he could, and attempted to transfer her social attentions from me to himself; but it would not do. Perhaps she thought I had a headache, and could not bear to talk; at any rate, she saw that her loquacious vivacity annoyed me, as I could tell by the malicious pertinacity with which she persisted. But I checked it effectually by putting into her hand the book I had been trying to read, on the fly-leaf of which I had hastily scribbled, –

"I am too well acquainted with your character and conduct to feel any real friendship for you, and as I am without your talent for dissimulation, I cannot assume the appearance of it. I must, therefore, beg that hereafter all familiar intercourse may cease between us; and if I still continue to treat you with civility, as if you were a woman worthy of consideration and respect, understand that it is out of regard for your cousin Milicent's feelings, not for yours."

Upon perusing this she turned scarlet, and bit her lip. Covertly tearing away the leaf, she crumpled it up and put it in the fire, and then employed herself in turning over the pages of the book, and, really or apparently, perusing its contents. In a little while Milicent announced it her intention to repair to the nursery, and asked if I would accompany her.

"Annabella will excuse us," said she; "she's busy reading."

"No, I won't," cried Annabella, suddenly looking up, and throwing her book on the table; "I want to speak to Helen a minute. You may go, Milicent, and she'll follow in a while." (Milicent went.) "Will you oblige me, Helen?" continued she.

Her impudence astounded me; but I complied, and followed her into the library. She closed the door, and walked up to the fire.

"Who told you this?" said she.

"No one: I am not incapable of seeing for myself."

"Ah, you are suspicious!" cried she, smiling, with a gleam of hope. Hitherto there had been a kind of desperation in her hardihood; now she was evidently relieved.

"If I were suspicious," I replied, "I should have discovered your infamy long before. No, Lady Lowborough, I do not found my charge upon suspicion."

"On what do you found it, then?" said she, throwing herself into an arm-chair, and stretching out her feet to the fender, with an obvious effort to appear composed.

"I enjoy a moonlight ramble as well as you," I answered, steadily fixing my eyes upon her; "and the shrubbery happens to be one of my favourite resorts."

She coloured again excessively, and remained silent, pressing her finger against her teeth, and gazing into the fire. I watched her a few moments with a feeling of malevolent gratification; then, moving towards the door, I calmly asked if she had anything more to say.

"Yes, yes!" cried she eagerly, starting up from her reclining posture. "I want to know if you will tell Lord Lowborough?"

"Suppose I do?"

"Well, if you are disposed to publish the matter, I cannot dissuade you, of course – but there will be terrible work if you do – and if you don't, I shall think you the most generous of mortal beings – and if there is anything in the world I can do for you – anything short of –" she hesitated.

"Short of renouncing your guilty connection with my husband, I suppose you mean?" said I.

She paused, in evident disconcertion and perplexity, mingled with anger she dared not show.

"I cannot renounce what is dearer than life," she muttered, in a low, hurried tone. Then, suddenly raising her head and fixing her gleaming eyes upon me, she continued earnestly: "But, Helen – or Mrs. Huntingdon, or whatever you would have me call you – will you tell him? If you are generous, here is a fitting opportunity for the exercise of your magnanimity: if you are proud, here am I – your rival – ready to acknowledge myself your debtor for an act of the most noble forbearance."

"I shall not tell him."

"You will not!" cried she, delightedly. "Accept my sincere thanks, then!"

She sprang up, and offered me her hand. I drew back.

"Give me no thanks; it is not for your sake that I refrain. Neither is it an act of any forbearance: I have no wish to publish your shame. I should be sorry to distress your husband with the knowledge of it."

"And Milicent? Will you tell her?"

"No: on the contrary, I shall do my utmost to conceal it from her. I would not for much that she should know the infamy and disgrace of her relation!"

"You use hard words, Mrs. Huntingdon, but I can pardon you."

"And now, Lady Lowborough," continued I, "let me counsel you to leave this house as soon as possible. You must be aware that your continuance here is excessively disagreeable to me – not for Mr. Huntingdon's sake," said I, observing the dawn of a malicious smile of triumph on her face – "you are welcome to him, if you like him, as far as I am concerned – but because it is painful to be always disguising my true sentiments respecting you, and straining to keep up an appearance of civility and respect towards one for whom I have not the most distant shadow of esteem; and because, if you stay, your conduct cannot possibly remain concealed much longer from the only two persons in the house who do not know it already. And, for your husband's sake, Annabella, and even for your own, I wish – I earnestly advise and entreat you to break off this unlawful connection at once, and return to your duty while you may, before the dreadful consequences –"

"Yes, yes, of course," said she, interrupting me with a gesture of impatience. "But I cannot go, Helen, before the time appointed for our departure. What possible pretext could I frame for such a thing? Whether I proposed going back alone – which Lowborough would not hear of – or taking him with me, the very circumstance itself would be certain to excite suspicion – and when our visit is so nearly at an end too – little more than a week – surely you can endure my presence so long! I will not annoy you with any more of my friendly impertinences."

"Well, I have nothing more to say to you."

"Have you mentioned this affair to Huntingdon?" asked she, as I was leaving the room.

"How dare you mention his name to me!" was the only answer I gave.

No words have passed between us since, but such as outward decency or pure necessity demanded.

Chapter Thirty-Five

NINETEENTH. – In proportion as Lady Lowborough finds she has nothing to fear from me, and as the time of departure draws nigh, the more audacious and insolent she becomes. She does not scruple to speak to my husband with affectionate familiarity in my presence, when no one else is by, and is particularly fond of displaying her interest in his health and welfare, or in anything that concerns him, as if for the purpose of contrasting her kind solicitude with my cold indifference. And he rewards her by such smiles and glances, such whispered words, or boldly-spoken insinuations, indicative of his sense of her goodness and my neglect, as make the blood rush into my face, in spite of myself – for I would be utterly regardless of it all – deaf and blind to everything that passes between them, since the more I show myself sensible of their wickedness the more she triumphs in her victory, and the more he flatters himself that I love him devotedly still, in spite of my pretended indifference. On such occasions I have sometimes been startled by a subtle, fiendish suggestion inciting me to show him the contrary by a seeming encouragement of Hargrave's advances; but such ideas are banished in a moment with horror and self-abasement; and then I hate him tenfold more than ever for having brought me to this! – God pardon me for it and all my sinful thoughts! Instead of being humbled and purified by my afflictions, I feel that they are turning my nature into gall. This must be my fault as much as theirs that wrong me. No true Christian could cherish such bitter feelings as I do against him and her, especially the latter: him, I still feel that I could pardon – freely, gladly – on the slightest token of repentance; but she – words cannot utter my abhorrence. Reason forbids, but passion urges strongly; and I must pray and struggle long ere I subdue it.

It is well that she is leaving tomorrow, for I could not well endure her presence for another day. This morning she rose earlier than usual. I found her in the room alone, when I went down to breakfast.

"Oh, Helen! Is it you?" said she, turning as I entered.

I gave an involuntary start back on seeing her, at which she uttered a short laugh, observing, "I think we are both disappointed."

I came forward and busied myself with the breakfast things.

"This is the last day I shall burden your hospitality," said she, as she seated herself at the table. "Ah, here comes one that will not rejoice at it!" she murmured, half to herself, as Arthur entered the room.

He shook hands with her and wished her good morning: then, looking lovingly in her face, and still retaining her hand in his, murmured pathetically, "The last – last day!"

"Yes," said she with some asperity; "and I rose early to make the best of it – I have been here alone this half-hour, and you – you lazy creature –"

"Well, I thought I was early too," said he; "but," dropping his voice almost to a whisper, "you see we are not alone."

"We never are," returned she. But they were almost as good as alone, for I was now standing at the window, watching the clouds, and struggling to suppress my wrath.

Some more words passed between them, which, happily, I did not overhear; but Annabella had the audacity to come and place herself beside me, and even to put her hand upon my shoulder and say softly, "You need not grudge him to me, Helen, for I love him more than ever you could do."

This put me beside myself. I took her hand and violently dashed it from me, with an expression of abhorrence and indignation that could not be suppressed. Startled, almost appalled, by this sudden outbreak, she recoiled in silence. I would have given way to my fury and said more, but Arthur's low laugh recalled me to myself. I checked the half-uttered invective, and scornfully turned away, regretting that I had given him so much amusement. He was still laughing when Mr. Hargrave made his appearance. How much of the scene he had witnessed I do not know, for the door was ajar when he entered. He greeted his host and his cousin both coldly, and me with a glance intended to express the deepest sympathy mingled with high admiration and esteem.

"How much allegiance do you owe to that man?" he asked below his breath, as he stood beside me at the window, affecting to be making observations on the weather.

"None," I answered. And immediately returning to the table, I employed myself in making the tea. He followed, and would have entered into some kind of conversation with me, but the other guests were now beginning to assemble, and I took no more notice of him, except to give him his coffee.

After breakfast, determined to pass as little of the day as possible in company with Lady Lowborough, I quietly stole away from the company and retired to the library. Mr. Hargrave followed me thither, under pretence of coming for a book; and first, turning to the shelves, he selected a volume, and then quietly, but by no means timidly, approaching me, he stood beside me, resting his hand on the back of my chair, and said softly, "And so you consider yourself free at last?"

"Yes," said I, without moving, or raising my eyes from my book, "free to do anything but offend God and my conscience."

There was a momentary pause.

"Very right," said he, "provided your conscience be not too morbidly tender, and your ideas of God not too erroneously severe; but can you suppose it would offend that benevolent Being to make the happiness of one who would die for yours? – To raise a devoted heart from purgatorial torments to a state of heavenly bliss, when you could do it without the slightest injury to yourself or any other?"

This was spoken in a low, earnest, melting tone, as he bent over me. I now raised my head; and steadily confronting his gaze, I answered calmly, "Mr. Hargrave, do you mean to insult me?"

He was not prepared for this. He paused a moment to recover the shock; then, drawing himself up and removing his hand from my chair, he answered, with proud sadness, – "That was not my intention."

I just glanced towards the door, with a slight movement of the head, and then returned to my book. He immediately withdrew. This was better than if I had answered with more words, and in the passionate spirit to which my first impulse would have prompted. What a good thing it is to be able to command one's temper! I must labour to cultivate this inestimable quality: God only knows how often I shall need it in this rough, dark road that lies before me.

In the course of the morning I drove over to the Grove with the two ladies, to give Milicent an opportunity for bidding farewell to her mother and sister. They persuaded her to stay with them the rest of the day, Mrs. Hargrave promising to bring her back in the evening and remain till the party broke up on the morrow. Consequently, Lady Lowborough and I had the pleasure of returning *tête-à-tête* in the carriage together. For the first mile or two we kept silence, I looking out of my window, and she leaning back in her corner. But I was not going to restrict myself to any particular position for her; when I was tired of leaning forward, with the cold, raw wind in my face, and surveying the russet hedges and the damp, tangled grass of their banks, I gave it up and leant back too. With her usual impudence, my companion then made some attempts to get up a conversation; but the monosyllables 'yes,' or 'no' or 'humph,' were the utmost her several remarks could elicit from me. At last, on her asking my opinion upon some immaterial point of discussion, I answered, – "Why do you wish to talk to me, Lady Lowborough? You must know what I think of you."

"Well, if you will be so bitter against me," replied she, "I can't help it; but I'm not going to sulk for anybody." Our short drive was now at an end. As soon as the carriage door was opened, she sprang out, and went down the park to meet the gentlemen, who were just returning from the woods. Of course I did not follow.

But I had not done with her impudence yet: after dinner, I retired to the drawing room, as usual, and she accompanied me, but I had the two children with me, and I gave them my whole attention, and determined to keep them till the gentlemen came, or till Milicent arrived with her mother. Little Helen, however, was soon tired of playing, and insisted upon going to sleep; and while I sat on the sofa with her on my knee, and Arthur seated beside me, gently playing with her soft, flaxen hair, Lady Lowborough composedly came and placed herself on the other side.

"Tomorrow, Mrs. Huntingdon," said she, "you will be delivered from my presence, which, no doubt, you will be very glad of – it is natural you should; but do you know I have rendered you a great service? Shall I tell you what it is?"

"I shall be glad to hear of any service you have rendered me," said I, determined to be calm, for I knew by the tone of her voice she wanted to provoke me.

"Well," resumed she, "have you not observed the salutary change in Mr. Huntingdon? Don't you see what a sober, temperate man he is become? You saw with regret the sad habits he was contracting, I know: and I know you did your utmost to deliver him from them, but without success, until I came to your assistance. I told him in few words that I could not bear to see him degrade himself so, and that I should cease to – no matter what I told him, but you see the reformation I have wrought; and you ought to thank me for it."

I rose and rang for the nurse.

"But I desire no thanks," she continued; "all the return I ask is, that you will take care of him when I am gone, and not, by harshness and neglect, drive him back to his old courses."

I was almost sick with passion, but Rachel was now at the door. I pointed to the children, for I could not trust myself to speak: she took them away, and I followed.

"Will you, Helen?" continued the speaker.

I gave her a look that blighted the malicious smile on her face, or checked it, at least for a moment, and departed. In the ante-room I met Mr. Hargrave. He saw I was in no humour to be spoken to, and suffered me to pass without a word; but when, after a few minutes' seclusion in the library, I had regained my composure, and was returning to join Mrs. Hargrave and Milicent, whom I had just heard come downstairs and go into the drawing room, I found him there still lingering in the dimly-lighted apartment, and evidently waiting for me.

"Mrs. Huntingdon," said he as I passed, "will you allow me one word?"

"What is it then? Be quick, if you please."

"I offended you this morning; and I cannot live under your displeasure."

"Then go, and sin no more," replied I, turning away.

"No, no!" said he, hastily, setting himself before me. "Pardon me, but I must have your forgiveness. I leave you tomorrow, and I may not have an opportunity of speaking to you again. I was wrong to forget myself and you, as I did; but let me implore you to forget and forgive my rash presumption, and think of me as if those words had never been spoken; for, believe me, I regret them deeply, and the loss of your esteem is too severe a penalty: I cannot bear it."

"Forgetfulness is not to be purchased with a wish; and I cannot bestow my esteem on all who desire it, unless they deserve it too."

"I shall think my life well spent in labouring to deserve it, if you will but pardon this offence – will you?"

"Yes."

"Yes! But that is coldly spoken. Give me your hand and I'll believe you. You won't? Then, Mrs. Huntingdon, you do not forgive me!"

"Yes; here it is, and my forgiveness with it: only, *sin no more*."

He pressed my cold hand with sentimental fervour, but said nothing, and stood aside to let me pass into the room, where all the company were now assembled. Mr. Grimsby was seated near the door: on seeing me enter, almost immediately followed by Hargrave, he leered at me with a glance of intolerable significance, as I passed. I looked him in the face, till he sullenly turned away, if not ashamed, at least confounded for the moment. Meantime Hattersley had seized Hargrave by the arm, and was whispering something in his ear – some coarse joke, no doubt, for the latter neither laughed nor spoke in answer, but, turning from him with a slight curl of the lip, disengaged himself and went to his mother, who was telling Lord Lowborough how many reasons she had to be proud of her son.

Thank heaven, they are all going tomorrow.

Chapter Thirty-Six

DECEMBER 20TH, 1824. – This is the third anniversary of our felicitous union. It is now two months since our guests left us to the enjoyment of each other's society; and I have had nine weeks' experience of this new phase of conjugal life – two persons living together, as master and mistress of the house, and father and mother of a winsome, merry little child, with the mutual understanding that there is no love, friendship, or sympathy between them. As far as in me lies, I endeavour to live peaceably with him: I treat him with unimpeachable civility, give up my convenience to his, wherever it may reasonably be done, and consult him in a business-like way on household affairs, deferring to his pleasure and judgment, even when I know the latter to be inferior to my own.

As for him, for the first week or two, he was peevish and low, fretting, I suppose, over his dear Annabella's departure, and particularly ill-tempered to me: everything I did was wrong; I was cold-hearted, hard, insensate; my sour, pale face was perfectly repulsive; my voice made him shudder; he knew not how he could live through the winter with me; I should kill him by inches. Again I proposed a separation, but it would not do: he was not going to be the talk of all the old gossips in the neighbourhood: he would not have it said that he was such a brute his wife could not live with him. No; he must contrive to bear with me.

"I must contrive to bear with you, you mean," said I; "for so long as I discharge my functions of steward and house-keeper, so conscientiously and well, without pay and without thanks, you cannot afford to part with me. I shall therefore remit these duties when my bondage becomes intolerable." This threat, I thought, would serve to keep him in check, if anything would.

I believe he was much disappointed that I did not feel his offensive sayings more acutely, for when he had said anything particularly well calculated to hurt my feelings, he would stare me searchingly in the face, and then grumble against my 'marble heart' or my 'brutal insensibility.' If I had bitterly wept and deplored his lost affection, he would, perhaps, have condescended to pity me, and taken me into favour for a while, just to comfort his solitude and console him for the absence of his beloved Annabella, until he could meet her again, or some more fitting substitute. Thank heaven, I am not so weak as that! I was infatuated once with a foolish, besotted affection, that clung to him in spite of his unworthiness, but it is fairly gone now – wholly crushed and withered away; and he has none but himself and his vices to thank for it.

At first (in compliance with his sweet lady's injunctions, I suppose), he abstained wonderfully well from seeking to solace his cares in wine; but at length he began to relax his virtuous efforts, and now and then exceeded a little, and still continues to do so; nay, sometimes, not a little. When he is under the exciting influence of these excesses, he sometimes fires up and attempts to play the brute; and then I take little pains to suppress my scorn and disgust. When he is under the depressing influence of the after-consequences, he bemoans his sufferings and his errors, and charges them both upon me; he knows such indulgence injures his health, and does him more harm than good; but he says I drive him to it by my unnatural, unwomanly conduct; it will be the ruin of him in the end, but it is all my fault; and then I am roused to defend myself, sometimes with bitter recrimination. This is a kind of injustice I cannot patiently endure. Have I not laboured long and hard to save him from this very vice? Would I not labour still to deliver him from it if I could? But could I do so by fawning upon him and caressing him when I know that he scorns me? Is it my fault that I have lost my influence with him, or that he has forfeited every claim to my regard? And should I seek a reconciliation with him, when I feel that I abhor him, and that he despises me? And while he continues still to correspond with Lady Lowborough, as I know he does? No, never, never, never! He may drink himself dead, but it is *not* my fault!

Yet I do my part to save him still: I give him to understand that drinking makes his eyes dull, and his face red and bloated; and that it tends to render him imbecile in body and mind; and if Annabella were to see him as often as I do, she would speedily be disenchanted; and that she certainly will withdraw her favour from him, if he continues such courses. Such a mode of admonition wins only coarse abuse for me – and, indeed, I almost feel as if I deserved it, for I hate to use such arguments; but they sink into his stupefied heart, and make him pause, and ponder, and abstain, more than anything else I could say.

At present I am enjoying a temporary relief from his presence: he is gone with Hargrave to join a distant hunt, and will probably not be back before tomorrow evening. How differently I used to feel his absence!

Mr. Hargrave is still at the Grove. He and Arthur frequently meet to pursue their rural sports together: he often calls upon us here, and Arthur not unfrequently rides over to him. I do not think either of these soi-disant friends is overflowing with love for the other; but such intercourse serves to get the time on, and I am very willing it should continue, as it saves me some hours of discomfort in Arthur's society, and gives him some better employment than the sottish indulgence of his sensual appetites. The only objection I have to Mr. Hargrave's being in the neighbourhood, is that the fear of meeting him at the Grove prevents me from seeing his sister so often as I otherwise should; for, of late, he has conducted himself towards me with such unerring propriety, that I have almost forgotten his former conduct. I suppose he is striving to 'win my esteem.' If he continue to act in this way, he may win it; but what then? The moment he attempts to demand anything more, he will lose it again.

February 10th. – It is a hard, embittering thing to have one's kind feelings and good intentions cast back in one's teeth. I was beginning to relent towards my wretched partner; to pity his forlorn, comfortless condition, unalleviated as it is by the consolations of intellectual resources and the answer of a good conscience towards God; and to think I ought to sacrifice my pride, and renew my efforts once again to make his home agreeable and lead him back to the path of virtue; not by false professions of love, and not by pretended remorse, but by mitigating my habitual coldness of manner, and commuting my frigid civility into kindness wherever an opportunity occurred; and not only was I beginning to think so, but I had already begun to act upon the thought – and what was the result? No answering spark of kindness, no awakening penitence, but an unappeasable ill-humour, and a spirit of tyrannous exaction that increased with indulgence, and a lurking gleam of self-complacent triumph at every detection of relenting softness in my manner, that congealed me to marble again as often as it recurred; and this morning he finished the business: – I think the petrifaction is so completely effected at last that nothing can melt me again. Among his letters was one which he perused with symptoms of unusual gratification, and then threw it across the table to me, with the admonition, –

"There! Read that, and take a lesson by it!"

It was in the free, dashing hand of Lady Lowborough. I glanced at the first page; it seemed full of extravagant protestations of affection; impetuous longings for a speedy reunion – and impious defiance of God's mandates, and railings against His providence for having cast their lot asunder, and doomed them both to the hateful bondage of alliance with those they could not love. He gave a slight titter on seeing me change colour. I folded up the letter, rose, and returned it to him, with no remark, but –

"Thank you, I will take a lesson by it!"

My little Arthur was standing between his knees, delightedly playing with the bright, ruby ring on his finger. Urged by a sudden, imperative impulse to deliver my son from that contaminating influence, I caught him up in my arms and carried him with me out of the room. Not liking this abrupt removal, the child began to pout and cry. This was a new stab to my already tortured heart. I would not let him go; but, taking him with me into the library, I shut the door, and, kneeling on the floor beside him, I embraced him, kissed him, wept over with him with passionate fondness. Rather frightened than consoled by this, he turned struggling from me, and cried out aloud for his papa. I released him from my arms, and never were more bitter tears than those that now concealed him from my blinded, burning eyes. Hearing his cries, the father came to the room. I instantly turned away, lest he should see and misconstrue my emotion. He swore at me, and took the now pacified child away.

It is hard that my little darling should love him more than me; and that, when the well-being and culture of my son is all I have to live for, I should see my influence destroyed by one whose selfish affection is more injurious than the coldest indifference or the harshest tyranny could be. If I, for his good, deny him some trifling indulgence, he goes to his father, and the latter, in spite of his selfish indolence, will even give himself some trouble to meet the child's desires: if I attempt to curb his will, or look gravely on him for some act of childish disobedience, he knows his other parent will smile and take his part against me. Thus, not only have I the father's spirit in the son to contend against, the germs of his evil tendencies to search out and eradicate, and his corrupting intercourse and example in after-life to counteract, but already he counteracts my arduous labour for the child's advantage, destroys my influence over his tender mind, and robs me of his very love; I had no earthly hope but this, and he seems to take a diabolical delight in tearing it away.

But it is wrong to despair; I will remember the counsel of the inspired writer to him 'that feareth the Lord and obeyeth the voice of his servant, that sitteth in darkness and hath no light; let him trust in the name of the Lord, and stay upon his God!'

Chapter Thirty-Seven

DECEMBER 20TH, 1825. – Another year is past; and I am weary of this life. And yet I cannot wish to leave it: whatever afflictions assail me here, I cannot wish to go and leave my darling in this dark and wicked world alone, without a friend to guide him through its weary mazes, to warn him of its thousand snares, and guard him from the perils that beset him on every hand. I am not well fitted to be his only companion, I know; but there is no other to supply my place. I am too grave to minister to his amusements and enter into his infantile sports as a nurse or a mother ought to do, and often his bursts of gleeful merriment trouble and alarm me; I see in them his father's spirit and temperament, and I tremble for the consequences; and too often damp the innocent mirth I ought to share. That father, on the contrary, has no weight of sadness on his mind; is troubled with no fears, no scruples concerning his son's future welfare; and at evenings especially, the times when the child sees him the most and the oftenest, he is always particularly jocund and open-hearted: ready to laugh and to jest with anything or anybody but me, and I am particularly silent and sad: therefore, of course, the child dotes upon his seemingly joyous amusing, ever-indulgent papa, and will at any time gladly exchange my company for his. This disturbs me greatly; not so much for the sake of my son's affection (though I do prize that highly, and though I feel it is my right, and know I have done much to earn it) as for that influence over him which, for his own advantage, I would strive to purchase and retain, and which for very spite his father delights to rob me of, and, from motives of mere idle egotism, is pleased to win to himself; making no use of it but to torment me and ruin the child. My only consolation is, that he spends comparatively little of his time at home, and, during the months he passes in London or elsewhere, I have a chance of recovering the ground I had lost, and overcoming with good the evil he has wrought by his wilful mismanagement. But then it is a bitter trial to behold him, on his return, doing his utmost to subvert my labours and transform my innocent, affectionate, tractable darling into a selfish, disobedient, and mischievous boy; thereby preparing the soil for those vices he has so successfully cultivated in his own perverted nature.

Happily, there were none of Arthur's 'friends' invited to Grassdale last autumn: he took himself off to visit some of them instead. I wish he would always do so, and I wish his friends were numerous and loving enough to keep him amongst them all the year round. Mr. Hargrave, considerably to my annoyance, did not go with him; but I think I have done with that gentleman at last.

For seven or eight months he behaved so remarkably well, and managed so skilfully too, that I was almost completely off my guard, and was really beginning to look upon him as a friend, and even to treat him as such, with certain prudent restrictions (which I deemed scarcely necessary); when, presuming upon my unsuspecting kindness, he thought he might venture to overstep the bounds of decent moderation and propriety that had so long restrained him. It was on a pleasant evening at the close of May: I was wandering in the park, and he, on seeing me there as he rode past, made bold to enter and approach me, dismounting and leaving his horse at the gate. This was the first time he had ventured to come within its inclosure since I had been left alone, without the sanction of his mother's or sister's company, or at least the excuse of a message from them. But he managed to appear so calm and easy, so respectful and self-possessed in his friendliness, that, though a little surprised, I was neither alarmed nor offended at the unusual liberty, and he walked with me under the ash-trees and by the water-side, and talked, with considerable animation, good taste, and intelligence, on many subjects, before I began to think about getting rid of him. Then, after a pause, during which we both stood gazing on the calm, blue water – I revolving in my mind the best means of politely dismissing my companion, he, no doubt, pondering other matters equally alien to the sweet sights and sounds that alone were present to his senses, – he suddenly electrified me by beginning, in a peculiar tone, low, soft, but perfectly distinct, to pour forth the most unequivocal expressions of earnest and passionate love; pleading his cause with all the bold yet artful eloquence he could summon to his aid. But I cut short his appeal, and repulsed him so determinately, so decidedly, and with such a mixture of scornful indignation, tempered with cool, dispassionate sorrow and pity for his benighted mind, that he withdrew, astonished, mortified, and discomforted; and, a few days after, I heard that he had departed for London. He returned, however, in eight or nine weeks, and did not entirely keep aloof from me, but comported himself in so remarkable a manner that his quick-sighted sister could not fail to notice the change.

"What have you done to Walter, Mrs. Huntingdon?" said she one morning, when I had called at the Grove, and he had just left the room after exchanging a few words of the coldest civility. "He has been so extremely ceremonious and stately of late, I can't imagine what it is all about, unless you have desperately offended him. Tell me what it is, that I may be your mediator, and make you friends again."

"I have done nothing willingly to offend him," said I. "If he is offended, he can best tell you himself what it is about."

"I'll ask him," cried the giddy girl, springing up and putting her head out of the window: "he's only in the garden – Walter!"

"No, no, Esther! You will seriously displease me if you do; and I shall leave you immediately, and not come again for months – perhaps years."

"Did you call, Esther?" said her brother, approaching the window from without.

"Yes; I wanted to ask you –"

"Good morning, Esther," said I, taking her hand and giving it a severe squeeze.

"To ask you," continued she, "to get me a rose for Mrs. Huntingdon." He departed. "Mrs. Huntingdon," she exclaimed, turning to me and still holding me fast by the hand, "I'm quite shocked at you – you're just as angry, and distant, and cold as he is: and I'm determined you shall be as good friends as ever before you go."

"Esther, how can you be so rude!" cried Mrs. Hargrave, who was seated gravely knitting in her easy-chair. "Surely, you never will learn to conduct yourself like a lady!"

"Well, mamma, you said yourself –" But the young lady was silenced by the uplifted finger of her mamma, accompanied with a very stern shake of the head.

"Isn't she cross?" whispered she to me; but, before I could add my share of reproof, Mr. Hargrave reappeared at the window with a beautiful moss-rose in his hand.

"Here, Esther, I've brought you the rose," said he, extending it towards her.

"Give it her yourself, you blockhead!" cried she, recoiling with a spring from between us.

"Mrs. Huntingdon would rather receive it from you," replied he, in a very serious tone, but lowering his voice that his mother might not hear. His sister took the rose and gave it to me.

"My brother's compliments, Mrs. Huntingdon, and he hopes you and he will come to a better understanding by-and-by. Will that do, Walter?" added the saucy girl, turning to him and putting her arm round his neck, as he stood leaning upon the sill of the window – "or should I have said that you are sorry you were so touchy? Or that you hope she will pardon your offence?"

"You silly girl! You don't know what you are talking about," replied he gravely.

"Indeed I don't: for I'm quite in the dark!"

"Now, Esther," interposed Mrs. Hargrave, who, if equally benighted on the subject of our estrangement, saw at least that her daughter was behaving very improperly, "I must insist upon your leaving the room!"

"Pray don't, Mrs. Hargrave, for I'm going to leave it myself," said I, and immediately made my adieux.

About a week after Mr. Hargrave brought his sister to see me. He conducted himself, at first, with his usual cold, distant, half-stately, half-melancholy, altogether injured air; but Esther made no remark upon it this time: she had evidently been schooled into better manners. She talked to me, and laughed and romped with little Arthur, her loved and loving playmate. He, somewhat to my discomfort, enticed her from the room to have a run in the hall, and thence into the garden. I got up to stir the fire. Mr. Hargrave asked if I felt cold, and shut the door – a very unseasonable piece of officiousness, for I had meditated following the noisy playfellows if they did not speedily return. He then took the liberty of walking up to the fire himself, and asking me if I were aware that Mr. Huntingdon was now at the seat of Lord Lowborough, and likely to continue there some time.

"No; but it's no matter," I answered carelessly; and if my cheek glowed like fire, it was rather at the question than the information it conveyed.

"You don't object to it?" he said.

"Not at all, if Lord Lowborough likes his company."

"You have no love left for him, then?"

"Not the least."

"I knew that – I knew you were too high-minded and pure in your own nature to continue to regard one so utterly false and polluted with any feelings but those of indignation and scornful abhorrence!"

"Is he not your friend?" said I, turning my eyes from the fire to his face, with perhaps a slight touch of those feelings he assigned to another.

"He was," replied he, with the same calm gravity as before; "but do not wrong me by supposing that I could continue my friendship and esteem to a man who could so infamously, so impiously forsake and injure one so transcendently – well, I won't speak of it. But tell me, do you never think of revenge?"

"Revenge! No – what good would that do? – It would make him no better, and me no happier."

"I don't know how to talk to you, Mrs. Huntingdon," said he, smiling; "you are only half a woman – your nature must be half human, half angelic. Such goodness overawes me; I don't know what to make of it."

"Then, sir, I fear you must be very much worse than you should be, if I, a mere ordinary mortal, am, by your own confession, so vastly your superior; and since there exists so little sympathy between us, I think we had better each look out for some more congenial companion." And forthwith moving to the window, I began to look out for my little son and his gay young friend.

"No, I am the ordinary mortal, I maintain," replied Mr. Hargrave. "I will not allow myself to be worse than my fellows; but you, Madam – I equally maintain there is nobody like you. But are you happy?" he asked in a serious tone.

"As happy as some others, I suppose."

"Are you as happy as you desire to be?"

"No one is so blest as that comes to on this side eternity."

"One thing I know," returned he, with a deep sad sigh; "you are immeasurably happier than I am."

"I am very sorry for you, then," I could not help replying.

"Are you, indeed? No, for if you were you would be glad to relieve me."

"And so I should if I could do so without injuring myself or any other."

"And can you suppose that I should wish you to injure yourself? No: on the contrary, it is your own happiness I long for more than mine. You are miserable now, Mrs. Huntingdon," continued he, looking me boldly in the face. "You do not complain, but I see – and feel – and know that you are miserable – and must remain so as long as you keep those walls of impenetrable ice about your still warm and palpitating heart; and I am miserable, too. Deign to smile on me and I am happy: trust me, and you shall be happy also, for if you are a woman I can make you so – and I will do it in spite of yourself!" he muttered between his teeth; "and as for others, the question is between ourselves alone: you cannot injure your husband, you know, and no one else has any concern in the matter."

"I have a son, Mr. Hargrave, and you have a mother," said I, retiring from the window, whither he had followed me.

"They need not know," he began; but before anything more could be said on either side, Esther and Arthur re-entered the room. The former glanced at Walter's flushed, excited countenance, and then at mine – a little flushed and excited too, I daresay, though from far different causes. She must have thought we had been quarrelling desperately, and was evidently perplexed and disturbed at the circumstance; but she was too polite or too much afraid of her brother's anger to refer to it. She seated herself on the sofa, and putting back her bright, golden ringlets, that were scattered in wild profusion over her face, she immediately began to talk about the garden and her little playfellow, and continued to chatter away in her usual strain till her brother summoned her to depart.

"If I have spoken too warmly, forgive me," he murmured on taking his leave, "or I shall never forgive myself." Esther smiled and glanced at me: I merely bowed, and her countenance fell. She thought it a poor return for Walter's generous concession, and was disappointed in her friend. Poor child, she little knows the world she lives in!

Mr. Hargrave had not an opportunity of meeting me again in private for several weeks after this; but when he did meet me there was less of pride and more of touching melancholy in his manner than before. Oh, how he annoyed me! I was obliged at last almost entirely to remit my visits to the Grove, at the expense of deeply offending Mrs. Hargrave and seriously afflicting poor Esther, who really values my society for want of better, and who ought not to suffer for the fault of her brother. But that indefatigable foe was not yet vanquished: he seemed to be always on the watch. I frequently saw him riding lingeringly past the premises, looking searchingly round him as he went – or, if I did not, Rachel did. That sharp-sighted woman soon guessed how matters stood between us, and descrying the enemy's movements from her elevation at the nursery-window, she would give me a quiet intimation if she saw me preparing for a walk when she had reason to believe he was about, or to think it likely that he would meet or overtake me in the way I meant to traverse. I would then defer my ramble, or confine myself for that day to the park and gardens, or, if the proposed excursion was a matter of importance, such as a visit to the sick or afflicted, I would take Rachel with me, and then I was never molested.

But one mild, sunshiny day, early in November, I had ventured forth alone to visit the village school and a few of the poor tenants, and on my return I was alarmed at the clatter of a horse's feet behind me, approaching at a rapid, steady trot. There was no stile or gap at hand by which I could escape into the fields, so I walked quietly on, saying to myself, 'It may not be he after all; and if it is, and if he do annoy me, it shall be for the last time, I am determined, if there be power in words and looks against cool impudence and mawkish sentimentality so inexhaustible as his.'

The horse soon overtook me, and was reined up close beside me. It was Mr. Hargrave. He greeted me with a smile intended to be soft and melancholy, but his triumphant satisfaction at having caught me at last so shone through that it was quite a failure. After briefly answering his salutation and inquiring after the ladies at the Grove, I turned away and walked on; but he followed and kept his horse at my side: it was evident he intended to be my companion all the way.

"Well! I don't much care. If you want another rebuff, take it – and welcome," was my inward remark. "Now, sir, what next?"

This question, though unspoken, was not long unanswered; after a few passing observations upon indifferent subjects, he began in solemn tones the following appeal to my humanity:

"It will be four years next April since I first saw you, Mrs. Huntingdon – you may have forgotten the circumstance, but I never can. I admired you then most deeply, but I dared not love you. In the following autumn I saw so much of your perfections that I could not fail to love you, though I dared not show it. For upwards of three years I have endured a perfect martyrdom. From the anguish of suppressed emotions, intense and fruitless longings, silent sorrow, crushed hopes, and trampled affections, I have suffered more than I can tell, or you imagine – and you were the cause of it, and not altogether the innocent cause. My youth is wasting away; my prospects are darkened; my life is a desolate blank; I have no rest day or night: I am become a burden to myself and others, and you might save me by a word – a glance, and will not do it – is this right?"

"In the first place, I don't believe you," answered I; "in the second, if you will be such a fool, I can't hinder it."

"If you affect," replied he, earnestly, "to regard as folly the best, the strongest, the most godlike impulses of our nature, I don't believe you. I know you are not the heartless, icy being you pretend to be – you had a heart once, and gave it to your husband. When you found him utterly unworthy of the treasure, you reclaimed it; and you will not pretend that you loved that sensual, earthly-minded profligate so deeply, so devotedly, that you can never love another? I know that there are feelings in your nature that have never yet been called forth; I know, too, that in your present neglected lonely state you are and must be miserable. You have it in your power to raise two human beings from a state of actual suffering to such unspeakable beatitude as only generous, noble, self-forgetting love can give (for you can love me if you will); you may tell me that you scorn and detest me, but, since you have set me the example of plain speaking, I will answer that I do not believe you. But you will not do it! You choose rather to leave us miserable; and you coolly tell me it is the will of God that we should remain so. You may call this religion, but I call it wild fanaticism!"

"There is another life both for you and for me," said I. "If it be the will of God that we should sow in tears now, it is only that we may reap in joy hereafter. It is His will that we should not injure others by the gratification of our own earthly passions; and you have a mother, and sisters, and friends who would be seriously injured by your disgrace; and I, too, have friends, whose peace of mind shall never be sacrificed to my enjoyment, or yours either, with my consent; and if I were alone in the world, I have still my God and my religion, and I would sooner die than disgrace my calling and break my faith with heaven to obtain a few brief years of false and fleeting happiness – happiness sure to end in misery even here – for myself or any other!"

"There need be no disgrace, no misery or sacrifice in any quarter," persisted he. "I do not ask you to leave your home or defy the world's opinion." But I need not repeat all his arguments. I refuted them to the best of my power; but that power was provokingly small, at the moment, for I was too much flurried with indignation – and even shame – that he should thus dare to address me, to retain sufficient command of thought and language to enable me adequately to contend against his powerful sophistries. Finding, however, that he could not be silenced by reason, and even covertly exulted in his seeming advantage, and ventured to deride those assertions I had not the coolness to prove, I changed my course and tried another plan.

"Do you really love me?" said I, seriously, pausing and looking him calmly in the face.

"Do I love you!" cried he.

"Truly?" I demanded.

His countenance brightened; he thought his triumph was at hand. He commenced a passionate protestation of the truth and fervour of his attachment, which I cut short by another question:

"But is it not a selfish love? Have you enough disinterested affection to enable you to sacrifice your own pleasure to mine?"

"I would give my life to serve you."

"I don't want your life; but have you enough real sympathy for my afflictions to induce you to make an effort to relieve them, at the risk of a little discomfort to yourself?"

"Try me, and see."

"If you have, never mention this subject again. You cannot recur to it in any way without doubling the weight of those sufferings you so feelingly deplore. I have nothing left me but the solace of a good conscience and a hopeful trust in heaven, and you labour continually to rob me of these. If you persist, I must regard you as my deadliest foe."

"But hear me a moment –"

"No, sir! You said you would give your life to serve me; I only ask your silence on one particular point. I have spoken plainly; and what I say I mean. If you torment me in this way any more, I must conclude that your protestations are entirely false, and that you hate me in your heart as fervently as you profess to love me!"

He bit his lip, and bent his eyes upon the ground in silence for a while.

"Then I must leave you," said he at length, looking steadily upon me, as if with the last hope of detecting some token of irrepressible anguish or dismay awakened by those solemn words. "I must leave you. I cannot live here, and be for ever silent on the all-absorbing subject of my thoughts and wishes."

"Formerly, I believe, you spent but little of your time at home," I answered; "it will do you no harm to absent yourself again, for a while – if that be really necessary."

"If that be really possible," he muttered; "and can you bid me go so coolly? Do you really wish it?"

"Most certainly I do. If you cannot see me without tormenting me as you have lately done, I would gladly say farewell and never see you more."

He made no answer, but, bending from his horse, held out his hand towards me. I looked up at his face, and saw therein such a look of genuine agony of soul, that, whether bitter disappointment, or wounded pride, or lingering love, or burning wrath were uppermost, I could not hesitate to put my hand in his as frankly as if I bade a friend farewell. He grasped it very hard, and immediately put spurs to his horse and galloped away. Very soon after, I learned that he was gone to Paris, where he still is; and the longer he stays there the better for me.

I thank God for this deliverance!

Volume Three

Chapter Thirty-Eight

DECEMBER 20TH, 1826. – The fifth anniversary of my wedding-day, and, I trust, the last I shall spend under this roof. My resolution is formed, my plan concocted, and already partly put in execution. My conscience does not blame me, but while the purpose ripens let me beguile a few of these long winter evenings in stating the case for my own satisfaction: a dreary amusement enough, but having the air of a useful occupation, and being pursued as a task, it will suit me better than a lighter one.

In September, quiet Grassdale was again alive with a party of ladies and gentlemen (so called), consisting of the same individuals as those invited the year before last, with the addition of two or three others, among whom were Mrs. Hargrave and her younger daughter. The gentlemen and Lady Lowborough were invited for the pleasure and convenience of the host; the other ladies, I suppose, for the sake of appearances, and to keep me in check, and make me discreet and civil in my demeanour. But the ladies stayed only three weeks; the gentlemen, with two exceptions, above two months: for their hospitable entertainer was loth to part with them and be left alone with his bright intellect, his stainless conscience, and his loved and loving wife.

On the day of Lady Lowborough's arrival, I followed her into her chamber, and plainly told her that, if I found reason to believe that she still continued her criminal connection with Mr. Huntingdon, I should think it my absolute duty to inform her husband of the circumstance – or awaken his suspicions at least – however painful it might be, or however dreadful the consequences. She was startled at first by the declaration, so unexpected, and so determinately yet calmly delivered; but rallying in a moment, she coolly replied that, if I saw anything at all reprehensible or suspicious in her conduct, she would freely give me leave to tell his lordship all about it. Willing to be satisfied with this, I left her; and certainly I saw nothing thenceforth particularly reprehensible or suspicious in her demeanour towards her host; but then I had the other guests to attend to, and I did not watch them narrowly – for, to confess the truth, I feared to see anything between them. I no longer regarded it as any concern of mine, and if it was my duty to enlighten Lord Lowborough, it was a painful duty, and I dreaded to be called to perform it.

But my fears were brought to an end in a manner I had not anticipated. One evening, about a fortnight after the visitors' arrival, I had retired into the library to snatch a few minutes' respite from forced cheerfulness and wearisome discourse, for after so long a period of seclusion, dreary indeed as I had often found it, I could not always bear to be doing violence to my feelings, and goading my powers to talk, and smile and listen, and play the attentive hostess, or even the cheerful friend: I had just ensconced myself within the bow of the window, and was looking out upon the west, where the darkening hills rose sharply defined against the clear amber light of evening, that gradually blended and faded away into the pure, pale blue of the upper sky, where one bright star was shining through, as if to promise – 'When that dying light is gone, the world will not be left in darkness, and they who trust in God, whose minds are unbeclouded by the mists of unbelief and sin, are never wholly comfortless,' – when I heard a hurried step approaching, and Lord Lowborough entered. This room was still his favourite resort. He flung the door to with unusual violence, and cast his hat aside regardless where it fell. What could be the matter with him? His face was ghastly pale; his eyes were fixed upon the ground; his teeth clenched: his forehead glistened with the dews of agony. It was plain he knew his wrongs at last!

Unconscious of my presence, he began to pace the room in a state of fearful agitation, violently wringing his hands and uttering low groans or incoherent ejaculations. I made a movement to let him know that he was not alone; but he was too preoccupied to notice it. Perhaps, while his back was towards me, I might cross the room and slip away unobserved. I rose to make the attempt, but then he perceived me. He started and stood still a moment; then wiped his streaming forehead, and, advancing towards me, with a kind of unnatural composure, said in a deep, almost sepulchral tone, – "Mrs. Huntingdon, I must leave you tomorrow."

"Tomorrow!" I repeated. "I do not ask the cause."

"You know it then, and you can be so calm!" said he, surveying me with profound astonishment, not unmingled with a kind of resentful bitterness, as it appeared to me.

"I have so long been aware of –" I paused in time, and added, "of my husband's character, that nothing shocks me."

"But this – how long have you been aware of this?" demanded he, laying his clenched hand on the table beside him, and looking me keenly and fixedly in the face.

I felt like a criminal.

"Not long," I answered.

"You knew it!" cried he, with bitter vehemence – "and you did not tell me! You helped to deceive me!"

"My lord, I did not help to deceive you."

"Then why did you not tell me?"

"Because I knew it would be painful to you. I hoped she would return to her duty, and then there would be no need to harrow your feelings with such –"

"O God! How long has this been going on? How long has it been, Mrs. Huntingdon? – Tell me – I must know!" exclaimed, with intense and fearful eagerness.

"Two years, I believe."

"Great heaven! And she has duped me all this time!" He turned away with a suppressed groan of agony, and paced the room again in a paroxysm of renewed agitation. My heart smote me; but I would try to console him, though I knew not how to attempt it.

"She is a wicked woman," I said. "She has basely deceived and betrayed you. She is as little worthy of your regret as she was of your affection. Let her injure you no further; abstract yourself from her, and stand alone."

"And you, Madam," said he sternly, arresting himself, and turning round upon me, "you have injured me too by this ungenerous concealment!"

There was a sudden revulsion in my feelings. Something rose within me, and urged me to resent this harsh return for my heartfelt sympathy, and defend myself with answering severity. Happily, I did not yield to the impulse. I saw his anguish as, suddenly smiting his forehead, he turned abruptly to the window, and, looking upward at the placid sky, murmured passionately, "O God, that I might die!" – and felt that to add one drop of bitterness to that already overflowing cup would be ungenerous indeed. And yet I fear there was more coldness than gentleness in the quiet tone of my reply: – "I might offer many excuses that some would admit to be valid, but I will not attempt to enumerate them –"

"I know them," said he hastily: "you would say that it was no business of yours: that I ought to have taken care of myself; that if my own blindness has led me into this pit of hell, I have no right to blame another for giving me credit for a larger amount of sagacity than I possessed –"

"I confess I was wrong," continued I, without regarding this bitter interruption; "but whether want of courage or mistaken kindness was the cause of my error, I think you blame me too severely. I told Lady Lowborough two weeks ago, the very hour she came, that I should certainly think it my duty to inform you if she continued to deceive you: she gave me full liberty to do so if I should see anything reprehensible or suspicious in her conduct; I have seen nothing; and I trusted she had altered her course."

He continued gazing from the window while I spoke, and did not answer, but, stung by the recollections my words awakened, stamped his foot upon the floor, ground his teeth, and corrugated his brow, like one under the influence of acute physical pain.

"It was wrong, it was wrong!" he muttered at length. "Nothing can excuse it; nothing can atone for it, – for nothing can recall those years of cursed credulity; nothing obliterate them! – Nothing, nothing!" he repeated in a whisper, whose despairing bitterness precluded all resentment.

"When I put the case to myself, I own it was wrong," I answered; "but I can only now regret that I did not see it in this light before, and that, as you say, nothing can recall the past."

Something in my voice or in the spirit of this answer seemed to alter his mood. Turning towards me, and attentively surveying my face by the dim light, he said, in a milder tone than he had yet employed, – "You, too, have suffered, I suppose."

"I suffered much, at first."

"When was that?"

"Two years ago; and two years hence you will be as calm as I am now, and far, far happier, I trust, for you are a man, and free to act as you please."

Something like a smile, but a very bitter one, crossed his face for a moment.

"You have not been happy, lately?" he said, with a kind of effort to regain composure, and a determination to waive the further discussion of his own calamity.

"Happy?" I repeated, almost provoked at such a question. "Could I be so, with such a husband?"

"I have noticed a change in your appearance since the first years of your marriage," pursued he: "I observed it to – to that infernal demon," he muttered between his teeth; "and he said it was your own sour temper that was eating away your bloom: it was making you old and ugly before your time, and had already made his fireside as comfortless as a convent cell. You smile, Mrs. Huntingdon; nothing moves you. I wish my nature were as calm as yours."

"My nature was not originally calm," said I. "I have learned to appear so by dint of hard lessons and many repeated efforts."

At this juncture Mr. Hattersley burst into the room.

"Hallo, Lowborough!" he began – "Oh! I beg your pardon," he exclaimed on seeing me. "I didn't know it was a *tête-à-tête*. Cheer up, man," he continued, giving Lord Lowborough a thump on the back, which caused the latter to recoil from him with looks of ineffable disgust and irritation. "Come, I want to speak with you a bit."

"Speak, then."

"But I'm not sure it would be quite agreeable to the lady what I have to say."

"Then it would not be agreeable to me," said his lordship, turning to leave the room.

"Yes, it would," cried the other, following him into the hall. "If you've the heart of a man, it would be the very ticket for you. It's just this, my lad," he continued, rather lowering his voice, but not enough to prevent me from hearing every word he said, though the half-closed door stood between us. "I think you're an ill-used man – nay, now, don't flare up; I don't want to offend you: it's only my rough way of talking. I must speak right out, you know, or else not at all; and I'm come – stop now! Let me explain – I'm come to offer you my services, for though Huntingdon is my friend, he's a devilish scamp, as we all know, and I'll be your friend for the nonce. I know what it is you want, to make matters straight: it's just to exchange a shot with him, and then you'll feel yourself all right again; and if an accident happens – why, that'll be all right too, I daresay, to a desperate fellow like you. Come now, give me your hand, and don't look so black upon it. Name time and place, and I'll manage the rest."

"That," answered the more low, deliberate voice of Lord Lowborough, "is just the remedy my own heart, or the devil within it, suggested – to meet him, and not to part without blood. Whether I or he should fall, or both, it would be an inexpressible relief to me, if –"

"Just so! Well then, –"

"No!" exclaimed his lordship, with deep, determined emphasis. "Though I hate him from my heart, and should rejoice at any calamity that could befall him, I'll leave him to God; and though I abhor my own life, I'll leave that, too, to Him that gave it."

"But you see, in this case," pleaded Hattersley –

"I'll not hear you!" exclaimed his companion, hastily turning away. "Not another word! I've enough to do against the fiend within me."

"Then you're a white-livered fool, and I wash my hands of you," grumbled the tempter, as he swung himself round and departed.

"Right, right, Lord Lowborough," cried I, darting out and clasping his burning hand, as he was moving away to the stairs. "I begin to think the world is not worthy of you!" Not understanding this sudden ebullition, he turned upon me with a stare of gloomy, bewildered amazement, that made me ashamed of the impulse to which I had yielded; but soon a more humanised expression dawned upon his countenance, and before I could withdraw my hand, he pressed it kindly, while a gleam of genuine feeling flashed from his eyes as he murmured, "God help us both!"

"Amen!" responded I; and we parted.

I returned to the drawing room, where, doubtless, my presence would be expected by most, desired by one or two. In the ante-room was Mr. Hattersley, railing against Lord Lowborough's poltroonery before a select audience, viz. Mr. Huntingdon, who was lounging against the table, exulting in his own treacherous villainy, and laughing his victim to scorn, and Mr. Grimsby, standing by, quietly rubbing his hands and chuckling with fiendish satisfaction.

In the drawing room I found Lady Lowborough, evidently in no very enviable state of mind, and struggling hard to conceal her discomposure by an overstrained affectation of unusual cheerfulness and vivacity, very uncalled-for under the circumstances, for she had herself given the company to understand that her husband had received unpleasant intelligence from home, which necessitated his immediate departure, and that he had suffered it so to bother his mind that it had brought on a bilious headache, owing to which, and the preparations he judged necessary to hasten his departure, she believed they would not have the pleasure of seeing him tonight. However, she asserted, it was only a business concern, and so she did not intend it should trouble her. She was just saying this as I entered, and she darted upon me such a glance of hardihood and defiance as at once astonished and revolted me.

"But I am troubled," continued she, "and vexed too, for I think it my duty to accompany his lordship, and of course I am very sorry to part with all my kind friends so unexpectedly and so soon."

"And yet, Annabella," said Esther, who was sitting beside her, "I never saw you in better spirits in my life."

"Precisely so, my love: because I wish to make the best of your society, since it appears this is to be the last night I am to enjoy it till heaven knows when; and I wish to leave a good impression on you all," – she glanced round, and seeing her aunt's eye fixed upon her, rather too scrutinizingly, as she probably thought, she started up and continued: "To which end I'll give you a song – shall I, aunt? Shall I, Mrs. Huntingdon? Shall I ladies and gentlemen all? Very well. I'll do my best to amuse you."

She and Lord Lowborough occupied the apartments next to mine. I know not how she passed the night, but I lay awake the greater part of it listening to his heavy step pacing monotonously up and down his dressing room, which was nearest my chamber. Once I heard him pause and throw something out of the window with a passionate ejaculation; and in the morning, after they were gone, a keen-bladed clasp-knife was found on the grass-plot below; a razor, likewise, was snapped in two and thrust deep into the cinders of the grate, but partially corroded by the decaying embers. So strong had been the temptation to end his miserable life, so determined his resolution to resist it.

My heart bled for him as I lay listening to that ceaseless tread. Hitherto I had thought too much of myself, too little of him: now I forgot my own afflictions, and thought only of his; of the ardent affection so miserably wasted, the fond faith so cruelly betrayed, the – no, I will not attempt to enumerate his wrongs – but I hated his wife and my husband more intensely than ever, and not for my sake, but for his.

They departed early in the morning, before any one else was down, except myself, and just as I was leaving my room Lord Lowborough was descending to take his place in the carriage, where his lady was already ensconced; and Arthur (or Mr. Huntingdon, as I prefer calling him, for the other is my child's name) had the gratuitous insolence to come out in his dressing-gown to bid his 'friend' Goodbye.

"What, going already, Lowborough!" said he. "Well, good morning." He smilingly offered his hand.

I think the other would have knocked him down, had he not instinctively started back before that bony fist quivering with rage and clenched till the knuckles gleamed white and glistening through the skin. Looking upon him with a countenance livid with furious hate, Lord Lowborough muttered between his closed teeth a deadly execration he would not have uttered had he been calm enough to choose his words, and departed.

"I call that an unchristian spirit now," said the villain. "But I'd never give up an old friend for the sake of a wife. You may have mine if you like, and I call that handsome; I can do no more than offer restitution, can I?"

But Lowborough had gained the bottom of the stairs, and was now crossing the hall; and Mr. Huntingdon, leaning over the banisters, called out, "Give my love to Annabella! And I wish you both a happy journey," and withdrew, laughing, to his chamber.

He subsequently expressed himself rather glad she was gone. "She was so deuced imperious and exacting," said he. "Now I shall be my own man again, and feel rather more at my ease."

Chapter Thirty-Nine

MY GREATEST source of uneasiness, in this time of trial, was my son, whom his father and his father's friends delighted to encourage in all the embryo vices a little child can show, and to instruct in all the evil habits he could acquire – in a word, to 'make a man of him' was one of their staple amusements; and I need say no more to justify my alarm on his account, and my determination to deliver him at any hazard from the hands of such instructors. I first attempted to keep him always with me, or in the nursery, and gave Rachel particular injunctions never to let him come down to dessert as long as these 'gentlemen' stayed; but it was no use: these orders were immediately countermanded and overruled by his father; he was not going to have the little fellow moped to death between an old nurse and a cursed fool of a mother. So the little fellow came down every evening in spite of his cross mamma, and learned to tipple wine like papa, to swear like Mr. Hattersley, and to have his own way like a man, and sent mamma to the devil when she tried to prevent him. To see such things done with the roguish naïveté of that pretty little child, and hear such things spoken by that small infantile voice, was as peculiarly piquant and irresistibly droll to them as it was inexpressibly distressing and painful to me; and when he had set the table in a roar he would look round delightedly upon them all, and add his shrill laugh to theirs. But if that beaming blue eye rested on me, its light would vanish for a moment, and he would say, in some concern, "Mamma, why don't you laugh? Make her laugh, papa – she never will."

Hence was I obliged to stay among these human brutes, watching an opportunity to get my child away from them instead of leaving them immediately after the removal of the cloth, as I should always otherwise have done. He was never willing to go, and I frequently had to carry him away by force, for which he thought me very cruel and unjust; and sometimes his father would insist upon my letting him remain; and then I would leave him to his kind friends, and retire to indulge my bitterness and despair alone, or to rack my brains for a remedy to this great evil.

But here again I must do Mr. Hargrave the justice to acknowledge that I never saw him laugh at the child's misdemeanours, nor heard him utter a word of encouragement to his aspirations after manly accomplishments. But when anything very extraordinary was said or done by the infant profligate, I noticed, at times, a peculiar expression in his face that I could neither interpret nor define: a slight twitching about the muscles of the mouth; a sudden flash in the eye, as he darted a sudden glance at the child and then at me: and then I could fancy there arose a gleam of hard, keen, sombre satisfaction in his countenance at the look of impotent wrath and anguish he was too certain to behold in mine. But on one occasion, when Arthur had been behaving particularly ill, and Mr. Huntingdon and his guests had been particularly provoking and insulting to me in their encouragement of him, and I particularly anxious to get him out of the room, and on the very point of demeaning myself by a burst of uncontrollable passion – Mr. Hargrave suddenly rose from his seat with an aspect of stern determination, lifted the child from his father's knee, where he was sitting half-tipsy, cocking his head and laughing at me, and execrating me with words he little knew the meaning of, handed him out of the room, and, setting him down in the hall, held the door open for me, gravely bowed as I withdrew, and closed it after me. I heard high words exchanged between him and his already half-inebriated host as I departed, leading away my bewildered and disconcerted boy.

But this should not continue: my child must not be abandoned to this corruption: better far that he should live in poverty and obscurity, with a fugitive mother, than in luxury and affluence with such a father. These guests might not be with us long, but they would return again: and he, the most injurious of the whole, his child's worst enemy, would still remain. I could endure it for myself, but for my son it must be borne no longer: the world's opinion and the feelings of my friends must be alike unheeded here, at least – alike unable to deter me from my duty. But where should I find an asylum, and how obtain subsistence for us both? Oh, I would take my precious charge at early dawn, take the coach to M—, flee to the port of —, cross the Atlantic, and seek a quiet, humble home in New England, where I would support myself and him by the labour of my hands. The palette and the easel, my darling playmates once, must be my sober toil-fellows now. But was I sufficiently skilful as an artist to obtain my livelihood in a strange land, without friends and without recommendation? No; I must wait a little; I must labour hard to improve my talent, and to produce something worth while as a specimen of my powers, something to speak favourably for me, whether as an actual painter or a teacher. Brilliant success, of course, I did not look for, but some degree of security from positive failure was indispensable: I must not take my son to starve. And then I must have money for the journey, the passage, and some little to support us in our retreat in case I should be unsuccessful at first: and not too little either: for who could tell how long I might have to struggle with the indifference or neglect of others, or my own inexperience or inability to suit their tastes?

What should I do then? Apply to my brother and explain my circumstances and my resolves to him? No, no: even if I told him all my grievances, which I should be very reluctant to do, he would be certain to disapprove of the step: it would seem like madness to him, as it would to my uncle and aunt, or to Milicent. No; I must have patience and gather a hoard of my own. Rachel should be my only confidante – I thought I could persuade her into the scheme; and she should help me, first, to find out a picture-dealer in some distant town; then, through her means, I would privately sell what pictures I had on hand that would do for such a purpose, and some of those I should thereafter paint. Besides this, I would contrive to dispose of my jewels, not the family jewels, but the few I brought with me from home, and those my uncle gave me on my marriage. A few months' arduous toil might well be borne by me with such an end in view; and in the interim my son could not be much more injured than he was already.

Having formed this resolution, I immediately set to work to accomplish it, I might possibly have been induced to wax cool upon it afterwards, or perhaps to keep weighing the pros and cons in my mind till the latter overbalanced the former, and I was driven to relinquish the project altogether, or delay the execution of it to an indefinite period, had not something occurred to confirm me in that determination, to which I still adhere, which I still think I did well to form, and shall do better to execute.

Since Lord Lowborough's departure I had regarded the library as entirely my own, a secure retreat at all hours of the day. None of our gentlemen had the smallest pretensions to a literary taste, except Mr. Hargrave; and he, at present, was quite contented with the newspapers and periodicals of the day. And if, by any chance, he should look in here, I felt assured he would soon depart on seeing me, for, instead of becoming less cool and distant towards me, he had become decidedly more so since the departure of his mother and sisters, which was just what I wished. Here, then, I set up my easel, and here I worked at my canvas from daylight till dusk, with very little intermission, saving when pure necessity, or my duties to little Arthur, called me away: for I still thought proper to devote some portion of every day exclusively to his instruction and amusement. But, contrary to my expectation, on the third morning, while I was thus employed, Mr. Hargrave did look in, and did not immediately withdraw on seeing me. He apologized for his intrusion, and said he was only come for a book; but when he had got it, he condescended to cast a glance over my picture. Being a man of taste, he had something to say on this subject as well as another, and having modestly commented on it, without much encouragement from me, he proceeded to expatiate on the art in general. Receiving no encouragement in that either, he dropped it, but did not depart.

"You don't give us much of your company, Mrs. Huntingdon," observed he, after a brief pause, during which I went on coolly mixing and tempering my colours; "and I cannot wonder at it, for you must be heartily sick of us all. I myself am so thoroughly ashamed of my companions, and so weary of their irrational conversation and pursuits – now that there is no one to humanize them and keep them in check, since you have justly abandoned us to our own devices – that I think I shall presently withdraw from amongst them, probably within this week; and I cannot suppose you will regret my departure."

He paused. I did not answer.

"Probably," he added, with a smile, "your only regret on the subject will be that I do not take all my companions along with me. I flatter myself, at times, that though among them I am not of them; but it is natural that you should be glad to get rid of me. I may regret this, but I cannot blame you for it."

"I shall not rejoice at your departure, for you can conduct yourself like a gentleman," said I, thinking it but right to make some acknowledgment for his good behaviour; "but I must confess I shall rejoice to bid adieu to the rest, inhospitable as it may appear."

"No one can blame you for such an avowal," replied he gravely: "not even the gentlemen themselves, I imagine. I'll just tell you," he continued, as if actuated by a sudden resolution, "what was said last night in the dining room, after you left us: perhaps you will not mind it, as you're so very philosophical on certain points," he added with a slight sneer. "They were talking about Lord Lowborough and his delectable lady, the cause of whose sudden departure is no secret amongst them; and her character is so well known to them all, that, nearly related to me as she is, I could not attempt to defend it. Curse me!" he muttered, par parenthese, "if I don't have vengeance for this! If the villain must disgrace the family, must he blazon it abroad to every low-bred knave of his acquaintance? I beg your pardon, Mrs. Huntingdon. Well, they were talking of these things, and some of them remarked that, as she was separated from her husband, he might see her again when he pleased."

"'Thank you,' said he; 'I've had enough of her for the present: I'll not trouble to see her, unless she comes to me.'

"'Then what do you mean to do, Huntingdon, when we're gone?' said Ralph Hattersley. 'Do you mean to turn from the error of your ways, and be a good husband, a good father, and so forth; as I do, when I get shut of you and all these rollicking devils you call your friends? I think it's time; and your wife is fifty times too good for you, you know –'

"And he added some praise of you, which you would not thank me for repeating, nor him for uttering; proclaiming it aloud, as he did, without delicacy or discrimination, in an audience where it seemed profanation to utter your name: himself utterly incapable of understanding or appreciating your real excellences. Huntingdon, meanwhile, sat quietly drinking his wine, – or looking smilingly into his glass and offering no interruption or reply, till Hattersley shouted out, – 'Do you hear me, man?'

"'Yes, go on,' said he.

"'Nay, I've done,' replied the other: 'I only want to know if you intend to take my advice.'

"'What advice?'

"'To turn over a new leaf, you double-dyed scoundrel,' shouted Ralph, 'and beg your wife's pardon, and be a good boy for the future.'

"'My wife! What wife? I have no wife,' replied Huntingdon, looking innocently up from his glass, 'or if I have, look you, gentlemen: I value her so highly that any one among you, that can fancy her, may have her and welcome: you may, by Jove, and my blessing into the bargain!'

"I – hem – someone asked if he really meant what he said; upon which he solemnly swore he did, and no mistake. What do you think of that, Mrs. Huntingdon?" asked Mr. Hargrave, after a short pause, during which I had felt he was keenly examining my half-averted face.

"I say," replied I, calmly, "that what he prizes so lightly will not be long in his possession."

"You cannot mean that you will break your heart and die for the detestable conduct of an infamous villain like that!"

"By no means: my heart is too thoroughly dried to be broken in a hurry, and I mean to live as long as I can."

"Will you leave him then?"

"Yes."

"When: and how?" asked he, eagerly.

"When I am ready, and how I can manage it most effectually."

"But your child?"

"My child goes with me."

"He will not allow it."

"I shall not ask him."

"Ah, then, it is a secret flight you meditate! But with whom, Mrs. Huntingdon?"

"With my son: and possibly, his nurse."

"Alone – and unprotected! But where can you go? What can you do? He will follow you and bring you back."

"I have laid my plans too well for that. Let me once get clear of Grassdale, and I shall consider myself safe."

Mr. Hargrave advanced one step towards me, looked me in the face, and drew in his breath to speak; but that look, that heightened colour, that sudden sparkle of the eye, made my blood rise in wrath: I abruptly turned away, and, snatching up my brush, began to dash away at my canvas with rather too much energy for the good of the picture.

"Mrs. Huntingdon," said he with bitter solemnity, "you are cruel – cruel to me – cruel to yourself."

"Mr. Hargrave, remember your promise."

"I must speak: my heart will burst if I don't! I have been silent long enough, and you must hear me!" cried he, boldly intercepting my retreat to the door. "You tell me you owe no allegiance to your husband; he openly declares himself weary of you, and calmly gives you up to anybody that will take you; you are about to leave him; no one will believe that you go alone; all the world will say, 'She has left him at last, and who can wonder at it? Few can blame her, fewer still can pity him; but who is the companion of her flight?' Thus you will have no credit for your virtue (if you call it such): even your best friends will not believe in it; because it is monstrous, and not to be credited but by those who suffer, from the effects of it, such cruel torments that they know it to be indeed reality. But what can you do in the cold, rough world alone? you, a young and inexperienced woman, delicately nurtured, and utterly –"

"In a word, you would advise me to stay where I am," interrupted I. "Well, I'll see about it."

"By all means, leave him!" cried he earnestly; "but *not* alone! Helen! Let me protect you!"

"Never! While heaven spares my reason," replied I, snatching away the hand he had presumed to seize and press between his own. But he was in for it now; he had fairly broken the barrier: he was completely roused, and determined to hazard all for victory.

"I must not be denied!" exclaimed he, vehemently; and seizing both my hands, he held them very tight, but dropped upon his knee, and looked up in my face with a half-imploring, half-imperious gaze. "You have no reason now: you are flying in the face of heaven's decrees. God has designed me to be your comfort and protector – I feel it, I know it as certainly as if a voice from heaven declared, 'Ye twain shall be one flesh' – and you spurn me from you –"

"Let me go, Mr. Hargrave!" said I, sternly. But he only tightened his grasp.

"Let me go!" I repeated, quivering with indignation.

His face was almost opposite the window as he knelt. With a slight start, I saw him glance towards it; and then a gleam of malicious triumph lit up his countenance. Looking over my shoulder, I beheld a shadow just retiring round the corner.

"That is Grimsby," said he deliberately. "He will report what he has seen to Huntingdon and all the rest, with such embellishments as he thinks proper. He has no love for you, Mrs. Huntingdon – no reverence for your sex, no belief in virtue, no admiration for its image. He will give such a version of this story as will leave no doubt at all about your character, in the minds of those who hear it. Your fair fame is gone; and nothing that I or you can say can ever retrieve it. But give me the power to protect you, and show me the villain that dares to insult!"

"No one has ever dared to insult me as you are doing now!" said I, at length releasing my hands, and recoiling from him.

"I do not insult you," cried he: "I worship you. You are my angel, my divinity! I lay my powers at your feet, and you must and shall accept them!" he exclaimed, impetuously starting to his feet. "I will be your consoler and defender! And if your conscience upbraid you for it, say I overcame you, and you could not choose but yield!"

I never saw a man go terribly excited. He precipitated himself towards me. I snatched up my palette-knife and held it against him. This startled him: he stood and gazed at me in astonishment; I daresay I looked as fierce and resolute as he. I moved to the bell, and put my hand upon the cord. This tamed him still more. With a half-authoritative, half-deprecating wave of the hand, he sought to deter me from ringing.

"Stand off, then!" said I; he stepped back. "And listen to me. I don't like you," I continued, as deliberately and emphatically as I could, to give the greater efficacy to my words; "and if I were divorced from my husband, or if he were dead, I would not marry you. There now! I hope you're satisfied."

His face grew blanched with anger.

"I am satisfied," he replied, with bitter emphasis, "that you are the most cold-hearted, unnatural, ungrateful woman I ever yet beheld!"

"Ungrateful, sir?"

"Ungrateful."

"No, Mr. Hargrave, I am not. For all the good you ever did me, or ever wished to do, I most sincerely thank you: for all the evil you have done me, and all you would have done, I pray God to pardon you, and make you of a better mind." Here the door was thrown open, and Messrs. Huntingdon and Hattersley appeared without. The latter remained in the hall, busy with his ramrod and his gun; the former walked in, and stood with his back to the fire, surveying Mr. Hargrave and me, particularly the former, with a smile of insupportable meaning, accompanied as it was by the impudence of his brazen brow, and the sly, malicious, twinkle of his eye.

"Well, sir?" said Hargrave, interrogatively, and with the air of one prepared to stand on the defensive.

"Well, sir," returned his host.

"We want to know if you are at liberty to join us in a go at the pheasants, Walter," interposed Hattersley from without. "Come! There shall be nothing shot besides, except a puss or two; I'll vouch for that."

Walter did not answer, but walked to the window to collect his faculties. Arthur uttered a low whistle, and followed him with his eyes. A slight flush of anger rose to Hargrave's cheek; but in a moment he turned calmly round, and said carelessly:

"I came here to bid farewell to Mrs. Huntingdon, and tell her I must go tomorrow."

"Humph! You're mighty sudden in your resolution. What takes you off so soon, may I ask?"

"Business," returned he, repelling the other's incredulous sneer with a glance of scornful defiance.

"Very good," was the reply; and Hargrave walked away. Thereupon Mr. Huntingdon, gathering his coat-laps under his arms, and setting his shoulder against the mantel-piece, turned to me, and, addressing me in a low voice, scarcely above his breath, poured forth a volley of the vilest and grossest abuse it was possible for the imagination to conceive or the tongue to utter. I did not attempt to interrupt him; but my spirit kindled within me, and when he had done, I replied, "If your accusation were true, Mr. Huntingdon, how dare you blame me?"

"She's hit it, by Jove!" cried Hattersley, rearing his gun against the wall; and, stepping into the room, he took his precious friend by the arm, and attempted to drag him away. "Come, my lad," he muttered; "true or false, you've no right to blame her, you know, nor him either; after what you said last night. So come along."

There was something implied here that I could not endure.

"Dare you suspect me, Mr. Hattersley?" said I, almost beside myself with fury.

"Nay, nay, I suspect nobody. It's all right, it's all right. So come along, Huntingdon, you blackguard."

"She can't deny it!" cried the gentleman thus addressed, grinning in mingled rage and triumph. "She can't deny it if her life depended on it!" and muttering some more abusive language, he walked into the hall, and took up his hat and gun from the table.

"I scorn to justify myself to you!" said I. "But you," turning to Hattersley, "if you presume to have any doubts on the subject, ask Mr. Hargrave."

At this they simultaneously burst into a rude laugh that made my whole frame tingle to the fingers' ends.

"Where is he? I'll ask him myself!" said I, advancing towards them.

Suppressing a new burst of merriment, Hattersley pointed to the outer door. It was half open. His brother-in-law was standing on the front without.

"Mr. Hargrave, will you please to step this way?" said I.

He turned and looked at me in grave surprise.

"Step this way, if you please!" I repeated, in so determined a manner that he could not, or did not choose to resist its authority. Somewhat reluctantly he ascended the steps and advanced a pace or two into the hall.

"And tell those gentlemen," I continued – "these men, whether or not I yielded to your solicitations."

"I don't understand you, Mrs. Huntingdon."

"You do understand me, sir; and I charge you, upon your honour as a gentleman (if you have any), to answer truly. Did I, or did I not?"

"No," muttered he, turning away.

"Speak up, sir; they can't hear you. Did I grant your request?"

"You did not."

"No, I'll be sworn she didn't," said Hattersley, "or he'd never look so black."

"I'm willing to grant you the satisfaction of a gentleman, Huntingdon," said Mr. Hargrave, calmly addressing his host, but with a bitter sneer upon his countenance.

"Go to the deuce!" replied the latter, with an impatient jerk of the head. Hargrave withdrew with a look of cold disdain, saying, – "You know where to find me, should you feel disposed to send a friend."

Muttered oaths and curses were all the answer this intimation obtained.

"Now, Huntingdon, you see!" said Hattersley. "Clear as the day."

"I don't care what he sees," said I, "or what he imagines; but you, Mr. Hattersley, when you hear my name belied and slandered, will you defend it?"

"I will."

I instantly departed and shut myself into the library. What could possess me to make such a request of such a man I cannot tell; but drowning men catch at straws: they had driven me desperate between them; I hardly knew what I said.

There was no other to preserve my name from being blackened and aspersed among this nest of boon companions, and through them, perhaps, into the world; and beside my abandoned wretch of a husband, the base, malignant Grimsby, and the false villain Hargrave, this boorish ruffian, coarse and brutal as he was, shone like a glow-worm in the dark, among its fellow worms.

What a scene was this! Could I ever have imagined that I should be doomed to bear such insults under my own roof – to hear such things spoken in my presence; nay, spoken to me and of me; and by those who arrogated to themselves the name of gentlemen? And could I have imagined that I should have been able to endure it as calmly, and to repel their insults as firmly and as boldly as I had done? A hardness such as this is taught by rough experience and despair alone.

Such thoughts as these chased one another through my mind, as I paced to and fro the room, and longed – oh, how I longed – to take my child and leave them now, without an hour's delay! But it could not be; there was work before me: hard work, that must be done.

"Then let me do it," said I, "and lose not a moment in vain repinings and idle chafings against my fate, and those who influence it."

And conquering my agitation with a powerful effort, I immediately resumed my task, and laboured hard all day.

Mr. Hargrave did depart on the morrow; and I have never seen him since. The others stayed on for two or three weeks longer; but I kept aloof from them as much as possible, and still continued my labour, and have continued it, with almost unabated ardour, to the present day. I soon acquainted Rachel with my design, confiding all my motives and intentions to her ear, and, much to my agreeable surprise, found little difficulty in persuading her to enter into my views. She is a sober, cautious woman, but she so hates her master, and so loves her mistress and her nursling, that after several ejaculations, a few faint objections, and many tears and lamentations that I should be brought to such a pass, she applauded my resolution and consented to aid me with all her might: on one condition only: that she might share my exile: otherwise, she was utterly inexorable, regarding it as perfect madness for me and Arthur to go alone. With touching generosity, she modestly offered to aid me with her little hoard of savings, hoping I would 'excuse her for the liberty, but really, if I would do her the favour to accept it as a loan, she would be very happy.' Of course I could not think of such a thing; but now, thank heaven, I have gathered a little hoard of my own, and my preparations are so far advanced that I am looking forward to a speedy emancipation. Only let the stormy severity of this winter weather be somewhat abated, and then, some morning, Mr. Huntingdon will come down to a solitary breakfast-table, and perhaps be clamouring through the house for his invisible wife and child, when they are some fifty miles on their way to the Western world, or it may be more: for we shall leave him hours before the dawn, and it is not probable he will discover the loss of both until the day is far advanced.

I am fully alive to the evils that may and must result upon the step I am about to take; but I never waver in my resolution, because I never forget my son. It was only this morning, while I pursued my usual employment, he was sitting at my feet, quietly playing with the shreds of canvas I had thrown upon the carpet; but his mind was otherwise occupied, for, in a while, he looked up wistfully in my face, and gravely asked, – "Mamma, why are you wicked?"

"Who told you I was wicked, love?"

"Rachel."

"No, Arthur, Rachel never said so, I am certain."

"Well, then, it was papa," replied he, thoughtfully. Then, after a reflective pause, he added, "At least, I'll tell you how it was I got to know: when I'm with papa, if I say mamma wants me, or mamma says I'm not to do something that he tells me to do, he always says, 'Mamma be damned,' and Rachel says it's only wicked people that are damned. So, mamma, that's why I think you must be wicked: and I wish you wouldn't."

"My dear child, I am not. Those are bad words, and wicked people often say them of others better than themselves. Those words cannot make people be damned, nor show that they deserve it. God will judge us by our own thoughts and deeds, not by what others say about us. And when you hear such words spoken, Arthur, remember never to repeat them: it is wicked to say such things of others, not to have them said against you."

"Then it's papa that's wicked," said he, ruefully.

"Papa is wrong to say such things, and you will be very wrong to imitate him now that you know better."

"What is imitate?"

"To do as he does."

"Does he know better?"

"Perhaps he does; but that is nothing to you."

"If he doesn't, you ought to tell him, mamma."

"I have told him."

The little moralist paused and pondered. I tried in vain to divert his mind from the subject.

"I'm sorry papa's wicked," said he mournfully, at length, "for I don't want him to go to hell." And so saying he burst into tears.

I consoled him with the hope that perhaps his papa would alter and become good before he died – ; but is it not time to deliver him from such a parent?

Chapter Forty

JANUARY 10TH, 1827. – While writing the above, yesterday evening, I sat in the drawing room. Mr. Huntingdon was present, but, as I thought, asleep on the sofa behind me. He had risen, however, unknown to me, and, actuated by some base spirit of curiosity, been looking over my shoulder for I know not how long; for when I had laid aside my pen, and was about to close the book, he suddenly placed his hand upon it, and saying, – "With your leave, my dear, I'll have a look at this," forcibly wrested it from me, and, drawing a chair to the table, composedly sat down to examine it: turning back leaf after leaf to find an explanation of what he had read. Unluckily for me, he was more sober that night than he usually is at such an hour.

Of course I did not leave him to pursue this occupation in quiet: I made several attempts to snatch the book from his hands, but he held it too firmly for that; I upbraided him in bitterness and scorn for his mean and dishonourable conduct, but that had no effect upon him; and, finally, I extinguished both the candles, but he only wheeled round to the fire, and raising a blaze sufficient for his purposes, calmly continued the investigation. I had serious thoughts of getting a pitcher of water and extinguishing that light too; but it was evident his curiosity was too keenly excited to be quenched by that, and the more I manifested my anxiety to baffle his scrutiny, the greater would be his determination to persist in it besides it was too late.

"It seems very interesting, love," said he, lifting his head and turning to where I stood, wringing my hands in silent rage and anguish; "but it's rather long; I'll look at it some other time; and meanwhile I'll trouble you for your keys, my dear."

"What keys?"

"The keys of your cabinet, desk, drawers, and whatever else you possess," said he, rising and holding out his hand.

"I've not got them," I replied. The key of my desk, in fact, was at that moment in the lock, and the others were attached to it.

"Then you must send for them," said he; "and if that old devil, Rachel, doesn't immediately deliver them up, she tramps bag and baggage tomorrow."

"She doesn't know where they are," I answered, quietly placing my hand upon them, and taking them from the desk, as I thought, unobserved. "I know, but I shall not give them up without a reason."

"And I know, too," said he, suddenly seizing my closed hand and rudely abstracting them from it. He then took up one of the candles and relighted it by thrusting it into the fire.

"Now, then," sneered he, "we must have a confiscation of property. But, first, let us take a peep into the studio."

And putting the keys into his pocket, he walked into the library. I followed, whether with the dim idea of preventing mischief, or only to know the worst, I can hardly tell. My painting materials were laid together on the corner table, ready for tomorrow's use, and only covered with a cloth. He soon spied them out, and putting down the candle, deliberately proceeded to cast them into the fire: palette, paints, bladders, pencils, brushes, varnish: I saw them all consumed: the palette-knives snapped in two, the oil and turpentine sent hissing and roaring up the chimney. He then rang the bell.

"Benson, take those things away," said he, pointing to the easel, canvas, and stretcher; "and tell the housemaid she may kindle the fire with them: your mistress won't want them any more."

Benson paused aghast and looked at me.

"Take them away, Benson," said I; and his master muttered an oath.

"And this and all, sir?" said the astonished servant, referring to the half-finished picture.

"That and all," replied the master; and the things were cleared away.

Mr. Huntingdon then went up-stairs. I did not attempt to follow him, but remained seated in the arm-chair, speechless, tearless, and almost motionless, till he returned about half-an-hour after, and walking up to me, held the candle in my face and peered into my eyes with looks and laughter too insulting to be borne. With a sudden stroke of my hand I dashed the candle to the floor.

"Hal-lo!" muttered he, starting back; "she's the very devil for spite. Did ever any mortal see such eyes? – They shine in the dark like a cat's. Oh, you're a sweet one!" So saying, he gathered up the candle and the candlestick. The former being broken as well as extinguished, he rang for another.

"Benson, your mistress has broken the candle; bring another."

"You expose yourself finely," observed I, as the man departed.

"I didn't say I'd broken it, did I?" returned he. He then threw my keys into my lap, saying, – "There! You'll find nothing gone but your money, and the jewels, and a few little trifles I thought it advisable to take into my own possession, lest your mercantile spirit should be tempted to turn them into gold. I've left you a few sovereigns in your purse, which I expect to last you through the month; at all events, when you want more you will be so good as to give me an account of how that's spent. I shall put you upon a small monthly allowance, in future, for your own private expenses; and you needn't trouble yourself any more about my concerns; I shall look out for a steward, my dear – I won't expose you to the temptation. And as for the household matters, Mrs. Greaves must be very particular in keeping her accounts; we must go upon an entirely new plan –"

"What great discovery have you made now, Mr. Huntingdon? Have I attempted to defraud you?"

"Not in money matters, exactly, it seems; but it's best to keep out of the way of temptation."

Here Benson entered with the candles, and there followed a brief interval of silence; I sitting still in my chair, and he standing with his back to the fire, silently triumphing in my despair.

"And so," said he at length, "you thought to disgrace me, did you, by running away and turning artist, and supporting yourself by the labour of your hands, forsooth? And you thought to rob me of my son, too, and bring him up to be a dirty Yankee tradesman, or a low, beggarly painter?"

"Yes, to obviate his becoming such a gentleman as his father."

"It's well you couldn't keep your own secret – ha, ha! It's well these women must be blabbing. If they haven't a friend to talk to, they must whisper their secrets to the fishes, or write them on the sand, or something; and it's well, too, I wasn't over full tonight, now I think of it, or I might have snoozed away and never dreamt of looking what my sweet lady was about; or I might have lacked the sense or the power to carry my point like a man, as I have done."

Leaving him to his self-congratulations, I rose to secure my manuscript, for I now remembered it had been left upon the drawing room table, and I determined, if possible, to save myself the humiliation of seeing it in his hands again. I could not bear the idea of his amusing himself over my secret thoughts and recollections; though, to be sure, he would find little good of himself therein indited, except in the former part; and oh, I would sooner burn it all than he should read what I had written when I was such a fool as to love him!

"And by-the-by," cried he, as I was leaving the room, "you'd better tell that d—d old sneak of a nurse to keep out of my way for a day or two; I'd pay her her wages and send her packing tomorrow, but I know she'd do more mischief out of the house than in it."

And as I departed, he went on cursing and abusing my faithful friend and servant with epithets I will not defile this paper with repeating. I went to her as soon as I had put away my book, and told her how our project was defeated. She was as much distressed and horrified as I was – and more so than I was that night, for I was partly stunned by the blow, and partly excited and supported against it by the bitterness of my wrath. But in the morning, when I woke without that cheering hope that had been my secret comfort and support so long, and all this day, when I have wandered about restless and objectless, shunning my husband, shrinking even from my child, knowing that I am unfit to be his teacher or companion, hoping nothing for his future life, and fervently wishing he had never been born, – I felt the full extent of my calamity, and I feel it now. I know that day after day such feelings will return upon me. I am a slave – a prisoner – but that is nothing; if it were myself alone I would not complain, but I am forbidden to rescue my son from ruin, and what was once my only consolation is become the crowning source of my despair.

Have I no faith in God? I try to look to Him and raise my heart to heaven, but it will cleave to the dust. I can only say, "He hath hedged me about, that I cannot get out: He hath made my chain heavy. He hath filled me with bitterness – He hath made me drunken with wormwood." I forget to add, "But though He cause grief, yet will He have compassion according to the multitude of His mercies. For He doth not afflict willingly nor grieve the children of men." I ought to think of this; and if there be nothing but sorrow for me in this world, what is the longest life of misery to a whole eternity of peace? And for my little Arthur – has he no friend but me? Who was it said, "It is not the will of your Father which is in heaven that one of these little ones should perish?"

Chapter Forty-One

MARCH 20TH. – Having now got rid of Mr. Huntingdon for a season, my spirits begin to revive. He left me early in February; and the moment he was gone, I breathed again, and felt my vital energy return; not with the hope of escape – he has taken care to leave me no visible chance of that – but with a determination to make the best of existing circumstances. Here was Arthur left to me at last; and rousing from my despondent apathy, I exerted all my powers to eradicate the weeds that had been fostered in his infant mind, and sow again the good seed they had rendered unproductive. Thank heaven, it is not a barren or a stony soil; if weeds spring fast there, so do better plants. His apprehensions are more quick, his heart more overflowing with affection than ever his father's could have been, and it is no hopeless task to bend him to obedience and win him to love and know his own true friend, as long as there is no one to counteract my efforts.

I had much trouble at first in breaking him of those evil habits his father had taught him to acquire, but already that difficulty is nearly vanquished now: bad language seldom defiles his mouth, and I have succeeded in giving him an absolute disgust for all intoxicating liquors, which I hope not even his father or his father's friends will be able to overcome. He was inordinately fond of them for so young a creature, and, remembering my unfortunate father as well as his, I dreaded the consequences of such a taste. But if I had stinted him, in his usual quantity of wine, or forbidden him to taste it altogether, that would only have increased his partiality for it, and made him regard it as a greater treat than ever. I therefore gave him quite as much as his father was accustomed to allow him; as much, indeed, as he desired to have – but into every glass I surreptitiously introduced a small quantity of tartar-emetic, just enough to produce inevitable nausea and depression without positive sickness. Finding such disagreeable consequences invariably to result from this indulgence, he soon grew weary of it, but the more he shrank from the daily treat the more I pressed it upon him, till his reluctance was strengthened to perfect abhorrence. When he was thoroughly disgusted with every kind of wine, I allowed him, at his own request, to try brandy-and-water, and then gin-and-water, for the little toper was familiar with them all, and I was determined that all should be equally hateful to him. This I have now effected; and since he declares that the taste, the smell, the sight of any one of them is sufficient to make him sick, I have given up teasing him about them, except now and then as objects of terror in cases of misbehaviour. "Arthur, if you're not a good boy I shall give you a glass of wine," or "Now, Arthur, if you say that again you shall have some brandy-and-water," is as good as any other threat; and once or twice, when he was sick, I have obliged the poor child to swallow a little wine-and-water without the tartar-emetic, by way of medicine; and this practice I intend to continue for some time to come; not that I think it of any real service in a physical sense, but because I am determined to enlist all the powers of association in my service; I wish this aversion to be so deeply grounded in his nature that nothing in after-life may be able to overcome it.

Thus, I flatter myself, I shall secure him from this one vice; and for the rest, if on his father's return I find reason to apprehend that my good lessons will be all destroyed – if Mr. Huntingdon commence again the game of teaching the child to hate and despise his mother, and emulate his father's wickedness – I will yet deliver my son from his hands. I have devised another scheme that might be resorted to in such a case; and if I could but obtain my brother's consent and assistance, I should not doubt of its success. The old hall where he and I were born, and where our mother died, is not now inhabited, nor yet quite sunk into decay, as I believe. Now, if I could persuade him to have one or two rooms made habitable, and to let them to me as a stranger, I might live there, with my child, under an assumed name, and still support myself by my favourite art. He should lend me the money to begin with, and I would pay him back, and live in lowly independence and strict seclusion, for the house stands in a lonely place, and the neighbourhood is thinly inhabited, and he himself should negotiate the sale of my pictures for me. I have arranged the whole plan in my head: and all I want is to persuade Frederick to be of the same mind as myself. He is coming to see me soon, and then I will make the proposal to him, having first enlightened him upon my circumstances sufficiently to excuse the project.

Already, I believe, he knows much more of my situation than I have told him. I can tell this by the air of tender sadness pervading his letters; and by the fact of his so seldom mentioning my husband, and generally evincing a kind of covert bitterness when he does refer to him; as well as by the circumstance of his never coming to see me when Mr. Huntingdon is at home. But he has never openly expressed any disapprobation of him or sympathy for me; he has never asked any questions, or said anything to invite my confidence. Had he done so, I should probably have had but few concealments from him. Perhaps he feels hurt at my reserve. He is a strange being; I wish we knew each other better. He used to spend a month at Staningley every year, before I was married; but, since our father's death, I have only seen him once, when he came for a few days while Mr. Huntingdon was away. He shall stay many days this time, and there shall be more candour and cordiality between us than ever there was before, since our early childhood. My heart clings to him more than ever; and my soul is sick of solitude.

April 16th. – He is come and gone. He would not stay above a fortnight. The time passed quickly, but very, very happily, and it has done me good. I must have a bad disposition, for my misfortunes have soured and embittered me exceedingly: I was beginning insensibly to cherish very unamiable feelings against my fellow-mortals, the male part of them especially; but it is a comfort to see there is at least one among them worthy to be trusted and esteemed; and doubtless there are more, though I have never known them, unless I except poor Lord Lowborough, and he was bad enough in his day. But what would Frederick have been, if he had lived in the world, and mingled from his childhood with such men as these of my acquaintance? And what will Arthur be, with all his natural sweetness of disposition, if I do not save him from that world and those companions? I mentioned my fears to Frederick, and introduced the subject of my plan of rescue on the evening after his arrival, when I presented my little son to his uncle.

"He is like you, Frederick," said I, "in some of his moods: I sometimes think he resembles you more than his father; and I am glad of it."

"You flatter me, Helen," replied he, stroking the child's soft, wavy locks.

"No, you will think it no compliment when I tell you I would rather have him to resemble Benson than his father." He slightly elevated his eyebrows, but said nothing.

"Do you know what sort of man Mr. Huntingdon is?" said I.

"I think I have an idea."

"Have you so clear an idea that you can hear, without surprise or disapproval, that I meditate escaping with that child to some secret asylum, where we can live in peace, and never see him again?"

"Is it really so?"

"If you have not," continued I, "I'll tell you something more about him"; and I gave a sketch of his general conduct, and a more particular account of his behaviour with regard to his child, and explained my apprehensions on the latter's account, and my determination to deliver him from his father's influence.

Frederick was exceedingly indignant against Mr. Huntingdon, and very much grieved for me; but still he looked upon my project as wild and impracticable. He deemed my fears for Arthur disproportioned to the circumstances, and opposed so many objections to my plan, and devised so many milder methods for ameliorating my condition, that I was obliged to enter into further details to convince him that my husband was utterly incorrigible, and that nothing could persuade him to give up his son, whatever became of me, he being as fully determined the child should not leave him, as I was not to leave the child; and that, in fact, nothing would answer but this, unless I fled the country, as I had intended before. To obviate that, he at length consented to have one wing of the old hall put into a habitable condition, as a place of refuge against a time of need; but hoped I would not take advantage of it unless circumstances should render it really necessary, which I was ready enough to promise: for though, for my own sake, such a hermitage appears like paradise itself, compared with my present situation, yet for my friends' sakes, for Milicent and Esther, my sisters in heart and affection, for the poor tenants of Grassdale, and, above all, for my aunt, I will stay if I possibly can.

July 29th. – Mrs. Hargrave and her daughter are come back from London. Esther is full of her first season in town; but she is still heart-whole and unengaged. Her mother sought out an excellent match for her, and even brought the gentleman to lay his heart and fortune at her feet; but Esther had the audacity to refuse the noble gifts. He was a man of good family and large possessions, but the naughty girl maintained he was old as Adam, ugly as sin, and hateful as – one who shall be nameless.

"But, indeed, I had a hard time of it," said she: "mamma was very greatly disappointed at the failure of her darling project, and very, very angry at my obstinate resistance to her will, and is so still; but I can't help it. And Walter, too, is so seriously displeased at my perversity and absurd caprice, as he calls it, that I fear he will never forgive me – I did not think he could be so unkind as he has lately shown himself. But Milicent begged me not to yield, and I'm sure, Mrs. Huntingdon, if you had seen the man they wanted to palm upon me, you would have advised me not to take him too."

"I should have done so whether I had seen him or not," said I; "it is enough that you dislike him."

"I knew you would say so; though mamma affirmed you would be quite shocked at my undutiful conduct. You can't imagine how she lectures me: I am disobedient and ungrateful; I am thwarting her wishes, wronging my brother, and making myself a burden on her hands. I sometimes fear she'll overcome me after all. I have a strong will, but so has she, and when she says such bitter things, it provokes me to such a pass that I feel inclined to do as she bids me, and then break my heart and say, 'There, mamma, it's all your fault!'"

"Pray don't!" said I. "Obedience from such a motive would be positive wickedness, and certain to bring the punishment it deserves. Stand firm, and your mamma will soon relinquish her persecution; and the gentleman himself will cease to pester you with his addresses if he finds them steadily rejected."

"Oh, no! Mamma will weary all about her before she tires herself with her exertions; and as for Mr. Oldfield, she has given him to understand that I have refused his offer, not from any dislike of his person, but merely because I am giddy and young, and cannot at present reconcile myself to the thoughts of marriage under any circumstances: but by next season, she has no doubt, I shall have more sense, and hopes my girlish fancies will be worn away. So she has brought me home, to school me into a proper sense of my duty, against the time comes round again. Indeed, I believe she will not put herself to the expense of taking me up to London again, unless I surrender: she cannot afford to take me to town for pleasure and nonsense, she says, and it is not every rich gentleman that will consent to take me without a fortune, whatever exalted ideas I may have of my own attractions."

"Well, Esther, I pity you; but still, I repeat, stand firm. You might as well sell yourself to slavery at once, as marry a man you dislike. If your mother and brother are unkind to you, you may leave them, but remember you are bound to your husband for life."

"But I cannot leave them unless I get married, and I cannot get married if nobody sees me. I saw one or two gentlemen in London that I might have liked, but they were younger sons, and mamma would not let me get to know them – one especially, who I believe rather liked me – but she threw every possible obstacle in the way of our better acquaintance. Wasn't it provoking?"

"I have no doubt you would feel it so, but it is possible that if you married him, you might have more reason to regret it hereafter than if you married Mr. Oldfield. When I tell you not to marry without love, I do not advise you to marry for love alone: there are many, many other things to be considered. Keep both heart and hand in your own possession, till you see good reason to part with them; and if such an occasion should never present itself, comfort your mind with this reflection, that though in single life your joys may not be very many, your sorrows, at least, will not be more than you can bear. Marriage may change your circumstances for the better, but, in my private opinion, it is far more likely to produce a contrary result."

"So thinks Milicent; but allow me to say I think otherwise. If I thought myself doomed to old-maidenhood, I should cease to value my life. The thoughts of living on, year after year, at the Grove – a hanger-on upon mamma and Walter, a mere cumberer of the ground (now that I know in what light they would regard it), is perfectly intolerable; I would rather run away with the butler."

"Your circumstances are peculiar, I allow; but have patience, love; do nothing rashly. Remember you are not yet nineteen, and many years are yet to pass before any one can set you down as an old maid: you cannot tell what Providence may have in store for you. And meantime, remember you have a right to the protection and support of your mother and brother, however they may seem to grudge it."

"You are so grave, Mrs. Huntingdon," said Esther, after a pause. "When Milicent uttered the same discouraging sentiments concerning marriage, I asked if she was happy: she said she was; but I only half believed her; and now I must put the same question to you."

"It is a very impertinent question," laughed I, "from a young girl to a married woman so many years her senior, and I shall not answer it."

"Pardon me, dear madam," said she, laughingly throwing herself into my arms, and kissing me with playful affection; but I felt a tear on my neck, as she dropped her head on my bosom and continued, with an odd mixture of sadness and levity, timidity and audacity, – "I know you are not so happy as I mean to be, for you spend half your life alone at Grassdale, while Mr. Huntingdon goes about enjoying himself where and how he pleases. I shall expect my husband to have no pleasures but what he shares with me; and if his greatest pleasure of all is not the enjoyment of my company, why, it will be the worse for him, that's all."

"If such are your expectations of matrimony, Esther, you must, indeed, be careful whom you marry – or rather, you must avoid it altogether."

Chapter Forty-Two

SEPTEMBER 1ST. – No Mr. Huntingdon yet. Perhaps he will stay among his friends till Christmas; and then, next spring, he will be off again. If he continue this plan, I shall be able to stay at Grassdale well enough – that is, I shall be able to stay, and that is enough; even an occasional bevy of friends at the shooting season may be borne, if Arthur get so firmly attached to me, so well established in good sense and principles before they come that I shall be able, by reason and affection, to keep him pure from their contaminations. Vain hope, I fear! But still, till such a time of trial comes I will forbear to think of my quiet asylum in the beloved old hall.

Mr. and Mrs. Hattersley have been staying at the Grove a fortnight: and as Mr. Hargrave is still absent, and the weather was remarkably fine, I never passed a day without seeing my two friends, Milicent and Esther, either there or here. On one occasion, when Mr. Hattersley had driven them over to Grassdale in the phaeton, with little Helen and Ralph, and we were all enjoying ourselves in the garden – I had a few minutes' conversation with that gentleman, while the ladies were amusing themselves with the children.

"Do you want to hear anything of your husband, Mrs. Huntingdon?" said he.

"No, unless you can tell me when to expect him home."

"I can't. – You don't want him, do you?" said he, with a broad grin.

"No."

"Well, I think you're better without him, sure enough – for my part, I'm downright weary of him. I told him I'd leave him if he didn't mend his manners, and he wouldn't; so I left him. You see, I'm a better man than you think me; and, what's more, I have serious thoughts of washing my hands of him entirely, and the whole set of 'em, and comporting myself from this day forward with all decency and sobriety, as a Christian and the father of a family should do. What do you think of that?"

"It is a resolution you ought to have formed long ago."

"Well, I'm not thirty yet; it isn't too late, is it?"

"No; it is never too late to reform, as long as you have the sense to desire it, and the strength to execute your purpose."

"Well, to tell you the truth, I've thought of it often and often before; but he's such devilish good company, is Huntingdon, after all. You can't imagine what a jovial good fellow he is when he's not fairly drunk, only just primed or half-seas-over. We all have a bit of a liking for him at the bottom of our hearts, though we can't respect him."

"But should you wish yourself to be like him?"

"No, I'd rather be like myself, bad as I am."

"You can't continue as bad as you are without getting worse and more brutalised every day, and therefore more like him."

I could not help smiling at the comical, half-angry, half-confounded look he put on at this rather unusual mode of address.

"Never mind my plain speaking," said I; "it is from the best of motives. But tell me, should you wish your sons to be like Mr. Huntingdon – or even like yourself?"

"Hang it! No."

"Should you wish your daughter to despise you – or, at least, to feel no vestige of respect for you, and no affection but what is mingled with the bitterest regret?"

"Oh, no! I couldn't stand that."

"And, finally, should you wish your wife to be ready to sink into the earth when she hears you mentioned; and to loathe the very sound of your voice, and shudder at your approach?"

"She never will; she likes me all the same, whatever I do."

"Impossible, Mr. Hattersley! You mistake her quiet submission for affection."

"Fire and fury –"

"Now don't burst into a tempest at that. I don't mean to say she does not love you – she does, I know, a great deal better than you deserve; but I am quite sure, that if you behave better, she will love you more, and if you behave worse, she will love you less and less, till all is lost in fear, aversion, and bitterness of soul, if not in secret hatred and contempt. But, dropping the subject of affection, should you wish to be the tyrant of her life – to take away all the sunshine from her existence, and make her thoroughly miserable?"

"Of course not; and I don't, and I'm not going to."

"You have done more towards it than you suppose."

"Pooh, pooh! She's not the susceptible, anxious, worriting creature you imagine: she's a little meek, peaceable, affectionate body; apt to be rather sulky at times, but quiet and cool in the main, and ready to take things as they come."

"Think of what she was five years ago, when you married her, and what she is now."

"I know she was a little plump lassie then, with a pretty pink and white face: now she's a poor little bit of a creature, fading and melting away like a snow-wreath. But hang it! – That's not my fault."

"What is the cause of it then? Not years, for she's only five-and-twenty."

"It's her own delicate health, and confound it, madam! What would you make of me? – And the children, to be sure, that worry her to death between them."

"No, Mr. Hattersley, the children give her more pleasure than pain: they are fine, well-dispositioned children –"

"I know they are – bless them!"

"Then why lay the blame on them? – I'll tell you what it is: it's silent fretting and constant anxiety on your account, mingled, I suspect, with something of bodily fear on her own. When you behave well, she can only rejoice with trembling; she has no security, no confidence in your judgment or principles; but is continually dreading the close of such short-lived felicity; when you behave ill, her causes of terror and misery are more than any one can tell but herself. In patient endurance of evil, she forgets it is our duty to admonish our neighbours of their transgressions. Since you will mistake her silence for indifference, come with me, and I'll show you one or two of her letters – no breach of confidence, I hope, since you are her other half."

He followed me into the library. I sought out and put into his hands two of Milicent's letters: one dated from London, and written during one of his wildest seasons of reckless dissipation; the other in the country, during a lucid interval. The former was full of trouble and anguish; not accusing him, but deeply regretting his connection with his profligate companions, abusing Mr. Grimsby and others, insinuating bitter things against Mr. Huntingdon, and most ingeniously throwing the blame of her husband's misconduct on to other men's shoulders. The latter was full of hope and joy, yet with a trembling consciousness that this happiness would not last; praising his goodness to the skies, but with an evident, though but half-expressed wish, that it were based on a surer foundation than the natural impulses of the heart, and a half-prophetic dread of the fall of that house so founded on the sand, – which fall had shortly after taken place, as Hattersley must have been conscious while he read.

Almost at the commencement of the first letter I had the unexpected pleasure of seeing him blush; but he immediately turned his back to me, and finished the perusal at the window. At the second, I saw him, once or twice, raise his hand, and hurriedly pass it across his face. Could it be to dash away a tear? When he had done, there was an interval spent in clearing his throat and staring out of the window, and then, after whistling a few bars of a favourite air, he turned round, gave me back the letters, and silently shook me by the hand.

"I've been a cursed rascal, God knows," said he, as he gave it a hearty squeeze, "but you see if I don't make amends for it – d—n me if I don't!"

"Don't curse yourself, Mr. Hattersley; if God had heard half your invocations of that kind, you would have been in hell long before now – and you cannot make amends for the past by doing your duty for the future, inasmuch as your duty is only what you owe to your Maker, and you cannot do more than fulfil it: another must make amends for your past delinquencies. If you intend to reform, invoke God's blessing, His mercy, and His aid; not His curse."

"God help me, then – for I'm sure I need it. Where's Milicent?"

"She's there, just coming in with her sister."

He stepped out at the glass door, and went to meet them. I followed at a little distance. Somewhat to his wife's astonishment, he lifted her off from the ground, and saluted her with a hearty kiss and a strong embrace; then placing his two hands on her shoulders, he gave her, I suppose, a sketch of the great things he meant to do, for she suddenly threw her arms round him, and burst into tears, exclaiming, – "Do, do, Ralph – we shall be so happy! How very, very good you are!"

"Nay, not I," said he, turning her round, and pushing her towards me. "Thank her; it's her doing."

Milicent flew to thank me, overflowing with gratitude. I disclaimed all title to it, telling her her husband was predisposed to amendment before I added my mite of exhortation and encouragement, and that I had only done what she might, and ought to have done herself.

"Oh, no!" cried she; "I couldn't have influenced him, I'm sure, by anything that I could have said. I should only have bothered him by my clumsy efforts at persuasion, if I had made the attempt."

"You never tried me, Milly," said he.

Shortly after they took their leave. They are now gone on a visit to Hattersley's father. After that they will repair to their country home. I hope his good resolutions will not fall through, and poor Milicent will not be again disappointed. Her last letter was full of present bliss, and pleasing anticipations for the future; but no particular temptation has yet occurred to put his virtue to the test. Henceforth, however, she will doubtless be somewhat less timid and reserved, and he more kind and thoughtful. – Surely, then, her hopes are not unfounded; and I have one bright spot, at least, whereon to rest my thoughts.

Chapter Forty-Three

OCTOBER 10TH. – Mr. Huntingdon returned about three weeks ago. His appearance, his demeanour and conversation, and my feelings with regard to him, I shall not trouble myself to describe. The day after his arrival, however, he surprised me by the announcement of an intention to procure a governess for little Arthur: I told him it was quite unnecessary, not to say ridiculous, at the present season: I thought I was fully competent to the task of teaching him myself – for some years to come, at least: the child's education was the only pleasure and business of my life; and since he had deprived me of every other occupation, he might surely leave me that.

He said I was not fit to teach children, or to be with them: I had already reduced the boy to little better than an automaton; I had broken his fine spirit with my rigid severity; and I should freeze all the sunshine out of his heart, and make him as gloomy an ascetic as myself, if I had the handling of him much longer. And poor Rachel, too, came in for her share of abuse, as usual; he cannot endure Rachel, because he knows she has a proper appreciation of him.

I calmly defended our several qualifications as nurse and governess, and still resisted the proposed addition to our family; but he cut me short by saying it was no use bothering about the matter, for he had engaged a governess already, and she was coming next week; so that all I had to do was to get things ready for her reception. This was a rather startling piece of intelligence. I ventured to inquire her name and address, by whom she had been recommended, or how he had been led to make choice of her.

"She is a very estimable, pious young person," said he; "you needn't be afraid. Her name is Myers, I believe; and she was recommended to me by a respectable old dowager: a lady of high repute in the religious world. I have not seen her myself, and therefore cannot give you a particular account of her person and conversation, and so forth; but, if the old lady's eulogies are correct, you will find her to possess all desirable qualifications for her position: an inordinate love of children among the rest."

All this was gravely and quietly spoken, but there was a laughing demon in his half-averted eye that boded no good, I imagined. However, I thought of my asylum in —shire, and made no further objections.

When Miss Myers arrived, I was not prepared to give her a very cordial reception. Her appearance was not particularly calculated to produce a favourable impression at first sight, nor did her manners and subsequent conduct, in any degree, remove the prejudice I had already conceived against her. Her attainments were limited, her intellect noways above mediocrity. She had a fine voice, and could sing like a nightingale, and accompany herself sufficiently well on the piano; but these were her only accomplishments. There was a look of guile and subtlety in her face, a sound of it in her voice. She seemed afraid of me, and would start if I suddenly approached her. In her behaviour she was respectful and complaisant, even to servility: she attempted to flatter and fawn upon me at first, but I soon checked that. Her fondness for her little pupil was overstrained, and I was obliged to remonstrate with her on the subject of over-indulgence and injudicious praise; but she could not gain his heart. Her piety consisted in an occasional heaving of sighs, and uplifting of eyes to the ceiling, and the utterance of a few cant phrases. She told me she was a clergyman's daughter, and had been left an orphan from her childhood, but had had the good fortune to obtain a situation in a very pious family; and then she spoke so gratefully of the kindness she had experienced from its different members, that I reproached myself for my uncharitable thoughts and unfriendly conduct, and relented for a time, but not for long: my causes of dislike were too rational, my suspicions too well founded for that; and I knew it was my duty to watch and scrutinize till those suspicions were either satisfactorily removed or confirmed.

I asked the name and residence of the kind and pious family. She mentioned a common name, and an unknown and distant place of abode, but told me they were now on the Continent, and their present address was unknown to her. I never saw her speak much to Mr. Huntingdon; but he would frequently look into the school-room to see how little Arthur got on with his new companion, when I was not there. In the evening, she sat with us in the drawing room, and would sing and play to amuse him or us, as she pretended, and was very attentive to his wants, and watchful to anticipate them, though she only talked to me; indeed, he was seldom in a condition to be talked to. Had she been other than she was, I should have felt her presence a great relief to come between us thus, except, indeed, that I should have been thoroughly ashamed for any decent person to see him as he often was.

I did not mention my suspicions to Rachel; but she, having sojourned for half a century in this land of sin and sorrow, has learned to be suspicious herself. She told me from the first she was 'down of that new governess,' and I soon found she watched her quite as narrowly as I did; and I was glad of it, for I longed to know the truth: the atmosphere of Grassdale seemed to stifle me, and I could only live by thinking of Wildfell Hall.

At last, one morning, she entered my chamber with such intelligence that my resolution was taken before she had ceased to speak. While she dressed me I explained to her my intentions and what assistance I should require from her, and told her which of my things she was to pack up, and what she was to leave behind for herself, as I had no other means of recompensing her for this sudden dismissal after her long and faithful service: a circumstance I most deeply regretted, but could not avoid.

"And what will you do, Rachel?" said I; "will you go home, or seek another place?"

"I have no home, ma'am, but with you," she replied; "and if I leave you I'll never go into place again as long as I live."

"But I can't afford to live like a lady now," returned I: "I must be my own maid and my child's nurse."

"What signifies!" replied she, in some excitement. "You'll want somebody to clean and wash, and cook, won't you? I can do all that; and never mind the wages: I've my bits o' savings yet, and if you wouldn't take me I should have to find my own board and lodging out of 'em somewhere, or else work among strangers: and it's what I'm not used to: so you can please yourself, ma'am." Her voice quavered as she spoke, and the tears stood in her eyes.

"I should like it above all things, Rachel, and I'd give you such wages as I could afford: such as I should give to any servant-of-all-work I might employ: but don't you see I should be dragging you down with me when you have done nothing to deserve it?"

"Oh, fiddle!" ejaculated she.

"And, besides, my future way of living will be so widely different to the past: so different to all you have been accustomed to –"

"Do you think, ma'am, I can't bear what my missis can? Surely I'm not so proud and so dainty as that comes to; and my little master, too, God bless him!"

"But I'm young, Rachel; I sha'n't mind it; and Arthur is young too: it will be nothing to him."

"Nor me either: I'm not so old but what I can stand hard fare and hard work, if it's only to help and comfort them as I've loved like my own bairns: for all I'm too old to bide the thoughts o' leaving 'em in trouble and danger, and going amongst strangers myself."

"Then you sha'n't, Rachel!" cried I, embracing my faithful friend. "We'll all go together, and you shall see how the new life suits you."

"Bless you, honey!" cried she, affectionately returning my embrace. "Only let us get shut of this wicked house, and we'll do right enough, you'll see."

"So think I," was my answer; and so that point was settled.

By that morning's post I despatched a few hasty lines to Frederick, beseeching him to prepare my asylum for my immediate reception: for I should probably come to claim it within a day after the receipt of that note: and telling him, in few words, the cause of my sudden resolution. I then wrote three letters of adieu: the first to Esther Hargrave, in which I told her that I found it impossible to stay any longer at Grassdale, or to leave my son under his father's protection; and, as it was of the last importance that our future abode should be unknown to him and his acquaintance, I should disclose it to no one but my brother, through the medium of whom I hoped still to correspond with my friends. I then gave her his address, exhorted her to write frequently, reiterated some of my former admonitions regarding her own concerns, and bade her a fond farewell.

The second was to Milicent; much to the same effect, but a little more confidential, as befitted our longer intimacy, and her greater experience and better acquaintance with my circumstances.

The third was to my aunt: a much more difficult and painful undertaking, and therefore I had left it to the last; but I must give her some explanation of that extraordinary step I had taken: and that quickly, for she and my uncle would no doubt hear of it within a day or two after my disappearance, as it was probable that Mr. Huntingdon would speedily apply to them to know what was become of me. At last, however, I told her I was sensible of my error: I did not complain of its punishment, and I was sorry to trouble my friends with its consequences; but in duty to my son I must submit no longer; it was absolutely necessary that he should be delivered from his father's corrupting influence. I should not disclose my place of refuge even to her, in order that she and my uncle might be able, with truth, to deny all knowledge concerning it; but any communications addressed to me under cover to my brother would be certain to reach me. I hoped she and my uncle would pardon the step I had taken, for if they knew all, I was sure they would not blame me; and I trusted they would not afflict themselves on my account, for if I could only reach my retreat in safety and keep it unmolested, I should be very happy, but for the thoughts of them; and should be quite contented to spend my life in obscurity, devoting myself to the training up of my child, and teaching him to avoid the errors of both his parents.

These things were done yesterday: I have given two whole days to the preparation for our departure, that Frederick may have more time to prepare the rooms, and Rachel to pack up the things: for the latter task must be done with the utmost caution and secrecy, and there is no one but me to assist her. I can help to get the articles together, but I do not understand the art of stowing them into the boxes, so as to take up the smallest possible space; and there are her own things to do, as well as mine and Arthur's. I can ill afford to leave anything behind, since I have no money, except a few guineas in my purse; and besides, as Rachel observed, whatever I left would most likely become the property of Miss Myers, and I should not relish that.

But what trouble I have had throughout these two days, struggling to appear calm and collected, to meet him and her as usual, when I was obliged to meet them, and forcing myself to leave my little Arthur in her hands for hours together! But I trust these trials are over now: I have laid him in my bed for better security, and never more, I trust, shall his innocent lips be defiled by their contaminating kisses, or his young ears polluted by their words. But shall we escape in safety? Oh, that the morning were come, and we were on our way at least! This evening, when I had given Rachel all the assistance I could, and had nothing left me but to wait, and wish and tremble, I became so greatly agitated that I knew not what to do. I went down to dinner, but I could not force myself to eat. Mr. Huntingdon remarked the circumstance.

"What's to do with you now?" said he, when the removal of the second course gave him time to look about him.

"I am not well," I replied: "I think I must lie down a little; you won't miss me much?"

"Not the least: if you leave your chair, it'll do just as well – better, a trifle," he muttered, as I left the room, "for I can fancy somebody else fills it."

"Somebody else may fill it tomorrow," I thought, but did not say. "There! I've seen the last of you, I hope," I muttered, as I closed the door upon him.

Rachel urged me to seek repose at once, to recruit my strength for tomorrow's journey, as we must be gone before the dawn; but in my present state of nervous excitement that was entirely out of the question. It was equally out of the question to sit, or wander about my room, counting the hours and the minutes between me and the appointed time of action, straining my ears and trembling at every sound, lest someone should discover and betray us after all. I took up a book and tried to read: my eyes wandered over the pages, but it was impossible to bind my thoughts to their contents. Why not have recourse to the old expedient, and add this last event to my chronicle? I opened its pages once more, and wrote the above account – with difficulty, at first, but gradually my mind became more calm and steady. Thus several hours have passed away: the time is drawing near; and now my eyes feel heavy and my frame exhausted. I will commend my cause to God, and then lie down and gain an hour or two of sleep; and then! –

Little Arthur sleeps soundly. All the house is still: there can be no one watching. The boxes were all corded by Benson, and quietly conveyed down the back stairs after dusk, and sent away in a cart to the M— coach-office. The name upon the cards was Mrs. Graham, which appellation I mean henceforth to adopt. My mother's maiden name was Graham, and therefore I fancy I have some claim to it, and prefer it to any other, except my own, which I dare not resume.

Chapter Forty-Four

OCTOBER 24TH. – Thank heaven, I am free and safe at last. Early we rose, swiftly and quietly dressed, slowly and stealthily descended to the hall, where Benson stood ready with a light, to open the door and fasten it after us. We were obliged to let one man into our secret on account of the boxes, etc. All the servants were but too well acquainted with their master's conduct, and either Benson or John would have been willing to serve me; but as the former was more staid and elderly, and a crony of Rachel's besides, I of course directed her to make choice of him as her assistant and confidant on the occasion, as far as necessity demanded, I only hope he may not be brought into trouble thereby, and only wish I could reward him for the perilous service he was so ready to undertake. I slipped two guineas into his hand, by way of remembrance, as he stood in the doorway, holding the candle to light our departure, with a tear in his honest grey eye, and a host of good wishes depicted on his solemn countenance. Alas! I could offer no more: I had barely sufficient remaining for the probable expenses of the journey.

What trembling joy it was when the little wicket closed behind us, as we issued from the park! Then, for one moment, I paused, to inhale one draught of that cool, bracing air, and venture one look back upon the house. All was dark and still: no light glimmered in the windows, no wreath of smoke obscured the stars that sparkled above it in the frosty sky. As I bade farewell for ever to that place, the scene of so much guilt and misery, I felt glad that I had not left it before, for now there was no doubt about the propriety of such a step – no shadow of remorse for him I left behind. There was nothing to disturb my joy but the fear of detection; and every step removed us further from the chance of that.

We had left Grassdale many miles behind us before the round red sun arose to welcome our deliverance; and if any inhabitant of its vicinity had chanced to see us then, as we bowled along on the top of the coach, I scarcely think they would have suspected our identity. As I intend to be taken for a widow, I thought it advisable to enter my new abode in mourning: I was, therefore, attired in a plain black silk dress and mantle, a black veil (which I kept carefully over my face for the first twenty or thirty miles of the journey), and a black silk bonnet, which I had been constrained to borrow of Rachel, for want of such an article myself. It was not in the newest fashion, of course; but none the worse for that, under present circumstances. Arthur was clad in his plainest clothes, and wrapped in a coarse woollen shawl; and Rachel was muffled in a grey cloak and hood that had seen better days, and gave her more the appearance of an ordinary though decent old woman, than of a lady's-maid.

Oh, what delight it was to be thus seated aloft, rumbling along the broad, sunshiny road, with the fresh morning breeze in my face, surrounded by an unknown country, all smiling – cheerfully, gloriously smiling in the yellow lustre of those early beams; with my darling child in my arms, almost as happy as myself, and my faithful friend beside me: a prison and despair behind me, receding further, further back at every clatter of the horses' feet; and liberty and hope before! I could hardly refrain from praising God aloud for my deliverance, or astonishing my fellow-passengers by some surprising outburst of hilarity.

But the journey was a very long one, and we were all weary enough before the close of it. It was far into the night when we reached the town of L—, and still we were seven miles from our journey's end; and there was no more coaching, nor any conveyance to be had, except a common cart, and that with the greatest difficulty, for half the town was in bed. And a dreary ride we had of it, that last stage of the journey, cold and weary as we were; sitting on our boxes, with nothing to cling to, nothing to lean against, slowly dragged and cruelly shaken over the rough, hilly roads. But Arthur was asleep in Rachel's lap, and between us we managed pretty well to shield him from the cold night air.

At last we began to ascend a terribly steep and stony lane, which, in spite of the darkness, Rachel said she remembered well: she had often walked there with me in her arms, and little thought to come again so many years after, under such circumstances as the present. Arthur being now awakened by the jolting and the stoppages, we all got out and walked. We had not far to go; but what if Frederick should not have received my letter? or if he should not have had time to prepare the rooms for our reception, and we should find them all dark, damp, and comfortless, destitute of food, fire, and furniture, after all our toil?

At length the grim, dark pile appeared before us. The lane conducted us round by the back way. We entered the desolate court, and in breathless anxiety surveyed the ruinous mass. Was it all blackness and desolation? No; one faint red glimmer cheered us from a window where the lattice was in good repair. The door was fastened, but after due knocking and waiting, and some parleying with a voice from an upper window, we were admitted by an old woman who had been commissioned to air and keep the house till our arrival, into a tolerably snug little apartment, formerly the scullery of the mansion, which Frederick had now fitted up as a kitchen. Here she procured us a light, roused the fire to a cheerful blaze, and soon prepared a simple repast for our refreshment; while we disencumbered ourselves of our travelling-gear, and took a hasty survey of our new abode. Besides the kitchen, there were two bedrooms, a good-sized parlour, and another smaller one, which I destined for my studio, all well aired and seemingly in good repair, but only partly furnished with a few old articles, chiefly of ponderous black oak, the veritable ones that had been there before, and which had been kept as antiquarian relics in my brother's present residence, and now, in all haste, transported back again.

The old woman brought my supper and Arthur's into the parlour, and told me, with all due formality, that 'the master desired his compliments to Mrs. Graham, and he had prepared the rooms as well as he could upon so short a notice; but he would do himself the pleasure of calling upon her tomorrow, to receive her further commands.'

I was glad to ascend the stern-looking stone staircase, and lie down in the gloomy, old-fashioned bed, beside my little Arthur. He was asleep in a minute; but, weary as I was, my excited feelings and restless cogitations kept me awake till dawn began to struggle with the darkness; but sleep was sweet and refreshing when it came, and the waking was delightful beyond expression. It was little Arthur that roused me, with his gentle kisses. He was here, then, safely clasped in my arms, and many leagues away from his unworthy father! Broad daylight illumined the apartment, for the sun was high in heaven, though obscured by rolling masses of autumnal vapour.

The scene, indeed, was not remarkably cheerful in itself, either within or without. The large bare room, with its grim old furniture, the narrow, latticed windows, revealing the dull, grey sky above and the desolate wilderness below, where the dark stone walls and iron gate, the rank growth of grass and weeds, and the hardy evergreens of preternatural forms, alone remained to tell that there had been once a garden, – and the bleak and barren fields beyond might have struck me as gloomy enough at another time; but now, each separate object seemed to echo back my own exhilarating sense of hope and freedom: indefinite dreams of the far past and bright anticipations of the future seemed to greet me at every turn. I should rejoice with more security, to be sure, had the broad sea rolled between my present and my former homes; but surely in this lonely spot I might remain unknown; and then I had my brother here to cheer my solitude with his occasional visits.

He came that morning; and I have had several interviews with him since; but he is obliged to be very cautious when and how he comes; not even his servants or his best friends must know of his visits to Wildfell – except on such occasions as a landlord might be expected to call upon a stranger tenant – lest suspicion should be excited against me, whether of the truth or of some slanderous falsehood.

I have now been here nearly a fortnight, and, but for one disturbing care, the haunting dread of discovery, I am comfortably settled in my new home: Frederick has supplied me with all requisite furniture and painting materials: Rachel has sold most of my clothes for me, in a distant town, and procured me a wardrobe more suitable to my present position: I have a second-hand piano, and a tolerably well-stocked bookcase in my parlour; and my other room has assumed quite a professional, business-like appearance already. I am working hard to repay my brother for all his expenses on my account; not that there is the slightest necessity for anything of the kind, but it pleases me to do so: I shall have so much more pleasure in my labour, my earnings, my frugal fare, and household economy, when I know that I am paying my way honestly, and that what little I possess is legitimately all my own; and that no one suffers for my folly – in a pecuniary way at least. I shall make him take the last penny I owe him, if I can possibly effect it without offending him too deeply. I have a few pictures already done, for I told Rachel to pack up all I had; and she executed her commission but too well – for among the rest, she put up a portrait of Mr. Huntingdon that I had painted in the first year of my marriage. It struck me with dismay, at the moment, when I took it from the box and beheld those eyes fixed upon me in their mocking mirth, as if exulting still in his power to control my fate, and deriding my efforts to escape.

How widely different had been my feelings in painting that portrait to what they now were in looking upon it! How I had studied and toiled to produce something, as I thought, worthy of the original! What mingled pleasure and dissatisfaction I had had in the result of my labours! – Pleasure for the likeness I had caught; dissatisfaction, because I had not made it handsome enough. Now, I see no beauty in it – nothing pleasing in any part of its expression; and yet it is far handsomer and far more agreeable – far less repulsive I should rather say – than he is now: for these six years have wrought almost as great a change upon himself as on my feelings regarding him. The frame, however, is handsome enough; it will serve for another painting. The picture itself I have not destroyed, as I had first intended; I have put it aside; not, I think, from any lurking tenderness for the memory of past affection, nor yet to remind me of my former folly, but chiefly that I may compare my son's features and countenance with this, as he grows up, and thus be enabled to judge how much or how little he resembles his father – if I may be allowed to keep him with me still, and never to behold that father's face again – a blessing I hardly dare reckon upon.

It seems Mr. Huntingdon is making every exertion to discover the place of my retreat. He has been in person to Staningley, seeking redress for his grievances – expecting to hear of his victims, if not to find them there – and has told so many lies, and with such unblushing coolness, that my uncle more than half believes him, and strongly advocates my going back to him and being friends again. But my aunt knows better: she is too cool and cautious, and too well acquainted with both my husband's character and my own to be imposed upon by any specious falsehoods the former could invent. But he does not want me back; he wants my child; and gives my friends to understand that if I prefer living apart from him, he will indulge the whim and let me do so unmolested, and even settle a reasonable allowance on me, provided I will immediately deliver up his son. But heaven help me! I am not going to sell my child for gold, though it were to save both him and me from starving: it would be better that he should die with me than that he should live with his father.

Frederick showed me a letter he had received from that gentleman, full of cool impudence such as would astonish any one who did not know him, but such as, I am convinced, none would know better how to answer than my brother. He gave me no account of his reply, except to tell me that he had not acknowledged his acquaintance with my place of refuge, but rather left it to be inferred that it was quite unknown to him, by saying it was useless to apply to him, or any other of my relations, for information on the subject, as it appeared I had been driven to such extremity that I had concealed my retreat even from my best friends; but that if he had known it, or should at any time be made aware of it, most certainly Mr. Huntingdon would be the last person to whom he should communicate the intelligence; and that he need not trouble himself to bargain for the child, for he (Frederick) fancied he knew enough of his sister to enable him to declare, that wherever she might be, or however situated, no consideration would induce her to deliver him up.

30th. – Alas! My kind neighbours will not let me alone. By some means they have ferreted me out, and I have had to sustain visits from three different families, all more or less bent upon discovering who and what I am, whence I came, and why I have chosen such a home as this. Their society is unnecessary to me, to say the least, and their curiosity annoys and alarms me: if I gratify it, it may lead to the ruin of my son, and if I am too mysterious it will only excite their suspicions, invite conjecture, and rouse them to greater exertions – and perhaps be the means of spreading my fame from parish to parish, till it reach the ears of some one who will carry it to the Lord of Grassdale Manor.

I shall be expected to return their calls, but if, upon inquiry, I find that any of them live too far away for Arthur to accompany me, they must expect in vain for a while, for I cannot bear to leave him, unless it be to go to church, and I have not attempted that yet: for – it may be foolish weakness, but I am under such constant dread of his being snatched away, that I am never easy when he is not by my side; and I fear these nervous terrors would so entirely disturb my devotions, that I should obtain no benefit from the attendance. I mean, however, to make the experiment next Sunday, and oblige myself to leave him in charge of Rachel for a few hours. It will be a hard task, but surely no imprudence; and the vicar has been to scold me for my neglect of the ordinances of religion. I had no sufficient excuse to offer, and I promised, if all were well, he should see me in my pew next Sunday; for I do not wish to be set down as an infidel; and, besides, I know I should derive great comfort and benefit from an occasional attendance at public worship, if I could only have faith and fortitude to compose my thoughts in conformity with the solemn occasion, and forbid them to be for ever dwelling on my absent child, and on the dreadful possibility of finding him gone when I return; and surely God in His mercy will preserve me from so severe a trial: for my child's own sake, if not for mine, He will not suffer him to be torn away.

November 3rd. – I have made some further acquaintance with my neighbours. The fine gentleman and beau of the parish and its vicinity (in his own estimation, at least) is a young....

* * *

Here it ended. The rest was torn away. How cruel, just when she was going to mention me! For I could not doubt it was your humble servant she was about to mention, though not very favourably, of course. I could tell that, as well by those few words as by the recollection of her whole aspect and demeanour towards me in the commencement of our acquaintance. Well! I could readily forgive her prejudice against me, and her hard thoughts of our sex in general, when I saw to what brilliant specimens her experience had been limited.

Respecting me, however, she had long since seen her error, and perhaps fallen into another in the opposite extreme: for if, at first, her opinion of me had been lower than I deserved, I was convinced that now my deserts were lower than her opinion; and if the former part of this continuation had been torn away to avoid wounding my feelings, perhaps the latter portion had been removed for fear of ministering too much to my self-conceit. At any rate, I would have given much to have seen it all – to have witnessed the gradual change, and watched the progress of her esteem and friendship for me, and whatever warmer feeling she might have; to have seen how much of love there was in her regard, and how it had grown upon her in spite of her virtuous resolutions and strenuous exertions to – but no, I had no right to see it: all this was too sacred for any eyes but her own, and she had done well to keep it from me.

Chapter Forty-Five

WELL, HALFORD, what do you think of all this? And while you read it, did you ever picture to yourself what my feelings would probably be during its perusal? Most likely not; but I am not going to descant upon them now: I will only make this acknowledgment, little honourable as it may be to human nature, and especially to myself, – that the former half of the narrative was, to me, more painful than the latter, not that I was at all insensible to Mrs. Huntingdon's wrongs or unmoved by her sufferings, but, I must confess, I felt a kind of selfish gratification in watching her husband's gradual decline in her good graces, and seeing how completely he extinguished all her affection at last. The effect of the whole, however, in spite of all my sympathy for her, and my fury against him, was to relieve my mind of an intolerable burden, and fill my heart with joy, as if some friend had roused me from a dreadful nightmare.

It was now near eight o'clock in the morning, for my candle had expired in the midst of my perusal, leaving me no alternative but to get another, at the expense of alarming the house, or to go to bed, and wait the return of daylight. On my mother's account, I chose the latter; but how willingly I sought my pillow, and how much sleep it brought me, I leave you to imagine.

At the first appearance of dawn, I rose, and brought the manuscript to the window, but it was impossible to read it yet. I devoted half an hour to dressing, and then returned to it again. Now, with a little difficulty, I could manage; and with intense and eager interest, I devoured the remainder of its contents. When it was ended, and my transient regret at its abrupt conclusion was over, I opened the window and put out my head to catch the cooling breeze, and imbibe deep draughts of the pure morning air. A splendid morning it was; the half-frozen dew lay thick on the grass, the swallows were twittering round me, the rooks cawing, and cows lowing in the distance; and early frost and summer sunshine mingled their sweetness in the air. But I did not think of that: a confusion of countless thoughts and varied emotions crowded upon me while I gazed abstractedly on the lovely face of nature. Soon, however, this chaos of thoughts and passions cleared away, giving place to two distinct emotions: joy unspeakable that my adored Helen was all I wished to think her – that through the noisome vapours of the world's aspersions and my own fancied convictions, her character shone bright, and clear, and stainless as that sun I could not bear to look on; and shame and deep remorse for my own conduct.

Immediately after breakfast I hurried over to Wildfell Hall. Rachel had risen many degrees in my estimation since yesterday. I was ready to greet her quite as an old friend; but every kindly impulse was checked by the look of cold distrust she cast upon me on opening the door. The old virgin had constituted herself the guardian of her lady's honour, I suppose, and doubtless she saw in me another Mr. Hargrave, only the more dangerous in being more esteemed and trusted by her mistress.

"Missis can't see any one today, sir – she's poorly," said she, in answer to my inquiry for Mrs. Graham.

"But I must see her, Rachel," said I, placing my hand on the door to prevent its being shut against me.

"Indeed, sir, you can't," replied she, settling her countenance in still more iron frigidity than before.

"Be so good as to announce me."

"It's no manner of use, Mr. Markham; she's poorly, I tell you."

Just in time to prevent me from committing the impropriety of taking the citadel by storm, and pushing forward unannounced, an inner door opened, and little Arthur appeared with his frolicsome playfellow, the dog. He seized my hand between both his, and smilingly drew me forward.

"Mamma says you're to come in, Mr. Markham," said he, "and I am to go out and play with Rover."

Rachel retired with a sigh, and I stepped into the parlour and shut the door. There, before the fire-place, stood the tall, graceful figure, wasted with many sorrows. I cast the manuscript on the table, and looked in her face. Anxious and pale, it was turned towards me; her clear, dark eyes were fixed on mine with a gaze so intensely earnest that they bound me like a spell.

"Have you looked it over?" she murmured. The spell was broken.

"I've read it through," said I, advancing into the room, – "and I want to know if you'll forgive me – if you can forgive me?"

She did not answer, but her eyes glistened, and a faint red mantled on her lip and cheek. As I approached, she abruptly turned away, and went to the window. It was not in anger, I was well assured, but only to conceal or control her emotion. I therefore ventured to follow and stand beside her there, – but not to speak. She gave me her hand, without turning her head, and murmured in a voice she strove in vain to steady, – "Can you forgive me?"

It might be deemed a breach of trust, I thought, to convey that lily hand to my lips, so I only gently pressed it between my own, and smilingly replied, – "I hardly can. You should have told me this before. It shows a want of confidence –"

"Oh, no," cried she, eagerly interrupting me; "it was not that. It was no want of confidence in you; but if I had told you anything of my history, I must have told you all, in order to excuse my conduct; and I might well shrink from such a disclosure, till necessity obliged me to make it. But you forgive me? – I have done very, very wrong, I know; but, as usual, I have reaped the bitter fruits of my own error, – and must reap them to the end."

Bitter, indeed, was the tone of anguish, repressed by resolute firmness, in which this was spoken. Now, I raised her hand to my lips, and fervently kissed it again and again; for tears prevented any other reply. She suffered these wild caresses without resistance or resentment; then, suddenly turning from me, she paced twice or thrice through the room. I knew by the contraction of her brow, the tight compression of her lips, and wringing of her hands, that meantime a violent conflict between reason and passion was silently passing within. At length she paused before the empty fire-place, and turning to me, said calmly – if that might be called calmness which was so evidently the result of a violent effort, – "Now, Gilbert, you must leave me – not this moment, but soon – and you must never come again."

"Never again, Helen? Just when I love you more than ever."

"For that very reason, if it be so, we should not meet again. I thought this interview was necessary – at least, I persuaded myself it was so – that we might severally ask and receive each other's pardon for the past; but there can be no excuse for another. I shall leave this place, as soon as I have means to seek another asylum; but our intercourse must end here."

"End here!" echoed I; and approaching the high, carved chimney-piece, I leant my hand against its heavy mouldings, and dropped my forehead upon it in silent, sullen despondency.

"You must not come again," continued she. There was a slight tremor in her voice, but I thought her whole manner was provokingly composed, considering the dreadful sentence she pronounced. "You must know why I tell you so," she resumed; "and you must see that it is better to part at once: – if it be hard to say adieu for ever, you ought to help me." She paused. I did not answer. "Will you promise not to come? – If you won't, and if you do come here again, you will drive me away before I know where to find another place of refuge – or how to seek it."

"Helen," said I, turning impatiently towards her, "I cannot discuss the matter of eternal separation calmly and dispassionately as you can do. It is no question of mere expedience with me; it is a question of life and death!"

She was silent. Her pale lips quivered, and her fingers trembled with agitation, as she nervously entwined them in the hair-chain to which was appended her small gold watch – the only thing of value she had permitted herself to keep. I had said an unjust and cruel thing; but I must needs follow it up with something worse.

"But, Helen!" I began in a soft, low tone, not daring to raise my eyes to her face, "that man is not your husband: in the sight of heaven he has forfeited all claim to –" She seized my arm with a grasp of startling energy.

"Gilbert, don't!" she cried, in a tone that would have pierced a heart of adamant. "For God's sake, don't you attempt these arguments! No fiend could torture me like this!"

"I won't, I won't!" said I, gently laying my hand on hers; almost as much alarmed at her vehemence as ashamed of my own misconduct.

"Instead of acting like a true friend," continued she, breaking from me, and throwing herself into the old arm-chair, "and helping me with all your might – or rather taking your own part in the struggle of right against passion – you leave all the burden to me; – and not satisfied with that, you do your utmost to fight against me – when you know that! –" she paused, and hid her face in her handkerchief.

"Forgive me, Helen!" pleaded I. "I will never utter another word on the subject. But may we not still meet as friends?"

"It will not do," she replied, mournfully shaking her head; and then she raised her eyes to mine, with a mildly reproachful look that seemed to say, "You must know that as well as I."

"Then what must we do?" cried I, passionately. But immediately I added in a quieter tone – "I'll do whatever you desire; only don't say that this meeting is to be our last."

"And why not? Don't you know that every time we meet the thoughts of the final parting will become more painful? Don't you feel that every interview makes us dearer to each other than the last?"

The utterance of this last question was hurried and low, and the downcast eyes and burning blush too plainly showed that she, at least, had felt it. It was scarcely prudent to make such an admission, or to add – as she presently did – "I have power to bid you go, now: another time it might be different," – but I was not base enough to attempt to take advantage of her candour.

"But we may write," I timidly suggested. "You will not deny me that consolation?"

"We can hear of each other through my brother."

"Your brother!" A pang of remorse and shame shot through me. She had not heard of the injury he had sustained at my hands; and I had not the courage to tell her. "Your brother will not help us," I said: "he would have all communion between us to be entirely at an end."

"And he would be right, I suppose. As a friend of both, he would wish us both well; and every friend would tell us it was our interest, as well as our duty, to forget each other, though we might not see it ourselves. But don't be afraid, Gilbert," she added, smiling sadly at my manifest discomposure; "there is little chance of my forgetting you. But I did not mean that Frederick should be the means of transmitting messages between us – only that each might know, through him, of the other's welfare; – and more than this ought not to be: for you are young, Gilbert, and you ought to marry – and will some time, though you may think it impossible now: and though I hardly can say I wish you to forget me, I know it is right that you should, both for your own happiness, and that of your future wife; – and therefore I must and will wish it," she added resolutely.

"And you are young too, Helen," I boldly replied; "and when that profligate scoundrel has run through his career, you will give your hand to me – I'll wait till then."

But she would not leave me this support. Independently of the moral evil of basing our hopes upon the death of another, who, if unfit for this world, was at least no less so for the next, and whose amelioration would thus become our bane and his greatest transgression our greatest benefit, – she maintained it to be madness: many men of Mr. Huntingdon's habits had lived to a ripe though miserable old age. "And if I," said she, "am young in years, I am old in sorrow; but even if trouble should fail to kill me before vice destroys him, think, if he reached but fifty years or so, would you wait twenty or fifteen – in vague uncertainty and suspense – through all the prime of youth and manhood – and marry at last a woman faded and worn as I shall be – without ever having seen me from this day to that? – You would not," she continued, interrupting my earnest protestations of unfailing constancy, – "or if you would, you should not. Trust me, Gilbert; in this matter I know better than you. You think me cold and stony-hearted, and you may, but –"

"I don't, Helen."

"Well, never mind: you might if you would: but I have not spent my solitude in utter idleness, and I am not speaking now from the impulse of the moment, as you do. I have thought of all these matters again and again; I have argued these questions with myself, and pondered well our past, and present, and future career; and, believe me, I have come to the right conclusion at last. Trust my words rather than your own feelings now, and in a few years you will see that I was right – though at present I hardly can see it myself," she murmured with a sigh as she rested her head on her hand. "And don't argue against me any more: all you can say has been already said by my own heart and refuted by my reason. It was hard enough to combat those suggestions as they were whispered within me; in your mouth they are ten times worse, and if you knew how much they pain me you would cease at once, I know. If you knew my present feelings, you would even try to relieve them at the expense of your own."

"I will go – in a minute, if that can relieve you – and *never* return!" said I, with bitter emphasis. "But, if we may never meet, and never hope to meet again, is it a crime to exchange our thoughts by letter? May not kindred spirits meet, and mingle in communion, whatever be the fate and circumstances of their earthly tenements?"

"They may, they may!" cried she, with a momentary burst of glad enthusiasm. "I thought of that too, Gilbert, but I feared to mention it, because I feared you would not understand my views upon the subject. I fear it even now – I fear any kind friend would tell us we are both deluding ourselves with the idea of keeping up a spiritual intercourse without hope or prospect of anything further – without fostering vain regrets and hurtful aspirations, and feeding thoughts that should be sternly and pitilessly left to perish of inanition."

"Never mind our kind friends: if they can part our bodies, it is enough; in God's name, let them not sunder our souls!" cried I, in terror lest she should deem it her duty to deny us this last remaining consolation.

"But no letters can pass between us here," said she, "without giving fresh food for scandal; and when I departed, I had intended that my new abode should be unknown to you as to the rest of the world; not that I should doubt your word if you promised not to visit me, but I thought you would be more tranquil in your own mind if you knew you could not do it, and likely to find less difficulty in abstracting yourself from me if you could not picture my situation to your mind. But listen," said she, smilingly putting up her finger to check my impatient reply: "in six months you shall hear from Frederick precisely where I am; and if you still retain your wish to write to me, and think you can maintain a correspondence all thought, all spirit – such as disembodied souls or unimpassioned friends, at least, might hold, – write, and I will answer you."

"Six months!"

"Yes, to give your present ardour time to cool, and try the truth and constancy of your soul's love for mine. And now, enough has been said between us. Why can't we part at once?" exclaimed she, almost wildly, after a moment's pause, as she suddenly rose from her chair, with her hands resolutely clasped together. I thought it was my duty to go without delay; and I approached and half extended my hand as if to take leave – she grasped it in silence. But this thought of final separation was too intolerable: it seemed to squeeze the blood out of my heart; and my feet were glued to the floor.

"And must we never meet again?" I murmured, in the anguish of my soul.

"We shall meet in heaven. Let us think of that," said she in a tone of desperate calmness; but her eyes glittered wildly, and her face was deadly pale.

"But not as we are now," I could not help replying. "It gives me little consolation to think I shall next behold you as a disembodied spirit, or an altered being, with a frame perfect and glorious, but not like this! – And a heart, perhaps, entirely estranged from me."

"No, Gilbert, there is perfect love in heaven!"

"So perfect, I suppose, that it soars above distinctions, and you will have no closer sympathy with me than with any one of the ten thousand thousand angels and the innumerable multitude of happy spirits round us."

"Whatever I am, you will be the same, and, therefore, cannot possibly regret it; and whatever that change may be we know it must be for the better."

"But if I am to be so changed that I shall cease to adore you with my whole heart and soul, and love you beyond every other creature, I shall not be myself; and though, if ever I win heaven at all, I must, I know, be infinitely better and happier than I am now, my earthly nature cannot rejoice in the anticipation of such beatitude, from which itself and its chief joy must be excluded."

"Is your love all earthly, then?"

"No, but I am supposing we shall have no more intimate communion with each other than with the rest."

"If so, it will be because we love them more, and not each other less. Increase of love brings increase of happiness, when it is mutual, and pure as that will be."

"But can you, Helen, contemplate with delight this prospect of losing me in a sea of glory?"

"I own I cannot; but we know not that it will be so; – and I do know that to regret the exchange of earthly pleasures for the joys of heaven, is as if the grovelling caterpillar should lament that it must one day quit the nibbled leaf to soar aloft and flutter through the air, roving at will from flower to flower, sipping sweet honey from their cups, or basking in their sunny petals. If these little creatures knew how great a change awaited them, no doubt they would regret it; but would not all such sorrow be misplaced? And if that illustration will not move you, here is another: – We are children now; we feel as children, and we understand as children; and when we are told that men and women do not play with toys, and that our companions will one day weary of the trivial sports and occupations that interest them and us so deeply now, we cannot help being saddened at the thoughts of such an alteration, because we cannot conceive that as we grow up our own minds will become so enlarged and elevated that we ourselves shall then regard as trifling those objects and pursuits we now so fondly cherish, and that, though our companions will no longer join us in those childish pastimes, they will drink with us at other fountains of delight, and mingle their souls with ours in higher aims and nobler occupations beyond our present comprehension, but not less deeply relished or less truly good for that, while yet both we and they remain essentially the same individuals as before. But, Gilbert, can you really derive no consolation from the thought that we may meet together where there is no more pain and sorrow, no more striving against sin, and struggling of the spirit against the flesh; where both will behold the same glorious truths, and drink exalted and supreme felicity from the same fountain of light and goodness – that Being whom both will worship with the same intensity of holy ardour – and where pure and happy creatures both will love with the same divine affection? If you cannot, never write to me!"

"Helen, I can! If faith would never fail."

"Now, then," exclaimed she, "while this hope is strong within us –"

"We will part," I cried. "You shall not have the pain of another effort to dismiss me. I will go at once; but –"

I did not put my request in words: she understood it instinctively, and this time she yielded too – or rather, there was nothing so deliberate as requesting or yielding in the matter: there was a sudden impulse that neither could resist. One moment I stood and looked into her face, the next I held her to my heart, and we seemed to grow together in a close embrace from which no physical or mental force could rend us. A whispered "God bless you!" and "Go – go!" was all she said; but while she spoke she held me so fast that, without violence, I could not have obeyed her. At length, however, by some heroic effort, we tore ourselves apart, and I rushed from the house.

I have a confused remembrance of seeing little Arthur running up the garden-walk to meet me, and of bolting over the wall to avoid him – and subsequently running down the steep fields, clearing the stone fences and hedges as they came in my way, till I got completely out of sight of the old hall and down to the bottom of the hill; and then of long hours spent in bitter tears and lamentations, and melancholy musings in the lonely valley, with the eternal music in my ears, of the west wind rushing through the overshadowing trees, and the brook babbling and gurgling along its stony bed; my eyes, for the most part, vacantly fixed on the deep, chequered shades restlessly playing over the bright sunny grass at my feet, where now and then a withered leaf or two would come dancing to share the revelry; but my heart was away up the hill in that dark room where she was weeping desolate and alone – she whom I was not to comfort, not to see again, till years or suffering had overcome us both, and torn our spirits from their perishing abodes of clay.

There was little business done that day, you may be sure. The farm was abandoned to the labourers, and the labourers were left to their own devices. But one duty must be attended to; I had not forgotten my assault upon Frederick Lawrence; and I must see him to apologise for the unhappy deed. I would fain have put it off till the morrow; but what if he should denounce me to his sister in the meantime? No, no! I must ask his pardon today, and entreat him to be lenient in his accusation, if the revelation must be made. I deferred it, however, till the evening, when my spirits were more composed, and when – oh, wonderful perversity of human nature! – Some faint germs of indefinite hopes were beginning to rise in my mind; not that I intended to cherish them, after all that had been said on the subject, but there they must lie for a while, uncrushed though not encouraged, till I had learnt to live without them.

Arrived at Woodford, the young squire's abode, I found no little difficulty in obtaining admission to his presence. The servant that opened the door told me his master was very ill, and seemed to think it doubtful whether he would be able to see me. I was not going to be baulked, however. I waited calmly in the hall to be announced, but inwardly determined to take no denial. The message was such as I expected – a polite intimation that Mr. Lawrence could see no one; he was feverish, and must not be disturbed.

"I shall not disturb him long," said I; "but I must see him for a moment: it is on business of importance that I wish to speak to him."

"I'll tell him, sir," said the man. And I advanced further into the hall and followed him nearly to the door of the apartment where his master was – for it seemed he was not in bed. The answer returned was that Mr. Lawrence hoped I would be so good as to leave a message or a note with the servant, as he could attend to no business at present.

"He may as well see me as you," said I; and, stepping past the astonished footman, I boldly rapped at the door, entered, and closed it behind me. The room was spacious and handsomely furnished – very comfortably, too, for a bachelor. A clear, red fire was burning in the polished grate: a superannuated greyhound, given up to idleness and good living, lay basking before it on the thick, soft rug, on one corner of which, beside the sofa, sat a smart young springer, looking wistfully up in its master's face – perhaps asking permission to share his couch, or, it might be, only soliciting a caress from his hand or a kind word from his lips. The invalid himself looked very interesting as he lay reclining there, in his elegant dressing-gown, with a silk handkerchief bound across his temples. His usually pale face was flushed and feverish; his eyes were half closed, until he became sensible of my presence – and then he opened them wide enough: one hand was thrown listlessly over the back of the sofa, and held a small volume, with which, apparently, he had been vainly attempting to beguile the weary hours. He dropped it, however, in his start of indignant surprise as I advanced into the room and stood before him on the rug. He raised himself on his pillows, and gazed upon me with equal degrees of nervous horror, anger, and amazement depicted on his countenance.

"Mr. Markham, I scarcely expected this!" he said; and the blood left his cheek as he spoke.

"I know you didn't," answered I; "but be quiet a minute, and I'll tell you what I came for." Unthinkingly, I advanced a step or two nearer. He winced at my approach, with an expression of aversion and instinctive physical fear anything but conciliatory to my feelings. I stepped back, however.

"Make your story a short one," said he, putting his hand on the small silver bell that stood on the table beside him, "or I shall be obliged to call for assistance. I am in no state to bear your brutalities now, or your presence either." And in truth the moisture started from his pores and stood on his pale forehead like dew.

Such a reception was hardly calculated to diminish the difficulties of my unenviable task. It must be performed however, in some fashion; and so I plunged into it at once, and floundered through it as I could.

"The truth is, Lawrence," said I, "I have not acted quite correctly towards you of late – especially on this last occasion; and I'm come to – in short, to express my regret for what has been done, and to beg your pardon. If you don't choose to grant it," I added hastily, not liking the aspect of his face, "it's no matter; only I've done my duty – that's all."

"It's easily done," replied he, with a faint smile bordering on a sneer: "to abuse your friend and knock him on the head without any assignable cause, and then tell him the deed was not quite correct, but it's no matter whether he pardons it or not."

"I forgot to tell you that it was in consequence of a mistake," – muttered I. "I should have made a very handsome apology, but you provoked me so confoundedly with your —. Well, I suppose it's my fault. The fact is, I didn't know that you were Mrs. Graham's brother, and I saw and heard some things respecting your conduct towards her which were calculated to awaken unpleasant suspicions, that, allow me to say, a little candour and confidence on your part might have removed; and, at last, I chanced to overhear a part of a conversation between you and her that made me think I had a right to hate you."

"And how came you to know that I was her brother?" asked he, in some anxiety.

"She told me herself. She told me all. She knew I might be trusted. But you needn't disturb yourself about that, Mr. Lawrence, for I've seen the last of her!"

"The last! Is she gone, then?"

"No; but she has bid adieu to me, and I have promised never to go near that house again while she inhabits it." I could have groaned aloud at the bitter thoughts awakened by this turn in the discourse. But I only clenched my hands and stamped my foot upon the rug. My companion, however, was evidently relieved.

"You have done right," he said, in a tone of unqualified approbation, while his face brightened into almost a sunny expression. "And as for the mistake, I am sorry for both our sakes that it should have occurred. Perhaps you can forgive my want of candour, and remember, as some partial mitigation of the offence, how little encouragement to friendly confidence you have given me of late."

"Yes, yes – I remember it all: nobody can blame me more than I blame myself in my own heart; at any rate, nobody can regret more sincerely than I do the result of my brutality, as you rightly term it."

"Never mind that," said he, faintly smiling; "let us forget all unpleasant words on both sides, as well as deeds, and consign to oblivion everything that we have cause to regret. Have you any objection to take my hand, or you'd rather not?" It trembled through weakness as he held it out, and dropped before I had time to catch it and give it a hearty squeeze, which he had not the strength to return.

"How dry and burning your hand is, Lawrence," said I. "You are really ill, and I have made you worse by all this talk."

"Oh, it is nothing; only a cold got by the rain."

"My doing, too."

"Never mind that. But tell me, did you mention this affair to my sister?"

"To confess the truth, I had not the courage to do so; but when you tell her, will you just say that I deeply regret it, and – ?"

"Oh, never fear! I shall say nothing against you, as long as you keep your good resolution of remaining aloof from her. She has not heard of my illness, then, that you are aware of?"

"I think not."

"I'm glad of that, for I have been all this time tormenting myself with the fear that somebody would tell her I was dying, or desperately ill, and she would be either distressing herself on account of her inability to hear from me or do me any good, or perhaps committing the madness of coming to see me. I must contrive to let her know something about it, if I can," continued he, reflectively, "or she will be hearing some such story. Many would be glad to tell her such news, just to see how she would take it; and then she might expose herself to fresh scandal."

"I wish I had told her," said I. "If it were not for my promise, I would tell her now."

"By no means! I am not dreaming of that; – but if I were to write a short note, now, not mentioning you, Markham, but just giving a slight account of my illness, by way of excuse for my not coming to see her, and to put her on her guard against any exaggerated reports she may hear, – and address it in a disguised hand – would you do me the favour to slip it into the post-office as you pass? For I dare not trust any of the servants in such a case."

Most willingly I consented, and immediately brought him his desk. There was little need to disguise his hand, for the poor fellow seemed to have considerable difficulty in writing at all, so as to be legible. When the note was done, I thought it time to retire, and took leave, after asking if there was anything in the world I could do for him, little or great, in the way of alleviating his sufferings, and repairing the injury I had done.

"No," said he; "you have already done much towards it; you have done more for me than the most skilful physician could do: for you have relieved my mind of two great burdens – anxiety on my sister's account, and deep regret upon your own: for I do believe these two sources of torment have had more effect in working me up into a fever than anything else; and I am persuaded I shall soon recover now. There is one more thing you can do for me, and that is, come and see me now and then – for you see I am very lonely here, and I promise your entrance shall not be disputed again."

I engaged to do so, and departed with a cordial pressure of the hand. I posted the letter on my way home, most manfully resisting the temptation of dropping in a word from myself at the same time.

Chapter Forty-Six

I FELT STRONGLY tempted, at times, to enlighten my mother and sister on the real character and circumstances of the persecuted tenant of Wildfell Hall, and at first I greatly regretted having omitted to ask that lady's permission to do so; but, on due reflection, I considered that if it were known to them, it could not long remain a secret to the Millwards and Wilsons, and such was my present appreciation of Eliza Millward's disposition, that, if once she got a clue to the story, I should fear she would soon find means to enlighten Mr. Huntingdon upon the place of his wife's retreat. I would therefore wait patiently till these weary six months were over, and then, when the fugitive had found another home, and I was permitted to write to her, I would beg to be allowed to clear her name from these vile calumnies: at present I must content myself with simply asserting that I knew them to be false, and would prove it some day, to the shame of those who slandered her. I don't think anybody believed me, but everybody soon learned to avoid insinuating a word against her, or even mentioning her name in my presence. They thought I was so madly infatuated by the seductions of that unhappy lady that I was determined to support her in the very face of reason; and meantime I grow insupportably morose and misanthropical from the idea that every one I met was harbouring unworthy thoughts of the supposed Mrs. Graham, and would express them if he dared. My poor mother was quite distressed about me; but I couldn't help it – at least I thought I could not, though sometimes I felt a pang of remorse for my undutiful conduct to her, and made an effort to amend, attended with some partial success; and indeed I was generally more humanised in my demeanour to her than to any one else, Mr. Lawrence excepted. Rose and Fergus usually shunned my presence; and it was well they did, for I was not fit company for them, nor they for me, under the present circumstances.

Mrs. Huntingdon did not leave Wildfell Hall till above two months after our farewell interview. During that time she never appeared at church, and I never went near the house: I only knew she was still there by her brother's brief answers to my many and varied inquiries respecting her. I was a very constant and attentive visitor to him throughout the whole period of his illness and convalescence; not only from the interest I took in his recovery, and my desire to cheer him up and make the utmost possible amends for my former 'brutality,' but from my growing attachment to himself, and the increasing pleasure I found in his society – partly from his increased cordiality to me, but chiefly on account of his close connection, both in blood and in affection, with my adored Helen. I loved him for it better than I liked to express: and I took a secret delight in pressing those slender white fingers, so marvellously like her own, considering he was not a woman, and in watching the passing changes in his fair, pale features, and observing the intonations of his voice, detecting resemblances which I wondered had never struck me before. He provoked me at times, indeed, by his evident reluctance to talk to me about his sister, though I did not question the friendliness of his motives in wishing to discourage my remembrance of her.

His recovery was not quite so rapid as he had expected it to be; he was not able to mount his pony till a fortnight after the date of our reconciliation; and the first use he made of his returning strength was to ride over by night to Wildfell Hall, to see his sister. It was a hazardous enterprise both for him and for her, but he thought it necessary to consult with her on the subject of her projected departure, if not to calm her apprehensions respecting his health, and the worst result was a slight relapse of his illness, for no one knew of the visit but the inmates of the old Hall, except myself; and I believe it had not been his intention to mention it to me, for when I came to see him the next day, and observed he was not so well as he ought to have been, he merely said he had caught cold by being out too late in the evening.

"You'll never be able to see your sister, if you don't take care of yourself," said I, a little provoked at the circumstance on her account, instead of commiserating him.

"I've seen her already," said he, quietly.

"You've seen her!" cried I, in astonishment.

"Yes." And then he told me what considerations had impelled him to make the venture, and with what precautions he had made it.

"And how was she?" I eagerly asked.

"As usual," was the brief though sad reply.

"As usual – that is, far from happy and far from strong."

"She is not positively ill," returned he; "and she will recover her spirits in a while, I have no doubt – but so many trials have been almost too much for her. How threatening those clouds look," continued he, turning towards the window. "We shall have thunder-showers before night, I imagine, and they are just in the midst of stacking my corn. Have you got yours all in yet?"

"No. And, Lawrence, did she – did your sister mention me?"

"She asked if I had seen you lately."

"And what else did she say?"

"I cannot tell you all she said," replied he, with a slight smile; "for we talked a good deal, though my stay was but short; but our conversation was chiefly on the subject of her intended departure, which I begged her to delay till I was better able to assist her in her search after another home."

"But did she say no more about me?"

"She did not say much about you, Markham. I should not have encouraged her to do so, had she been inclined; but happily she was not: she only asked a few questions concerning you, and seemed satisfied with my brief answers, wherein she showed herself wiser than her friend; and I may tell you, too, that she seemed to be far more anxious lest you should think too much of her, than lest you should forget her."

"She was right."

"But I fear your anxiety is quite the other way respecting her."

"No, it is not: I wish her to be happy; but I don't wish her to forget me altogether. She knows it is impossible that I should forget her; and she is right to wish me not to remember her too well. I should not desire her to regret me too deeply; but I can scarcely imagine she will make herself very unhappy about me, because I know I am not worthy of it, except in my appreciation of her."

"You are neither of you worthy of a broken heart, – nor of all the sighs, and tears, and sorrowful thoughts that have been, and I fear will be, wasted upon you both; but, at present, each has a more exalted opinion of the other than, I fear, he or she deserves; and my sister's feelings are naturally full as keen as yours, and I believe more constant; but she has the good sense and fortitude to strive against them in this particular; and I trust she will not rest till she has entirely weaned her thoughts –" he hesitated.

"From me," said I.

"And I wish you would make the like exertions," continued he.

"Did she tell you that that was her intention?"

"No; the question was not broached between us: there was no necessity for it, for I had no doubt that such was her determination."

"To forget me?"

"Yes, Markham! Why not?"

"Oh, well!" was my only audible reply; but I internally answered, – "No, Lawrence, you're wrong there: she is not determined to forget me. It would be wrong to forget one so deeply and fondly devoted to her, who can so thoroughly appreciate her excellencies, and sympathise with all her thoughts, as I can do, and it would be wrong in me to forget so excellent and divine a piece of God's creation as she, when I have once so truly loved and known her." But I said no more to him on that subject. I instantly started a new topic of conversation, and soon took leave of my companion, with a feeling of less cordiality towards him than usual. Perhaps I had no right to be annoyed at him, but I was so nevertheless.

In little more than a week after this I met him returning from a visit to the Wilsons'; and I now resolved to do him a good turn, though at the expense of his feelings, and perhaps at the risk of incurring that displeasure which is so commonly the reward of those who give disagreeable information, or tender their advice unasked. In this, believe me, I was actuated by no motives of revenge for the occasional annoyances I had lately sustained from him, – nor yet by any feeling of malevolent enmity towards Miss Wilson, but purely by the fact that I could not endure that such a woman should be Mrs. Huntingdon's sister, and that, as well for his own sake as for hers, I could not bear to think of his being deceived into a union with one so unworthy of him, and so utterly unfitted to be the partner of his quiet home, and the companion of his life. He had had uncomfortable suspicions on that head himself, I imagined; but such was his inexperience, and such were the lady's powers of attraction, and her skill in bringing them to bear upon his young imagination, that they had not disturbed him long; and I believe the only effectual causes of the vacillating indecision that had preserved him hitherto from making an actual declaration of love, was the consideration of her connections, and especially of her mother, whom he could not abide. Had they lived at a distance, he might have surmounted the objection, but within two or three miles of Woodford it was really no light matter.

"You've been to call on the Wilsons, Lawrence," said I, as I walked beside his pony.

"Yes," replied he, slightly averting his face: "I thought it but civil to take the first opportunity of returning their kind attentions, since they have been so very particular and constant in their inquiries throughout the whole course of my illness."

"It's all Miss Wilson's doing."

"And if it is," returned he, with a very perceptible blush, "is that any reason why I should not make a suitable acknowledgment?"

"It is a reason why you should not make the acknowledgment she looks for."

"Let us drop that subject if you please," said he, in evident displeasure.

"No, Lawrence, with your leave we'll continue it a while longer; and I'll tell you something, now we're about it, which you may believe or not as you choose – only please to remember that it is not my custom to speak falsely, and that in this case I can have no motive for misrepresenting the truth –"

"Well, Markham, what now?"

"Miss Wilson hates your sister. It may be natural enough that, in her ignorance of the relationship, she should feel some degree of enmity against her, but no good or amiable woman would be capable of evincing that bitter, cold-blooded, designing malice towards a fancied rival that I have observed in her."

"Markham!"

"Yes – and it is my belief that Eliza Millward and she, if not the very originators of the slanderous reports that have been propagated, were designedly the encouragers and chief disseminators of them. She was not desirous to mix up your name in the matter, of course, but her delight was, and still is, to blacken your sister's character to the utmost of her power, without risking too greatly the exposure of her own malevolence!"

"I cannot believe it," interrupted my companion, his face burning with indignation.

"Well, as I cannot prove it, I must content myself with asserting that it is so to the best of my belief; but as you would not willingly marry Miss Wilson if it were so, you will do well to be cautious, till you have proved it to be otherwise."

"I never told you, Markham, that I intended to marry Miss Wilson," said he, proudly.

"No, but whether you do or not, she intends to marry you."

"Did she tell you so?"

"No, but –"

"Then you have no right to make such an assertion respecting her." He slightly quickened his pony's pace, but I laid my hand on its mane, determined he should not leave me yet.

"Wait a moment, Lawrence, and let me explain myself; and don't be so very – I don't know what to call it – inaccessible as you are. – I know what you think of Jane Wilson; and I believe I know how far you are mistaken in your opinion: you think she is singularly charming, elegant, sensible, and refined: you are not aware that she is selfish, cold-hearted, ambitious, artful, shallow-minded –"

"Enough, Markham – enough!"

"No; let me finish: – you don't know that, if you married her, your home would be rayless and comfortless; and it would break your heart at last to find yourself united to one so wholly incapable of sharing your tastes, feelings, and ideas – so utterly destitute of sensibility, good feeling, and true nobility of soul."

"Have you done?" asked my companion quietly.

"Yes; – I know you hate me for my impertinence, but I don't care if it only conduces to preserve you from that fatal mistake."

"Well!" returned he, with a rather wintry smile – "I'm glad you have overcome or forgotten your own afflictions so far as to be able to study so deeply the affairs of others, and trouble your head so unnecessarily about the fancied or possible calamities of their future life."

We parted – somewhat coldly again: but still we did not cease to be friends; and my well-meant warning, though it might have been more judiciously delivered, as well as more thankfully received, was not wholly unproductive of the desired effect: his visit to the Wilsons was not repeated, and though, in our subsequent interviews, he never mentioned her name to me, nor I to him, – I have reason to believe he pondered my words in his mind, eagerly though covertly sought information respecting the fair lady from other quarters, secretly compared my character of her with what he had himself observed and what he heard from others, and finally came to the conclusion that, all things considered, she had much better remain Miss Wilson of Ryecote Farm than be transmuted into Mrs. Lawrence of Woodford Hall. I believe, too, that he soon learned to contemplate with secret amazement his former predilection, and to congratulate himself on the lucky escape he had made; but he never confessed it to me, or hinted one word of acknowledgment for the part I had had in his deliverance, but this was not surprising to any one that knew him as I did.

As for Jane Wilson, she, of course, was disappointed and embittered by the sudden cold neglect and ultimate desertion of her former admirer. Had I done wrong to blight her cherished hopes? I think not; and certainly my conscience has never accused me, from that day to this, of any evil design in the matter.

Chapter Forty-Seven

ONE MORNING, about the beginning of November, while I was inditing some business letters, shortly after breakfast, Eliza Millward came to call upon my sister. Rose had neither the discrimination nor the virulence to regard the little demon as I did, and they still preserved their former intimacy. At the moment of her arrival, however, there was no one in the room but Fergus and myself, my mother and sister being both of them absent, 'on household cares intent'; but I was not going to lay myself out for her amusement, whoever else might so incline: I merely honoured her with a careless salutation and a few words of course, and then went on with my writing, leaving my brother to be more polite if he chose. But she wanted to tease me.

"What a pleasure it is to find you at home, Mr. Markham!" said she, with a disingenuously malicious smile. "I so seldom see you now, for you never come to the vicarage. Papa, is quite offended, I can tell you," she added playfully, looking into my face with an impertinent laugh, as she seated herself, half beside and half before my desk, off the corner of the table.

"I have had a good deal to do of late," said I, without looking up from my letter.

"Have you, indeed! Somebody said you had been strangely neglecting your business these last few months."

"Somebody said wrong, for, these last two months especially, I have been particularly plodding and diligent."

"Ah! Well, there's nothing like active employment, I suppose, to console the afflicted; – and, excuse me, Mr. Markham, but you look so very far from well, and have been, by all accounts, so moody and thoughtful of late, – I could almost think you have some secret care preying on your spirits. Formerly," said she timidly, "I could have ventured to ask you what it was, and what I could do to comfort you: I dare not do it now."

"You're very kind, Miss Eliza. When I think you can do anything to comfort me, I'll make bold to tell you."

"Pray do! – I suppose I mayn't guess what it is that troubles you?"

"There's no necessity, for I'll tell you plainly. The thing that troubles me the most at present is a young lady sitting at my elbow, and preventing me from finishing my letter, and, thereafter, repairing to my daily business."

Before she could reply to this ungallant speech, Rose entered the room; and Miss Eliza rising to greet her, they both seated themselves near the fire, where that idle lad Fergus was standing, leaning his shoulder against the corner of the chimney-piece, with his legs crossed and his hands in his breeches-pockets.

"Now, Rose, I'll tell you a piece of news – I hope you have not heard it before: for good, bad, or indifferent, one always likes to be the first to tell. It's about that sad Mrs. Graham –"

"Hush-sh-sh!" whispered Fergus, in a tone of solemn import. "We never mention her; her name is never heard." And glancing up, I caught him with his eye askance on me, and his finger pointed to his forehead; then, winking at the young lady with a doleful shake of the head, he whispered – "A monomania – but don't mention it – all right but that."

"I should be sorry to injure any one's feelings," returned she, speaking below her breath. "Another time, perhaps."

"Speak out, Miss Eliza!" said I, not deigning to notice the other's buffooneries: "you needn't fear to say anything in my presence."

"Well," answered she, "perhaps you know already that Mrs. Graham's husband is not really dead, and that she had run away from him?" I started, and felt my face glow; but I bent it over my letter, and went on folding it up as she proceeded. "But perhaps you did not know that she is now gone back to him again, and that a perfect reconciliation has taken place between them? Only think," she continued, turning to the confounded Rose, "what a fool the man must be!"

"And who gave you this piece of intelligence, Miss Eliza?" said I, interrupting my sister's exclamations.

"I had it from a very authentic source."

"From whom, may I ask?"

"From one of the servants at Woodford."

"Oh! I was not aware that you were on such intimate terms with Mr. Lawrence's household."

"It was not from the man himself that I heard it, but he told it in confidence to our maid Sarah, and Sarah told it to me."

"In confidence, I suppose? And you tell it in confidence to us? But I can tell you that it is but a lame story after all, and scarcely one-half of it true."

While I spoke I completed the sealing and direction of my letters, with a somewhat unsteady hand, in spite of all my efforts to retain composure, and in spite of my firm conviction that the story was a lame one – that the supposed Mrs. Graham, most certainly, had not voluntarily gone back to her husband, or dreamt of a reconciliation. Most likely she was gone away, and the tale-bearing servant, not knowing what was become of her, had conjectured that such was the case, and our fair visitor had detailed it as a certainty, delighted with such an opportunity of tormenting me. But it was possible – barely possible – that some one might have betrayed her, and she had been taken away by force. Determined to know the worst, I hastily pocketed my two letters, and muttered something about being too late for the post, left the room, rushed into the yard, and vociferously called for my horse. No one being there, I dragged him out of the stable myself, strapped the saddle on to his back and the bridle on to his head, mounted, and speedily galloped away to Woodford. I found its owner pensively strolling in the grounds.

"Is your sister gone?" were my first words as I grasped his hand, instead of the usual inquiry after his health.

"Yes, she's gone," was his answer, so calmly spoken that my terror was at once removed.

"I suppose I mayn't know where she is?" said I, as I dismounted, and relinquished my horse to the gardener, who, being the only servant within call, had been summoned by his master, from his employment of raking up the dead leaves on the lawn, to take him to the stables.

My companion gravely took my arm, and leading me away to the garden, thus answered my question, – "She is at Grassdale Manor, in —shire."

"Where?" cried I, with a convulsive start.

"At Grassdale Manor."

"How was it?" I gasped. "Who betrayed her?"

"She went of her own accord."

"Impossible, Lawrence! She could not be so frantic!" exclaimed I, vehemently grasping his arm, as if to force him to unsay those hateful words.

"She did," persisted he in the same grave, collected manner as before; "and not without reason," he continued, gently disengaging himself from my grasp. "Mr. Huntingdon is ill."

"And so she went to nurse him?"

"Yes."

"Fool!" I could not help exclaiming, and Lawrence looked up with a rather reproachful glance. "Is he dying, then?"

"I think not, Markham."

"And how many more nurses has he? How many ladies are there besides to take care of him?"

"None; he was alone, or she would not have gone."

"Oh, confound it! This is intolerable!"

"What is? That he should be alone?"

I attempted no reply, for I was not sure that this circumstance did not partly conduce to my distraction. I therefore continued to pace the walk in silent anguish, with my hand pressed to my forehead; then suddenly pausing and turning to my companion, I impatiently exclaimed, "Why did she take this infatuated step? What fiend persuaded her to it?"

"Nothing persuaded her but her own sense of duty."

"Humbug!"

"I was half inclined to say so myself, Markham, at first. I assure you it was not by my advice that she went, for I detest that man as fervently as you can do, – except, indeed, that his reformation would give me much greater pleasure than his death; but all I did was to inform her of the circumstance of his illness (the consequence of a fall from his horse in hunting), and to tell her that that unhappy person, Miss Myers, had left him some time ago."

"It was ill done! Now, when he finds the convenience of her presence, he will make all manner of lying speeches and false, fair promises for the future, and she will believe him, and then her condition will be ten times worse and ten times more irremediable than before."

"There does not appear to be much ground for such apprehensions at present," said he, producing a letter from his pocket. "From the account I received this morning, I should say –"

It was her writing! By an irresistible impulse I held out my hand, and the words, "Let me see it," involuntarily passed my lips. He was evidently reluctant to grant the request, but while he hesitated I snatched it from his hand. Recollecting myself, however, the minute after, I offered to restore it.

"Here, take it," said I, "if you don't want me to read it."

"No," replied he, "you may read it if you like."

I read it, and so may you.

Grassdale, Nov. 4th.

Dear Frederick, – I know you will be anxious to hear from me, and I will tell you all I can. Mr. Huntingdon is very ill, but not dying, or in any immediate danger; and he is rather better at present than he was when I came. I found the house in sad confusion: Mrs. Greaves, Benson, every decent servant had left, and those that were come to supply their places were a negligent, disorderly set, to say no worse – I must change them again, if I stay. A professional nurse, a grim, hard old woman, had been hired to attend the wretched invalid. He suffers much, and has no fortitude to bear him through. The immediate injuries he sustained from the accident, however, were not very severe, and would, as the doctor says, have been but trifling to a man of temperate habits, but with him it is very different. On the night of my arrival, when I first entered his room, he was lying in a kind of half delirium. He did not notice me till I spoke, and then he mistook me for another.

"Is it you, Alice, come again?" he murmured. "What did you leave me for?"

"It is I, Arthur – it is Helen, your wife," I replied.

"My wife!" said he, with a start. "For heaven's sake, don't mention her – I have none. Devil take her," he cried, a moment after, "and you, too! What did you do it for?"

I said no more; but observing that he kept gazing towards the foot of the bed, I went and sat there, placing the light so as to shine full upon me, for I thought he might be dying, and I wanted him to know me. For a long time he lay silently looking upon me, first with a vacant stare, then with a fixed gaze of strange growing intensity. At last he startled me by suddenly raising himself on his elbow and demanding in a horrified whisper, with his eyes still fixed upon me, "Who is it?"

"It is Helen Huntingdon," said I, quietly rising at the same time, and removing to a less conspicuous position.

"I must be going mad," cried he, "or something – delirious, perhaps; but leave me, whoever you are. I can't bear that white face, and those eyes. For God's sake go, and send me somebody else that doesn't look like that!"

I went at once, and sent the hired nurse; but next morning I ventured to enter his chamber again, and, taking the nurse's place by his bedside, I watched him and waited on him for several hours, showing myself as little as possible, and only speaking when necessary, and then not above my breath. At first he addressed me as the nurse, but, on my crossing the room to draw up the window-blinds, in obedience to his directions, he said, "No, it isn't nurse; it's Alice. Stay with me, do! That old hag will be the death of me."

"I mean to stay with you," said I. And after that he would call me Alice, or some other name almost equally repugnant to my feelings. I forced myself to endure it for a while, fearing a contradiction might disturb him too much; but when, having asked for a glass of water, while I held it to his lips, he murmured, "Thanks, dearest!" I could not help distinctly observing, "You would not say so if you knew me," intending to follow that up with another declaration of my identity; but he merely muttered an incoherent reply, so I dropped it again, till some time after, when, as I was bathing his forehead and temples with vinegar and water to relieve the heat and pain in his head, he observed, after looking earnestly upon me for some minutes, "I have such strange fancies – I can't get rid of them, and they won't let me rest; and the most singular and pertinacious of them all is your face and voice – they seem just like hers. I could swear at this moment that she was by my side."

"She is," said I.

"That seems comfortable," continued he, without noticing my words; "and while you do it, the other fancies fade away – but this only strengthens. – Go on – go on, till it vanishes, too. I can't stand such a mania as this; it would kill me!"

"It never will vanish," said I, distinctly, "for it is the truth!"

"The truth!" he cried, starting, as if an asp had stung him. "You don't mean to say that you are really she?"

"I do; but you needn't shrink away from me, as if I were your greatest enemy: I am come to take care of you, and do what none of them would do."

"For God's sake, don't torment me now!" cried he in pitiable agitation; and then he began to mutter bitter curses against me, or the evil fortune that had brought me there; while I put down the sponge and basin, and resumed my seat at the bedside.

"Where are they?" said he: "have they all left me – servants and all?"

"There are servants within call if you want them; but you had better lie down now and be quiet: none of them could or would attend you as carefully as I shall do."

"I can't understand it at all," said he, in bewildered perplexity. "Was it a dream that –" and he covered his eyes with his hands, as if trying to unravel the mystery.

"No, Arthur, it was not a dream, that your conduct was such as to oblige me to leave you; but I heard that you were ill and alone, and I am come back to nurse you. You need not fear to trust me: tell me all your wants, and I will try to satisfy them. There is no one else to care for you; and I shall not upbraid you now."

"Oh! I see," said he, with a bitter smile; "it's an act of Christian charity, whereby you hope to gain a higher seat in heaven for yourself, and scoop a deeper pit in hell for me."

"No; I came to offer you that comfort and assistance your situation required; and if I could benefit your soul as well as your body, and awaken some sense of contrition and –"

"Oh, yes; if you could overwhelm me with remorse and confusion of face, now's the time. What have you done with my son?"

"He is well, and you may see him some time, if you will compose yourself, but not now."

"Where is he?"

"He is safe."

"Is he here?"

"Wherever he is, you will not see him till you have promised to leave him entirely under my care and protection, and to let me take him away whenever and wherever I please, if I should hereafter judge it necessary to remove him again. But we will talk of that tomorrow: you must be quiet now."

"No, let me see him now, I promise, if it must be so."

"No –"

"I swear it, as God is in heaven! Now, then, let me see him."

"But I cannot trust your oaths and promises: I must have a written agreement, and you must sign it in presence of a witness: but not today – tomorrow."

"No, today; now," persisted he: and he was in such a state of feverish excitement, and so bent upon the immediate gratification of his wish, that I thought it better to grant it at once, as I saw he would not rest till I did. But I was determined my son's interest should not be forgotten; and having clearly written out the promise I wished Mr. Huntingdon to give upon a slip of paper, I deliberately read it over to him, and made him sign it in the presence of Rachel. He begged I would not insist upon this: it was a useless exposure of my want of faith in his word to the servant. I told him I was sorry, but since he had forfeited my confidence, he must take the consequence. He next pleaded inability to hold the pen. "Then we must wait until you can hold it," said I. Upon which he said he would try; but then he could not see to write. I placed my finger where the signature was to be, and told him he might write his name in the dark, if he only knew where to put it. But he had not power to form the letters. "In that case, you must be too ill to see the child," said I; and finding me inexorable, he at length managed to ratify the agreement; and I bade Rachel send the boy.

All this may strike you as harsh, but I felt I must not lose my present advantage, and my son's future welfare should not be sacrificed to any mistaken tenderness for this man's feelings. Little Arthur had not forgotten his father, but thirteen months of absence, during which he had seldom been permitted to hear a word about him, or hardly to whisper his name, had rendered him somewhat shy; and when he was ushered into the darkened room where the sick man lay, so altered from his former self, with fiercely flushed face and wildly-gleaming eyes – he instinctively clung to me, and stood looking on his father with a countenance expressive of far more awe than pleasure.

"Come here, Arthur," said the latter, extending his hand towards him. The child went, and timidly touched that burning hand, but almost started in alarm, when his father suddenly clutched his arm and drew him nearer to his side.

"Do you know me?" asked Mr. Huntingdon, intently perusing his features.

"Yes."

"Who am I?"

"Papa."

"Are you glad to see me?"

"Yes."

"You're not!" replied the disappointed parent, relaxing his hold, and darting a vindictive glance at me.

Arthur, thus released, crept back to me and put his hand in mine. His father swore I had made the child hate him, and abused and cursed me bitterly. The instant he began I sent our son out of the room; and when he paused to breathe, I calmly assured him that he was entirely mistaken; I had never once attempted to prejudice his child against him.

"I did indeed desire him to forget you," I said, "and especially to forget the lessons you taught him; and for that cause, and to lessen the danger of discovery, I own I have generally discouraged his inclination to talk about you; but no one can blame me for that, I think."

The invalid only replied by groaning aloud, and rolling his head on a pillow in a paroxysm of impatience.

"I am in hell, already!" cried he. "This cursed thirst is burning my heart to ashes! Will nobody – ?"

Before he could finish the sentence I had poured out a glass of some acidulated, cooling drink that was on the table, and brought it to him. He drank it greedily, but muttered, as I took away the glass, – "I suppose you're heaping coals of fire on my head, you think?"

Not noticing this speech, I asked if there was anything else I could do for him.

"Yes; I'll give you another opportunity of showing your Christian magnanimity," sneered he: "set my pillow straight, and these confounded bed-clothes." I did so. "There: now get me another glass of that slop." I complied. "This is delightful, isn't it?" said he with a malicious grin, as I held it to his lips; "you never hoped for such a glorious opportunity?"

"Now, shall I stay with you?" said I, as I replaced the glass on the table: "or will you be more quiet if I go and send the nurse?"

"Oh, yes, you're wondrous gentle and obliging! But you've driven me mad with it all!" responded he, with an impatient toss.

"I'll leave you, then," said I; and I withdrew, and did not trouble him with my presence again that day, except for a minute or two at a time, just to see how he was and what he wanted.

Next morning the doctor ordered him to be bled; and after that he was more subdued and tranquil. I passed half the day in his room at different intervals. My presence did not appear to agitate or irritate him as before, and he accepted my services quietly, without any bitter remarks: indeed, he scarcely spoke at all, except to make known his wants, and hardly then. But on the morrow, that is to say, in proportion as he recovered from the state of exhaustion and stupefaction, his ill-nature appeared to revive.

"Oh, this sweet revenge!" cried he, when I had been doing all I could to make him comfortable and to remedy the carelessness of his nurse. "And you can enjoy it with such a quiet conscience too, because it's all in the way of duty."

"It is well for me that I am doing my duty," said I, with a bitterness I could not repress, "for it is the only comfort I have; and the satisfaction of my own conscience, it seems, is the only reward I need look for!"

He looked rather surprised at the earnestness of my manner.

"What reward did you look for?" he asked.

"You will think me a liar if I tell you; but I did hope to benefit you: as well to better your mind as to alleviate your present sufferings; but it appears I am to do neither; your own bad spirit will not let me. As far as you are concerned, I have sacrificed my own feelings, and all the little earthly comfort that was left me, to no purpose; and every little thing I do for you is ascribed to self-righteous malice and refined revenge!"

"It's all very fine, I daresay," said he, eyeing me with stupid amazement; "and of course I ought to be melted to tears of penitence and admiration at the sight of so much generosity and superhuman goodness; but you see I can't manage it. However, pray do me all the good you can, if you do really find any pleasure in it; for you perceive I am almost as miserable just now as you need wish to see me. Since you came, I confess, I have had better attendance than before, for these wretches neglected me shamefully, and all my old friends seem to have fairly forsaken me. I've had a dreadful time of it, I assure you: I sometimes thought I should have died: do you think there's any chance?"

"There's always a chance of death; and it is always well to live with such a chance in view."

"Yes, yes! But do you think there's any likelihood that this illness will have a fatal termination?"

"I cannot tell; but, supposing it should, how are you prepared to meet the event?"

"Why, the doctor told me I wasn't to think about it, for I was sure to get better if I stuck to his regimen and prescriptions."

"I hope you may, Arthur; but neither the doctor nor I can speak with certainty in such a case; there is internal injury, and it is difficult to know to what extent."

"There now! You want to scare me to death."

"No; but I don't want to lull you to false security. If a consciousness of the uncertainty of life can dispose you to serious and useful thoughts, I would not deprive you of the benefit of such reflections, whether you do eventually recover or not. Does the idea of death appal you very much?"

"It's just the only thing I can't bear to think of; so if you've any –"

"But it must come some time," interrupted I, "and if it be years hence, it will as certainly overtake you as if it came today, – and no doubt be as unwelcome then as now, unless you –"

"Oh, hang it! Don't torment me with your preachments now, unless you want to kill me outright. I can't stand it, I tell you. I've sufferings enough without that. If you think there's danger, save me from it; and then, in gratitude, I'll hear whatever you like to say."

I accordingly dropped the unwelcome topic. And now, Frederick, I think I may bring my letter to a close. From these details you may form your own judgment of the state of my patient, and of my own position and future prospects. Let me hear from you soon, and I will write again to tell you how we get on; but now that my presence is tolerated, and even required, in the sick-room, I shall have but little time to spare between my husband and my son, – for I must not entirely neglect the latter: it would not do to keep him always with Rachel, and I dare not leave him for a moment with any of the other servants, or suffer him to be alone, lest he should meet them. If his father get worse, I shall ask Esther Hargrave to take charge of him for a time, till I have reorganised the household at least; but I greatly prefer keeping him under my own eye.

I find myself in rather a singular position: I am exerting my utmost endeavours to promote the recovery and reformation of my husband, and if I succeed, what shall I do? My duty, of course, – but how? No matter; I can perform the task that is before me now, and God will give me strength to do whatever He requires hereafter. Goodbye, dear Frederick.

Helen Huntingdon.

"What do you think of it?" said Lawrence, as I silently refolded the letter.

"It seems to me," returned I, "that she is casting her pearls before swine. May they be satisfied with trampling them under their feet, and not turn again and rend her! But I shall say no more against her: I see that she was actuated by the best and noblest motives in what she has done; and if the act is not a wise one, may heaven protect her from its consequences! May I keep this letter, Lawrence? – You see she has never once mentioned me throughout – or made the most distant allusion to me; therefore, there can be no impropriety or harm in it."

"And, therefore, why should you wish to keep it?"

"Were not these characters written by her hand? And were not these words conceived in her mind, and many of them spoken by her lips?"

"Well," said he. And so I kept it; otherwise, Halford, you could never have become so thoroughly acquainted with its contents.

"And when you write," said I, "will you have the goodness to ask her if I may be permitted to enlighten my mother and sister on her real history and circumstance, just so far as is necessary to make the neighbourhood sensible of the shameful injustice they have done her? I want no tender messages, but just ask her that, and tell her it is the greatest favour she could do me; and tell her – no, nothing more. You see I know the address, and I might write to her myself, but I am so virtuous as to refrain."

"Well, I'll do this for you, Markham."

"And as soon as you receive an answer, you'll let me know?"

"If all be well, I'll come myself and tell you immediately."

Chapter Forty-Eight

FIVE OR SIX DAYS after this Mr. Lawrence paid us the honour of a call; and when he and I were alone together – which I contrived as soon as possible by bringing him out to look at my cornstacks – he showed me another letter from his sister. This one he was quite willing to submit to my longing gaze; he thought, I suppose, it would do me good. The only answer it gave to my message was this:

"Mr. Markham is at liberty to make such revelations concerning me as he judges necessary. He will know that I should wish but little to be said on the subject. I hope he is well; but tell him he must not think of me."

I can give you a few extracts from the rest of the letter, for I was permitted to keep this also – perhaps, as an antidote to all pernicious hopes and fancies.

* * *

He is decidedly better, but very low from the depressing effects of his severe illness and the strict regimen he is obliged to observe – so opposite to all his previous habits. It is deplorable to see how completely his past life has degenerated his once noble constitution, and vitiated the whole system of his organization. But the doctor says he may now be considered out of danger, if he will only continue to observe the necessary restrictions. Some stimulating cordials he must have, but they should be judiciously diluted and sparingly used; and I find it very difficult to keep him to this. At first, his extreme dread of death rendered the task an easy one; but in proportion as he feels his acute suffering abating, and sees the danger receding, the more intractable he becomes. Now, also, his appetite for food is beginning to return; and here, too, his long habits of self-indulgence are greatly against him. I watch and restrain him as well as I can, and often get bitterly abused for my rigid severity; and sometimes he contrives to elude my vigilance, and sometimes acts in opposition to my will. But he is now so completely reconciled to my attendance in general that he is never satisfied when I am not by his side. I am obliged to be a little stiff with him sometimes, or he would make a complete slave of me; and I know it would be unpardonable weakness to give up all other interests for him. I have the servants to overlook, and my little Arthur to attend to, – and my own health too, all of which would be entirely neglected were I to satisfy his exorbitant demands. I do not generally sit up at night, for I think the nurse who has made it her business is better qualified for such undertakings than I am; – but still, an unbroken night's rest is what I but seldom enjoy, and never can venture to reckon upon; for my patient makes no scruple of calling me up at an hour when his wants or his fancies require my presence. But he is manifestly afraid of my displeasure; and if at one time he tries my patience by his unreasonable exactions, and fretful complaints and reproaches, at another he depresses me by his abject submission and deprecatory self-abasement when he fears he has gone too far. But all this I can readily pardon; I know it is chiefly the result of his enfeebled frame and disordered nerves. What annoys me the most, is his occasional attempts at affectionate fondness that I can neither credit nor return; not that I hate him: his sufferings and my own laborious care have given him some claim to my regard – to my affection even, if he would only be quiet and sincere, and content to let things remain as they are; but the more he tries to conciliate me, the more I shrink from him and from the future.

"Helen, what do you mean to do when I get well?" he asked this morning. "Will you run away again?"

"It entirely depends upon your own conduct."

"Oh, I'll be very good."

"But if I find it necessary to leave you, Arthur, I shall not 'run away': you know I have your own promise that I may go whenever I please, and take my son with me."

"Oh, but you shall have no cause." And then followed a variety of professions, which I rather coldly checked.

"Will you not forgive me, then?" said he.

"Yes, – I have forgiven you: but I know you cannot love me as you once did – and I should be very sorry if you were to, for I could not pretend to return it: so let us drop the subject, and never recur to it again. By what I have done for you, you may judge of what I will do – if it be not incompatible with the higher duty I owe to my son (higher, because he never forfeited his claims, and because I hope to do more good to him than I can ever do to you); and if you wish me to feel kindly towards you, it is deeds not words which must purchase my affection and esteem."

His sole reply to this was a slight grimace, and a scarcely perceptible shrug. Alas, unhappy man! Words, with him, are so much cheaper than deeds; it was as if I had said, 'Pounds, not pence, must buy the article you want.' And then he sighed a querulous, self-commiserating sigh, as if in pure regret that he, the loved and courted of so many worshippers, should be now abandoned to the mercy of a harsh, exacting, cold-hearted woman like that, and even glad of what kindness she chose to bestow.

"It's a pity, isn't it?" said I; and whether I rightly divined his musings or not, the observation chimed in with his thoughts, for he answered – "It can't be helped," with a rueful smile at my penetration.

* * *

I have seen Esther Hargrave twice. She is a charming creature, but her blithe spirit is almost broken, and her sweet temper almost spoiled, by the still unremitting persecutions of her mother in behalf of her rejected suitor – not violent, but wearisome and unremitting like a continual dropping. The unnatural parent seems determined to make her daughter's life a burden, if she will not yield to her desires.

"Mamma does all she can," said she, "to make me feel myself a burden and incumbrance to the family, and the most ungrateful, selfish, and undutiful daughter that ever was born; and Walter, too, is as stern and cold and haughty as if he hated me outright. I believe I should have yielded at once if I had known, from the beginning, how much resistance would have cost me; but now, for very obstinacy's sake, I will stand out!"

"A bad motive for a good resolve," I answered. "But, however, I know you have better motives, really, for your perseverance: and I counsel you to keep them still in view."

"Trust me I will. I threaten mamma sometimes that I'll run away, and disgrace the family by earning my own livelihood, if she torments me any more; and then that frightens her a little. But I will do it, in good earnest, if they don't mind."

"Be quiet and patient a while," said I, "and better times will come."

Poor girl! I wish somebody that was worthy to possess her would come and take her away – don't you, Frederick?

* * *

If the perusal of this letter filled me with dismay for Helen's future life and mine, there was one great source of consolation: it was now in my power to clear her name from every foul aspersion. The Millwards and the Wilsons should see with their own eyes the bright sun bursting from the cloud – and they should be scorched and dazzled by its beams; – and my own friends too should see it – they whose suspicions had been such gall and wormwood to my soul. To effect this I had only to drop the seed into the ground, and it would soon become a stately, branching herb: a few words to my mother and sister, I knew, would suffice to spread the news throughout the whole neighbourhood, without any further exertion on my part.

Rose was delighted; and as soon as I had told her all I thought proper – which was all I affected to know – she flew with alacrity to put on her bonnet and shawl, and hasten to carry the glad tidings to the Millwards and Wilsons – glad tidings, I suspect, to none but herself and Mary Millward – that steady, sensible girl, whose sterling worth had been so quickly perceived and duly valued by the supposed Mrs. Graham, in spite of her plain outside; and who, on her part, had been better able to see and appreciate that lady's true character and qualities than the brightest genius among them.

As I may never have occasion to mention her again, I may as well tell you here that she was at this time privately engaged to Richard Wilson – a secret, I believe, to every one but themselves. That worthy student was now at Cambridge, where his most exemplary conduct and his diligent perseverance in the pursuit of learning carried him safely through, and eventually brought him with hard-earned honours, and an untarnished reputation, to the close of his collegiate career. In due time he became Mr. Millward's first and only curate – for that gentleman's declining years forced him at last to acknowledge that the duties of his extensive parish were a little too much for those vaunted energies which he was wont to boast over his younger and less active brethren of the cloth. This was what the patient, faithful lovers had privately planned and quietly waited for years ago; and in due time they were united, to the astonishment of the little world they lived in, that had long since declared them both born to single blessedness; affirming it impossible that the pale, retiring bookworm should ever summon courage to seek a wife, or be able to obtain one if he did, and equally impossible that the plain-looking, plain-dealing, unattractive, unconciliating Miss Millward should ever find a husband.

They still continued to live at the vicarage, the lady dividing her time between her father, her husband, and their poor parishioners, – and subsequently her rising family; and now that the Reverend Michael Millward has been gathered to his fathers, full of years and honours, the Reverend Richard Wilson has succeeded him to the vicarage of Linden-hope, greatly to the satisfaction of its inhabitants, who had so long tried and fully proved his merits, and those of his excellent and well-loved partner.

If you are interested in the after fate of that lady's sister, I can only tell you – what perhaps you have heard from another quarter – that some twelve or thirteen years ago she relieved the happy couple of her presence by marrying a wealthy tradesman of L—; and I don't envy him his bargain. I fear she leads him a rather uncomfortable life, though, happily, he is too dull to perceive the extent of his misfortune. I have little enough to do with her myself: we have not met for many years; but, I am well assured, she has not yet forgotten or forgiven either her former lover, or the lady whose superior qualities first opened his eyes to the folly of his boyish attachment.

As for Richard Wilson's sister, she, having been wholly unable to recapture Mr. Lawrence, or obtain any partner rich and elegant enough to suit her ideas of what the husband of Jane Wilson ought to be, is yet in single blessedness. Shortly after the death of her mother she withdrew the light of her presence from Ryecote Farm, finding it impossible any longer to endure the rough manners and unsophisticated habits of her honest brother Robert and his worthy wife, or the idea of being identified with such vulgar people in the eyes of the world, and took lodgings in — the county town, where she lived, and still lives, I suppose, in a kind of close-fisted, cold, uncomfortable gentility, doing no good to others, and but little to herself; spending her days in fancy-work and scandal; referring frequently to her 'brother the vicar,' and her 'sister, the vicar's lady,' but never to her brother the farmer and her sister the farmer's wife; seeing as much company as she can without too much expense, but loving no one and beloved by none – a cold-hearted, supercilious, keenly, insidiously censorious old maid.

Chapter Forty-Nine

THOUGH MR. LAWRENCE'S health was now quite re-established, my visits to Woodford were as unremitting as ever; though often less protracted than before. We seldom talked about Mrs. Huntingdon; but yet we never met without mentioning her, for I never sought his company but with the hope of hearing something about her, and he never sought mine at all, because he saw me often enough without. But I always began to talk of other things, and waited first to see if he would introduce the subject. If he did not, I would casually ask, "Have you heard from your sister lately?" If he said "No," the matter was dropped: if he said "Yes," I would venture to inquire, "How is she?" but never "How is her husband?" though I might be burning to know; because I had not the hypocrisy to profess any anxiety for his recovery, and I had not the face to express any desire for a contrary result. Had I any such desire? – I fear I must plead guilty; but since you have heard my confession, you must hear my justification as well – a few of the excuses, at least, wherewith I sought to pacify my own accusing conscience.

In the first place, you see, his life did harm to others, and evidently no good to himself; and though I wished it to terminate, I would not have hastened its close if, by the lifting of a finger, I could have done so, or if a spirit had whispered in my ear that a single effort of the will would be enough, – unless, indeed, I had the power to exchange him for some other victim of the grave, whose life might be of service to his race, and whose death would be lamented by his friends. But was there any harm in wishing that, among the many thousands whose souls would certainly be required of them before the year was over, this wretched mortal might be one? I thought not; and therefore I wished with all my heart that it might please heaven to remove him to a better world, or if that might not be, still to take him out of this; for if he were unfit to answer the summons now, after a warning sickness, and with such an angel by his side, it seemed but too certain that he never would be – that, on the contrary, returning health would bring returning lust and villainy, and as he grew more certain of recovery, more accustomed to her generous goodness, his feelings would become more callous, his heart more flinty and impervious to her persuasive arguments – but God knew best. Meantime, however, I could not but be anxious for the result of His decrees; knowing, as I did, that (leaving myself entirely out of the question), however Helen might feel interested in her husband's welfare, however she might deplore his fate, still while he lived she must be miserable.

A fortnight passed away, and my inquiries were always answered in the negative. At length a welcome "yes" drew from me the second question. Lawrence divined my anxious thoughts, and appreciated my reserve. I feared, at first, he was going to torture me by unsatisfactory replies, and either leave me quite in the dark concerning what I wanted to know, or force me to drag the information out of him, morsel by morsel, by direct inquiries. "And serve you right," you will say; but he was more merciful; and in a little while he put his sister's letter into my hand. I silently read it, and restored it to him without comment or remark. This mode of procedure suited him so well, that thereafter he always pursued the plan of showing me her letters at once, when 'inquired' after her, if there were any to show – it was so much less trouble than to tell me their contents; and I received such confidences so quietly and discreetly that he was never induced to discontinue them.

But I devoured those precious letters with my eyes, and never let them go till their contents were stamped upon my mind; and when I got home, the most important passages were entered in my diary among the remarkable events of the day.

The first of these communications brought intelligence of a serious relapse in Mr. Huntingdon's illness, entirely the result of his own infatuation in persisting in the indulgence of his appetite for stimulating drink. In vain had she remonstrated, in vain she had mingled his wine with water: her arguments and entreaties were a nuisance, her interference was an insult so intolerable that, at length, on finding she had covertly diluted the pale port that was brought him, he threw the bottle out of the window, swearing he would not be cheated like a baby, ordered the butler, on pain of instant dismissal, to bring a bottle of the strongest wine in the cellar, and affirming that he should have been well long ago if he had been let to have his own way, but she wanted to keep him weak in order that she might have him under her thumb – but, by the Lord Harry, he would have no more humbug – seized a glass in one hand and the bottle in the other, and never rested till he had drunk it dry. Alarming symptoms were the immediate result of this 'imprudence,' as she mildly termed it – symptoms which had rather increased than diminished since; and this was the cause of her delay in writing to her brother. Every former feature of his malady had returned with augmented virulence: the slight external wound, half healed, had broken out afresh; internal inflammation had taken place, which might terminate fatally if not soon removed. Of course, the wretched sufferer's temper was not improved by this calamity – in fact, I suspect it was well nigh insupportable, though his kind nurse did not complain; but she said she had been obliged at last to give her son in charge to Esther Hargrave, as her presence was so constantly required in the sick-room that she could not possibly attend to him herself; and though the child had begged to be allowed to continue with her there, and to help her to nurse his papa, and though she had no doubt he would have been very good and quiet, she could not think of subjecting his young and tender feelings to the sight of so much suffering, or of allowing him to witness his father's impatience, or hear the dreadful language he was wont to use in his paroxysms of pain or irritation.

The latter (continued she) most deeply regrets the step that has occasioned his relapse; but, as usual, he throws the blame upon me. If I had reasoned with him like a rational creature, he says, it never would have happened; but to be treated like a baby or a fool was enough to put any man past his patience, and drive him to assert his independence even at the sacrifice of his own interest. He forgets how often I had reasoned him 'past his patience' before. He appears to be sensible of his danger; but nothing can induce him to behold it in the proper light. The other night, while I was waiting on him, and just as I had brought him a draught to assuage his burning thirst, he observed, with a return of his former sarcastic bitterness, "Yes, you're mighty attentive now! I suppose there's nothing you wouldn't do for me now?"

"You know," said I, a little surprised at his manner, "that I am willing to do anything I can to relieve you."

"Yes, now, my immaculate angel; but when once you have secured your reward, and find yourself safe in heaven, and me howling in hell-fire, catch you lifting a finger to serve me then! No, you'll look complacently on, and not so much as dip the tip of your finger in water to cool my tongue!"

"If so, it will be because of the great gulf over which I cannot pass; and if I could look complacently on in such a case, it would be only from the assurance that you were being purified from your sins, and fitted to enjoy the happiness I felt. – But are you determined, Arthur, that I shall not meet you in heaven?"

"Humph! What should I do there, I should like to know?"

"Indeed, I cannot tell; and I fear it is too certain that your tastes and feelings must be widely altered before you can have any enjoyment there. But do you prefer sinking, without an effort, into the state of torment you picture to yourself?"

"Oh, it's all a fable," said he, contemptuously.

"Are you sure, Arthur? Are you quite sure? Because, if there is any doubt, and if you should find yourself mistaken after all, when it is too late to turn –"

"It would be rather awkward, to be sure," said he; "but don't bother me now – I'm not going to die yet. I can't and won't," he added vehemently, as if suddenly struck with the appalling aspect of that terrible event. "Helen, you must save me!" And he earnestly seized my hand, and looked into my face with such imploring eagerness that my heart bled for him, and I could not speak for tears.

* * *

The next letter brought intelligence that the malady was fast increasing; and the poor sufferer's horror of death was still more distressing than his impatience of bodily pain. All his friends had not forsaken him; for Mr. Hattersley, hearing of his danger, had come to see him from his distant home in the north. His wife had accompanied him, as much for the pleasure of seeing her dear friend, from whom she had been parted so long, as to visit her mother and sister.

Mrs. Huntingdon expressed herself glad to see Milicent once more, and pleased to behold her so happy and well. She is now at the Grove, continued the letter, but she often calls to see me. Mr. Hattersley spends much of his time at Arthur's bedside. With more good feeling than I gave him credit for, he evinces considerable sympathy for his unhappy friend, and is far more willing than able to comfort him. Sometimes he tries to joke and laugh with him, but that will not do; sometimes he endeavours to cheer him with talk about old times, and this at one time may serve to divert the sufferer from his own sad thoughts; at another, it will only plunge him into deeper melancholy than before; and then Hattersley is confounded, and knows not what to say, unless it be a timid suggestion that the clergyman might be sent for. But Arthur will never consent to that: he knows he has rejected the clergyman's well-meant admonitions with scoffing levity at other times, and cannot dream of turning to him for consolation now.

Mr. Hattersley sometimes offers his services instead of mine, but Arthur will not let me go: that strange whim still increases, as his strength declines – the fancy to have me always by his side. I hardly ever leave him, except to go into the next room, where I sometimes snatch an hour or so of sleep when he is quiet; but even then the door is left ajar, that he may know me to be within call. I am with him now, while I write, and I fear my occupation annoys him; though I frequently break off to attend to him, and though Mr. Hattersley is also by his side. That gentleman came, as he said, to beg a holiday for me, that I might have a run in the park, this fine frosty morning, with Milicent and Esther and little Arthur, whom he had driven over to see me. Our poor invalid evidently felt it a heartless proposition, and would have felt it still more heartless in me to accede to it. I therefore said I would only go and speak to them a minute, and then come back. I did but exchange a few words with them, just outside the portico, inhaling the fresh, bracing air as I stood, and then, resisting the earnest and eloquent entreaties of all three to stay a little longer, and join them in a walk round the garden, I tore myself away and returned to my patient. I had not been absent five minutes, but he reproached me bitterly for my levity and neglect. His friend espoused my cause.

"Nay, nay, Huntingdon," said he, "you're too hard upon her; she must have food and sleep, and a mouthful of fresh air now and then, or she can't stand it, I tell you. Look at her, man! She's worn to a shadow already."

"What are her sufferings to mine?" said the poor invalid. "You don't grudge me these attentions, do you, Helen?"

"No, Arthur, if I could really serve you by them. I would give my life to save you, if I might."

"Would you, indeed? No!"

"Most willingly I would."

"Ah! That's because you think yourself more fit to die!"

There was a painful pause. He was evidently plunged in gloomy reflections; but while I pondered for something to say that might benefit without alarming him, Hattersley, whose mind had been pursuing almost the same course, broke silence with, "I say, Huntingdon, I would send for a parson of some sort: if you didn't like the vicar, you know, you could have his curate, or somebody else."

"No; none of them can benefit me if she can't," was the answer. And the tears gushed from his eyes as he earnestly exclaimed, "Oh, Helen, if I had listened to you, it never would have come to this! And if I had heard you long ago – oh, God! How different it would have been!"

"Hear me now, then, Arthur," said I, gently pressing his hand.

"It's too late now," said he despondingly. And after that another paroxysm of pain came on; and then his mind began to wander, and we feared his death was approaching: but an opiate was administered: his sufferings began to abate, he gradually became more composed, and at length sank into a kind of slumber. He has been quieter since; and now Hattersley has left him, expressing a hope that he shall find him better when he calls tomorrow.

"Perhaps I may recover," he replied; "who knows? This may have been the crisis. What do you think, Helen?" Unwilling to depress him, I gave the most cheering answer I could, but still recommended him to prepare for the possibility of what I inly feared was but too certain. But he was determined to hope. Shortly after he relapsed into a kind of doze, but now he groans again.

There is a change. Suddenly he called me to his side, with such a strange, excited manner, that I feared he was delirious, but he was not. "That was the crisis, Helen!" said he, delightedly. "I had an infernal pain here – it is quite gone now. I never was so easy since the fall – quite gone, by heaven!" and he clasped and kissed my hand in the very fulness of his heart; but finding I did not participate in his joy, he quickly flung it from him, and bitterly cursed my coldness and insensibility. How could I reply? Kneeling beside him, I took his hand and fondly pressed it to my lips – for the first time since our separation – and told him, as well as tears would let me speak, that it was not that that kept me silent: it was the fear that this sudden cessation of pain was not so favourable a symptom as he supposed.

I immediately sent for the doctor: we are now anxiously awaiting him. I will tell you what he says. There is still the same freedom from pain, the same deadness to all sensation where the suffering was most acute.

My worst fears are realised: mortification has commenced. The doctor has told him there is no hope. No words can describe his anguish. I can write no more.

* * *

The next was still more distressing in the tenor of its contents. The sufferer was fast approaching dissolution – dragged almost to the verge of that awful chasm he trembled to contemplate, from which no agony of prayers or tears could save him. Nothing could comfort him now; Hattersley's rough attempts at consolation were utterly in vain. The world was nothing to him: life and all its interests, its petty cares and transient pleasures, were a cruel mockery. To talk of the past was to torture him with vain remorse; to refer to the future was to increase his anguish; and yet to be silent was to leave him a prey to his own regrets and apprehensions. Often he dwelt with shuddering minuteness on the fate of his perishing clay – the slow, piecemeal dissolution already invading his frame: the shroud, the coffin, the dark, lonely grave, and all the horrors of corruption.

"If I try," said his afflicted wife, "to divert him from these things – to raise his thoughts to higher themes, it is no better: – 'Worse and worse!' he groans. 'If there be really life beyond the tomb, and judgment after death, how can I face it?' – I cannot do him any good; he will neither be enlightened, nor roused, nor comforted by anything I say; and yet he clings to me with unrelenting pertinacity – with a kind of childish desperation, as if I could save him from the fate he dreads. He keeps me night and day beside him. He is holding my left hand now, while I write; he has held it thus for hours: sometimes quietly, with his pale face upturned to mine: sometimes clutching my arm with violence – the big drops starting from his forehead at the thoughts of what he sees, or thinks he sees, before him. If I withdraw my hand for a moment it distresses him.

"'Stay with me, Helen,' he says; 'let me hold you so: it seems as if harm could not reach me while you are here. But death will come – it is coming now – fast, fast! – and – oh, if I could believe there was nothing after!'

"'Don't try to believe it, Arthur; there is joy and glory after, if you will but try to reach it!'

"'What, for me?' he said, with something like a laugh. 'Are we not to be judged according to the deeds done in the body? Where's the use of a probationary existence, if a man may spend it as he pleases, just contrary to God's decrees, and then go to heaven with the best – if the vilest sinner may win the reward of the holiest saint, by merely saying, 'I repent!''

"'But if you sincerely repent –'

"'I can't repent; I only fear.'

"'You only regret the past for its consequences to yourself?'

"'Just so – except that I'm sorry to have wronged you, Nell, because you're so good to me.'

"'Think of the goodness of God, and you cannot but be grieved to have offended Him.'

"'What is God? – I cannot see Him or hear Him. – God is only an idea.'

"'God is Infinite Wisdom, and Power, and Goodness – and *Love*; but if this idea is too vast for your human faculties – if your mind loses itself in its overwhelming infinitude, fix it on Him who condescended to take our nature upon Him, who was raised to heaven even in His glorified human body, in whom the fulness of the Godhead shines.'

"But he only shook his head and sighed. Then, in another paroxysm of shuddering horror, he tightened his grasp on my hand and arm, and, groaning and lamenting, still clung to me with that wild, desperate earnestness so harrowing to my soul, because I know I cannot help him. I did my best to soothe and comfort him.

"'Death is so terrible,' he cried, 'I cannot bear it! You don't know, Helen – you can't imagine what it is, because you haven't it before you! And when I'm buried, you'll return to your old ways and be as happy as ever, and all the world will go on just as busy and merry as if I had never been; while I –' He burst into tears.

"'You needn't let that distress you,' I said; 'we shall all follow you soon enough.'

"'I wish to God I could take you with me now!' he exclaimed: 'you should plead for me.'

"'No man can deliver his brother, nor make agreement unto God for him,' I replied: 'it cost more to redeem their souls – it cost the blood of an incarnate God, perfect and sinless in Himself, to redeem us from the bondage of the evil one: – let Him plead for you.'

"But I seem to speak in vain. He does not now, as formerly, laugh these blessed truths to scorn: but still he cannot trust, or will not comprehend them. He cannot linger long. He suffers dreadfully, and so do those that wait upon him. But I will not harass you with further details: I have said enough, I think, to convince you that I did well to go to him."

* * *

Poor, poor Helen! Dreadful indeed her trials must have been! And I could do nothing to lessen them – nay, it almost seemed as if I had brought them upon her myself by my own secret desires; and whether I looked at her husband's sufferings or her own, it seemed almost like a judgment upon myself for having cherished such a wish.

The next day but one there came another letter. That too was put into my hands without a remark, and these are its contents:

Dec. 5th. He is gone at last. I sat beside him all night, with my hand fast looked in his, watching the changes of his features and listening to his failing breath. He had been silent a long time, and I thought he would never speak again, when he murmured, faintly but distinctly, – "Pray for me, Helen!"

"I do pray for you, every hour and every minute, Arthur; but you must pray for yourself."

His lips moved, but emitted no sound; – then his looks became unsettled; and, from the incoherent, half-uttered words that escaped him from time to time, supposing him to be now unconscious, I gently disengaged my hand from his, intending to steal away for a breath of air, for I was almost ready to faint; but a convulsive movement of the fingers, and a faintly whispered "Don't leave me!" immediately recalled me: I took his hand again, and held it till he was no more – and then I fainted. It was not grief; it was exhaustion, that, till then, I had been enabled successfully to combat. Oh, Frederick! None can imagine the miseries, bodily and mental, of that death-bed! How could I endure to think that that poor trembling soul was hurried away to everlasting torment? It would drive me mad. But, thank God, I have hope – not only from a vague dependence on the possibility that penitence and pardon might have reached him at the last, but from the blessed confidence that, through whatever purging fires the erring spirit may be doomed to pass – whatever fate awaits it – still it is not lost, and God, who hateth nothing that He hath made, will bless it in the end!

His body will be consigned on Thursday to that dark grave he so much dreaded; but the coffin must be closed as soon as possible. If you will attend the funeral, come quickly, for I need help.

Helen Huntingdon.

Chapter Fifty

ON READING THIS I had no reason to disguise my joy and hope from Frederick Lawrence, for I had none to be ashamed of. I felt no joy but that his sister was at length released from her afflictive, overwhelming toil – no hope but that she would in time recover from the effects of it, and be suffered to rest in peace and quietness, at least, for the remainder of her life. I experienced a painful commiseration for her unhappy husband (though fully aware that he had brought every particle of his sufferings upon himself, and but too well deserved them all), and a profound sympathy for her own afflictions, and deep anxiety for the consequences of those harassing cares, those dreadful vigils, that incessant and deleterious confinement beside a living corpse – for I was persuaded she had not hinted half the sufferings she had had to endure.

"You will go to her, Lawrence?" said I, as I put the letter into his hand.

"Yes, immediately."

"That's right! I'll leave you, then, to prepare for your departure."

"I've done that already, while you were reading the letter, and before you came; and the carriage is now coming round to the door."

Inly approving his promptitude, I bade him good morning, and withdrew. He gave me a searching glance as we pressed each other's hands at parting; but whatever he sought in my countenance, he saw there nothing but the most becoming gravity – it might be mingled with a little sternness in momentary resentment at what I suspected to be passing in his mind.

Had I forgotten my own prospects, my ardent love, my pertinacious hopes? It seemed like sacrilege to revert to them now, but I had not forgotten them. It was, however, with a gloomy sense of the darkness of those prospects, the fallacy of those hopes, and the vanity of that affection, that I reflected on those things as I remounted my horse and slowly journeyed homewards. Mrs. Huntingdon was free now; it was no longer a crime to think of her – but did she ever think of me? Not now – of course it was not to be expected – but would she when this shock was over? In all the course of her correspondence with her brother (our mutual friend, as she herself had called him) she had never mentioned me but once – and that was from necessity. This alone afforded strong presumption that I was already forgotten; yet this was not the worst: it might have been her sense of duty that had kept her silent: she might be only trying to forget; but in addition to this, I had a gloomy conviction that the awful realities she had seen and felt, her reconciliation with the man she had once loved, his dreadful sufferings and death, must eventually efface from her mind all traces of her passing love for me. She might recover from these horrors so far as to be restored to her former health, her tranquillity, her cheerfulness even – but never to those feelings which would appear to her, henceforth, as a fleeting fancy, a vain, illusive dream; especially as there was no one to remind her of my existence – no means of assuring her of my fervent constancy, now that we were so far apart, and delicacy forbade me to see her or to write to her, for months to come at least. And how could I engage her brother in my behalf? How could I break that icy crust of shy reserve? Perhaps he would disapprove of my attachment now as highly as before; perhaps he would think me too poor – too lowly born, to match with his sister. Yes, there was another barrier: doubtless there was a wide distinction between the rank and circumstances of Mrs. Huntingdon, the lady of Grassdale Manor, and those of Mrs. Graham, the artist, the tenant of Wildfell Hall. And it might be deemed presumption in me to offer my hand to the former, by the world, by her friends, if not by herself; a penalty I might brave, if I were certain she loved me; but otherwise, how could I? And, finally, her deceased husband, with his usual selfishness, might have so constructed his will as to place restrictions upon her marrying again. So that you see I had reasons enough for despair if I chose to indulge it.

Nevertheless, it was with no small degree of impatience that I looked forward to Mr. Lawrence's return from Grassdale: impatience that increased in proportion as his absence was prolonged. He stayed away some ten or twelve days. All very right that he should remain to comfort and help his sister, but he might have written to tell me how she was, or at least to tell me when to expect his return; for he might have known I was suffering tortures of anxiety for her, and uncertainty for my own future prospects. And when he did return, all he told me about her was, that she had been greatly exhausted and worn by her unremitting exertions in behalf of that man who had been the scourge of her life, and had dragged her with him nearly to the portals of the grave, and was still much shaken and depressed by his melancholy end and the circumstances attendant upon it; but no word in reference to me; no intimation that my name had ever passed her lips, or even been spoken in her presence. To be sure, I asked no questions on the subject; I could not bring my mind to do so, believing, as I did, that Lawrence was indeed averse to the idea of my union with his sister.

I saw that he expected to be further questioned concerning his visit, and I saw too, with the keen perception of awakened jealousy, or alarmed self-esteem, or by whatever name I ought to call it, that he rather shrank from that impending scrutiny, and was no less pleased than surprised to find it did not come. Of course, I was burning with anger, but pride obliged me to suppress my feelings, and preserve a smooth face, or at least a stoic calmness, throughout the interview. It was well it did, for, reviewing the matter in my sober judgment, I must say it would have been highly absurd and improper to have quarrelled with him on such an occasion. I must confess, too, that I wronged him in my heart: the truth was, he liked me very well, but he was fully aware that a union between Mrs. Huntingdon and me would be what the world calls a mesalliance; and it was not in his nature to set the world at defiance; especially in such a case as this, for its dread laugh, or ill opinion, would be far more terrible to him directed against his sister than himself. Had he believed that a union was necessary to the happiness of both, or of either, or had he known how fervently I loved her, he would have acted differently; but seeing me so calm and cool, he would not for the world disturb my philosophy; and though refraining entirely from any active opposition to the match, he would yet do nothing to bring it about, and would much rather take the part of prudence, in aiding us to overcome our mutual predilections, than that of feeling, to encourage them. 'And he was in the right of it,' you will say. Perhaps he was; at any rate, I had no business to feel so bitterly against him as I did; but I could not then regard the matter in such a moderate light; and, after a brief conversation upon indifferent topics, I went away, suffering all the pangs of wounded pride and injured friendship, in addition to those resulting from the fear that I was indeed forgotten, and the knowledge that she I loved was alone and afflicted, suffering from injured health and dejected spirits, and I was forbidden to console or assist her: forbidden even to assure her of my sympathy, for the transmission of any such message through Mr. Lawrence was now completely out of the question.

But what should I do? I would wait, and see if she would notice me, which of course she would not, unless by some kind message intrusted to her brother, that, in all probability, he would not deliver, and then, dreadful thought! She would think me cooled and changed for not returning it, or, perhaps, he had already given her to understand that I had ceased to think of her. I would wait, however, till the six months after our parting were fairly passed (which would be about the close of February), and then I would send her a letter, modestly reminding her of her former permission to write to her at the close of that period, and hoping I might avail myself of it – at least to express my heartfelt sorrow for her late afflictions, my just appreciation of her generous conduct, and my hope that her health was now completely re-established, and that she would, some time, be permitted to enjoy those blessings of a peaceful, happy life, which had been denied her so long, but which none could more truly be said to merit than herself – adding a few words of kind remembrance to my little friend Arthur, with a hope that he had not forgotten me, and perhaps a few more in reference to bygone times, to the delightful hours I had passed in her society, and my unfading recollection of them, which was the salt and solace of my life, and a hope that her recent troubles had not entirely banished me from her mind. If she did not answer this, of course I should write no more: if she did (as surely she would, in some fashion), my future proceedings should be regulated by her reply.

Ten weeks was long to wait in such a miserable state of uncertainty; but courage! It must be endured! And meantime I would continue to see Lawrence now and then, though not so often as before, and I would still pursue my habitual inquiries after his sister, if he had lately heard from her, and how she was, but nothing more.

I did so, and the answers I received were always provokingly limited to the letter of the inquiry: she was much as usual: she made no complaints, but the tone of her last letter evinced great depression of mind: she said she was better: and, finally, she said she was well, and very busy with her son's education, and with the management of her late husband's property, and the regulation of his affairs. The rascal had never told me how that property was disposed, or whether Mr. Huntingdon had died intestate or not; and I would sooner die than ask him, lest he should misconstrue into covetousness my desire to know. He never offered to show me his sister's letters now, and I never hinted a wish to see them. February, however, was approaching; December was past; January, at length, was almost over – a few more weeks, and then, certain despair or renewal of hope would put an end to this long agony of suspense.

But alas! It was just about that time she was called to sustain another blow in the death of her uncle – a worthless old fellow enough in himself, I daresay, but he had always shown more kindness and affection to her than to any other creature, and she had always been accustomed to regard him as a parent. She was with him when he died, and had assisted her aunt to nurse him during the last stage of his illness. Her brother went to Staningley to attend the funeral, and told me, upon his return, that she was still there, endeavouring to cheer her aunt with her presence, and likely to remain some time. This was bad news for me, for while she continued there I could not write to her, as I did not know the address, and would not ask it of him. But week followed week, and every time I inquired about her she was still at Staningley.

"Where is Staningley?" I asked at last.

"In —shire," was the brief reply; and there was something so cold and dry in the manner of it, that I was effectually deterred from requesting a more definite account.

"When will she return to Grassdale?" was my next question.

"I don't know."

"Confound it!" I muttered.

"Why, Markham?" asked my companion, with an air of innocent surprise. But I did not deign to answer him, save by a look of silent, sullen contempt, at which he turned away, and contemplated the carpet with a slight smile, half pensive, half amused; but quickly looking up, he began to talk of other subjects, trying to draw me into a cheerful and friendly conversation, but I was too much irritated to discourse with him, and soon took leave.

You see Lawrence and I somehow could not manage to get on very well together. The fact is, I believe, we were both of us a little too touchy. It is a troublesome thing, Halford, this susceptibility to affronts where none are intended. I am no martyr to it now, as you can bear me witness: I have learned to be merry and wise, to be more easy with myself and more indulgent to my neighbours, and I can afford to laugh at both Lawrence and you.

Partly from accident, partly from wilful negligence on my part (for I was really beginning to dislike him), several weeks elapsed before I saw my friend again. When we did meet, it was he that sought me out. One bright morning, early in June, he came into the field, where I was just commencing my hay harvest.

"It is long since I saw you, Markham," said he, after the first few words had passed between us. "Do you never mean to come to Woodford again?"

"I called once, and you were out."

"I was sorry, but that was long since; I hoped you would call again, and now I have called, and you were out, which you generally are, or I would do myself the pleasure of calling more frequently; but being determined to see you this time, I have left my pony in the lane, and come over hedge and ditch to join you; for I am about to leave Woodford for a while, and may not have the pleasure of seeing you again for a month or two."

"Where are you going?"

"To Grassdale first," said he, with a half-smile he would willingly have suppressed if he could.

"To Grassdale! Is she there, then?"

"Yes, but in a day or two she will leave it to accompany Mrs. Maxwell to F— for the benefit of the sea air, and I shall go with them." (F— was at that time a quiet but respectable watering-place: it is considerably more frequented now.)

Lawrence seemed to expect me to take advantage of this circumstance to entrust him with some sort of a message to his sister; and I believe he would have undertaken to deliver it without any material objections, if I had had the sense to ask him, though of course he would not offer to do so, if I was content to let it alone. But I could not bring myself to make the request, and it was not till after he was gone, that I saw how fair an opportunity I had lost; and then, indeed, I deeply regretted my stupidity and my foolish pride, but it was now too late to remedy the evil.

He did not return till towards the latter end of August. He wrote to me twice or thrice from F—, but his letters were most provokingly unsatisfactory, dealing in generalities or in trifles that I cared nothing about, or replete with fancies and reflections equally unwelcome to me at the time, saying next to nothing about his sister, and little more about himself. I would wait, however, till he came back; perhaps I could get something more out of him then. At all events, I would not write to her now, while she was with him and her aunt, who doubtless would be still more hostile to my presumptuous aspirations than himself. When she was returned to the silence and solitude of her own home, it would be my fittest opportunity.

When Lawrence came, however, he was as reserved as ever on the subject of my keen anxiety. He told me that his sister had derived considerable benefit from her stay at F— that her son was quite well, and – alas! that both of them were gone, with Mrs. Maxwell, back to Staningley, and there they stayed at least three months. But instead of boring you with my chagrin, my expectations and disappointments, my fluctuations of dull despondency and flickering hope, my varying resolutions, now to drop it, and now to persevere – now to make a bold push, and now to let things pass and patiently abide my time, – I will employ myself in settling the business of one or two of the characters introduced in the course of this narrative, whom I may not have occasion to mention again.

Some time before Mr. Huntingdon's death Lady Lowborough eloped with another gallant to the Continent, where, having lived a while in reckless gaiety and dissipation, they quarrelled and parted. She went dashing on for a season, but years came and money went: she sunk, at length, in difficulty and debt, disgrace and misery; and died at last, as I have heard, in penury, neglect, and utter wretchedness. But this might be only a report: she may be living yet for anything I or any of her relatives or former acquaintances can tell; for they have all lost sight of her long years ago, and would as thoroughly forget her if they could. Her husband, however, upon this second misdemeanour, immediately sought and obtained a divorce, and, not long after, married again. It was well he did, for Lord Lowborough, morose and moody as he seemed, was not the man for a bachelor's life. No public interests, no ambitious projects, or active pursuits, – or ties of friendship even (if he had had any friends), could compensate to him for the absence of domestic comforts and endearments. He had a son and a nominal daughter, it is true, but they too painfully reminded him of their mother, and the unfortunate little Annabella was a source of perpetual bitterness to his soul. He had obliged himself to treat her with paternal kindness: he had forced himself not to hate her, and even, perhaps, to feel some degree of kindly regard for her, at last, in return for her artless and unsuspecting attachment to himself; but the bitterness of his self-condemnation for his inward feelings towards that innocent being, his constant struggles to subdue the evil promptings of his nature (for it was not a generous one), though partly guessed at by those who knew him, could be known to God and his own heart alone; – so also was the hardness of his conflicts with the temptation to return to the vice of his youth, and seek oblivion for past calamities, and deadness to the present misery of a blighted heart a joyless, friendless life, and a morbidly disconsolate mind, by yielding again to that insidious foe to health, and sense, and virtue, which had so deplorably enslaved and degraded him before.

The second object of his choice was widely different from the first. Some wondered at his taste; some even ridiculed it – but in this their folly was more apparent than his. The lady was about his own age – i.e., between thirty and forty – remarkable neither for beauty, nor wealth, nor brilliant accomplishments; nor any other thing that I ever heard of, except genuine good sense, unswerving integrity, active piety, warm-hearted benevolence, and a fund of cheerful spirits. These qualities, however, as you way readily imagine, combined to render her an excellent mother to the children, and an invaluable wife to his lordship. He, with his usual self-depreciation, thought her a world too good for him, and while he wondered at the kindness of Providence in conferring such a gift upon him, and even at her taste in preferring him to other men, he did his best to reciprocate the good she did him, and so far succeeded that she was, and I believe still is, one of the happiest and fondest wives in England; and all who question the good taste of either partner may be thankful if their respective selections afford them half the genuine satisfaction in the end, or repay their preference with affection half as lasting and sincere.

If you are at all interested in the fate of that low scoundrel, Grimsby, I can only tell you that he went from bad to worse, sinking from bathos to bathos of vice and villainy, consorting only with the worst members of his club and the lowest dregs of society – happily for the rest of the world – and at last met his end in a drunken brawl, from the hands, it is said, of some brother scoundrel he had cheated at play.

As for Mr. Hattersley, he had never wholly forgotten his resolution to 'come out from among them,' and behave like a man and a Christian, and the last illness and death of his once jolly friend Huntingdon so deeply and seriously impressed him with the evil of their former practices, that he never needed another lesson of the kind. Avoiding the temptations of the town, he continued to pass his life in the country, immersed in the usual pursuits of a hearty, active, country gentleman; his occupations being those of farming, and breeding horses and cattle, diversified with a little hunting and shooting, and enlivened by the occasional companionship of his friends (better friends than those of his youth), and the society of his happy little wife (now cheerful and confiding as heart could wish), and his fine family of stalwart sons and blooming daughters. His father, the banker, having died some years ago and left him all his riches, he has now full scope for the exercise of his prevailing tastes, and I need not tell you that Ralph Hattersley, Esq., is celebrated throughout the country for his noble breed of horses.

Chapter Fifty-One

WE WILL NOW turn to a certain still, cold, cloudy afternoon about the commencement of December, when the first fall of snow lay thinly scattered over the blighted fields and frozen roads, or stored more thickly in the hollows of the deep cart-ruts and footsteps of men and horses impressed in the now petrified mire of last month's drenching rains. I remember it well, for I was walking home from the vicarage with no less remarkable a personage than Miss Eliza Millward by my side. I had been to call upon her father, – a sacrifice to civility undertaken entirely to please my mother, not myself, for I hated to go near the house; not merely on account of my antipathy to the once so bewitching Eliza, but because I had not half forgiven the old gentleman himself for his ill opinion of Mrs. Huntingdon; for though now constrained to acknowledge himself mistaken in his former judgment, he still maintained that she had done wrong to leave her husband; it was a violation of her sacred duties as a wife, and a tempting of Providence by laying herself open to temptation; and nothing short of bodily ill-usage (and that of no trifling nature) could excuse such a step – nor even that, for in such a case she ought to appeal to the laws for protection. But it was not of him I intended to speak; it was of his daughter Eliza. Just as I was taking leave of the vicar, she entered the room, ready equipped for a walk.

"I was just coming to see, your sister, Mr. Markham," said she; "and so, if you have no objection, I'll accompany you home. I like company when I'm walking out – don't you?"

"Yes, when it's agreeable."

"That of course," rejoined the young lady, smiling archly.

So we proceeded together.

"Shall I find Rose at home, do you think?" said she, as we closed the garden gate, and set our faces towards Linden-Car.

"I believe so."

"I trust I shall, for I've a little bit of news for her – if you haven't forestalled me."

"I?"

"Yes: do you know what Mr. Lawrence is gone for?" She looked up anxiously for my reply.

"Is he gone?" said I; and her face brightened.

"Ah! Then he hasn't told you about his sister?"

"What of her?" I demanded in terror, lest some evil should have befallen her.

"Oh, Mr. Markham, how you blush!" cried she, with a tormenting laugh. "Ha, ha, you have not forgotten her yet. But you had better be quick about it, I can tell you, for – alas, alas! – She's going to be married next Thursday!"

"No, Miss Eliza, that's false."

"Do you charge me with a falsehood, sir?"

"You are misinformed."

"Am I? Do you know better, then?"

"I think I do."

"What makes you look so pale then?" said she, smiling with delight at my emotion. "Is it anger at poor me for telling such a fib? Well, I only 'tell the tale as 'twas told to me:' I don't vouch for the truth of it; but at the same time, I don't see what reason Sarah should have for deceiving me, or her informant for deceiving her; and that was what she told me the footman told her: – that Mrs. Huntingdon was going to be married on Thursday, and Mr. Lawrence was gone to the wedding. She did tell me the name of the gentleman, but I've forgotten that. Perhaps you can assist me to remember it. Is there not some one that lives near – or frequently visits the neighbourhood, that has long been attached to her? – a Mr.— oh, dear! Mr.—"

"Hargrave?" suggested I, with a bitter smile.

"You're right," cried she; "that was the very name."

"Impossible, Miss Eliza!" I exclaimed, in a tone that made her start.

"Well, you know, that's what they told me," said she, composedly staring me in the face. And then she broke out into a long shrill laugh that put me to my wit's end with fury.

"Really you must excuse me," cried she. "I know it's very rude, but ha, ha, ha! – Did you think to marry her yourself? Dear, dear, what a pity! – Ha, ha, ha! Gracious, Mr. Markham, are you going to faint? Oh, mercy! Shall I call this man? Here, Jacob –" But checking the word on her lips, I seized her arm and gave it, I think, a pretty severe squeeze, for she shrank into herself with a faint cry of pain or terror; but the spirit within her was not subdued: instantly rallying, she continued, with well-feigned concern, "What can I do for you? Will you have some water – some brandy? I daresay they have some in the public-house down there, if you'll let me run."

"Have done with this nonsense!" cried I, sternly. She looked confounded – almost frightened again, for a moment. "You know I hate such jests," I continued.

"Jests indeed! I wasn't jesting!"

"You were laughing, at all events; and I don't like to be laughed at," returned I, making violent efforts to speak with proper dignity and composure, and to say nothing but what was coherent and sensible. "And since you are in such a merry mood, Miss Eliza, you must be good enough company for yourself; and therefore I shall leave you to finish your walk alone – for, now I think of it, I have business elsewhere; so good evening."

With that I left her (smothering her malicious laughter) and turned aside into the fields, springing up the bank, and pushing through the nearest gap in the hedge. Determined at once to prove the truth – or rather the falsehood – of her story, I hastened to Woodford as fast as my legs could carry me; first veering round by a circuitous course, but the moment I was out of sight of my fair tormentor cutting away across the country, just as a bird might fly, over pasture-land, and fallow, and stubble, and lane, clearing hedges and ditches and hurdles, till I came to the young squire's gates. Never till now had I known the full fervour of my love – the full strength of my hopes, not wholly crushed even in my hours of deepest despondency, always tenaciously clinging to the thought that one day she might be mine, or, if not that, at least that something of my memory, some slight remembrance of our friendship and our love, would be for ever cherished in her heart. I marched up to the door, determined, if I saw the master, to question him boldly concerning his sister, to wait and hesitate no longer, but cast false delicacy and stupid pride behind my back, and know my fate at once.

"Is Mr. Lawrence at home?" I eagerly asked of the servant that opened the door.

"No, sir, master went yesterday," replied he, looking very alert.

"Went where?"

"To Grassdale, sir – wasn't you aware, sir? He's very close, is master," said the fellow, with a foolish, simpering grin. "I suppose, sir –"

But I turned and left him, without waiting to hear what he supposed. I was not going to stand there to expose my tortured feelings to the insolent laughter and impertinent curiosity of a fellow like that.

But what was to be done now? Could it be possible that she had left me for that man? I could not believe it. Me she might forsake, but not to give herself to him! Well, I would know the truth; to no concerns of daily life could I attend while this tempest of doubt and dread, of jealousy and rage, distracted me. I would take the morning coach from L— (the evening one would be already gone), and fly to Grassdale – I must be there before the marriage. And why? Because a thought struck me that perhaps I might prevent it – that if I did not, she and I might both lament it to the latest moment of our lives. It struck me that someone might have belied me to her: perhaps her brother; yes, no doubt her brother had persuaded her that I was false and faithless, and taking advantage of her natural indignation, and perhaps her desponding carelessness about her future life, had urged her, artfully, cruelly, on to this other marriage, in order to secure her from me. If this was the case, and if she should only discover her mistake when too late to repair it – to what a life of misery and vain regret might she be doomed as well as me; and what remorse for me to think my foolish scruples had induced it all! Oh, I must see her – she must know my truth even if I told it at the church door! I might pass for a madman or an impertinent fool – even she might be offended at such an interruption, or at least might tell me it was now too late. But if I could save her, if she might be mine! – It was too rapturous a thought!

Winged by this hope, and goaded by these fears, I hurried homewards to prepare for my departure on the morrow. I told my mother that urgent business which admitted no delay, but which I could not then explain, called me away.

My deep anxiety and serious preoccupation could not be concealed from her maternal eyes; and I had much ado to calm her apprehensions of some disastrous mystery.

That night there came a heavy fall of snow, which so retarded the progress of the coaches on the following day that I was almost driven to distraction. I travelled all night, of course, for this was Wednesday: tomorrow morning, doubtless, the marriage would take place. But the night was long and dark: the snow heavily clogged the wheels and balled the horses' feet; the animals were consumedly lazy; the coachman most execrably cautious; the passengers confoundedly apathetic in their supine indifference to the rate of our progression. Instead of assisting me to bully the several coachmen and urge them forward, they merely stared and grinned at my impatience: one fellow even ventured to rally me upon it – but I silenced him with a look that quelled him for the rest of the journey; and when, at the last stage, I would have taken the reins into my own hand, they all with one accord opposed it.

It was broad daylight when we entered M— and drew up at the 'Rose and Crown.' I alighted and called aloud for a post-chaise to Grassdale. There was none to be had: the only one in the town was under repair. "A gig, then – a fly – car – anything – only be quick!" There was a gig, but not a horse to spare. I sent into the town to seek one: but they were such an intolerable time about it that I could wait no longer – I thought my own feet could carry me sooner; and bidding them send the conveyance after me, if it were ready within an hour, I set off as fast as I could walk. The distance was little more than six miles, but the road was strange, and I had to keep stopping to inquire my way; hallooing to carters and clodhoppers, and frequently invading the cottages, for there were few abroad that winter's morning; sometimes knocking up the lazy people from their beds, for where so little work was to be done, perhaps so little food and fire to be had, they cared not to curtail their slumbers. I had no time to think of them, however; aching with weariness and desperation, I hurried on. The gig did not overtake me: and it was well I had not waited for it; vexatious rather, that I had been fool enough to wait so long.

At length, however, I entered the neighbourhood of Grassdale. I approached the little rural church – but lo! There stood a train of carriages before it; it needed not the white favours bedecking the servants and horses, nor the merry voices of the village idlers assembled to witness the show, to apprise me that there was a wedding within. I ran in among them, demanding, with breathless eagerness, had the ceremony long commenced? They only gaped and stared. In my desperation, I pushed past them, and was about to enter the churchyard gate, when a group of ragged urchins, that had been hanging like bees to the window, suddenly dropped off and made a rush for the porch, vociferating in the uncouth dialect of their country something which signified, "It's over – they're coming out!"

If Eliza Millward had seen me then she might indeed have been delighted. I grasped the gate-post for support, and stood intently gazing towards the door to take my last look on my soul's delight, my first on that detested mortal who had torn her from my heart, and doomed her, I was certain, to a life of misery and hollow, vain repining – for what happiness could she enjoy with him? I did not wish to shock her with my presence now, but I had not power to move away. Forth came the bride and bridegroom. Him I saw not; I had eyes for none but her. A long veil shrouded half her graceful form, but did not hide it; I could see that while she carried her head erect, her eyes were bent upon the ground, and her face and neck were suffused with a crimson blush; but every feature was radiant with smiles, and gleaming through the misty whiteness of her veil were clusters of golden ringlets! Oh, heavens! It was not my Helen! The first glimpse made me start – but my eyes were darkened with exhaustion and despair. Dare I trust them? Yes – it is not she! It was a younger, slighter, rosier beauty – lovely indeed, but with far less dignity and depth of soul – without that indefinable grace, that keenly spiritual yet gentle charm, that ineffable power to attract and subjugate the heart – my heart at least. I looked at the bridegroom – it was Frederick Lawrence! I wiped away the cold drops that were trickling down my forehead, and stepped back as he approached; but, his eyes fell upon me, and he knew me, altered as my appearance must have been.

"Is that you, Markham?" said he, startled and confounded at the apparition – perhaps, too, at the wildness of my looks.

"Yes, Lawrence; is that you?" I mustered the presence of mind to reply.

He smiled and coloured, as if half-proud and half-ashamed of his identity; and if he had reason to be proud of the sweet lady on his arm, he had no less cause to be ashamed of having concealed his good fortune so long.

"Allow me to introduce you to my bride," said he, endeavouring to hide his embarrassment by an assumption of careless gaiety. "Esther, this is Mr. Markham; my friend Markham, Mrs. Lawrence, late Miss Hargrave."

I bowed to the bride, and vehemently wrung the bridegroom's hand.

"Why did you not tell me of this?" I said, reproachfully, pretending a resentment I did not feel (for in truth I was almost wild with joy to find myself so happily mistaken, and overflowing with affection to him for this and for the base injustice I felt that I had done him in my mind – he might have wronged me, but not to that extent; and as I had hated him like a demon for the last forty hours, the reaction from such a feeling was so great that I could pardon all offences for the moment – and love him in spite of them too).

"I did tell you," said he, with an air of guilty confusion; "you received my letter?"

"What letter?"

"The one announcing my intended marriage."

"I never received the most distant hint of such an intention."

"It must have crossed you on your way then – it should have reached you yesterday morning – it was rather late, I acknowledge. But what brought you here, then, if you received no information?"

It was now my turn to be confounded; but the young lady, who had been busily patting the snow with her foot during our short sotto-voce colloquy, very opportunely came to my assistance by pinching her companion's arm and whispering a suggestion that his friend should be invited to step into the carriage and go with them; it being scarcely agreeable to stand there among so many gazers, and keeping their friends waiting into the bargain.

"And so cold as it is too!" said he, glancing with dismay at her slight drapery, and immediately handing her into the carriage. "Markham, will you come? We are going to Paris, but we can drop you anywhere between this and Dover."

"No, thank you. Goodby – I needn't wish you a pleasant journey; but I shall expect a very handsome apology, some time, mind, and scores of letters, before we meet again."

He shook my hand, and hastened to take his place beside his lady. This was no time or place for explanation or discourse: we had already stood long enough to excite the wonder of the village sight-seers, and perhaps the wrath of the attendant bridal party; though, of course, all this passed in a much shorter time than I have taken to relate, or even than you will take to read it. I stood beside the carriage, and, the window being down, I saw my happy friend fondly encircle his companion's waist with his arm, while she rested her glowing cheek on his shoulder, looking the very impersonation of loving, trusting bliss. In the interval between the footman's closing the door and taking his place behind she raised her smiling brown eyes to his face, observing, playfully, – "I fear you must think me very insensible, Frederick: I know it is the custom for ladies to cry on these occasions, but I couldn't squeeze a tear for my life."

He only answered with a kiss, and pressed her still closer to his bosom.

"But what is this?" he murmured. "Why, Esther, you're crying now!"

"Oh, it's nothing – it's only too much happiness – and the wish," sobbed she, "that our dear Helen were as happy as ourselves."

"Bless you for that wish!" I inwardly responded, as the carriage rolled away – "and heaven grant it be not wholly vain!"

I thought a cloud had suddenly darkened her husband's face as she spoke. What did he think? Could he grudge such happiness to his dear sister and his friend as he now felt himself? At such a moment it was impossible. The contrast between her fate and his must darken his bliss for a time. Perhaps, too, he thought of me: perhaps he regretted the part he had had in preventing our union, by omitting to help us, if not by actually plotting against us. I exonerated him from that charge now, and deeply lamented my former ungenerous suspicions; but he had wronged us, still – I hoped, I trusted that he had. He had not attempted to cheek the course of our love by actually damming up the streams in their passage, but he had passively watched the two currents wandering through life's arid wilderness, declining to clear away the obstructions that divided them, and secretly hoping that both would lose themselves in the sand before they could be joined in one. And meantime he had been quietly proceeding with his own affairs; perhaps, his heart and head had been so full of his fair lady that he had had but little thought to spare for others. Doubtless he had made his first acquaintance with her – his first intimate acquaintance at least – during his three months' sojourn at F—, for I now recollected that he had once casually let fall an intimation that his aunt and sister had a young friend staying with them at the time, and this accounted for at least one-half his silence about all transactions there. Now, too, I saw a reason for many little things that had slightly puzzled me before; among the rest, for sundry departures from Woodford, and absences more or less prolonged, for which he never satisfactorily accounted, and concerning which he hated to be questioned on his return. Well might the servant say his master was 'very close.' But why this strange reserve to me? Partly, from that remarkable idiosyncrasy to which I have before alluded; partly, perhaps, from tenderness to my feelings, or fear to disturb my philosophy by touching upon the infectious theme of love.

Chapter Fifty-Two

THE TARDY GIG had overtaken me at last. I entered it, and bade the man who brought it drive to Grassdale Manor – I was too busy with my own thoughts to care to drive it myself. I would see Mrs. Huntingdon – there could be no impropriety in that now that her husband had been dead above a year – and by her indifference or her joy at my unexpected arrival I could soon tell whether her heart was truly mine. But my companion, a loquacious, forward fellow, was not disposed to leave me to the indulgence of my private cogitations.

"There they go!" said he, as the carriages filed away before us. "There'll be brave doings on yonder today, as what come tomorra. – Know anything of that family, sir? Or you're a stranger in these parts?"

"I know them by report."

"Humph! There's the best of 'em gone, anyhow. And I suppose the old missis is agoing to leave after this stir's gotten overed, and take herself off, somewhere, to live on her bit of a jointure; and the young 'un – at least the new 'un (she's none so very young) – is coming down to live at the Grove."

"Is Mr. Hargrave married, then?"

"Ay, sir, a few months since. He should a been wed afore, to a widow lady, but they couldn't agree over the money: she'd a rare long purse, and Mr. Hargrave wanted it all to hisself; but she wouldn't let it go, and so then they fell out. This one isn't quite as rich, nor as handsome either, but she hasn't been married before. She's very plain, they say, and getting on to forty or past, and so, you know, if she didn't jump at this hopportunity, she thought she'd never get a better. I guess she thought such a handsome young husband was worth all 'at ever she had, and he might take it and welcome, but I lay she'll rue her bargain afore long. They say she begins already to see 'at he isn't not altogether that nice, generous, perlite, delightful gentleman 'at she thought him afore marriage – he begins a being careless and masterful already. Ay, and she'll find him harder and carelesser nor she thinks on."

"You seem to be well acquainted with him," I observed.

"I am, sir; I've known him since he was quite a young gentleman; and a proud 'un he was, and a wilful. I was servant yonder for several years; but I couldn't stand their niggardly ways – she got ever longer and worse, did missis, with her nipping and screwing, and watching and grudging; so I thought I'd find another place."

"Are we not near the house?" said I, interrupting him.

"Yes, sir; yond's the park."

My heart sank within me to behold that stately mansion in the midst of its expansive grounds. The park as beautiful now, in its wintry garb, as it could be in its summer glory: the majestic sweep, the undulating swell and fall, displayed to full advantage in that robe of dazzling purity, stainless and printless – save one long, winding track left by the trooping deer – the stately timber-trees with their heavy-laden branches gleaming white against the dull, grey sky; the deep, encircling woods; the broad expanse of water sleeping in frozen quiet; and the weeping ash and willow drooping their snow-clad boughs above it – all presented a picture, striking indeed, and pleasing to an unencumbered mind, but by no means encouraging to me. There was one comfort, however, – all this was entailed upon little Arthur, and could not under any circumstances, strictly speaking, be his mother's. But how was she situated? Overcoming with a sudden effort my repugnance to mention her name to my garrulous companion, I asked him if he knew whether her late husband had left a will, and how the property had been disposed of. Oh, yes, he knew all about it; and I was quickly informed that to her had been left the full control and management of the estate during her son's minority, besides the absolute, unconditional possession of her own fortune (but I knew that her father had not given her much), and the small additional sum that had been settled upon her before marriage.

Before the close of the explanation we drew up at the park-gates. Now for the trial. If I should find her within – but alas! She might be still at Staningley: her brother had given me no intimation to the contrary. I inquired at the porter's lodge if Mrs. Huntingdon were at home. No, she was with her aunt in —shire, but was expected to return before Christmas. She usually spent most of her time at Staningley, only coming to Grassdale occasionally, when the management of affairs, or the interest of her tenants and dependents, required her presence.

"Near what town is Staningley situated?" I asked. The requisite information was soon obtained. "Now then, my man, give me the reins, and we'll return to M—. I must have some breakfast at the 'Rose and Crown,' and then away to Staningley by the first coach for —."

At M—I had time before the coach started to replenish my forces with a hearty breakfast, and to obtain the refreshment of my usual morning's ablutions, and the amelioration of some slight change in my toilet, and also to despatch a short note to my mother (excellent son that I was), to assure her that I was still in existence, and to excuse my non-appearance at the expected time. It was a long journey to Staningley for those slow-travelling days, but I did not deny myself needful refreshment on the road, nor even a night's rest at a wayside inn, choosing rather to brook a little delay than to present myself worn, wild, and weather-beaten before my mistress and her aunt, who would be astonished enough to see me without that. Next morning, therefore, I not only fortified myself with as substantial a breakfast as my excited feelings would allow me to swallow, but I bestowed a little more than usual time and care upon my toilet; and, furnished with a change of linen from my small carpet-bag, well-brushed clothes, well-polished boots, and neat new gloves, I mounted 'The Lightning,' and resumed my journey. I had nearly two stages yet before me, but the coach, I was informed, passed through the neighbourhood of Staningley, and having desired to be set down as near the Hall as possible, I had nothing to do but to sit with folded arms and speculate upon the coming hour.

It was a clear, frosty morning. The very fact of sitting exalted aloft, surveying the snowy landscape and sweet sunny sky, inhaling the pure, bracing air, and crunching away over the crisp frozen snow, was exhilarating enough in itself; but add to this the idea of to what goal I was hastening, and whom I expected to meet, and you may have some faint conception of my frame of mind at the time – only a faint one, though: for my heart swelled with unspeakable delight, and my spirits rose almost to madness, in spite of my prudent endeavours to bind them down to a reasonable platitude by thinking of the undeniable difference between Helen's rank and mine; of all that she had passed through since our parting; of her long, unbroken silence; and, above all, of her cool, cautious aunt, whose counsels she would doubtless be careful not to slight again. These considerations made my heart flutter with anxiety, and my chest heave with impatience to get the crisis over; but they could not dim her image in my mind, or mar the vivid recollection of what had been said and felt between us, or destroy the keen anticipation of what was to be: in fact, I could not realise their terrors now. Towards the close of the journey, however, a couple of my fellow-passengers kindly came to my assistance, and brought me low enough.

"Fine land this," said one of them, pointing with his umbrella to the wide fields on the right, conspicuous for their compact hedgerows, deep, well-cut ditches, and fine timber-trees, growing sometimes on the borders, sometimes in the midst of the enclosure: "very fine land, if you saw it in the summer or spring."

"Ay," responded the other, a gruff elderly man, with a drab greatcoat buttoned up to the chin, and a cotton umbrella between his knees. "It's old Maxwell's, I suppose."

"It was his, sir; but he's dead now, you're aware, and has left it all to his niece."

"All?"

"Every rood of it, and the mansion-house and all! Every hatom of his worldly goods, except just a trifle, by way of remembrance, to his nephew down in —shire, and an annuity to his wife."

"It's strange, sir!"

"It is, sir; and she wasn't his own niece neither. But he had no near relations of his own – none but a nephew he'd quarrelled with; and he always had a partiality for this one. And then his wife advised him to it, they say: she'd brought most of the property, and it was her wish that this lady should have it."

"Humph! She'll be a fine catch for somebody."

"She will so. She's a widow, but quite young yet, and uncommon handsome: a fortune of her own, besides, and only one child, and she's nursing a fine estate for him in —. There'll be lots to speak for her! 'fraid there's no chance for uz' – (facetiously jogging me with his elbow, as well as his companion) – "ha, ha, ha! No offence, sir, I hope?" – (to me). "Ahem! I should think she'll marry none but a nobleman myself. Look ye, sir," resumed he, turning to his other neighbour, and pointing past me with his umbrella, "that's the Hall: grand park, you see, and all them woods – plenty of timber there, and lots of game. Hallo! What now?"

This exclamation was occasioned by the sudden stoppage of the coach at the park-gates.

"Gen'leman for Staningley Hall?" cried the coachman and I rose and threw my carpet-bag on to the ground, preparatory to dropping myself down after it.

"Sickly, sir?" asked my talkative neighbour, staring me in the face. I daresay it was white enough.

"No. Here, coachman!"

"Thank'ee, sir. – All right!"

The coachman pocketed his fee and drove away, leaving me, not walking up the park, but pacing to and fro before its gates, with folded arms, and eyes fixed upon the ground, an overwhelming force of images, thoughts, impressions crowding on my mind, and nothing tangibly distinct but this: My love had been cherished in vain – my hope was gone for ever; I must tear myself away at once, and banish or suppress all thoughts of her, like the remembrance of a wild, mad dream. Gladly would I have lingered round the place for hours, in the hope of catching at least one distant glimpse of her before I went, but it must not be – I must not suffer her to see me; for what could have brought me hither but the hope of reviving her attachment, with a view hereafter to obtain her hand? And could I bear that she should think me capable of such a thing? – Of presuming upon the acquaintance – the love, if you will – accidentally contracted, or rather forced upon her against her will, when she was an unknown fugitive, toiling for her own support, apparently without fortune, family, or connections; to come upon her now, when she was reinstated in her proper sphere, and claim a share in her prosperity, which, had it never failed her, would most certainly have kept her unknown to me for ever? And this, too, when we had parted sixteen months ago, and she had expressly forbidden me to hope for a re-union in this world, and never sent me a line or a message from that day to this. No! The very idea was intolerable.

And even if she should have a lingering affection for me still, ought I to disturb her peace by awakening those feelings? To subject her to the struggles of conflicting duty and inclination – to whichsoever side the latter might allure, or the former imperatively call her – whether she should deem it her duty to risk the slights and censures of the world, the sorrow and displeasure of those she loved, for a romantic idea of truth and constancy to me, or to sacrifice her individual wishes to the feelings of her friends and her own sense of prudence and the fitness of things? No – and I would not! I would go at once, and she should never know that I had approached the place of her abode: for though I might disclaim all idea of ever aspiring to her hand, or even of soliciting a place in her friendly regard, her peace should not be broken by my presence, nor her heart afflicted by the sight of my fidelity.

"Adieu then, dear Helen, forever! Forever adieu!"

So said I – and yet I could not tear myself away. I moved a few paces, and then looked back, for one last view of her stately home, that I might have its outward form, at least, impressed upon my mind as indelibly as her own image, which, alas! I must not see again – then walked a few steps further; and then, lost in melancholy musings, paused again and leant my back against a rough old tree that grew beside the road.

Chapter Fifty-Three

WHILE STANDING thus, absorbed in my gloomy reverie, a gentleman's carriage came round the corner of the road. I did not look at it; and had it rolled quietly by me, I should not have remembered the fact of its appearance at all; but a tiny voice from within it roused me by exclaiming, "Mamma, mamma, here's Mr. Markham!"

I did not hear the reply, but presently the same voice answered, "It is indeed, mamma – look for yourself."

I did not raise my eyes, but I suppose mamma looked, for a clear melodious voice, whose tones thrilled through my nerves, exclaimed, "Oh, aunt! Here's Mr. Markham, Arthur's friend! Stop, Richard!"

There was such evidence of joyous though suppressed excitement in the utterance of those few words – especially that tremulous, 'Oh, aunt' – that it threw me almost off my guard. The carriage stopped immediately, and I looked up and met the eye of a pale, grave, elderly lady surveying me from the open window. She bowed, and so did I, and then she withdrew her head, while Arthur screamed to the footman to let him out; but before that functionary could descend from his box a hand was silently put forth from the carriage window. I knew that hand, though a black glove concealed its delicate whiteness and half its fair proportions, and quickly seizing it, I pressed it in my own – ardently for a moment, but instantly recollecting myself, I dropped it, and it was immediately withdrawn.

"Were you coming to see us, or only passing by?" asked the low voice of its owner, who, I felt, was attentively surveying my countenance from behind the thick black veil which, with the shadowing panels, entirely concealed her own from me.

"I – I came to see the place," faltered I.

"The place," repeated she, in a tone which betokened more displeasure or disappointment than surprise.

"Will you not enter it, then?"

"If you wish it."

"Can you doubt?"

"Yes, yes! He must enter," cried Arthur, running round from the other door; and seizing my hand in both his, he shook it heartily.

"Do you remember me, sir?" said he.

"Yes, full well, my little man, altered though you are," replied I, surveying the comparatively tall, slim young gentleman, with his mother's image visibly stamped upon his fair, intelligent features, in spite of the blue eyes beaming with gladness, and the bright locks clustering beneath his cap.

"Am I not grown?" said he, stretching himself up to his full height.

"Grown! Three inches, upon my word!"

"I was seven last birthday," was the proud rejoinder. "In seven years more I shall be as tall as you nearly."

"Arthur," said his mother, "tell him to come in. Go on, Richard."

There was a touch of sadness as well as coldness in her voice, but I knew not to what to ascribe it. The carriage drove on and entered the gates before us. My little companion led me up the park, discoursing merrily all the way. Arrived at the hall-door, I paused on the steps and looked round me, waiting to recover my composure, if possible – or, at any rate, to remember my new-formed resolutions and the principles on which they were founded; and it was not till Arthur had been for some time gently pulling my coat, and repeating his invitations to enter, that I at length consented to accompany him into the apartment where the ladies awaited us.

Helen eyed me as I entered with a kind of gentle, serious scrutiny, and politely asked after Mrs. Markham and Rose. I respectfully answered her inquiries. Mrs. Maxwell begged me to be seated, observing it was rather cold, but she supposed I had not travelled far that morning.

"Not quite twenty miles," I answered.

"Not on foot!"

"No, Madam, by coach."

"Here's Rachel, sir," said Arthur, the only truly happy one amongst us, directing my attention to that worthy individual, who had just entered to take her mistress's things. She vouchsafed me an almost friendly smile of recognition – a favour that demanded, at least, a civil salutation on my part, which was accordingly given and respectfully returned – she had seen the error of her former estimation of my character.

When Helen was divested of her lugubrious bonnet and veil, her heavy winter cloak, etc., she looked so like herself that I knew not how to bear it. I was particularly glad to see her beautiful black hair, unstinted still, and unconcealed in its glossy luxuriance.

"Mamma has left off her widow's cap in honour of uncle's marriage," observed Arthur, reading my looks with a child's mingled simplicity and quickness of observation. Mamma looked grave and Mrs. Maxwell shook her head. "And aunt Maxwell is never going to leave off hers," persisted the naughty boy; but when he saw that his pertness was seriously displeasing and painful to his aunt, he went and silently put his arm round her neck, kissed her cheek, and withdrew to the recess of one of the great bay-windows, where he quietly amused himself with his dog, while Mrs. Maxwell gravely discussed with me the interesting topics of the weather, the season, and the roads. I considered her presence very useful as a check upon my natural impulses – an antidote to those emotions of tumultuous excitement which would otherwise have carried me away against my reason and my will; but just then I felt the restraint almost intolerable, and I had the greatest difficulty in forcing myself to attend to her remarks and answer them with ordinary politeness; for I was sensible that Helen was standing within a few feet of me beside the fire. I dared not look at her, but I felt her eye was upon me, and from one hasty, furtive glance, I thought her cheek was slightly flushed, and that her fingers, as she played with her watch-chain, were agitated with that restless, trembling motion which betokens high excitement.

"Tell me," said she, availing herself of the first pause in the attempted conversation between her aunt and me, and speaking fast and low, with her eyes bent on the gold chain – for I now ventured another glance – "Tell me how you all are at Linden-hope – has nothing happened since I left you?"

"I believe not."

"Nobody dead? Nobody married?"

"No."

"Or – or expecting to marry? – No old ties dissolved or new ones formed? No old friends forgotten or supplanted?"

She dropped her voice so low in the last sentence that no one could have caught the concluding words but myself, and at the same time turned her eyes upon me with a dawning smile, most sweetly melancholy, and a look of timid though keen inquiry that made my cheeks tingle with inexpressible emotions.

"I believe not," I answered. "Certainly not, if others are as little changed as I." Her face glowed in sympathy with mine.

"And you really did not mean to call?" she exclaimed.

"I feared to intrude."

"To intrude!" cried she, with an impatient gesture. "What –" but as if suddenly recollecting her aunt's presence, she checked herself, and, turning to that lady, continued – "Why, aunt, this man is my brother's close friend, and was my own intimate acquaintance (for a few short months at least), and professed a great attachment to my boy – and when he passes the house, so many scores of miles from his home, he declines to look in for fear of intruding!"

"Mr. Markham is over-modest," observed Mrs. Maxwell.

"Over-ceremonious rather," said her niece – "over – well, it's no matter." And turning from me, she seated herself in a chair beside the table, and pulling a book to her by the cover, began to turn over the leaves in an energetic kind of abstraction.

"If I had known," said I, "that you would have honoured me by remembering me as an intimate acquaintance, I most likely should not have denied myself the pleasure of calling upon you, but I thought you had forgotten me long ago."

"You judged of others by yourself," muttered she without raising her eyes from the book, but reddening as she spoke, and hastily turning over a dozen leaves at once.

There was a pause, of which Arthur thought he might venture to avail himself to introduce his handsome young setter, and show me how wonderfully it was grown and improved, and to ask after the welfare of its father Sancho.

Mrs. Maxwell then withdrew to take off her things. Helen immediately pushed the book from her, and after silently surveying her son, his friend, and his dog for a few moments, she dismissed the former from the room under pretence of wishing him to fetch his last new book to show me. The child obeyed with alacrity; but I continued caressing the dog. The silence might have lasted till its master's return, had it depended on me to break it; but, in half a minute or less, my hostess impatiently rose, and, taking her former station on the rug between me and the chimney corner, earnestly exclaimed –

"Gilbert, what is the matter with you? – Why are you so changed? It is a very indiscreet question, I know," she hastened to add: "perhaps a very rude one – don't answer it if you think so – but I hate mysteries and concealments."

"I am not changed, Helen – unfortunately I am as keen and passionate as ever – it is not I, it is circumstances that are changed."

"What circumstances? Do tell me!" Her cheek was blanched with the very anguish of anxiety – could it be with the fear that I had rashly pledged my faith to another?

"I'll tell you at once," said I. "I will confess that I came here for the purpose of seeing you (not without some monitory misgivings at my own presumption, and fears that I should be as little welcome as expected when I came), but I did not know that this estate was yours until enlightened on the subject of your inheritance by the conversation of two fellow-passengers in the last stage of my journey; and then I saw at once the folly of the hopes I had cherished, and the madness of retaining them a moment longer; and though I alighted at your gates, I determined not to enter within them; I lingered a few minutes to see the place, but was fully resolved to return to M— without seeing its mistress."

"And if my aunt and I had not been just returning from our morning drive, I should have seen and heard no more of you?"

"I thought it would be better for both that we should not meet," replied I, as calmly as I could, but not daring to speak above my breath, from conscious inability to steady my voice, and not daring to look in her face lest my firmness should forsake me altogether. "I thought an interview would only disturb your peace and madden me. But I am glad, now, of this opportunity of seeing you once more and knowing that you have not forgotten me, and of assuring you that I shall never cease to remember you."

There was a moment's pause. Mrs. Huntingdon moved away, and stood in the recess of the window. Did she regard this as an intimation that modesty alone prevented me from asking her hand? And was she considering how to repulse me with the smallest injury to my feelings? Before I could speak to relieve her from such a perplexity, she broke the silence herself by suddenly turning towards me and observing –

"You might have had such an opportunity before – as far, I mean, as regards assuring me of your kindly recollections, and yourself of mine, if you had written to me."

"I would have done so, but I did not know your address, and did not like to ask your brother, because I thought he would object to my writing; but this would not have deterred me for a moment, if I could have ventured to believe that you expected to hear from me, or even wasted a thought upon your unhappy friend; but your silence naturally led me to conclude myself forgotten."

"Did you expect me to write to you, then?"

"No, Helen – Mrs. Huntingdon," said I, blushing at the implied imputation, "certainly not; but if you had sent me a message through your brother, or even asked him about me now and then –"

"I did ask about you frequently. I was not going to do more," continued she, smiling, "so long as you continued to restrict yourself to a few polite inquiries about my health."

"Your brother never told me that you had mentioned my name."

"Did you ever ask him?"

"No; for I saw he did not wish to be questioned about you, or to afford the slightest encouragement or assistance to my too obstinate attachment." Helen did not reply. "And he was perfectly right," added I. But she remained in silence, looking out upon the snowy lawn. "Oh, I will relieve her of my presence," thought I; and immediately I rose and advanced to take leave, with a most heroic resolution – but pride was at the bottom of it, or it could not have carried me through.

"Are you going already?" said she, taking the hand I offered, and not immediately letting it go.

"Why should I stay any longer?"

"Wait till Arthur comes, at least."

Only too glad to obey, I stood and leant against the opposite side of the window.

"You told me you were not changed," said my companion: "you are – very much so."

"No, Mrs. Huntingdon, I only ought to be."

"Do you mean to maintain that you have the same regard for me that you had when last we met?"

"I have; but it would be wrong to talk of it now."

"It was wrong to talk of it then, Gilbert; it would not now – unless to do so would be to violate the truth."

I was too much agitated to speak; but, without waiting for an answer, she turned away her glistening eye and crimson cheek, and threw up the window and looked out, whether to calm her own, excited feelings, or to relieve her embarrassment, or only to pluck that beautiful half-blown Christmas-rose that grew upon the little shrub without, just peeping from the snow that had hitherto, no doubt, defended it from the frost, and was now melting away in the sun. Pluck it, however, she did, and having gently dashed the glittering powder from its leaves, approached it to her lips and said:

"This rose is not so fragrant as a summer flower, but it has stood through hardships none of them could bear: the cold rain of winter has sufficed to nourish it, and its faint sun to warm it; the bleak winds have not blanched it, or broken its stem, and the keen frost has not blighted it. Look, Gilbert, it is still fresh and blooming as a flower can be, with the cold snow even now on its petals. – Will you have it?"

I held out my hand: I dared not speak lest my emotion should overmaster me. She laid the rose across my palm, but I scarcely closed my fingers upon it, so deeply was I absorbed in thinking what might be the meaning of her words, and what I ought to do or say upon the occasion; whether to give way to my feelings or restrain them still. Misconstruing this hesitation into indifference – or reluctance even – to accept her gift, Helen suddenly snatched it from my hand, threw it out on to the snow, shut down the window with an emphasis, and withdrew to the fire.

"Helen, what means this?" I cried, electrified at this startling change in her demeanour.

"You did not understand my gift," said she – "or, what is worse, you despised it. I'm sorry I gave it you; but since I did make such a mistake, the only remedy I could think of was to take it away."

"You misunderstood me cruelly," I replied, and in a minute I had opened the window again, leaped out, picked up the flower, brought it in, and presented it to her, imploring her to give it me again, and I would keep it for ever for her sake, and prize it more highly than anything in the world I possessed.

"And will this content you?" said she, as she took it in her hand.

"It shall," I answered.

"There, then; take it."

I pressed it earnestly to my lips, and put it in my bosom, Mrs. Huntingdon looking on with a half-sarcastic smile.

"Now, are you going?" said she.

"I will if – if I must."

"You are changed," persisted she – "you are grown either very proud or very indifferent."

"I am neither, Helen – Mrs. Huntingdon. If you could see my heart –"

"You must be one, – if not both. And why Mrs. Huntingdon? – Why not Helen, as before?"

"Helen, then – dear Helen!" I murmured. I was in an agony of mingled love, hope, delight, uncertainty, and suspense.

"The rose I gave you was an emblem of my heart," said she; "would you take it away and leave me here alone?"

"Would you give me your hand too, if I asked it?"

"Have I not said enough?" she answered, with a most enchanting smile. I snatched her hand, and would have fervently kissed it, but suddenly checked myself, and said, –

"But have you considered the consequences?"

"Hardly, I think, or I should not have offered myself to one too proud to take me, or too indifferent to make his affection outweigh his worldly goods."

Stupid blockhead that I was! – I trembled to clasp her in my arms, but dared not believe in so much joy, and yet restrained myself to say, –

"But if you should repent!"

"It would be your fault," she replied: "I never shall, unless you bitterly disappoint me. If you have not sufficient confidence in my affection to believe this, let me alone."

"My darling angel – my own Helen," cried I, now passionately kissing the hand I still retained, and throwing my left arm around her, "you never shall repent, if it depend on me alone. But have you thought of your aunt?" I trembled for the answer, and clasped her closer to my heart in the instinctive dread of losing my new-found treasure.

"My aunt must not know of it yet," said she. "She would think it a rash, wild step, because she could not imagine how well I know you; but she must know you yourself, and learn to like you. You must leave us now, after lunch, and come again in spring, and make a longer stay, and cultivate her acquaintance, and I know you will like each other."

"And then you will be mine," said I, printing a kiss upon her lips, and another, and another; for I was as daring and impetuous now as I had been backward and constrained before.

"No – in another year," replied she, gently disengaging herself from my embrace, but still fondly clasping my hand.

"Another year! Oh, Helen, I could not wait so long!"

"Where is your fidelity?"

"I mean I could not endure the misery of so long a separation."

"It would not be a separation: we will write every day: my spirit shall be always with you, and sometimes you shall see me with your bodily eye. I will not be such a hypocrite as to pretend that I desire to wait so long myself, but as my marriage is to please myself, alone, I ought to consult my friends about the time of it."

"Your friends will disapprove."

"They will not greatly disapprove, dear Gilbert," said she, earnestly kissing my hand; "they cannot, when they know you, or, if they could, they would not be true friends – I should not care for their estrangement. Now are you satisfied?" She looked up in my face with a smile of ineffable tenderness.

"Can I be otherwise, with your love? And you do love me, Helen?" said I, not doubting the fact, but wishing to hear it confirmed by her own acknowledgment. "If you loved as I do," she earnestly replied, "you would not have so nearly lost me – these scruples of false delicacy and pride would never thus have troubled you – you would have seen that the greatest worldly distinctions and discrepancies of rank, birth, and fortune are as dust in the balance compared with the unity of accordant thoughts and feelings, and truly loving, sympathising hearts and souls."

"But this is too much happiness," said I, embracing her again; "I have not deserved it, Helen – I dare not believe in such felicity: and the longer I have to wait, the greater will be my dread that something will intervene to snatch you from me – and think, a thousand things may happen in a year! – I shall be in one long fever of restless terror and impatience all the time. And besides, winter is such a dreary season."

"I thought so too," replied she gravely: "I would not be married in winter – in December, at least," she added, with a shudder – for in that month had occurred both the ill-starred marriage that had bound her to her former husband, and the terrible death that released her – "and therefore I said another year, in spring."

"Next spring?"

"No, no – next autumn, perhaps."

"Summer, then?"

"Well, the close of summer. There now! Be satisfied."

While she was speaking Arthur re-entered the room – good boy for keeping out so long.

"Mamma, I couldn't find the book in either of the places you told me to look for it" (there was a conscious something in mamma's smile that seemed to say, 'No, dear, I knew you could not'), "but Rachel got it for me at last. Look, Mr. Markham, a natural history, with all kinds of birds and beasts in it, and the reading as nice as the pictures!"

In great good humour I sat down to examine the book, and drew the little fellow between my knees. Had he come a minute before I should have received him less graciously, but now I affectionately stroked his curling locks, and even kissed his ivory forehead: he was my own Helen's son, and therefore mine; and as such I have ever since regarded him. That pretty child is now a fine young man: he has realised his mother's brightest expectations, and is at present residing in Grassdale Manor with his young wife – the merry little Helen Hattersley of yore.

I had not looked through half the book before Mrs. Maxwell appeared to invite me into the other room to lunch. That lady's cool, distant manners rather chilled me at first; but I did my best to propitiate her, and not entirely without success, I think, even in that first short visit; for when I talked cheerfully to her, she gradually became more kind and cordial, and when I departed she bade me a gracious adieu, hoping ere long to have the pleasure of seeing me again.

"But you must not go till you have seen the conservatory, my aunt's winter garden," said Helen, as I advanced to take leave of her, with as much philosophy and self-command as I could summon to my aid.

I gladly availed myself of such a respite, and followed her into a large and beautiful conservatory, plentifully furnished with flowers, considering the season – but, of course, I had little attention to spare for them. It was not, however, for any tender colloquy that my companion had brought me there: –

"My aunt is particularly fond of flowers," she observed, "and she is fond of Staningley too: I brought you here to offer a petition in her behalf, that this may be her home as long as she lives, and – if it be not our home likewise – that I may often see her and be with her; for I fear she will be sorry to lose me; and though she leads a retired and contemplative life, she is apt to get low-spirited if left too much alone."

"By all means, dearest Helen! – Do what you will with your own. I should not dream of wishing your aunt to leave the place under any circumstances; and we will live either here or elsewhere as you and she may determine, and you shall see her as often as you like. I know she must be pained to part with you, and I am willing to make any reparation in my power. I love her for your sake, and her happiness shall be as dear to me as that of my own mother."

"Thank you, darling! You shall have a kiss for that. Goodbye. There now – there, Gilbert – let me go – here's Arthur; don't astonish his infantile brain with your madness."

* * *

But it is time to bring my narrative to a close. Any one but you would say I had made it too long already. But for your satisfaction I will add a few words more; because I know you will have a fellow-feeling for the old lady, and will wish to know the last of her history. I did come again in spring, and, agreeably to Helen's injunctions, did my best to cultivate her acquaintance. She received me very kindly, having been, doubtless, already prepared to think highly of my character by her niece's too favourable report. I turned my best side out, of course, and we got along marvellously well together. When my ambitious intentions were made known to her, she took it more sensibly than I had ventured to hope. Her only remark on the subject, in my hearing, was –

"And so, Mr. Markham, you are going to rob me of my niece, I understand. Well! I hope God will prosper your union, and make my dear girl happy at last. Could she have been contented to remain single, I own I should have been better satisfied; but if she must marry again, I know of no one, now living and of a suitable age, to whom I would more willingly resign her than yourself, or who would be more likely to appreciate her worth and make, her truly happy, as far as I can tell."

Of course I was delighted with the compliment, and hoped to show her that she was not mistaken in her favourable judgment.

"I have, however, one request to offer," continued she. "It seems I am still to look on Staningley as my home: I wish you to make it yours likewise, for Helen is attached to the place and to me – as I am to her. There are painful associations connected with Grassdale, which she cannot easily overcome; and I shall not molest you with my company or interference here: I am a very quiet person, and shall keep my own apartments, and attend to my own concerns, and only see you now and then."

Of course I most readily consented to this; and we lived in the greatest harmony with our dear aunt until the day of her death, which melancholy event took place a few years after – melancholy, not to herself (for it came quietly upon her, and she was glad to reach her journey's end), but only to the few loving friends and grateful dependents she left behind.

To return, however, to my own affairs: I was married in summer, on a glorious August morning. It took the whole eight months, and all Helen's kindness and goodness to boot, to overcome my mother's prejudices against my bride-elect, and to reconcile her to the idea of my leaving Linden Grange and living so far away. Yet she was gratified at her son's good fortune after all, and proudly attributed it all to his own superior merits and endowments.

I bequeathed the farm to Fergus, with better hopes of its prosperity than I should have had a year ago under similar circumstances; for he had lately fallen in love with the Vicar of L—'s eldest daughter – a lady whose superiority had roused his latent virtues, and stimulated him to the most surprising exertions, not only to gain her affection and esteem, and to obtain a fortune sufficient to aspire to her hand, but to render himself worthy of her, in his own eyes, as well as in those of her parents; and in the end he was successful, as you already know. As for myself, I need not tell you how happily my Helen and I have lived together, and how blessed we still are in each other's society, and in the promising young scions that are growing up about us. We are just now looking forward to the advent of you and Rose, for the time of your annual visit draws nigh, when you must leave your dusty, smoky, noisy, toiling, striving city for a season of invigorating relaxation and social retirement with us.

Till then, farewell,
Gilbert Markham.

Staningley: *June* 10*th*, 1847.

Biographies

Charlotte & Anne Brontë

The intrigue surrounding Charlotte Brontë (1816–55) and Anne Brontë (1820–49), authors of some of the most well-known and loved British novels, still entices fans more than 150 years after their works' publication. As for many writers, childhood lay the groundwork for both Anne's and Charlotte's writing.

Early Lives of The Brontë Sisters

Charlotte and Anne and and their four siblings (altogether five girls and one boy) grew up in Haworth, West Yorkshire when the family moved there in 1820 for their father, Patrick (1777–1861), to take up the position of curate. At a young age, their mother, Maria (1783–1821), died of cancer, leaving the children under the care of Patrick and his sister, Elizabeth Branwell (1776–1842). The losses Anne and Charlotte were to suffer during childhood were not yet over. In 1824 four of the sisters, Maria (1814–25), Elizabeth (1815–25), Charlotte and Emily were sent away to the Clergy Daughters' School in Lancashire, a psychologically dark time that also resulted in the deaths the two elder sisters, Maria and Elizabeth – tuberculosis took them both in June 1825. Charlotte and Emily then returned home to their sister, Anne, and brother, Branwell, clearly marked by these formative experiences. The four siblings found mental relief by creating romantic, imaginary worlds, which they populated with complex characters and elaborate events, these exercises in fantasy equipping the Brontë sisters for later literary efforts. Their time at school, however brief, taught the sisters that life could be harsh and bleak, having a profound effect on Charlotte especially, as seen in her most famous novel, *Jane Eyre* (1847).

Charlotte's Writing Career

It was at Haworth in the 1840s that Charlotte began to make her first steps into the world of professional writing. She worked on various pieces, and achieved her first publication – a book of poems, co-authored with Emily and Anne, though only two copies sold. Then, in 1847, Charlotte's first novel *Jane Eyre* was published. It was an instant sensation, and changed her life and reputation forever.

Charlotte wrote other novels, although *Jane Eyre* is by far her most popular. *Shirley* (1849) and *Villette* (1853) received moderate acclaim, as did *The Professor*, published posthumously in 1857. Brontë also started a novel called *Emma*, of which only around 20 pages were written. *Villette* shares several themes with *Jane Eyre*, especially regarding women struggling to live on their own terms, despite the straightjackets of gender conventions. But while Jane ends up happily married, *Villette* ends with the protagonist, Lucy Snowe, being independently secure yet without the man she loves. In Shirley, Brontë also wrestled with the theme of women's struggle for independence, but blended this into broader reflections on the nature of exploitation in industrial society.

After the publication of *Jane Eyre*, Charlotte's publisher persuaded her to reveal her true identity, whereupon she travelled to London regularly, becoming friends with authors Elizabeth Gaskell (1810–65), William Makepeace Thackeray (1811–63) and Harriet Martineau (1802–76), among others. Accounts of Charlotte's time in London, however, describe her as a serious, shy and quiet woman, not the dynamic personality expected by society. How this seemingly quiet, inexperienced country girl wrote works of such acute society commentary, emotion and passion remains an enduring mystery.

Charlotte married Arthur Bell Nichols, her father's curate – thought by many to be the basis for Rochester's character – in June 1854. Soon after their marriage, she fell pregnant but died from tuberculosis, along with her unborn child, aged 38. Charlotte was interred in the family vault in Haworth.

Anne's Writing Career

Anne was educated at home and worked as a governess for a number of years before publishing her first book of poetry in 1846 along with Charlotte and Emily under the pseudonyms Acton, Currer, and Ellis Bell. Only two copies sold, yet Anne was undeterred from writing. One year later, Anne published her first novel, *Agnes Grey*, which closely mirrored her experience as a governess, exposing the cruel reality of human nature. Although written at the same time as Charlotte's *Jane Eyre*, Anne was accused of copying her sister due to her novel being published later. Her second novel, *The Tenant of Wildfell Hall*, was published in three volumes in 1848 and was instantly successful despite being criticized for its morbid subject and outspokenness. That same year, Anne and Charlotte visited Charlotte's publisher, George Smith, to reveal their true identities.

Within the next year, both Branwell and Emily died of illness despite their young age, and this tragedy deeply affected Anne. She soon fell ill with tuberculosis and died in Scarborough on 28 May 1849 at the age of 29. Charlotte decided to bury Anne at the location where she died rather than the family vault, and she and Anne's former schoolmistress were the only mourners at the funeral.

Sophie Franklin (Foreword)

Sophie Franklin is currently completing her PhD at Durham University, which focuses on the violences of Anne, Charlotte, and Emily Brontë's writings in relation to nineteenth-century perceptions of violence. She graduated from the University of St Andrews in 2013 and gained an MA from Durham University in 2014. Before starting her PhD in 2015, she worked in an editorial capacity for a small publishing house and in bookselling. Her first book, *Charlotte Brontë Revisited: A View from the Twenty-First Century*, was published by Saraband in April 2016; and her thesis is supported by an AHRC Northern Bridge studentship.

Original Publication

Jane Eyre by Charlotte Brontë

Originally Published (under the pseudonym 'Currer Bell') by Smith, Elder and Co., London, 1847

The Tenant of Wildfell Hall by Anne Brontë

Originally Published (under the pseudonym 'Acton Bell') by Thomas Cautley Newby, London, 1848

New & Classic Writing

Other Romantic Fantasy titles from FLAME TREE PUBLISHING include

Jane Austen: Pride & Prejudice | Emma
Jane Austen: Sense & Sensibility | Mansfield Park
Brontë Sisters: Wuthering Heights | Villette

Flame Tree's Gothic Fantasy books offer a carefully curated series of new titles, each with combinations of original and classic writing:

Chilling Horror Short Stories
Chilling Ghost Short Stories
Science Fiction Short Stories
Murder Mayhem Short Stories
Crime & Mystery Short Stories
Swords & Steam Short Stories
Dystopia Utopia Short Stories
Supernatural Horror Short Stories
Lost Worlds Short Stories
Time Travel Short Stories
Heroic Fantasy Short Stories
Agents & Spies Short Stories
Pirates & Ghosts Short Stories

as well as new companion titles which offer rich collections of classic fiction from masters of the gothic fantasy genres:

H.G. Wells Short Stories
Lovecraft Short Stories
Edgar Allan Poe Collection
Sherlock Holmes Collection
Knights of the Round Table

Available from all good bookstores, worldwide, and online at
flametreepublishing.com

Romantic Fantasy

For our books, calendars, blog
and latest special offers please see:
flametreepublishing.com